ALICE SKYE SERIES

BOOKS 1-3

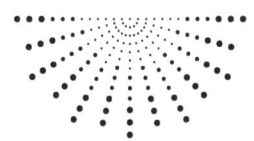

TAYLOR ASTON WHITE

DISCLAIMER - Written in British English including spelling and grammar.

Copyright © 2020 by Taylor Aston White

All rights reserved.

No part of this book may be reproduced in any form or by any electronic or mechanical means, including information storage and retrieval systems, without written permission from the author, except for the use of brief quotations in a book review.

Edited by Michael Evan

Alice Skye

Witch's Sorrow
Druid's Storm
Rogue's Mercy
Elemental's Curse
Book Five coming soon

Alice Skye Short Story

Witch's Bounty

ACKNOWLEDGMENTS

I would like to start by thanking my good friends Mitchell Kelby and Hayley Morland, who helped and encouraged me at the very early stages of writing.

While we haven't known each other as long, I'd like to thank Michael Evan for your ability to make me laugh and 'go all Emo.'

His friendship means more than he knows.

Lastly, a special thank you to my mother, Nadine, who without her this book(s) wouldn't have been possible.

Her guidance and inspiration will stick with me forever.

Your FREE short story is waiting...

Witch's Bounty

When the wrong man's framed, and the Metropolitan Police don't care. Paladin Agent Alice Skye takes it on herself to find the real culprit.

Check out this free short story and follow Alice in the modern world of magic.

Get your free copy of Witch's Bounty here:
    www.taylorastonwhite.com

This book is written in British English, including spelling and grammar.

WITCH'S SORROW

BOOK ONE

PROLOGUE

What was that?
She opened her eyes and stared at the ceiling, the luminescent glow of the many stars and moons barely lighting up the dark room. Another loud bang resonated up through the floorboards, forcing a squeak in panic. She grabbed her teddy, covering herself in a pink fluffy blanket with her eyes squeezed shut.

Wait... She opened her eyes, peeking past the pink fluff.

It was probably Kyle being stupid, trying to scare her again.

She reached over to click on the lamp, a pink glow emitting from the unicorn patterned lampshade.

"Kyle?" she called, her brother's room only next door. Lifting a small fist, she knocked three times against the wall.

"Kyle?" she called again, this time louder.

She shrugged the covers away before swinging her legs off the side of the bed, careful to not let her feet get too close to the darkness beneath. Her door creaked open as she timidly peered into the hallway, noticing Kyle's bedroom door slightly ajar, his 'DO NOT CROSS' yellow tape torn from the wood.

"Kyle," she whispered, "you're going to be in so much trouble." She quickly glanced into his room, noticing his empty bed, the sheets and duvet a messy bundle at the bottom.

Something creaked behind her.

She swivelled to look further down the hallway, squinting her eyes in the dim light.

"Mum?" Her parent's door was wide open, the bed just as empty as Kyle's.

Creak. Creak. Creak.

She ran over to the banister, her heart a rabbit in her chest as she peered down into the darkness below. She wasn't fond of the dark.

"Mum?" she shouted now. "Dad?" No response. Nothing. Her hand shook as she gripped the banister, her feet making no noise as she took a few steps down.

Something shattered, a crash, glass.

"Mum?" she called once more, her voice wobbling as tears threatened. She clutched her bear close to her chest as she walked the last few steps of the staircase, her bare feet cold against the hardwood. Another crash. The lights flicked ahead before turning off, covering her in complete darkness.

"Kyle if that's you, it's not funny."

Still no response, she couldn't even hear the usual hum of the heating, the darkness a void of silence.

She padded down the hallway, pushing the kitchen door gently as soft light flickered beneath the frame.

CHAPTER ONE

Alice groaned as she turned slightly, the cheap bed creaking beneath her. A yawn escaped as she absently reached towards the nightstand, her hand touching the familiar coolness of her phone. Light streamed through the cheap curtains, forcing her to squint through tired eyes.

"What the?" she groaned as she brought the mobile phone closer to her face, confused with why it wasn't lighting up. The dark screen caused her stress to spike, especially when shaking the phone violently did nothing. Not that shaking anything violently ever worked.

The phone wasn't on charge, the white wire mocking her beside the bed.

"FUCK!" Alice bounced off the mattress, running half-naked into her living room to squint at the small analogue clock on her TV.

7:56 am

"Fuck. Fuck. Fuck." She grabbed the closest clothes, pulling them on while she tried to brush through the nest she called hair. Hopping on one foot she pulled on her ankle boots, stretching to grab her jacket and satchel before she ran through the front door a few seconds later.

It had to be today, Alice groaned to herself as she hurriedly made her way down several floors to the street below. *The one day I can't bloody be late.*

The door separating the foyer to the road was already open as she half-jogged out, her attention on the small parking space to the side of the building. Her 'vintage,' as she liked to call it, Volkswagen Beetle sat like it always did in its dedicated parking space. The pale blue colouring more silver than it should be, the rust and scrapes flaking away at the paint. The hubcaps were gone, stolen yet again and some smartarse had scraped a bad luck spell into the back bumper. The joke was on them though, they had done one of the symbols wrong.

She dropped her bag onto the bonnet before she frantically searched for the car keys.

"You have got to be kidding me!" she muttered, searching every pocket. The keys were not in her bag like they were supposed to be. They were probably still sitting beside the kettle where she had left them last. Her eyes rolled over to the clumsy curves of the bad luck spell.

It seemed they didn't get it wrong after all.

I don't have time for this, she thought as she grabbed the satchel and hitched it high on her shoulder.

The bus stop was roughly a ten-minute walk up the road. Her light jog made it in four with only a few minutes' wait. The doors screeched open as the bus driver barely looked up, his long greasy hair hiding most of his face.

"Central Caverns please," she asked politely, her voice surprisingly strong considering she hadn't had time for her morning caffeine.

With barely a grunt the driver accepted her money before starting the bus. She sat towards the front, scooting over to the window seat so she could watch the buildings blur together as the bus manoeuvred through the residential area towards the central part of the city. The steady vibration centred her as she stared blankly, her brain on override as she tried to figure out why she had to go to a meeting.

One day was not enough warning.

Her role as a Paladin was something she was proud of, something she was good at if she said so herself. She was trained to track and detain Breed, also known as anyone not one hundred percent human, by any means necessary.

Well, within reason of course.

Witches, vampires, shifters, faeries and the occasional selkie was what she was skilled in. Unfortunately, the pay wasn't as you would expect a high-risk job would have, especially considering Paladin Agents had a marginally higher mortality rate compared to other jobs. Which wasn't surprising when the subject she was in charge of bringing to justice was twice her size, had large fangs and the tendency to rip one's throat out.

Most people who hired her through Supernatural Intelligence, the organisation created as a Breed partnership with the local metropolitan police, were genuinely tight-arsed. So she wasn't allowed to use flashy spells or show off because the contracts wouldn't pay for it. Don't even get her started on the internal contracts, ones assigned by the Met themselves when they found themselves in over their heads. They paid even less.

What the hell have I done? She pressed her hand against the window, allowing the cool glass to comfort her clammy palms. She hadn't done anything wrong.

At least, not recently.

"Central Caverns," a husky voice called from the front, someone that smoked fifty a day.

"Stop it, Alice." She shook her head, clearing her thoughts as she climbed out the bus, barely stepping off before the doors closed and accelerated away. Alice groaned to herself when she noticed the Starbucks wasn't very busy next to S.I. tower, her mouth salivating as she forced her feet to walk past the green canopy and towards the rotating doors.

Conscious of the time she grabbed her security pass from her jacket pocket, barely giving herself time to wave to the security guards before she headed towards an empty lift, her nerves a flutter. She waited patiently for the floor numbers to rise, the obnoxious music not helping with her anxiety. She hated being late.

With a deep, calming breath, she squinted at the reflective surface of the chrome doors, trying to decide if she looked presentable or not. Her hair wasn't awful, the blonde strands up in a half bun that looked almost purposely styled, in a sexy messy way. Last night's makeup was still there, the eyeliner smudged enough that it looked like smoky eye shadow around her emerald eyes. Her lips were cracked, but not obviously so. She looked like she'd had an all-nighter, not ready for a meeting with her boss.

It could be worse.

The lift beeped, the doors opened to reveal the general bustle of the forty-second floor. Alice ignored the stares from her colleagues as she manoeuvred through the cubicles, heading towards the back of the building where the meeting would take place.

"Ah, there you are," a high-pitched voice laughed from the corner. "I thought you weren't going to turn up."

Alice turned to Barbara the receptionist, intending to reply with a snarky comment. Instead, she decided to bite her tongue and be polite. It would do her no good to piss off her boss's favourite receptionist, even if it would be satisfying. Barbara, also known as Barbie due to her likeness to the plastic doll, had worked for Dread for as long as Alice could remember, and considering Dread had brought her into work as a small child that was quite a long time.

"I woke up late," was all she said as she went to stand beside the window, staring down at the many floors below. The view was beautiful. London, a city with thousands of years of history blended seamlessly with the steel and glass of the modern world. Alice sighed as she settled herself into a seat, the clock on the wall showing she had made it in time, with just a few minutes to spare.

The leather cushion squeaked as she relaxed and watched a blue flame dance between her fingertips, the ball of fire common when she was feeling extreme emotion. Or for no reason at all. It was a peculiar little thing.

"If you don't put that fire thingy out you are going to set off the sprinklers," Barb sniggered, her baby blue eyes narrowed.

Alice pursed her lips, concentrating on the pretty blue flame, green sparkles bursting at intervals. With a barely audible pop the ball disappeared, leaving her looking at her hands, her nails short and broken, the black nail polish starting to chip.

What have I fucked up now?

The blue flame burst to life once more, energised by her spike in nerves. She tried to bat it away, but it happily glided along the air. Only she had the luck to be cursed with teenage acne, mood swings *and* spontaneous balls of flame. She pondered the mechanics of the small twinkly flame, trying to remember a time when the little thing didn't pop into existence.

"You shouldn't slouch, it's bad for your posture," Barb snidely commented, her long, perfectly manicured nails tapping loudly against the keyboard on her desk.

Alice automatically sat up as her eyes darted to the bottled blonde witch who didn't have many friends in the office. The woman dressed in the most provocative clothes she could find, her perky implanted breasts on full show. Barb was easily pushing late forties, yet she spent all her money on magic infused jewellery that helped cover her wrinkles.

"Barbie, why am I here?"

Barb's eyes narrowed at the nickname, but didn't comment. "You know Commissioner Grayson loves a good meeting." She pouted her lips, a slight curve at the edge. She knew why she was here, but wouldn't say.

"This is a joke right?" Barb ignored her, her attention back to the computer, but the sinister smile still in place.

Alice still hadn't figured out why she was there. She had only three assignments over the past month, and they all had gone well. The black witch who was caught selling curses and black amulets online was an easy tag. She was stupid enough to have her return address on the parcels.

The second was the wolf shifter that made a scene at the bar, one that was wrecked in the process. What pissed her off was the fact they had banned *her* from the bar, as if it was somehow her fault they had a destructive wolf that trashed two chairs and an ugly looking painting. Her last assignment involved a Vamp, one where his psychological condition wasn't considered when he applied to be turned. He was only three-years-old in undead terms when he was found bathing in blood, not his own, with his trousers around his ankles. It wasn't a pretty sight.

"Tick tock, it's almost time," Barbie giggled. It would have sounded cute on a small child; on her it was just creepy. She flicked her hair over her shoulder, making sure to pout her bright pink lips even more. It was people like Barbie who gave witches a bad name. She smelt like a sickly mixture of roses and doughnuts, not ozone like other witches, ones who actually practised the art of magic.

Something vibrated next to the computer, followed with a shrill whine that had Barbie reaching over to the old grey-corded phone. The phone was so old compared to the modern computer it was almost prehistoric, which made no sense in a company benefitting from the latest technology and equipment. *'If it isn't broke, don't fix it'* was a favoured saying amongst Breed over a hundred.

"Yes sir," Barbie breathed sexily into the receiver, her voice taking on the perfect phone sex rumble, unlike her normal high-pitched soprano.

"Why yes sir, I will send her in immediately." With a click, she put down the phone before she swivelled to face Alice, a smirk plastered across her face. "Commissioner Grayson will see you now."

With a pensive nod, Alice entered through the large oak door, pushing against the heavy metal handle. The room beyond was dark, almost pitch black as she stumbled inside.

"Alice," a deep voice greeted, Dread's whole body hidden in shadow. "Please, take a seat." A hand stretched into the sliver of light created by the open door, his fingers, long and pale, were decorated with a diamond and ruby encrusted ring that encircled his middle finger. She closed the door behind her, the room in complete darkness.

Dread's window, the one that would have just an amazing view of London to the one in reception, was blocked out with a blackout blind, the man preferring to sit in the dark.

Alice stepped forward, feeling for the chair she luckily noticed before she closed the door. She wasn't afraid of the dark, she just wasn't happy with it. She didn't trust the complete absence of sight, especially as the man sitting quietly before her could see perfectly while she couldn't even see her hand in front of her face.

She heard a click, the room illuminated by a chrome lamp that perched on the corner of his oversized wooden desk, clean of everything other than the lamp, a piece of paper and a single gold pen that he had positioned perfectly along the natural grooves of the wood. She tried to hide her jump as his eyes settled on her, ones that were just as dark as the room. Obsidian ovals in a white face, ones so dark you couldn't tell where the irises started and pupils began.

Well, she thought to herself. *This is disconcerting.* She had known him all her life, could read him better than anyone, and he wasn't happy.

Drum. Drum. Drum.

Dread's fingers tapped against the top of his desk in an annoying sequence.

Drum. Drum. Drum.

Dread Grayson has held his position as Commissioner of the Supernatural Intelligence Bureau since it was first built around three hundred years ago. The man sitting before her, who still drummed his fingers across the wood, was one of the most powerful people in the city, not counting The Council. He just stared at her, his face worryingly composed, the grooves, which he received before the turn, seemed etched from stone, not one facial muscle moving. He continued to stare at her unblinking, his dark hair cut close to the scalp, almost bald. Large bushy eyebrows dominated his otherwise hair-free face, the dark hair highlighting his incredibly pale complexion.

"You cut your hair recently. Looks nice," Alice nervously commented as she brushed her own blonde strands from her face. *Why am I here?*

He finally blinked at her as a vein started to pulse in his forehead.

"What are you wearing?" he asked, voice clipped.

Alice looked down, seemingly confused by his comment.

Oh shit.

She bit her lip, heat against her cheeks as she only just noticed what she had thrown on. Her shirt was pure white with two strategically placed avocados on the front. Tucked into her black jeans it looked relatively clean. She was grateful it was one of her politer shirts.

She folded her arms over her chest, trying to hide the design as if nothing was wrong. That gained her a small, familiar smile, just the tip at the corner of his mouth. Dread had always moaned about her choice in clothing, ever since he took over as her legal parental guardian all those years ago. He still moaned regularly, even though she constantly reminded him she was twenty-three.

He thought she was acting up.

She thought the shirts were cool.

The smile vanished, his face immobile once again. His eyes were something he often used to scare people, the creepiness of them enough to force anyone to behave. It was uncomfortable, to say the least.

The door at her back opened, allowed some extra light to creep into the still too dark room. She fought not to turn, Dread holding her gaze until the door shut once again.

"Now Alice, you will remain quiet until asked a direct question. Do you understand?" Dread betrayed no emotion, he had become the Commissioner of the Supernatural Intelligence Bureau, leader of the Paladins. Not her parental figure.

She just nodded back, deciding it was better not to open her mouth at all. She didn't always have a conscious thought on what came out.

"Okay then, when Mr Wild takes a seat we can start this meeting." His obsidian eyes broke their connection, allowing her to breathe for a second before Mr Wild sat in the seat beside her.

The man was tall, around six feet with long light brown hair that hid the expression on his face in a straight curtain.

She looked back at Dread in confusion. *Why am I here?* she asked silently while his eyes stayed blank. He knew what she had asked, but refused to respond. She huffed to herself as she chanced another glance to her right. Piercing blue eyes met hers for a fleeting second before she forced herself to look away.

Fuck. Fuck. Fuck. She had recognised those eyes, eyes of a shifter, someone that was part man, part animal. One that was *pissed*.

"Let's get on with this then," the man beside her complained, his voice deep but emotionless. Monotone even.

She turned to look at him again as his irises changed, the brightness dimming to a darker blue, ones that showed even less emotion, if that was even possible. It was like staring at a wall.

Alice observed him as he swept his long hair over his shoulder, revealing an unusually narrow nose compared to his broad chin. His facial hair was messy, as if he was used to being clean shaven but hadn't had the time or just couldn't be bothered. She continued to stare at him even as he looked at Dread expectantly, ignoring her for the moment. He had been the wolf shifter she had tagged a week ago, the one who had helped wreck the bar and had gotten her banned.

"Let's begin then, shall we?" Dread tapped once more on the desk. "Agent Alice Skye, do you know why you have been asked to attend this meeting?"

"No," she murmured, even as she struggled to figure out what was going on.

"Do you remember the gentleman next to you?"

Alice gritted her teeth. "Yes."

"Then can you explain to me why you arrested the Alpha of White Dawn?"

"White Dawn?" Alice opened her mouth in a silent gasp. *Oh shit,* she cursed herself. White Dawn was the largest wolf pack in London, if not Europe. She had royally fucked up. "It was a contract, amber level retrieval." She strained to remember the exact details.

"Who gave you the contract?" Dread asked as he studied her carefully.

"It was emailed across to me. Nothing suspicious about it." She tried to shrug without moving her arms from her chest, which made her look even more unprofessional.

"How did you even find me?" the Alpha next to her growled. His irises flashed the brighter blue, barely a second before returning to the darker shade. From her experience with shifters it was his animal's response, their emotions and instincts rawer than their human counterpart.

Alice refused to face him, not wanting to aggravate his beast. "I'm good at my job."

"What happened Alice?" Dread leaned forward, the light from the chrome lamp giving him an ethereal glow.

"I was waiting outside the bar where I had tracked the wolf…" A small snarl to her right. "I mean, Mr Wild," she corrected. "He held a man up by his throat, against a wall."

"You held a man against a wall? In a human bar?" Dread's unnerving eyes turned to the Alpha. His fangs punched below his bottom lip in a show of uncharacteristic annoyance.

"Pack business." Was the Alpha's only response, his tone absolute.

Alice continued. "The man had started to shift, bones were breaking, and his fur started to erupt from his ripped flesh, but it was wrong." She knew it, she had seen enough shifts from human to animal and back again to recognise the difference in the transition.

"Wrong?" Dread questioned her.

"I have seen people shift, and this man was wrong, sick maybe. He changed into a half state, his legs bent at the wrong angle and half his body exposing muscle. He ran from the bar and the…" Alice hesitated, deciding to correct herself. "the Alpha, chased after him. So I followed."

"And because of you, he got away." Mr Wild started to snarl before he caught himself, his face shocked before it relaxed back into its impassivity.

"He wasn't my target." She observed him from the corner of her eye, wary.

"It took me three months to track him. I needed the information he could give me. Because of you…" The Alpha started to stand, his voice deepening as violence threatened.

"ENOUGH!" Dread slammed his hand down onto the table, rattling his pen onto the floor. The vein in his head pulsed violently, attempting to escape his porcelain skin. "I have heard enough." He stared down Mr Wild until he had returned to his seat. "After discussing the details with both yourself and Agent Skye, I have come to a decision that my Paladin was acting correctly in these circumstances."

The Alpha started to protest until Dread held up his hand.

"However, I will personally investigate how a warrant for your arrest was issued. We both know you're not S.I. jurisdiction."

That caught Alice's attention. The only authority above S.I. was The Council.

"I'm not happy with this," Mr Wild said as he settled himself into a more relaxed position. It looked forced. "It took all my resources to track that wolf and then your Paladin went and fucked it up."

"Be that as it may, she did her job correctly." Dread caught her eye, showing her he was still angry.

But I didn't do anything wrong. Dread's eyes glittered as if he could read exactly what she was thinking, which he could. His own eyes replied *shut up and sit still.* So she bit her lip, deciding to take his advice.

"Now let's turn to another matter at hand, Alice mentioned the wolf being sick? Is there a disease going around that we should be concerned about?"

Alice turned to look at the Alpha once more, watching his jaw clench before he replied. "No."

Body language was something she was trained in, and the wolf just lied. *Now that's interesting.*

"Is there anything else you would like to discuss?" Dread reached down to his pen that had fallen, taking his time to line it back up with the grooves of the wood.

"Not at this present time," Mr Wild rumbled, annoyed but hiding the emotion.

"Great, so that matter can be put to rest." Dread pressed a hidden button beneath his desk. The door opened silently, allowing light to penetrate the tense room.

"Alice, we need to discuss your recent assignments. However, I will wait until we do not have an audience." He stood up before placing his hand over the breast pocket of his jacket, a sign of respect. It looked sarcastic. "Until next we meet Mr Wild. Please contact Supernatural Intelligence if you require anything further."

Mr Wild said nothing. Instead, he stormed out the door as a flustered Barbie spoke to him in hushed tones. Alice stood, but decided to wait, watching Dread carefully.

"Alice, you should probably escort our guest down." He concentrated on the pen.

"Why did you do that?" she asked, confused. "You knew he was lying. Why didn't you say anything?"

"And say what?" He finally looked up, his eyes still angry but more composed. "If you think I'm doing an inadequate job, why don't you tell me what you would have done?"

Alice hesitated, thinking about her response carefully. "I don't know, ask him more questions?"

"He is the Alpha, Alice. Sickness among his wolves has nothing to do with us. Shifters, in general, have nothing to do with us unless they pay for our services. You know as well as I do they are self-governed ever since Xavier took over on The Council."

His forehead furrowed, his expression stolid. Alice didn't know what to say, The Council being a subject she knew little about. The Council of five, or technically six when counting the Fae twins stayed out of the media, reigning over Breed silently. Dread, on the other hand, had met them all, and he wasn't a fan.

"I'll escort Mr Wild out of the building." She turned toward the door.

"Oh, and Alice," he started, forcing her to pause. "Make sure Mr Wild doesn't break anything on his way down."

CHAPTER TWO

The lighting in the hallway blinded as Alice walked past Barbie, the receptionist glaring as she adjusted her top to show more of her breasts.

"Mr Wild, if you are finished with the show would you please follow me," Alice said politely, not needing to explain what she meant by the *show*.

She felt his tension behind her a second later, an ominous presence that stormed past her towards the lifts at the back of the floor, easily manoeuvring through the maze of drab grey cubicles spotted around in a confusing labyrinth. The only way to distinguish each cubicle from one another was the bursts of colour pinned to the walls, individuals trying to personalise their little space in a sea of grey.

The Supernatural Intelligence Bureau, also known as The Tower, was on constant speed, everyone having something to do or somewhere to be. The forty-second floor was the main operation for the Paladins, a small desk to prepare for contracts as well as their boss, Commissioner Dread Grayson's office. The other floors contained I.T. technicians, weapons specialists, mailmen, just to name a few. There were even a whole five floors dedicated to a specialist hospital team who worked alongside the London Hope Hospital, England's largest medical facility specialising in holistic magic as well as general medicine.

Alice stood for a moment, trying to catch her breath.

Well, it wasn't awful, she groaned, covering her face with the palms of her hands. *Fuck. Fuck. Fuck.* The only good thing that came out of that meeting was, A: Dread admitted she actually did a good job. *Sort of anyway*. And B: He didn't mention any warnings or disciplinary meetings. Which was always a bonus.

"Oh Alice," a sing-song voice called to her.

She spun to look at Barbie, a feral smile on her pink painted lips.

"Just to let you know your disciplinary meeting has been scheduled for Tuesday at ten-thirty." Her eyes twinkled as she smiled. "Make sure you're here on time." With a last giggle, she turned back towards her desk.

"Great," Alice whispered to herself. "Just great." A lump in her gut, nerves attacking. "Maybe I could get a job with Sam at the bar?" she muttered to herself.

"You can't do that, you hate people," a chirpy voice replied.

Alice smiled when she noticed two people hanging around her cubicle. "What are you guys doing here?"

What sort of friends would hang around to see if she was fired or not?

"I thought you guys were both out on a contract?" Rose and Danton (or D as he was known to his friends) looked at her expectantly, waiting for the gossip.

"We were ma petite sorcière. But I missed your belle smile," D sighed dramatically, his long black hair scraped back off his face.

Rose elbowed him in the chest. "Ignore him, we finished it up early."

"Mon amie you wound me." He feigned hurt, his pale hand draped dramatically over his heart.

"As Roselyn was saying, we finished our expèdition early. But enough of that, I would like to know how ma petite sorcière is doing?"

"Yeah Alice, are you okay? Isn't that the Alpha? Oh my god, are you fired?" Rose asked in her usual cheery voice.

At a tall five feet, eleven inches, topping Alice's mundane height by a good seven inches, she looked like a cheerleader, one who could rip your throat out and smile sweetly the whole time. She was a panther shifter, a sleek cat the same dark shade as her hair.

"Oui, how are you?" D asked as his dark eyes turned towards the Alpha on the other side of the room. "Why is that wolf storming around? You piss him off, non?"

"How did you guys even know about that?"

"You know how nobody here can keep secrets." Rose fluffed up her dark hair. "So is it true? Did you arrest the Alpha?"

"Maybe." The Alpha in question paced in front of the lifts, his eyes flicking towards her every few seconds.

"Well then ma petite sorcière, in case you have to leave the tower in a more permanent fashion I would like to say how edible you look. Délicieuse," he said, with a sensual curve of his lips. "I'm sure there are things we could do to cheer you up? Non?"

Alice couldn't help but laugh. "I'm busy." She looked up at D's laughing face, his skin perfect, common amongst the older Vamps. The exception, like Dread, was when they had scars, wrinkles or skin imperfections before their turn.

"One day I will own your heart." He said this to her regularly, enough that she knew he didn't mean it. D didn't do relationships, didn't like being 'tied down'. Unless 'tied down' involved satin bed sheets and velvet rope.

He really liked to talk after a few drinks, or a lot of drinks as it was in his case.

"Well, not any day soon." A ding behind her, the lift doors opening as Mr Wild's patience wore thin. "I have to escort him down. I'll catch up with you guys soon." With a quick wave, she jogged to the lift, barely squeezing in with the Alpha as the doors closed.

The typical lift music couldn't drown out the tension in the small metal box. The picture on the wall showed ten people being able to fit into the small space, yet the air was thick with just the two of them.

Well, this is awkward.

Mr Wild didn't seem to feel the same tension, his arms loosely hooked onto his forearms as he leaned against one of the silver panels, casually staring at her. Alice tried desperately not to stare back, instead counting down the floors.

39. 38. 37. 36.

"How long have you been a Paladin?" he asked, the question sounding genuine. Strange considering his face looked anything but, his brow low over his eyes.

"Around five years."

"Not long then."

"Long enough." Alice frowned, looking up at him then. His eyes flashed a pale blue as she held his gaze, his animal taking a look.

She had never met someone who could morph so quickly and so

often. She held his stare, desperate to read him. He didn't look angry anymore, more curious. The annoyance was still there, not that his face gave anything away. She just knew it, could feel the underlying pressure in the air. So she didn't look away, just as curious as his wolf seemed to be. His nostrils flared, as if he was scenting the lift, scenting her. She finally dropped her eyes.

"How long have you been Alpha?" she asked, keeping her tone light.

He ignored her question. "Did you train as a Paladin?"

"How is that any of your business?" she asked before she could think of something polite to say. She opened her mouth to apologise as the lift door pinged open on the twentieth floor, a group of three people looked at the tension in the small space, deciding to wait until the next one.

Mr Wild waited until the door closed fully, and the lift began moving again before replying. "Just curious. Never met a Paladin quite like you."

She didn't know whether that was a compliment or not. Probably not. Alice considered it for a few seconds before replying.

"Yes, I trained at the academy."

"Not at the university?"

"No." Alice fidgeted, feeling uncomfortable, the subject a sore spot. She had been accepted into the University of London studying magic crafts, something she had been excited about. Dread was the one who convinced her to become a Paladin, to go to the academy instead. It meant her magic knowledge was basic and self-taught.

"Don't you have to gain a degree to become a recognised witch by the Magika?"

"No." *Yes. Dammit.* "I don't see what point you're trying to make." She felt her cheeks begin to burn as she concentrated hard on the lights dancing in the seam of the tarnished brass doors.

10. 9. 8.

The lift finally creaked to a stop, opening to show the marble floor and columns of the lobby, a beautiful mosaic of crushed browns, golds and beiges. The metallic elements glittered as light reflected from the revolving doors, hitting the specs in the stone.

Without pause she exited the lift and quickly walked towards the front desk, having to fish out her pass from her bag and scanning the screen on the turnstile to sign herself out. The front desk was large, almost the same width as the whole atrium apart from a couple of inches each side.

There were four members of security on the desk at all times. Vince Cooker, the head of security was waving enthusiastically. He was a mage, a human touched with magic. While not as powerful as a full-blooded witch he could still do a few tricks, which he enjoyed showing Alice on as many occasions as he could.

"Hey, Vince."

"Hey there, Alice. I didn't get to say hi earlier, you seemed to be in a bit of a rush," the old security guard chuckled, his dark skin wrinkling even further. "Who's the gentleman by the glass?"

Alice chanced a look behind her, expecting the Alpha to have already left. He surprised her by waiting just outside the doors.

"He is..." Well, she couldn't just tell him she arrested the guy. "A friend."

"Well, he isn't a happy friend." His smile turned to a frown, his grey eyebrows pulled together in concern.

"He's just having a bad day," she said as she signed Mr Wild out too.

She waved goodbye as she felt cold air brush across her skin, summer having long ago disappeared into autumn, the temperature dropping uncomfortably low as the trees continued to lose their colour.

"Mr Wild." She nodded to the man standing to the side of the entrance. "I'm sure it's been a pleasure." He just stared at her, his eyes once again unreadable.

"How do you do that?" she asked, deciding that she had nothing to lose.

"Do what?"

"Control your emotions." She studied his eyes carefully, noting the flare of shock before he concealed it once again.

How can he conceal his emotions so easily? What did he have to hide?

He stared back, his eyes lingering for a second longer than they should before he turned and walked away.

CHAPTER THREE

The bus screeched as it peeled away from the bus stop a short walk away from her flat, a billow of black smoke chasing it down the street. Alice strode past the *'Welcome to Midnight Glade'* sign, a wide metal rectangle hanging loosely from a lamppost. Fangs and large eyes had been added to several of the letters, the neighbourhood kids playing around. It would take a trained eye and someone with decent magic knowledge to notice the small symbols carved along the bottom, anti-violence hexes and protection spells created by overly concerned residents.

Midnight Glade North was like every other suburb surrounding London, an incredibly large community with modest houses painted in whites, beiges, blues and even a few gaudy pinks. Picket fences, neatly trimmed shrubs and flowerbeds decorate paved driveways with well taken care of lawns. People walked their dogs, children played happily in the community park and cars parked neatly along the roads.

The area looked the same as any other residential zone, the exception being that seventy percent of the community was Breed. While it was no longer a shock to have kids in school with shifter children, or a work colleague who had an unusual liquid diet, most humans felt uncomfortable in a majority Breed area. It was almost like an age-old instinct not to hang around with someone who could see you as lunch.

Humans (commonly referred to as Norms) wouldn't notice the small differences in the neighbourhood compared to their 'ordinary' ones unless they knew what they were looking for. Children drew with chalk on the streets, their patterns specific to enchantments rather than daisies and hearts. Windows painted black, giving protection from the sunlight or that a front door had an oversized 'doggy' door fitted where homeowners who had paws could enter easily.

"Hey, that's mine!" a little girl shouted, running in front of Alice as she chased after her brother who had stolen her doll, the head that which had already been ripped off and thrown into a neighbours garden. "I'm telling mum!" the little girl cried as her small hands sharpened into claws as her body reacted to her frustration.

Alice continued to walk as she flicked her collar up to protect her exposed cheeks, the air bitter cold. Slowly, the houses started to become less maintained, flats boarded up from fire damage. Flower beds, if at all planted, had died, the bushes left untrimmed and a few houses needing a good paint, if not completely abandoned. Some teenagers lurked at the street corners, sitting on the street signs passing cigarettes between them like a shifty drug deal. Potholes didn't get filled and cars became less expensive.

The flat Alice shared with her best friend Sam was in one of the less maintained buildings, one that was built in the seventies and hadn't been updated since. The walls were paper-thin and Alice could already hear an argument from apartment 1C as she made her way up the stairs, quickly followed by banging and shouting. The walls were brown with red squares, although not as garish compared to the putrid green carpet that could have once been a shag pile but had flattened and discoloured over years of use. There was no lift, having been broken years before Alice had moved in.

Her neighbour, Mrs Finch in 3A, explained a few years back that Mr Tucker, the caretaker and resident in 1A refused to fix the *'damn thing'* because a group of shifters decided to use it as a place to party and the jumping up and down broke the mechanics. Mr Tucker, on the other hand, explained Mrs Finch was *'talking out of her arse'* and in fact, one of her many dogs had pissed on the exposed wires and ruined the electrics. So Alice took the stairs to the third floor, her place right at the end of the corridor.

"Oh Alice, it's so nice to have caught you," Mrs Finch called from her open doorway as she held a small black dog that shook in her arms. Alice hid her sigh as she turned around, a fake smile pasted on her face.

"I need you to tell that boy of yours that he shouldn't tease my babies like that." Several barks in agreement from behind her as the dog in her arm stayed silent, his eyes bulging.

"What has Sam done now?" Alice asked, bemused. Sam had a love, hate relationship with Mrs Finch. He loved to wind her up, and she hated him for it.

"I'll have you know that boy prowled outside my door, in his *other form*." She made it sound like he did it on purpose. Which admittedly, he did. "It makes my babies upset to know there's a cat outside." The small dog in her arm continued to shake.

Alice bit the inside of her cheek, "I'll ask Sam to refrain from standing outside your door when he's a leopard."

With an awkward wave Alice turned hastily towards her door. *I can't be bothered with this crap.*

"Now Alice, I'm not finished," Mrs Finch said, her neck prickling a pale pink in irritation. "I saw another woman sneak away from your apartment the other night. A *different* one from the last time." The revulsion was clear.

"What has that got to do with me?" she asked, her temper getting thin as the day started to take its toll on her mood.

"Well, he shouldn't just bring home every girl he's just met. It's unsanitary." She sniffed in disgust.

"I'll let Sam know you don't appreciate his partners. Now if you would excuse me." Alice lifted her fist to knock, only just remembering she still didn't have her keys. Hoping Sam was in and she didn't have to ask someone to break it down she knocked hard, the door swinging open easily.

"Sam?" She called as she closed the door behind her. "Sam, what's wrong with the door?"

"Oh, hey babe girl," Sam smiled, his white blonde head appearing from the kitchen archway, the area leading off from the living room. "Small technical issue in that someone broke in."

"What? Again?" Alice groaned as she walked past the bathroom on the left to the surprisingly decent sized kitchen in the back. She dropped her bag on the small table before facing him, her arms crossed. "Isn't that the second time this month?"

"Aye," he replied cheerily in a soft Irish lilt, his accent only pronounced on certain words and phrases, having died down from years of living in England. "But I have replaced the lock, and it seems like nothing is missing." He wiggled his eyebrows at her, the same colour as his natural white blonde hair, a long straight curtain that's cut several inches beneath his shoulders.

"That's because there's nothing here to steal."

Sam had been her best friend since they met as kids in a support group. She had sat in the circle amongst the other children who had gone through their own traumas, scared and lonely. He had tugged on her plaited hair one day and asked her how to braid his own long, unmanageable locks. She couldn't help but smile at his impish grin with a small dimple in one cheek.

"No comment," he shouted from the kitchen.

"I don't know why we stay here." Alice sat heavily in one of the two foldable chairs she got for ten pounds at one of the cheap furniture chains.

"I've already suggested we go stay at your house."

"It's not my house." Alice settled her chin on her palm, watching Sam potter around the kitchen. Her house, or parents' house, was a boarded up building on the other side of the city. "And you know I can't."

"I know." He softened his voice. "I'm just tired of this place. Did you know Mrs Finch called me a whore today?" He fluttered his eyelashes in mock horror. "I don't know whether to be offended or flattered."

"Offended," Alice smiled. "She told me in the hallway. She also mentioned you should stay away from her dogs."

"Those wee shits shouldn't be called dogs. What's the small black one called? Sooty? Or is it Sunny?" He turned his back to her, stirring a black pot on the stove. Cooking utensils hung neatly on the wall in front of him, some on hooks and others on a magnetic strip. The kitchen tiles were yellow and broken, the spider web of cracks giving the dull wall a sad type of decoration.

"Sooty is the black Chihuahua, Sunny is the ginger Pomeranian."

"It's sad that you know their names."

"I don't know all of them." Alice got up to investigate the contents of the pot. "Only the ones I see the most. She usually stops me to show me the pictures of them she keeps in her purse." The dark brown liquid bubbled angrily, various unidentifiable meats and vegetables floating around. "She has about seven dogs in there now."

"I don't even see how that's allowed." Reaching up he grabbed two white plates from the cupboard.

"What ya cooking?" Alice asked. "It smells... interesting."

"I'll have you know I am a master chef." He gave her a teasing smile, pouring some brown sludge with various meats onto the plate. He threw the spoon back into the pot, causing the brown liquid to jump out onto the wall.

"Bloody hell Sam, you've gotten it all over me." Alice rubbed the side of her arm, the brown stuff scalding hot.

Sam snorted. "That's what she said."

"So funny," she murmured as she picked up her own plate and followed him to the small two-seater table.

"So..." Sam started, a spoonful of his masterpiece halfway to his lips. "Why the long face?"

Alice scooped a mixture of the rice and sauce onto her fork, her taste buds exploding as she placed it on her tongue. "Hey, this is really good." She ate another mouthful, moaning as she bit into a particularly juicy piece of chicken. Well, she thought it was chicken.

"Stop stalling. What happened?" His amber eyes rolled over to her, the colour the same as the leopard that was his other half. He thought it made him look badass. She actually agreed, but would never admit that to his face. Shifters were born with two parts, both a human, and an animal. It was his animal, the leopard, that gave him his attitude, its instincts rawer compared to the human. It was unusual amongst shifters to have the same eyes as their counterpart, a result of his harsh childhood.

Alice chewed the chicken for longer than needed. "I fucked up."

"You what?" He spluttered some of his food. "What did you do?"

"I may, or may not have arrested the Alpha of White Dawn."

"The Alpha?" Sam burst out laughing, clutching his stomach. "Why did you do that?"

"Well, I didn't personally go after him or anything. It was a contract. There was a warrant and everything."

"Was he hot?"

"SAM!" She threw an unused spoon at his head, he ducked and it clattered to the floor.

"Now that wasn't very nice." He suppressed a laugh, his lips trembling at the effort.

"My career is over and all you can do is laugh." She lifted her arms, exasperated.

"You're being dramatic. What did the dark overlord say?"

Alice smiled at Sam's nickname for Dread. "He didn't really say anything." She looked down at what was left on her plate. "I have a disciplinary meeting with him in a couple of days."

"See," Sam said as he added more food to his plate. "If it was that serious the meeting would have been immediate."

"Maybe." Alice looked out onto the small ledge the landlord called a balcony. Small terracotta pots stood along the edge, some hanging over the railing with a selection of herbs she used for potions. "What about you? You not at work today?"

"Graveyard shift," he moaned as he leant against the metal sink, his empty plate soaking.

Alice suppressed a laugh when she noticed his t-shirt, the words *'I tried to be normal once. Worst two minutes of my life'* written in bold typography across the black cloth. They both shared a humour for quirky tees.

"Why don't you come with me tonight? Let your hair down, have a few drinks. It could be fun."

"Not tonight." No, she had to practise her sorry face. "But I'm definitely up for it soon."

"You need it." He finished up at the sink. "I need to get changed, feel free to change your mind and meet me later. The new boss is in town and I want you to meet him."

Her eyebrows creased. "Meet him? Why?"

"Because you have no social life outside of work. You won't even go on a date with that Vamp."

"Hey, I have a social life," she pouted. "And Danton isn't serious when he asks me out." She also wasn't interested.

"Baby girl, I don't count as your social life."

Alice stuck her tongue out at him.

"And besides, he's also hot," Sam continued, ignoring her childish reaction.

"You think anybody with a pulse is hot."

"And that's why I have an amazing social life."

"I don't think you banging hundreds of people counts," she pointed out. He just laughed as he exited the kitchen towards his bedroom. Alice followed, flopping onto her stomach on his bed, her head balanced in her hands. "What's your job like?"

Sam twisted as he pulled off his t-shirt, scars crisscrossing his abs and back. Small pale lines barely visible from age, the biggest ones high on his shoulder blades. His golden skin tone an advantage in hiding the worst marks.

"Why are you asking?" He grabbed his work shirt, a black cotton tee with the name *'Blood Bar'* written in dark red across the back and left pec. "Looking for a career change?"

"Maybe." She sighed, rolling onto her back to stare at the ceiling. The once white paint had peeled in places, the artex cracked.

"Stop brooding. You love your job." He threw a sock at her. "You could always become one of those phone sex operators?" Sam's eyes lit up with excitement.

"You give the worst advice." She changed into a sitting position as he plaited his long hair. "I need a pay rise."

"Don't we all," he tutted, checking his appearance in the small mirror above his chest of drawers, the top drawer having broken off a few months back leaving a gaping hole. His bedroom, like hers, was small and compact, Sam's bed a large double with baby blue duvet and pillow, the sheets always messy and never made.

He came to sit beside her, his arms coming around in a hug.

"You screamed last night," he said, matter-of-factly. "Scared the living shit out of me."

"Did I?" She could never remember her dreams.

"Do you want to talk about your nightmares, baby girl?"

"No." She concentrated on her hands, twisting them in her lap.

"They're getting worse."

"They always do this close to the anniversary." She hugged him hard, resulting in him purring against her cheek, the vibration comforting. Releasing him with a final squeeze, she got up. "You know how it goes. I get some nightmares, I brood, and then it's all over." Every year.

"We both know that isn't healthy." He leant back on his arms.

"And your obsession with sleeping with every living thing is?"

Sam narrowed his eyes.

"Shit, I'm sorry, I didn't mean it." She was just tired and angry.

"Maybe you should go speak to Dr Lemington again?"

Dr Lemington was their psychiatrist as children. He didn't help either of them then, so how could he help her now?

"I don't need any help. I deal with everything just fine."

"Yeah, sure."

Alice could almost hear the eye roll. "Look, I don't want to fight. You need to get to work, and I need to go soak in the tub with a pot of ice cream."

"Aye, I do." He stood, adjusting his skinny jeans. "You sure you don't want to hang with me tonight?" The look of worry on his face made her turn away. He had his own demons, he didn't need to fight hers too.

"No it's cool, I'll be fine." With a kiss on the cheek Sam walked out, the front door shutting a moment later.

Once she heard the lock click she walked into the living room, heading towards the bathroom when a photograph caught her eye. She stared at the picture, the two adults and two kids smiling towards the camera, the only picture she had of her family, the others having been lost or packed away at the house. The house that Alice still hadn't dealt with, still hadn't visited. She tilted her head as she looked at her mother, her emerald green eyes shining with happiness.

Alice reached up, fingertips' touching the glass, tracing her mother's smiling face before moving onto her father, a tall man who only had eyes for his wife. While her mum was the light with bright hair and eyes, her dad was the dark, black hair and deep mahogany eyes. Kyle, her older brother was a mixture of both, dark brown hair with emerald eyes while Alice, the little girl holding her dad's hand was a perfect copy of her mother.

Alice choked back emotion as she dropped her hand, her family gone. Taking a moment to herself she turned to the bathroom, a hot bubble bath sounded like the perfect distraction.

CHAPTER FOUR

Alice flicked the dirt from underneath her fingernails, the soil having embedded itself from spending most of her morning tending her few plants and herbs on her balcony. She usually used gardening to calm her temper, but it hadn't worked today. The contract she had been assigned igniting her irritation.

How could they do this to me? she thought to herself. *It's barely above intern level.*

Alice audibly sighed, annoyed that she could hear herself whining in her own head. Frustrated she clicked through her phone, double checking the contract, assuring herself the small guy at the bar was indeed the right target.

Target: 347680
Mr Scoolie Smitt – Fae – Leprechaun. 4ft tall – long brown hair.
Sells dud charm spells to young adults who use them to get high.
Alcoholic
Aggression level – green
Retrieval fee – Basic

She had been training to become a Paladin for as long as she could remember, Dread having prepared her since she was a little girl. It made her great at her job, yet there she was, on a contract with a leprechaun.

Not even an interesting leprechaun, one who liked to sell crappy charms.

The screen flashed as she analysed all the information, confirming the details with her research.

The Fang
Red Lion
The Cock Ring

Three pubs the alcoholic leprechaun liked to frequent. As she had already been to The Fang and The Cock Ring, (The Cock Ring having, disappointingly, just a rooster as its logo,) she now sat grumpily in The Red Lion Pub just off Angel.

"Give me n'other one then," Mr Smitt called to the bar staff, his high-pitched voice carrying across the room. A large rucksack sat at his feet, almost the same size as him. It was just luck he was the only leprechaun in tonight, otherwise she was out of options. She tried to examine his clothing, looking for the telltale sign he belonged to one of the two Fae courts. Which honestly were more like cults, or some ridiculous frat/sorority.

The Seelie court, also known as the Light Fae, were relatively nice compared to their darker brethren. In her experience, at least. They usually wore an emerald somewhere on their body to symbolise their connection to Seelie. On the other end was the Unseelie court, also known as the Dark Fae, who were a lot less friendly. Their traditions were more barbaric than their light siblings and were often on S.I.'s wanted list. They liked to use the ruby as their emblem.

As Mr Smitt wasn't wearing any gemstones, he probably wasn't registered with either court, which made paperwork a hell of a lot easier.

From his increasing volume she gathered he was only a few drinks away from toppling over, or leaving. So she decided to wait until she detained him.

With time on her hands she looked down at the newspaper left on her table, she might as well relax and make the most out of the evening. Someone had clearly read through it already, the paper torn in places, the crossword completed and artistic penis symbols were drawn on almost every page.

The main headline on the first page was of a body mysteriously disappearing from the morgue. Most of the story had lovely dicks drawn over the writing, but Alice understood the general idea. As she flipped through the pages a picture of a smiling man caught her eye, one of the few photos without pen marks all over it. The title explained he was the youngest witch to accept a position in the Magika, the highest members of the magic world.

The Magika, much like The Council, were a board of witches that specifically govern their own race. They specialised in a tiered system to determine how powerful someone was in each main class, earth, arcane and black.

Earth magic was classified simply as someone who used natural ingredients to create potions, amulets and charms. Arcane was slightly different, using their chi to physically manipulate their power. The witch would use incantation words to throw spells at people and objects and was known to be one of the harder classifications to master. Most witches mixed a little of both classes, however, there was one more class of magic.

Black magic was the worst, and yet the most powerful of the three classes. Those witches use blood and death to create spells and potions, something that had been made illegal for obvious reasons.

Within each class there were several branches, such as herbalist within earth and sorcerer within arcane. Inside each branch a witch could be tiered between one and three, one being the highest and three being the lowest. However, most witches just went by their class heading unless they personally specialised in a particular branch.

Tier four was reserved for mages, humans who were touched by magic. Normally born from a witch and a human they were treated like second-class citizens in the magic community. No mage had ever gotten to tier one even though some were pretty powerful in their own right.

Alice snorted at the picture. "It doesn't take a pretty piece of paper to decide how much of a witch I am."

A loud smash brought her attention up to the stage, a drunken man apologising profusely to the amp he had bumped into. He stood there for a good few minutes, his apology turning into a full-blown conversation. Distracted, Alice lifted her drink to her lips, the bubbles going down the wrong hole until she choked loudly, her hand snapping up to cover her mouth. Throat still raw from the coughing she pushed her glass away, sitting straighter in her chair as her boot squeaked across the threadbare carpet.

What the...? Beneath the table she checked her boot, frowning at the noise. *Oh gross.* Her boot squeaked again, the spongy carpet having soaked in a generous amount of liquid. It's probably safe to say over the years alcohol, vomit and other bodily fluids had helped decorate it.

Alice looked down.

It was probably what all the brown patterns were.

Gag.

The décor unsurprisingly matched the disgusting carpet, brown and blue striped walls with paint peeling straight from the brick. Black and white photographs had been nailed to the surface to try and add some decoration. A portrait showed a group of men smiling, a wide angled shot of the outside of the pub and one of a serene woman, her once pretty face having received similar treatment as the newspaper.

The man over to the left continued to chat animatedly to the amp, one foot planted on the ledge of the poor excuse for a stage, and his other placed on the carpet. He leaned forward to caress the black felt of the speaker, his empty glass placed haphazardly on top. A waitress walked past and picked up the glass, causing him to mutter something at her before he staggered off, collapsing onto a table nearby.

Pints clinked as two bartenders served drinks at the bar, the wood a lot cleaner than the tables and chairs dotted around the room. The old wood scratched beyond redemption, the top's sticky, like a fine layer of glue engraved into the grooves of the wood. There was a deep open fireplace, the fire protected by an ornate iron grate cracking happily to the left, the warmth from the flames a pleasant sensation. Unfortunately, the heat cooked the odd smell in the air, a mixture of mould, damp and old beer.

Something shattered against the bar, dark amber liquid pouring down the front.

"Stoopid fecking bitch," the leprechaun shouted, trying unsuccessfully to stop the drink from soaking into his rucksack, the bag now having been placed on the counter. Alice looked over at the ugly clock ticking loudly above the bar.

It was getting late.

With a sullen look at her glass she returned her attention to the room, deciding if it was quiet enough to just snatch her target and call it a night. It wasn't like it was busy, the bar reasonably empty apart from a few drunken men. A handful sat around drinking quietly, some chatting with their friends and some alone, watching the football game on the painfully old television in the corner.

A laugh came from the pool table, a welcoming sound compared to the dull background noise. A thwack as a billiard ball was hit too hard, the ball smashing to the floor. White fangs flashed as the men laughed again.

Blade tight to her back she stood, making sure it remained hidden beneath her jacket, but within easy reach. Glass in hand she walked over to the bar, sitting on the stool next to her target.

"Hi," she greeted, flashing her most sensual smile. He warily looked her over, taking in her leather knee-high boots, tight jeans and a black t-shirt. His eyes lingered on her breasts for a moment before deciding his Guinness was more interesting.

Eyebrows creased, Alice looked down at her cleavage, deciding she needed to invest in a good push-up bra.

How pathetic.

"Can I get a Guinness please?" she asked the barmaid, a shifter Alice would guess from the amount of hair on the back of her hands.

"A fellow Guinness drinker then miss?" Mr Smitt smiled over at her, his eyes actually rolling over her with appreciation this time.

"Maybe," she said, thanking the barmaid before sipping a bit of the liquid, trying not to cough as it went down.

"What ya lookin' for? I may look small but some parts of me are anyfin' but," he chuckled to himself, pushing his rucksack out the way so he could see her better.

"I was actually looking for someone to sell me some..." Alice hesitated, trying to sound unsure. "Charms," she ended in a whisper.

"Aye, well, sellin' charms is what I do second best." He winked at her to make sure she understood the innuendo. "Well, are you lookin' for a good time? I have charms for that, ones that make you irresistible to the opposite sex, or the same sex, depending on what you're into." He looked at her expectantly.

"So you admit you do sell charms?"

"Aye miss. Best there is." He proudly smacked the top of his rucksack.

"Brilliant." She stood up, reaching to the back of her jeans to unhook her handcuffs. "Mr Smitt, I have a warrant for your arrest for selling dud and illegal charms, you do not have to say anything, but what..."

His mouth did a great impression of a fish. "Feck off."

Arsehole. "I have a warrant for your arrest. You will come with me quietly..."

He turned on his stool and pointed his chubby finger towards her, the motion causing him to fall face first onto the carpet. Using his confusion, Alice snapped her cuffs onto both of his wrists, the cuff automatically tightening to his wrist size.

"Hey, what the 'ell do you think you're doin'?" he shouted, dazed.

"I told you, you're under arrest." Alice huffed as she leant down to grab his rucksack, finding the bag full of hundreds of different wooden disks. She pushed the disks out the way, finding several vials of blood and a couple bags of salt.

Idiot. Most of the disks were useless. The salt from his fingers ruining the charms before they could even be invoked. Alice picked up a vial of blood, watching it move as she tilted it to the light.

He started to panic, scrambling as he tried to release his wrists. "Oi!" he called. "They're mine!"

She ignored him, instead zipping up the bag and placing it onto the bar.

"Please," he started to beg, turning to one of the bartenders. "Someone call the cops, this bitch is robbin' me"

"Hey, you need to take this outside." The barmaid pointed her finger at Alice. "We don't want any trouble in 'ere. Leave or I'll call the Met."

Alice stifled a laugh. *What was the Met police going to do?* They had no jurisdiction when a Paladin had a warrant. Besides, they were normally the ones that issued the bloody thing.

From inside her jacket pocked she pulled out her Paladin license, the evidence enough for the barmaid to growl and walk away. The Metropolitan Police dealt with the investigations and boring part of law enforcement, dealing with Breed unless the situation was serious or required a specialist.

She was the specialist.

"There would be no use calling the cops. I have a valid warrant."

Mr Smitt's face fell, the colour draining from his cheeks. "I'll give you anyfin', anyfin' you want. Remember I can find the end of the rainbow!"

"Come on." She went to grab him, but he jumped out of reach.

"I have money." He licked his lips nervously. "Pots of gold. More gold than you could ever want."

She ignored him, grabbing him by the scruff.

"Hey, bloodsuckers..." he shouted behind him. "Get rid of this whore for me an' I'll give ya some cash."

The Vamps stopped their game of pool, turning to look at them in unison, as if they were one person and not three individuals. Their eyes dark in their pale emotionless faces, all hint of fun and humour gone.

Vampires could be really creepy fuckers sometimes.

"Now boys," Alice began. "We're not going to do something stupid are we?"

They smiled, a wide grin showing the edges of their very sharp teeth. A threat.

Oh shit.

She released Mr Smitt's scruff as she faced the Vamps, analysing her options. One: Run away. *Not really an option.* Two: Ignore them and hope they go away. *Unlikely.* Three: Humiliate them with her badass skills but also hope they give up before she does.

The first Vamp calmly walked around the table, his sinister smile still in place as he looked her up and down.

Option three it is then.

Alice pulled out her sword, a sharp blade from her back sheath, ignoring the gun on her hip. Vampires were normally too fast to aim a gun at and get an accurate hit, so it meant close quarters with a blade to take them on.

"Any attack against a Paladin warrants an immediate arrest. I WILL use deadly force." The vampires laughed at her threat. They actually laughed.

Bastards.

A blue flame bobbed around the hilt, not as threatening as she would have liked but at least it was something. The vampires stopped laughing, the one closest to her hissed, his fangs elongating in his jaw as he snarled at her.

Fuck, fuck, fuck.

Vamps were fast, like ridiculously fast. She may have trained, but she could never match the speed and strength of even a baby Vamp. It was why Paladins normally partnered on vampire contracts.

Alice breathed in, steadying her weight on her legs as she waited.

"I SAID TAKE THIS OUTSIDE!" the barmaid shouted.

"Shut up, Mary." A man grabbed and pulled her to the back of the bar, pushing her through a door.

"Yes, shut up Mary," the Vamp at the back of the pool table echoed, his head tilted to the side as he watched her carefully. His hair was dark, dyed Alice thought, his pale roots showing. He smiled, showing off his large fangs.

The three Vamps were serious Goth rejects, all wearing black trench coats with metal studs. One wore black lipstick, making his skin look even sicklier than it should. The mouthpiece of the group seemed to be content to stand and watch, his relaxed posture unthreatening as he leant against the wall towards the side.

He wasn't a threat just yet, so she turned to the other two, tutting at their appearance as they made their way around the pool table. "Don't you boys know that Vamps have joined the modern world? They don't just wear all black now," she teased.

None of them smiled. *Tough crowd.*

"You're no match for us, witch," the one on the left snarled. He even made the word 'witch' sound dirty.

She turned her attention to him, pointing her blade as she smiled sweetly. "I'm sorry Metal face, I couldn't understand you with all that stuff hanging out of your mouth." That got her a small chuckle from one of the other Vamps.

"Shut it Greig," Metal face growled, shooting his friend a dark look.

Alice turned to the one called Greig. "I don't know what you're smiling about, you're wearing more makeup than the whole of the French renaissance combined." That stopped his chuckle. "Hey, I have a joke for you." They all look at her like she had lost it. "What happened to the two mad Vamps?"

The three guys looked at each other warily. Not sure how to take her.

"What's the answer?" Someone from the back of the pub drunkenly shouted, followed by a bunch of murmurs.

"Well, they both went a bit batty." A cacophony of laughs from behind, the Vamps not reacting at all. "What?" she asked them, shrugging. "That was a good joke."

"Enough of this," Metal Face shouted, leaning over to grab her.

"*Adolebitque.*" She threw her hand towards Metal Face, his shoes catching alight with a bang before he even touched her. He let out a shrill cry, hopping from one foot to the next to stifle the flames.

A fist blurred, just catching her cheek as the hit resonated through her teeth. She flicked her tongue against the inside of her mouth, making sure all her teeth were still present and standing.

Fucking, ow.

In no time at all Greig hit out again, his fist only just missing as she bent out the way.

Fuck me, he's fast, she thought, moving so her back was backed against the bar.

She needed him angry.

"Is that all you got?" she sneered.

That did it.

Timing it perfectly she moved out of the way at the last possible moment, Grieg throwing himself headfirst into the solid wood bar, knocking himself out cold.

One down.

Chants came from behind, mostly encouragement for her but some for Metal Face. Much to his annoyance his new nickname seemed to have caught on. Mr Smitt was one of the people not on her side.

Alice knew as soon as the flames died, the air shifting behind her. "I have another joke," she said as she turned to Metal Face.

He just snarled, fangs flashing.

"What's a vampire's favourite sport?" The crowd behind were clapping along, even calling out guesses. "Batminton."

His hand a blur he grabbed a pool cue and threw it at her, barely missing her head before he jumped forward, fangs bared. The cue stuck into the wall, the end trembling. Her free hand grabbed his neck inches before he could bite her throat. His skin pale, with red blemishes, pimples ready to burst spread chaotically around his young face.

Vampires used to be humans who had had a blood exchange with another vampire, the virus attacking the human DNA and mutating the strands creating an almost immortal. The virus was very temperamental, only certain humans survived the transition. The ones that did lived off of special proteins commonly found in fresh blood. His skin was yet to settle down into its perfection, meaning he was very young in undead terms.

A nail scraped down her neck, warm liquid leaving a trail down her throat. His nostrils flared wildly as her arm blocked his attacks, jaws grinding together as his own fangs cut into his lips, pearls of blood dripping down his chin.

Brown eyes swirled, pupils growing before encompassing the whole eye.

Fuck.

A Vamp attacking was one thing, one in the throes of bloodlust was something entirely different.

Alice held him at arm's length, a nail scratching down her

outstretched arm, clawing to get to her throat. Her arm strained as he started to thrash, his eyes never leaving her pulse as it beat heavily against her neck, his senses all attuned to that one point.

She lifted her sword, impaling it into his chest in one clean move. His mouth opened in shock, the silver penetrating his heart. The crowd gasped, shocked at the sudden turn of events.

Alice twisted the blade, knowing the pain would distract Metal Face enough to think straight, the blade not enough to give him true death. Fairy tales throughout history had gotten that part correct, the only thing that could kill vampires was wood or fire. One thing Hollywood had embellished was that they didn't turn to dust when stabbed. They rotted and smelt like everyone else, which also meant the older the Vamp the worse the smell. It was a shame their affliction to the sun wasn't true either, just a little extra sensitive skin.

Real life was forever disappointing.

"Holy shite!" Mr Smitt cried.

"Now we both know this blade alone isn't enough to kill you." She looked him in the eye, the pupils shrinking, showing more of his natural brown. "But as you can see, I can manipulate fire." She waited, allowing it to sink in. "And we both know what will happen if I put fire in the nice hole in your chest." She let that knowledge bleed into her eyes.

"Enough," the last Vamp said, his eyes flickering between them as he walked around the table. "We'll go."

"Yes. You will." She smiled sweetly, making him pale even more than his natural skin tone. With a quick move she removed the blade from Metal Face's chest, holding it loosely at her side. The crowd erupted into applause as all three vampires left, glasses clinking as they cheered and congratulated each other as if they had a great part in it all.

"Shite, shite, shite," her leprechaun jabbered to himself, fighting against the special cuffs. He looked up at her, eyes wide. "Please, please, I've got gold, lots of gold. I've..."

Blade sheathed she grabbed him, interrupting his babbling as he tried desperately to fight her hold. Black rucksack in hand she started to leave as Mary the bartender blocked the exit.

"You missy are barred. Look at this mess." She waved at the dented bar with the cue still sticking out the wall. "Who will pay for this?"

Alice fought a snappy response, instead pushing past with a screaming leprechaun.

She plopped him on the curb, opening the back of her car before throwing him inside. The handcuffs clicked into a special metal plate embedded into the seats, making Mr Smitt unable to escape.

She turned to him as she got in the driving side, making sure he wasn't trying to damage anything. Snot was smeared across his chubby face, his fists, the size of a three-year-old child's, were clenched together, trying to pull out of the magic infused cuffs.

"Please," his muffled voice begged. "Please, I'm sorry, I really am." He choked like he was going to be sick. She glared at him until he stopped. "Ple... as... se?" he hiccupped.

"Shut up." She leaned back in her chair, closing her eyes to drown out the sobbing.

Blood hell. I'm definitely going to be blamed for this.

CHAPTER FIVE

One. Two. Three. Four.
Alice counted the metal beams running along the ceiling of the studio, several halogen lights hanging from each one. A bird sat and watched from beam number three, his beady eyes judging her as she lay on the mat.

How the bloody hell did a bird get in here?

"Alice, get up," Rose moaned, tapping her foot.

"No." Alice rolled her head to look up at her friend's annoyed expression.

"You're being childish."

"If I get up, you'll beat me up again."

"That's the point." Rose reached down to pull Alice to her feet. "You need to stop letting anger control your fighting. You're making stupid mistakes."

Alice glared as she adjusted her ponytail, several strands of hair already escaped.

Without warning Rose kicked out, aiming high.

"Shit." Alice ducked out the way, swinging her own leg around to hit her opponent's flank.

Rose flashed teeth when the kick connected, spinning her before she regained her balance. "Better." With a right hook she hit out, feigning the movement while she kicked out with her leg, easily tricking Alice and tripping her back onto the mat. With a small jump she pinned her, Rose's forearm pressed into the back of her neck. "But not good enough."

"Fuck," Alice growled, double tapping the mat. "You tricked me."

Rose just shrugged. "You weren't paying attention."

Alice continue her glare before sighing, her chest pumping up and down as she settled her pulse. "You're right. I can't believe I didn't see your thigh tense."

"You need to act, not react."

"Yeah, yeah." Alice balanced on her knees, tilting her head back to stare at the damn bird. It just chirped quietly, flapping its wings before settling down. Rose sat beside her, offering her the water bottle.

"What happened? You're normally a much better opponent."

Alice accepted the bottle. "I don't know, maybe I'm distracted?"

"About the meeting?"

"No." She thought about it. "Maybe? I don't know."

"I think you should talk to someone."

Alice stared at her friend, eyes narrowing when Rose wouldn't keep eye contact. "You need to stop talking to Sam."

"He's just worried. He said the nightmares are getting worse."

"They're fine. I'm fine." With an irritated growl she moved to her feet, her eyes focusing as she noticed a punching bag not being used at the side. Fist clenched she smacked it, her frustration pushing it back to whack against the brick wall.

Rose loudly exhaled. "We love you, you know that?" She went to stand next to the bag, holding it in place.

Alice stopped her assault, her knuckles red and sore. "I know."

"Even after you get fired today and become a stripper that can make slightly above average love charms." Rose ducked at the towel thrown at her head, laughing.

"Very funny." She pressed her cheek against the bag, the sand inside not very comfortable. "We both know I would make brilliant love charms."

Rose tilted her head. "Sure, whatever." With a towel she wiped the sweat from her face. "So, anybody interesting in your life at the moment?"

Alice groaned. "Oh god, please stop talking to Sam. We both know I don't."

"I'm just asking." She lifted her hands up in defence. "I think a good ol' rut is just what you need."

"A good ol' rut?" Alice laughed. "Is that what it's called these days?"

"Well, you wouldn't know." Rose wiggled her eyebrows. "Seriously, I'm sure it will act as a great tension release."

"When you find the other half to that particular equation, let me know." With that she walked towards the locker rooms, moving around the other couples sparring.

The studio was large, several offices converted into the wide, open space. Mats were placed erratically around the floor, each person pulling their own one from the large pile in the corner.

"Oh Alice, I'm glad I bumped into you." A man walked up to her, his white workout shirt see-through from sweat. "I heard from a little birdie that you've been fired," Michael smirked, his ginger hair tied up in a terrible topknot, giving the impression of a single horn. "I'm hardly surprised, considering."

"I can see you're still an arsehole," Alice muttered beneath her breath before she turned with a grimace. "Nice to see you too, Mickey." She started to walk around him when he blocked her path.

"It's Michael." He sniffed at her, his dark green eyes narrowing. She had no idea why he was an arsehole, but decided years ago that was just his personality.

"Well Mickey, I can see your nipples." She pointed at his shirt. As he looked down she slipped past him, continuing her way to the locker rooms.

Where did he hear that? Alice asked herself, slowly getting worried. If rumours were already going around the office, maybe it was possible and her job wasn't safe.

"Hey, wait up." Rose jogged to catch up, her arm coming round Alice's shoulders as they walked. "Ignore dick weed. You know you can't trust anything that comes out his mouth. Only last week he was telling someone how he tagged a bunch of black witches all on his lonesome with his makeshift wand." Rose patted her on the back before moving away. "We both know he hasn't got the skills to make a wand, never mind the funds."

Wands were ridiculously expensive, the small pointy wood able to concentrate a spell a lot easier for the caster, resulting in fewer accidents.

"He even told everyone how he is going to be given a special recognition for it from the Magika!" Rose continued with a snort. "Yeah, maybe recognition for the worst witch in town. He has one of the worst track records in Paladin history."

"Yeah, you're right." Alice said, not quite believing it herself.

"Come on blondie." Rose put her arm around her again. "Let's get you to your meeting. Don't want you to piss off Grayson any more than he already is."

"I'm sure I can manage it."

Adjusting her neatly pressed collar, Alice stared at the clock on her grey cubicle wall, it was one of those Chinese novelty cats that every minute or so looked in the other direction.

The realisation that something could go very wrong in the meeting was dawning on her. Not once in the last five years working under Dread had she been called into an official disciplinary meeting. Yes, she had had more than one warning over the years, but nothing as official as an actual meeting.

The cat's eyes moved to the left, its tail swinging beneath it. Swatting at the blue ball floating lazily around her head she continued to stare at the cat, the eyes swapping to the right once more.

Stupid bloody thing. She swatted at the blue flame again, giving a better impression of a cat than the actual cat clock. *Why do I get a drunken Tinkerbell every time my emotions go to shit?* Alice sighed. *It's probably a physical manifestation of my insanity.*

The blue flame floated over her face, dancing happily, unaware of her less than kind thoughts.

Eyes closed she breathed in, letting the air out slowly, concentrating carefully to calm her nerves, stopping herself from surrendering to a full-blown panic attack.

Okay. I can do this.

She stood up, tucking her white shirt into her black pencil skirt, the outfit chosen specifically to look professional. She even added a black leather necklace, the one Dread bought for her for her nineteenth birthday.

"You can just walk in," Barb drawled from her seated position behind her desk, her attention more on manicuring her nails than her actual job. "It's not like this will take long," she smiled nastily.

Alice hesitated in front of the door, her fingers grasping the handle.

"Well go in then," Barb urged. "You look like an idiot just standing there staring."

Biting her tongue Alice plunged the door open, stepping into the surprisingly light room and closing the latch behind her.

"Alice," Dread greeted, his face unreadable as he sat at his desk. "Take a seat." The blind behind him had been raised slightly, allowing a little sunlight into the room.

Alice looked around with curiosity, never before seeing the office in daylight. The room was framed with dark oak bookshelves, each shelf looking like it had been carved straight from the wall, every one full of books. Alice squinted as she tried to recognise some of the titles, most being in an unfamiliar language. Photographs lined the back wall, some of Dread shaking hands with important people such as members of The Council, London's Mayor as well as few select celebrities.

Looking back at him, she took a seat in the only chair available, the chrome back making her sit as straight as possible.

Dread's eyes drifted to her necklace, his face softening for a second before hardening once more. Alice waited patiently for him to speak first, her hands sweaty as she rested them on her lap. A million scenarios raced through her head as she stared at him, possibilities of outcomes she didn't want to happen. Dread's hand disappeared underneath his desk, something thumping onto the wooden surface a second later.

"A Folder?" Alice felt her whole body turn cold. Dread had pulled out a red manila folder with her name scrawled across the front. It was a thick folder.

"So where shall we start?" Dread flipped over the first page, reading a little before looking up at her. "Ah yes, here we go. December 19th 2011, you turned a Norm into a dwarf."

Oh, crap.

"I did," she replied carefully. "He was stealing the presents under the tree in the shopping mall." The Met thought it was hilarious, a fitting punishment.

"He wasn't a contract."

"He was still stealing." It was only an illusion. She hadn't actually turned him into a dwarf. "I gave him over to the cops didn't I?"

"The point is that it wasn't your job to deal with it. You are not a police officer."

"But..."

"What about August 2012? You used a sleep potion to capture a black witch."

"I'm allowed to use charms, amulets and potions."

"You put to sleep the whole first row of people in that cinema."

"It may have had a weird area of effect."

Won't be buying a cheap potion again.

"September 2013 you almost drowned a kelpie." He looked up at her from over the folder. "I didn't even know you could do that."

Alice began to comment, but he had already continued.

"July 2015 you stabbed a shifter to the point they had to be rushed to the hospital because of silver poisoning."

"How was I supposed to know he had an above average allergy to silver?"

"That's not the point I'm making and you know it. November 2015 you captured a vampire by giving him sunburn."

"He wasn't in any real danger. He was new, he didn't realise the sun wouldn't actually kill him." Alice tried and failed not to smile at the memory, the vampire in question sobbing when she opened the curtain, not realising he wouldn't die from a little vitamin D. It wasn't her fault he was uneducated.

"Alice this isn't a joke." The smile dropped from her face. "You recently had a full-blown fight with three vampires, in front of a room full of people."

"Now that seriously wasn't my fault."

"Not according to the owner. She wants compensation for the damage."

"I never started that fight." Alice leant forward, pressing her palms face down onto the desk.

"So you didn't goad them with jokes?" Dread glared at her hands until she removed them, her sweaty fingertips leaving marks.

"Errr."

Bugger.

"You don't take your job seriously."

"Of course I do! I have the highest success rate in the branch than any other Paladin."

"Highest success rate, but also the highest damage rate." He slammed the folder closed with an audible slap. "I'm giving you a formal warning. You should be grateful it's not worse considering there are plenty more examples where these come from."

Alice pressed her lips together, excuses bubbling up her throat.

"No comment? That's a first."

Alice just stared at him, trying not to piss him off any more than she already was.

Leaning back in his chair he stared back, his eyes squinting suspiciously at her. "Now that the unpleasantries are over with there are a few things I would like to discuss." His cufflinks clunk on the table as he straightened his gold pen. Alice noticed the cufflinks were black, matching the rest of his black suit. The only suit he owned, apparently.

"Okay," Alice replied warily.

"I have a contract for you. One that has had the fee paid in full."

"Really?" she asked, startled. "Private or autho?" Private was someone who personally hired directly through the organisation for a substantial fee.

It's where they got their nicknames as bounty hunters. They weren't bounty hunters, at least, that's not what her Paladin license said.

Autho were contracts passed on through the Met. In those situations the government helped fund the work, being as it technically classed as police work. It was the private jobs that kept S.I. running smoothly, as authority contracts were categorised as government work, which meant minimal funding.

"Private. It seems you made an impression with the local Alpha."

"Seriously?" Alice felt excitement bubble, the thrill of a new contract exhilarating. "What for?"

"This is a very unusual situation. He didn't give me much choice in the matter."

"Didn't give you much choice?"

Dread leant over to his phone, clicking a button on the receiver before a deep grumbling voice filled the room.

"*Commissioner Grayson,*" the phone's speaker squeaked. "*While it is in my interest to take matters further regarding the misunderstanding with one of your Paladins, I have an offer that will please both of us. I would like to hire Alice exclusively for a contract regarding pack business. I've emailed across the appropriate details and will meet with Alice personally for the rest. I look forward to hearing from you.*" The receiver clicked off as the message ended.

"Why me?" That wasn't how S.I. worked. You couldn't pick and choose who worked on a case.

"Like I said, it's unusual, but we don't need the attention of The

Council right now. His threats might be idle, but we cannot take the risk." Dread reached into a drawer, bringing out another folder, this time yellow. Pushing it across the desk he handed it to her. "Mr Wild has your details and will contact you further with any more information."

Picking up the folder she held it to her chest. "Anything else?"

"Don't do anything reckless."

CHAPTER SIX

The car rattled to a stop with a puff of smoke, barely making it into the designated parking space. The Beetle always seemed to sigh once it was turned off, as if it overexerted itself simply by driving around town.

Reaching over she grabbed the folder as a loud bang echoed above her. Without thought, she flung the folder towards the suddenly open car door, holding her palm up in what she hoped was a threatening way. She was just glad she didn't squeal.

"You are late, Miss Skye."

"Huh?" She moved her palm out of the way, having to stretch her neck to see the man standing sullen by her door. He had the folder in one hand, having caught it when she threw it. His other hand was resting on the top of the car, with his body slightly stooped so he could catch her eye.

The Alpha had changed since she last saw him a few days ago, his eyes, as always, shielding any thoughts filtering through his brain. His face was clean-shaven, smooth enough to show his blemish free skin. From what she could see he wore a white buttoned up shirt, with the first couple buttons opened to reveal a tanned chest. His jaw was clenched as if he couldn't control the slight annoyance that she was either late, or that she threw his own folder at him. Probably both.

"How am I late?"

"You left The Tower precisely two hours ago, you don't live that far away."

"You followed me?" she steamed as pushed out with her hand so she could get out the car. He moved enough for her to get out, but not enough that she didn't have to brush against him slightly. She felt even more irritated. "How do you even know where I live?"

"You're intelligent enough to understand how I know where you live, considering you just accused me of following you." He leaned against her car, arms folded as he stared down at her.

She slammed the door shut, internally laughing when the noise and vibrations made him move away.

"As you are in possession of the folder, I assume you have accepted the contract?" He knew he hadn't given her much choice, so she said nothing. "Can we go up to your place so we can discuss it in more detail?"

"Why couldn't we have met at one of the conference rooms?"

"I prefer a more... personal setting." When she hesitated, he handed her back the folder. "Miss Skye, you must understand that this contract is strictly pack business. That means anyone under contract by the pack would come under pack jurisdiction. Do you understand?"

"There's a nice little coffee shop around the corner."

"No. This is private."

Alice weighed her options. "Fine."

She started to make her way towards her home, assuming he would follow. When she opened her door a few minutes later he walked past, his gaze taking in the ruined carpet, cracks in the walls, and mould on the ceiling in one quick sweep. She had the urge to apologise for the state of the place, but didn't.

He was the one who invited himself.

There was a loud techno beat pumping from one of her neighbours, the random thumps and pulses annoying. Alice whacked her hand against the living room wall, something she did regularly. There was no point shouting at them to turn it down, they couldn't hear her anyway.

As Mr Wild went to look at her limited collection of books on her homemade shelf, she heard a knock. It took her a second to realise it wasn't her neighbour whacking the wall back.

"Hello?" A woman's voice called through the front door. "Alice, are you in there?"

Oh god, really?

"Mrs Finch," Alice greeted as she opened the door slightly, blocking the view with her body. "Now is not a good time."

"Oh Alice, turn this awful music down." The old woman pushed the door open further, letting herself in along with one of her dogs. "Oh!" She stopped when she noticed Mr Wild. "I didn't know you had company." She turned her attention back to Alice, the glasses she normally kept secured around her neck sitting on the bridge of her nose, making her chestnut eyes huge in her too-small face. "Alice you should have said you had a young man over. I never see you with anyone, I would have brought over my famous tea."

"He's just a work colleague, Mrs Finch."

"Oh, pity." Her dog cowered by her legs, letting out a tiny growl as it faced the Alpha. "Now stop it Mr Toodle's," she scolded the dog. "I'm sorry, he is never this rude." She grabbed the shaking poodle. "Remember my dear, you would make a great wife." She made sure she looked back at Mr Wild for the last part.

"Goodbye, Mrs Finch." She gently closed the front door behind the old woman. Alice always thought it was strange that she encouraged her to marry any man that would take her, yet Sam wasn't allowed alone with a partner. Admittedly, he did bring home a lot of partners.

"Make sure you turn this music down," she called through the door.

"Nice neighbours," Mr Wild murmured.

"She's okay when she isn't propositioning everyone to be my husband." She thought she heard a slight laugh, but when she turned to face him she decided she must have heard wrong. She threw the folder onto the side table before taking a seat on the sofa. "Now, Mr Wild..."

"It's Rex," he interrupted, distracted. "Do you have cats?" he asked as he perched himself on the chair's arm.

"Cats?" She looked around in case she hadn't realised a cat had somehow gotten in. "Oh, my roommates a leopard."

"Ah." He folded his arms across his chest, nose wrinkled.

Great, she thought to herself. *Not only does the place look awful, it stinks too.*

"So, you don't get many male visitors then?"

No way was she going to touch that.

"Shall we start?" she asked in her most professional voice. She opened the folder, frowning when she noticed only three small Polaroid photographs inside. She tipped the folder upside down just in case there was something stuck, but nothing else came out. She laid out the three photographs neatly, looking at each in turn.

All three were pictures of deaths, two male and one female. They were all different people, yet all three photos were eerily similar. In every one the skin and muscle of the deceased had been peeled from the bone, blood a stark contrast as it congealed along the wounds around their arms and throats.

Alice looked closer, deciding they looked self-inflicted. The female photograph clearly showed skin and blood beneath her fingernails, the size and shape matching the ligature marks around the larger wounds.

"This is all the evidence you need. This is what happens when we don't find my wolf."

"Find?" She looked up at the Alpha then, noticing how he wouldn't look at the photographs, instead watching her. "Is one of your wolves missing?"

"Yes. These are previous wolves that, over the last year, have gone missing. They all end up the same way."

Alice silently gasped, wondering if he was serious. He had said it without an ounce of emotion so it was hard to decide. "Could they not have just decided to leave?" *And had really bad luck*, she wanted to add.

"Pack life is very different Miss Skye, and difficult to understand if you're not a shifter. They are allowed their own lives but they must be part of the pack structure. There are no lone wolves in my territory."

"Have they been autopsied?" She would be interested to confirm how they got some of their wounds.

"No. It wasn't needed."

"Wasn't needed? Something in the report could've helped..."

"It wouldn't have." He wouldn't budge.

She pursed her lips. "How long has your wolf been missing?"

"His name is Roman, and it's been about four weeks."

"Four weeks?" She felt her eyebrows rise. "That's a long time..."

"He isn't dead yet Miss Skye." He quickly looked away. "I would know."

"I didn't mean..." *Fuck.* What could she say to that? "Do you have any other useful information?"

"None that is relevant."

Relevant?

"Do you have any leads for me?"

He scanned her face for a second before answering. His eyes dark enough to tell her it was the man looking at her reactions and not the wolf. "Yes, there is a male wolf in my territory that has become a person of interest. He has been seen on several occasions talking to my men." He glanced down at the photographs before coming back to her. "I hear he will be in Underworld tonight."

"The club?" Alice's ears perked up, she had never been to the upscale Breed nightclub. "It takes months to get on the list…"

"It'll be your job to get in then, wouldn't it?"

She narrowed her eyes. "So you want me to find this mystery man and what?"

"Your job will be to get as much information from him as possible. By any means necessary."

"I can't just torture him." *Also illegal as hell.*

"You will do everything in your power to get the job done. Remember who is paying your wage at the moment Miss Skye."

"It's Agent, Mr Wild. Make sure you remember that." She had about enough of his attitude.

"My men call me Sire."

Alice just heard white noise. He couldn't possibly be asking her to call him Sire? Could he? "That's nice for you." *No way in hell.*

"Fine *Agent* Skye, you may call me Rex." He started to get up.

"Then you may call me Alice." She also stood, feeling uncomfortable to continue sitting when he towered over her.

She flipped the photographs over, not wanting to look at them anymore.

"This is your target." He handed her another Polaroid, this time from his jeans pocket.

She analysed it as he opened her front door. "Wait, will you be there tonight?"

"No, I have prior engagements." He seemed to hesitate at the threshold. "I have instructed my pack to stay away also, I don't want them to interfere." He patted down his pockets before finding a leather scrap. "Before I forget, this is for you." He reached over and grabbed her arm, his thumb stroking the underside of her wrist as he double knotted the leather. "It's a charm, a warning to any shifters that you are off limits."

She stared at the leather plaited bracelet, noticing a crescent moon pendant attached in the middle. "Will this not warn the lone wolf I'm hunting tonight?"

He looked at her as if it was a stupid question. "I will contact you tomorrow regarding any information you discover. Do not miss my phone call." With that he walked away.

CHAPTER SEVEN

The night air felt electric as Alice waited patiently outside the club, the bright red 'Underworld' sign illuminating the line of people waiting behind the long red rope.

"I knew I would get you on a date ma petite sorcière," Danton smiled devilishly.

"It's not a date," she said, rolling her eyes.

"Ah, that's what you think." D just chuckled, adjusting his white shirt to show as much skin of his chest as possible. The colour made his skin even more ghostly pale, bringing out his dark eyes and hair in contrast.

"I appreciate you getting me into the club, although, I think we're both overdressed," she mused, playing with the hem of her dress as she gazed across the crowd of people waiting. The dress she had chosen was provocative enough to show off her limited assets, her breasts considered on the small side. The black fabric was cut low at the front, hinting at a slow curve of flesh with the hem just above her knee. Twin knives were strapped high on her thighs, small blades unlike the one she normally carried down her spine, her favoured sword not able to hide in the backless garment.

"You, my dear petite sorcière..." D touched her bare back in reassurance, leaning down to whisper in her ear. "Look breathtaking." His breath teased her throat. "These women have nothing on your beautè."

"They also have nothing on," Alice noted, shocked at the women's, and even some men's choice of attire. People were pushing the rule of appropriate clothing allowed in public, some only wearing a G-string and a smile, while others had taken hi-vis on to a whole new level. "What sort of club is this?"

Danton didn't even look at them, his interest only for her. "Come, Alice, our table is booked inside." His hand pressed into her back.

"This is a job, not a date." Alice quickly felt under her dress for her knives, making sure the leather holsters were tight to her thighs. If someone happened to glance over they would think she was flashing the crowd, but who were they to judge? "I'm looking for someone..."

"Oui oui, I know, a man with black spiky hair. Can you give me any more information?"

"Only this." She opened her clutch to grab the Polaroid, allowing D to study the grainy photograph of the man.

"Dark hair, dark eyes with pale skin." D looked up at her, his flirtatiousness gone, replaced with professionalism. He could do that, use his sexuality to tease, get his own way. How could you trust someone who could turn it on and off like a light switch?

This was why she didn't date.

"You sure he isn't a vampire?" A direct question.

She shook her head. "You're here to be my spotter."

"Of course. Let me be your arm candy tonight then."

"Lead the way."

Underworld was situated in the Breed district, an old warehouse turned club with a waiting list as long as her arm. The building was painted charcoal grey straight over the brick, with black painted windows looking more like an abandoned asylum than the nightclub apparently hidden inside. Alice stood underneath the large, red neon sign above the metal door, the clubs name manipulated in the glass as a faint beat vibrated through the pavement.

"Come on." D guided her towards the Bouncer, ignoring the glares from the line.

"Evening Mr Knight," the Bouncer welcomed, a huge man of at least six feet, five inches. "Your usual table is ready." He lifted the red rope blocking the door, biceps bulging.

"Welcome to Underworld, where all your darkest desires come true," the woman behind the desk greeted, a fake smile plastered on her face. Her dark hair was tied up into twin peaks at the top of her head, the strands hair-sprayed into fake horns. Her too white teeth flashed beneath blood red lips. "Mr Knight," she nodded towards D, the politeness forced.

"Maggie." He turned on his seductive smile. "How have you been?"

She ignored him, her smile wavering before she recovered. "Ma'am, have you been to our venue before?"

"Oh, no I haven't." Alice tried to ignore the tension.

"Then I will recite the rules. There is no shifting or magic on the premises. Anybody shifting or conducting magic, even something small, will be immediately removed and banned." She pointedly looked at Alice as if she was secretly accusing her of something. "Sharing blood is allowed only as long as it's consented and kept clean. Sex is also allowed as long as it's consented but you can only do that in the booths. Not on the dance floor."

"Sex? That's a joke right?" She looked at D for confirmation. "Bloody hell, really?"

"If someone doesn't leave you alone you are allowed to contact a bodyguard who will assess the situation and decide if one or both of you need removing. Bodyguards can be found hanging around the edges."

"Okay." Alice tried not to worry. She didn't really know what she was getting herself into.

"You may enter through the curtain, enjoy."

"Did you kill her cat or something?" Alice whispered to him as they passed through the thick curtain.

D just laughed, the noise muted compared to the music pumping through the speakers placed strategically across the dance floor. The pulsating beat thumped, the sea of dancers thrusting to the rhythm, sweat a glossy sheen across their bodies.

"Wow." Alice blinked, blinded by the flashing lights. "It's smaller than I imagined."

The room was perfectly square, walls raw, scrapes marking the concrete showing the history of the warehouse. Metal beams lined the ceiling, a string of multicoloured spotlights strung across them. A metal cage hung from the same beams, strategically placed right above the dance floor, holding an almost naked woman dancing provocatively around a pole. To the left was a bar, the entire length of the room with a seating area opposite.

"This way." D grabbed her hand, squeezing his palm against hers as he manoeuvred them through the dancers towards the lounge.

He pushed her into a seat. "What are you doing?" she scolded as she scooted further into the booth.

"We're on a date." He looked genuinely confused.

"This is work." She batted at his hand as he attempted to caress her face.

"Femme stupide. We're here to attract a man? Non? Then we need to make him see you, make him…" He seemed to struggle with his words. "Jaloux. Oui, jealous. He needs to see you above all the other women. You understand?"

"I think so?" *Nope. Not at all.*

"Oh non. Do you know nothing of shifter men? They want what they can't have. Look around the room Alice, what do you see?"

She humoured him, not really understanding. "I don't get it."

"Look at the men, staring hungrily into the throngs of dancers. Staring at women already taken." His eyes flashed in challenge as he leaned down, laying a soft kiss against her throat, just above her pulse. She froze, unsure how to react.

"A drink Mr Knight?" A waitress interrupted, her hair teased into the same twin peaks as the receptionist. Alice broke the contact, shimmying over in the booth to create a barrier of air between them, giving her time to breathe, to think.

The waitress noticed the move, her lips tilting up into a sensual smile. She flashed her neck, making sure he saw her scars. The blood kiss was an addiction, people doing anything to get their next fix of the euphoria a vampire bite could give. They didn't seem to understand the predator they had at their throats, the ecstasy they felt was a pheromone the fangs secreted into tricking their prey into feeling pleasure, not pain as they drain your lifeblood. Poetic really.

The waitress bent to put the bottle of champagne into the icebox, making sure her short skirt became even shorter.

"Would you like anything else, sir?" she said, arousal heavy in her eyes.

"That would be all," he dismissed, his eyes hard as he looked at Alice. Pouting, the waitress walked away, adding an extra sway to her hips. "Now where were we?"

D reached for the bottle, pouring two glasses before setting it back down.

"The most basic instinct is desire, we need these men in the room to desire you. To notice you. If this man you are after is here, he must pick you above the rest."

"What has you kissing me got to do with anything?"

"Trust me..." Gently grabbing her face he leaned down to press a soft kiss.

When she didn't move, he added a slight pressure, licking gently along the seam of her lips.

"Let me in." His lips were talented as he kissed her again, enticing her into joining in. A subtle movement of her jaw and he groaned, rewarding her with another lick.

She kissed him back, their tongues fighting for dominance. She started to enjoy herself, teasing him with quick movements of her tongue. Feeling brave she wrapped her hands in his hair, angling his face for a better...

Blood on her tongue, her gasp breaking the contact.

"Mon ami, you can ask me to be your spotter anytime," he grinned, showing fangs tipped in red.

Alice stared at his lips, deciding whether to kiss him again. The feeling quickly passed. D wasn't her type. Neither was the Alpha, yet she wished it was him she had been kissing.

Bloody hell. She really needed to get laid.

D's eyes glittered as he looked at her, his gaze drifting as something behind caught his attention. "Ah, the kiss worked."

Subtly, Alice looked over her shoulder, quickly surveying the eyes staring at their little corner in the lounge. "You were right." Picking up her glass she downed the rest of her champagne, not wanting the good stuff to go to waste.

"Of course, like I would trick you into a kiss without having a plan." A dark chuckle. "I'm just waiting for you to confess your undying love."

"You're funny."

"Oui, oui," he dramatically sighed. "My heart bleeds."

"I'm sure one of the waitresses could help with that."

"C'était méchant. Go look tempting elsewhere. I have women to talk to."

She leaned in close, whispering in his ear. "Remember the picture, he has black spiky hair." She made it look as sensual as she could, feeling eyes prickle across her skin. With those words she stood up from the table, feeling him watch her as she made her way across the room towards the bar.

Fighting her way along the dance floor she sat on an empty stool at the end, swinging so she could see along the long length. Hundreds of coloured bottles lined the shelving stacked against the wall, all lit up with a spotlight. A huge floor-to-ceiling mirror stood behind the bottles, dancers replicated onto the surface.

She watched the dancers spin around, dancers who were lost to the music, eyes closed and drinks held high up the air as they swung their hips.

She scanned their faces, trying to find anyone who matched the photograph.

"Now what I find peculiar..." Alice spun her stool, trying to hide her disappointment at the blonde standing behind her. "Is what are you doing with a Vamp?" The man smiled, a sensual curve of his lip as his eyes fell to her cleavage. He flared his chi, a greeting, a test among witches to see who was more powerful. The sensation an electric current across her flesh.

Alice concentrated on not flaring her own chi, something that was almost instinct when greeting another witch. She didn't want to encourage him, or gain any more unwanted attention from the wrong man.

"Not interested," she said, turning away.

A hand came down on her shoulder, spinning her back. "What? Your own Breed not good enough then?" He sat beside her, seemingly unaware of her disinterest. "You want to stay with fang-face?" He nodded towards the lounge. "I'm pretty sure he's busy."

Alice couldn't help but look, spotting D in the same booth she had kissed him in earlier, but this time he was joined by two other women.

"He's an adult." An adult who was supposed to be paying attention.

"You need a real man." He gripped her chin in his free hand, forcing her to look at him. "Someone who can show you a real good time." He flicked his hair, the dark blond razor cut at the sides.

"I said I'm not interested." She added an extra bit of bite to her words, breaking his hold.

"Is this gentleman bothering you?" A large hand came down on the blonde's shoulder, squeezing gently.

"Fuck off man, I saw her first," the witch sneered.

The new stranger leant forward. "She says she isn't interested. So fuck off." The blonde witch paled.

The stranger turned to look at her, his eyes dark, the iris covering most his eye, leaving barely any white.

Holy crap.

"Has he offended you?" His dark eyebrows came low on his face, the same shade on his head, hair spiked up with gel in every direction possible.

She appraised him quickly before smiling, making sure to bite her lip seductively. Well, as seductively as she could manage. "He was just leaving."

"No, I fucking wasn't," the blonde witch scowled. "I wanted to buy you a drink."

"Excuse me." He grabbed the scruff of the blonde and started dragging him towards the emergency exit. "Stay there pretty lady, I'll be back in a moment."

Alice hesitated, her instinct and training telling her to follow them, but her brain telling her to wait. *Shit.*

She couldn't break cover.

Cursing under her breath she turned to the lounge, the booth now completely empty. "Great." She scanned the crowd, looking for Danton. "Dammit." Inside her clutch she grabbed her phone, sending a quick text instead.

A drink was plopped in front of her, a pink sparkly concoction with a long straw and an orange paper umbrella. She jumped as it cracked against the bar, her attention elsewhere.

"See, I said I would be back." The dark haired stranger gently pushed the glass of pink liquid toward her, his knuckles red and scraped.

"Is that other guy okay?" she asked, staring at his hand as she ignored the drink.

"He's fine. Just dandy."

He started rolling up the sleeves of his black dress shirt, the hair on his arms black and baby fine. Thick veins pulsated beneath his skin, like snakes stretching beneath the flesh.

"I bought you the drink to apologise for how you were treated."

"I appreciate it," Alice said as he grinned. "But I don't accept drinks from strangers."

"If you don't want it, I'm sure I can find someone else," he sniffed before he clutched the glass.

Shit. Shit. Shit.

She needed to keep his attention.

"What's your name?" she asked quickly. "If I know your name, then we're not strangers."

"Name's Tomlin, but you can call me Tom. What's yours?" His hand fanned out, his nails a sickly blue as if blood struggled to get to the fingertips.

The hairs on the back of her neck stood on edge. "Leela." Her palm touched his outstretched hand, the skin ice cold.

"Nice to meet you." His eyes watched her, like onyx. The look similar to a vampire close to bloodlust, yet, Alice knew he wasn't a vampire. She didn't even get a shifter vibe from him.

Could Rex have gotten his Breed wrong?

Trying not to stare she sucked the straw between her lips, groaning as a small amount of the summer berries hit her tongue, the alcohol burning deliciously down her throat. She was careful only to sip, conscious that she didn't order it herself.

The music renewed, a dance anthem pulsating through the speakers. The crowd continued to dance, all the bodies thrusting and swaying in tempo with the music.

"Hey, this is really good," she shouted at him over the music.

"Of course it is," he smiled, showing a row of sharper than usual teeth.

Alice tried to keep her shudder to herself. It wasn't exactly uncommon for some shifters to file their teeth, but it was creepy.

"So, you come here often?" He leaned in close, his breath just as cold as his skin against her cheek.

"My first time." She tried to lean away, using her drink as an excuse as she sipped, the alcohol helping against his intense cold. "I'm from out of town."

"You here alone?" He watched her throat swallow, his leg vibrating, fidgeting.

"I'm actually here with someone, but he seems to be more interested in other women than me." Alice stuck her bottom lip out, feigning disappointment. "Good thing you're here to keep me company."

He encouraged her to swallow faster. "Drink up, I want to dance."

"I can't dance," she said around the straw. She lazily sucked up the last of the liquid, her head spinning before she blinked the blurriness away.

Why was she here again? *Oh yeah.* She needed to ask him questions, or get him into a more private area. "Do you want to...?"

He grabbed her hand before she finished the question, pulling her towards the dance floor.

She felt herself drifting, not able to feel her legs.

"You can dance with me."

Alice didn't feel the hem of her dress rise before his cold hands touched her bare skin, fingers kneading into the flesh as he pulled her flush against his chest. Hands tight, he matched their movements to the heavy beat of the music.

"See, you can dance." He twirled her around so her back was now to his chest, his hands coming up to hold her waist.

"I feel sick." She fought the sudden nausea. She had only taken a few sips, why was she nauseous?

"Don't be silly." He continued to move them, his hands exploring her body through her thin dress. Pulling free she turned around, clutching her head as his face blurred.

"Leela, come here." He grabbed her arm, the pain sharp as his nails dug in.

Who the fuck is Leela?

"Ow." She pushed out, barely moving him.

"ALICE!" A voice called through the crowd. Lights flashed as she tried to look for the source, her head groggy.

Hands grabbed her, yanking her away from the dance floor as she was pushed through the crowd.

"ALICE...MERDE. MOVE OUT THE WAY!" That voice again, yelling.

Alice felt herself fall to her knees, the music pounding in her head as she tried not to be sick. She was suddenly lifted, her stomach pressed against something hard as she felt fresh air against her skin, the stench of rotten food assaulting her nose a moment later.

"Put me down." She tried to wiggle free, the movement painfully slow. "I'm going to be sick." She was roughly settled onto her feet. "Oh my god." She closed her eyes, the cold air amazing against her fevered skin.

"I thought we could speak more privately out here." A cage of arms surrounded her, pushing her against the brick wall.

Concentrating, she looked at her surroundings, trying desperately to figure out where she was through the haze. Huge dustbins lined the brick walls on both sides, each one under a streetlamp. A cat hissed, eyes reflective as it scuttled away.

"Where are we?" Her breathing became laboured as she felt exhaustion taking over, her heart beating faster than usual.

She had to think fast.

Hand stiff she released a blade, the familiar weight settling into her palm.

Tom leaned forward, not noticing her knife as his lips began assaulting hers, shoving his tongue into her mouth. A hand wrapped around her neck, slamming her head against the brick wall hard enough she saw stars. His eyes were wide, watching her as his pupils narrowed to slits, like a snake.

Disorientated, Alice struggled against him, exciting him further as his lips travelled down the side of her neck.

"Ever heard of the word no?" The words came out slurred, her tongue thick in her mouth. Slowly she brought up the knife, the blade sharp enough to sear into his chest with little effort.

"FUCK!" He leapt back, snarling with his sharp teeth. Lifting a hand he backhanded her, causing her to collapse almost unconscious against the wall. "You'll pay for that," he growled, pulling the blade out of his chest as if it was nothing.

Using the knife, he bent down to cut the straps off her dress, the black material sagging against her skin. Hands gripped in the material, he lifted and pushed her face first against the wall.

"Stop struggling." He settled his weight, her legs pinned with his own.

Something warm against her neck, a tongue lapping across her flesh. His hands ripped more of the fabric, searching beneath under her skirt.

"Fuck me. How many knives do you have?" he growled, chest vibrating. Her head was wretched to the side, held at an angle as he wrapped her blonde strands around his fist.

"Stop," Alice whispered, legs heavy as a sharp pain sliced into her neck. Heat poured from her throat, dripping down her back.

Tom groaned, his teeth tearing through her flesh much like her knife did his chest.

Abruptly, Alice collapsed, Tom's body no longer there to keep her up. Her knees screamed in shock as they connected with the stone floor, the pain dull and throbbing in time with her pulse. Groggily, Alice leant onto her hands, her head hanging low as she struggled to stay awake, arms shaking violently at the weight.

Something burned against her neck, the pain intense as it ripped through the numbness that threatened to take over her body.

A familiar voice, the words incoherent as the world went dark.

"**M**um?" she called once more, her voice wobbling. Bear clutched tight to her chest, she walked further down the staircase, her bare feet cold against the hard wood.

Another crash. The lights flicker ahead before turning off, covering her in complete darkness.

"Kyle if that's you, it's not funny."

Still no response.

Padding down the hallway she pushed the kitchen door, soft light flickering beneath the frame.

"Mummy?" Her voice wet, close to tears. Door heavy, she pushed it harder. "Daddy?" She stepped forward, the light from the window creating a weird glow across the floor, like it was shiny.

A growl vibrated through the air behind her.

In a panic she ran further into the kitchen, her ankle twisting as she slipped on something wet. "Ahhhh," she cried, using her hand to help her sit up before slipping back into the warm liquid.

Drip. Drip. Drip.

She lifted her hand, the dark substance drizzling down her wrist to her elbow in a hot stream. Holding her breath, she listened, not hearing anything in the room with her.

Thwack. Thwack. Thwack.

Tears left a warm trail down her face. "Mummy?" she whispered.

Something walked down the hallway.

Thwack. Thwack. Thwack.

Scrambling against the tiles she tore open a cupboard, squeezing her body into the small space, pushing the bottles of bleach and detergent out the way.

Door shut, she placed her hand over her mouth, the warm liquid tasting coppery against her lips. Blood pumped in her ears, making it hard to concentrate on any sounds outside as darkness surrounded her.

CHAPTER EIGHT

Alice jumped awake, a scream caught in her throat, the nightmare fading as her head ached, a rhythmic pounding inside her temple. Closing her eyes, she tried to remember the dream, visualising a shadow standing over her, the face obscured by darkness.

Her nightmares were a shattered memory created by a scared child, too broken to be pieced together.

Something licked her fingers, the tongue rough. Turning her head she stared at the leopard half lying across her legs, Sam's huge eyes staring back at her expectantly.

"Sam?" she asked the leopard, her voice harsh, even to her ears. Sam purred in response, curling further onto her legs so his fur came into focus. His leopard was a glorious gold, his rosettes a deep black that turned into a warm brown. It made him pretty, and he knew it.

THUMP, THUMP, THUMP.

Sam jumped up, his hackles rising as a growl erupted from his throat.

THUMP, THUMP, THUMP.

In one motion she swung her legs off the bed, her knees giving out immediately. "Bloody hell!" Her arms slapped against the side table as she tried to stop her fall.

"FEMALE?" A voice shouted in the distance.

THUMP, THUMP, THUMP.

"SHUT THE FUCK UP!" A different voice, this one further away. Probably one of her neighbours.

Sam paced in front of her bedroom door, shooting through the opening once she turned the handle. He quickly ran to the front door and sniffed along the edge, peering back at her anxiously with amber eyes before disappearing into his bedroom.

"ALICE! ARE YOU IN?"

THUMP, THUMP, THUMP.

She unlocked the front door and opened it, only then realising she was wearing just a sleep shirt, one barely covering her underwear, but it was already too late. Rex stared, a blush burning the back of her neck as his gaze leisurely rolled over her ruffled hair and bare legs. Alice felt herself fidget as he looked at the length of her body, his eyes hardening as he noticed the bruises.

"Can I help you?" she asked politely, pretending everything was normal and she didn't have a hangover from hell.

Silently he walked in, slamming the front door behind him. "Do you ever answer your bloody phone?"

Head pounding, she closed her eyes, trying not to throw up as pain resonated through her skull.

A warm hand gripped the top of her arm.

"You okay?"

"Does she bloody look okay?" Sam leaned against the wall, wearing only a pair of boxers. His long blond hair swept over one shoulder, draped elegantly across his bare chest. Clicking his tongue Sam pointedly looked Rex up and down, his face clearly unimpressed. "You must be the Alpha."

"You must be her cat," Rex replied, ignoring Sam's scowl. He turned back to Alice, dismissing the leopard. "What happened?" He reached out to touch her face, his eyes betraying nothing, yet his hand was feather light on her skin.

"Danton brought her back from the club," Sam stated, bringing their attention back to him. "He said she was attacked, he had to seal her wounds." Sam licked out his tongue in demonstration.

Alice jumped when Rex leaned down to sniff her neck, his clean-shaven cheek rubbing against hers.

"Get off my girl," Sam growled, stepping between them and forcing Rex to move back.

"Your girl, huh?" Rex tilted his head, nostrils flaring.

"Both of you stop it." She put her hand on Sam's arm, quieting him down. "Did D say anything else?"

Sam stared at Rex for a few seconds more, the warning clear. "Not really."

Sam caught Alice's gaze. *How do you feel?* he silently asked, not wanting the Alpha to understand his concern. It was a trick they had learnt from Dread, being able to read someone's eyes.

Could be better, she replied the same way.

"I'll put the kettle on," she said aloud before turning to the kitchen. Her headache thumped, someone clearly dancing the foxtrot across her brain. Painkiller in hand, she swallowed it dry as she turned on the kettle, waiting for it to boil. Her foot tapped as she waited, the motion causing the headache to radiate so she stopped, closing her eyes instead.

"Your boyfriend's getting ready for work," Rex said, a telltale squeak as he settled himself onto one of her flimsy chairs. "Right after he threatened me, of course."

Alice turned then, hearing slight humour in his voice. She still couldn't decipher him, his face relaxed, his eyelashes low across his eyes, shielding his thoughts. Did he know she was trying to read him? Everyone had tells, facial twitches, rapid blinking, smiles that didn't reach their eyes. All subtle indicators of emotion, even deception. She could read people well.

Yet, she couldn't read him, at least, not when the man was in control. His beast, as she was beginning to learn, was rawer in his emotions. How was she supposed to know what he was thinking if he was constantly in control?

Deciding not to acknowledge his last statement she grabbed a mug, pouring him a drink.

"Here." She handed it over to Rex, suppressing a smile when he lifted it to his lips, revealing the hidden joke.

'*TWAT*' was written neatly in white along the bottom, only visible when someone tipped the mug at a certain angle.

"Thanks," he grumbled, setting the mug down. "Do you remember anything from last night?"

Alice took a sip of her own tea before answering, the painkiller working miracles as it soothed down her throat. "I was dancing..." She shook her head, trying to remember but stopped when her brain threatened to explode. "I was carried outside," she continued, her eyes closed as she tried to remember.

"Anything else?" A whisper, his voice closer than it was before. Startled she opened her eyes, his face only a centimetre away, his lashes low, eyes watching her mouth. Heart racing, she licked her dry lips, his gaze following the action before he looked up at her, his blue eyes radiating something she couldn't read.

"Erm."

"Baby girl, have you seen my work shirt?" Sam walked in, taking in the situation with a quick sweep of his eyes. Alice jumped back, heat burning across her cheeks. "Well, don't let me interrupt you."

"You didn't interrupt anything," Alice stuttered.

"Sure I didn't," Sam smirked, jumping up onto the kitchen counter, his chest still bare as he swung his denim clad legs. "Nice mug," he commented.

Rex frowned, still not understanding the joke. "Tyler, my second is on his way over, he might know some more information."

"What about how you guys let Alice be attacked?" Sam smiled sweetly, his eyes staring at the floor as he baited Rex.

Alice just audibly sighed. "I need to shower." She stretched her arms up, enjoying the click before she realised both men were staring at her. "I won't be long." She called behind as she hurried to the bathroom.

She tried not to think of them alone, as the possibility of walking out with the kitchen in ruins ran through her head.

They were adults, they could behave themselves.

Deciding to make the shower quick, she stepped in front of the mirror, groaning when she saw the top she was wearing. She thought she had on one of her sleeping shirts.

Apparently not.

The words *'Things to do with a pussy...'* was written across her chest. *'Play with it'* was on the left breast and *'Lick it'* was on the right, both placed either side of the image of a black cat, its paws reaching down to play with the bottom hem.

Yes, the Alpha of one of the largest packs in Britain had seen her wear nothing but an obscene t-shirt. In her defence, it wasn't hers.

Hopefully he saw the humour in it. Which was doubtful.

Bloody hell.

In one swift movement she pulled off the t-shirt, throwing it into the corner of the small bathroom. She risked a look in the mirror, the harsh bathroom light highlighting the bruises across her skin.

"Shit." She bared her throat, remembering the sharp pain the night before. The skin had a purplish tone that was starting to turn a sickly yellow. Hesitantly she reached up, the skin smooth and unbroken.

A vampire's saliva was famous for its healing qualities, a few licks and they could close most superficial wounds, which made sense evolutionarily speaking, considering they have to cut someone to feed. Better to be able to heal them afterwards rather than let their dinner bleed to death.

It's was just lucky her bite wasn't deep enough to cause more damage, and even luckier she had D around to close it.

Turning to the shower she operated the dial. The old shower head wheezed, sputtering before water poured from the many holes. The bathroom, just like the rest of the place, was old and broken. They had painted over the tiles when they first moved in, the colour now an off white unlike the bright green it was before. The shower hung above the old bath, the panels avocado coloured and cracked.

The water was scalding when she stepped into the stream, the water unknotting the tangle of hair as bits of debris and flakes of brick began to fall out. Lathering her lavender soap, she stroked down her arms, across her breasts and lower over her stomach. The water at her feet was a rusty red, the colour becoming paler before disappearing altogether. Startled, she searched over her body for an open wound, not finding anything. She turned to look at herself in the mirror, able to just see if she leaned slightly. Dried blood, mostly washed away was patched across her shoulder blades and back.

Her hand went up to her neck again, reassuring herself that her throat was whole.

A loud crash, followed by a shout.

Wiping the water from her face she listened, thinking she had imagined it.

Another crash, this time the door vibrating as something smashed against it.

"Fuck." She hopped out of the shower, steadying herself as she started to slip on the tiled floor.

Grabbing a towel from the rack she opened the door, almost running into the back of Sam. He stood in the way, his shoulders bunched as he stood guard.

"Sam?" she asked, trying to peer around his shoulders. "What's happening?"

"Dominance issues." He turned so she couldn't see. "I wouldn't come out."

She ducked underneath his arm, her gaze narrowing as she noticed a vase smashed on the floor. One of the small things she actually liked.

"What the hell is going on?"

A loud growl turned her head, the sofa having been pushed across the room. Rex was crouched on the floor, it took her a few seconds to see the man underneath.

"What are you doing?" She took a step forward, stopping when she heard a warning bark. Rex leant forward, his hands on either side of the stranger with his teeth bared. "Enough!" she shouted.

Rex snarled, jumping up to stand in the corner, his eyes gone completely wolf. The wolf watched her, anger, desire, and vengeance flashing across his eyes too fast to read.

"Alice stay back." She felt Sam grab her arm, pulling her away. "Be careful," he whispered in her ear. "Rex's beast is in control." Shifters were one with their beasts, sharing the same body but two personalities, the beast half being the more savage of the temperaments.

"What happened?" she asked, whispering back. The stranger on the floor slowly came to his knees, his head still tilted painfully to the side.

"His second needs to show submission."

"What? Why?"

Sam shrugged against her. "The pack has a hierarchy. Stops them from fighting amongst themselves."

"You're not like that," she commented, continuing to stare at the man on his knees. Confused, she looked up at Rex, his eyes like ice, the wolf having its own internal dilemma. She had no idea what to say to calm the situation, especially to a wolf in human skin. She would describe herself as experienced with shifter culture, having lived with and worked with many. She knew the higher the dominance, the better control over their beast. An Alpha had complete control. Yet, Rex didn't seem to.

"I'm not a wolf." Sam fidgeted next to her, his own beast reacting to the uncomfortable atmosphere.

Rex was pulling an aura, something all Alphas or dominant shifters could do to get weaker shifters to submit. Sam might not be a wolf, but his animal was fighting instinct not to succumb to the power. She could feel it across her chi, the essence of her magic connected to her own aura. It was like a gentle river across her senses, persuasive and calming. It was trying to quiet the room, control the beasts.

She wasn't a beast.

"Are we done here?" she asked the wolf, showing him he wasn't the only Alpha here. At least, if there was such a thing as a witch Alpha.

Rex continued to stare, unblinking focus as he took a step forward. Sam tensed, ready to intervene.

"Go get dressed." Rex's gaze roamed over her exposed flesh, the towel only just covering the important bits. "I'll clean up the mess." His voice was strained, deeper than usual. Looking through her lashes she watched him, his face immobile, jaw still clenched.

He was fighting for control.

Sam pulled her into the bedroom, using his larger body to block the door. Shifters kept their human consciousness when shifted, they were able to see through the eyes of their animal and help decide what actions to take. That's what Sam had told her once. He had also explained that when they shift, the animal can take over. They were a more animalistic personality, more unpredictable. That's what she had felt staring at Rex, his animal reacting to something she couldn't see, the man having no control over his animal's instincts.

"He has little control over his beast," Sam commented as she started to dress, a steady growl vibrating across his bare chest. "How can someone as powerful as that have no control?"

She knew it was rhetorical, but felt herself answering anyway. "I don't know." But she sure as hell was going to figure it out. "Go to work Sam."

"And leave you with the granny killer? I don't think so baby girl."

"Granny killer?" She threw him one of his work shirts that had been mixed with her own clothes. He quickly pulled it on.

"My, what big teeth you have," he mocked in a high girly voice. "Better to eat you with my dear." He gnashed his teeth together.

Alice let out a snort. Sam, forever dramatic. "He's hired me for a job…"

"He looks at you like you're dinner."

"This is stupid." She wasn't going to admit what she saw in his eyes. Didn't even want to think about it. "You know I have to do this."

Sam pressed his lips together. "Call me if you need me." He opened the bedroom door, storming out. She heard the front door slam a moment later.

Great, now Sam is pissed. Frustrated, she pulled at her hair, tying it up into a relatively neat ponytail before she walked back into her living room.

The stranger was standing in the corner, his arms crossed as his eyes followed her. His hair was dark, darker than the mahogany of his skin and shaved close to his skull, military style. His nose was the only thing ruining his otherwise perfectly symmetrical face, a too large nose that had clearly been broken at least once or twice.

"Hi," Alice greeted, "you must be Tyler." The man just replied with a shallow nod. He openly stared at her, his hazel eyes tracing details across her face. "You don't talk much do you?" That got her a head tilt, otherwise no other reaction.

This was Rex's second?

"You challenging my second, Alice?"

She turned to the man in question, his eyes once again in control. *Challenging him?*

"No."

"Then why were you staring?"

"I was watching his eyes, they're almost as unreadable as yours," she confessed. Rex pursed his lips, nodding to Tyler. The other man left quietly a second later. Alice scrutinised the whole scene, not understanding. "I thought we needed him?"

"We do, he will be meeting us at the club."

"So we're going back?"

"Yes." Rex watched her neck, his eyes tracing the bruises.

She moved into the kitchen, noticing how nothing was broken or misplaced. Even the grains of her pentagram she had forgotten to clean up were undisturbed, the salt teased into a five-pointed star within a circle. Pulling her spelling pot from the cupboard, she set it gently onto the pentagram, careful not to smudge the lines. Rex stood silently, leaning against the doorway.

"I can't walk around like this," she gestured to her neck before opening a drawer next to the sink and grabbing a small wooden disk.

Complexion spells were one of the few amulet charms she could create from memory. However, it was expensive to create, so like everybody else with a tight budget she bought ready-made ones. They weren't as good.

Rex just grunted.

"So what's the plan?" she asked while placing the wooden disk into the bowl, pouring the store bought complexion potion over the disk gently. It would create an amulet, specifically designed for skin imperfections, freckles, blemishes, discolouration and even bruises. They would all be covered with the complexion veil, magic that concealed the imperfections under a shroud.

"The plan is to see if we can track that wolf." Rex had walked quietly behind her, peering inquisitively into the pot.

"How would you track him?"

"Tyler is a tracker. One of the best."

"Like a bloodhound?" She turned her back, gently turning the wooden disk to soak up the potion. *"Ignis."* The disk burst into flame, eating up the remaining liquid.

"An accurate description. However, I wouldn't call him that to his face." The flame died out, turning the wooden disk a few shades darker. With a knife she cut a small line along the tip of her thumb.

"What are you doing?" Rex grabbed her arm, his tongue licking out to catch the drop of blood.

"Seriously, that's the second time in less than twelve hours someone has sucked or licked me." Rex's eyes flashed, his reaction unsettling her. "I need to activate the charm." She tugged against him until he released her arm. Watching him suspiciously from the corner of her eye she squeezed her thumb, letting a single drop of blood hit the disk. Instantly there was a little fizzle, the scent of ozone strong in her nose.

"Why your blood?"

"I have special enzymes, it's used as a reagent that reacts with the ingredients to turn on the magic's effect." Spinning the wood she smiled, feeling the magic thrum into her fingertips. She slipped the disk between the leather bracelet Rex had given her and tightened the cord, anchoring the disk flat to her skin.

"It's gone." A warm hand stroked across her neck, the skin unusually soft for a man. She remained still, not able to see who was in control.

"Yes, that's the point." She stepped back from Rex's palm, unsure of her feelings. Butterflies attacked her stomach, a confusing reaction considering he wasn't usually her type. Yes, she found him fairly attractive, but the reaction she felt was more than just attraction. It was an intense longing, like she couldn't breathe unless he was beside her. She had never felt like that with anyone, was confused by it. Lust, yes, endless desire? No. That's what worried her.

She swallowed, Rex's eyes following the movement. That was the problem with dominant shifters, you never knew if you were prey or not.

Her libido didn't seem to care.

"So are we going?" she asked, distracting him, or maybe it was herself. With a slow nod he turned away, assuming she would follow.

CHAPTER NINE

The nightclub looked creepy in the daylight, just a drab grey building with black painted windows, more like a drug den than the upscale Breed club she knew to be hidden inside.

White and blue police tape blocked them from entering the shadowed opening to the side. Alice hesitated at the tape, staring at the array of police officers talking animatedly to one another. One took a photograph behind a dumpster, the flash momentarily washing the alley in white.

"Excuse me," someone asked, stepping around them so they could bend beneath the tape. Alice automatically moved out the way, her eyes fixated on the 'coroner' embroidery on their black jumpsuits.

"Shit." Rex widened his stance, folding his arms over his chest. "What are they doing here?"

"I don't know." Alice tried to peer down the alley, the police officers blocking everything. "Can you see anything?"

"No civilians," a man barked.

Alice spun towards the voice. "Excuse me?"

"I said no civilians." The man tapped his pen to the white notebook clutched in his hands. "You should move along now."

"What happened?" Rex asked, his body language closed off.

"Are you, or are you not a civilian?" The man absently tapped the breast of his shirt, scowling when he realised the shirt had no pockets as if he was used to wearing a coat or jacket.

"I'm Agent Alice Skye from..."

"With S.I.?" he frowned, turning towards the alley. "Hey, who called the freaks in?"

"No one called us," she interrupted, grinding her molars. "We were just passing by."

"Hmmm," he gawked at her, taking in her blonde hair and height. "You don't look like a Paladin." He glared at Rex. "You don't look like one either."

"Well, what do we look like Officer?"

"It's Detective, Detective O'Neil."

"Fine, Detective. Would you rather just tell us what's happened or do I call this in and officially report it?"

"You can't do that. This is my case." He eyes narrowed as he scanned her up and down.

"So from the coroner's van I assume there is a body?" she politely asked, changing tactics.

The Detective grumbled. "Yes, you assume correctly. John Doe found around six this morning."

"Breed?"

"Not sure," he answered as his hand absently stroked his dark goatee, the hair peppered with grey. "Which is why we haven't called you guys yet." He glared between them, his eyes lingering on Rex. "You have any ID?"

She pulled out her phone, showing him the document and ID proving her Paladin status. He grunted as he checked the details. Charming man.

"Fine. You can come take a look, but only you." Rex tensed, not saying anything. "I don't need civilians walking all over my crime scene."

"Okay."

"This way Alice..."

"It's Agent Skye."

"Skye then."

Detective O'Neil guided her past the array of people, ignoring the distasteful looks from the other Officers.

"Like I said, John Doe was found around six. We can't be sure, but we have been given an estimated death of around eleven the previous evening."

"Who found him?" Alice questioned, her mind already looking for details. From the number of men standing over in the corner, she guessed that was where the body was. There were spots of blood along the floor, small, only specks across the concrete. More blood was spotted across the walls, as if someone was hit with such force blood exploded from an open wound, or an orifice such as the mouth.

"The Bouncer." He got out an e-cigarette from his trouser pocket, slipping it between his lips he sucked it hard. It caused the end light to flare orange, giving the impression of a real cigarette. "He's standing over there giving a statement to Officer Palmer." He nodded in the general direction.

Alice looked behind her, recognising the large man.

"The deceased is over here."

She followed him to the body half hidden behind the dumpster, bin bags and rubbish half covering the male. Kneeling, she looked closer, her breath catching as she recognised the witch from the night before, the blonde who kept pestering her.

"You have a positive ID yet?" she asked, proud her voice didn't show how unnerved she was at the realisation. It was one thing to see a dead body, it was another to see one that she saw alive only hours earlier. She felt her face scrunch up, annoyed and disappointed with herself.

Should have followed my gut. I shouldn't have let this happen.

"Not yet." The Detective watched her face carefully, noting her reaction. She quickly calmed her face, relaxing it to impassivity. He slowly sucked from his fake cigarette, holding it in before looking at the end with disgust. "Nothing in his pockets."

"It's clear he was dumped here, but wasn't killed." She raised her hand to the blood splatters against the brick, her fingertips tracing the formation gently. "He was punched first, possibly in the face."

"What makes you say that?" He watched her face again.

It made her uncomfortable.

"The blood specks behind us, quite a distance away from the main pool of blood around the body. Something hit him, hard. There is no spray over here even through it's clear he had his throat cut."

"That's what we thought," he agreed, nodding at her. "Impressive, I didn't realise Paladins did this type of work." He turned the cigarette off, putting it back into his pocket.

"You would have to cross-reference the autopsy but I would give money that it wasn't the initial throat slit that killed him." When he didn't correct her she continued. "The blood surrounding the body is not enough, even added to the initial spray behind us it wouldn't be enough to kill him. The wound around his neck is congealed, dried. Are there any bite marks?" She bent to touch the body, pulling her hand back when she remembered she wasn't wearing gloves.

"Why would you ask about bite marks?" He handed her a pair of plastic gloves from his pocket. She slipped them on before kneeling back beside the body, careful to not touch any of the blood.

"The throat is slit to the bone..." She pulled the head up gently, showing the spinal cord clearly through an open wound. "Carotid artery is cleanly cut, all his lifeblood should have flowed onto the floor. But it hasn't, so my first thought would be he was drained of blood first." She softly felt along the neck of the deceased, eventually finding a row of holes in the hollow between his neck and shoulder. "His throat was slit to try to hide the bite. Have you found the weapon?"

"My boys are looking." He accepted the gloves back when she handed them over. He assessed her, it was nothing sexual, more like a man who was evaluating his prized horse. He nodded to himself as if she passed some invisible line into acceptance.

"Yours or ours?"

"He's a witch, or maybe a mage." She quickly continued when he raised an eyebrow. "I felt some magic residue when I touched him. No human could have made those bite marks." She stared down at the body, most of it covered in tin cans, crisp packets and discarded waste. Hidden. John Doe's eyes are wide open as well as his mouth, a silent scream forever on his face.

"I agree. I'll contact The Tower to get assistance." He patted his invisible pocket again, frowning until he reached up to the left side of his head, grabbing a real cigarette tucked behind his ear. He was obviously trying to quit, but failing.

"You should ask the gentleman I was with over."

"Why?" He slanted his eyes suspiciously.

"He's a wolf, their sense of smell can pick up things we could not."

"A wolf, huh?" He searched over the officers until he saw Rex, who stood in the distance. O'Neil thought hard on the idea before confirming with a passing colleague. "There's also more blood further up the alley."

"More blood? From the deceased?"

"We're not sure yet, have to get forensics to check but my gut says no. There isn't any trail leading between them."

Alice lifted her hand up to her throat, remembering the dull pain. "Someone else's?"

"We're leaving the option open."

"Detective?" A young man walked over, his face sweaty with a green tinge. "Mr Sullivan would like to speak to the woman." He blinked over at Alice, his eyes wide.

"Thank you, Officer Gordon." O'Neil lit the cigarette he had been holding, placing it on the tip of his lips. "Agent Skye why don't you go speak to Mr Sullivan. He hasn't been very forthcoming with any information." He savoured a drag of his cigarette, blowing a billow of smoke out his nostrils like a dragon.

"Yeah, sure."

"Hey lady, over here." Alice followed the officer to the Bouncer she met the night before, the six foot plus man clearly angry at being detained.

"Hello. You wanted to speak to me?" she smiled at the Bouncer, lips wavering when she watched his eyes flick to the officer then back. "Hey," she turned to the Officer, "Detective O'Neil needs help with the body."

"Really?" It was almost a squeak, his face turning even greener. "Okay." He ran off.

"You're Alice right?"

"And you were on the door last night."

"Aye. Danton wanted me to give you a message." He crossed his large arms across his chest, veins straining against his skin.

"D?" She looked around, seeing if anybody was near enough to overhear.

"Not here lass, follow me." He walked through an open doorway, the corridor leading into a small office. Sullivan moved to stand behind the small black desk, a silver laptop sitting on top. "This room is more secure." He gestured to the only chair in the room.

"No, it's fine." She decided to stand, not wanting him to tower over her. "This your office?"

"No, just a generic office." He looked around the room like it was the first time he had been there. "Sometimes the boss sits in here, it's soundproof." He flipped open the little laptop, the light glowing over his face, highlighting his impressive cheekbones. "Danton does us favours from time to time." Little clicks on the trackpad, his fingers moving incredibly slow as if he wasn't used to using the equipment. "So we owe him, he asked the boss to ask around and find out some information."

"Information?" She raised her eyebrows.

"Aye, he left before we could relay the information to him so we were advised to give it to you." He clicked a few more times. "Here." He moved the laptop around, a static image of a man tied to a chair on the screen.

"What is this?" She leant on the table, trying to get a better look. Without a word Sullivan reached around and clicked a button, turning on the video. The screen flashed a few times, the image blurry.

"Are you ready to talk yet?" a voice off camera asked.

The man in the chair just smiled, revealing white teeth. His hands flexed, stretching his fingertips as he tested the strength of the rope on his wrists and ankles.

"Nothing? Pity." The screen went black for a few seconds, screams echoing from the speakers.

Alice continued to watch the screen, the black changing to a pale pink before the image came back. The video revealed the man tied to the chair again, blood dripping from his lips, the smile no longer in place. Reaching over she clicked a button on the keyboard, pausing the video.

"What is this?" she asked again.

"Danton asked for backup when you were forcibly removed from the club. We found you in the alley with the dark man, just before he ran off."

"You find the body then too?"

"No lass, that was later."

Alice hesitated on the play button. "You called him a 'dark man'?"

"Aye, we call them dark men when we can't identify the Breed. They are normally from the Dark Court, dark Fae with expensive glamour."

"So he's an Unseelie caste?" She couldn't remember him wearing anything to give that away. Fae were proud of their courts, would normally want to show it off.

"Relative," was his reply.

"What do you mean?"

He ignored the question. "We promised Danton we would help find you, we did. However, as the situation was more severe than we initially realised Danton now owes us the favour." He turned his eyes to her, they were a deep brown with a fleck of green. "I'm sure you will let him know."

"What would this favour be?"

Sullivan smiled, showing crooked teeth. "We tagged his friend. We have decided it would be relevant information for Danton. You will also pass this on."

"His friend?"

Sullivan reached over and continued the video.

"I think you should start answering my questions," the voice off camera asked again, his voice angry.

"Fuck you." Blood splattered as the man in the chair muttered.

"That's the wrong answer." A hand could be visibly seen as a palm covered the camera lens, the screen going dark. After a few muffled shouts the palm moved back, showing the tied up man slumped down in the chair, his head resting on his chest. *"Shall I ask again?"*

The man in the chair slowly and painfully shook his head.

"Okay then, let's start." Alice heard a crack, knuckles clicking. *"What's your name?"*

"Louis." He rolled his head to the side, his cheek still resting on his shoulder. His eyes were a piercing black, the orbs looking straight at the camera as if he could see right through it.

"You have a partner. Yes?"

"Yes." With a grunt, he lifted his head.

"What have you been doing in my club? Dealing drugs?"

"No!" The man coughed, blood splashing down his once white shirt.

"Then what? We have had complaints you and your partner have been trying to sell something."

Louis laughed. *"We were recruiting."*

"Recruiting?"

"For the cause."

"Cause?"

"The Becoming."

"The fucking what? A cult?"

"No." He started to pull violently at his bonds. *"You are not worthy, you wouldn't understand."* He spat towards someone hidden from the camera.

"What I understand is that you have been forcing yourself on people. Your partner has just been caught with his pants down, pockets full of date rape herbs and a dead body."

"WHERE IS HE?" The rope at his ankle snapped.

"He isn't here."

The lights flickered, another rope snapping as the man ferociously shook the wooden chair. His arms bulged, black veins pulsating against his skin. With a screech the remaining ropes burst open, one flicking out to clip the camera, causing it to fall to the floor. The screen cracked, screams erupting through the microphone before the image went dark.

Sullivan silently closed the lid, pushing the laptop to the side of the table.

"What happened?"

No answer.

"When was this filmed?"

Sullivan had stepped back to lean against the wall, using shadow to cover his face. She was grateful, he was huge, like wrestler huge. His hands were as big as her head.

"Last night."

"Where is he now?"

Sullivan remained silent, giving her all the answer she needed.

"Anything else I need to know?"

"Yes. The drug we found on him was agrimony."

"The date rape drug?"

Agrimony was a herb used specifically for people with sleep disorders, or in severe cases as a date rape drug. It was supposedly tasteless, and in small quantities could make anybody dangerously drowsy, unable to fight back.

"Yep, my boss isn't happy. Not good biz if you have people dropping that shit into lass's drinks. We have never heard of this 'Becoming.' If it is something that directly influences our business we would appreciate any information."

Alice just nodded, she would need information herself before she could even share any. Back down the corridor she finally found the exit into the alley, the noise of all the police officers loud compared to the soundproofed corridor. She walked quickly past everyone and ducked under the police tape, looking around for Rex.

"Agent." Detective O'Neil came over, a new cigarette hanging from his lips, the end yet to be lit. "Did Mr Sullivan tell you anything interesting?"

"No, he just thought he recognised me. Honest mistake." She looked around again, unable to see Rex. "Have you seen the man I was with?"

"Over there somewhere." He finally lit his cigarette, a look of ecstasy lighting up his face before being replaced with his usual grimace. "Take this..." He handed her a card. "It's my contact details, ring me if you suddenly remember something interesting Mr Sullivan said."

She crushed the card in her hand.

"Of course."

With one last hard look he dismissed her.

Exhaling, she scanned the crowd again, finally spotting Rex's head. "Why are you over here?" she asked as she walked over, watching him straighten up at her approach.

"I had to get out the way for Tyler to catch the scent."

"Where is Tyler?" She still hadn't seen him in the crowd.

"He's gone. Good call to get someone over to sniff the body. I was waiting for you before we catch up with him. He mentioned the scent is strong, he isn't far." He tilted his head to look at her. "What did the ursine want?"

Ursine? Oh. "Bear?" she asked, confused.

"The Bouncer."

She quickly relayed what the Bouncer told her. Rex's face had been unreadable the whole time, like his face was carved from granite. "The Becoming mean anything..."

"No, never heard of it," Rex said before she even finished the question.

"He didn't really talk much about it, just the fact he was recruiting people..."

"Alice we better be going." He started to move away.

"But it's a good place to start."

"A better place would be to track down that rogue wolf. Are you coming or not?"

Alice gritted her teeth. "Fine."

CHAPTER TEN

The walk to Tyler took less time than she thought it would, the general busyness that was London calmer than usual. They found him pacing in front of a large abandoned warehouse, the door and windows covered up half-heartedly with wooden planks, decorated in various multicoloured graffiti.

"What is this place?" she asked, staring up at the huge double storey building.

The front was boarded up, something about a male's large appendage in neon pink graffiti sprawled artistically across it. Alice looked up at the drab building, two sizable windows placed beside the door, both closed off and decorated with similar artistry. Four more windows spotted along the upper storey with two more circular windows at the top. They had no boards, just shadowed over with dust and grime. Several broken shards stuck out, an impenetrable blackness oozing out from the holes. Something moved in her peripheral vision, a shape running across a window.

"It's creepy."

"Must have been an old factory," Rex stated.

No shit Sherlock.

Brushing her hand across the wooden panel she tried to find somewhere weak, something easy enough to pull off. A loud screech as Rex pulled off a board effortlessly, long rusted nails sticking from the wood.

"Move please." Tyler budged past her, grabbing another board and pulling it off. Alice moved back, surprised by his deep bass voice. Tyler ignored her, his attention on the removing of the boards quickly and efficiently.

Bloody hell, he does speak.

Once the hole was large enough Alice nudged past them, turning at an angle so she could fit.

"Alice wait…" Rex said as her sleeve got caught on a nail sticking out. "It might be dangerous, let one of us go first."

She tugged her sleeve free, groaning when she noticed the massive hole in the cotton. "Fuck."

"Are you alright?" Rex came up next to her, his hand roaming across her arm as he looked for any damage.

"I just caught my sleeve." She scowled at her shirt before taking in the building surrounding her. It was huge, even bigger than she initially thought. "This must once have been an old textile factory," she muttered to herself, walking behind them into the dark, dusty room.

Around a dozen tables were lined up neatly in rows of four, all evenly spaced. Piles of fabrics and papers sprawled carelessly over the table tops. Mannequins and tailors dummies lined the walls, all seemingly frozen into place, backs stiff, some with arms and heads, and some without. Eyes seemed to follow her every movement, seeing nothing yet seeing everything.

As she walked further into the room the mannequins became more grotesque, more non-human. Porcelain and fabric creatures once resembling humans warped into faceless monsters, bodies burnt and deformed, eyes having been scratched off their once pretty faces, mutilated. The spray can artists had somehow gotten in there too, offensive words and images painted onto the pale flesh.

Alice felt disturbed, almost repulsed at the sight, not quite wanting to turn her back to the army of dolls. A bird squawked, making her glance up as a black shadow flew out through one of the cracks in the windows, the large room having no second floor.

"Tyler can you smell that?" Rex kept his voice low.

Tyler lifted his nose to the air, but didn't confirm or deny. He started to pace the room, his face scrunched up in concentration before storming over to the back end of the abandoned building.

Alice followed quickly behind, almost slamming into the back of

Tyler when she followed his eyesight, her eyes unable to make out what he was watching until sunlight finally shone through a broken window.

Hung from a beam was the wolf they were tracking, Tom. His once black eyes misted over in death. Rope was knotted around each of his arms, anchored to the wooden beams running parallel along the ceiling.

Alice felt bile rise up her throat, the creak of the rope against the wood too much. The room was full of old dusty fabrics, rolls of cotton, linen and organza piled high against the walls, dark blue paint peeling off the brick. Dust hovered in the air, creating bursts of sparkle as they reflected off the rays of light from the cracked windows high above. A couple of industrial sewing machines had been pushed to the far corners of the derelict room. The once working machines had rusted with age, their needles dulled.

Blood dripped to the floor, leaving a red splash across the concrete. Looking back at the body Alice hesitantly walked forward, feeling the urge to check for a pulse, to check for any sense of life. A stupid notion considering his intestines were on show, hanging precariously by his feet, the blood dripping off in an irritating patter.

"Alice," warned Rex, as she felt a warm hand on her shoulder.

"Let me do my job." She shrugged him off.

Tom's head was slumped down, chin to chest, his hair covering his barely recognisable face. Pale skin decorated in bursts of blue, purple and yellow.

"He has broken ribs," she mumbled to herself, hovering her hand over the patterns decorating his chest, next to the large lacerations so deep she could see muscle. Black moved underneath his skin, veins and arteries continuing to leak through his various wounds. The ropes creaked again, the body swaying slightly in the non-existent breeze.

The guys hadn't spoken a word, their attention on the swaying corpse. Concerned, she looked at them, their faces pale as they continued to stare at the body.

"Hey, are you both okay?" They didn't even look at her, their eyes trained on Tom's chest. Taking a step back her breath caught at the back of her throat, blood turning to ice in her veins.

The phrase *'Time's up'* was carved neatly into his flesh.

"Rex?" she asked. "What does that mean?"

He didn't say anything for a few minutes, his eyes never leaving the body before he turned to her, his eyes bright, the wolf prowling behind his irises. "A warning. A threat."

"From who? What aren't you telling me?"

"I don't know." He moved towards Tyler, starting a low conversation between them. She couldn't even tell Tyler was speaking but for the gentle vibrations of his throat, his mouth barely moving. He seemed angry, his movements agitated. His eyes connected with hers when he noticed her staring, they flared wolf, a bright yellow before he turned his back to her.

"I'll call the forensics in."

"We don't need them." Rex stormed across the floor towards her, his stride powerful and irritated. Even his face was surprisingly angry. "I'll call in my wolves."

"No, that's not how this works." She stood her ground as he glowered over her. "We need to run blood work and look into what carved that warning in his chest. Your wolves are not trained…"

"I said no," he growled.

"It's part of the package. When you hired me…"

"I hired you to listen to me."

"You hired me for my experience and advice." She felt her own irritation ignite, could feel an intense heat low in her stomach. Her fingers twitched, fire prickling her skin.

"Let her contact them." Tyler intervened. "We could find something out that benefits us." Rex turned to Tyler, full wolf in his eyes. Tyler dropped the eye contact instantly, his throat tilted to the side in submission.

"Rex, it makes sense." He didn't want to listen, his ice eyes bright in the dark room. She could feel the power behind them, could feel the authority that was bred into all Alphas.

She lifted a hand to his chest as he stepped into her, his skin hot beneath his shirt. "Stop it." He pushed against her hand, the wolf in his eyes excited. She released her pent-up energy, allowing a thin wall of flame to line her either side. She didn't want to hurt him, but she wasn't one of his sheep to manipulate and control.

His nose flared, his head tilting as his wolf studied her. She was running out of ideas fast, she had never seen him react this way. His wolf was still excited, almost playing with her as he showed her his teeth.

"Sire." Tyler whispered beside her. She hadn't even heard him move.

Rex let out a deep growl, one that started at the bottom of his chest and erupted out of his mouth. "Contact them." He pushed away from her, storming out of the warehouse.

Extinguishing the flames she grabbed her phone, texting the appropriate team. The reply was almost instant.

Sending out to your coordinates now. Please standby.

"You shouldn't challenge him," Tyler stated.

"I didn't," Alice said, confused. Not intentionally anyway. "What was that even about?" She waited for the reply, not expecting an answer. She knew shifter etiquette, knew that another animal shouldn't look into a dominants eyes. But surely he knew she wasn't an animal?

"No one has ever challenged him."

CHAPTER ELEVEN

Alice had never seen anything like it before, and was happy to never see anything like it again.

"As you can see, the organs have been moved towards the back, pressed against the spine," Dr Miko Le'Sanza, Head Pathologist for London Hope Hospital stated as he opened the chest captivity of Tomlin, the wolf they had found hanging crucifix style only a few days earlier. She had pulled as many favours as she could to get the autopsy pushed through, knowing Rex was on a time limit.

"What does that mean?" Alice asked as she followed Miko around the lab. She was told to meet Tyler at the reception desk, but instead turned up early to have a catch up with her old friend. Although, he was more interested in showing her as many gory details as possible.

"You will see." His slightly upturned eyes shone in excitement, a gift from his Asian mother. His father, on the other hand, gave him his dark curly hair and naturally tanned skin. The combination made him beautiful, in a delicate feminine way.

He moved around the body with a metal cart, full of instruments that would be better suited to a torture chamber than a hospital morgue.

"If you look here..." Using a sharp knife he sliced a few layers of skin beside several vertebrae, peeling back the skin.

"What am I looking at?" She walked towards the table.

"There are unusual patterns along the underside of the ribcage, almost like a spider web." Grabbing an instrument, Miko pointed to one of the black vein-like tubes that crisscrossed underneath the skin.

"What are they?" she asked, having no clue what she was looking at. Not that she had the first idea about forensic science.

"I have no idea. But once your friend turns up, you will learn that this particular cadaver is anything but normal." He poked one of the black tubes, the spider web seeming to pulsate before settling.

"That's disgusting."

"Is this a bad time?" a voice asked from behind. She knew who it was immediately, but turned anyway.

"Oh, hey." She blinked up at Rex, surprised to see him dressed so casually. He wore a plain white t-shirt with khakis, compared to his usual dress shirts and expensive jeans. He even wore trainers. "Where's Tyler?"

"He's preoccupied." He looked towards the Doctor, his face cold. "Alice seems to believe you might give something of relevance."

"Relevance?" Miko chuckled, grabbing a clipboard from the corner of one of the desks and handing it to Alice. "I'll have you know I'm always relevant."

Alice glanced at the paper before she heard a weird, forced laugh. Surprised, she faced Rex who gave her a quick smile, one that didn't reach his eyes.

"What's that?" Rex asked, pointedly looking at the paper on her clipboard, the fake smile fading from his lips.

"Oh." She checked the paperwork again, reading the report a few times over before she understood all the letters and numbers. "This can't be right." A frown creased her brow.

"I've run the tests several times just to check, the DNA matches up. I've never seen anything like it." Miko grabbed the report from Alice before handing it to Rex.

"This is unbelievable."

"What are you guys on about?" He read through the paperwork, not understanding the report.

Miko walked over with a handful of vials and syringes, each already filled with various substances. "What it means is that the blood we extracted is unique and believed to be impossible."

"You're still not making any sense."

"What the report says is that the DNA matches with a shifter, but a couple of unusual strands have appeared in the blood-works." Miko clapped his hands together excitedly before going over to a cabinet and opening a metal cupboard, cool air floating out before he closed the door again. "So when we opened him up it was very unusual."

"Unusual how?" Rex asked. His face stone as he leant carefully on the wall next to the door, his nose turned away from the selection of chemicals and formaldehyde.

"This." Miko shook the large jar in his hands, something pink inside hitting the glass wall before settling in the middle.

"What the fuck is that?" Alice stepped closer, trying to look into the jar with condensation rolling down the glass.

"This, my dear friends is a heart."

"That is not a heart." Alice eyed the bulbous flesh in the water, the shape similar to a heart but at least twice the size.

"This is actually the heart of the wolf you brought in. As you can see it is clearly oversized."

"Clearly," Rex said dryly.

Miko shook the glass again, the water becoming murky before clearing as the heart thudded against the glass. With a few pops, the heart contorted, constricting before releasing, causing bubbles to pop out of several holes and floating to the top.

"Holy shit did that thing move?" Alice went to touch the jar, snapping her hand back as the heart pumped again.

"Yes, believe it or not, it is still pumping." Miko put the jar down. "And it's not even a delayed muscle spasm, like a chicken who would continue to run around even after losing his head. I've been watching it for the last couple days since you brought the body in. It is somehow still living."

"Why is it so large?"

Miko shrugged. "No idea, I can tell it's deformed, most Breeds, at least humanoid have a heart with four valves. A mitral valve and tricuspid valve, they control the blood flow from the atria to the ventricles. We also have an aortic valve and a pulmonary valve that controls the flow out of the ventricles. Now this heart has eight valves."

"Eight? Why would you need eight?"

"That is the big question isn't it?" Miko tapped his nail against the glass, the heart continuing to pump every thirty seconds or so.

"So what does this all mean?" asked Rex, his attention on the pink flesh.

"I have been researching along with a couple of specialists," Miko started to move around the lab, grabbing bits of paper from various work surfaces. "Like I said before, it's almost impossible."

"Doc, what does it mean?"

"Well, between myself and several of my colleagues we have come to the decision that it could quite possibly be a Daemon transition."

"A Daemon?" Alice frowned, trying to remember the last time she had even heard of a Daemon sighting. Something clicked in her head, her nightmares starting to make sense.

Shit. Shit. Shit. Alice stepped back, facing the wall as her stomach rolled.

"Technically, there are no records that Daemons exist, they're not a registered Breed. However, there are medical archives going back hundreds of years depicting such transitions... Alice, are you okay?"

She sucked in a breath. "I'm fine." She was closer to knowing, to finding out what happened.

"Like I was saying, there have been autopsies of creatures that medical professionals at the time have named as Daemons due to their likeliness to the biblical stories, although they are nothing to do with religion."

He scanned through sheets of paper, seeming to forget he had company before looking up, surprised.

"Oh, yeah. There are also newspaper articles and police reports with matching descriptions, but as I said, because Daemons have never been actually classified as an official Breed, no one ever investigated further."

"So, in your professional opinion?" Alice asked, needing to confirm. "You believe that to be a Daemon?"

"I believe that is exactly what he was, or at least would be if the transition was complete." He pursed his lips.

"What can we do with this information?" Rex asked, putting the clipboard down on one of the shiny surfaces.

"Unfortunately not a lot. I'm currently getting my apprentices to look into unusual blood works in autopsy reports over the past year. I'm hoping once I have something to compare my results with I could work out how far the transition is and what actually killed him."

"You don't even know what killed him?" Rex said in his usual arctic tone. "His organs were on the floor."

"It isn't that simple," Miko snapped as he ruffled his hair. "I'm not exactly working on the usual body, now am I?"

"Do you mind if I come back tomorrow?" Alice asked, "I would like to look through some of the reports."

"Sure, ring me later to organise a pass." He absently waved his hand.

"So you haven't found anything useful." Rex crossed his arms. "This has been a waste of time."

Alice glared at him. "Did you find anything else unusual?" she asked the doctor.

Miko ignored Rex's comment. "Yes and no. His internals are messed up, like his lungs and stomach didn't know where to go when his heart grew." Miko pointedly gave her a look. She remembered him showing her the damaged tissue surrounding the spine.

Wonder what that could mean.

"He had blood in his stomach, but I can't really tell if that's unusual or not. I know some shifters drink blood through ceremonies and when hunting."

Alice glanced at Rex, looking for confirmation. "Rex?" she called.

No response, he seemed to be staring at the body.

"Rex?" she said again, slightly louder this time.

He looked up then, his face pale. "What?" His eyes flashed, his wolf reacting.

"Dr Le'Sanza was saying some shifters consume blood for ceremonies and stuff? That true?"

He seemed to shake himself, a full body vibration. "I need to go."

"Rex?"

He faced her, eyes glistening. "Contact me if you find anything else." With that he left the room.

What's up with him?

Alice leant against a stainless steel cabinet, waiting for Miko to be finished with whatever he was doing. She felt herself stare towards the body, his feet bare, with a white tag tied around his big toe.

What can I remember about Daemons? Alice bit the inside of her cheek, trying to think. Dread told her stories as a child, warnings. She didn't believe him. Why would she?

"Alice?"

What else did he say?

"Alice?"

She needed to learn more.

"ALICE!" Miko clicked his fingers.

"Huh?" She blinked at him.

"I've been calling your name." He raised an eyebrow. "What were you thinking about?"

"Nothing important." She cleared her throat.

"So, we going to talk about your wolf?"

"What? Rex isn't my wolf." She felt heat against her cheeks. "We're just working together."

"I meant him..." He pointed to the corpse. "But it's interesting you mentioned Rex now, isn't it." His brows knitted. "Have you seen the way he looks at you?"

"Looks at me?"

"He looks at you as if you're his."

"Excuse me?" *He doesn't really look at me like that, does he?* That confused things. "Anyway, what do we know about Daemons?" She didn't want to think about anything else right now.

"Other than the fact they are beyond rare? Not a lot." He gawked at the corpse. "They were more common in the nineteenth century, but have been hunted to near extinction."

"Hunted? Who has hunted them?"

"Well that's the interesting thing, I don't know." He threw his papers onto a counter. "I have asked anybody who should know and I got nowhere." He tugged at his hair. "Don't suppose you know anything?"

"No." She thought about it. "You said the body was transitioning? Is it magic? Or like a shifter?"

"Magic? That's interesting. Shifters in general, while not widely known, do actually have magic. It's how they are able to shift between their forms."

"So Daemon's could be a type of Shifter?"

"That's relative, they seem to shift from one form to another but there isn't any evidence to suggest that. There is also no evidence to suggest anything else either." With a pen he started to write notes on a piece of paper. "It's an interesting theory though, something I will definitely explore." He peeked at her over the paper. "I'm going to run the bloods again, see if I can break them down further." He turned back towards his work.

"I guess that's me dismissed."

Miko didn't respond, his attention on his new project.

"Bye then." Her voice was lost as she walked towards the lifts, just about to press the button when the door opened unexpectedly. A man stood in the centre as the doors opened, his face puzzled before recognition flowed across his features.

"Agent Skye," he greeted as he stepped out, letting the door close behind him before she could step in.

"Detective." She eyed the button to the left, analysing if she could reach around and not seem rude.

"What are you doing here?"

"Visiting a friend."

He played with the unlit cigarette on his left ear. "Interesting I found you, I was on my way to talk to someone about the body found behind the club. It seems that someone did bleed John Doe virtually dry before using a tin can lid to slice through his jugular."

"A tin can?" That was surprising, the cut looked too clean. She would have put money on a knife.

"That's what the professionals say. What was interesting was he was severely dehydrated. When the guys finally moved the body, a few of his bones disintegrated."

"What could have caused that?" She had never heard of anything like it.

"They're still looking into it." He checked his watch.

"Do you have any leads?"

"Only the extra blood found at the scene, it was magic infused. Identified as belonging to a witch."

"You sure it wasn't a mage?"

"No, the blood was too strong." He frowned, his eyes moving behind her.

"Alice," someone hissed to her back.

Alice spun, heart in her throat. "Dread, you almost gave me a heart attack." She hated that vampires were virtually silent in their movements.

"We have matters to discuss." His eyes flicked to the Detective. "O'Neil, haven't spoken to you in a while."

"Commissioner. Have you looked into the proposal I sent over?"

"About the liaison team? I'm currently working with my Paladins to decide who would be better suited."

"Good. The big bosses are pushing for a more blended variety in the workforce. Liaising with a Paladin would be a start."

"I agree, I believe it would benefit both sides. I will get back to you as soon as I have come to my decision. Now if you would excuse me." Dread grabbed her arm, escorting her further down the hallway.

"Dread what is this?" She dragged her feet until he stopped, making him face her. "Why are you even here?"

"I have just got the report about the wolf. I'm here to personally remove you from your recent contract. Starting now you will no longer be working for Mr Wild. I have organised Danton to replace you."

"Replace me? Wait… back up. Why am I being removed?"

He waited as someone walked past, not wanting anyone to overhear.

"We cannot discuss this in the open."

Mouth tight, she opened a door to their right, walking into the small cupboard before Dread could complain. "You wanted privacy?" She flicked the switch for the light, the bulb choking to life with a high-pitched whine.

Dread closed the door behind him, looking around the small room in disgust. It was literally a cleaning closet, several wooden brooms were stacked against each other on the left while the right wall was full of shelves holding cleaning supplies.

"This isn't what I had in mind, Alice."

"Start from the beginning. Why am I being removed from the case? I feel like I'm really starting to make a breakthrough…"

"The risk is too high."

"Dread, I'm a fucking Paladin…"

"Language!" he hissed, his obsidian eyes narrowing. "You're a Paladin who isn't trained to deal with Daemons, especially abominations like that."

"Then who deals with them?"

"There is an organisation that specialises in such things."

"An organisation? Who?" She needed to speak to them.

"I do not have to explain myself to you Alice. There's a reason behind every story I have ever told you. You should try to remember that." He exhaled, calming himself. "I can't risk any of them finding you, if they found out…" He caught himself before he revealed anymore.

"If who found out?" Panic built in her blood. "What haven't you told me?"

"You were never supposed to know," he murmured quietly, almost to himself.

"Dread…" She wanted to tell him about her nightmares, but couldn't seem to get the words out of her mouth.

"Alice..." he sighed. "You must understand, I see you like a daughter, one I want to protect." He hesitated, trying to find the right words. "No, this isn't the right time."

Alice let out a little scream, frustration creasing her features. "I don't understand, you demand I leave something alone but you don't explain why." Her eyes blurred.

Alice dropped her lashes, shocked as moisture filled her eyes.

"You *will* drop the case." He paused as the closet door rattled, as if someone knocked it as they walked past. "This is over Alice. My decision is final." Dread paused, almost as if he was going to say something else.

She turned her head and held his gaze, seeing if she could read through his evasion.

"I'm pulling you off this case. Mr Wild will just have to deal with it." He moved to put his hand on the handle, his back to her. "I know this is hard but my priority is your safety. It's what I promised..." He cleared his throat. "The risk is too high. Not when it's your life."

The door creaked open before he disappeared.

Alice let her head rest against the wall, her eyes closed, refusing to let her tears fall. She wasn't stupid, she knew her broken nightmares that haunted her were memories.

It didn't matter how many years went by, Alice still felt the empty ache in her chest when she thought about her family, her mother, father and brother who were all brutally murdered late one night in their family home. The only exception was her, a small child who had been woken up by a strange noise. A child who had ran and hid when she saw a monster, a shadow.

CHAPTER TWELVE

"He can't take me off the case," Alice grumbled into her polystyrene cup early the next morning. She had checked her Paladin status on the S.I. database at dawn, delighted to see the paperwork hadn't gone through. That gave her at least two days. Until then, she wouldn't be contactable by The Tower.

Blowing along the top of her coffee she stared at the large converted townhouse that housed the local hospital. The front of the building was made up of five-story townhouses that have been connected to the sleek glass and steel structure built behind. Alice quickly moved past row of ambulances, walking into the general reception area. The smell assaulted her nose almost instantly, the strong mixture of copper and disinfectant polluting the air strong enough to choke on. The accident and emergency centre was situated directly behind the reception, rows of benches lined the white lino flooring, almost every available space taken up by someone moaning, bleeding or clutching some part of their anatomy.

"Morning, I'm here to see Dr Le'sanza," she politely asked the tired looking receptionist behind the desk. "He should be expecting me."

"Name?" the woman, Betty according to her name tag, asked.

"Alice Skye."

Betty nodded before scanning through a book in front of her, a frown creasing her brow.

"Is there a problem?" *Was I too early?* She looked up at the clock on the wall, noting how it was only just past eight. She had been too wound up to sleep.

"If you could please excuse me Ma'am, I need to make a phone call." Without waiting for a response Betty grabbed the handset by her computer, clicking a few buttons before murmuring into the phone. Alice could feel the eyes on her back, an accusation of impatient people having to wait too long.

As if it was her fault they had to wait.

"Miss Skye, was it?"

"Yes, that would be me. I spoke to Le'Sanza yesterday..."

"Yes Miss Skye, he has confirmed your meeting. He just didn't follow the proper protocol to register a visitor, doctors do that sometimes." Leaning down into one of her drawers she pulled out a long lanyard with *'VISITOR'* written across it. "Please wear this at all times," she said, passing it over. "It will gain you access to the lower levels of the hospital, please do not go into any patient's rooms unless supervised. If you walk to the large lift and press 'B1', you will find Dr Miko Le'Sanza's office. Take a left, down the corridor and it's right at the end, you can't miss it. Any questions?"

"I've been there before, thank you."

"Have a great day." With that practised smile, she turned to the next person in line.

Clearly dismissed, Alice walked to the lift, waiting patiently in line with the other people. With a bing the lift doors opened, allowing everyone to squish themselves into the small space.

"Press floor one please," a woman asked politely as she read from her clipboard. Pushing the hair away from her face Alice obeyed, pressing the two floors and stood quietly beside the woman. The lift music started almost instantly, an annoying raucous of instruments as if the orchestra all stood up and took a step to the right, playing an instrument they were not familiar with.

A few stops and people started to filter out, leaving more space to move around.

Stepping back she allowed someone to pass, placing her at the back of the lift with the metal banister digging into her back. An annoying ringing broke through the music, adding an obnoxious tone to the already terrible song. A man who wore all black answered his phone, flipping the front open and putting it to his ear. Alice couldn't help but stare, surprised to see a flip phone in this day and age.

"Yes?" the man barked into the receiver. "Yes, we have already found the appropriate information. No, but we haven't got access yet." The man stopped his conversation, turning to glare at Alice. "Excuse me." He held his hand over the microphone, his palm bigger than the black handset.

Alice blinked up at him stupidly. "Oh, sorry."

He just tutted and faced the doors.

"Sorry about that. Yes, of course. I will keep you updated." He tucked his phone into his front pocket, grabbing his sunglasses and planting them on his nose.

The lift dinged once more, signalling that she had reached her desired floor. The door moaned, revealing a very similar white corridor layout. It must be a rule somewhere that all hospitals must be painted a sickly white colour. Shoulders stiff, she walked out, barely stopping herself from looking back at the man, her gut telling her something was wrong.

Dr Miko Le'Sanza's office was right at the end of the corridor, his name embossed on a gold plated sign hanging on the solid wood, unsurprisingly painted white. She knocked gently before walking in.

"Miko?"

"Hello?" Miko swivelled his head towards the door, a surprised look on his face. "Hi Alice, didn't expect you today."

"What are you on about? I said yesterday I was coming?"

"Well yes, but Commissioner Grayson said..."

"Dread came in?" She felt the blood rush from her face. *Shit. Shit. Shit.*

"Well, yes."

Miko shuffled the papers in his hands as he stood up, a tower of envelopes and coloured folders engulfing what she knew to be his desk, various pens and pencils thrown vicariously across the pile. "He wanted to organise a team to take over examining the body," he smirked. "I politely told him to shove it. No way was I letting anybody take this over."

"You said what?" She really wished she could have seen Dread's face. "How did he even know about it?"

"No idea. I told him I'm not letting some buffoons come over and mess up my research. So he had no choice but to hire me directly under

The Tower until further notice." He sniffed as if displeased, but grinned at the same time. "Which means I also know you're no longer the Paladin on this case."

"So you're not letting me see the reports?" She felt the energy leave her. What would she do now? That was her main lead.

"Of course I am. What he doesn't know won't hurt him."

She beamed, looking around the small office. His desk has been pushed to the far wall, under a light box showing someone's broken bone. The computer sat on the left corner, the screen showing a black screensaver with a pink square bouncing from one corner to the other.

"When's the last time you cleaned?" She sat on the pile of folders on the one chair available in the room.

"I call it an organised mess." He pulled out a few boxes from under his desk, planting them on her lap. "These are the files you were after."

"Really?" She pushed the top box off, letting it land on the floor at her feet. "Oh man, I think I owe you dinner." She smiled at the number of folders, hoping some of them contained something helpful.

"Actually, you owe about six people dinner. We have all agreed on steak." His eyes sparkled. "These particular reports are based on unusual deaths with no known family," he shrugged. "Normally in these situations they are never re-opened, just closed once all the leads go dead. So any unusual abnormalities aren't investigated further."

"Have you read these?" She nodded to the pile on her lap.

"I skimmed them last night. There's one I think you should see." He went to the mess on his desk, shuffling through layers of paperwork before he found what he was looking for. Accepting the report she opened the first page.

Office of the medical examiner
London

Report of examination
Decedent: Maxi L. Swanson
Case Number: RF 12466-892029
Cause of death: Unknown
Identified by: Teeth were used to check medical records. Concluded with the nuclear DNA comparison done by medical staff laboratory. (Skeletal specimen for identification: Right Tibia) *
*Disclosure – Unusual strands in DNA

Age: *Bones are consistent with an age of around 32 years*
Sex: *Male*   ***Race:*** *Caucasian*
Date of death: *(Found) 10/11/2010 (Estimate) 8/11/2010*
....
Date of Examination: *12th November 2010 through to 20th November 2010*
Examination and summary analysis performed by: UNDISCLOSED
Cause of death: *Exsanguination (Loss of blood to a degree sufficient to cause death)*
....

Findings

¥ *Blood found in the body was less than 40%*
¥ *Unusual substance found in the blood inside the body*
¥ *Bite marks around throat and wrists*
¥ *Found in same clothes reported last wearing.*
¥ *Wounds consistent with self-harm*
¥ *Blood under fingernails – own DNA*
¥ *Reported missing on the 20th of October 2010*
¥ *No proof of struggle*
¥ *Toxicology detects no drugs but cannot determine substance found in blood.*
¥ *Shifter DNA – Species unknown*
¥ *Unknown substance also found in the back of the throat*
¥ *Internal organs larger than usual.*
....

Conclusion:

The subject's self-inflicted wounds have tiny incisions consistent with fang marks.
The unknown substance found in his blood was also found in the back of the throat, ingested.
Died from blood loss and sepsis caused by the open wounds across the body. Little medical history can be found. The front teeth were deformed but the molars towards the back of the throat were used in conjunction with the DNA check.
Due to the limited proof and evidence of third party, the cause of death cannot be completely determined with certainty. The manner of death is

unknown.

"Unusual strands in DNA?" She flicked through the pages.

"His blood is similar to the wolf you brought in, the abnormalities matching."

"What does that mean?"

"Not really sure yet. But if more of these files match it would be a breakthrough."

BEEP. BEEP. BEEP.

The lights above flashed several times.

BEEP. BEEP. BEEP.

"Shit!" Miko ran to his door, peering out into the corridor.

BEEP. BEEP. BEEP.

"Miko, what is it?" Alice chased behind him, the one file clutched to her chest. The lights overhead turned off for a few seconds before fluttering back to life, the backup generator kicking in.

"Someone has set off the alarm," he replied in between the obnoxious beeps. He started to move towards the stairs, following the crowd of mildly panicked people as they passed beneath a violently flashing red light.

"As in a fire test?" she questioned, following quickly behind.

"Not that I know of."

"Dr Le'Sanza!" someone called. "Doctor..." Miko turned to the sound of his name. "Doctor I'm glad I caught you, someone set the fire alarm off from the morgue."

"The morgue? Wasn't Dr Washington down there?"

"No, sir. Dr Washington got called to a meeting. Security is trying to reset the alarm but it could take a few minutes."

"So there is no fire?"

"No, CCTV has just confirmed."

"Thank you James, could you please go up to reception to help settle the patients?"

"But Dr, I should go help clear up the morgue..."

"It's fine, I have someone to help." James's eyes flashed to Alice. "Oh, of course." He started to run off, his white lab coat flying behind him.

Alice waited a few seconds while the beeping cleared, the sound resonating inside her skull. "What did he mean clean up the morgue?"

Miko turned to her, his face pale. "Shit."

The mortuary was empty by the time they both descended the stairs, having to calm several people on the way down, reassuring them everything was fine.

The corridor leading to the main autopsy room was eerily quiet, nothing like how it normally was. Metal trolleys abandoned, paperwork scattered across the floor.

"Miko, who did you tell about the heart?" Alice heard herself whisper, her eyes scanning the rooms breaking off from the corridor. The emergency lighting was still activated, making everywhere darker than it should be, allowing shadows to swallow up the corners of the rooms.

Ignoring her, he walked past the main autopsy room and through a side door where floor to ceiling metal squares patterned the walls. One of the squares was open, the metal door open with a silver gurney half hanging out. A white cloth draped from the metal, the fabric caught on the edge of the door. A large fridge was at the back, next to a few racks with vials of different coloured liquids.

"It's not here." Miko panicky moved over everything on the shelves, even bending to check behind the rack. "It's not here." He opened the fridge next, closing the heavy door only moments later. "Shit. Alice, it isn't here."

"What about the body?" she asked.

He turned to the only open mortuary refrigerator, pushing the gurney violently with a high screech. "Someone has taken it," he said hopelessly.

"Miko..." She went to stand in front of him, his attention on the black hole in the wall. "Who did you tell about the heart?" He didn't seem to hear her, his attention still on the hole where the body should have been. "MIKO." She clicked her fingers, causing him to blink and shake his head. "Who did you tell?"

"No one I couldn't trust," he said, voice croaking. "Alice why would someone break into a hospital for it?"

"I don't know." The room suddenly brightened, the main power kicking back in. "How can someone just stroll in here and leave with a body and no one notice?"

Miko finally met her eyes, the pupils narrowed. "I don't know." He turned to punch a cabinet. "FUCK!" The sound resonated as Miko grabbed his fist, swearing.

Alice ignored him, instead picking up some debris off the floor and placing them on the side. She had noticed all the rooms, ones that normally locked with a key card, were unlocked. Going over to the double doors she peered at the black box on the wall, one that looked completely undamaged. Frowning she went to touch it, pulling her hand back at the last second when a spark flashed.

What the fuck?

"Miko? What would set off the fire alarm if there was no fire?"

He walked to stand beside her, frowning at the wall. "Someone could have pulled the fire alarm?"

"What about if something tripped the electric?" The black box sparked again, making them step back.

"Not normally, but a slight smoke from the spark could affect the sensitive detectors."

"How long does it take for the alarm to be reset?"

Miko thought about it for a few seconds. "Up to ten minutes."

"So they had ten minutes from when the alarm went off to grab what they came for and escape through the confusion." That was obviously plenty of time.

"The alarm could have been planned."

"Possible." She checked another door, noticing it also had the same treatment.

"Do you..."

Alice held up her hand to silence him, concentrating on a sound from the corner of the room. She heard it again, a soft moan.

"Hello?"

The sound again, slightly louder.

"Shit." Miko walked to an overturned gurney. "Over here." Together they gently moved the obstacle, spotting someone lying along the floor, their back towards a metal cabinet. "Hey, can you hear me?" He gently ran his hands over the unconscious woman, checking her body for any damage.

"She was thrown into the cabinet," Alice commented as she pulled some broken glass away. The woman's face was swollen, the skin around her eye swelling to the point her eye was forced closed. "She must have gotten in the way."

"Barbarians, this is a bloody hospital for goodness sake." Miko gently helped her up as the woman slowly regained consciousness. "Hello, it's Dr Le'Sanza, can you tell me your name?" The woman just stared blankly through her one clear eye. "She's probably concussed. We need to get her upstairs."

"I'll call for help."

The air was chilly when Alice left the hospital, happy to leave the woman with a series of doctors. She had to leave the reports with Miko, who promised to contact her if he found anything. She wanted to stay but couldn't risk running into anybody from the office. They wouldn't have the body to study anymore but someone would definitely be investigating its disappearance, as well as the heart.

The floor squelched under her shoes as she paused outside the doors, water from the heavy rain leaving the floor and roads dangerously wet, the cold weather discouraging the water to evaporate. Eyes dry and gritty she wiped her face with her hands, her breath coming out in a long sigh. It was like they were a step ahead of them, first with killing the wolf and now with his body. Was that their plan all along? To leave the dead with a warning and then recover it?

Rex wasn't telling her something.

A vibration in her pocket. Alice quickly peeked at the phone screen, ignoring the text from Dread. Her finger hovered over Rex.

This wasn't just about his wolf anymore.

A sudden screech made her jump, her phone leaping from her hand to land in a heap on the ground. Heat scorched across her face, her body weightless as she was thrown back, her arms catching her fall as she was hurled to the wet concrete.

Screams rattled, surrounding her from all angles followed by heavy footsteps.

BANG!

Disorientated, she pushed herself up onto her arms and lifted her head, trying to make out the chaos that surrounded her.

"HELP, SOMEONE PLEASE!"

She shakily climbed to her feet, looking around at the carnage, blood a harsh red against the dark ground. A car had crashed into an ambulance, the white metal destroyed, crushing both vehicles completely. The impact had pushed the ambulance into the road, causing a few cars to swerve dangerously to avoid a collision, one being unlucky and crashing head on.

"MUMMY!"

"CALL THE DOCTORS!"

"THIS IS A HOSPITAL FOR FUCK SAKE!"

Voices shouted in the chaos, getting louder as cars continued to avoid adding further carnage. She felt the heat on her face intensify as something caught fire, igniting the first car instantly.

"PLEASE. SOMEONE. SHE'S TRAPPED!"

Alice moved through the crowd, running towards the people desperately trying to free the woman trapped in the car. The door had been caved in, people unable to pull the lock open as they scrambled to gain purchase. The woman groaned and rolled her head to one side of the airbag, blood dripping down her face.

"It won't open." Alice desperately searched for something she could use to help open the door. "Try the other door," she cried to anyone who would listen.

She could feel the heat lick her skin, the scent of oil and petrol strong in her nose as it leaked across the asphalt.

"Hey, we're just getting you out," she spoke calmly to the woman in the car, her eyes glazed over in pain. "Can you undo your seatbelt for me?" The woman stared before sluggishly reaching over, trying desperately to release the belt.

"It won't open." The woman started to cry, violently tugging at the belt. "Why won't it open?"

"It's okay, we can cut it open. It's not a problem." The heat at her back was getting worse, smoke a thick plume surrounding them.

"Ma'am please step away from the car." A fireman rushed over, his suit protecting him from the intense heat. "Ma'am I need you to get back from the car, it's dangerous." He pushed her out the way, and began to frantically work on the metal door with one of his instruments.

Alice stumbled back as coughs constricted her lungs, the smoke thick enough to obscure her vision. She thought she could see the red fire engine in the distance, but couldn't make out the details.

"EVERYONE GET DOWN."

A pop as petrol ignited, causing a fireball only meters away. Metal creaked against the heat, a car becoming engulfed as the flames raced to devour everything in its path. Another firefighter became immersed in smoke beside her, his friends struggling for control, ignoring her as she stood motionless. Burning flesh assaulted her nose, choking as it became hard to breath.

Without thought she approached the flame, the orange and yellow element dancing, fighting against the breeze and the water being poured from the hose.

"It's not working," she whispered to herself, watching the fire grow rather than die. She couldn't understand why, but she felt the biggest urge to touch the fire. She thrust her hand into the blaze, coating her skin with her own blue power.

A cyclone of sound surrounded her, voices and screams she couldn't distinguish as she concentrated on the flame. The fire reacted, surrounding her completely rather than following its desired destination along the oil. Alice peeked over her shoulder, making sure the fireman was still working on the car door, prioritising the injured.

"DON'T MOVE!" Another fireman mouthed at her, unable to hear him above the roar of the flames.

Alice threw her head back, a scream breaking free from her throat, her chi electric as she tried to fight the fire, absorbing its energy. Her hair whipped around her head as her fingertips started to burn, blue fire meeting the red. Slowly the blue conquered, swallowing the danger as her own power burned past her elbows. With one last pop the last of the flame went out, taking with it her breath.

Lungs tight, she held her hands to her chest, her arms still holding her blue flame, the edges licked with green. With a last thought, Alice extinguished the flame, turning off her power like a faucet.

The abrupt emptiness staggered her, causing her to fall to her knees below the smoke. Blood pumped in her ears, breath struggling as her lungs struggled to move in and out. Her hand shook as she reached to her face, her fingertips coming back red as she felt something warm drip down her face.

She surrendered to the sudden exhaustion.

CHAPTER THIRTEEN

Beep. Beep. Beep.
What the bloody hell is that?
Alice reached over blindly, trying to turn off the annoying sound.

Beep. Beep. Beep.

Unable to find the source of the sound she stretched, feeling something in her hand tug.

"Keep still please."

"OW!" Alice jumped into a sitting position, staring at the red hole that was now in her hand. "What was that?"

"Just removing your drip," a woman in white and blue answered, her attention completely on the task of cleaning the small cut quickly and efficiently. "You might feel slightly disorientated, we had to sedate you because you kept burning my colleagues."

Beep. Beep. Beep.

Alice groggily blinked the remnant of sleep from her eyes, trying to pay attention to the surrounding details. Panic slowly settled in as she recognised the room, an adjustable bed with itchy wool blankets, a single wooden chair at the foot and ugly blue curtains. A TV was on in the top corner, an old small box with a huge heavy back.

Beep. Beep. Beep.

"Oh, let me get that." The nurse clicked a few buttons, stopping the repetitive noise.

"Why...why..." she stuttered, her throat dry. She heard a loud commotion towards the gap in her door, could just make out Dread arguing.

"You did an amazing thing you know."

"I'm... I'm sorry, what?" Confused by the statement she twisted to face the nurse.

"Because of you, that woman and possibly more survived that inferno." With that statement she left, allowing Dread to enter.

"Wow, private room. Snazzy." She coughed, clearing her throat.

Dread just stared, his face creased in worry before he began pacing back and forth.

"Dread, seriously, I'm fine." He just continued to pace, the action making her nervous. He was the calmest and most collected person she knew. He did not pace. "What was I supposed to do? Let her die? The water wasn't working..." she started to babble.

"What you did was brave and stupid." He stopped pacing, his black eyes scary as he reassured himself she was okay. "Mostly stupid."

"But..."

"You were caught on camera."

"Camera?" she asked, confused.

"On a phone, someone caught footage of you absorbing all that fire."

"So?" She swung her legs off the hospital bed.

Dread was suddenly in front of her, his body blocking her from getting off. "Do not move."

"Is that why you're pissed at me? I don't understand."

"I'm not angry, I'm just..." Dread looked around the room, searching for an explanation. "Alice you can't get caught doing things like that on camera."

"What? Why?" She lifted her chin defiantly.

"Since I found out Daemons have been sniffing around," he snapped at her, his burst of irritation and worry evident from the vibration of his pulse. "We both know your affiliation with fire is unusual, that alone would gain you unwanted attention. Add that to the fact..."

"The fact what?" She wiggled her toes, satisfied that she felt every movement.

"I have already said too much." Dread cleared his throat.

"Were you going to say that Daemons killed my family?" She watched the surprise flash across his face before he looked away. That was all the confirmation she needed. She knew she would never get him to admit it out loud, yet that one look gained her a little more of the missing puzzle.

Instead of replying he took a moment to compose himself, the move bringing the small TV in the corner into view, 'BREAKING NEWS' flashing across the screen.

Alice leant forward to watch the poor quality video, clearly recorded on a mobile phone. The image shook but showed a blonde woman in a circle of fire, blue power a river flowing from her hands, eating up the flame. The video cut off just before she collapsed.

"Turn the volume up," she asked, watching the screen.

Dread turned it off instead. "Alice, you must never tell anyone about this. It could put you in danger."

"Why did you never tell me?" she quietly asked. He knew she wanted to know everything about that night, wanted to understand why.

"And what would you have done with the knowledge?"

Her mouth opened to reply, but nothing came out. She didn't know what she would have done.

"I have brought you up the only way I knew how…"

"Knock, knock." A man wearing a white coat walked in, interrupting their conversation.

"Alice, I would like you to meet Dr Richards. He will be your physician." Dread lifted his palm, shaking hands with the doctor.

"Please. Call me Dave," the doctor replied smoothly, a friendly smile on his face.

"It's nice to meet you Dr Dave, but why do I need a doctor?" She looked between the two men.

"It's just a precaution," the doctor smiled, making Alice stare at the several rings pierced into his lip.

"Do you not set off every metal detector you go through?" she asked as she assessed the rest of his piercings. Along with the lip rings, he had a ring through his nose, like a bull. He also had a bar through his left eyebrow while his right eyebrow had a tattoo of an eagle soaring above it. The small artwork impressively detailed.

"Sometimes." A close-lipped smile. "I have even more piercings below the coat."

Alice blushed as she fought not to look down, interested to see if she could see anything through the fabric of his clothing. "That's nice," she said, concentrating very hard on his face. "So why do I need a doctor again?"

"Like Dr Richards said it's just a precaution," Dread answered. "You shouldn't have been able to absorb that fire, but you did. You also collapsed afterwards."

"I'll be based at The Tower, I just want you to visit me once a week to check your vitals." He grabbed her chart, reading the paper clipped to the front. "How are you feeling?"

"I feel fine."

"Any aches or pains? Headache?"

"No." *Surprisingly*.

"How often have you been having power flares?" He caught her eye, watching her reactions.

She bit her lip, thinking about her answer. "Not often. I just lose some control, it takes more effort than normal to calm down."

"Is it when you get angry?"

Alice hesitated. "Sometimes."

"Ok," he said carefully as he flared his chi.

Feeling the electric across her aura she flared her own back, shocked at how desensitised it had become.

"My chi..." she cried.

"Will return to normal in a few hours, I think you just over stimulated yourself. Magic is like a muscle, it needs to be trained otherwise it will become exhausted, especially with how much you made it stretch today. I wouldn't panic, it feels normal, but I wouldn't go around absorbing any amount of fire for a while," he chuckled to himself.

She couldn't argue. "Sound advice."

"I'm just going to assess your development over the next few months. We need to find out why you fainted." He took out what she thought was a pen from his coat pocket, clicking it to reveal a small light. He shone it into her eyes a few times, checking her pupils intently. "You also started bleeding from your ears and nose. You don't need a doctor to tell you that's bad." He clicked off the light. "Physically you're healthy, the only damage you seem to have sustained were a couple grazes when you collapsed."

"Hey, did anybody call for a ride?" a familiar voice called.

"SAM!" Alice ran into his arms, thankful to see him. Sam didn't do hospitals.

"Oh, hey baby girl, you giving the docs a run for their money?" he chuckled, hugging her close. "You okay?" he whispered against her hair.

"She's fine." Dr Dave replied, overhearing. "She just needs to rest for a few days."

"Of course she's fine." He stepped back, checking her from head to toe.

"Alice you have already been discharged," Dr Dave said. "But please come see me next week."

"Of course she will doctor," Sam tugged her towards the door. "I'll make sure she goes to every appointment."

CHAPTER FOURTEEN

Alice cradled her third glass, Sam topping up her vodka and cranberry mix whenever she was getting low. He had convinced her she needed to come and relax, enjoy a night out at the bar he worked at. So far it was working.

"Don't you think you've had enough?" he asked, pouring her yet another new glass. Sam looked great in his tight black work t-shirt, his long beautiful hair flowing free around his shoulders. His eyes were serious, mouth tense with concern.

"Nope." She sipped the liquid again, sighing at the burning sensation.

"When I invited you to hang out I didn't realise you would drink like a fish." He eyed her almost empty glass once more.

"You said I should drink and have fun."

"Yes, *have* fun. Baby girl, your face says anything but." He twirled a finger around a curl of her hair. "You look stunning yet you haven't even stepped on the dance floor."

"I'm taking my time," she pouted.

She had enjoyed getting dressed in the dark red satin midi dress she bought years ago but had never worn, matched with the same shade lipstick. She just wasn't yet ready to immerse herself with the other dancers, pretty dress or not.

"You're sulking." He pulled away her glass, folding his arms across his chest.

"Am not." She knew she sounded like a child, but her deliciously fuzzy brain didn't care. "Why aren't you doing bartender-y things?"

"'Bartender-y' things? Bloody hell, I think you need to stop drinking."

"Just one more?" She smiled cheekily. She wasn't sulking, she was thinking, two entirely different things.

He just stared at her.

"There's plenty more bartenders."

"We shall see," he sighed, handing her drink back. "What are you going to do about the contract?"

"I can't just drop it. I've learnt more in the last few days than I have my entire life."

"Did you really want to know though?"

"What do you mean?"

"Like, does it make it any easier? Knowing?" He waved as someone shouted for his attention.

Alice hesitated. "I don't know." She downed the last of her drink. "Sam I don't know what to do."

"You should stay away from anything that involves the D word."

That made her chuckle. "We both know I don't get any."

"Aye, very funny. You know what I mean." He leant forward on his elbow, half climbing onto the shiny black worktop as he whispered above the music. "Daemons."

"Yes." Things really did go bump in the night, she would know. "It's busy in here." She changed the subject.

"Yeah, since the new management it's been hectic." He squinted down the bar, someone as called for him once again. "Babe, I have to go serve, you just going to hang here?"

"For a while longer." His look of concern didn't change. "Then I'm going to go dance."

"Good, go enjoy yourself." He kissed her cheek. "Last one." He stole her cup and replaced it with a tall glass that was orange juice mixed with cranberry. "Sex on the beach." With a wink he walked towards the throngs of people at the other side of the bar, his sway in full swing.

Sam had worked in the Blood Bar for a few years, always enjoying the social life that came with being a bartender. He was right with the new management making the place busier, changing the old generic bar into something more stylish and modern. Gone were the cheap seating and sticky floors, replaced with high-end leather stools with chrome detailing and shiny wooden flooring. A stage was newly built from the same dark wood, designed as if it just erupted from the floor.

Blood Bar was notorious for its blood infused cocktails that brought in mainly Vamp clientele, but never really catered to anyone else. The new menu kept to its original taste from where the bar got its name, plus it included a wider range of beverages tailored to almost every Breed.

It was definitely a pleasant place to sit and contemplate her interesting life. Well, at least decide what her next step would be. She needed to know more, as if the more she knew the more she could unlock her memories, unlock her nightmares.

Flaring her chi she gave a satisfied sigh, feeling the usual electric undercurrent from the room. Over the last few hours she had felt her magic restore back to its natural level, like a bottle slowly refilling. Content, she continued to drink her cocktail as she enjoyed the music coming from the beautiful tenor of the singer on the small stage. The band behind filling the room with a steady beat that had most of the bar on their feet dancing.

Something brushed across her chi.

"Maybe you should stop drinking," a husky voice said next to her.

Ready to turn around and tell the person where to shove it, she hesitated, blinking stupidly at the tall man leaning against the bar. His chi continued to stroke hers as his steel grey eyes appraised her face. She had never felt anything like it, sparkles teasing across her aura. She couldn't decide if she liked it or not.

"Excuse me?" she asked, staring at him as she quickly adjusted her own chi. "I didn't realise you were my keeper."

The man smiled, a slight curve of his lips at her comment. He folded his heavily tattooed arms over his chest, a black shirt showing the bars logo across his left pec.

He must work here.

"Maybe you should mind your own business?" She searched desperately along the bar for Sam.

The man chuckled darkly, unfolding his arms from his chest. "Come on sweetheart, you need to go home."

"I'm good here thanks." She knocked the bar for emphasis. That got her another chuckle. "Go play with those lovely ladies over there..." She pointed in a vague direction behind her. "They seem to want your attention."

He followed her finger, frowning when he noticed the group of women staring at him, his eyes narrowing before he looked back at her, his face serious, the flirtatious arrogance gone.

She slipped off the stool, stumbling on her heels before his arm snapped out, steadying her.

"Oh, thanks." His hand didn't move off hers, his skin radiating heat. She tapped his hand, failing to not stare at his tattoos. "I'm not drunk." She could even dictate the alphabet backwards. Probably.

"That's not what a drunk person would say at all." He released her arm.

"Crap." He had her there. "Well, I'm going to dance." She turned and stumbled again, barely catching herself on the bar. So she may have had a few more drinks than she initially thought.

Fighting a blush, she pretended nothing happened and straightened, yanking her skirt back down to an appropriate height. With a nod she walked unsteadily towards the dancing crowd, the musician now singing a heavy ballad.

Letting the music take over she felt herself start to sway, her arms rising in the air with her eyes closed. The beat changed and she altered her moved to match, her hips curling in tempo with the rhythm. She allowed the music to calm her inner turmoil.

Arms wrap around her from behind, a body pasting itself against her back as she danced. His hips moved in rhythm with hers before a hand came round to her stomach, controlling.

His breath against her ear. "What the bloody hell do you think you're doing?" Rex asked.

She knew who it was almost the instant she felt his presence. Twisting her hips she danced against him, feeling his breath hitch, his palm tightening against her stomach.

"I'm having fun." She tried to turn in his grip but he kept her back pressed against his front, his own hips continuing their dance. "Rex, let me turn."

He bent her head slightly instead, his nose pressed against the side of her throat before she finally twisted in his arms, enough to see his white shirt, blood dried into the collar.

"You're drunk." His hands travelled down to hold the bottom of her back, pressing gently.

"I'm an adult." She continued to dance, allowing the music to move her muscles against him. She thought he would tense up, retreat into his intensity as he had done every time before, but he surprised her, instead matching her rhythm with his own.

"You don't think I know that?" he growled. That statement stopped her short, making her gaze up into his eyes. They were electric, clear as anything yet, just as unreadable, as if he didn't understand himself either.

"Why are you here?" she asked, not trusting her own eyes. "How did you find me?"

He pulled her toward him, placing her hands on his shoulders so he could bend down to her ear. "I'm here to ask why *my* Paladin is here getting drunk."

"I *am not* drunk!" She laughed loud enough to disturb the other dancers. "Am I seriously not allowed to enjoy myself without being judged by people?" She clenched her fists. "Haven't you heard? I'm off the case."

"I know." His fingers dug into her back, his voice intimate against her skin. "You think I take orders from anyone?"

She stopped dancing. "What are you saying?"

"I already said you're my Paladin." His eyes traced her lips, their natural blue flashing pale.

She gasped, finally able to read his emotions.

Hunger.

Lust.

The raw openness should shock her, but didn't.

"Why don't you ever smile?" She licked the edge of her suddenly dry lips, his eyes following the action carefully.

"I smile."

"Not at me."

"You just don't see it." She felt his heat against her as he pushed into her personal space. "I have never quite met a female like you." His mouth came down to slant across her own, tongue pushing unapologetically between her lips. She felt the roughness of his kiss, the raw emotions leaking as he gave into his wilder nature, breaking free from his constant control. She pulled his head against her, moaning as she lets him devour her lips.

Her front door was barely closed before Rex was on her, his hands under her dress to lift her up against the hard wall. His freshly shaven skin brushed across her cheek, his tongue licking, teasing along her tongue. She knew in the back of her head it was wrong, but apparently her body didn't care.

She clawed at his shirt, buttons popping in every direction as she pulled it apart to stroke her nails across his chest. He growled into her mouth, his hand boldly pressing against her breast before he pinched a nipple through the thin material of her dress. Her brain short-circuited, arousal heating her up from the inside out as liquid heat grew between her legs.

"Bed?" Rex growled, kissing her again.

Alice just nodded against his mouth, her lungs fighting for air. Lifting her up he carried her into her bedroom, throwing her on the bed as soon as he entered. She bounced in the middle, her hands scrambling against the duvet for support. Rex looked intently down at her, his face hard to read.

Nerves burst through her arousal, confusion. "Wait..." She couldn't finish, her eyes widening when he reached beneath his shirt, pulling it over his head in one sweep. Mouth dry Alice stared at his gorgeous wide chest, over his chiselled abs down the line of thin hair leading into his dress trousers.

He was on her in the next instant, his mouth on hers as his hands roamed under her dress, his touch an amazing contrast to her sensitive flesh. Lifting her dress he pulled it over her head, wrapping the fabric around her wrists, pinning them above her head.

"Rex?" she breathed, feeling vulnerable. It was going too fast...

He kissed down her neck, her wrists still pinned above her head, pushing her breasts together seductively. His tongue licked around her nipple, blowing against the wetness. Alice let out a small noise, almost a sob as he bit down on the sensitive nub, tugging it between his teeth. She pushed at his wrist, writhing underneath him.

Fuck!

The dress burst into flames, the threads burning into smithereens within seconds.

"Shit." He released her.

She hooked her leg around, pushing against his shoulder as he stared confused at the remains of the fabric. The sudden distraction gave her a sudden advantage, flipping them so she was straddling him, his erection continuing to strain. He just sat back up, biting down on the neglected nipple.

"Oh," she sighed, her voice low, husky with arousal.

With a snarl he twisted them, gaining dominance once again. Undulating on the bed she rubbed her thighs together in anticipation, excitement running over her. She had never felt like this, never wanted something so much.

A quick flick of a claw and he cut the edges of her underwear, tearing it clean from her hips in one clean motion.

"That was my favourite pair," Alice moaned up to him, his face expressionless, his eyes too intense as he gripped her, pulling her down the bed.

"No talking." He released her for a second, removing his trousers in a quick movement before his hot body was once again over her. Reaching down, he slipped one finger inside her, teasing the moisture, checking her readiness. He brushed the pad of his thumb against the small bundle of nerves that begged for his attention.

"Yes," she almost begged. Lifting her knee he placed it over his shoulder, opening her to him. She felt the head nudge at her opening, just teasing the entrance. "REX!" she shouted, his cock impaling her seconds later.

Growling low in his throat he started to thrust, powerful movements that pushed her up the sheets. Gripping his arms she held herself in place, her nerve endings screaming at the onslaught. Suddenly pulling out he pushed her hip, tossing her onto her stomach. Lifting her back up on to her knees he thrust into her once more.

He gave her no time to get used to him before he started moving again. Pumping his cock in and out in powerful thrusts. Alice braced herself, taking every inch of him. He grunted as he pumped, reaching below to rub her bundle of nerves, flicking his finger over it in time with his thrusts. Feeling the tell-tale signs of her tightening around him he pumped impossibly faster, spilling himself into her as she moaned his name.

S neaking a peak she opened the cupboard slowly, seeing nothing through the small gap. The door swung open violently, a shadow standing over the opening. "Come here, little girl," the shadow snarled.

She screamed as a hand grabbed her ankle, pulling her from her safe place. Her head hit the floor with a crack, creating bursts of light behind her eyes.

"You trying to hide from me, little girl?"

With a squeal, she pulled from the stranger's grasp, the warm liquid lubricant against the strong hand. In a rush she threw herself against the back door, the wood groaning from the impact. In her panic she stumbled with the doorknob, turning it at the right angle. The door opened a sliver, catching on the security chain.

She squeezed through the small gap as suddenly a hand snaked out, grabbing her nightgown.

"Got you," the voice growled, the shadow's eyes glowing red in the darkness.

CHAPTER FIFTEEN

After what felt like forever, Alice finally pulled into a parking space in the busy high street, her car choking as it settled.

She had woken up with a silent scream, her pulse racing as the remnants of her nightmare faded. The dread had felt so real, so vivid compared to usual. Realisation of what the creature was, the shadow making her subconscious go wild.

Yet, the nightmares were still in faded puzzle pieces, repeats of the same story, over and over with no context.

She hit her hand on the steering wheel in frustration.

What was worse was she had woken up alone.

From the absence of heat on the other side of the bed, she had been alone for a while.

Stupid. Stupid. Stupid. She hit the steering wheel again, calming herself.

She had never expected she would end up in bed with Rex, he just happened to be at the right time and place. Yet she felt hurt, embarrassed that she woke up alone in bed after everything that happened.

A dirty secret.

Her body ached, muscles that were rarely used protesting as she shifted in her seat. He had been rough, she had wanted it that way, but could she forgive him for using her and then leaving? No note. Just an empty, cold place beside her in bed?

"I used him too," she admitted to herself. Which was true, she wanted to be able to feel something, wanted someone to make her feel alive. Wanted something constant as her life seemed to be derailing around her.

With a sigh she flipped down the mirror, tilting her neck up into the light.

He had to bite me, didn't he? she cursed him.

She had used the last of her potion to create that amulet, so the red sore on the side of her neck, just above her shoulder blade wouldn't stand out in stark contrast to her pale skin.

Annoyed at Rex she jumped out of the car, the door swinging shut leaving her standing in the busy high street. Someone nudged her, causing her to step straight into a puddle.

"Hey lady, move out the fucking way," a young man shouted as he continued his fast pace further up the high street, shopping bags swinging violently by his side.

She replied automatically with a hand gesture as she moved towards the magic shop, deciding that from now on she would be nothing less than professional.

But first, she needed to hide the bite.

The black washed out 'Mystic Medlock's Magic Shop' sign hung from the old wall, squeaking as it flapped gently in the breeze. The outside of the shop had two large glass pane windows, one side advertising novelty magic tricks for the Norms, and the other showing around three different sized chests with drawers Alice knew to be filled with different amulets and herbs. She walked past the large stone gargoyle that guarded the entrance and into the deserted shop.

The shop was empty other than a bored looking man in a blue apron, who leant against the wall. His algae green eyes lit up as he noticed her enter, his back straightening and his hands patting down his front.

"Welcome," he greeted, smiling with his teeth. He gave a slight flare of his chi before retreating back behind the counter.

"Hello," she smiled back.

The shop was decorated with novelty witch hats and pumpkins that grinned with sharp teeth. A fat black cat sat in the corner, licking its paw lazily, not even looking up to see who entered. A display unit had been moved recently from the scratches on the floor, to be replaced with a cardboard box holding different Hallows Eve cards.

"Isn't it a bit early to be selling Samhain decorations?" The week long festivities were over a month away, the twenty-fifth to the thirty-first of October a huge Breed event where most of the world partied for a week straight in celebration of Breed becoming recognised citizens over three hundred years ago.

"You can blame the card companies. They try to squeeze as much money as they can out of the holidays," the clerk chuckled.

He was just shy of six feet tall with short lank brown hair, his face was pale and Alice noticed faint freckles spotted across his high cheekbones. His mouth was full, turned up at the corners as his green eyes glittered underneath the artificial light. He obviously thought he was hilarious.

"Anything I can help you with?" he asked politely.

"I need a concealer charm, I seem to have run out." She watched as he moved around the shop, opening drawers and looking in cabinets. "Er, are you new here?" she squinted at him.

"Not exactly." His eyes flashed slightly. "My father owns the shop and he needed someone to help out, so I came back home." He shrugged as if it was no big deal.

"Oh, Mr Medlock?"

"Yes, you know him?"

"I do." Alice smiled, having known the old man for years. He was always complaining the bigger chains were going to put him out of business, yet Alice couldn't shop anywhere else. "How is he?"

"He's fine, thinking about retiring." The man continued to search absently for the charms. It was clear he had no idea where he was looking. With a chuckle she walked towards the south wall, opening a drawer clearly marked 'cosmetic charms' and grabbing one of the small cylindrical disks.

The cat in the corner hissed at something before jumping to the floor, slowly hobbling to Alice's feet to look up at her with large yellow eyes. Letting out a yowl the cat waddled past, passing through the beaded curtain into the back.

"He can't retire, he knows everything." She smiled when the man finally turned, holding the disk gently between her fingertips so he could see.

The man grinned back. "Trust me, he doesn't know everything." He coughed, clearing his throat. "The name's Alistair, but my friends call me Al." He held out his hand.

"Alice." She brushed her own hand across his before handing over the disk.

"So where have you been hiding? I wasn't even aware Mr Medlock had a son."

"I've been studying abroad, just finished my degree when my father called asking for me to help out in the shop." He started to ring up her purchase on an old vintage looking cash register. Each button released a loud ping noise, the vibrations gently echoing against the various glass displays set behind.

"What did you study?" She found herself asking, suddenly interested.

"Engineering."

"Engineering?" She noticed the scraps of metal and screws on the desk.

"Yes, The mechanics of magic in machinery. It sounded cool at the time," he smiled gently, almost shy. "Working here has given me some time to play around with some ideas. The shop isn't as busy as I remember it."

"Yeah, the new chain came in down the street…"

"Ah yes, my father is always standing outside shaking his fist at them. Like it would help." Wrapping up the charm he handed it back over, the price flashing up.

Swallowing, she handed over the correct money, wondering if she gave the receipt to the expenses team she could claim it back. She was sure she could make up a decent excuse for why she needed the particular charm.

"Thank you."

"You're welcome. It's one my father made personally so I know it will definitely cover up that nasty bite on your neck. You need to find a boyfriend who doesn't treat you like food."

Alice's hand automatically covered the mark, her cheeks heating in embarrassment. "He's not my boyfriend," she replied before quickly shutting her mouth. Like that didn't make her sound worse.

"Then things just got a lot more interesting." Al leant across the desk, accidentally brushing some metal and screws onto the floor. "Shit!"

A loud buzz filled the shop before a whirling sound dashed across the floor. Alice stepped out of the way as a small circular black contraption began greedily sucking up the debris through a nose at the front. It was the size of a small plate and resembled a strange elephant. The back looked broken, or maybe even unfinished as she could see all the mechanics working inside its open shell, like a clock. The metal and screws it was trying to clean up kept shooting out its back onto the floor behind it, making it turn to collect them again and again.

"What is that?" She watched in awe, never having seen anything like it.

"Shit, shit, shit." Al scrambled to catch it as it whirled around his feet, happily chatting away to itself. "SIM STOP!" he shouted at the metal thing. The mechanical elephant halted, twirling to face Al almost expectantly. "SIM, off," Al declared in clear words before leaning down and picking it up.

"Well, that's curious."

"This is SIM, Suck. It. Mechanics. It's a working name." He hugged SIM to his chest, scowling down at it.

"Well, your degree just got a whole lot more interesting." She clutched her purchase. "I have to go to work, good luck with SIM."

She smiled to herself as she left the store, listening to the fading sound of Al scolding the mechanical elephant hoover.

Having already applied the charm, the small wooden disk hidden beneath her bracelet, Alice felt herself finally begin to relax as she sat down in her small workspace. Each cubicle was made up of three grey felt walls with a desk, every single one identical in their uniformity. It was up to the owners of the desks to personalise their small little space, and that is exactly what Alice had done.

Her desk, just like the others, was a pale wood with two drawers on each side. Mostly filled with pens and notepads, normal stationary things you would expect from a desk. A computer sat on the right corner, still turned on from the last time she had sat there with nothing to do, her game of solitaire patiently waiting for her to finish.

The grey walls had various pictures pinned to the felt, photographs of Sam, old contracts as well as her Chinese knock-off cat clock. Sam liked to buy her things that had a cat theme, her newest addition was a poster with a sleeping cat curled on the front, and the words *'Don't talk to me'* printed underneath.

She closed the solitaire game that always popped up when she turned on the computer and clicked open her emails. "Why am I getting emails about Viagra?" she muttered to herself, clicking through the various correspondences about penis extensions, amazing weight loss pills and badly written pleas from princes asking for help to move their millions. "Aha." She finally opened the email she was looking for.

Alice,

Considering you discharged yourself at the hospital before I could come visit I'm going to assume you are okay. Which is good but don't do something like that again.
I have attached my notes regarding the reports in the last year, most are a waste of time but a few should be of interest.

I have managed to stay on the case and will be liaising with the Paladin in charge, Danton, so you will see me more in The Tower. I will try to give you any more information I come across.
Don't get caught.

Kind regards,
Miko
P.S. Feel free to give me Dr Richards number.

Alice smiled at the email. Only Miko would turn something this important into something he could get a date from.

Actually, she corrected, Sam would probably do the same. Her mood lifted as she opened the attachment and clicked print, hearing the printer roar to life a few cubicles over.

Notes-
John Doe – Unknown
• Elongated canines, blood found in the stomach. Scratch marks across the torso. Skull deformed, bone protruding through skin on top of the head.
John Doe – Unknown shifter
• Elongated canines, blood found in the stomach. Shifter DNA doesn't match blood in the stomach
Maxi L. Swanson - Unknown
• Elongated canines, blood found in the back of throat. Self-inflicted wounds.

John Doe - Unknown shifter
• Elongated canines, blood found in the stomach. Scratch marks across the torso. Shifter DNA
Sahari Mooner – Unknown
• All teeth have been forcibly removed. Blood found in the stomach and back of the throat
Jane Doe – Human
• Bruises on the wrists and ankles. Sticky residue around the mouth (Awaiting analysis). Broken teeth. Blood found in the back of the throat
Mischa Palmer - Unknown shifter
• Elongated canines, blood found in the stomach. Skull cracked
Rachel Langly - Fae
• Teeth completely deformed, blood found in the stomach. Nails torn from the fingertips.
Francis Carter – Lion shifter
• Teeth deformed, DNA came back with unusual strains.
Alesha Morgan – Human
• Paper ripped – No formal information
Bobby Dust – Hyena shifter
• Head had been cut clean off
Tomlin (Surname unknown) – Wolf shifter
• Purposely killed?

Reading the notes she typed the names into the S.I. database, the screen flashing between pages, the police directory searching through hundreds of thousands of records. If any of these people had had any trouble with the police, even just a parking ticket a record should flash up.

Sitting back she closed her eyes, the screen flashing through the pages too fast for her to read. Relaxing into the chair she thought back to the hospital, running all the conversations through her head over and over again. She hadn't exactly lied to the doctor, she just hadn't told the whole truth. It was only once that she had ever lost control to the point her own power had almost consumed her, but it wasn't uncommon for her to lose a little bit of control. Her annoying dancing ball of flame was proof of that.

An audible beep made her jump, knocking her cup of tea onto the floor with a crash. "Shit." She quickly picked up the cracked cup and placed it back on her worktop, using a tissue to dab at the spill. The computer beeped again, waiting for attention. Using the mouse she navigated through all the information.

Rachel Langly – Water Fae (Siren) – Reported missing 1974 – Arrested on 15th May 2016. Fraud.

Francis Carter – Shifter (Lion) – Sun Kiss Pride – Arrested on 27th July 2016. Possession of Class A drugs and charms.

Bobby Dust – NO RECORD.

Maxi L. Swanson – Reported missing 1999 – DUI 1987.

Sahari Mooner – Reported missing 2010.

Mischa Palmer – NO RECORD.

Alesha Morgan – Human – Arrested on January 10th 2015. Theft.

Rachel Langly was a beautiful woman, at six foot one she was all long legs, her red hair emphasizing her luscious lips and sharp cheekbones. She definitely looked like an epiphany of a male wet dream, a siren in every sense of the word.

Her supermodel looks showed just how easy it would be to sing men to their deaths at sea, just looking at her most men would bow at her feet. Even in the police mug shot she had a sensuality about her, her luscious lips tilting up at the corner, her eyes rimmed in black.

'No known family'

"Great." She clicked through the pictures, cringing. It was nice to know that when sirens died, the charms they used to survive on land disintegrated. Her long beautiful legs melted together like wax, pearlescent scales growing from her webbed feet up to her navel. Her neck developed gills, and her eyes became inhumanly large.

Alice closed the tab and returned her attention to the list. Using a pencil she crossed out Miss Langly's name, the pencil cutting through the paper from frustration.

"Fuck, Fuck, Fuck," she chanted to herself, rubbing her palms across her face.

She looked up from between her fingers, a photograph of a blonde male staring back. Alice clicked on Mr Francis Carter's photograph, enlarging the details. The dark chocolate eyes were void of any emotion, his emaciated cheeks stark against his natural tan.

"Francis Carter. Sun Kiss Pride, Lion Shifter... where is Sun Kiss?" Alice minimised the page, intending to search for local prides.

"What the fuck?" The computer cut out, the screen flashing before showing the login screen.

Error. Log in details incorrect. You have been blocked. See helpdesk for more information.

"Seriously?" Alice huffed.

This can't be happening.

She scribbled down Francis Carter's name and she tucked the paper into her jeans pocket. The I.T. guys were only a few floors down so she decided to take the stairs.

"Hello?" She knocked on the door leading to where the I.T. technicians work. Alice tried to fight a smile at the poster on the door, a giant A2 print of *'I.T. GUYS. HAVE YOU TURNED IT ON AND OFF AGAIN?'* written in bold typography.

"Hello?" She knocked louder, knowing someone would have to be in.

"It's open."

"Oh." Alice pushed the door, stepping over the threshold into what looked like a spaceship. Computer monitors were arranged around the large room, each screen showing something different. A half built computer tower sat in the middle of the room, bright wires attempting to escape.

"Hey, Alice." Lewis, one of the I.T. guys swung his chair around to give her a little wave. Crisps layered in his incredibly long beard, long enough that it covered most of his bright green t-shirt.

"You on the late shift, Lewis?" Alice asked, closing the door behind her gently.

"Yeah, me and Billy. He's gone to go get us some more crisps." He lifted up the empty crisp packet, even tipping it upside down just to emphasise how empty the packet was. "What can I do to help you doll? I don't normally see you down here."

"It's not letting me log in. Just keeps giving me an error message."

"Ah okay, let's take a look shall we." He spun his chair to face one of the monitors, his chubby fingers racing across the keys as he typed something into the computer. "It looks like you have been locked out."

"Locked out?" She leant over to look at the screen. "How can I be locked out?"

"Looks like..." He clicked some more buttons. "Commissioner Grayson has put you on medical leave. Look." He pointed to her picture on the screen, the one every member of the building had for security. Her picture was easy to spot, her blonde messy hair bright compared to the darker tones of her colleagues. It hadn't helped she wasn't aware it was picture day, so she had the previous night's makeup smudged across her face. They wouldn't let her retake it.

The words *'Medical leave until further notice'* flashed across the bottom of the picture.

"Shit. Is that why I can't access any systems?"

"Pretty much.," He read the small print. "Top restrictions too." He shrugged his shoulders, the motion causing some crisps to escape from his beard and land on his stomach.

"Okay." *Crap.* "Can you reverse it?"

"Not without risking my job."

"Fair enough." She lifted her hand to her face, wiping across her eyes. *Shit.*

"I might not be able to reinstate your restrictions, but..." he beamed at her. "I don't have such restriction."

"You sure you won't get into trouble?" she said hesitantly.

"I owe you. You helped me catch my cheating wife, if it wasn't for you, I would still be with the bitch. What do you need?"

"Thanks Lewis, you're a star," she grinned, grabbing the notes from her pocket.

CHAPTER SIXTEEN

This was a stupid idea, Alice thought to herself as she sat in her car outside a large derelict house, scowling at the crumpled map in her lap. Squinting her eyes, she double checked the roads that were supposed to lead to Sun Kiss Pride.

"This can't be right?"

The large Georgian house was set back in a few acres of land, the pale bricks crumbling. Green and brown ivy hugged the walls, hiding most of the damage. The surrounding trees and bushes were a spectrum of the same dire shades, a mixture of browns, reds and yellows, summer pushing into autumn. There were two large windows at the front of the house, all covered by heavy dark brocade curtains, an uncomfortable contrast to the dirty white of the window frames.

Black smoke darkened the sky above signalling someone was home, yet the drive was empty of all other vehicles but her own, which was parked slightly behind a large overgrown bush.

A shrill ring made her jump in her seat. Scrambling for her phone she checked the number before answering.

"Hello, you have reached the mobile of Alice, please leave a message after the..."

"Alice, you're not funny."

"Hi, Sam." She heard his small laugh at the end of the line.

"*Why are you in Little Birmingham?*" His voice took on a serious tone.

"Well, to be honest I'm currently staring at a house." She had actually been staring at the house for a while, waiting to see if anyone moved behind one of the windows. So far nothing. "Wait, how did you know where I was?" She sat up from her slouch, frowning at the phone.

"*Rex turned up and...*"

"Rex? What's he doing there?"

"*He... Rex... turn...*" he began, voice breaking up.

"Hello? Sam? I think I'm losing you."

"*Sorry about that,*" he said, voice strained.

"Just tell him I'm checking out this house, it's supposed to be the pride's den. But, I'm pretty sure Google lied."

Something moved in her peripheral vision, a twitch in the curtain. She watched carefully, waiting for it to move again. When it didn't she released a breath she didn't know she was holding.

"*Pride?*" a slightly deeper voice said, ending with a snarl, "*what the fuck do you think you're doing?*"

Alice could hear Sam arguing in the background, the microphone unable to pick up his exact words. "Why are you with Sam?" She felt her face scowl. "Put Sam back on."

He ignored her request. "*You were supposed to ring.*"

For a man that was emotionless, he sounded pissed.

"Well if you were there when I woke up I could have told you then couldn't I?" Okay, she was only a little bit sour.

"*Sun Kiss Pride?*" A growl. "*Don't do anything stupid and wait for me. You shouldn't have gone there alone.*"

"I'm not stupid Rex, I have thought this through." She hadn't, but she wasn't going to admit that. "I was only going to ask a few questions."

"*Wait for me. I'm leaving now, I'll be there in three hours.*" He would have to make up some serious speed to get to Little Birmingham in three hours. "How did you even know where I was?"

"*Just wait.*"

"Rex I don't need your help."

Another snarl. "*Wait.*" He wasn't giving her much choice. "*Meet you at Manor Green Park.*" He gave her the directions and once she confirmed she understood he hung up without a goodbye.

"Arsehole," she scolded the phone before throwing it onto the seat beside her. Laying the map back over her lap she checked where the park was, happy to see it was only a short drive away. Car in gear, she took one last look at the house. It probably wasn't the right place anyway.

Alice watched an old man walk painfully slow across the path towards the ducks, stale bread clutched under his free arm, the strong breeze doing nothing to stop his journey. Cold, Alice pulled her jacket around her tighter as she looked around the park, enjoying the sun's warmth between the gusts of wind. A group of shifter and human children were running around the grassy area, kicking a black and white football around. A shout as the ball went wide, heading towards the flock of ducks sitting by the pond. With a loud squawk the birds fluttered away, landing further up the pond and away from the children's ball.

The old man stopped his walk, puffing. With determination, he set off again towards the other side, back towards the ducks.

Alice smiled despite herself.

She'd been sitting for long enough for her arse to go numb. She had already walked around the park several times, resigning herself to just sitting and watching. It didn't help that anger still bubbled, not being able to let the conversation with Rex go. She was getting grumpy.

Flicking her phone on she scrolled to Sam's number, hitting the video call.

"Alice, I can't talk now." Sam lifted his phone to reveal half his face. "I'm still at work." She could just see the collar of his work t-shirt, his hair in his usual plaits.

"I want to know what happened with Rex? How did he know where I was?"

"He just turned up here," Sam propped the phone up on something, the angle revealing the top half of his torso. "Had to get him kicked out by the bouncers..."

"Sam, what is that on your face?" Alice tried to zoom in on the image. "Is that a bruise?"

Sam touched his cheekbone, brushing across the purple mark that was already healing, would be completely gone by tomorrow.

"It's nothing." He buffed a glass before placing it onto a shelf. "What do you even see in Rex?" He tossed the rag onto his shoulder. "He's getting a bit territorial."

"No, he's not." Alice quieted her voice as someone sat beside her. "It's nothing."

"*He's an Alpha...*"

"We're just working together."

"*Sure, baby girl.*" A sphinx smile. "*Don't ya think it's strange? The way you were hired for the job?*"

She hadn't given it much thought. He had lost three wolves, and had been hunting alone before he hired her. So what made him change his mind?

"*Look, I'm getting off in an hour, we'll talk then.*" A yawn, eyes sleepy as he bent to his phone. "*Love ya baby girl.*"

"Wait, Sam..." The phone went dark. "Dammit." Unable to sit any longer she started to walk the length of the park once more, heading towards the iron wrought bridge.

"Salve dominam," a voice gurgled as soon as she stepped onto the first step.

Startled, Alice searched around for the owner of the voice, seeing no one close enough to have spoken.

"Lonii pro troll?" the voice gargled once again.

"Toll for the troll?" she repeated in English, her Latin rusty. She still knew some basic words, Latin a language taught to all children, especially as it was used in spell-work as well as being favoured amongst the older Fae.

"Oh yes mistress, toll for the troll." Long black fingernails burst through the green sludge on the wall on the underside of the bridge. It grasped the sides, pulling the rest of its body through the small hole with a wet noise. Rust from the metal moulded itself into the sludge, hardening to become scaly skin as small black ovals popped out of the top, eyes staring. Trolls were the only Fae that iron didn't affect, indeed an annoyance to the High Lords of each caste considering they were classed as the lowest of the Fae possible.

Alice stepped off the bridge, making sure she stood in direct sunlight. "Why should I pay the toll when I haven't crossed your bridge?"

"Silly malefica, you always pay Muck."

"Muck?"

"Muck myself." He leant over an arm, bowing towards her. Well, as much as a bow as a creature with no bones could do.

"Hello, Muck, nice bridge you have." The troll slurped in response.

"I don't plan to cross your bridge, but I'll pay the toll if you answer some questions for me?"

"Questions?" His black eyes squinted in confusion.

Great. An intellectually challenged troll. "Questions as in...erm, interrogo?"

The troll smiled, showing a row of pointy nails along his jaw. His green skin swirled, melding into a calmer blue before hardening again. "Ask away mistress."

"Erm, okay." She tugged her jacket in thought. "Who are the local shifters?"

"Bestia leo."

"Lions?"

"Yes." Muck grinned even further, enjoying the game.

"Any other local bestias?"

"No local." He paused for a moment, thinking. "Visitors." He shook his head, sludge slopping across the floor. One bit reached her boot, the sludge sizzling before hardening in the sunlight. As subtle as possible she tried to dislodge it, but it was impossible.

"What sort of visitors?"

Muck smiled, showing even more teeth. "Toll." He held out his hand, stretching as far as possible without coming into direct sunlight. Alice removed one of her gold stud earrings, trying not to touch his skin as she dropped the gold into his hand. "Gratias mistress."

"You shouldn't be talking to the bridge dweller," a new voice said from behind.

Alice turned, watching the painfully thin man approach.

"They will tell you anything for some gold." The stranger stood a few feet away, his dirty blonde hair scruffy, his long stubble a shade darker.

"HSSSSSSSS LEO." Muck spat towards the man, the sludge barely reaching him as he gave a garbled growl. "Nec leo." Muck braced his arms on the iron, sludge splitting into two legs as he absorbed the surrounding water, gaining mass.

"Shit." Alice stepped back, not wanting to be anywhere near Muck when he reached his full size. "Muck, look at me." She waved her arms, trying to get his attention.

"Aut tu præterieris."

He wasn't listening.

"Muck, what visitors?" She tried again, but his attention was completely on the man walking towards them.

"I think you should step away from the..."

Alice grabbed the stranger's outstretched arm, twisting it behind his back.

"Owwww."

Alice knew the hold was painful, but it was hard to keep pressure with the height difference.

She slowly stood on her tiptoes, whispering into his ear. "I don't know who you are, but you shouldn't touch me." She put more weight on his bent elbow, getting her a hiss in return. With a last twist she released him, her eyes trained on his muscles, waiting to see if they tensed for an attack.

Muck made a thunderous noise, his skin becoming a sickly green, head and shoulders taking up almost the entire space underneath the small bridge. Without taking her eyes off the lion she reached to her other ear and removed her remaining earring, tossing it at him. It bounced off his hardened skin, landing in the sun. He would have to wait until dark to claim it.

"I don't think he likes you," she said to the tall man who held his arm protectively to his chest.

"No." A worried glance. "I'm Preston, from Sun Kiss. Coleman sent me."

"He did?" She felt her eyebrows rise, remembering from her research that Coleman Grant was the Pride Leader. *How did he even know I was here?*

A nod. "He's expecting you for dinner, if you would follow me I can take you..."

"How did you know who I was?" she interrupted.

"Mr Wild is at the manor..."

He couldn't possibly be calling the derelict house a manor? Surely she had the wrong place before.

"He told us you would be here." Preston looked at his watch. "We have to hurry, dinner will be ready soon and we can't be late." He shifted his eyes to look around the park, as if he was worried someone might overhear.

"That didn't answer my question," she pushed him. "How did you know who I was?"

"Mr Wild has a photograph of you in his wallet."

He does? Alice saved that information for later. "I'll follow you in my car."

"NO!" A panicked look. "Cole was specific, I have to drive."

"No thanks, I can drive myself." She folded her arms across her chest.

"Please let me drive you." The panic started to grow, his eyes darting around as he licked his dry lips.

Guilt settled in her stomach. "What about a compromise? I'll drive, but you can come in the passenger seat?"

"I suppose... yes. That should be okay." Open relief on his face.

"Okay."

She guided him towards the car park, making sure he walked slightly in front.

Lions were predators. Everything about this man, from the scruffiness of his clothes to the gauntness of his face suggested he was more prey.

CHAPTER SEVENTEEN

"Nice house," Alice commented as she pulled into the same large driveway she was in earlier, the only difference was there were around six other cars along its edge. Car parked at the end she stepped out onto the stones, glancing up at the neglected house. It was just as bad as it was earlier, the darker sky not hiding any of the damages.

Preston said nothing as he walked slowly towards the front of the house, or manor as he laughingly described it. The loose stones crunched beneath her shoes as she paused next to him, trying not to stare at the huge claw marks and cracks patterned along the inside of the columns. The large door opened at their approach, revealing a hollow cheeked young man dressed in a white shirt and slacks.

"Preston," the man greeted. His eyes roamed across her, taking in the black Chelsea boots, blue jeans and black t-shirt with *'Sorry I'm late, but I didn't want to be here'* written across it. Fitting really.

Alice tried not to crack a smile, knowing she looked severely under-dressed for a formal dinner.

He sniffed as if unimpressed. "We've been expecting you." He walked down the hallway, leaving the door open.

The walls, which she tried not to gawk at as she followed the man, weren't as bad as she would have guessed from the outside. The striped wallpaper looked freshly applied, albeit a bit badly and the paint was newly coated if she went by the strong smell.

"If you would wait in here," the nameless lion pointed into a room at the end of the hall. "My Pride Leader will join you shortly."

That wasn't weird at all, she though as he left her alone.

"Miss Skye."

She froze in the doorway, fisting her hands.

Rex sat at the large tale, watching her with pure focus. She held his gaze, letting him know from the tension of her shoulders that she was beyond angry. He had recently shaved, his skin smooth enough to caress. His light brown hair had been pulled into a bun, a few strands framing his face. She wasn't a fan of men with buns, yet she felt the strongest urge to stroke it, to paste her body against his like a dog in heat. She had never quite felt such a strange compulsion.

"Nice of you to join us." He stood, stalking towards her.

Alice allowed her nails to cut into her hand, the pain stopping her from pulling him against her. "Nice scratches." She stared at the trio of claw marks across his face, the wound already fading to a pale pink. "I wonder how you got them."

"You should have called me." He barked out the words like bullets, his hand coming up to her jaw.

She smacked the hand, breaking the connection. "Those scratches look like a cats."

"I'm impressed with your knowledge of cat scratches. Is that some sort of kink you're into?" a chuckle from the doorway.

"Careful Cole." A warning, Rex's jaw clenched as he fought for control. "She's mine."

"Well, isn't that interesting," Coleman murmured. He was an average looking guy, his blonde hair scraped back from his scalp, a rubber band holding the pale strands in a lank ponytail. His eyes were mean and narrow, constant frown lines indented into his forehead. His mouth a harsh line, hidden faintly behind his ginger beard. "You must be *his* Alice."

"Hmm, must be." She looked between the men, the tension palpable in the small room. They knew each other, and it wasn't friendly.

"You look fine to me." Cole leisurely checked her up and down, eyes glistening as he smiled at her shirt. "Not a mark on you. Those news stations are always exaggerating." He clicked his tongue.

"What does he mean?" Rex gripped her jaw once more, staring into her eyes.

She kept her face passive. "Nothing." Rex's eyes narrowed, he knew she was lying.

"Now, now children. No fighting, we are among friends." Cole clapped his hands and a group of men walked in as if called. They positioned themselves behind certain chairs, forcing Alice and Rex to split.

"Alice, take a seat." Cole motioned with his hand. "I saved this space for you, opposite me," he said with a toothy grin. She passed Rex as she sat in the seat Cole pulled out, tensing as he brushed his fingertips through her hair. "Such a pretty blonde. Like your mother's..." he whispered along her neck.

"Excuse me?" She whipped around to face him, his attention on the decanters on the bar.

"Boys," he proclaimed as he started to pour, the men sitting down in one fluid motion, practised in their precision.

She watched them carefully, knowing something was wrong, but unable to put her finger on it. They all sat there, all six of them, all different ages with no expression on their faces. No emotion in their eyes. It was like a blank canvas, a puppeteer pulling the strings. Their suits were all the same, almost uniform in their blandness, many of them too large for their small forms, cheekbones sharp against their skin.

Cole continued to meticulously pour a red liquid into a glass, repeating it several times as an uncomfortable silence filled the room. The lions were yet to react, all barely breathing as they stared blankly across the table. Moving slowly Cole handed one glass to Alice, his fingers lingering on her own before he went to Rex.

As if a spell was broken the young lions started to fidget, pulling at their lapels in panic. The three to her right started to squirm uncontrollably, their eyes mostly white as they frantically took in their surroundings.

"Hitting the alcohol already honey?" A woman strode in, her dramatic neckline leaving nothing to the imagination. She pouted, making her bright red lips, the same startling shade as her hair, look bigger, more sensual.

The atmosphere became thick, fear heavy as all the lions froze, becoming once again unmoving mannequins. The woman smiled seductively along the table, lingering slightly longer than she needed to on Rex before kissing Cole on the lips, leaving a red smear.

"This is my wife, Poliana." Cole smiled lovingly before helping her take a seat.

"Wife?" Rex raised his eyebrows. "Congratulations, I never knew. How long?"

"About a year," Poliana replied, her eyes slanted as she stroked the skin of the young man next to her, his face pale as he stayed completely still, his chest barely moving.

"Welcome pride members, new friends and old." Cole lifted one of the glasses up to the air, saluting the room. "I hope you enjoy your stay." He stared intently at Alice as he took a sip.

Picking up her own she brought it to her nose, a sour copper smell coming from the deep red liquid. She tensed, looking over at Rex as he sipped his own. He shook his head gently, almost imperceptibly as he placed his drink back down. Following suit she placed her hands beneath the table, careful not to get too close to the lion next to her.

Cole finally sat at the head of the table.

"So, please tell me. Why is the Alpha of White Dawn gracing my presence after all this time?" A slow smile. "Or better yet, why has he brought a Paladin into my home?"

She glanced away from the lion beside her, catching Cole's eye. His smile widened.

"She's a bit small for you isn't she?" He continued to openly glare at her, his eyes roaming across her face. "I get she has some curves, but she must break easily? Nothing like the women you used to have." With a tut he took another drink, sipping loudly on the rim.

Alice felt her face burn. "We're working together."

"Are you now, pretty lady?" A predator's smile, one showing his sharp teeth.

A bark of a sound. The man Poliana was caressing doubled over in pain, his forehead touching the table, a choking noise escaping from this throat.

Cole looked over angry. "Lukas, calm down."

"Sorry, sire." The man known as Lukas continued to cough, shaking as he gained control.

"Where was I? Oh yes, Miss Alice Skye. I knew of a family in London with that name once. Shame what happened, don't suppose you know anything of it?" A smirk.

She remained silent.

"What? You're not even going to deny it?"

"You seem to be talking enough for the both of us," she bit back.

Cole's eyes narrowed, his hand crushing the glass enough to leave a crack. "Hmm. I can see why he has taken you to his bed."

"You sound so sure."

"Concealer charms might cover up the bite, but I am the lion equivalent of Rex. Our sense of smell is beyond your comprehension, even my lions can smell him on you."

"Cole," Rex growled a warning.

"Interesting," Cole chuckled. "I suppose that would be a conversation for you to have in private." He sipped from the broken glass, red liquid leaking through the small crack.

Alice tried for patience, her fingers digging into her knees as she failed. "This isn't about me..."

"Is it not?" His face was impassive, eyes bright. "You are nothing. I'm just reminding you that you're just a pawn in something bigger than all of us."

"Cole that is enough," Rex stated, his fist coming down hard on the table, making the cutlery rattle. "You know I wouldn't have come here if I didn't need to." His eyes were serious as he glared.

Cole stared back, no smile on his face. "Interesting how you have come back. After all this time." The intensity between the two shifters, the two leaders was electric.

The lions started to murmur, their attention not on the Pride Leader but on Poliana, the only other woman at the table.

Where are the other females? Alice eyed the lion next to her, his face twitching as she watched him, frowning. He was pretty, apart from the clear malnourishment. His face was perfectly symmetrical with the straightest nose she had ever seen. The other lions too, Alice had noticed, were all handsome men.

"Where are the women?" she asked him, studying his reaction intently.

He flinched, his eyes darting wildly. "I'm not supposed to talk to you," he whispered back, his voice surprisingly deep.

"Why not?" she asked in the same volume. He just swallowed and shook his head, his attention on the Pride Leaders wife. She tried to speak to the lion on her other side, but his eyes widened in alarm before he faced the wall, away from her.

A cough brought her attention back to Lukas, his chest rattling as he wheezed in and out. He looked scared, the whites of his eyes huge as he stared straight ahead. Poliana had moved closer to him, her hand stroking his thigh, her tongue licking lazily along the side of his ear. The wheezing noise continued, an uncomfortable screeching sound that hitched in intervals, his breathing shallow.

Alice glanced around the table, not one lion would look her in the eye, all either concentrating on their plates or on Lukas, their eyes full of pain.

There's something wrong. Alice couldn't figure it out, but she just felt something in the air interfering with the lions, something she had never felt before.

Alice concentrated as her vision blurred, her third eye opening, allowing her to see perceptions beyond ordinary sight. Auras appeared in a burst of colour, a distinctive atmospheric film that surrounded any living being like a personal shield. What separated the humans from magic users was the ability to harness their aura, creating a chi.

The sounds in the room became a low hum, background noise as she focused on Rex and Cole who continued a conversation she could no longer hear.

Searching straight for Poliana she gasped, watching her aura swirl with a spectrum of colour Alice had never seen before. Most people have a dominant colour that is unique to them, with other colours spotted throughout to show sharp emotions. Poliana's was different. Hers was a burst of reds, oranges, yellows and greens that merged together in a beautiful concoction of colour.

Concentrating, Alice watched the hand Poliana stroked Lukas with, his aura an incredibly pale blue, almost transparent. Holes appeared wherever her hand touched, Lukas's aura becoming weaker, disappearing before her eyes. The blue colour whirled, crawling up Poliana's fingertips.

Alice sucked in a breath. She knew exactly what she was. A type of Fae whose sole purpose was to seduce men so they could feed. A Succubus.

Bloody Hell.

She was literally eating his aura, gaining sustenance by absorbing his life force. It must be why many of the lions were so malnourished and weak, she was slowly killing them.

Alice looked over the remaining lions, their auras just as damaged as Lukas's, holes floating across her vision, everyone except Cole. His aura was a dull grey, spotted with black but completely whole.

Letting her third eye slip she blinked the remnants of the sight away.

Intense anger bubbled in her blood, her eyes flicking across the lions, now noticing the bruises, new and old marked across their flesh like sirens of abuse. Cole had destroyed his pride, turning the strong, proud predators into prey, food for his wife.

"They're dying," she said quietly. The lion next to her finally turned towards her, an odd expression on his face. "You're killing them," she said louder, loud enough that everyone on the table heard.

"Excuse me?" Cole stood up, his eyebrows creased together.

"She's killing them, absorbing their aura." Poliana started to giggle as if she was a small five-year-old child, and not a full grown woman. "Look at your lions. Can you not see?" Alice gripped the edge of the table, blue sparks coming from her fingertips in irritation. She paused, calming down, willing the fire back inside. "You are their Pride leader, you're allowing them to be hurt."

"They are only giving what they can. We are in the process of enrolling some new blood into the pride."

"Where are all the females?" she quickly asked.

"They don't need any females," Poliana finally spoke up. "Do we boys?" The lions murmured back in agreement.

"You're a witch, how could you possibly understand what it's like to be part of a pride? My wife completes us, fills the void against the members we have lost."

"So you have lost members?"

"Yes." Genuine emotion in his eyes. "My wife feeding on them is a small price to pay for the pride to feel complete again. Whole."

"You're killing them," Alice repeated matter-of-factly.

"No one has gone missing or died since she arrived." He laughed, his eyes fevered, excited. "No one can touch us."

Alice stood up, the back of her chair falling to the floor with a crash.

"Alice I think we should go." Rex moved quickly to stand behind her, growling at the lions next to her in warning. "There's nothing here."

"Why are you even here?" Cole questioned, ignoring Rex. "Poli is stable, together we have learnt to control her cravings."

"Your pride came up in the investigation I'm working on. A lion was found dead with an interesting amount of similarities to another body."

"Which one?"

Which one? Exactly how many were there?

"Francis Carter," she replied, noting the lions recoil.

"Francis." A hollow chuckle. "He didn't listen to any advice. Thought he could control his urges." His eyes glazed over in thought.

"Urges?"

"Drugs, women. To anything and everything he would become addicted. He thought he was invincible."

"What happened?"

"He thought he could beat the system." Cole's eyes stared off into nothing. "How could a stupid boy try to beat *them* when I couldn't do it myself?" He shook his head, eyes flashing yellow. "He was a fool, one who nearly destroyed the whole pride. Without Poli everyone could have succumbed to the same fate." He gazed over his lions like a father would his children.

"Who's them?" Alice pushed.

Cole ignored her, instead turning to glare at Rex.

"This has been a pleasant evening. I apologise we have to cut it short." Cole started to leave, pausing at the threshold. "I might not be in the circle anymore, but I know you are."

Rex's eyes flashed in warning.

"Stop delaying the inevitable. They are growing impatient." He tugged at his lapels. "Is it worth the risk?" With that he left, Poliana and the lions following him out in perfect synchronisation.

Alice stared after them, confused. "What the actual fuck?" Rex was emitting an intense heat against her back, as if she could feel his anger.

"We need to leave." Without checking to see if she followed, he made his way out the house. Alice stomped after him, her temper still blaring.

Her boots started to slide on the loose stones of the driveway as she followed him towards a large black Range Rover.

"Get in," he said without turning. Opening a side door he shrugged off his jacket, throwing it into the back. With a small thwack something fell out of his pocket, landing on the floor by his tyre.

"I have my own car." She bent down to pick up the brown square, realising it was a wallet as she stroked the worn leather.

"You need to come back to the motel," he said, his tone leaving no room for argument.

But Alice liked to argue. "I said I have my own car. I can drive myself home tonight." Besides, it wasn't late.

She clutched the wallet to her, staring down at it intently before she opened the flap. A photograph was pinned with a paperclip to the left fold, a photograph of herself from a side angle, as if someone took the photo without her knowing. Her blonde hair was in a high ponytail, loose strands dancing around her flushed face as if she had just finished running. Her green eyes were looking off into the distance, a small private smile on her lips.

The photograph made her look delicate.

It made her feel uneasy.

Pulling the picture out she tried to take a closer look.

"Rex, why do you have a photo of..." she paused as she noticed another photo underneath, beneath the transparent plastic. Three men stood huddled together in the picture, Rex was on the left, the biggest grin as he smiled at the camera, his arm stretched behind two other men.

"Those are my brothers," Rex whispered, his voice full of an emotion Alice had never heard from him before. "That's Theo," he said pointing to the man furthest right. "He's my twin."

"Twin," she repeated back at him, only just realising the two men were identical. "And who's this?" She pointed to the younger man in the middle, their features similar, clearly brothers.

"And that," he pointed to the younger man in the middle. "Is Roman..." He took the wallet from her, staring at the picture for a few seconds before throwing it into the back of his car with his jacket.

"Roman? As in the wolf that's missing?" It all started to make sense. He slowly turned to face her, his eyes bright as the wolf prowled behind his irises, his emotions strong. "Why have you only just hired me?"

"What?"

"You've lost three wolves," Rex tried to hide his flinch. "And you've only just asked for outside help. Why?"

He stared at her for what felt like hours. "It's because I'm running out of time." With that he got in his car, closing the door behind him.

CHAPTER EIGHTEEN

They remained silent as Rex used the little key-card to open the motel door. According to Rex, who felt the need to apologise before even entering the building, it was the only place available in such a short time. Which didn't give her much confidence.

The room didn't look too awful in the dark, almost normal as Alice could just make out the bed in the back, the curtains drawn behind it. She flicked on the yellowing plastic light switch, waiting for something to happen. Nothing did. She flicked it a few more times, but it still didn't turn on, keeping the room gloomy. Instead, she pulled the curtain, allowing the harsh light of the street lamp outside to illuminate through the window.

"Wow," she said, appraising the room. "This is... nice." It wasn't.

Rex stayed by the door, his expression intense. The room was a typical motel room with a queen size bed and off-white linen. Taking a closer look Alice noticed the slight yellow rings, the stains being the result of years of sweat and other bodily fluids. She was definitely sleeping in all her clothes. Maybe even wrapped in a towel.

Lifting up the duvet sheet she pulled it off, relieved to notice the sheet underneath was clean. A sofa covered in a pink and blue paisley pattern sat in the corner of the room, opposite the old television that looked like it had seen better days, dust a fine layer across the screen.

The bathroom, which was right next to the front door, actually had a working light, even if it did flick on and off on its own accord. The porcelain tub with attached shower was an avocado green with a matching sink. There was even a large rectangular mirror positioned above, a spider web of cracks along its surface, interestingly growing from a hole the size of a fist.

Rex still hadn't moved from the door, his eyes watching as she wandered around the room.

"You fancy room service? We didn't get to eat at dinner," she asked absently.

"This place doesn't do room service."

She could have probably guessed that.

"Why did you come?" she asked.

"Why did you not call me?" he countered.

She clenched her teeth, not wanting to overreact. "I had it under control."

"Clearly not. If I wasn't there…"

"What? What could have happened?" She strode up to him, her anger vibrant. "You need to let me do my job."

"That *I* hired you for." His eyes flashed arctic. "I'm going to speak to Cole tomorrow morning."

"And ask him what? Why he's with a woman who's eating his people? Or how he could allow Francis Carter to become so entangled with darkness his body was ripped to shreds by his own hands?"

"It's his wife." A snarl.

"Who's killing his people." She crinkled her nose in disgust.

"How could you possibly understand their situation?"

"Understand?" She couldn't believe what she was hearing.

"She might give them protection," Rex laughed emotionlessly.

"Bullshit, protection from what?"

"Pack is everything. I can understand if keeping her around stabilised the pride."

"I'm not listening to this," she replied as she stormed past him, her hand touching the door handle before his palm smacked against the wood.

"You don't have a pack, you don't understand what you would do for them." His arm tensed as she tried to open the door, his strength unmoving. "My pack is everything. There is nothing I wouldn't do for them." He looked straight into her eyes. "My family, however, is my *life*."

Alice froze in place, the emotion coming off of him raw, powerful. "Rex..."

"I would kill for my brothers. I would die for them." His voice quivered, thick with hopelessness, pain.

Alice felt her own heartache, the emptiness her family left behind radiating. She understood, better than anyone else she understood the pain, something that never went away, but it wasn't enough. Her anger stronger, hotter.

"You didn't tell me that it was your brother we were searching for."

"It didn't matter."

"How can you say that?" She heard her voice rise even as she fought to control it. "I'm doing everything I can to help you and you didn't even give me all the information?"

"I said it didn't matter." He stepped forward, his height dwarfing hers as he crowded her against the door. "It's irrelevant information, knowing wouldn't have helped."

"It would give me somewhere else to search, more people to question. Your other brother..."

"Isn't available." He raised his own voice, his tone so close to Alpha she had to grit her teeth. "I have given you everything you need, kept nothing from you that I didn't feel relevant. Yet you still go off on your own, not giving me what I've paid for."

"Do not question my ability." She felt the intense heat in her stomach, rising with each breath as she fought for control. Relaxing into the power overload she calmed herself, keeping the power within limits.

"Is that a threat?" A whisper against her cheek, a hand twisted in her hair. "Do you think you're stronger than me?"

Alice let out a flame, a flash in front of his face in warning. "Don't push me."

Without warning his lips came down on her own, his tongue assaulting hers with teasing strokes. He released a growl as he grabbed her wrist, pulling her hand from the door and removing the concealer charm from where she had tucked it. The illusion immediately broke, revealing the bite mark. Rex licked across it, his chest grumbling as he nipped her skin.

It felt invigorating. It felt perfect. It felt...

"Stop this." She pulled her face away, stopping herself from taking it further, from pulling his lips back to her own.

He ignored her, assaulting her mouth once again.

"I said, no." She pushed against him, the intense lust dissipating the further apart they got. "I don't sleep with people who don't trust me." She pushed at him again, her thoughts clearer as her blue Tinkerbell floated around her wrist.

He looked angry before his face closed off. "It's just a fuck, Miss Skye."

Ice cold water. "It's Agent Skye." She blasted a space between them, making him jump back or risk being burned. "I don't really understand what this is," she pointed between them.

"Well if you need me to draw you a picture..."

"You think I don't see you? You think you hide behind this emotionless intensity, this mask, but you don't. It's a cold rage that your wolf is forcing you to confront." Her tone was husky, emotions running high. "What is so bad that you have to hide from me? Hide it from yourself?"

"You know nothing." A hiss. "You're just a stupid fucking female." He stood with his arms crossed, tension coiled up his spine.

"What do you want from me?"

"I want you to fix it." A shout.

"Fix what?"

"Everything," he snarled, turning to punch his fist through the wall. "I thought you would be the one. You seem alpha enough."

She gaped at the hole, unable to speak.

"But I don't know anymore." He stared at his hand, watching the blood ooze gently down his knuckles. "I don't know." With that he yanked open the front door, almost bringing it off its hinges before slamming it shut behind him.

Alice stood there, cold, unable to move until she heard his footsteps fade into the night.

Alice flipped the visor down as the early morning sun streamed through the windscreen. She had been sitting in the car park of the local market for a while, deciding whether to get out or not. She had been up all night, unsure what to say to Rex. Hours later she had gone down to her car, intending to drive home when she noticed him fast asleep in his 4X4. She felt anger at seeing him, anger at what he was trying to do, but mostly anger at his situation. She knew what a man looked like when he was out of options. So she decided to stay in the motel, her annoyance at the situation dissolving, at least until she read the text in the morning.

Agent Skye,
I'm sorry I wasn't there when you woke up, but I can't let you distract me from what needs to be done. Talking to Cole went well, he has given me a lead about a woman Francis was dating when he went AWOL. She owns a shop in the market a few miles up the road, I'm going to head there now. Will talk when we get back.
Rexley Wild.

"Distract?" Alice closed off her phone, throwing it into the glove compartment. How was she distracting him? *Bullshit.*

Voices filtered in through the gap in the window, couples arguing about who was driving, an old woman gushing over a recent purchase and even a small child wailing at being denied sweets. A few rows down Rex's huge car gleamed, standing out against the other less expensive cars and bikes. She opened her door, the sun instantly warming her skin.

The market was bustling with colour, rows and rows of wooden and concrete stalls selling everything from handmade jewellery and clothes to basic concealer charms and amulets. The air vibrated with energy, the exhilaration infectious. A woman bellowed how fresh her fruit and vegetables were, thrusting her treasures at anybody walking too close to her stall. Apples, kiwis, lychees, pineapples, all layered one on top of each other, all glistening in their ripeness. Alice fought not to get sidetracked, her eyes scanning everyone as she searched for Rex.

She had no idea where to start.

At a loss in the busy crowd she searched for someone to ask directions, deciding on one of the stall owners.

Manoeuvring through the crowd Alice found a beautiful collection of stones and crystals sitting elegantly atop velvet cloth and oak slices. Touching one she felt it sing, begging to be bought. Crystals were greedy things, natural formations created by the earth used by magic users for spells, the smooth stones able to store a small amount of chi. Alice reached out and touched another crystal, a beautiful pendant, the rock almost glowing with the attention, the small gold flecks shining against the dark blue of the raw stone.

"That crystal was made for you by the song it's projecting," the stall owner mused, smiling over at Alice, her multicoloured head turban complementing the colours of all her stones and crystals. Taking the pendant from Alice she held it up to the sun, the gold specks sparkling. "Lapis Lazuli. Nice choice, a protection stone that protects against physical and psychic attacks. Great for protection circles, would you like to buy it?"

"Yes please," Alice smiled, stroking the cold surface. Handing over the money she allowed the woman to tie a leather knot at the back of her neck, letting the crystal sit in the hollow of her throat. "Thank you."

"You're welcome, my dear. I love it when my crystals find their rightful owners."

Alice nodded, bringing up her hand to hold the crystal gently, the smooth texture incredibly comforting.

"Oh, my." The woman grabbed her wrist, twisting it so she could see her bracelet better. "What is that?" Her brows furrowed as she stared at the moon pendant, a frown on her face.

"Alice?" a voice shouted. Alice turned just as Rex stormed towards her, his face annoyed. "What are you doing here?" He pulled her away.

"What, I'm Alice again?" He ignored her. "I was looking for you," she said through clenched teeth. Turning back to the stall owner she started to apologise.

"Do you know what that is?" the woman asked frantically, trying to grab her wrist again. "Do you understand?"

"Thank you but we should be going." Rex pulled her through the crowd, towards the car park. "You shouldn't be here," he snarled.

"What?" Alice dug her heel in, pulling her arm free with a tug. Her eyes narrowed as she noticed his slight smirk, knowing she could only get him to let go because he allowed it. She preferred him when he was emotionless. "I'm supposed to be helping."

"I said we would talk back home."

"Well, I'm already here." She stared at him, watching his pissed off expression smooth out into one of complete detachment. *Ah,* there was the emotionless she was used to.

"Have you found this lady yet?" she questioned.

"Yes," he replied, reserved. "She's in a cabin at the back."

"Have you spoken to her?"

"Not yet."

Nodding her head Alice turned back to the crowd, the number of people thinning as the sun hid behind the clouds, the temperature dropping.

"It's this way." Rex walked beside her, his movements frigid as he controlled his anger the only way he knew how. Deciding not to antagonise him further she quietly walked towards the corner of the market square, following to the half concrete half wood cabins.

Beautiful tapestries hung from the top of the concrete shop to the furthest left, flowing down to separate into sections. Each tapestry was handmade to create different scenes, everything from a field of tulips to a feast in a great hall. Inside, the handcrafted scenes became darker, the once beautiful tulips burning, their beautiful colours twisted and warped from the heat. Further inside one showed a scene with people bowing to a horned beast, blood oozing from bite marks across their flesh. Another showed people burning at the stake, their faces distorted in pain in such detail you could almost hear them scream.

"Can I help you?" asked a woman who had walked into the room and begun draping a semi-finished tapestry over an old wooden chair. Rex remained quiet, his muscles bunched as she went to stand beside him.

"Yes, we wanted to ask some questions."

"Questions?" she frowned, her eyes drifting between them. "I'm sorry, who are you?"

The woman was around the same height as Alice, her hair jet black and tied in twin plaits draped over her shoulders. It was her eyes that held Alice's attention, she had never seen eyes so dark, even darker than Dread's, like charcoal orbs surrounded by lashes. Alice swore she could even see flicks of red as the woman appraised Rex.

"I know you," the woman almost purred as she walked over and dragged one of her long nails across his chest. "You have some 'splaining to do." A sharp cackle.

"We need to ask questions." Rex finally said, his voice cold, no recognition on his face, yet he didn't step back.

"Fine." With a twist of her wrist the front of the shop closed, a lock clicking into place. Once she was happy the door was secure she lifted a tapestry, revealing a hidden archway. "No one will disturb us. Please follow me into my office." Without a backwards glance the woman sauntered through, her black braids swinging behind her.

The hidden room was faintly lit with red candles, the flames creating shadows dancing across the black and white portraits adorning the walls. Not one face was smiling.

"Take a seat." The woman threw her hand out in the rough direction of the table, her attention on the shelf by the back wall. With a little click, the lights above turned on.

Alice carefully studied the room, warily eyeing the shelves along the walls.

She felt something stare.

Turning around she eyed the portraits hanging on the walls, their eyes dead. Yet, when she moved, they seemed to follow. A clatter as the woman removed something from a shelf, dropping it onto the table. Deciding against the vulnerability of being seated, Alice chose to stand behind Rex as he folded himself into one of the chairs, arms braced on the table.

"So why are you here?" the woman asked Rex, completely ignoring Alice.

"I need to talk about Francis Carter."

"Francis?" The woman's smirk that was etched on her face started to fade, a black look replacing it. "Francis is dead."

"We know. We want to know how."

"How?" Barely a whisper this time. "You want to know how?" A dry laugh. "He was chosen, gifted. He wanted the power, craved it."

"What power?" Alice moved from behind Rex.

"But he was unable to control it. So it consumed him." The woman continued as if she hadn't heard Alice.

"Annie." Rex tapped his knuckles against the table. "I remember. Your name is Annie."

"Ah, so you do know me," she laughed.

"More heard of you. You're the gatekeeper."

"Precisely." Turning away from the shelf she sat at the other end of the table, opposite to Rex.

Sensing movement in the corner of her eye, Alice looked past Annie and regarded the shelves behind, an array of creatures forever frozen in position. A taxidermy rat was bent at an impossible angle along its backbone, beside it an owl with its head turned one-eighty and a boar's head with a rabbit's carcass impaled on one of its tusks.

This place was next level creepy. "What's a gatekeeper?"

Annie glared over at Alice as if she had forgotten she was even there. "I find people worthy enough for the cause."

"The cause?" Alice frowned, where had she heard that phrase before? "Wait." Alice thought back, remembering her conversation with the bouncer. "The cause? Are you talking about The Becoming?"

Rex tensed, refusing to look at her.

"Rexley Wild, who have you brought with you?" Annie stepped closer, her chi electric as she flared, testing Alice's magic against her own. "A witch? Why have you brought me a witch?" She looked at Rex for an answer. "They're not going to be pleased."

"Who? Who isn't going to be pleased?" Alice asked.

"Alice we need to go." Rex stood to leave, his movements edgy.

"Wait, your name's Alice?" Annie's eyes narrowed. "They're not going to be pleased at all."

"Alice, please," Rex begged, his voice urgent.

"Yes, Alice, white magic is so boring isn't it? Never thought about going to the dark side."

"Dark side?" Alice frowned, flicking her attention to Rex, then back again. "No, never."

"No?" Annie stalked closer, her movements slow. "Not even a little bit?" Lifting up her sleeve she showed her scarification tattoo, a ram's head entangled in a pentagram. Twisting her wrist she held out her hand, beckoning Alice to touch.

Alice almost did. Almost. "Rex let's go." As soon as the words left her mouth, he had pulled her back into the market, the crowd having completely dispersed.

"We need to get out of here." His eyes darted around the crowd.

The cold air hit her, clearing her thoughts. "What the fuck was that? This is more than a normal lost person case..."

"Calm down," Rex leant down to hiss in her face.

"Calm down?" She moved towards the car park, deciding only a few steps in that she wasn't finished. "You know what? I can't help you. You hired me to help and yet keep vital information from me."

"I'm not..."

"Don't." She cut him off with a hand gesture. "You knew that witch. You knew what The Becoming was." She barely paused to take a breath. "What even is The Becoming? Some sort of cult?"

"Alice, you have to understand..." He slowly backed her away from the cabin.

"Understand? UNDERSTAND WHAT?" Her voice rose again, anger a vibration beneath her skin. "I'm good at my job but you're giving me nothing. How am I supposed to help you?" She felt lost as she faced him, her energy zapped.

"I don't know what to say..." His eyes widened, flicking behind her.

Annie stood in the doorframe, her head tilted as she watched them argue.

"You can't leave." She stepped out, a smirk tilting her lips. "We were just getting acquainted."

"Alice, please." His eyes darted back to Annie. "We'll discuss it back home."

"I said," Annie twirled her hand, a black ball of aura coating her skin. "You can't leave." The air became static.

Alice felt for her own power, bringing it to the surface as blue flames flashed from her fingertips. She could taste Annie's magic, the strength of it like an acid on her tongue.

A cackle. "Stupid bitch." Annie flung her aura.

Alice rolled, her own spell leaving her lips. "*ADOLEBITQUE!*"

A high-pitched screech as the incantation hit.

"Come on Alice." Rex pulled at her wrist, pulling her attention.

Something burned across her back, sending her careening into Rex, sprawling them onto the floor. Gritting her teeth, she spun, throwing everything she had from her hand.

"*ARDENTI TURRIS!*" Her aura pulsed, pain across her back.

"Alice, she's gone." White noise, flames cracking from her fingertips. "Alice…"

She turned, his face trying desperately to remain blank, but his eyes were anything but. They flashed ice, his wolf at the forefront, appraising her with heat. Heat and worry. He was cautious of her.

"We need to leave."

Alice blinked, trying to control the excess.

"It isn't safe."

She was unable to speak, the pain radiating across her shoulder blades.

Her nightgown ripped, allowing her to stumble into the dirt, her knees hitting the ground hard.

A loud bang as something crashed into the door.

The wood around the lock began to splinter.

She looked around the darkness, the earth feeling familiar against her bare feet as she climbed up. Following the pathway down she ran behind the giant oak tree, using the bushes to hide.

Another bang as the door finally gave, a low cuss as the shadow staggered out the door. "Come here little girl," he snarled. "Come here... your parents are inside, they need you."

She cowered against the tree, holding her hand against her mouth to stop the sobs.

A high pitch scream.

Fear twisted her, leaving her immobile as more tortured shrieks filled the air.

"You hear that little girl?" the monster laughed. "Your mamma needs you, come out, come out where ever you are."

CHAPTER NINETEEN

Alice jerked awake, her dream dissipating sluggishly, the nightmare leaving a cold essence deep in her stomach. It was as if her memories were blocked, a DVD that had been scratched or software corrupted. Flickers of the same thing over and over again, every year without fail. It was almost like her brain was trying to tell her something, but panicked at the last moment and decided she wasn't ready to see, wasn't ready to understand.

Her grief counsellor had once explained she had never gotten past step two of the five stages of grief, never getting past anger. Alice hated to admit it, but always thought the woman was right, she had never felt the other stages, bargaining, denial and then acceptance. Especially the acceptance.

How could they expect a six-year-old child to accept that?

How could they ask a twenty-three-year-old woman to accept it either?

Rolling over on her mattress she stared at the sun's rays breaking through the blinds, a welcoming sight compared to the last couple of days, the continuing deep ache an annoying reminder. Stretching out her arm her breath escaped in a rush, pain resonating down her back enough to allow a little squeal of discomfort to escape.

"Alice?" A soft knock on her door before it pushed open, revealing Sam who stood there with a mug in his hand, steam billowing from the top. Closing the door, he set the mug on her side table, pulling his legs up onto the bed to sit beside her.

Her eyes narrowed on him instantly, one: he never knocked before entering anywhere, just waltzed in like he owned the place. Two: he closed the door behind him.

"You're staring," Sam fidgeted.

"Sam…" she started before she heard a distinctive click of the front door locking. "Sam?" she asked. "Who was that?"

"No one." He shrugged, a secret smile on his face. Alice was about to question him further when she heard a faint knocking. Sam's eyes went wide as Alice scrambled off the bed, pretty much throwing him to the side as she raced him to the front door. "Alice wait…"

"Oh hello," Alice greeted the blushing man standing on the threshold, his fist held up as if he was going to knock again. "How can I help you?" She smiled at the man, taking in his messy red hair, shorter at the sides than the top, crudely buttoned shirt and black skinny jeans.

"Oh…erm." The man blushed impossibly further, almost the same shade as his amazing hair. "I seem to have left my…"

"Here you go." Sam thrust a wallet at him.

"Oh, thanks." Freckles, the guy had freckles. "So, errr, call me?" An invitation had never sounded so meek.

"Sure," Sam nodded, slowly closing the door so Alice could no longer see the redhead. "I will definitely call you." With that the door closed, turning to her. "Don't comment."

"Comment about what? He's cute." She leant against the wall. "Where did you meet?"

"At the club." Amber eyes met hers. "You do realise you answered the door in nothing but your underwear and a smile?"

Alice fought not to look down, only just realising she could feel a pleasant breeze across her skin. She must have yanked her clothes off before collapsing into bed the night before. The redhead was lucky she had been too tired to figure out the clasp of her bra, or he would have seen a lot more than he bargained for.

"Don't change the subject."

He smiled at the door as if he could see through it. "He's proper cute though."

"Very." Alice couldn't stop her cheek-cracking grin.

"How is this funny?" Sam chuckled as he pulled her into his arms, scraping his stubbled cheek against her wild unkempt hair. She groaned, sucking in a pained breath as her back ignited in a series of aches when his aura touched hers. "Alice?" Concern in his voice. "You okay?" He leaned down into her hair. "You smell different."

"Do I?" She leant back, the ache lessening the further away she was. "I seem to have burned some of my aura."

"Burned it?" Sam's eyes went wide as he looked her up and down, unable to see auras. "What does that even mean?"

"I think I'm missing some." She huffed as pain shot down her back once again. "I need to replace it before it gets worse."

"Worse?" Panic obvious in his voice. "What do you mean worse? Who do we call for that? Can the hospital deal with that?" He went to pick up the telephone sitting on a side table by the sofa, putting the handset back in its cradle when he remembered they hadn't paid the bill for the landline in months. They never really used it anyway.

"No, we can't go to the hospital. Dread will figure out I haven't dropped the Daemons. He can't find out."

"Wait, wait, wait. Back up. You damaged your aura while searching for Daemons?"

"I wasn't technically searching for Daemons..."

"Alice what the fuck!" Sam shouted, his voice getting higher in pitch. "If Overlord finds out, he will kill you!"

"I know!" Obviously, he wouldn't kill her, but he could make her life a living hell. "We need to find a specialist."

"A specialist? Where do we find that? On www.Ifuckedupmyaura.com?"

"So funny. I was thinking I could even do it."

"You? How? You don't know anything about auras? You even fucked up that shaving spell."

"Did not." Alice scowled, she didn't 'fuck it up' exactly. The spell had worked, it just had a surprising area of effect. Besides, Rose had forgiven her when her hair finally grew back.

"Whatever," Sam snorted. "Where do you think you can find the spell?"

"I was thinking, maybe my mum would have had something?"

"Your mum?" He raised an eyebrow. "Wasn't your mum a gardener?"

"Well yes." She bit her lip, thinking. "Dread used to tell me when I was young how my mum could stir anything. Give her a recipe and she would be able to do it." He used to tell her stories of her parents when she was still young and scared. Every night he would sit on her new bed and tell her about how amazing they were.

The stories were like crack to a junkie, something a small broken child would cling to for hope.

'Alice, get into bed.'

'But the monsters?' Alice felt her bottom lip quiver, a cold hand squeezing her heart.

'Shhh,' Dread stroked across her cheek. 'Don't worry child, Uncle Dread is here.' He tugged up her new duvet set they had chosen together that day, pink with unicorns.

Alice had giggled when she saw his face, he wanted her to have the superheroes one.

'Do you know what your mum said to me when you were first born?'

'No.' Alice sat up slightly, resting forward on her elbows.

The last few weeks had been a blur, doctors, psychiatrists and specialists all wanted to poke and prod. She wouldn't speak, wouldn't even cry.

She had just sat comatose, barely responding. It was only when a young boy at one of the many grief meetings, a boy with the longest hair she had ever seen, had asked her how she had done her plait did she finally speak. Replying with a story about her mum. That's when Dread started telling her stories about her parents, ones that made her heart hurt and yet fill with joy at the same time.

'She said to me...' Dread tucked a piece of her hair behind her ear. 'That this little girl will be the most amazing person anyone has ever seen.'

"Alice?"

She shook her head. "Huh?"

"Where did you go?" Sam smiled gently, worry still blatant in his amber eyes.

"Back to when I was a kid." She smiled at the memory. Dread had taught her how to cope, how to be strong. He was always there for her, even though he still treated her like the little girl he took under his wing all those years ago. "I remember my mum sitting with lots of books, reading spells. Maybe the books are still there?"

"Where?" Sam thought for a second. "At the house? You haven't been there in years."

"Exactly. No one has."

"Let me get dressed, I'll come with you."

"No." She pushed her palm against his chest. "I need to do this myself."

"You sure?" He grabbed her in a hug again, his chest vibrating in a soft purr, the gentle noise and vibration instantly comforting. "I don't want you to hurt."

"I know." She snuggled into his warmth. "But I need to do this."

The house had aged in the last few years, the white paint peeling off in chunks to reveal the dark brick underneath. The windows weren't boarded up as she had initially thought, but had white smears across the glass that shops had when refurbishing. The windows themselves seemed in pretty good shape, the decent area having kept the kids from breaking in or vandalising the glass. The bushes around the house, while overgrown, were also surprisingly decent considering no one had lived there for close to seventeen years. The neighbour's obviously didn't want the house to be a total eyesore in the well-kept neighbourhood.

Sam had been asking her for a while if they could talk about moving in, *'anything is better than here'* he had said, complaining about their flat once again. Not that she didn't complain just as much, but the thought of her moving back to her childhood home...

A shiver started to rattle her bones. Shaking the feeling she continued to stare at the old house, irrational fear threatening to choke her, the nightmare the night before not helping the sense of foreboding. Blinking past the black spot invading her vision she walked carefully up to the front, the porch light off. She checked the bulb, noticing a huge crack along the side, a bird's nest neatly hidden inside.

Her hand shook as she inserted the key into the lock, the click echoing through the empty lounge as the door squeaked open. Dust glittered in the air as streams of light shone into the dark house, a musty smell thick and suffocating. Alice could feel her heart beat against her ribs, hard enough it began to hurt. Swallowing her sense of panic she stepped inside, noticing how her footsteps left marks in the dust.

Alice knew exactly where to look, knew she didn't have to go anywhere near the kitchen, nowhere near the window where she could see the garden.

The stairs creaked as she slowly made her way up, the light better upstairs, the windows not having had the same white smear treatment. Her parents' bedroom was the last door on the left, the door ajar.

The vanity had been pushed at an angle against the wall, adjacent to the bed that was a simple metal frame and mattress. Walking over she tugged it back into place from her memory, beside the window that faced the front drive.

Bottles lined up like soldiers against the grime covered mirror. Picking one up she examined it closer, trying to read the worn label before giving up and putting it back in its place. The two drawers turned out to be empty of anything helpful, just old out of date makeup and lotions.

Strange.

Starting to lose hope Alice continued to search frantically through her parent's things, checking under the bed frame, inside the wardrobe and even in the en-suite. Other than the necessities, nothing signalled her parents were magic users. No candles, runes or crystals. Nothing. It's as if the room was purposely staged to look normal, human.

She sat at the edge of the bed, careful to not put her full weight on the frame as it creaked. In fact, she hadn't seen anything witch-wise in the house at all. Admittedly, she had only checked one room and the lounge, but all witches had runes and protection spells carved into the walls. It was part of their nature.

Maybe she made a mistake? Maybe she didn't remember her mother as much as she thought. Her childhood memories were rusty at best, shadowed with trauma.

No.

Alice knew something wasn't right. Going back into the wardrobe she pushed against the hung fabrics, most of them half eaten by moths. When they didn't move she pulled them off the rack, letting them crumble into a pile on the floor.

"There's got to be something..." Fingers blindly searched. "Aha." She finally found the small indent she was looking for. Pushing with the tip of her finger she heard a small click.

'Ready or not, here I come.'

"Ready or not, here I come," Alice repeated her memory, remembering playing hide-and-seek with her brother years ago. Eight years her senior, Kyle was the usual moody teen in the family, his mood worsening when their parents made him play with her.

The cupboard had been Alice's favourite hiding place, somewhere she had found by accident one day and a place Kyle had never located. Alice suppressed a grin as the hidden door squeaked open, the space so dark it absorbed light. Reaching inside she felt a cold hard surface, something wooden.

With a grunt she pulled the heavy box out into the open and picked it up, placing it onto the vanity table so it was in the natural light. The box itself was nondescript. Not wood like she first thought but made of a thick cardboard. There were no markings, no dents, no stains. Nothing to indicate what was inside.

The lid came off easily enough, the movement letting the dust fly up into the air and into Alice's face. Coughing and waving to disperse the grime she finally peeked inside, a smile cracking her face at what she found. A large leather bound book. A grimoire.

This is exactly what she was searching for, it was...

A light flashed at the corner of her eye.

Looking out through the window she noticed a man standing on the street, his face covered over with a hood. She blinked, the phantom disappearing.

Confused, she searched down the street, wondering if she really did see someone standing there or if it was her imagination.

CHAPTER TWENTY

"So, let me get this right..." Sam began as his legs trembled against the kitchen counter. "You're going to read a random book and hope something in there will repair your aura?" He sipped from what must be his fifth coffee, his hands juddering from the overload of caffeine.

"It's not random," she muttered. "It's also a grimoire." Alice stroked across the leather-bound cover.

"What if there isn't a spell?" Sam continued to swing his legs back and forth, his denim covered hips barely perched on the kitchen counter. He must have been on another late shift from the amount of coffee he was guzzling, his chest bare as he scratched across his pecs hard enough to leave marks. "What will you do then?"

"I don't know." She frowned, not wanting to accept it wouldn't work. "But I'll think of something." She watched him from the corner of her eye, his edgy movements concerning her. "Are you okay?"

He ignored her, instead turning to the kettle to refill his cup. Sam took everything to the extreme, including drinking, smoking, caffeine and even sex. It was lucky that he had never been into drugs, his personality that of an addict.

"I think you've had enough coffee."

Sam slid his eyes to her, the amber narrowed as he flicked his plaited hair over a shoulder. "Let's have a look at this book then," he commented instead.

Alice tried to hide her own shaking hand as she opened to the first page, pictures of stars and moons drawn across the stained paper. Flipping through she started to find spells written messily throughout, some written in a strong, curvy handwriting in the middle of a page and others she found written rough and squished together, as if it was rushed. There were random phrases painted in some corners and dramatic drawings scribbled on others.

"This is a mess," Alice remarked as she tried to decipher all the nonsense.

"You find anything?" A thump as he jumped from the counter, his bare feet making little noise as he padded across the lino.

"What about this one..." Alice squinted as she tried to read the small print.

"This is gonna be interesting," he said mockingly from behind her shoulder, close enough that she could feel his breath against her bare nape. She fought not to glare at him.

"'How to transmute into a badger'."

"What. The. Actual. Fuck. Why would someone want that?" Sam started to laugh.

"I don't actually know." Alice couldn't really believe it herself. "Here's another one, 'For the love of your life'."

"A love spell?"

Alice read through the notes. "Seems to be. Also illegal as hell." What was her mother doing with an illegal spell? "'How to remove a soul from a body.'" Both Alice and Sam just stared at each other, deciding not to comment. "'Eternal happiness.' 'The black mark.' 'Age definer.'"

"Wait... fold that page over!" Sam leant across to bend the corner of the page himself. "We could use that spell in a few years' time."

She batted him away. "'Illusionarium.' 'Aura feeder...'"

"Wait, go back."

"Okay, it says here...'When the integrity of the aura is compromised, the person will experience draining of energy and magic. This can manifest in many ways, for example, a depleted and sudden energy loss, a sharp change of mood, headache as well as acute pain over the area affected. Other, more unusual symptoms could be nausea or loss of consciousness. Unhealed holes in the aura can often lead to serious and permanent *consequences. Moreover, the presence of holes in the aura greatly increases the risk of attachment or invasion of negative entities.'"*

"I have no idea what you just said."

"It means I have left my aura open to nasties." The idea made her feel both ill and dirty at the same time. "The spell seems simple enough. A circle, candles, I can't muck that up."

"Suuuureeee." Sam dodged the tea towel she threw at his head. "It will be alright baby girl, if not Overlord can save the day like he usually does."

"We haven't had to call for Dread's help since we were kids."

Sam sighed in delight. "And I still remember his face when he saw how many cocktails you had drunk. You threw up everywhere."

"It was graduation and I seem to remember you threw up first."

"Well, you have a defective memory," Sam grinned.

Alice couldn't help but chuckle back. They had been awful kids, even worse teenagers. "No threats. Like I said the spell is simple enough." She quickly re-read the instructions. "Okay, I need my candles back."

"Candles?"

"Yes." She narrowed her eyes at him. "You used them last didn't you?"

"Well," he said, looking away, "the funny thing is..."

A bus skidded as it pulled into the bus stop outside Mystic Medlock's Magic Emporium, splashing them as they walked along the pavement, the torrential rain pretty much killing the open aired high street. Jumping away from the cold water Alice ran into the magic shop, trying and failing to dodge the rain.

"I don't know why I had to come," Sam said as he shook the loose rain from his hair, the water droplets showering over the gargoyle guarding the door.

"Because you're paying for my new candles," she huffed, still annoyed. She couldn't believe he ruined her candles. That was the last time she'd lend him anything.

"It was an accident! I didn't realise they would melt so fast!" He sulked behind her.

"What were you even doing with them?" No reply, just a chuckle. "Okay, I don't want to know."

She shook her head, leaving him by the door as she stalked towards the wall of candles. Browsing, Alice found the soy versions she preferred.

"SAM!" she shouted in his vague direction, "GET YOUR WALLET OUT!" She heard him snigger, and followed the sound until she found him standing in the corner of the shop. "What are you looking at?" she asked as she stepped beside him.

"That thing is moving." Sam pointed to beside the large paradise palm.

"Moving? What?" Sam had finally lost it.

Walking over Alice lifted a leaf, revealing a very happy gnome. At thirty centimetres tall, the gnome didn't make much of an impact in size, but the hollow eyes and creepy smile caused the hairs on the back of her neck to stand on edge. His blue coat contrasted against his luminous green belt and red-capped hat. A fisherman's pole was clutched in his chubby palms, hidden slightly by his pure white beard.

"Wow, creepy."

"I swear Alice, he moved."

She watched the gnome carefully, feeling stupid until she noticed a pair of big, yellow, unblinking eyes staring at them from behind the fern. "Look, it's just the cat."

"I know the cat was there." His nostrils flared to prove his point. "I swear he moved."

"Leave the nice fisherman alone and help me find the chalk."

"Hello, can I help you? Oh, Alice isn't it?" a friendly voice called.

Alice turned, algae green eyes smiling down at her. "Oh, Alistair."

"Please, call me Al." He touched his fringe, pushing the strands away from his eyes. "You want chalk? It's by the register." He smiled towards Sam. "Hi mate, haven't met you before."

Sam smirked.

"This is my roommate, Sam." Alice purposely coughed, bringing Sam's attention to her. *Stop it,* she warned with her eyes.

He's cute, Sam replied back, his amber ovals glinting mischievously.

Don't you even think about it.

"Nice to meet you Al," Sam greeted. "You got a girlfriend?" He batted his eyelashes, testing the situation. "Or a boyfriend."

"Sam," Alice hissed.

"Ah, no. I don't have a girlfriend," Al answered to Alice, her face flushing at the attention. "I'm definitely available."

"That's interesting, did you know my friend Alice..." Sam squealed mid-sentence as she pinched the fleshy part of his arm. Turning to rub the small mark he scowled before changing subject. "What's up with the weird gnome?"

"Oh, you mean Jordan?" Al smiled friendly.

"You named your gnome Jordan?" Alice asked, bewildered.

"Well, I didn't name him. He came with that name."

"I think he moved," Sam said, his attention towards the palm at the corner of the room.

"Yeah, he does that." He finished wrapping the last candle, placing all the merchandise into a paper bag along with a single chalk.

"And that's normal?" Alice pulled a face.

Al just shrugged, smiling at her. "Cash or card?"

"Pay up Sam."

With a small growl he handed over his card. "I'm just saying, but being your friend is expensive."

"That will teach you not to ruin my stuff." She grinned as she accepted the bag. "Thanks Al, see you around." She turned to leave, not wanting Sam to make it any more uncomfortable.

"Wait." Al held out his arm to stop them. "You okay?" He jumped over the counter and walked towards her.

"Excuse me?"

"You have holes in your aura."

"Do I?" She played ignorance. "I haven't noticed." Her back spasmed at that moment, making her squeak in pain while dropping the bag.

"Shit." Sam grabbed the candles as they rolled away. "You okay?"

"Fine," she replied through clenched teeth.

"Seriously, you have holes all over your aura," Al said again, looking concerned.

"I'm fixing it," she replied as the spasm subsided.

"You should have used your crystal. It would have stopped your aura from getting this bad." Al eyed the raw Lapis around her throat. "Have you not activated it?"

"Activated?" Her brows came together in confusion.

"It's a Lapis Lazuli, isn't it? A protection crystal, you can use it as a source for a protection circle. You just need to do the ritual to train the crystal to react to an incantation or trigger word."

"Oh, really?" She gently gripped it between two fingers, the crystal warm. "Is it easy to do?"

"Well, it isn't particularly hard, I took a few side classes in protection when I was studying engineering. I think we could do it."

Alice thought for a second, weighing up the options. "Can we do it now?"

"I haven't got the space here, you need to draw a protection circle. Besides, your friend has already left." He nodded to the front where she could see Sam lighting up a cigarette.

"What time do you close here?" she asked as she spun back to Al.

"Five."

"Did you want to come over to my place when you finish? I have space in my kitchen."

"You asking me on a date?" he flirted, eyes smiling.

"A date?" Alice flustered. "Oh, no. I just…"

"I can be over around six. But only if you promise me our second date will be something proper." He patted his apron, finding a piece of paper and writing down his details. "Here's my number, text me your address." With a wink he let go, his smile never breaking as she rushed out of the shop.

CHAPTER TWENTY-ONE

Alice smiled at her neatly drawn pentagram, happy with the lines and symmetry.

"Why do you always use salt chalk?" Sam questioned, his legs fidgeting as he sat on his favourite counter by the sink. After an uncomfortable car ride home in which she stared daggers at him at every traffic light possible, he had happily declared he was going to watch and help. Not that he could actually do anything.

"The salt acts as a catalyst, it controls the chemical reaction without itself being affected, almost like a barrier. If you actually mix salt, on the other hand, it does the opposite, it completely breaks the spell and dissipates the magic. So if you ever get spelled or want to break an amulet just dunk it in a vat of strong salty water."

"Is that why you are using the salt-chalk and not actual salt?"

"Pretty much, if I was to cook with my copper pots I would use proper salt to draw my pentagrams as it has no risk of mixing. I use the chalk when I'm going to be in the centre of the spell as it's harder to rub the chalk off and interrupt the flow than accidentally kicking over granules."

"Is that what went wrong with your other spells?"

"What other spells?" she frowned.

Sam lifted his hand. "Protection ward," he pointed to his pinkie. "Waxing spell," he pointed to his ring finger. "The one where you…"

"Okay, I get it," she scowled. He was always bringing up every time she buggered something up. Sticking her tongue out she reached for the bag of candles, unwrapping them carefully before grabbing a knife. Sam gently tugged her hair, brushing strands through his fingertips over and over again as she carefully carved the first candle.

The symbol for earth was an equilateral triangle with a line vertically through the middle. Once the carving was finished she blew off the excess wax, placing the candle at the bottom left of the small pentagram's star drawn in the centre of their kitchen. Earth, as well as fire, were fixed points within a pentagram, with air and water situated towards the top.

The second sign was fire, an upside down equilateral triangle with two waves on each of the sides. She placed the candle on the bottom right of the star. The third was water, simply three horizontal wavy lines that went on the furthest right point with air being three vertical wavy lines, placed on the furthest left point.

The last symbol was spirit, a simple circle symbolizing infinity and eternity. Sitting in the centre pentagram she lit a match, lighting earth first, then fire, water, air and lastly spirit.

"Does it matter which candle you light first?" Sam asked, genuinely interested. This wasn't the first spell he had witnessed, but probably the most interesting. Watching someone create vanity charms and amulets in an old copper pot was pretty boring compared to a physical circle. She looked down at her pentagram again, hoping it hadn't damaged the already worn lino flooring so they didn't lose their security deposit.

"You're supposed to anchor the protection circle by lighting the two fixed points which are fire and earth, you then light air and water to flow into the centre and lastly spirit, which closes it."

"Why do you even need a circle?"

"It's safer. It's a barrier that protects your aura when you mix it with the spell to consummate." She shrugged, not actually knowing the exact details why you couldn't do it without a circle. She wasn't curious enough to try.

"Being a shifter is so much easier." A smile. "It's also why I enjoy watching you try not to screw up."

Alice replied with her middle finger before she let out a breath, concentrating. Once her mind was empty she opened her third eye, checking to make sure the circle was whole. A thin gold and green shimmery film covered the pentagram in a dome, the circle perfect, bigger than she predicted. Pretty impressive for her first try, not that she was gloating.

"The circle is done," she exclaimed as her face broke into a smile, her cheeks straining from the excitement.

"So what's the next stage?"

"Shit." Alice looked at her neat circle, the gold and green morphing into a blue before changing back. "I might have left the instructions by the sink." Which was outside her circle.

"Can't you just go get it?"

"If I touch the circle it will fall, I'll have to start all over again." Once she touched the outside, her aura would rebound back to her.

"Oh, okay." Sam jumped down from the counter and grabbed the leather grimoire. "Want me to read the instructions?"

"Yeah, I'm not sure I should push anything through the circle," she told him, squinting at the dome.

"Okay, give me a second... it says to create a salt circle, light the candles, yadda yadda yadda, okay here it is. *'To realign your aura to its original state, excluding any permanent damage gained, you must quicken the flames with a blood donation.'*"

"A blood donation?"

"That's what it says." He flipped through the pages.

"Oh, okay." Alice grabbed the burnt match and broke it in half. Carefully, she poked the pad of her thumb with the sharp edge, a pearl of blood appearing at the tip.

"Alice?"

"I need to quicken the flames." She squeezed her thumb, letting a single drop of blood drop into each candle, ending with spirit. "Right, what's next?"

"It says you say the incantation and your aura will just replenish."

"Just like that?" That seemed too easy.

"Just like that." Sam squinted as he read through the book once more. "Ready to repeat after me?"

"Ready."

"Anima ad animam."

"Anima ad animam," she began, nervous.

"Ut aura erat aura."

"Ut aura erat aura."

"Putabas sanare capitii textile."

"*Putabas sanare capitii textile.*" Alice sucked in a breath, her lungs burning as she gasped for air.

"Alice?" Sam asked as pain ripped through every cell in her body. "ALICE!?"

"What happened?" A deep snarl followed by an inaudible reply.

Frowning, Alice opened her eyes, blinking blindly at the light above.

How can eyelashes hurt?

"Is she going to be okay?"

"How am I supposed to know? I felt something was wrong and..."

Noise assaulted her ears, different pitches, voices that were muffled, almost as if she was underwater. Blinking a couple more times her eyes started to adjust, the kitchen ceiling coming into focus.

What the hell was that stain?

She watched as the green hue of her circle changed, mixing with blue like a sea mist, disorientating the suspicious ceiling mark.

"What do you mean you felt something was wrong? That's impossible, you're not even mated."

"That is none of your concern."

"Who the fuck..."

Alice rolled her neck, squinting at the two men arguing in her kitchen doorway. It took a few seconds to recognise them through the circle, the moving colours making it look like she was viewing them through a smeared window.

Sam, she realised, was only an inch or so shorter than Rex, his finger angrily pointing at the Alpha's chest. His mouth was slightly open, his breaths coming in short pants as he tasted the surrounding aggression, his leopard close to the surface. Rex, on the other hand, looked like he was made from granite, his muscles bunched, tense as he snarled at her best friend. They both turn to look at her when she finally crawled to her knees.

"Wow. That hurt." She took in a shaky breath, flexing her muscles.

"Baby girl?" Sam knelt beside her as close as he could get without touching the circle. "Open the circle."

"What?" Her head rolled on her shoulders as her neck clicked. She felt... good. Really good.

"Open the bloody circle," Rex barked, tension still obvious along his shoulders.

Sam snarled, his already prominent canines extending. "Don't speak to her like that." She could visibly see his skin tremble, fur threatening to break through the surface.

"Stop it," she tried to say, but it came out more like a croak. Flicking her hand out she touched the dome, voltage as her aura raced up her arm, breaking the circle.

"What were you thinking?" Rex crouched beside her, the opposite side of Sam. "You could have killed yourself."

"What are you even doing here?" she shot back accusingly.

"Yeah, what are you even doing here? I didn't call you," Sam said, eyes narrowed.

Rex ignored them. "You could have killed yourself."

"Don't be stupid," Alice replied as Rex's eyes flashed arctic. "I know exactly what I'm doing. It's you who hasn't got any trust."

"Careful." Rex's voice was a warning, his wolf close to the edge.

"I think you should leave." She stood up, her back feeling great, energised even. Inside she felt whole, her core aura electric. As she clicked her fingers her chi rippled, coating her hand with blue flames. It was effortless, the little power she used barely touching her chi reserve.

"Remember who hired you." Rex stared at the flame, eyes still ice.

"You don't let me forget." She made the flame grow before extinguishing it. "I'm just going to be researching, so if I get any information that could help I'll contact you."

His face softened for a second, barely a glimpse as he thought it over. "Fine." A shallow nod. "I didn't realise how bad the necromancer hurt you, for that I apologise."

"It's fine, no harm done."

Alice fought not to touch him, her hand almost reaching up to Rex's skin on its own accord before she clenched it into a fist. It was a weird reaction she couldn't explain. She stepped back into Sam, the distance between them helping the weird magnetic pull.

"Ah, I'll keep you updated."

Sam purred low in his chest, his hand stroking through the strands in her hair as he centred himself with touch.

"You do that." Rex went to stretch towards her before he caught himself, his eyes following Sam's lazy movements as he continued to stroke her hair.

Shifters were tactile creatures, needing the physical response to calm their animals. Rex was itching to touch her, reassure his beast that she wasn't hurt. But she couldn't bring herself to close the gap, allow him some comfort.

She couldn't explain her weird attraction, and until she could, she wouldn't allow herself to indulge in what her body was begging her for. She clenched her fists harder.

"Why are you here Rex?" He seemed to be everywhere.

"I came to inform you that time is running out. Another one of my wolves has gone missing."

"What?" she gasped. "When? How?"

"Not important. What is important is that we need to find a new lead."

"How is the time frame not important...?"

"It isn't relevant," Rex interrupted.

"There you go again, keeping information from me..."

"Look, I need to go. They need me at the den." Ice eyes met her own. "You *will* call me." He growled as he slammed the front door, not giving her time to reply.

"Fuck." She smacked her hand against the wood.

"He's such an arsehole." Sam stood to the side with his arms crossed.

"You have no idea." She stared at her hand, tracing the little crescent moon indents her nails left. "Fuck, fuck, fuck." He had done it again, left her in the dark and expected her to find her way out.

"I don't trust him, he acts like he has something to hide."

"I know he has." She knew as soon as he recognised the necromancer, she just wasn't sure what he was hiding. Yet she couldn't drop the case, not until she found out the answers she didn't even know she was searching for.

"Then what's the plan?"

Oh, I don't know, figure out what the hell is going on before my resistance gives up and I jump back into bed with him.

She knew she sounded crazy even in her own head, so instead she said, "I need to research this cult."

And pray to the many gods that it was going to lead somewhere.

CHAPTER TWENTY-TWO

"You didn't have to come." Alice crossed the road, dodging past impatient back cabs that couldn't care less that it was a pedestrian's right of way.

"My spidey senses are tingling." Sam walked beside her. "I just feel like..." he paused, unable to explain.

"You know in every situation it would be me, protecting you right?" She glanced to her left, smirking.

"Yeah, but I look scarier." He showed her his canines.

She couldn't argue with that. "Seriously, what can go wrong in a library?"

"A book could fall on you." He shrugged as he peered at her from the corner of his eye. "Or Rex could turn up." He stretched his hand out to stop her. "You need to stay away from him."

"You don't need to worry." A car screeched against the wet asphalt as it dodged a cyclist. Beeps and horns a daily occurrence in a city.

"He's taking way too much interest in you," Sam said, anxious.

"I'm figuring it out." She turned them towards the mammoth Victorian style building located just off the west district. The intricate, architectural structure was a stunning contrast to the neighbouring skyscrapers, and the hundreds of original glass windows reflecting different patterns in a kaleidoscope of colour.

The rain had calmed down to a trickle rather than the downpour that pummelled earlier, the sun breaking through the coal grey clouds to shine bleakly.

"What are we here for?" Sam asked as they walked through the two storey wooden door that led into the main atrium of the library.

"Research."

Sam laughed. "It's called the internet."

"What I want to research can't be tracked."

"Ah, you don't want Dread to find out." Sam's face turned solemn. "Don't get yourself in over your head. I don't know what Rex has hired you for, but you seem to be at a crossroads."

Alice didn't know what to say, the seriousness of the statement unsettling. "I know what I'm doing." She hoped.

The library was the oldest across the British Isles, with the most amount of literature under one roof since before the Great War. Floor-to-ceiling bookcases lined each wall, curving in great arrangements to create a chaotic labyrinth of books, tapestries and paintings. The place smelt dusty with a hint of wood polish, which wasn't completely unpleasant.

Wooden benches and tables were placed neatly in the centre, underneath the glass ceiling Alice knew to be several floors above. Various busts were randomly placed around the different floors, everything from the monarchy to authors such as Shakespeare and Jane Austen to Winston Churchill and Charlie Chaplin. Most were in reasonable condition depending on their age, others were cracked and vandalised.

"Where do we start?" Sam asked nonchalantly, his hand brushing against the top of an armchair, the old brown leather cracked across the seat, the cushion long gone.

"Oh, erm…" she hesitated. She hadn't thought that far ahead. Biting her lip she looked around, hoping an idea would spring to mind. "What about simply starting at 'C'?"

"And look for what?"

"Cults?" She shrugged. "I'm interested in the ideologies behind The Becoming."

"The Becoming?"

"Yes, have you heard of it before?"

"No." A frown. "This isn't the normal thing you do Alice," he moaned as she began leading them towards the bookshelf headed 'C'. "Daemons, cults. It's pretty hard core compared to your usual stuff."

"My usual stuff hasn't helped me with my dreams, have they?"

"You mean your nightmares? The ones that have been worse since you started this?" He picked up a book, slamming it back in its slot after he read the title. "You're hurting yourself and you don't even see it."

"Has it not occurred to you that maybe I need to break before I can grow?" *Before I can understand.* "You would do anything you could to find your dad. To get back at him."

"That isn't the same." A low growl, his amber eyes glowing.

"The hell it is," she hissed back. "I need to find out what happened that night, and this research is helping. Working with Rex is helping." She felt her voice quiver. "Instead of questioning me, can't you support me?" She met his eyes. "I support you."

He held her gaze. "I do support you." He grabbed her into a hug, his chin resting on her head. "I can't lose you."

"You won't." She hugged him tightly before stepping back.

A nod towards the shelf, his usual mischievous smile in place. "So, where would you like to start?"

"All I have to go with is that cult, The Becoming." She started to scan the hundreds if not thousands of books along the shelves.

"How are you sure it's even a cult?" He leant against the opposite shelf, arms crossed.

"Just a guess, what else could it be?" She selected a book titled, '*Age old Cults affecting modern society*' and began scanning through the pages.

"What else have you got to go on?"

She slammed the book shut.

"Not a lot. I have the autopsy reports showing possible signs of Daemon transitions, but it isn't based on solid evidence. I can't even compare them to the wolves because Rex didn't get any autopsies performed." She blew out in frustration, looking for any other books that could give an insight into a mysterious cult that could, or couldn't help.

"This is why I'm not a Paladin, it seems boring when you spend your time in mind-numbing libraries." His attention wandered as Alice continued looking through the books. "You found anything yet? How long is this going to take?"

"I said you didn't have to come," she huffed, her own patience becoming thin.

"We've already discussed this."

"And I have already told you, I'm fine." Annoyed, she grabbed several books from the shelf, stacking them into Sam's arms before grabbing some more. "Let's take these to a table it'll be easier to study them."

Back stiff she walked to an empty wooden table towards the centre of the atrium, directly underneath the glass roof. The table was marked beyond redemption, a green and gold plastic lamp was drilled into the centre giving some artificial light that didn't seem to have an off option.

"Here." Sam thumped the books down, sitting himself at the edge. "I think I have something for you," he smirked as he flicked through one of the books.

"You do?"

Sam dramatically cleared his throat. "'*His bulging cock penetrated as she moaned his name,*'" he read loudly. "'*Leaning down he kissed along her throat as he increased his thrusts, her tunnel squeezing his thick shaft...*'"

"BLOODY HELL!" Alice knocked the book out of his hand, her face burning as she looked to see if anyone had overheard. Sam just chuckled, his dimples dancing across his cheeks. "If you're not going to help, leave me alone." When he didn't answer she glanced up at him, his attention on one of the aisles as a woman wearing a dangerously short skirt bent over to pick something from the floor. "Sam," she called. "Sam," Still no answer. "Earth to Samion."

"Huh?" He reluctantly turned to her.

"I'm going to be sitting here a while, why don't you go prowl somewhere else."

"You sure?" His brows came together.

Alice smirked. "Sure."

"Okay, see you in a while." He unsurprisingly walked towards the bent woman, one who was happily fluffing her dark hair and pouting her lips at the sudden attention.

Rolling her eyes Alice picked up the next book, the title stating '*Ancient Art of Magic the Personification of Cults.*'

Flipping through the first few pages she frowned, the paper in poor condition with some sheets completely ripped out. A mixture of English, Latin, Gaelic as well as other languages she didn't recognise filled the pages, seemingly nonsense. Squinting, she tried to read the headings in English, stopping when she noticed '*B.e.c.o*' before disappointingly seeing the rest of the word was smudged by ink.

Licking her dry lips she read the small print underneath,

'For one to 'Become,' an age old one must sacrifice a vessel of clean magic. Doing so will give the bearer the ability to transcend into the next stage, giving unbelievable power over the darker arts, their body reflecting the great power bestowed on them by the mother of everything.'

Alice blinked, re-reading the passage over several times, trying to make sense of the words. The passage stated it was written in *'The Ancient Kingdom Third Century, now Europe.'*

"Third century?" she mused to herself. "What was around in Europe in the third century?"

"Celts," a light voice answered from behind her.

Startled, Alice accidentally pushed the book onto the floor, her mouth agape as the mystery man bent to gently pick it up.

"Interesting read," he mused, his voice musical. Taking a seat beside her he flicked back to the same page before reading the small paragraph. "Yes, it's definitely the Celts, I believe specifically the druids." He handed her back the book.

"Excuse me?" She cleared her throat as she stared at his eyes, purple iridescent orbs that matched the pastel of his shoulder length hair. She assumed he was a man, but she wasn't actually sure, his features that of complete androgyny. Either way, it was definitely Fae.

"Look here," he said as his long fingers traced across the passage, "It says *'bestowed on them by the mother of everything.'* Druids worshiped nature, specifically mother Gaia who they, at least, used to believe was their source of magic. The time frame is around the same but your best bet would be to ask a druid."

"Maybe." The Fae was actually making a lot of sense. "If it was druids, wouldn't it state Great Britain rather than Europe?"

"Oh, so you know something about druids?" His iridescent eyes sparkled.

"Some. It also says in the same paragraph about *'sacrificing a vessel of clean magic'*. Druids are notoriously famous for their passivity, peaceful people who gained their magic from the earth and atmosphere."

"Passiveness?" The Fae laughed, the sound like little bells tinkling through the air. "When was the last time you met a passive druid? You can't associate an entire race into an expectation. That's the same as saying all witches own black cats, or all faeries eat small children." He smiled, amused at his own joke.

"Okay, point made."

"You're also assuming the *'vessel of clean magic'* is something sinister when it could easily be something as simple as a plant. There is nothing else in here to state otherwise."

"You obviously know more than me on this subject."

"I wouldn't take it to heart, I'm a professor at the local University specialising in atmospheric magic. I have to know the basics of all magic based Breeds to really understand how to take certain aspects of magic further," the professor stated, his eyelashes the same pastel shade as his hair. "You a student? They have a study on the original history of magic based Breeds in the next semester. You could really benefit from it."

"Oh, no I'm not. I'm just really interested in the history."

"Alice, you find anything?" Sam walked over to the table, interrupting the Fae. "I tried to look for books about Daemon's but couldn't find anything." His amber eyes narrowed to slits as he appraised the professor, his nostrils flaring as he tried to scent his Breed.

"Oh Sam, this is..." She didn't know his name.

"Professor Luanou, but I'm afraid I must be going." The Fae stood up, his black shirt and trousers reminding her more of something a sensei would wear rather than a university professor. "I must have made a mistake in suggesting you should attend the history of magic based Breed's next semester. We do not tolerate any practitioners of the dark arts." His eyes flashed to her numerous books about cults as well as the inappropriate erotica before he walked away.

"What is the faerie on about?" Sam frowned as he took the now vacant seat.

"Wait..." she called after him. "I DON'T PRACTICE BLACK MAGIC!" The professor didn't acknowledge her statement. "I really don't." She sighed, noticing the audience of people watching her outburst.

"So what was that about?" Sam rolled a cigarette between his fingertips, the end creased as if he had stubbed it against something.

"He now thinks I'm studying black magic since you came over and mentioned the Daemon books."

"Really?" Sam chuckled. "You at least find anything interesting?"

"A little. I think I found the description of The Becoming." She turned the page so he could read. "And after speaking to the professor it does sound like something that's druid in origin."

"Druid? Like your Da?"

"Maybe. The professor made some solid comments but I would really need to ask another druid, other than my dad's appreciation for nature I don't know much about his history."

"What about Overlord?"

"He might know something." Dread had been best friends with her father, and while he never admitted his true age, she knew he was old.

Alice closed the books, stacking them up and putting them on a tray for the librarian to put back into place.

"Did you find anything?" she asked.

"Found nothing. The word Daemon is completely missing if the books were in alphabetical order."

"I thought you were checking out the skirt girl?" She crossed her arms, smirking up at Sam.

"Aye, but it's a complete turn off when my nose itches from the amount of glamour that Fae was wearing." He reached up to scratch his nose as if it still was irritated. "So what now?"

Alice looked up at the clock on the wall. "We have time to pop to The Tower, might as well ask Dread the questions before Al gets to our place."

"What about the Daemon books?"

"We can ask the receptionist, maybe we're missing something."

The clerk was right by the front entrance, the small queue having completely dissipated by the time they got there. The desk an oversized mahogany monstrosity, seeming even bigger than possible compared the frail old woman sitting behind.

"How may I help you, young lady?" she asked, her small eyes magnified through her thick circular glasses.

"I'm looking for anything to do with Daemons. We can't seem to find anything."

"Daemons?" Her eyes widened slightly. "Oh, let me check." She tapped her keyboard. "I'm sorry but we do not keep those types of books here."

"Really? We are in the biggest library I have ever seen and there isn't one book about Daemons?" Sam asked dryly. "Bit weird don't you think?"

"Have you checked under 'D,' my dear?"

Alice tried to smile sweetly, ignoring the question. "We are looking more specifically into daemonic transitions."

"I just told you we do not hold those sort of books here."

"Well, where would we find those sort of books then?"

"Not here."

"What about some history on them, maybe?" Alice asked, changing tactics.

"We have nothing like that here." The woman's voice was getting sterner.

"You didn't check your computer," Alice said sardonically, starting to lose her temper.

The old woman tapped one button. "Nothing."

"I don't understand why this is so difficult, we're only interested," Sam interjected.

"We don't practice black magic." Alice had never had to defend herself so much. "It's just for a project we're working on."

"I have already said we do not have those types of books here." She sniffed unpleasantly.

"Then where are they?"

"Not here. You shouldn't even be looking at that sort of stuff. It's dangerous."

"What's so dangerous about books?" Sam growled. "This is ridiculous."

The woman's eyes slowly bled into panic, the pulse in her throat beating visibly against her skin.

"What do you know about Daemons?" Alice asked as a heavy hand landed on her shoulder. Turning slightly she eyed the security guard. "Is there a problem here?"

"I'm going to have to ask you to leave," the guard grumbled, his fingers digging in.

Sam swore in the background, snarling at his own personal security guard.

"Why? We haven't done anything wrong."

"If you don't vacate the premises immediately, we will remove you."

Alice removed the hand from her shoulder. "Fine. Sam, we're leaving." She pulled at an angry Sam before they were escorted through the door.

"What a load of bullshit," Sam shouted at the guards, flashing them some interesting hand gestures.

Alice looked behind her shoulder, three security guards standing ominously near the entrance. The clerk spoke in hushed tones into the phone at her desk, trying desperately not to make eye contact.

"What was that about?" Sam asked, turning his attention back to Alice as they stood under the alcove.

"She knows something." Alice knew it, the look in the clerk's eyes was pure panic as well as guilt. But what could make an old woman react in fear like that?

The Tower was busy as they made their way up to the forty-second floor, the noise and chaotic rumblings of her colleagues a pleasant comfort.

"It's getting late." Sam looked around the large room into all the different cubicles, eyes lighting up when he noticed the cat-themed novelty gifts he had gotten her over the years. "You have a date, remember."

"It's not a date." Alice just sighed. "I'm not going to be long, you could have waited outside."

Sam had dated a few of her colleagues over the years, and not one ended well.

"Oh, Alice," a shrill voice called from beside her. "I see you haven't been fired yet." Michael swanned over wearing a green velvet jacket over an off-white shirt, his ginger hair had been recently cut just above his ears. "Shame," he sniggered.

She didn't have the patience. "Bye Mickey."

His arm snaked out, pulling her against his chest, close enough she could smell the coffee on his tongue. She immediately turned and broke his hold, stepping back just as Sam snarled past, his arm extended as he forced Mickey against the wall.

"SAM, NO!"

"Now we're gonna have a little chat," Sam hissed directly into Michael's face, claws erupting from his fingertips as he kneaded them across the sensitive skin of his throat.

"Alice," Mickey choked, sweat dripping into his eyes. "Control your pussy."

"Aye, pussy." Sam purred low in his chest as he rubbed the side of his face against his. "You want to see what this pussycat can do?"

"Sam, please." Alice caught his eye, the amber glowing to the point she could almost see the leopard looking back. He always reacted badly, ever since they were kids he took it upon himself to be her protector, as if she couldn't protect herself.

Don't do this. He isn't worth it, she begged with her eyes, not wanting Mickey to understand.

He hurt you, Sam replied in the same way.

There was only a handful of people she could have a wordless conversation with, have a strong enough bond to be able read their expression. Sam more than a brother to her, regardless of blood.

No one should be able to touch you like that. Years of abuse flashed across his eyes, uncontrollable pain before he calmed himself. She had never asked for details about his past, knowing only a small amount based on the history of scars decorating his body. A long time ago she decided she never would.

I'm not breakable.

No you're fucking not. His eyes lost their electricity, the leopard still present but not running the show.

With his face still pressed to Mickey's he gently nipped his ear, purring at the flinch. "If you wanted my number precious, you should have just asked." Pushing away he turned back towards the lifts, a cigarette already placed between his lips as he disappeared through the metal doors.

Mickey made an unrecognizable sound, sweat still pouring down his face. "I'm going to report him for that, assaulting a Paladin is a criminal offence."

"I'm sure you will. Make sure to note how you grabbed me first." Watching his face turn various shades of red she turned towards Dread's office, happily noticing the absence of his secretary, Barbie. Lifting her hand she knocked against his closed door. "Dread?" she called.

"Alice? What are you doing here? I haven't released you from medical leave."

"Oh, yes, well I have had some time to think and wanted to ask some questions."

"What questions?" He gestured to a chair before his own. The room bright from the window behind him, the blackout blind he normally preferred rolled to the top to show the amazing view of the city. "Why is Sam here?"

"Sam?" *How does he even know that?*

"He didn't make a scene did he?" Dread raised a dark eyebrow, his bottomless eyes almost laughing as if he knew exactly what had happened. He probably did, knowing him.

"He's waiting outside."

"Hmm." He tapped his ring against the table. "What can I help you with?"

"I wanted to know more about druids."

Dread paused. "Why?"

"I realised I didn't know much about dad's heritage. I was hoping you could tell me."

"Why the sudden interest?"

"The anniversary is coming up again." She didn't have to fake the emotion clogging her throat. "I want to remember them better than blurry memories or old photographs." Which wasn't a complete lie.

He nodded, accepting her explanation. "Well, what do you want to know?"

"I want to know how often druids practiced dark magic?" She watched his face tick, his expression remaining unchanged as he took a few seconds to answer. "I was just at the library and I read about some druids choosing dark magic compared to earth."

"What have you been reading?"

"Just a book."

He glared at her for a few seconds. "Anybody can choose dark magic, regardless of their Breed, background or religion."

Pretty much what the Professor had said. "So they weren't more prone to dark magic?" She bit her lip, waiting on the answer.

"Not any more than anyone else. Your father was strictly clean, high in The Order, as you already know. A respected man." She knew little about The Order, Dread having explained to her it was an organisation strictly of druids for which her father worked. He never told her what they did exactly, always saying it was *'top secret stuff'* when she asked as a child.

"Would anybody from The Order be willing to talk to me?"

"Stay away from them Alice, they're dangerous people."

"Then why did dad work with them?" Alice pointed out.

Dread just continued to glare, the vein in his forehead pulsing. "You need to drop this, I don't know what you have been reading, but it is clearly inaccurate."

"Fine." She leant back in her chair, staring out the window. "I saw something interesting at the library today."

"Interesting?" His fingers tapped against the top of his desk.

"While I was there someone asked about Daemons, but they were escorted out by security." Only a small lie.

Dread narrowed his eyes to slits, akin to a python watching its prey. "Whom have you been talking to?"

"No one." She tried not to react to his gaze. "I just thought it was weird."

"Daemons are dark magic, so the media has represented them as mythological tales since The Change. All literature based on black, dark or death magic was removed around the same time to stop mundane people becoming infatuated." He shook his head as if remembering something.

"So they lied to the public and said Daemons weren't real?"

"Nobody has ever said they weren't real, it was always up to the general public to make their own decision. Admittedly those decisions were persuaded along the way. Daemons are rare enough that in all my years I have only had to deal with a handful. It is believed that the process to become a Daemon has a high failure rate. The Council doesn't want people going around trying to summon Daemons to gain access to ancient dark knowledge."

"What even is a Daemon, exactly?"

Dread tapped his knuckles against his desk. "Those who choose dark magic. Alice I'm very busy, you should be at home resting."

"Okay, but what about the literature, was it all destroyed?"

Dread shook his head. "To my knowledge they were just moved from the public floors. Only a select few have access to the restricted section of the library."

"Restricted section? How comes I didn't know there even was a restricted section?"

"Because you don't have access."

Touché. "Thanks Dread."

CHAPTER TWENTY-THREE

Sam mumbled to himself as he paced across the kitchen, his movements agitated as he took his usual seat on the kitchen counter, his legs swinging. He had been uncharacteristically quiet on their way home, a scowl carved onto his beautiful face.

Alice eyed him warily as she prepared the circle she had used earlier, the marking still perfect. She checked each candle separately, making sure the carvings were all still clear.

Sam's voice broke through her concentration. "Did Overlord give you anything to go on?"

"Maybe." She placed the candle marked with fire back down, setting it delicately into its place. "I have a plan." When he just frowned she continued. "There's apparently a private wing in the library."

"How do you expect to get into this private wing? We just got kicked out."

She folded her arms. "Go in after hours. It's a library, all I have to do is dodge some security guards, open a locked door, look around and leave. Easy."

Sam opened his mouth to reply.

Knock. Knock. Knock.

"That's not exactly a detailed plan. We'll sort this out later," he murmured as he opened the front door.

"Evening Alice. Sam."

Sam nodded a greeting to Alistair before sitting in his usual spot on the counter, out of the way.

"Hey, I've already set up the circle. I wasn't sure what you would need." Alice awkwardly scratched her head, desperately trying not to embarrass herself with her lack of knowledge.

"It looks perfect." Al smiled wide as he placed his backpack on the floor. "Impressive circle."

"I used it earlier."

Sam huffed something underneath his breath. She glared at him until he looked away, his poor mood starting to grate against her. He was always dramatic, sulking for hours when he was annoyed at something, or someone.

"It's really well done, I thought you weren't used to this sort of thing?" He walked over and checked out the placements.

"I'm not."

"Impressive," he said again. "Right, do you have the crystal?" He took off his coat, revealing a dark blue shirt neatly buttoned to the top. His sleeves were rolled to his elbows, grease smeared along his arms.

"I do." She lifted it from under her t-shirt. The instant it was in the open air it started to hum.

"It will stop making that noise once we activate the aegis."

"So, what are we actually going to do?"

"We are going to put a little of your aura within the crystal, once you say the invocation it will create an aegis, a molecule thin shield created from your aura."

"Should I be taking notes?" Alice joked.

Al continued as if he hadn't heard her, instead getting his own chalk out of his bag and scribbling symbols around her own. "Are you ready?" His eyes lit up in excitement.

"Sure…" Alice took a step into her pentagram, her bare feet cold against the hard floor.

Al began to whisper, the runes and symbols beginning to glow as he rummaged through his bag. "Light the candles," he said as he handed her a small mirror.

Earth, fire, water, air then spirit. The circle cracked into place around her. A gasp, her smile dropping as she noticed Al's shocked face.

"What? What?" Alice panicked. "Did I do something wrong?"

How could I fuck this up?

"No, I've never seen a circle like yours." His eyes glazed, a sign he was looking through his third eye. *"Flaminco."* A larger circle erupted around them both, eclipsing her own.

Sam looked at her at that moment, his eyes easily readable. *Someone wants to show off.*

Shut up. She looked through her own third eye, noticing how Al's circle was an unappealing orange. "Okay. What do I do now?"

"Put the crystal onto the mirror, then push your aura from your hand onto the crystal. The mirror will act as a catalyst, a block. It stops your aura from leaking into other objects and helps the concentration on the pendant."

"How do I do that? You can't see your own aura."

"Just concentrate, I will tell you how it is going."

"Okay. Okay. Okay," she whispered underneath her breath.

Sitting down onto the floor she crossed her legs, using her knees as a table with the mirror balanced between them. She carefully placed her crystal on the mirror's glass, hovering her hand over it before she began to chant loudly in her head.

Move. Move. Now. Do something. Anything.

She let out a frustrated growl. "It's not working."

"Alice stop overthinking it. Close your eyes."

She obeyed.

"Now envision a cloud around your hand, imagine the cloud flowing over your fingers and towards the mirror."

Pins and needles over her elbow, flowing down her right arm into her palm. Uncomfortable.

"That's it, keep going."

Alice wiggled her fingers, the tips aching without the warmth of her aura.

"Okay, now hold your aura over the crystal, and say this phrase, followed by the word you will use as your incantation. *In hac sphaera absorbet meam commisisse.*"

"Okay..." She concentrated on holding her place, her eyes still closed. *"In hac sphaera."* Numbness swept across her fingertips. *"Absorbet meam."* Sudden pain through her hand. *"Commisisse."*

Her hand spasmed closed over the pendant.

"ARMA!"

Her aura rebounded back like an elastic band. With a yelp Alice jumped up, knocking the mirror from her lap with a crash. Her step back brought her in contact with her circle, breaking the dome with a pop.

"Shit, are you okay?" Al walked over, careful to not break his own circle until she was ready.

"I'm fine, it was just a shock." She looked over at the shards on the floor. "Your mirror," she cried.

He laughed "It's okay." He picked up the necklace through the broken glass, handing it to Alice.

"Did it work?" she asked, eyeing the crystal suspiciously. It didn't look any different.

"I'm going to drop my circle, once it's dropped put the necklace on and say your incantation." He pushed against the invisible wall surrounding them, another soft pop signalling his circle had opened.

Alice held the necklace carefully in her palm, the raw stone warm in her hand, familiar. Slipping it over her head she placed it neatly in the hollow of her throat.

"Arma." An instant circle formed around her, the whole three-hundred and sixty degrees. A thin shield made of a mixture of green, blue with specks of gold.

"Wow Alice, that's really cool," Sam said with awe, his mood suddenly changing. "Is that what your aura looks like?" He jumped off the counter to press his hand gently against the opaque surface. With a hiss, he pulled his hand back. "Ow."

"Erm," Al mumbled. "It shouldn't be that big."

"What do you mean?" Warmth drained from her face.

"An aegis is only supposed to be a shield in front of you. You have made a complete circle, and without a drawn pentagram." His eyebrows creased as he walked around it, touching the barrier in different areas. "I've never seen anything like this." He poked the circle again. "Have you studied arcane magic?"

"No." She eyed the dome. "Is this not normal?" She touched the barrier to drop the circle.

"There's nothing wrong with it, I'm just surprised is all." He clapped his hands together. "You should really practise with arcane energy, I think you're a natural. Can you manipulate a ball of energy?"

"Yeah." *Sort of anyway.*

"Great." He grabbed his coat and rucksack. "By the way, I get to choose our next date." With a wink he let himself out.

"See, I told you it was a date." Sam padded across to her, his fingers playing with the crystal at her throat.

"Hardly a date." She rolled her eyes. "Now let's get back to planning."

From the radio came an eerily detached voice. "Check. One. Two. Three. Check. Alice, can you hear me?"

"Hear you loud and clear, over," Alice replied, holding down the little button on the side. Placing the walkie-talkie radio back on her belt she looked around the empty street, checking to see if anyone was looking.

"There's a staff door on the side of the building, you will then need to go across the atrium towards the back of the building. There will be a large double door to the left. Go through that towards the private corridors."

"Where the bloody hell are you getting this information?"

"There's an interactive map of the whole library on their website," Sam replied dryly.

Alice burst out laughing, softening the noise with her black leather glove. "Even the private wings?"

"Nah. I've checked the whole map and there are a couple of doors you can't look into which are through that corridor."

Static before she turned the radio down slightly. It was hard to sneak around in a city that doesn't really sleep, the lights illuminated the street enough to make it difficult to look inconspicuous. Acting as casual as possible she walked towards the alley at the side of the building, her black leather catsuit helping her to hide amongst the little shadows available.

"Okay, I've found the staff entrance, no names from now on. Over." Re-attaching the radio to her belt she picked up her small knife hidden in a loop within her boot. Grabbing a pin from her hair she placed both in the keyhole, turning one slowly until she heard a series of clicks, each pin clicking into its correct height. With a little more pressure the final pin clicked into place, allowing her to turn the lock mechanism.

Suppressing a smirk she put her knife back into her boot, her fingers tingling as she pressed down on the handle gently, peering through the small gap. Satisfied that no one was there she crawled through, closing the door gently behind her before checking the room for cameras.

Must be the staff cloakroom. Squinting in the poor light she noticed hangers lining one side of the room while a selection of ugly armchairs and a small table sat against the opposite wall. A coloured photograph of a smiling woman was the only decoration on the otherwise bland walls, *'Employee of the Month'* written in gold across the top.

She searched every corner of the room and saw no tell-tale cameras. Happy, she stood to her full height, adjusting the leather straps under her breasts and stomach that held her sword flush against her back. She usually wore the straps beneath her clothing, but they were uncomfortable against the catsuit, forcing her to wear them over the top. She probably should have left it at home. What could go wrong in a library?

Walking to the only door available she passed a mirror, her face a stark contrast to the darkness. Blonde strands had escaped her black beanie hat, creating a halo around her face, accentuating the thick black eyeshadow and eyeliner she decided to put on to help her blend in. Sam had laughed his arse off when he saw her. *'You look like a gothic panda gimp.'* he had said.

She pretended to be annoyed, explaining she had to wear the outfit otherwise her blonde hair and pale skin, courtesy of her mother's Nordic heritage, would have stuck out like a sore thumb. He just laughed harder. She didn't want to admit he was right.

Moving past the mirror she opened the door, the lock on the inside easily turning as she made her way quietly into the atrium. All the artificial lights had been turned off, leaving only the streetlights to leak through the stained glass windows, creating a dissonant pattern across the already ugly carpet. She kept to the walls, blending into the darkness as much as possible as she walked through.

A noise came from the left.

Dropping to her knees, she quickly crawled towards the clerk's desk.

"So how was your wife's birthday party last week?" one of the security guards asked, sweeping his torch across the patterned floor.

"Terrible, apparently I got the wrong bracelet for her. Ungrateful bitch," the other guy replied.

Alice stayed hidden, controlling her breathing until their voices were distant murmurs across the room. When confident they were far enough away she peeked over the desk, noticing a small green glow across the other side of the large atrium. Careful to not make any noise she sneaked towards the first bookshelf.

"Have you got to the door yet?"

She hushed the speaker.

"Steve, did you hear that?"

"Hear what?"

"A noise, over there..." He swept the torch in her direction, the light creeping under the bookshelf towards her feet.

OH SHIT. She hid amongst the other bookcases, her thick-soled boots making no noise on the plush carpet.

"George it's nothing, your imagination's going wild again."

"Maybe..." Alice picked up a small book, throwing it across the room, creating a soft bang in the opposite direction. "Over there." A jingle of keys as the men ran towards the distraction.

She rushed towards the private corridor, the light turning out to be a 'restricted area' sign. Alice pushed at the door, but it didn't budge.

Fuck.

Noise close behind.

Running past she entered the only other door available, the door swinging shut just as light swept from beneath the frame. Alice stared, heart in her throat. The light eventually moved away, the footsteps disappearing with it.

"You almost got me caught," she whispered into the radio.

"*Sorry.*"

"I'm in the men's room." She kept her voice low. "It had to be the bloody men's bathroom, didn't it?"

"*Babe, if you needed to go you should have just said.*"

"Funny. Is there any way out of here other than the bathroom door?"

"*Give me a second, there's no other exit, but it does back up to another bathroom. Is there a grate or something?*"

Alice moved her hand gently across the walls, careful not to touch the urinals. "There's a vent." Getting her knife back out of her boot she used it to unscrew the corners, catching the vent as it sagged off the wall. Leaning it gently against the tiles she peered in, unable to see anything. "I'm going to try it."

She climbed into the small metal hole and pulled the vent back across the opening. No one would notice it was loose until the morning.

Ouch. Her head smacked into the opposite grate. Mouth twisted in a snarl she peeked through the small gap.

Nothing.

Just another bathroom.

Turning slightly she planted both her palms across the metal, pushing. A squeak, the metal resisting. Pushing even harder the metal started to groan, bending at the top and bottom. The corners screeched as the screws were forced out, warping before crashing to the floor.

Fuck. Fuck. Fuck.

She held her breath, and counted.

60. 59. 58. 57.

No tell-tale noise, just a low hum.

25. 24. 23.

No footsteps. No noisy keys.

10. 9. 8.

Crawling out from the hole she stood up, stretching her muscles. The low hum was slightly louder towards the door, more of an annoyance than anything. Pushing the door soft light flooded in, the lighting strips on the ceiling the reason for the hum. Stepping through she planted herself to the wall, blinking her eyes to help readjust to the sudden light.

The corridor seemed to hold a couple of doors, light shining through the small windows. A buzz from above. In the corner she noticed a blinking red light, hidden. Keeping herself low and against the wall she watched it as it slowly turned, sweeping the corridor.

"*Adolebitque.*" The camera sizzled, melting before the little red light flickered off. "Okay." Happy that there were no other cameras she checked through the first door, the window allowing her to see into the surprisingly small room. Metal and glass cabinets lined the back, diamonds and jewels placed underneath the glass.

The second room held paintings, some on the walls while others were just gently stacked against each other on the floor. The third room held some vandalised busts, floating heads that had some bad artwork painted across them, but no books. Alice reached for the fourth door.

"I think I've found the basement," she whispered into the black radio. "Is there any information on the website?" The door opened onto small spiral stairs, leading into darkness. "Hello?" she asked again, making sure the frequency was correct.

Static.

Crap, something must be interfering.

Grabbing a small torch from one of her pockets she clicked the button, the tiny light bright enough to see the ends of the step's reflective strips. Following the curved stairs down to the bottom, she stepped onto the concrete floor.

The light from the torch struggled, flickering on and off before dying completely. With a sigh she dropped the useless device into her bag and reached for a couple of glow sticks. With a satisfying crack she snapped them in half, shaking the liquid before throwing them across the room, lighting up the large square concrete space with an eerie green glow. Holding one stick in her hand she held it before her, scanning the room.

It was bare, nothing against the dark walls. The only thing was a cage sitting dead in the centre.

Weird.

With nothing in the room, she turned back to the stairs.

Alice gasped. "Where are the fucking stairs?" She exhaled as she frantically reached her hand out, her brain refusing to believe the stairs could just disappear. Her palm connected to the brick, the surface intensely cold, even through the gloves.

"Sam?" she asked the radio, panic in her tone. "Sam? Are you there?" No response, not even static. "Fuck." With nowhere else to go she moved towards the cage.

A high-pitched noise filled the room, a shattering sound that made her jump back with a cry. The noise stopped just as suddenly as it started, almost as if she had imagined it. She waited, concentrating.

Nothing. She heard no bugs scattering across the floor, no water droplets. There wasn't even a smell. If it wasn't for the glow sticks, the room would be pitch dark, giving out no sensory output. Hesitantly she stepped forward, the piercing noise screeching again as lights danced beneath her feet. Another step forward and the noise stopped.

She looked down at the floor, not recognising the small patterns lighting up in the concrete.

What the fuck?

Cautiously, she reached down, touching a rune to the left of the light. A pierce shrill filled the air before lighting up, a spectrum of colours breaking through the concrete with a rainbow glow. *Shit. Shit. Shit.* Sweeping her gaze across the carvings she checked the different runes and symbols, each one slightly different from the last, surrounding the cage in a perfect circle. An educated guess would say a circle had been engraved into the concrete, but not a circle she had ever seen. Taking a closer look she tried to make out more of the runes, starting to understand one slightly.

A hiss.

Scrambling back she froze, blood rushing in her ears as she strained once again to hear anything. Her sudden panic excited her Tinkerbell, the little blue ball bouncing happily around her head. Fluffing it away from her face she peered into the dark, seeing nothing but black.

I'm losing my mind.

The cage was around ten square feet, all sides covered in thick metal bars, an intricate mesh patterned in between. The lattice climbed around the whole structure, including the top. No chance of just climbing over. Peering through the small holes in the mesh Alice saw nothing, almost like a void, absorbing any light. Lifting the lock she studied it, her blue ball of flame allowing her to read more runes that were scribed all over the heavy metal. With her pin and knife she started to pick the lock, and with a click it turned.

Yes.

The knife snapped.

Alice stared at the knife dumbfounded as something clattered to the ground.

What the fuck? A metal shard by her boot. *Did that lock just spit it out?* The pin launched itself out in a similar fashion, clanking to the ground next to the remnants of the small blade.

A hiss again, but closer.

She threw the handle, it disappearing into the shadows. She squinted further into the darkness, trying desperately to listen for any movement as she stepped back over the runes.

Drip. Drip. Drip.

Drops of liquid against the concrete floor, sizzling on contact, like acid.

Slowly she reached back and unsheathed her sword, her senses on high alert as she felt the air move to her left. Instinctually she moved out of the way, rolling backwards and across the runes. They lit up un a burst of rainbow.

Another hiss, something being spat in her direction.

With a scratchy sound a long black leg stepped over the light line, long hairs swaying at the movement. Another leg, movements jarred as bones clicked into place.

Click. Click. Click.

A third leg came into sight, accidentally touching an un-activated rune, causing further light to illuminate the dark space. The sudden shrill noise made the legs flinch.

What. The. Actual. Fuck?

Alice felt her mouth snap open, her sword wavering as she watched the three legs click as they moved.

Click. Click. Click.

The thing leant forward, balancing on what she assumed were its front legs, slowly, almost wary of the symbols embedded into the concrete floor. Alice stood frozen, seeing her wide-eyed reflection, mouth agape in the hundreds of dark eyes staring back at her.

Sluggishly, the giant creature opened its own mouth, huge white fangs protruding from black gums. Drool ran like a river between its smaller, razor-like teeth, dropping onto the floor with a sizzle. Another step forward and a fourth leg appeared, slowly scraping its claw against the floor like nails on a chalkboard, leaving a scar across the concrete.

Fast as a whip one leg shot towards her, making her jump out of the way, slashing out blindly with her sword. Something wet landed beside her, big enough that it made an uncomfortable noise when she kicked it away with her boot. Pulse beating impossibly loud in her head she tensed, waiting for it to strike again before a hiss screeched from the darkness only a few meters from where she stood, spittle landing on her leg.

Reacting, she ran towards the cage, activating several runes as she went. The high-pitched noise vibrated against the walls, loud enough to make even Alice flinch, wanting to hold her hands over her ears. The beast roared, spittle landing in front of it before it writhed in pain, its long legs trying to claw at the lights.

"Shit." Holes appeared in the leather, one just above her breast, one on her stomach and a couple along her left leg, exactly where the creature's spit had landed. Flesh peeking through, she faced the creature, the extra light providing a better look even as it continued to fight against the rainbow.

A spider.

Of course it would be a giant fucking spider.

The monster spider was twice the size Alice originally thought. Its head dwarfed by its giant hairy body, three legs against the floor, one held up in the air dripping black liquid into a puddle. Four more legs spaced evenly against the wall, making its body face Alice at an angle. Slowly the spider pushed one of its uninjured legs against the light, pushing past the runes, testing.

Concentrating, she felt the deep heat in her chest expand into her hands. It felt electric as she allowed the overload to manifest, her focus on the spider.

"*Ignis*," she screamed, satisfied when the intense ball of flame formed around her fingertips. "Die fucker." She launched her ball, gasping when it just popped, crashing to the floor as if it had hit an invisible wall.

The spider seemed to chuff through its fangs, amusement in its gaze. "Oh bugger."

Hand tight on her blade she ran to the unactivated runes, watching as she pressed her foot against the grooves, the light and noise an instant reaction. In a panic the spider tried to claw into the wall, failing to escape the onslaught of raucous sound. Without warning the spider launched itself across the room, a claw at the end of a long leg scraping against her stomach. Doubling over she clutched her midsection, blood pooling beneath her fingers. Another leg hit her from behind, causing her to fly into the cage head first, her blade dropping from her hands.

Alice climbed shakily to her feet, crying out as her shoulder protested.

Another hiss, a patter as liquid was sprayed across her back. Instant burning, bubbles eating away at the leather before starting on her exposed skin. Gritting her teeth, she turned, feeling her burnt skin peeling. At a run Alice shot towards the runes, dragging her foot in an arc around the cage, illuminating every single one.

A chorus of sound, a cacophony of deafening shrills. The noise trembled the floors, causing her to fall against the cage, exhausted. She grabbed the metal lock for stability as it taunted her, laughing. Or it could have been the blood loss.

A glint of light, her blade lying useless against the cold concrete floor. In a burst of energy she rolled towards it, swinging it in the air at the same instant a leg came crashing down. With an inhuman screech the creature reared back, black blood spraying past her face, barely missing her. Before she could react another leg came from the darkness, pinning her against the cage with a sharp claw to her shoulder. With a scream she ripped the claw from her flesh, moving towards the cage door, waiting.

"Come here you fucker," she taunted, no real energy behind the words.

Alice swapped her sword to her left hand, her right badly damaged. The ridiculous blue flame innocently floated by her shoulder, just a spark at the corner of her eye, neither helping the situation nor hindering.

"I'M GOING TO SQUISH YOU INTO A SMALL INSIGNIFICANT BLOB YOU BUG!" It would have sounded so much more threatening if she hadn't slurred most of the speech, her brain slowing down as her blood decorated the floor.

The spider reared around, threatening Alice with his fangs.

"YOU. YOU. FUCKER. YOU." It was best to keep the threats simple and effective, especially if nothing coherent was going to come out.

Alice held the blade up, pointing it unsteadily at the spiders face. With a shriek, the spider spat. She danced out of the way at the last minute, the spittle hitting the heavy lock, searing and smoking at the contact. With a scream Alice brought her blade down, the acidic spit having weakened the metal enough for the lock to disintegrate on impact. She launched herself into the cage door, swinging it closed behind her.

Alice closed her eyes, waiting for the spider to crash through the unlocked gate.

Nothing.

She quickly peered through the gaps behind her, into nothing. Darkness. No lights from the runes. No burn marks on the concrete. No giant murderous spider. It was as if it had been when she was outside the cage, looking in. A void. Absorbing all the light.

Her legs gave out, collapsing beneath her into an unsteady pile. Blood poured from her stomach and shoulder, an impossible amount leaking across the floor. Her sword clattered to the ground, her hand limp at her side. She blinked several times, each time the room brightened before darkening around the corners. Head heavy, she looked up at the chandelier that lit up the white ceiling, wooden beams shooting in a pattern from the centre.

Blink.

A cage, an intricate latticework of metal mesh revealing only darkness above her.

Blink.

White ceiling, pale walls with colourful paintings. A statue stood in the corner, its modesty covered by a leaf beside a bookshelf full of old leather-bound books. Black invaded her vision, creeping from the corners once again.

Her head slumped against something cold.

CHAPTER TWENTY-FOUR

Oh god, my head.
Alice moved to brush her hair from her face, her wrist stopping short with a rattle. She pulled her arm again, pain shooting through her shoulder sharp enough she hissed.

What the fuck?

She opened her eyes, the harsh light causing her to squint. "What?" She looked down. "Where the hell are my clothes?"

Her catsuit had been removed along with her bag, radio and sword. Her black lace bra, underwear and harness the only things covering her.

How the fuck did they remove my catsuit without removing the harness?

Wiggling her toes she looked further down, her legs cuffed carefully to a wooden chair. She pulled at her wrists again, her arms having been tied behind her back.

"If you pull anymore you might hurt your wrists," a deep voice chuckled. She stopped tugging, her muscles going rigid.

Who the fuck is that? Blowing her hair from her face she peered through the blonde strands. A huge male stood against the wall, one foot on the floor and one against the wall, bent at the knee.

"Excuse me?" she questioned while pulling at her bonds again.

The male just crossed his heavily tattooed arms across his chest. Waiting.

Fighting a snarl Alice calmed herself, thinking. She couldn't burn through metal, and she didn't have access to her bag or sword. "Fuck."

He sniggered, the sound echoing across the room.

"Who are you?" she asked, staring at the stranger. Nothing. No answer. "Why am I tied up?" A thump as his other foot landed on the floor. "Are you going to talk or not?" A small chuckle, but he remained hidden.

Great, she thought. *He has a sense of humour.*

Alice tested her leg restraints. No budge.

"Why were you in the basement?" he asked with a penetrating glance.

"Where's the spider?"

"So you're scared of spiders?" Another dark, irritating chuckle. "That was the Somnlin. Our deterrent against thieves and curious librarians."

"A Somnlin?"

"An illusion taken from your deepest fear."

"That was not an illusion, it almost sliced me in half."

Or did it? Alice peered down, noticing only smooth skin, no sign of the bloody gaping hole, no cuts or bruises.

"It was a physical manifestation taken from your imagination, it's as real as you believe it to be." He walked round to face her, his heavy biker boots making no noise on the wood. "The spell causes you to be delusional, makes you see things that aren't there."

So that's why my spell failed. It's not really there.

"So are you saying that if I just closed my eyes and believed it wasn't there, it couldn't have hurt me?"

"It never actually touched you." He was laughing at her.

"Yeah, well you're a shitty librarian." She blew at her hair again, the blonde strands tickling her cheek.

"Why were you in the basement?" His face morphed to blank, expressionless as he asked his questions.

"Why am I naked?" she countered.

His dark hair, longer on the top than the sides was pulled back from his angular face, the colour matching the long stubble along his strong jaw and neck. His too full lips were straight, all humour gone as his narrowed steel-grey eyes watched her carefully. A faint scar marked his otherwise blemish free skin, a pale pink line that curved gently from his high cheekbone to break into his top lip, accentuating his masculinity.

"You were passed out on the floor." His gaze slowly roamed across her skin, eyes lingering far longer than necessary. "I was checking you were okay."

"You didn't have to strip me."

"Probably, but it was fun." A cheeky grin. "Interesting knife you have."

"It's not a knife!" she sneered, the harness biting into her skin. "That's my…"

"Interesting runes along the blade." His eyes darted to hers. "You do them yourself?"

"Runes?" Alice strained her neck, trying to see her blade. It was alight with colour, patterns bright flaring down the steel. They seemed to brighten as the man stroked down the edge, wanting him to touch.

Her sword had runes?

"Why were you in the basement?" he asked again, his eyebrows pinched.

She ignored the question, instead flaring out her chi. If he wanted to interrogate her, she at least wanted to know what he was. Pushing out her chi she tested, sucking in a breath when her aura hit his, the feeling electric against her senses. His eyes flashed silver, lashes quickly coming down to hide them as his full lips curled in amusement. It was clear from his reaction he was a magic user, something she recognised, yet didn't.

"Are you a faerie?" She pulled her chi back, the connection too strong for her to concentrate. What was he? He wasn't a witch.

"No." Another curl of those lips. "But I know they prefer being called The Fae." He tilted his head slightly, causing some of his hair to cover his expression. "Are you going to answer my question?" He clicked his fingers, the tattoos on his arms illuminating gently against his skin before a ball of arcane encased his hand.

"Neat trick, do you do kids parties too?" Alice pulled once again against the bonds, sweat starting to drip down her skin as the arcane built against his hand.

Shit. Shit. Shit, she chanted, wiggling her bum, the wood uncomfortable against bare skin. *Wood*. Wood burned.

"*Adolebitque.*" She rattled her wrists to mask her voice.

"Are we going to do this the hard way?" He took a threatening step forward.

"Wait, what are you?" She hoped the question caught him off guard.

"A man."

She fought not to roll her eyes. "That's not what I asked." Another groan, the wood weakening.

"So I'm not a man?" He reached down to the zipper of his black jeans. "Shall we check that out, sweetheart?"

"WAIT!" She tried to stall him, feeling the wood continue to weaken beneath her. He hesitated at her outburst, the arcane on his hand hissing.

Alice licked her dry lips, staring at his arms. Black and red intricate patterns wrapped around most of his left arm and all of his right arm, symbols similar to the ones on the floor and locked in the library basement. Symbols she now recognised, her memory sluggish to catch up in her panic.

"I know what you are." The symbols were of Celtic origin, runes that were engraved to give a permanent anchor to a spell the same way she would use the five elements. Runes her father had tattooed around his wrists.

With a final creak the chair gave way. Muscles tensed, she pulled just as the chair collapsed, her feet ripping free from the wooden legs. Within an instant she was pushed against the wall, a strong arm against her throat, no sign of the arcane.

"Careful sweetheart," he breathed against her neck, loosening his hold enough to allow her to turn, pressing her shoulders flat against the wall. She glared up at him with controlled anger.

With a final push against her neck he stepped back, close enough to grab her but not close enough to touch. Her skin continued to burn where his hands once were, a phantom against her flesh.

"How did you move so fast?" She released a shaky breath.

"Why don't you tell me considering you know what I am?" he replied smugly.

She didn't miss a beat. "You're a druid."

"Gold fucking star." He stepped towards her, forcing her back against the wall. "Now, why were you in the fucking basement?"

"I don't know why," she hissed through her teeth, the pain in her wrists fuelling her anger. At least her legs were free, two separate cuffs hanging from each ankle.

The man didn't say anything for a minute, his face immobile. "I know you're a Paladin, you had your license in your bag." Her eyes flashed to his, but she remained silent, deciding to stare at the tattoo crawling up his throat instead. "What's your name?"

"You said yourself you've read my Paladin license. You know it's Alice."

"Progress." He stepped away, his eyes accusing. "Just making sure it's actually your license."

She didn't have to read minds to know he thought she was a burglar. To be fair to him, she was dressed like one.

"Now, I will not ask again. Why were you in the basement?"

"I was looking for literature on a cult."

"A cult?" His eyes narrowed. "What cult?"

Alice bit her lip, deciding what to tell him. "The Becoming." She watched his reaction, noticing his jaw clench.

"So you're chasing Daemons."

"Am I?" That at least confirmed the passage she read from the book. "Who are you?"

"Who I am is not important."

"I didn't ask your star sign, I want your name." She straightened her back, trying to look scarier than she actually was. Especially considering she was half naked with black makeup smeared across her face. She probably looked crazy.

"Fine, I'm Riley."

"Is that your first or last name?"

He just smiled in response. That smile made her frown, his face suddenly becoming more familiar.

"Do I know you?" she asked, trying to place him.

"Why would a Paladin be researching a cult? You on a contract?"

"Maybe." She kept the eye contact. "So do you have any literature I can read regarding this cult?"

Riley clicked his fingers, the cuffs around her wrists and ankles falling to the floor with a clink. Slowly pulling her hand from behind her back she flexed her fingers, but resisted the urge to rub her wrists.

"Your clothes are behind you on the table." He nodded to a table in the other corner. "Get dressed."

"Turn around." She didn't want to get dressed with him watching. He just crossed his arms over his chest, eyes darkening. Biting her tongue she stormed over to the table, noticing her destroyed catsuit. "You didn't have to cut it off." He ignored her, continuing to watch. Quickly stepping into the leather she tied the ripped parts across her breasts, covering her modesty as much as possible. "Give me my sword."

"Oh, this?" He stroked her blade again, watching the lights dance at his touch. "It's nice, never seen anything like it."

"It was a gift." Dread had given it to her when she completed the academy, had explained it was her mother's, passed down through the family. She had never asked how he had it.

"Hmm." He flipped it several times. "What do the runes mean?"

She had no idea. "Don't change the subject, talk." She found her beany, shoving it into her bag before slinging it over her shoulder.

"What do you know of this cult?"

"Nothing, which is why I'm here, researching." She eyed her sword, weighing the options whether she could just grab it back. The way he was expertly flipping it would suggest she probably couldn't.

"When did you first hear of it?"

"A woman attacked us, she said she was recruiting."

"Who's 'us'?" His eyes were piercing, as if he could see the answers through her skin. "Who hired you originally?" She refused to reply. "Maybe we could help each other."

Alice hesitated, not trusting him. Looking around the room she noticed it was decorated the same as all the other private rooms she saw earlier in the library. One wall was encased completely in a huge bookcase, old leather-bound books piled high.

"What do you know of this cult?" It wasn't like he was going to allow her to look at the documents behind.

"It's one of the oldest organisations known in daemonic history." He balanced her sword expertly on his finger.

"Yet fascinatingly enough, it's based on druid arts."

He stopped balancing the sword, instead placing the hilt into one of his fists. "So, you do know something."

"Are you part of The Order?"

"Who have you been talking to?" He threw her the sword, training only allowing her to spin and catch it by the hilt and not the blade. Chest pumping with how fast he could throw she gently sheathed it, feeling instantly better when the weight registered against her spine. She had noticed how, as soon as she touched the hilt, the lights disappeared, and the way his eyes narrowed told her he noticed it too.

Her aching limbs protested, her full bladder deciding to wake up. "Are we done here? You're clearly not going to help."

He jumped forward, crowding her against the back of the room. "You need to drop this subject, let the big boys deal with it." His cheeks creased at her slight flinch. He kept crowding her, enough that she could feel the heat radiate from his chest. Until she had to tilt her head up to keep him in view, his unusual eyes ablaze in challenge.

"You're clearly not doing a good enough job..." Her hand tingled, fingertips alight with blue flame as she pulled her hand up to stop him from coming any further. "Otherwise you wouldn't be just the security guard for a load of books."

That gained her a full-blown laugh. "We will definitely be seeing each other again."

CHAPTER TWENTY-FIVE

Alice twisted into the kick, knocking the hanging punching bag back. She had been taking her temper out on the bag for a while, allowing the energy to flow out of her fists and feet into the worn leather. The repetitive kicks and punches were relaxing, giving her some control in an otherwise irrepressible situation.

She had gotten home earlier to an empty flat, Sam having gone to work once he had finally heard from her. Apparently, according to the text she had received, he had been permanently banned from the library, having gone back hours later once it was open to try to find her. The idea he had scared people enough to get banned made her laugh.

The gym was quiet as she continued to work her frustration against the sand filled bag, only a few other people working out in the large open space. Another punch, the chain above the bag screeching as it pushed against its restraints.

Fuck my life. Feeling her fists start to ache she decided to take out her blade, the sword Dread had given her when she had graduated from the academy, somewhere he had persuaded her to go.

Apparently it was an heirloom from her mother's side, something that was supposed to be handed down in the family. She had thought it was a generic sword until he had explained the significance of it, a steel blade with a dark, well-worn hilt. It didn't glow when she touched it, which made it even more curious.

Twisting around the bag she did a series of exercises designed to control the blade as if it was simply part of her arm. Without encouragement the end erupted into flame, leaving a charred smell in the air as it swept across the cracked leather of the punching bag.

Shit.

She needed to get herself together. Her back still ached gently from where she had been tied to a chair, her shoulders clicking as she stretched and started a cool down routine. Swapping the sword to her left hand she practised a sweeping motion, angling her hand to reduce strain. Flipping it a couple times in the air she practised balancing before turning with speed to point it at the jugular of the man standing behind her.

"That's not very nice." Danton's Adam's apple bobbed as he talked, getting precariously close to the edge of her steel. "Your hand is too extended. It would be easier to swipe it off you."

She knew that, and she also knew he couldn't help himself but to comment.

She stood there with the sword still at his throat, a red pearl of blood sliding across the tip.

"D," she greeted, swiftly sheathing her blade in the custom sheath at her back. "Go away." Without a second glance she grabbed her sports bag, walking straight out into the sunlight. The workout had done nothing to calm her, her temper still bubbling as she noticed Danton walk casually beside her, his face slightly scrunched up as the sun shone down. With a grunt he reached into his coat pocket and brought out his sunglasses, letting the shaded glass protect his sensitive eyes. As usual, she was disappointed with the horror movie stereotypes. Vampires didn't turn crispy when they stepped into sunlight, even though Hollywood still liked to dramatise.

"We need to talk." D's accent wasn't as pronounced when he was serious.

"About what?" she asked disinterestedly as she walked to the other side of the road. He casually followed her, looking completely out of place in his matrix style black leather jacket. Alice in comparison was only in a pale blue t-shirt and black yoga pants with 'Cheeky' written across her butt. They looked quite the pair. "What do you want? I'm in no mood for company." Especially company who would repeat everything she said back to her boss.

"I'm here because you broke into the library last night."

Alice stopped, deciding whether or not to deny it. "How do you know that?" A few strands of hair had escaped from her hairband, flapping across her face from the wind. "Have you been following me?" She felt lead in her gut, the realisation she was right when he didn't defend himself. "Why?"

"I have been asked..."

"Since when do you listen to every order?"

D stood a few feet back, his pale fingers pulling his long hair away from his face in an uncharacteristic display of agitation.

"Did Dread send you?"

"Alice, you need to listen to me. This is important." He stepped toward her.

"Back off." She dropped her voice a few octaves.

He pulled the sunglasses from his face, showing her his dark eyes. "You threatening me petite sorcière?" An unfriendly smile.

"Whatever works." The wind whipped at her hair.

"You don't understand. You need to come with me." His leg tensed as he leant forward. "It isn't safe."

The moment she realised he was a threat she stumbled back, his long arm reaching before she managed a shout.

"*ARMA!*" With a hiss D was repelled as the aura shield touched him, burns appearing across any exposed flesh, healed over within the next second. "Were you actually going to jump me?" Alice felt all the anger leave her, replaced with shock. "Take me by force?"

Danton wasn't just her trainer or fellow Paladin, he was her friend. She didn't want to fight him. She wasn't confident who would win.

"Wow. Nice aegis." A whistle.

Stunned, Alice turned towards the voice, only just seeing the tall man poke at her bubble.

"This is impressive. Did you really make it all by yourself?" The man walked around the circle, appreciating its structure. "You can make this but you couldn't escape handcuffs?"

"Riley?" she gasped. Fate must have it really in for her. "What are you doing here?" She risked a glance at D, who was staring at the druid with a look of pure hate.

Riley poked at her shield again, sparks sprouting at the connection. "How are you, sweetheart? Your back okay from all the action last night?" Alice choked out a cough at the blatant innuendo.

She could hear D growl, his fangs releasing from the top of his jaw. "Do not speak to her."

"Oh. Vampire." Riley smiled, showing teeth. "Hop along now. Alice and I have something to discuss."

"Reculez enfant."

Riley laughed. "Attention aux insultes vieil homme," he replied in the same language.

French. Why didn't I bloody learn French?

"Alice, please." Danton slowly moved around the bubble, further away from Riley, almost as if he was worried, or scared. "You need to trust me."

"Trust you? You were about to grab her if I wasn't mistaken." Riley played his fingers along her shield, smirking as D stepped further away. "Vous devez reculer."

"Boys," Alice shouted, annoyed. "If you're gonna talk about me, make it English." She glared at both of them in turn.

"Sorry sweetheart, your Vamp friend was just leaving."

"Vous avez entendu mon ordre, druide."

"Ensuite, vous pouvez parler avec Le Conseil." D's face burned red at Riley's reply, his lip curled as he stalked off.

Alice watched him go. "What did you say?"

"Nothing important," Riley shrugged as he leant against a lamppost, his black t-shirt rising up before he pushed it down. Not before she noticed his tattoos went across the left side of his abs.

"Why are you here?" she asked.

"Would you believe it's a coincidence?" That smile again, one that lit up his face, highlighting his cheekbones. He studied the structure of her aegis, slowly walking around the dome. "So, are you going to pop this or what?" He poked at it again.

"Not until you tell me why you're here?" She crossed her arms, dropping them as soon as his eyes dropped to her breasts.

"You said something interesting last night..." He tilted his head to the side, some of his dark hair draping over his forehead. "Something I want to investigate."

"Well isn't that nice for you." She pressed her lips together.

Riley's face turned cold, his grey eyes flashing, almost mirrored.

It must be a trick of the light.

"Now what I want to know is why Jackson Skye's daughter is

researching Daemons?" A curve of his lip. "Looking to taste the dark side are we?"

Alice felt her mouth snap open. *How the fuck did he know that?*

"It wasn't hard to find out much about you sweetheart." He stopped directly in front of her. "You're supposed to be dead."

"And you didn't poof and disappear. The world is full of disappointments." Stomach churning she looked around, noticing how the street was empty.

"I want to go speak to this woman who was recruiting. Where can I find her?"

"Oh, so there is something you don't know." She widened her stance. "If you want anything from me we need to compromise."

"Compromise?" His brows came low over his face. It was clear he had always gotten his own way.

"I will tell you where to find the necromancer, if…"

"If?"

"If you take me with you." She watched his reaction carefully. She was so close to piecing her nightmares together she could taste it. Without Riley's perspective on things, she was out of options. She just had to deal with him first.

"You will only slow me down." She didn't budge. "I'll only agree on one condition."

"What condition?"

"We do this my way."

"We are not going on that." Alice eyed the shiny Harley motorcycle parked up on the curb, Riley gently leaning against it. "You'll kill us."

"Don't be stupid." He stoked across the shiny metal, his leather jacket draped over one of the handlebars. Alice just tapped her foot, observing the bike wearily.

No way in hell. She had changed into something more comfortable, something that didn't have the word 'cheeky' embroidered onto it. Tossing her ponytail off her shoulder she stalked towards him, swinging her car keys around her finger.

"I'm not doing a five hour drive on something with two wheels."

"We could make it in half that."

"No." She tapped her foot again. "I'll drive." Riley sombrely followed her as she guided him down the side road.

"That," Riley said as he looked over her beetle. "Isn't a car. It's a rust bucket."

Alice tried not to get offended. "Well, it has four wheels and a metal roof. Already safer than your death trap." She glanced over her car, admittedly it had seen better days. She hadn't actually realised the marks around the door were rust, she just thought it was dirt. "It gets the job done." She smacked the roof in reassurance, trying not to cringe as rust flaked off.

"Fine, I guess it will do." He went to open the driver's side. "I'll drive."

"I don't think so." She smiled at his annoyed face. "My car, my rules." He looked like he wanted to argue before allowing her to slide into the driving seat. He climbed into the passenger side, having to push the seat as far back as he could to fit his long legs in. Even then he had to bend his knees, his shoulders taking over half of the area available in the small space.

"Why are we taking your car again?" he grunted, closing the door.

"Because I'm not getting on the back of that bike. Besides, you don't even know where we're going." She inserted her key into the ignition, the car grumbling to life a second later.

"It's called a sat nav." Stretching, he took off his leather jacket, throwing it onto the small backseat.

"What's with your tattoos?" she asked, not looking at him.

"My tattoos?" He glanced over at her, her face burning at the attention. "They're special runes, but you already knew that."

"I'm more interested in what they mean and why you have so many?" Her father had always told them they were special tattoos, but he had never explained further.

Druids, from her very limited childhood knowledge, were similar to witches in that they were magic based Breeds. However, rather than just using their aura and chi they also could use the earths ley lines, natural forming earth energies that seemed to connect ancient sacred sites, undetectable to anybody who wasn't attuned to the earth. The rumours were that the tattoos were embedded with magic, not that any druid had ever confirmed it, not even her father.

"You're asking questions I'm not willing to answer." She peeked at him then, catching eyes that had gotten impossibly dark, the grey almost black. There was a hint of challenge in them, almost a dare. She looked away quickly.

"So, if you want to be friendly, what's with your dagger?"

"It's not a dagger," she quickly corrected.

"Yes, it is."

"No, it isn't." She couldn't help but look from the corner of her eye before concentrating on the road once again. "It's a sword."

"Sword?" He chuckled. "It's a very short sword."

"How observant of you." It actually wasn't that short, it was slightly longer than her forearm, giving her perfect balance in her swing.

"Does it have a name?"

"A name?" *Is he on something?*

"Don't all swords have names?" He clicked his tongue.

"No, it hasn't got a name."

"What about spiky?" Riley casually drew across the window with the tip of his finger. "Or maybe Pen?"

"Pen? What sort of name is that?"

"It's something small and pointy."

"That's not even a little bit funny." She drummed her fingers across the steering wheel in irritation.

Riley flashed her a smile before turning to stare out the window. "What about 'Phantom Iron Sword'? Or P.I.S. for short."

Alice snorted. "I'm not even going to comment." She opened a window slightly, letting the breeze play through her hair. "Why are you investigating the cult?"

"Why are you investigating it?" he countered.

She clutched the steering wheel hard, ignoring the slight squeal of the leather. If they were going to act like a cat and dog the whole journey, the drive would be unbearable.

"You're very small for a Paladin," he said, turning so his back was to the passenger door.

"What's my height got to do with anything?"

"It hasn't. I was just making an observation." He tilted his head to the side, his dark grey eyes staring at her intently. "I know for a fact Paladins don't get contracts based on Daemons."

"How would they know Daemons were involved?"

"You're ignoring my point."

"And you're ignoring mine." Alice blinked up at the traffic lights, waiting patiently for green. "Now why are you investigating the cult?"

"It's my job, I am the guy they call when they need something exterminated."

Alice hesitated, surprised he answered. "And who called you?"

A dark chuckle. "Are you going to tell me where we're going?"

"To a market in Hollow Creek."

A nod. "I know the place." He continued to stare, his eyes penetrating as she concentrated intently on the road.

This was a bad idea.

Why didn't she listen to the advice of never getting into a car with a stranger? Especially a stranger who wouldn't stop staring, his gaze leaving heat on the exposed skin of her arms and neck. She tried not to fidget, the harness against her back, hidden beneath her clothes rubbing against her in irritation. Riley just continued to chuckle beside her.

CHAPTER TWENTY-SIX

Car parked in an empty space, Alice climbed out, locking the door behind her. The entrance to the market was surprisingly empty of all pedestrians, the energy and colour of her previous visit a complete contrast to the dilapidated, malodorous state of the boarded up stalls.

"You sure this is the place?" Riley asked, his leather jacket back on to cover his black t-shirt.

"Yes." Alice led the way, trying to ignore the almost haunted looks of the closed stalls and shops. Graffiti was painted badly across the wood partitions, all in bland colours, as if life and colour had been sucked away, leaving behind just monotone. Numerous alleyways broke out from the centre atrium, many previously hidden from view by the bustling market. The sun strained against the thick clouds, shadowing the already dark alleyways.

The streetlights flickered on and off, confused by the lack of light, solar powered bulbs that were fuelled by the sun, but reacted to the darkness. Plastic bags danced in the wind, mingling with the other litter that had been carelessly tossed away.

Looking around, Alice hesitated, not recognising anything straight away. *Shit.* Maybe she had taken a wrong turn. "I think it's just over here." She pointed to the corner of the square.

The tapestry shop was boarded up, absent the same as the rest. A sign hung dangerously off its pivots, telling her it was the right place. Riley pushed against the heavy door, the locking mechanism not moving. Peering inside Alice checked the gaps in the boards, the interior too dark to see.

"Give me a second..." Alice began.

Riley kicked with his heavy boot, splintering the wood surrounding the solid lock.

"Ever heard of a locksmith?" she asked dryly.

"I smell blood." He pushed the door open, the hinges squeaking into the darkness.

"Holy shit, what happened?" A Putrid odour leaked from the open door, undertones of copper.

Riley didn't respond, instead walking into the room. He pushed the burnt tapestries across the floor, scorch marks smearing the hard concrete. "Looks like someone tried to destroy everything, but didn't finish."

Alice remained silent, swallowing the bile threatening her throat.

"You okay?" he asked when he noticed her face.

"Fine." She swallowed again. "Her office is over there." She flung her arm in the general direction of the hidden door, the tapestry barely hanging against the wall. The door opened easily, the noxious smell reaching its peak inside the small airless room.

"It's been ransacked," she stated, breathing carefully through her mouth.

"So it has." He wandered in, inspecting the remnants. "Stay there."

"What?" She took an automatic step inside, staring at the remains on the floor. "So that's what the smell is." She quipped, no humour in her voice. "It looks like she exploded."

"It's a 'he'."

Alice stared at him wide-eyed. "How can you even tell?" He didn't answer, instead looking around the room. Pulling her top to cover her nose and mouth she bent down to the floor, staring at the remains.

The skull was larger than she would have thought, humanoid with oversized canines. Patterns like a spider web cracked across the top, breaking into an eye socket.

"He was hit on the head numerous times with a blunt object. I can't tell if it was before or after he exploded," Alice murmured. Another chaotic pile of human tissue and organs sat in the corner of the room, half hidden by the overturned table. A femur stuck out from the pile, a shock of white against the browns and reds of the old congealed blood. "There's more than one body here."

"It's an ancient summoning spell. Normally someone is sacrificed around an inverted pentagram. The more men sacrificed the longer the connection."

"Willingly?" She couldn't see any evidence of restraints.

"I doubt it."

"What does it summon exactly?"

"There are a few possibilities, but probably Daemons, but only if you know their names. The summoner creates a circle from which the Daemon cannot escape, the blood from the victims fuelling the dark magic."

"People still summon Daemons?" That realisation floored her, Daemon summoning hadn't been reported since the early nineteenth century.

"Very rarely, not many people still have the knowledge. A Daemon also isn't willingly going to give up their freedom even if it is only while they're in the circle."

"What do you mean give up their freedom?"

"Once they have been summoned, they are magic bound to the summoner, at least, until the timer is up."

She knew nothing of this magic, but she could feel the remnants leak through the floor.

"Is there anything here?" she asked, her stomach recoiling as the black essence leaked from the corpses, almost like a tar caressing her skin, obstructing her airways.

"Nothing I can see." He kicked at the rubble, moving the table across the room. Leaning down he touched the floor, dry blood flaking beneath his fingertips.

The inverted pentagram was carved into the concrete, congealed blood from the three men soaking into every crack. "The spell's still leaking, probably because the bodies aren't even a day old."

Alice saw something out of the corner of her eye, reaching down she gently moved the table, frowning at the small object. "I've found something."

"Grab it, we need to burn this place down before someone else finds it. I don't want to risk someone syphoning off the remains."

Nodding, Alice grabbed the small rectangular object, shoving it in her pocket without giving it a second glance.

"*Scintillam.*" She lit up the walls, holding the flame steady as it slowly ate away at everything that wasn't concrete. The flesh of the bodies began to burn, a noxious cloud filling the air to the point she had to escape the room.

Walking out into the cold she left Riley to finish, the wind cool against her skin.

She was glad she didn't deal in death, didn't deal in the dark magic that was the opposite of her own. Magic was yin and yang, right and wrong, darkness and light. Newton's third law, for every action there was an equal and opposite reaction. Every spell required a sacrifice in various options of severity, whether it was a plant, her own blood or death. There were reasons being a black witch was illegal.

There were times when people actually protested against the use of living organisms in spells, bringing up the morality of killing a living being, even if it was just a plant. But it was quickly dismissed as being ludicrous. If people really got upset over killing plants, then a lot of people would be suffering from guilt when trimming houseplants or cutting their grass.

"Hello Miss," a small voice called.

"Hello?" she asked, looking around the abandoned market.

"Over here," the falsetto tone beckoned, coming from the alley opposite.

Alice hesitated, peering into the shadows. "Can I help you?"

"No, but I may be able to help you child." An old woman stepped forward, her multicoloured patchwork dress brushing the ground as she moved. "May I read your fortune?" She gave a toothy grin, her two front teeth missing.

"No, thank you. I don't believe in fortune telling," she answered, dismissing the woman.

"Very controversial for a witch."

Alice froze. "You sound so sure that I'm a witch?" Alice almost checked to see if she had a pointy hat on, which of course she didn't.

"Aye witch, can smell you a mile off. Come for a fortune." She held out a dark hand, encouraging Alice to come with her.

"Like I said, I don't believe in fortune telling."

"Please, no charge. I see the warnings in the cards."

"Warnings?"

"Yes. Warnings." She shook her head forward in a violent motion, her grey dreadlocks swinging intensely. "They are coming." She held out her hand again, her oversized rings catching the light. "You have seen him."

"Who is coming? Seen who?"

The old woman started to turn away.

"Wait..." Alice reached out. "You said 'you have seen him.' Seen who?"

"My cards can tell you." An oversized smile again. "Follow me." She moved away, no care for her dress as it mopped up the grime along the floor.

Alice wavered, debating what to do. *Fuck.* It went against her training, but she needed to know what she meant, so she followed after her.

"Please. Please. Sit." The woman pulled out a chair from the small round table, taking a seat on the throne opposite. The room was as you would predict a fortune teller's shop should look like. The walls draped artfully with velvet fabric, a mixture of reds, pinks and purples. A wooden freestanding bookcase leant against the wall, feathers, skulls, books and candles sitting neatly atop it. The flames flickered, making shadows dance against the drapes.

At least there wasn't a glass orb sitting neatly in the middle of the table, Alice joked to herself. *Because that would be total overkill.*

"Please child. Sit." She shuffled the cards in her hand, the noise sharp against the silence. Sitting in her chair she faced the old woman, her eyes matching her withered dark skin.

"Now, normally you would ask a question and the cards would answer, this time however I feel we need to do this slightly differently. Your first card," she said, shuffling the pack. "This is your past." She held the cards out, allowing Alice to pick one.

"Death," the old woman stated, as she placed the card face up on the wooden table. "The death card is wildly misunderstood. Most people worry at the prospect of death, but that is not what I see with you. The card portrays an armoured, skeletal figure astride a stallion, black. Death passes people from all walks of life and each is affected differently, you see on the card a man, a priest full of his faith rewarding the afterlife, rewarding death. A young woman turns away out of fear, yet kneels obediently, unable to control her destiny. Lastly a child, completely innocent lays dead flowers by the stallion's hooves, blissfully ignorant of the horrors that are happening."

Alice stared intently at the card, not understanding the meaning.

"Your second card. The present." She held out the pack again. "Ah, the high priestess." She placed the card next to death, tapping it gently with her finger. "The high priestess is you."

"Me?" Alice asked, confused.

"The high priestess indicates that you are seeking knowledge, but such knowledge requires great discipline." She tapped her finger against the woman's face. "The woman sits between two pillars, one light and one dark. One positive and one negative, you are drawn from outside influences, torn between two."

The woman shuffled the remaining cards further before grabbing another.

"The high priestess is not alone, the ace of wands helps guide her." She placed the ace of wands cards below the high priestess, overlapping. "The ace of wands is the element of fire within the tarot pack, the power of will, sexuality, full of passion, desire."

She slammed the cards on the table, making Alice jump at the sudden movement.

"What does this all mean?" Alice asked, still distracted by the death card. "This is ridiculous," she said, heading towards the door.

An arm grabbed her, nails digging into skin. Turning, Alice faced the woman, ice shooting through her chest. The woman's once dark eyes had glazed over, the pupil's pure white.

"Please child, take this." The woman thrust a card into her face. "We have the seven of swords. A man, as you can see is carrying five swords, two still at his feet. He's tiptoeing away, looking behind him to check if he's being caught, being followed. Betrayal or even deception on his face."

"What has he got to do with me?"

"Are you being deceived my child? It is up to you to decide who or what that may be. You are not thinking with your head, you should listen to your intuition."

Erm, what?

"Your last card." She held the card between two fingers. "We have the king of swords. An authority figure, a cold warrior who acts on his own judgments."

"Okay, I think this is enough." Alice grabbed the cards, crushing them in her hand before shoving them into her jacket pocket. Pulling away from the old woman she stormed out of the small shop, to turn face first into Riley's chest. "Oh."

Riley grabbed her arms before she stumbled back. "What are you doing down here?" He frowned, his thumbs rubbing soothing circles along her forearms.

"I was just..." She turned back to the shop, one that was completely closed, boarded up with old posters layered across where the door once was. "I was just..." *What the fuck?* The neon light fixture above the door was smashed, looking like it had been broken for a while. "I was doing nothing. Just needed to walk off the smell."

Riley stared intently, not believing her. Not wanting to get into a staring contest she turned her head further into the alley, stiffening as she noticed someone in a long cloak standing twenty feet away, a hood hiding its face.

"Alice?" Riley tugged to get her attention.

"Do you see it?" she asked quietly.

"See what?" He frantically looked around, his eyes narrowing as he searched for threats.

Alice continued to stare at the cloaked figure. "Nothing."

I'm going crazy. Batshit-la-la-land.

"It's nothing. It's been a long day." She tugged out of his grasp, shocked at the intense cold that instantly consumed his warmth. "We should go." She gently barged past him, walking in the vague direction of the car park.

"Alice, wait." Riley's long legs caught her up in no time.

"Did you get what you need?" she asked to the air, her emotions too raw to face him.

"What was that all about? I turned around and you were just gone."

"I said I needed some air." He didn't need to know she was losing it.

She turned the corner, skidding to a stop when she noticed four men standing by her car. Riley faced towards the empty car park, his eyes hardening at the sight of the men.

"Friends of yours?" he growled.

I'm going to have to add this to my list of other bad decisions. She knew better, was trained better. Yet she was desperate, an increasingly bad feeling that seemed to overshadow her judgement.

"Nope." She unsheathed her sword, pulling it free from underneath her shirt. Riley looked over approvingly. The men all stood on edge as they approached, fidgeting and looking around the car park warily, their eyes focusing when they walked closer, one gripping a baseball bat in his shaking hands.

"May we help you gentleman?" Riley asked, words like steel.

"Our Pride Leader wants a word." One of the men stepped forward, a scrap of dark greasy hair covering the majority of his face. His cheeks were hollow, veins visible beneath his pale skin. Several other men, just as malnourished as the first, stood a few feet behind their eyes vacant as they waited for instructions. She didn't recognise any of them.

"What's your name?" she nonchalantly asked.

He seemed confused for a second before replying. "Rupert."

"Well Rupert. You may tell Cole to go fuck himself for me," she taunted.

"You know we can't do that." His eyes flashed with worry before hardening.

"Who are these guys?" Riley whispered, his face like stone when he faced her.

"They're from the local pride."

"They don't look like lions."

"Enough," the dark haired man snarled, his nails elongating with his anger. The comment seemed to wake up the other guys, making them step together as a unit. "Come now, or we will force you."

"If you wanted a date, you should have just asked," she drawled, flipping her sword absently in the air. "But, you're not my type."

"Your mouth must get you into a lot of trouble." Riley murmured beside her, his fist clenching.

"You have no idea." She thought she heard a chuckle, but decided it must have been the wind.

"Fine." A silent signal passed between the men. The leader walked slowly towards Alice, an almost sad smile on his face. "You're leaving us no choice." His words slurred as his face slowly shifted in his anger, his control weakening.

His nose grew, pulling his face into a contorted point, his jaw clicking as it widened, allowing room for the large canines that had begun protruding from his mouth. With a snarl he launched towards her, his malnutrition not hindering his speed.

"*Arma!*" With a shout her aegis jumped into existence around her, the dark haired leader jumping straight into the side at full speed. The impact shook the shield, making Alice step back, straight into the side.

"Riley, don't kill them!" she shouted.

Riley dodged a punch to his head, bending at the waist while kicking out at the person behind.

"Why?" he growled, throwing more punches. The lion's head snapped back with an audible crack, falling into his friend.

Two down.

"Just please, don't..." Rupert rugby tackled her, pinning her to the floor.

Bringing her blade up she blocked his mouth as it aimed for her neck, the blade caught between his inhumanly long jaws. "For fuck sake, I'm trying..." She reached into her boot. "Not to..." Unsheathed a small dagger. "Hurt you." She slashed the blade down his side, deep enough to hurt but not enough to be fatal. He howled out in pain, dropping her sword from his mouth.

Kicking up she dislodged him just as a hand appeared around his throat, lifting his weight off of her. Riley threw the lion into his friend, a crash as they bumped into each other like bowling pins. Chasing after them Riley kicked one of them to the ground, making sure he wouldn't get up any time soon.

Jumping up Alice looked around at the chaos. Rupert was crushed against a dent in the driving side door, curled in on himself as he groaned. The last lion ran off, disappearing from view within seconds.

"Shit. Riley, you're hurt."

"Oh." He looked down at the twin tears across the front of his t-shirt, blood oozing from the holes. "Fuck sake, this was one of my favourite shirts."

Alice turned back to her car, ignoring the lion groaning and rubbing his head. "I can't believe you hit my car. I can't afford a new one." She kicked the bat lying absently by her wheel. She had no idea how it got there or how it had been snapped clean in half. She decided she didn't care.

Riley stalked over, pushing Rupert out of the way before leaning over and popping out the dent. "All new."

"Funny." She re-sheathed her sword, eyeing him warily. He just took down two full grown shifters with ease, a third if she counted Rupert who he effortlessly threw against her car. Her fingers tingled, her blade heavy on the back as she weighed her options. He was definitely more of a threat than she first thought.

"How many blades do you have in that small outfit of yours?" he asked, a playful smile on his face.

"Enough." She looked at him, feeling warmth grow in her stomach, her adrenaline reacting. He opened his mouth slightly, eyes narrowing. He stepped toward her as if he could feel the sudden connection.

Fuck.

Without a second thought she grabbed a spare knife from her other boot, and threw it at him.

"Oh shit!" She blinked stupidly, gaping at what she had just done. Riley held her knife in front of his face, a fist circled around the blade. Blood dripped gently down his wrist, hitting the asphalt. Riley glared at her as he dropped the knife, squeezing his hand to stop the blood flow.

What the fuck was that? His eyes seemed to say, but she couldn't be sure.

She had no idea what made her do that. He was fast, but not fast enough to catch the handle. She licked her dry lips, tensing when his eyes followed the nervous movement.

"You're driving," she said after a few moments, the energy in the air still obvious. He accepted the keys silently, getting into the car without another word. The car rumbled to life, the warmth of the heaters welcome.

What the fuck is wrong with me?

She slid a side look towards Riley, his mouth open slightly as if he was gently panting, his throat swallowing as he concentrated on the road.

Unable to stare at him any longer she turned to the window, counting the trees calmly between the streetlights. Feeling inside her jacket she pulled out the two tarot cards she had stashed in her pocket and ripped the death card in two, throwing it out the window. She felt the air move as Riley turned to see what she was doing, could even feel the air expel as he opened his mouth to speak before quickly turning to face the road once more.

Closing the window she looked down at her last card. The king of swords sat on a throne, a long sword in his left hand, an owl sitting obediently on his right. *'An authority figure'* the old woman had said, *'a cold warrior who acts on his own judgments.'* She peered closer at the card, bringing it right up to her face, the king, with jewels encrusted around his neck wore a cloak of grey.

Alice crushed the card in her hand.

CHAPTER TWENTY-SEVEN

The car slowed before coming to a gradual stop, the clouds, having released their weight on the drive back, beat against the roof in a comforting rhythm. Britain was famous for the rain, although it did seem worse than usual.

Riley had parked as close as he could to her place, the dark sky looming over them as she reached for the handle.

"We need to talk." Riley's deep voice almost shook the small car. The atmosphere was still there, something she couldn't describe, almost electric, like her chi was energised by simply being near him. It wasn't as strong as before, but still there. Unnerved to say the least she watched his reflection carefully in the glass, wondering if he felt it too.

Or was she simply losing her mind?

Probably the latter.

Sighing to herself she finally faced him, the lights from the dashboard creating a halo around his face, softening his masculine features.

"Talk, huh?" she tried a side smile, feeling her face crack at the fakeness of it.

"I need to see what you picked up from the cabin."

"What?" She felt it then, the weight of the rectangular box she picked up earlier. "Oh." She had completely forgotten, thought of her cloaked ghost figure playing around in her mind. Reaching for it Riley's hand snapped out, grabbing her wrist.

"Don't get it out here, we don't know who's watching." She looked at him like he had sprouted a second head. Snatching her wrist away she opened the car door, the cool rain hitting her instantly as she walked briskly to the front of her building.

The front door had been broken years ago when someone had forgotten their keys and decided to just kick the weak wood down. No one had bothered to fix it so she easily pushed the door open and started to climb the stairs.

"Alice, we're not finished."

She continued her way up, feeling the hair on the back of her head rise as he effortlessly followed behind. "I think we are." She felt anger grow, an unreasonable reaction considering it wasn't his fault. Squeezing her fists tight she fought the sparks that threatened to release. She had to calm herself before it started to leak.

"Alice?" Riley's weary voice beside her as she walked towards her door.

Techno music pumped through the hallway, broken up by the barks from Mrs Finch's dogs. She could feel the fire start to burn up her throat, feel it react to Riley.

"Keys, please." She let out a breath, almost tasting the smoke. The door creaked open enough for her to push herself through, but not quick enough for Riley's booted foot to shove the door the rest of the way open.

"What's wrong?" He spun her to face him, panic in her eyes as his hands held her shoulders. Air expelled out his throat, a growl erupting from his chest. Alice's breasts pumped against the restriction of her clothes, her body too hot as she fought for control of the power that had awakened. She could feel the flames want to absorb him, testing his energy against her own. If she didn't release it soon she might combust, or worse.

Like a tap, the built up energy dissipated, cooling to a simmer.

"Riley," her voice cracked as she met his eyes, a deep grey encircled by a thin black. Glints of blue floated through his irises, giving the illusion of a mirror. She stared at those eyes, ones that weren't just an illusion, they were actually mirroring her own image back at her. Her own eyes were heavy with a mixture of panic and arousal. Hair a mess, blonde strands circling her flushed face. "What did you do?"

He released her as abruptly as he had grabbed her, his face contorting as he controlled himself. "You will kill someone unless you learn to control yourself." His voice had dropped a few octaves, almost husky as he panted gently through his mouth. He stepped back, widening the space between them. "What are you?" he asked, no hint of humour in his voice.

"What am I?" Her voice was weak, an intense calm coming over her. "What are you? You just..." She had no idea what he had just done. "Took my magic away?"

His fists clenched as he ground his teeth. "How could you possibly hold that much chi and not know how to control it?" He mumbled something incoherently. "Touching you was like standing in a big fucking ley line." She couldn't feel ley lines so couldn't compare, however, she once heard it was like sticking your finger into a power socket.

Her pulse fluttered as she tried to remain calm, she couldn't speak, couldn't react. She felt drained as if he took something from her. Feeling suddenly too hot she pulled off her jacket, throwing it against the sofa where it missed and thudded to the ground. Riley's eyes automatically appraised her, his once silver mirrored irises returning to normal.

"Your eyes?" Those same eyes closed off, dark lashes coming down to hide.

"We need to look at the object you found. Everything you have done up to this point is meaningless unless we figure something out. You'll need something to tell your wolf..."

"My wolf?" She felt the fevered skin on her face drain, replaced with an intense cold. "So you knew who hired me in the first place?" *Of course he did, he knows fucking everything.* Needing to think and put some space between them she bent to grab her coat, storming into her small kitchen to place the jacket down on a counter, staring at the bulge in the pocket.

"What did you pick up?" he asked, his deep voice breaking the silence.

"I don't know," she replied to the jacket. If he believed she was solely doing this for Rex she had an advantage, something he didn't know.

"Alice, we need to know what you found at the witch's cabin."

"The necromancer," she corrected him.

"Semantics. All witches can become necromancers. It's the magic they study that gives them the name."

He was right but... still. Biting her tongue she answered. "I'm not sure what it is, I just picked it up and shoved it into a pocket."

"That's the first sign of kleptomania you know."

"Funny." She opened her pocket to reveal the rectangular object, staring at it intently. "It's a book."

The book was reasonably small, only slightly larger than her palm with wraparound brown leather. What she assumed were either privacy or protection runes scratched around the corners, the leather turning to suede at the deepest points. Alice squinted at the symbols, not recognising the harsh lines. Turning it in her hands she eyed the clasp, an off-bronze latch with a small circular indent. Looking it over she couldn't tell how to open it.

Pressing down onto the small indent she felt an intense cold, cold enough it stung her skin. With a small yelp, she dropped the book from her hands.

Riley snatched it before it hit the floor. Sucking her finger into her mouth she narrowed her eyes as he examined the book himself, seeming unaffected by the intense cold.

"It's locked."

No shit, she smirked to herself before taking her still throbbing finger out of her mouth. "Can you open it?"

"It's locked by a Pandora charm."

"A what?" she asked, genuinely confused.

"You know the story about Pandora's box? A box that wasn't supposed to be opened otherwise evil would reign down on earth. A Pandora charm literally stops people from opening things, such as chests, boxes, doors and in this case a book." He slammed said book down onto the counter. "It's attuned to blood."

"Blood?" *Of course, because nothing is ever simple.*

"Well, can you open it?" she asked, watching the book intently on the counter.

"Probably." He crushed the palm of his hand to his face. "Without the specific blood needed it is hard. But I should be able to do it." He caught her attention. "I'll need to take it with me." He reached forward.

"NO." She exploded from her position and knocked the book onto the floor. "It stays with me." She nudged the book with her foot, bringing it closer. She couldn't trust him, she had no idea who he was, what he was capable of or how to find him again.

"This is more important than your bloody contract," he growled.

Oh if he actually knew.

"It. Stays. Here."

"Stubborn." He unclenched his jaw. "Fine, at least let me void the tracking runes." *Tracking runes?* Alice stared at the book on the floor. *Who exactly was tracking it?* Alice bit her lip at the thought.

"Fine," she grudgingly accepted. Bending down she hesitantly picked up the book, careful to not touch the clasp. "I'm sure you can do it in my kitchen." Riley just glared with his unusual eyes.

"All I need is salt and a container." Riley glanced around the small kitchen, picking up her bag of salt from the corner.

"A container?" Reaching up to one of the top shelves she grabbed a Hello Kitty lunch box, smirking as she offered it to Riley.

"It will do." He opened the obscenely pink lunch box, tossing the book inside before closing the latch. Without turning he poured salt onto a counter around the lunchbox. He started teasing the grains into what looked like a Celtic knot, but one that ended in points rather than curves.

Alice stepped closer, watching the rune being drawn when she heard his voice whisper in a language she didn't recognise. Stepping even closer she strained her ears. She decides it might be an adaption of Latin? Or maybe Gaelic?

"Is it done?" she asked his shoulder.

She went on her tiptoes to have a better look, never having seen anything like it. Her knowledge of tracking runes, admittedly lacking, was nothing like this. She reached her hand across, intending to see if she could feel anything coming from the salt when Riley grabbed her arm.

"Don't touch it." He turned her away from the salt. "I haven't got time or the ingredients to void it so I have had to just block it. If you remove the box, the tracking runes will reignite. I don't think you really want whoever is tracking that book to find you in a... compromising position."

"I wasn't going to touch it." She wasn't, probably.

Riley broke into one of his smiles, the one that turned his face into something dangerous, highlighting his sharp cheekbones. She didn't trust that smile at all.

"Can I trust you not to try and open it without me?" He stepped towards her, crowding. She instinctively stepped back, right into one of the kitchen counters. He came further, caging her with his arms on each side. "Promise me you will not open the book." His gaze was intense.

"You said not to move the box." She bit out the words, the events of the day wearing thin on her temper. "It's just a book."

"If you try to open it the wrong way, you will ignite the Pandora charm." He leant forward even further, making her bend to keep away. "It turns deadly." He whispered the last part against her lips. Alice struggled to concentrate, the heat of him radiating against her as she felt the energy building within once again.

His eyes reacted, slowly swirling, becoming mirrored, yet not. His own breath became laboured, mixing with hers as she struggled to control herself. The energy spiked, making her want to moan before she caught the noise.

"ALICE?" A door slammed.

Her eyes widened in panic at the interruption. She pushed against Riley, forcing him to step back, the cuts across his chest glowing through the fabric of his t-shirt.

What the hell had just come over her?

"Looks like your wolf is back," Riley whispered a second before Rex appeared, his usual closed off face awash in anger.

"Who the fuck are you?" Rex snarled, releasing his claws.

"How did you get in?" she retorted, her early anger renewing from the embarrassment of Rex walking in on her. But she wasn't doing anything wrong? Was she?

"She's mine," Rex stated, ignoring Alice before trying to grab her. Only falling short when she quickly stepped away.

"Rex. Stop it." He wasn't listening. "This is Riley, he's a friend."

Riley leant against the worktop, his body relaxed but his eyes hard.

"He was helping me with research."

"She's mine," Rex groaned low in his throat, his eyes completely wolf. He shook his head like a dog, his teeth growing bigger inside his mouth, large canines protruding through his lips.

Alice turned back to Riley. "I think you should go."

At the mention of his name, he looked down at her, his eyes holding the unusual silver gleam in them, something ancient and animalistic staring out of those silver irises. Blinking, they returned to his normal grey.

"I don't think you should be left alone with him."

"I can take care of myself."

Riley hesitated before slowly nodding. "I will be back as soon as I can get the equipment." With that he quickly left.

"Oh, hey baby girl," Sam walked through the partially open front door. "Why did I just walk past...?"

A howl echoed through the flat.

They turned to the kitchen where Rex paced in the small space.

"Rex?" she asked again, concern and a question all in that one word. He snarled, spit spraying the room through his sharp teeth. Spinning he slammed his fist into the wall cabinet, a dent appearing around his hand.

Closing her eyes, she breathed through her anger, not wanting the fire to build to uncontrollable proportions again.

"Who the fuck is that?" he roared at her. Alice ignored him, continuing to just calm her temper with her eyes closed. "ALICE!"

"I already told you," she scowled, her tone like ice. "He's just a friend."

"Bullshit." His eyes were still an electric blue, his control fracturing, the wolf fighting for dominance.

"Who the hell are you to talk to me like that?" She met his eyes.

Sam tensed as he pulled them both down to their knees against the floor. "Be lower than his head," Sam whispered against her ear. "If you are not lower, the wolf will presume you are challenging his authority.

"But I'm a witch?" She didn't have to follow the same rules as shifters.

"He isn't acting rational," he said, worry underlying his tone. He caught her eye. *He's like a pup, how the fuck is he an Alpha?*

Alice shook her head. She didn't know.

"Who is that wolf?" Rex roared again.

"Wolf?" she asked, confused but keeping her voice calm. "He isn't a wolf." The next roar shook the room.

"He smells like one. A fucking predator in my territory."

He started to pace.

Alice stayed on the floor, the tiles cold against her bare knees. Enough time later for her calves to cramp, Rex finally stopped pacing, his movements less edgy. Taking that as an indication he was calmer she stood, staring daggers at him. She had finally hit her limit.

"What the fuck was that all about?" she seethed.

"He was challenging me," he replied matter-of-factly. As if that was a good enough reason to redecorate her kitchen.

"He isn't a wolf. He isn't even a shifter."

"Is that what he told you?" He laughed, rage in the lines of his body.

"Yes." She barely got the word out before Rex was on her, his hand gripping as he crushed his mouth to hers, the force bruising.

"You are mine," he snarled, nostrils flaring. "You smell like him." His voice went deeper. Electric blue swam across his irises as he kissed her again, a fang digging into her lip.

"Rex, back off," Sam hissed beside them, his own cat reacting to the situation.

She called for her aegis, not wanting Sam to make the situation worse. Her circle encased them, leaving Sam on the outside.

"Get. Off. Me!" she snarled against his mouth. Challenge in his eyes he grabbed her hand, sucking one of her fingers into his mouth, his tongue rolling around the tip.

She remained calm, watching the wolf tease across his features. She tuned out Sam's snarling, his hand banging against the circle.

"Are you finished?"

"You work for me." He put on his usual mask, and once again she found herself annoyed, yet amazed at his ability to control his emotions so fully.

Copper filled her mouth.

"Why was he here?"

"He isn't a shifter," she carefully replied, not wanting to set him off again.

"I know exactly what he is." Rex leant forward as if he was going to kiss her again.

"I think you should leave." She stared into his eyes, showing him her anger.

Rex stared back for a few seconds before turning away, facing the edge of her circle. "Miss Skye?"

She reached to the side, fingers connecting to her aegis before her chi resonated back. Rex stood for a moment, facing the wall before he quietly walked past a seething Sam and out of their flat.

"What the fuck was that about?" Sam quickly touched her face, checking her lip for any damage. Reaching for a paper towel he blotted the corner of her mouth, soaking up any excess blood.

"I don't know." Why would Rex react like that?

"Are we going to talk about the fact you left me outside the circle?" Sam threw the paper towel away.

No. She shook her head.

If he touches you again, I will kill him. Sam started to stroke her hair, purring gently in his chest.

"Why was Riley here?" Sam asked.

"Riley? You know Riley?" She leant back to look at his face. His eyes were slightly crazed, the leopard pacing.

"Of course I know him, he's the new owner of The Blood Bar." He tilted his head to the side. "Did you not recognise him?" Sam walked out the kitchen, returning within moments with a magazine underneath his arm. "Look."

Alice scanned over the front, her pulse loud in her ears. "You have got to be joking."

'London says hello to one of our top bachelors... Riley Storm.'

"That's Riley Storm."

He's a fucking Storm? Holy shit.

The Storm family was one of the most influential in London, owning a large chunk of the real estate. They casually touched elbows with high-end politicians and celebrities, one of those families that were just famous for having money. Looking down to the photograph Alice stared into Riley's grey eyes, his face in open joy, laughing at something the photographer must have said. His dark hair was dishevelled as if he had just run his fingers through the strands. He was bent slightly at the waist, his white shirt open revealing a tanned chest, his tattoos peeking through the gap.

'The Storms' only son Riley has returned from his travels to learn the family trade.'

Alice's eyes glazed as she read the article, confusion mixing with shock.

Things have just gotten even more interesting.

CHAPTER TWENTY-EIGHT

Alice paced in front of Dread's office, the rain battering against the large windows, aggravating her further.
I'm in over my head.
"You sound like an elephant stomping around like that," Barbie tutted to herself, her attention on the emery board she was pushing across her nails.

Alice decided to stomp even harder, continuing her course around the sitting area.

"You should have made an appointment," Barbie continued. "He's a busy man you know."

"It's an emergency." Likely, probably, she wasn't sure. Alice finally came to a chair, sitting down heavily. "I only need to speak to him quick."

"Yeah, well, he's in an important meeting. You'll have to wait." She sniffed before turning away. "You could have just called."

Alice sighed, sinking further into the chair as she closed her eyes. She concentrated on breathing, in and out, the fire inside aggravated, reacting the more upset she became. She needed to purge, her chi overwhelming.

But she was scared.

How could she possibly hold as much chi as she was without just combusting? Riley had said it was like standing in a ley line, but surely he was being dramatic?

She needed to speak to Dr Dave.

"Thank you sir, you will not regret it," a voice broke through her thoughts.

"It has been a pleasure Michael. Don't let me down." Dread's voice flowed through the sudden gap in his office door.

"I won't, sir." Mickey swaggered out of the office, a grin from ear to ear that stretched even further once he noticed Alice.

"Oh Alice babe, did you hear about my promotion?"

"Promotion?" she echoed, eyebrows drawn together. She hadn't heard about any promotions going?

"I have been specifically chosen by The Council for some liaison work. They only wanted the best."

"Well Michael, everyone knows you're the best," Barbie added, pushing her breasts out as she leant over her desk. "You obviously deserved it."

Oh, ew. Alice tried to hide her disgust. "Congratulations Mickey, will you be away from the office for a while?" *Please say yes.*

"Probably. I'm hoping to get my own office within The Council. Soon I might even be Commissioner." He smirked, pushing a hand through his slicked back, greasy red hair. Alice wanted to laugh, Mickey the weasel would never have the balls to run The Tower, never mind actually being in the room with all the members of The Council at once. Alice had never met any of The Council, but had heard the rumours.

Michael would probably piss himself, she mused to herself.

"Fascinating stuff." Alice leant forward so she could see Barbie, "Barbie can I go in now?"

"Oh, whatever Alice, can't you see I'm talking to Michael? You're so rude."

"Yes Alice, once I'm the boss you won't speak to Barbara like that at all. That's even if you're still here." They both shared a snigger.

Ignoring them she walked past to push open the heavy door, allowing it to close behind her gently. She stood by the entrance for a few seconds, waiting for Dread to acknowledge her. He knew she had been sitting there, waiting, just like he knew everything that happened in his Tower.

"Mickey is after your job by the way," she said instead of a greeting.

He hadn't even looked up, instead writing on a single piece of paper with his gold pen.

"I need to retire eventually," he commented. He signed the bottom of the paper before putting it into a hidden drawer on his desk.

She fought a chill that threatened to run down her spine as he looked up at her, his eyes, though usually dark, were the darkest she had ever seen. Bottomless pits that encased all the whites of his eyes.

"What's pissed you off?" Alice took a seat in front of him, careful to not stare directly into the abyss. The rumours about Vamps hypnotising their prey were widely spread in the eighteenth and nineteenth centuries, more than likely by the Vamps themselves. While not technically true, the older the Vamp the more influence they wield. It also depended on how susceptible their prey was.

"Language," he scolded. "I hope you're here to tell me why one of my best Paladins has gone AWOL. Danton was supposed to report back but has been uncontactable."

"How am I supposed to know?" she frowned.

"His last contact was with you."

"He's probably hiding with his tail between his legs after he failed to grab me." She crossed her arms.

"WHAT?" Dread almost floated out of his chair, the lamp on his desk somehow vibrating as the vein in his forehead burst, giving his pale complexion a flushed appeal. Alice felt the hair on the back of her neck stand on edge, she thought his eyes were uncomfortable before... "WHAT HAPPENED?"

"Wait..." Sudden realisation hit her. "If you didn't tell D to grab me, then who did?"

A feral sound came from Dread, his fangs punching through his gums to rest below his bottom lip. "Start from the beginning." He seemed to compose himself, his face marble as he waited for her to explain. "Did you say Riley Storm?" Something flashed across his eyes, but it was too fast for her to catch.

"Yes." She left out the part where she broke into the library, he didn't need to know that. "He interrupted D and..."

"How do you know Mr Storm?" Dread interrupted, his fingers like claws on his desk.

"I don't." His face said he didn't believe her. "It was just a coincidence, I hadn't met him before. I didn't even know he was a Storm until Sam recognised him."

"Sam?"

"Yeah, apparently Riley is the new owner of the bar Sam works at."

Dread's eyes finally narrowed, allowing some white to peek back through. "What a coincidence." He grabbed the handset from beside his desk, punching in numbers from memory. "Get me the Archdruid," he barked into the receiver. "This is Commissioner Grayson."

Alice strained to hear the conversation.

"Tell Mason if he doesn't call back within the next hour I will pay him a *friendly* visit tonight." With that he slammed the phone down, cracking the plastic.

"Who was that?" Alice chirpily asked. *And who's the Archdruid?*

"You need to stay away from Riley, Alice. He's a Guardian from The Order." Alice sat a little straighter, listening intently. He had never been exactly clear what The Order do. "He's one of the most dangerous men..."

"Well, I'm pretty dangerous too."

"Don't be a child." His severe face stopped her next comment. "He is the youngest ever to gain that rank. He is the judge, jury and executioner." He leant back in his chair, scraping his fingernails across the desk. "What are you even doing Alice?"

"What?"

"Do you think I don't know what you have been up to? Breaking into the library for what? Books on Daemons?"

Busted.

"I..."

"You're taking it too far. Do you think knowing will bring them back?" Alice sat there silenced, unsure what to say. It's not like she had a plan. "If the people you're hunting find out..."

"Find out what?" She tried to cover the tremor in her voice. "I don't even know who I'm hunting."

"And that is exactly why I'm worried."

Alice shuddered as the freezing cold rain battered down, soaking through her jacket quickly. She felt hollow as she walked out of his office and into the street forty floors below, the sky becoming dim as the clouds hid the disappearing sun.

"I don't know what I'm doing," she told the rain.

And who was the Archdruid? What does he have to do with anything? She had been so angry she even forgot to ask about her sword. *Fuck sake.*

A car squelched past at a blinding speed, making her back off from the pavement. Sighing, she looked down the usually busy street, noticing how empty it was. Feet slipping, she turned towards the bus stop and froze, her skin turning to the same temperature as the rain. A hooded figure stood a few feet away, the face hidden in shadow. She stared at it dumbfounded, wondering if she was hallucinating.

The phantom suddenly turned, quickly walking in the opposite direction.

"HEY!" Alice shouted to its back. "WAIT!" She splashed through puddles as she chased after it, following it down several streets until it finally turned down an alleyway. Ignoring the crazy looks from other pedestrians she stood in the mouth of the alley, staring at the figure.

"Hey." She tried again, wondering if the hallucination had the capability to speak back. "What are you?" Of course it didn't reply, instead it just stood at the brick wall at the back between two black bins. "Are you from my imagination?" She shook her head. *Yes, I did just ask that.* "Why are you following me?" She laughed at herself. "Why am I still asking questions?"

The phantom seemed to shake, its shoulders rising and falling in a fast sequence.

Great, my imaginary ghost is laughing at me.

With a huff she picked up a can, throwing it at the figure, watching as the metal sailed through to hit the brick wall as if no one stood there. Verification that she was crazy.

"Yeah, well. Fuck you." She turned to leave when the figure stepped forward. Halting, she watched it move slowly towards her, her back stiffening and the hairs on her arms stood to attention. The figure stopped when it was within a foot of her, within touching distance. The rain suddenly stopped, the wind no longer biting. The figure raised its cloaked arm, reaching out…

"Alice?" A feminine voice called from behind, making Alice jump back and turn at the same time.

"Why are you standing alone in the rain?" Rose held her gym bag above her head.

Alice spun back to the alley, blinking through the rain that she could feel once again, wanting to confront her cloaked phantom.

"I don't know."

C *hest tight, she carefully peered around the trunk of the oak tree, staring at the shadowed man, his large body covered in darkness.*
"Come here you little bitch."

Sudden light brightened the garden, the flash blinding her.

Blinking past the glare she peered over the trunk once again, gasping as she saw the monster standing by her house. His face was distorted into a scowl, twin horns protruding from the centre of his forehead, curling through his hair before finishing by his ears. An off-white teddy bear was clutched between his large palms, the fur speckled with pink.

"Come out, come out, where ever you are," the monster sang.

The light turned off once again, leaving only the moonlight. She felt her heart beat in her chest, a rabbit trying to escape. Salt on her tongue as tears streamed from her eyes, mixing with the snot against her upper lip.

"Shit. Where are you?" Shoes crunched as the monster moved closer.

CHAPTER TWENTY-NINE

Something's watching me.
 Alice woke to the sudden realisation she wasn't alone in her bedroom. She blinked, her eyes struggling to adjust to the darkness. A shadow stood ominously by her open door, taller than her phantom cloaked figure but a shadow, nonetheless.

Great. She rubbed her face with her hands, *I'm seeing other things now.* Flopping down onto her back she stared towards the ceiling, deciding it was just best to ignore it.

A squeak, the floorboards protesting.

What the fuck?

The air moved above her.

Acting on instinct she rolled quickly over as a hand came down, a rag pushed forcibly down into the pillow where her head should have been. Kicking out into the darkness her bare foot connected with something hard, someone or something grunting at the blow.

"You're real?" Scrambling out of her bed she fell to her knees, clenching her teeth at the shock of pain.

"SAM!?" she shouted, her heart turning to ice when he didn't respond. "SAM?" she shouted again as she rolled out the way of a kick. Launching to her feet she tackled the intruder, knocking them both to the floor in a heap. "FUCK!" She tried to get up but something clamped around her wrists.

She yanked herself free, scrambling across the floor in the dark.

A chuckle close behind. "Come here, bitch."

"*LUX PILA!*" A ball of light bursting into existence above her, illuminating the small bedroom with an eerie blue glow. She stood by her curtained window, sheets from her bed piled on the floor in her panic. The large shadow loomed by her doorframe once more, a pale cloth clutched in its big hands.

A fist flew towards her face, connecting with her cheek and throwing her head back. Crashing against the wall she clutched her cheek, the pain sharp as copper coated her tongue. Another fist came towards her holding the cloth, a sickly sweet smell emitting from the white fabric. Sliding out of the way she yanked at the curtain covering her window, throwing it in the vague direction of the attacker. The curtain landed on its head, disorientating it enough that she kicked out with her foot, connecting painfully with its groin.

Distracted with the pain he (it was definitely a he) clutched himself, her knee meeting his nose in the next instant.

A deep growl as the man pulled the curtain and threw it on the floor, his face scrunched up in a snarl as light leaked from the uncovered window. With a roar he leapt forward, picking her up by the top of her arms and throwing her straight through the open bedroom door. She landed hard on her tailbone, her head connecting with the edge of the side table. A weight settled on top of her, hands constricting her throat. She clawed at the man, his dark eyes bleeding into a vibrant red.

"*Ignis,*" she whispered from a strangled breath, sparks flying from her fingertips. His hands tightened impossibly further before suddenly loosening. With a yelp blisters appeared along his hands and arms, red welts that expanded to bursting point as the sparks ate away at his skin.

Alice wriggled, trying to get out from underneath him, her efforts useless as he reached over and grabbed another cloth from his back pocket. Holding it above her head he laughed, showing small pointy teeth along both jaws.

Calming herself she flipped onto her stomach, her sleep t-shirt riding up so her skin gripped the laminate floor uncomfortably. She stretched, trying to grab the side table...

A loud crash, the front door slamming open and ricocheting off the wall with such power it automatically shut itself. A black blur grabbed her intruder, throwing him against the wall between the bedrooms with such force the picture nailed to the wall smashed to the floor.

Alice clutched her throat, her body suddenly remembering how to breathe as she coughed violently, oxygen struggling to recirculate her system.

What the actual fuck?

She pulled herself to her knees, her head swimming. Feeling as if her skull was weighted she turned to look behind, her eyes taking too long to take in any details.

"Riley?" she coughed again, her throat protesting at any sort of speech. "How? Why are you here?" she wheezed in another painful gulp, successfully stopping herself from fainting.

Point to me.

Riley slammed the attacker against the wall, his legs flying wildly in panic. "I was watching the place, I didn't trust they hadn't already tracked the book."

"Did you see Sam?" she coughed again, the pain mingling with her growing headache.

"He isn't here."

Oh yeah. She finally remembered. *He was called into work.*

Alice leant against the sofa for support, attention on her attacker, the view better from the living room as the light from the balcony stretched through the kitchen archway. The guy was huge, easily double her size and wore all black. His red eyes were wide, the pupils slit, like a cat, or a snake.

"What is he?" she asked, her throat painful.

"Daemon."

The Daemon cackled deep in his chest, smiling with his teeth.

"A Daemon?" she parroted. She stared at the man, if she could even call it a man, as it struggled against the hand at its throat. The shadow in her nightmares was nothing compared to the real thing. Over six foot with bulging muscles overlaid with dark veins. Heavy features scrunched with pain, dark hair longer than her own styled to cover the small horns that had been sanded down.

"What are you doing here?" Riley snarled. The Daemon continued to laugh, blood bubbling around his lips. "What are you doing here?" Riley repeated, the words resonating with a power Alice had never heard.

The Daemon gurgled in response, his red eyes glazing over. A light from Riley's closed fist, a ball of arcane held against the Daemon's skin, the power licking against his clothing, almost teasing the flesh as it burned and melted.

Alice stared, her throat dry. Arcane magic was unpredictable, raw power manifested into a ball of light. It took incredible strength to control it so casually.

The Daemon hissed in pain, blood now pouring down his chin in a steady stream.

"I will ask you one last time. Why?" Riley leant in. "Are. You. Here?" The last word a breath against the Daemons face, almost intimate in its rage.

"She is the one," the Daemon gargled. "She is the last before The Becoming." A wet cough, its hands holding onto Riley's forearms so it didn't suffocate.

"Stop with the riddles," Alice responded, her voice hoarse, sore from the strangulation.

The Daemon laughed once again, the sound wet. Something dripped out of his ears, a sea of red across his dark skin.

"He is Becoming."

"Who is Becoming?" she asked.

A scream as the arcane ball slowly burrowed into his chest. Red tears leaking from his eyes.

"What do you want from Alice?" Riley asked.

"Dragon born. She's the dragon born." A hollow chuckle as his chest rattled. "With steady breaths, they ride towards the dawn. Mortals cower in the dark, defenceless, prepare to mourn. Shadows move across their souls, as darkness, corruption and power grows. The four elements, magnets against mortal breath. Generations of lies, of wrath. Power in its truest form, made physical with greed. Are they saviours who wish to lead? Famine destroys along the path, against Pestilence in his wrath. Death stares and waits his turn, as War's flames turn to burn. The apocalypse they bring to earth, destroying it for all it's worth."

"What's happening?" Alice asked, her face in open shock. The Daemon convulsed, shaking violently. Riley released his grip and the Daemon fell straight to his knees, blood pooling quickly around his body. His dark skin slowly turned red, as if he was combusting from the inside out.

"Blood's leaking out of his pores," Riley grunted, absorbing the arcane back into his hand.

"Death is coming, War." A wet snigger. "You are the catalyst." A smile showing red stained, pointy teeth. "With your ascent, the new beginning will start."

A deep inhale. His face crumpling, eyes sinking into his face as skin was absorbed into his body, a shock of white as his skull appeared through the flesh, cracking and disintegrating before their eyes. The body melting into itself, leaving nothing left, not even dust.

"Great," Riley snarled, staring down into what was left of the attacker. Red splashed across his shirt and face.

"What happened?" Alice asked for the third time, her face white.

"He was on a timer."

"A timer?"

"Yes, it's a delayed assassination spell. The spell went off because he was taking too long. If he succeeded and got you out of here the spell would have dissipated and he would've lived."

Riley turned to look at Alice, his face expressionless. "Where's the book?"

"Book?" A confused look. "Oh, it's still in the lunchbox."

Without another word he turned towards the kitchen, opening the lunchbox with a quick click.

Frowning at the book he reached to the bottom of his shirt, pulling it over his head revealing intricate black and red tattoos along the left side of his back. Scrunching the shirt in his fist he squeezed some red liquid onto the silver clasp, right above the circle indent. With a pop and sizzle, the book snapped open.

"It's done."

"How did you know that would work?" she asked, having followed him.

"I didn't."

She walked over to where he was standing, feeling the heat from his skin. "You have blood on your hands," she whispered, carefully taking the book out of his palms.

She scanned the book, flipping through pages.

"It's a list," she said a moment later.

"A list?" he asked, wiping the remaining blood off his face and chest with his destroyed shirt, throwing it into the bin in the corner of the room. Alice stared at the book, careful not to look at him.

Maxi Swanson – Dead – Survived only 2 weeks.
Samuel Lewis – Survived.

Sahari Mooner – Dead.
Stewart Leonard – Survived.
Ernest Rhodes – Infection started.
Alesha Morgan – Dead.
Bobby Dust – Dead – Did not take to the infection.
Mischa Palmer – Dead.
Jackie Nunez – Dead.
Alexus Pride – Survived – Rabid, had to be put down.
Francis Carter – Dead.
Louis Owen – M.I.A.
Tomlin Kar – Started infection – Got caught by target. Had to be made an example of.
Roman Wild – Started infection – Taken to infection perfectly, looks promising.

Alice stared at Rex's brother's name, a million questions forming at the forefront of her mind.

Does Rex know?

She flipped further through the book blindly, unsure how to deal with the information.

"Oh," she gasped, unable to speak past the lump in her throat. With shaking hands she traced the indents the pen had made on the page, the name circled many times. Her name. Repeated over and over.

"Anything?" Riley's voice made her jump.

She glanced at him, wide-eyed. "My name's in here." She held out the book, he accepted it before flipping through the pages.

"So it is," he grunted, tossing the book onto the counter.

Alice walked away to stare out the window of her balcony, the light of dawn threatening to break in the distance.

"May I use your shower?"

She nodded, still facing the window, her emotions too raw to reply. She felt him rather than heard him walk away, silent even though she knew he wore heavy leather boots. The shower started in the bathroom only minutes later. Grabbing a mug from beside the sink she poured in hot water, and simply held it in her hands, watching the water as it settled.

Riley re-entered the room a lifetime later, the mug now cool in her palms, his chest bare, jeans low on his hips. He leant against a cabinet opposite, his eyes reflective in the light.

"What happened to your cupboard?" He nodded towards the dent.

"Rex thought he would redecorate."

"Did he touch you?" A low growl.

Alice refused to reply, instead she looked up from her mug she caught his eyes. "What are you?"

"You know what I am." He turned his head at an angle, an animalistic gesture, something she was used to watching Rex do, or even Sam.

"You're more than that," she stated. Her eyes travelled across his chest, following the patterns that flowed across his left peck, further down his taut stomach before disappearing below his jeans. His right arm was completely covered in the beautifully intricate designs, his left only partially covered. A slight pink scratch marked his chest, the only evidence of the wound from the lions. He held her gaze, the silver sheen reflecting heat. "Rex called you a wolf."

"Did he?" No smile. Only eyes.

"Are you?"

"Am I what?"

"A wolf?"

Riley didn't hesitate. "It's complicated."

"It's a yes or no question."

"I'm not a shifter." Controlled words.

She refused to let him bend. "How can you lift a Daemon off the ground like that?"

"I work out."

"You were faster than those lions."

"They were lazy. Alice what do you want me to say? I am who I am."

"Then who are you?"

"I am me," he stated, face tense. "Now who are you?"

"Who am I?" she laughed. She didn't know the answer to that herself.

"He called you a dragon." He stepped closer.

Alice remained silent.

"What did he mean?"

She moved further from him, not liking the fact he was towering over her, her height giving her little advantage.

"I have no idea." She really didn't.

She had no idea why her name was in a book.

Why he called her a dragon.

Why her family was slaughtered and she was the only survivor.

Riley narrowed his eyes as he decided whether she was telling the truth. Alice stared back, daring him to comment, the lukewarm tea forgotten in her hand. What did he expect from her?

"You're not telling me something." A statement.

"Oh, like you haven't told me you're a Storm?" She watched something dark pass across his face. "Or was it just something you forgot to mention?"

"We're not talking about me."

"Like hell we are!" She felt her voice rise.

"You know nothing of me and my family," he said, annoyed as he backed towards the shadows, hiding his face, hiding his eyes.

"And I know *nothing* of mine." She moved up to him, trying to see his expression through the darkness.

She could feel his gaze on her face, could tell when he decided she was telling the truth, that she didn't know what the Daemon was talking about. A light suddenly reflected across his eyes, the iris turning silver in a flash before becoming hidden once again. Swallowing her emotions she stepped away, trying to get her thoughts together.

"What was he talking about? The poem?" She didn't recognise it.

"It's just a poem," Riley replied, his voice soft. "It supposedly depicts the four horsemen of the apocalypse."

She turned to the balcony, watching the pink sky.

"War, he called me war." She felt a warmth against her neck, butterflies in her stomach. Turning she looked up at his face. His eyes were inhuman, something ancient staring out. She didn't feel scared, only a sudden anticipation. It was different with Riley, a natural attraction compared to the torrential longing she felt for Rex. She didn't feel like she needed Riley beside her, but wanted him instead.

He stared down at her, his eyebrows pulled together in confusion. Slowly, he leaned down, giving her time to change her mind. He sighed her name as his lips came down on her own, the contact electric. She melted into the kiss, surprised by her sudden voracious hunger. Sliding his hands down her waist he bunched up her T-shirt, going beneath to touch his warm hands to the bottom of her back.

"Alice..." he groaned as if she were the greatest pleasure, or pain.

Lifting her up he moved her to sit on the edge of the sink, she could feel him through the fabric of his jeans, a large bulge against her most sensitive area, her underwear giving little protection.

She moaned into the kiss, nipping at his lip before he started to peck down her neck. She panted heavily, her brain overpowered with arousal as her chi danced from the electric current. With a small bite to her neck, he let her slide to the floor, her legs like jelly. He took step back, staring at her with a blank expression. In one slow movement he bent at the waist, light perspiration glittering along his back.

He walked out without looking back, leaving the cold to swarm into the space he just stood.

CHAPTER THIRTY

"Fucking stain," Alice scolded the blood that seemed to have permanently ingrained itself into the laminate flooring. "He had to bleed all over the place didn't he?" She pushed the cloth through the red liquid, squeezing the excess into the bucket next to her. Sighing, she scrubbed the floor, the supposedly 'magic' bleach doing little.

After what felt like hours Alice finally sat back, staring at the doomed flooring. It wasn't budging.

"Well, I guess this place needed a new rug anyway." She threw the destroyed rag into the bucket when a loud knock rocked her door. "Shit." She looked around the room for something to hide the stain. "JUST A MINUTE!" she shouted through the wood.

KNOCK. KNOCK. KNOCK.

"For fuck sake." She cringed at the blood. She did not want to explain anything to Mr Tucker or her landlord. "I SAID," she shouted even louder through the door. "JUST A MIN...."

The door swung open, two men dressed head to toe in black swarmed in, their faces covered by oversized black sunglasses.

On instinct she kicked the bucket, letting the mixture of water, bleach and bloody mucus shower the men. Their shocked faces were all she needed as she lifted her elbow up to meet the first man's nose, causing his head to flick back into the wall with a crack. The second one snarled as his arms encircled her, lifting her off her feet as he growled something inaudible in her ear. Chest constricting she threw her head back, catching his face and kicking out at the same time. The momentum threw them both back, hitting the wall with a thump his arms loosened around her. Turning with a snarl she called to her power, lighting up her palms...

"ENOUGH!"

Attention shifted to the older gentleman who closed the door gently behind him. His suit was clearly pricey, ironed to perfection with a silver clip holding his blood red tie in place. His face was aged, but in a way rich people age, someone who has never had to worry about where their next meal would come from. Fashionable laugh lines. His eyes were cruelly pinched, annoyed as he looked her up and down, and from the scowl she knew he was disappointed.

"Bruno. Marco. Please wait outside," he instructed the two men who had taken to stand beside him.

Sunglasses number one held his nose, blood pouring down his face, while sunglasses number two frowned at the broken glasses clenched in his big fist, intricate runes were tattooed around his left eye, pulsating in irritation before he followed his friend out the door. The bleach had already started to eat away at their black shirts, leaving white patterns like a badly designed tie-dye.

"I don't think we have been properly introduced," the older man started. "I am..."

"Mason Storm. You're Riley's father." She could clearly see it after she looked past his severe expression. He had the same high cheekbones as Riley, ones that seem to be chiselled from stone with a strong forehead and jaw. His skin was clean-shaven, hair the same dark tone as his son's but peppered with grey.

His eyes the same unusual shade, eyes of a predator.

"I see you have no manners," Riley's father tutted to himself. He folded his arms across his chest, bringing her attention to his expensive watch. "You may call me Councilman Storm."

Councilman?

That was something she didn't know. Dread had taught her to always be wary of The Council, of the people who believed they ruled everything.

"Why are you here?" Alice breathed heavily as her chest ached, her ribs protesting with every inhale. "Why did your bodyguards attack me?"

"Firstly they didn't attack you, they defended themselves." His eyes narrowed as he took in the bloodstains across the floor. "Secondly, I am here because my son seems to be fascinated with you, Miss Skye."

He appraised her once again, his face turning into a grimace as he noticed her black t-shirt. It just happened to be the one that said *'CLASSY AS FUCK!'* written in white across her breasts. She folded her arms to cover it.

"I like to take an interest in anything my son does. I personally don't see his fascination."

Okay, rude.

"Can I help you?" She tried to keep her voice civil.

"Your manners are atrocious, your father would be disappointed."

"Excuse me?" She dropped her arms. "You knew my father?" Alice fought for her voice not to break.

"Of course, he was my advisor, a high-ranking Vector. He left it all for your mother, the fool he was. Right until the very end." He tilted his nose up slightly. "He was corrupted by that woman. I will not let it happen to my son."

Alice narrowed her eyes. "So you're the Archdruid?"

"Well, of course, who else would it be?" he smirked, full of himself. It's nothing like the smirk Riley can do, a smile full of tease and laughter. This smile made her want to run for her blade.

"Now tell me, how did you survive when your family did not?"

Alice remained silent.

"You seem surprised I know that?" He chuckled as he tugged the ends of his black suit jacket. "I'm a man who knows secrets. So, are you going to tell me? No? I'm sure it is an amazing tale. But one for another time then?"

A blue flame burst across her fingertips, her irritation manifesting itself as she swallowed down the excess power.

I need to get myself together.

His eyes watched the flame in fascination. "So much like your mother. I wonder if you will learn to control it? Or allow it to consume you."

She frowned. "Consume me?"

He checked his watch. "Now this has been lovely but I really do need to be getting off. Important people and so on…"

He turned to the door, opening it slightly before looking back over his shoulder.

"Stay away from my son Alice, or else people close to you could get hurt."

He tugged something from his inner pocket, unfolding it before flinging it towards her.

"This is for you. I found it pinned to your front door. I'm sure you don't need any more enemies Miss Skye." With that he left, slamming the door shut behind him.

Alice clenched her hand, crinkling the paper he had handed her before she calmed herself, flipping it over. Her temper instantly cooled, acid coating her tongue as she studied the photograph. It was Sam, unconscious with his wrists and ankles painfully bound by silver, bruises pattered across his face and chest.

Below it was an address.

Sam's phone went to voicemail. Again.

Swallowing her dread she parked up the dirt road, a short walk away from the long driveway of a compound. The address was just out of the city, surrounded by land for miles on all sides.

There was an old manor house built at the end of the drive, surrounded by smaller, similarly designed buildings. Alice surveyed the area, noticing the house backed up to a dense forest. Several cars were parked along the drive, a mixture of cheap run-arounds and expensive 4X4s.

Crouching behind a black truck she analysed the house, squinting to see into any of the windows. There was clearly something happening, shadows moving erratically behind the curtains. She heard a howl, followed quickly by a loud growl.

The front door crashed open and a shirtless man stormed out, heading straight towards where Alice was hiding. Confused, she stood up from her crouch, arms folded across her chest as she made her way around the truck.

"What the fuck are you doing?" Rex snarled. "Why are you here?" He halted a few feet away, close enough for Alice to see a slight sheen of sweat across his skin, glistening next to the blood that had already started to clot from the deep abrasions.

"How did you know I was there?" she asked.

"Alice, I don't have time for this." He turned back to the house, expecting her to follow.

"Where's Sam?" She ran after him, her voice strained as panic began to rise. "Is he here?"

"Sam? What are you on about?"

She followed him down the hallway, her boots tapping on the wooden floor.

"I got a photo and it had this address on it." She pulled out the photograph, showing it to him when he finally stopped walking. "Where is he?"

Rex looked at it carefully, his lashes low when he handed it back. "I have no idea, he isn't here."

"But he has to be..."

"Oh look who it is," a voice mocked from an open doorway. "How is little Alice?"

She turned to the voice, her hand automatically drawing her sword when she noticed Cole. "What are you doing here?" she asked through clenched teeth, hand tightening on the hilt.

"Helping out my friend," he replied with a curl of amusement on his lips. "Has the little witch come to play?"

"Cole, enough." Rex held out his hand. "Alice, give me your sword. There are no weapons in the Den. This is a safe place, I will not have you walking around armed."

"No."

"Then we won't help you find Sam," Rex growled.

Panic built further as Alice took a moment to decide, calming herself as she surveyed the room. The calmer she made herself, the clearer she saw.

Cole stood behind Rex, leaning casually against the door jamb, his body language seemingly uninterested in the situation. His eyes, however, were burning, emotions intense.

Rex crossed his arms as he waited, his face grimacing as he opened one of the deep cuts across his chest. Blood trickled down his abdomen to drip on the floor, each drop slowing as his blood clotted once again.

Seemingly out of options she licked her dry lips.

"What happened here?"

Cole answered before Rex could. "Pack matters. We don't need assistance from a witch."

"You aren't pack," she bit back.

"Alice I haven't got all day…" A howl interrupted him, tightening his jaw he waited for the noise to finish before continuing. "Give me your sword, so we can help."

She hesitated, not wanting to be without her weapon. Blade hot against her palm she handed it over.

"Thank you." Rex nodded as he handed it to someone behind him.

She remained silent, not sure about the situation.

A shadow leapt through a doorway, smashing itself against the opposite wall.

Howls of pain erupted as the large man-wolf clawed at its own chest, deep enough to see bone. Alice moved out of the way, never seeing a shift so violent. The beast's snout elongated as razor-sharp teeth erupted from newly formed flesh. Black liquid oozed from open wounds across the creatures bare chest, the fluid thick and stringy. Bones cracked, skin stretched, growing, shrinking and rearranging as the body morphed. The fur looked to be absorbed back into the body, pink muscles and ligaments appearing underneath before hardening like leather, a burst of colour compared to the darkness of the fur.

This shifter's transformation was a violent metamorphosis of one form to another. The strange black liquid continued to pour out of the wounds that didn't seem to heal, the thick substance sticking to the floor.

She had seen enough shifts to know that it wasn't normal.

"Cole," Rex grabbed the scruff of the wolf. "Take Alice outside." He wrestled the wolf as it tried frantically to bite him, his claws digging into Rex's chest.

"What's happening?" She really wished she had never given up her sword.

A hand came down to clutch her shoulder, fingers pinching painfully. Alice turned, raising her elbow high enough she hit it straight into Cole's throat. He snarled, clutching his neck as he choked and gasped for breath.

Not caring about his damaged windpipe she stepped back onto the drive, not stopping until she was at the end of the row of cars. Hands shaking she crouched down, her own breath coming in pants as she tried to control her emotions.

Sam wasn't there.

Then where was he? Why would the paper show this address?

"That was mean." Cole coughed as he walked up beside her, his voice slightly strained.

"You shouldn't have touched me." She straightened, her gaze taking in the grassy areas that surrounded the house before disappearing into forest. "Where's your wife?"

"She's not allowed to leave our house." He coughed again, spitting onto the dirt floor.

"What's happened?" She nodded towards the house when she faced him, noting that his beard was shorter than last time.

"Rex is being punished. He never was good at taking my advice."

"Punished?"

"He's a fool, one that will eventually learn."

Alice watched his eyes. "What is he being punished for?"

"That is for him to tell, for him to decide." Cole looked towards the house as a wolf howled. "He just needed a little push."

Stupid lion, speaking in riddles.

"I need to speak to Rex, we need to get out a search party for Sam."

"Well isn't it your lucky day, he's walking over." With a sarcastic bow, Cole moved towards the house, passing Rex as he stormed towards her.

"You don't understand what's happening." He shot the words like bullets. "You have no idea what's going on."

"Rex I need help with Sam, he's been taken…"

"You just don't get it do you?" he shouted, eyes ablaze and angry. She had never seen him so angry. "You were supposed to help me, supposed to keep them away. My mate, this supposedly powerful witch…"

"Mate? Rex, what are you on about?"

Rex continued, almost in delirium. "They were wrong. You can't help." His voice broke, pain radiating from every word. "I didn't know what to do. They're my pack, my family."

"Rex, I…"

"You smell like them." His voice dropped, his wolf close to the surface.

Slowly he reached across the small space between them, closing his hand delicately on her throat, his thumb stroking gently across her skin.

"I'm sorry for everything." His hand began to tighten as he wrapped his other hand around her hair.

"REX?" She pulled away, her skull screaming as she felt the hair pulled straight from her scalp. She stared at the blonde strands clutched in his closed fist.

"I have no choice. They're giving me no choice."

"Choice? Rex, what are you talking about?" She eyed him carefully, her heart in her throat. He was a shifter, stronger and faster than her, an Alpha even more so. She was trained to track down his kind, yet she felt a slow terror ache her bones. She had never gone against someone with eyes that held the edge of sanity.

She needed to calm him down.

"Rex. REX, look at me." She kept eye contact, the beast within him unable to look away. "We can get through this, I can help if we talk about it." She slowly edged away, stopping when she noticed him tense.

"You can't help." His voice was no longer his own.

"Of course I can, I'm the big bad witch remember? You said so yourself." She swallowed to help her dry throat. "What was Cole talking about?"

"They're coming for them, for everybody."

"Who is?"

"I..."

The wind erupted around her, throwing her hair into her face and breaking the eye contact. She scrambled back, but not fast enough. All the air in her lungs was knocked out as she was crushed to the ground, Rex straddling her hips.

"Rex," she croaked. Pinned to the earth.

"I'm sorry." With one hand he held her down, with the other he reached into his back pocket.

Shit. Shit. Shit.

Lifting up her knee she kicked up, connecting to his groin with enough impact for him to be thrown back. With all her anger she released an arcane blast, a wall of flame against Rex's unprotected face.

A shout as he covered his skin, protecting his eyes from the sudden heat. With all her strength she pushed against him, hard enough she was able to wiggle out and half crawl away. He snarled, patting out the small flames from his hair as she gained her feet and ran straight into the protection of the wooded area surrounding the pack's land.

A chorus of howls erupted around her, a discord of noise from behind. Not daring to look back she continued running, dodging trees and jumping over roots and debris, trusting her reflexes to stop her falling. Alice reached for her back, searching for her blade that wasn't there, having given it to Rex earlier.

"Fuck." She stopped, her lungs burning. She quickly reached her back pocket and grabbed her phone, careful of the broken glass. "Fuck." She leant against a moss-covered tree, the howls getting closer. "Fuck. Fuck. Fuck."

She scrolled through her phone, the screen flickering before going black.

"Great, just fucking great."

A crunch to her left. A woman stood at the edge of the trees, her nails darkening, elongating and becoming razor sharp as she watched. "There you are," she whispered, her eyes glittering with excitement. "I've been looking for you." Without another word she launched herself across the clearing, her shifter speed carrying her almost effortlessly over the ground.

"*ARMA!*" Alice shouted as the woman closed in, the aegis of aura popping into existence just in time. She bounced off the circle and crashed into a tree, on her feet a second later.

The aegis flickered, disappearing then reforming.

"Shit."

Alice grabbed at her throat, the crystal pendant no longer there. It must have fallen off when she fought with Rex. The dome flickered again, taking all of her concentration to keep it formed without its anchor point.

The woman circled the dome, her skin darkening with her anger, teeth growing in her mouth.

Wiping the sweat from her face she ignored the pain shooting through her skull, taking everything to keep the shield formed. The aegis shimmered, the woman launching herself across the space as it went down.

A scream filled the woods.

Alice gasped, her arms completely covered in blue flames licked with emerald. The woman rolled around the ground, trying to put the fire out from her clothes, patting them with her bare hands, skin blistering as it started to consume her.

Alice blinked, blood rushing in her ears, something warm dripping down her face as copper coated her tongue. Wiping her face with her sleeve she saw red, blood dripping from her nose.

Arms grabbed her from behind, crushing her against a wide chest she recognised.

A short, sharp pain in her side.

Warmth grew from her abdomen, bubbling through her bloodstream.

Cotton at the back of her throat.

"I'm sorry it has to be this way."

She looked up at Rex, her legs giving out.

Her tongue felt heavy in her mouth, unable to form any words. She couldn't feel herself collapse, her knees hitting the earth with a thump. Her head rolled as she turned to stare into his eyes, blue spheres heavy with regret.

CHAPTER THIRTY-ONE

Head heavy, Alice groaned as she opened her eyes, shutting them quickly when the lights above burned. Squinting until her eyes adjusted to the bright light she looked up, noticing that her wrists were manacled together, linked with a chain attached to the ceiling. She stared at it for a few seconds, tugging her wrists gently to the sound of the chain rattling.

"Fuck," she exhaled, keeping her voice low. "Fuck, fuck, fuck." The light was coming from a single point in the ceiling, a spotlight aimed at her alone. Beyond the light she saw nothing, darkness being kept at bay from the single bulb.

Panic grew as she tried desperately to tug at the chains, testing their strength until the pain became too much. Lead in her stomach she lurched forward, nausea rising to the point bile choked her throat.

"You'll dislocate your shoulder if you lean anymore," a voice calmly uttered through the darkness.

Alice froze, straining to hear something other than the rattle of the chain and the blood pumping through her skull.

"Hello?" She tugged more desperately. "Rex?" she whispered hesitantly, shrinking back against the brick wall.

"Why would you call for him?" A quiet monotone replied. "He betrayed you."

Alice strained to hear where the voice was coming from, panic peaking when she finally saw something at the corner of her eye. Turning she watched as a figure walked into the circle of light, her veins turning to ice when she recognised the dark cloak.

"You're not real."

"You look like her," her imaginary phantom replied, voice soft, almost detached.

"You're not real," Alice cried once again.

"Real?" The phantom pondered it for a second. "Am I real?"

It slowly glided towards her, almost painfully as the black cloak swished gently. A pale hand emerged from the sleeve, boney with dark veins pulsating underneath paper-thin skin.

"I don't even know if I am real anymore." It pulled off its hood, pale skin stretched across a slim face.

"Have you found her?" another voice joined in, one that was familiar.

"Alice," her brother called "Alice. It's me. It's Kyle. Come out from where you are hiding."

The monster continued to check the bushes and flowerbeds, searching for her.

"She's not here," the monster growled. "I was promised the girl."

"Shut up," her brother whispered back. "Alice." He raised his voice. "You know how mum doesn't like you playing out here in the dark."

A click as he turned on a torch, the light landing on his shoes for a moment, dark red stains marking the pristine white trainers.

"Alice," he called once again, his voice scared.

Blinking suddenly through wet eyes Alice stared at what was once her brother, his features the same as the gangly fourteen-year-old too skinny for his frame, except he had grown into his shoulders. His cheeks were hollow, dark messy stubble speckled across his jaw as emerald eyes, the same as hers, as their mother's, stared at her blankly.

"Kyle?" Alice choked out, tears pouring down her face.

"Why are you crying?" he asked, confusion swirling in his eyes. His hand raised to touch her face, the skin ice cold.

"Why are you doing this?" She tried to shrink back, her head hitting brick. "I don't understand."

"I thought you were dead." His other hand came up to hold her face, his breath just as cold as he moved forward. "Then I saw you, igniting the dragon, saving that woman." His gaze searched for something, she wasn't sure what.

"Fuck this," the monster stormed into the kitchen, returning moments later with her mum screaming, dragged her by her hair as she flailed wildly.

"Mummy," Alice squealed, covering the noise at the last minute, as if she could stop the sound carrying. Light landed just a foot from where she was crouched, huddled by the bark.

"What are you doing?" Kyle shouted as the monster grabbed their mother's hair, wrapping it around his fist as she fought the bonds holding her.

"Please. Please," she begged. "Why?"

"NO, STOP!" Kyle grabbed the monster's arm.

"I knew this was a mistake." The monster pushed Kyle back effortlessly, turning to lift him by the throat with one arm. "Fucking kid." He flung Kyle away as if he were nothing.

Alice closed her eyes, hands shaking as she hid behind the tree. Screams echoed until they suddenly stopped.

She tried to control her tears, her sight watery as she struggled to see in the dark.

"Alice..."

She felt her heart beat in her chest, the sobs coming stronger as she struggled to control them.

"Alice..."

The monster slowly approached the tree, whispering over and over.

"Alice... Alice, come here little girl." Heavy legs beside the fern. "There you are," a growl as an arm reached down to grab her.

With a cry Alice absently grabbed a rock, throwing it with as much force as she could. The sharp edge hit the monster with a squishy noise, hard enough that he shrieked, grabbing his face as a pale liquid dripped down his skin.

"Mummy?" she sobbed, running across the garden to the curses of the monster. "Mum? Kyle?"

Her nightdress danced in the cold wind, trying to trip her up as she knelt beside her mother, Kyle nowhere in sight.

"Mum?" she whispered, her knees warm in the dirt. She patted her *mother's hair, her face hidden beneath it.* "Mummy, it's okay, I got him. Look... Mummy?"

She lifted up her mother's long blonde hair, confused by the sea of red decorating the front of her mother's nightgown.

A sharp pain along her scalp. "Alice," Kyle wrapped more hair around his fingers. "Don't go away again."

Go away?

Alice felt the nausea growing.

"KYLE!" a smoky voice growled, hidden behind the light. "Control yourself."

Kyle's eyes swam with black, pupils dilating as his mouth turned into a grimace.

"If you ignore him," he spoke against her cheek. "He will go away."

"KYLE!"

Kyle ripped away, nails clawing at his own face.

"WHAT?" he shouted towards the voice.

"Walk her down, the preparation has been finished."

Kyle turned back, eyes completely encased in black. "This way."

"What? Kyle STOP!" Her chains went taut as he started to drag her from the room. "PLEASE." He didn't respond, pulling her chain with agitation. "You don't have to do this."

A heinous putrid smell polluted the air, leaving her gagging as she struggled against the chains. Steel cells lined the hallway beyond the light, groans and whimpers leaking through the bars. One cell held a group of people, their clothes ripped, soaked in blood and their own urine. Scars decorated their skin in a disorganised pattern, white lines along their arms, legs and backs. They all scattered as Kyle dragged Alice through the hallway, their black eyes all rimmed with red, all open, terrified as their tongue-less mouths were agape in fear.

"Where's Sam?" she cried, her neck stretching as she searched into every cell.

"Who?"

The next cell held a naked man, his head sunk into his chest as his arms were locked into the wall, almost embedded into the brick. Black veins pulsated under his pale skin, matching the beat of his sluggish heart.

"That isn't Sam," she whispered to herself in relief.

Then where was he?

Tiles ran along the floor and partially up the wall, what once could have been white was a dirty brown, flaking like rust from the blood moulded into the surface.

"Why him?" Kyle growled, the softness of his voice edged with anger.

"What?" Alice snarled back, feeling her chi fill with her fire as she continued to fight the chains dragging her across the tile.

"The Alpha." He watched her from the corner of his eye. "He's wrong. Too weak," he said with disapproving tone. "He betrayed you."

"Yeah well, people betraying me seems to be a habit." She kicked out at his legs in frustration.

He stopped walking, impatient.

"You need to stop that." He angrily yanked the chains. The wolf in the corner snarled, making Kyle's head whip around with a sneer. "SHUT UP!" He stormed to the cell, smacking the metal with his palm.

Alice froze, realising he dropped the chain in his distraction.

Quietly, she started to pull it toward her, hesitating when a voice behind whispered in a weak voice.

"Ple... ase..." a woman's voice quivered. "Please, help me."

Alice turned to face a naked woman with dirty brown hair, her skin a sickly grey patterned with yellow bruises. One eye was swollen shut, blood stained down her face like tears. A pile of cloth lay to her right, a makeshift bed made from the scraps. A tray rested by the bars with a grey lumpy substance in a wooden bowl, green mould fluffy on top, flies buzzing around it greedily. Red smears decorated the walls, a series of parallel lines covering most of the wall space.

"Get the keys." She licked her lips nervously, the skin cracking open painfully.

Alice quickly checked Kyle, who was still distracted by the aggressive wolf. "Where?" Alice gently whispered back.

"Over there." The woman stretched her arm through the bars of her cell, the skin stretched tight to the bone. "He has it." She waved a hand toward Kyle frantically. "HE HAS IT!" she wailed.

"Shhhhh." Alice grabbed the woman's outstretched hand. "Shhh." She tried to calm her.

"He has it. He has it." Delirium took hold as the woman continued to chant. "He has it. He has it." She started to giggle hysterically. "HE HAS IT!"

"Alice come here, she's dangerous." Kyle grabbed Alice's shoulders, pulling her away from the woman who was now rocking, clawed hands trying to strike out.

Alice screamed as she was pulled, rocking her elbow back and hitting him in the stomach before twisting out of his grasp.

"Oomfff." He bent at the waist.

Breathing heavily, she gathered her chi, holding her flame in both hands. About to throw the fire she stopped, watching his eyes fight to become green.

"Kyle?" her voice tremored. "What happened to you?"

"Run." He dry heaved before screaming in pain, nails clawing at his own eyes. He bolted forward, grabbing the chain in his hand and yanking her off her feet. "Bad Alice." He pulled the chain with force, his eyes once again black.

"*CORUSCARE!*" she shouted, throwing her hand out towards his face, igniting the cloak.

A growl, the smoke clearing quickly as Kyle calmly shook off the robe as it turned to ash in his hands, his skin showing a history of abuse, pale scars crisscrossing almost every part of exposed skin.

Silver cuffs encircled his wrists, patterns engraved into the metal that seemed to pulsate along with the matching choker surrounding his neck.

Clicking his fingers she flinched, gasping when he held a ball of flame in his hand, green tinged with black.

"Don't do that," his voice was soft once again, black eyes fighting against the green as the flame danced between his fingertips.

"What are those cuffs?" she asked, stomach churning. "I can help."

He tilted his head, pain radiating across his face as he retched.

"NO!" He started to shake, throwing his head around as the cuffs glowed brightly.

Alice gathered the chain around her wrist, waiting for his next move when he turned to face her, eyes unfocused.

"They're coming," he whispered, leaning forward. "Run." He started to convulse, his eyes rolling in the back of his head before he fought back control. Groaning, he dragged himself to the exit, leaving the same way he had forced her in.

Alice stared after him, unable to move from the floor as exhaustion beat heavy on her. She dropped the chain with a rattle, concentring on calming her pulse, ignoring the manic crying from the woman and howling from the wolf. Looking down at her raw wrists she tried to squeeze her hands through, desperation taking hold when she felt someone watching her.

"He's coming," the delirious woman cackled. "60. 59. 58..."

"Shut up," Alice hissed, cursing as her fingers failed to fit. The manacles were heavy, locked tight.

"45. 44. 43..."

"Please, let me think."

Water dripped from the ceiling in the corner, hitting a shallow puddle on the cracked tile. The partial stonewalls were shiny, damp with a light green tinge and metal industrial supports that looked warped. A dirty orange cabinet was broken in the corner, the door hanging on one hinge with dust gathered on the empty shelves. Nothing that could help.

"Maybe something's in the cells," she whispered to herself as she crawled across the floor towards the third cell. The wolf paced, huffing and growling as she got closer.

"30. 29. 28..."

The inside of the cell was identical to the woman's, stonewalls with deep gouges and bloody marks. A tray that had been destroyed littered the floor, mixed in with sawdust, tufts of fur and bone. The wolf leapt at the bars with a snarl, part of his snout reaching out from a gap as he tried to bite his way through the metal.

"The bone." She cautiously watched the wolf. "I can pick the lock with a bone."

But how will I get it?

Unexpectedly, the bone skidded across the floor. Startled she glanced at the wolf, the beast calmly staring back as it pushed another bone underneath the small gap between the bars.

"23. 22. 21..."

"You can understand me?"

She wasn't confident how much of the person the wolf had retained. When shifters stayed in their animal form too long, it became hard to come back.

"Are you from White Dawn?" The wolf gave a sharp yip, pawing at the ground. Alice sucked in a breath, "Roman?" The wolf turned, growling at something as pain struck the back of her head.

CHAPTER THIRTY-TWO

"Brothers!" a voice boomed as the room erupted into applause. "It's time."
In igne comburetis. Cinis in nos exsurgent.
Alice's headache matched the rhythm of the chant, a tattoo dancing against the inside of her head. She squinted her eyes as she watched the series of cloaked men, surrounding her in a partial circle. Each acolyte held a single candle, the wax dripping onto their grey palms without a flinch. Swallowing bile she flexed her swollen fingers, the surface cold beneath her. She moved slowly, pulling at her wrists, shocked to feel no resistance.

Lashes low so they hid her eyes she tried to study the room, noticing how she was lying on a stone slab in the centre of what looked like an old storage facility. Steel beams held up the high ceiling, surrounded by large cabinets that were mostly closed. Hooks were planted into the walls, some broken, leaving dangerous spikes while others held old high-vis jackets.

Alice tried to keep her breathing steady, even as an intense cold prickled across her skin.

"Brothers," the smoky voice called. "How long we have waited."
Alice recognised the voice.
Where was Kyle?
He wasn't there, wasn't one of the acolytes. She was sure of it.

"Are we all prepared?"

In igne comburetis. Cinis in nos exsurgent.

Alice tried not to groan, the combined voices of the men rattling against her skull. The intense cold increased as she felt something glide slowly towards the pedestal, followed by a scraping sound across the concrete and tile.

Shit. Shit. Shit.

She couldn't see clearly enough in the candlelit room, she had no weapons, no known exits and the intense feeling of panic was getting greater with every passing second.

She was running out of time.

"You promised me Roman."

Alice's eyes opened wide at the voice.

"A deal is a deal."

She strained to turn her head, barely catching a glimpse of Rex as he intercepted her captor. How could she not have seen his deception? Was she that stupid?

"Did you hear that brothers?" the smokey voice called. "This Alpha is asking for his pup." A laugh as the cloaked men twitched in agitation.

"You said…"

"I *told* you to retrieve the dragon…"

"You implied that if I did this, you would release Roman." Rex's voice dropped, anger coming from his wolf.

"ENOUGH." Alice flinched at the shout. "Do not overstep." Rex was pushed against the wall, his eyes arctic.

"No, this…" Rex snarled as a hand grabbed his throat, stopping his words.

"Go back to your pack. Before they replace the weak Alpha that you are," the larger man threatened, releasing his clenched hand as Rex gasped for breath.

"Yes, master." Rex looked up, his eyes almost sorry before he turned away, leaving the room, leaving her.

Fuck! Alice squeezed her eyes shut.

"Ah, there she is." A hand brushed against her arm. It took everything in her to stay relaxed, not to tense up and give herself away. "I know you're awake." An intimate whisper.

Leaping up she flipped off the stone, landing heavy on the balls of her feet.

"*IGNIS!*" She flung out her arm, flame erupting from her palm like a whip. A high-pitched screech, pain radiating behind her eyes as the pierce shrill forced her to her knees, head in her hands.

Arms encased her, forcing her to stand.

"HOLD HER DOWN."

"NO!" Alice fought against the arms, pulling at the hoods covering their faces. She gasped as the cloth ripped away, showing empty eye sockets, lips sewn together, white thread a stark contrast against their dark skin.

In igne comburetis. Cinis in nos exsurgent.

The chorus of voices continued to chant, invading her head, needles across her brain. Alice felt her heartbeat in her throat, a cold terror filling her gut. A larger hand closed around her arm, throwing her back onto the stone slab with a thud. Arms and legs pinned she struggled, energy evaporating.

Eyes wide open, she quickly took in her surroundings.

She was wrong before, it wasn't a storage facility.

The stone pedestal was in the centre of an abandoned underground station.

Large gold candelabras stood in the corner, holding hundreds of candles, wax melting delicately onto the concrete floor. The white wax slowly turned a sickly pink, mixing with blood that was running along grooves etched into the floor. Old movie posters and train maps still decorated the walls, the once bright pictures muted over the years, covered in layers of dust. There was even a ticket station in the corner, runes written in blood smeared across the glass. The cavernous room trembled as a train passed overhead, dust and debris raining down. The acolytes stood patiently, holding her down.

"LOOK AT ME!"

Alice whipped her head towards the voice, freezing when she noticed the Daemon standing before her. Eyes that were pure red watched with slit pupils, a slow and satisfied smile creeping across his scarred face. Horns were filed down to the skull, barely visible beneath long black hair. Wide shoulders flexed as he gripped her chin, forcing her to meet his gaze.

Something moved in her peripheral view, a black sheet that scuffed across the floor.

Oh shit. They were wings, wings that were dragging behind him. *Of course he has fucking wings.* Black veins patterned like a spider web across the thin membrane, the arch protruding from his shoulders high above his head.

"Who are you?" she asked, yanking her jaw from his grasp.

"Is it really important?" A cold laugh.

"Why are you doing this?" He ignored her, his attention on the others. "What have you done to Kyle?"

In igne comburetis. Cinis in nos exsurgent.

"Today we meet here my brothers, to start The Becoming." He turned his back.

"Where's Kyle?"

"The blood of the dragon is the final catalyst before we take our power we rightfully deserve. Before we start the end of days."

In igne comburetis. Cinis in nos exsurgent.

"Dragon? What fucking dragon?" She pulled against her restraints.

The Daemon just smirked. "You're more ignorant than your parents, little dragon."

"My parents?"

He grabbed Alice's left wrist, holding it immobile in his large hand.

"The blood of your mother was corrupted by that druid, useless."

A long nail cut across the delicate flesh at the crease of her wrist, blood pooling along the wound.

"But with your life force, we will Become. The blood of the dragon, the blood of war." His head hovered over her wound, an intimate bloody kiss.

Alice screamed, pain searing through her arm. Her flesh tore as she pulled her arm free from his teeth.

A slow smile, his canines covered in red.

"Per ignem enim moriemur. Sanguinis sacrificii nos cogunt. Im igne comburetis. Cinis in nos exsurgent." He raised his arms, chanting towards the sky.

Fire erupted from her blood, a scalding pain that bubbled through her veins. Her life force pumped slowly from her wrist, a red trail across the stone. Head rolling to the side she watched as consciousness flickered, the blood dripping to the floor with her blue fire crackling as it followed the flow.

"Hoc sacrificium, absorbet. Et factus est."

"Fuck!" Alice shouted as pain throbbed through every nerve, flames scorching towards the runes, lighting up in intricate patterns along the concrete.

"In fire, we burn..."

"Why are you doing this?" Alice asked, her vision darkening at the corners, her lungs struggling.

"In ash, we rise," he finished, his arms still raised to the sky, before snake eyes moved to her, glittering with excitement. "Because I can."

A loud crash, the ceiling trembling as concrete and dust showered the room.

"ALICE!" a voice shouted.

The pain pulsated with the beat of her heart, darkness shrouding her.

"ALICE!" That voice, shouting from a distance again. "WAKE UP!"

Someone grabbed her, pulling her into a sitting position against something hard, a hand against her throat.

"ALICE!"

Her eyes slipped open, blurring as she struggled to make out the scene in front of her. Riley danced around the room, balls of arcane flashing into the acolytes as they scattered like skittles. A flash of steel, a head rolling off its shoulders as another man who was dressed identically to Riley fought the others. The stranger seemed just as impossibly fast, his sword blurring as he took down one acolyte after another. He wore wraparound sunglasses, his hair pure white compared to Riley's dark.

Her eyes became heavy, the pain dulling.

"They're too late." Smoke against her face, a mouth against her ear.

Gasping for a breath she struggled, lifting her hands to claw at his skin.

Flames continued to pour from her left wrist, strangely silent compared to the clang of metal and shouts surrounding her. She heard whispers in her ear, a desolate sound she couldn't make out as she watched the fire, oddly mesmerising as it flowed into the patterns along the floor.

She felt the hand tighten.

"Pay attention," he growled.

"Fuck you," she snarled through clenched teeth, blood fragrant at the back of her throat.

A crash, an acolyte thrown against the wall, head impaling into one of the hooks.

"ALICE, SHIELD!" Riley shouted from across the room.

"Fucking Guardians," the Daemon seethed, hand loosening as he watched the action.

"ALICE!" Riley moved towards them, jumping over the flames. "SHIELD!"

Shield?

"*Arma,*" she whispered, her aura solidifying into existence around her, a molecule thin film lasting only a second. The hand loosened against her, a shout of pain. With her last remaining energy, she pushed back.

A silver ball of arcane flew past the corner of her eye, landing straight into the Daemon as he stumbled. With a shriek, he scrabbled at his chest, scraping the energy from his skin with a snarl just as it started to eat into skin and bone.

Flames continued to pour from her wrist, her life burning up as she watched. She turned her head, seeing Riley and the Daemon circle each other. Riley raised a gun, pointing it steadily as the tattoos across his arms glowed.

"Is that all you got?" the Daemon mocked, his wings pulsating and curling around his shoulders in irritation.

Stepping forward he knocked the gun from Riley's hands, sending it skidding across the floor to land against a fallen acolyte. Alice eyed it, watching her hand reach for it in a painfully slow motion. She slipped off the stone, dragging herself through the flames to reach the weapon, leaving a trail of fire and blood behind her.

Riley stood motionless, his chest barely moving as he remained calm.

"You're too late," the Daemon taunted, blood still staining his teeth. "Only a matter of moments before she is gone, and we Become." His thigh tensed.

Riley moved with him, slashing out with his blade as it sliced across the Daemons chest with a hiss. The Daemon reared back, looking down in astonishment as Riley rushed forward, punching him straight in the face with a crunch. A hand came from out of nowhere, nails slicing across Riley's bare arm. Black foam bubbled from the gouges, acid burning through skin.

"Riley," Alice tried to warn, her voice making no noise against the cacophony of battle.

Her fingertips finally touched the metal.

The Daemon laughed again as he smirked into Riley's reflective eyes.

"I see your beast, it screams for release. You're just like me." A glint in his eyes before black flames rained down from the ceiling. "You just keep it better hidden."

Another ball of red tinged with black was thrown across the room, Riley intercepted it with a blast, returning the arcane with interest.

The spell went wild, crashing into the wall, shattering the tiles.

"Fuck," Riley growled as he turned his claymore blade carefully in his hand. Waiting.

The Daemon hissed, circling him slowly. "It's your own people that did that to you. Broke you as a child, forced you to share a spirit."

Alice tried to scream as a cloaked figure grabbed her ankle, his fist tightening before he became dust, Riley's arcane evaporating him into nothing. She heard Riley shout, his face annoyed as he kicked a minion with his boot, the cloaked figure collapsing into the carnage.

Swinging his blade in a wide arc he cut off its head.

"Enough of this," Riley called as he lifted his sword. "You can never win."

"Is that so? Then how come I already am?"

The Daemon stepped from the shadows, his fist powering through the air before Riley even noticed. The second punch doubled him over, causing him to suck in a breath. His sword clattered to the ground, the Daemon kicking it away as he approached.

Alice lifted the gun, her hand shaking from the weight.

"This is getting tiring. Join the cause or die."

"Fuck you," Riley snarled. Drawing back his arm he released his fist. The Daemon yowled, clutching his nose as Riley hit out again, the impact causing him to stumble back, almost tripping over the bodies.

She pulled the trigger.

A bead of blood appeared on the Daemons dark forehead, the bead growing from the centre between his eyes. Another shot. A hole appearing in his throat, a choked noise as blood gurgled. With a roar Riley jumped forward, pushing as much raw power as he could muster through the small hole in his head, searing him from the inside out.

"You could never win." Riley pushed, putting all his rage into that one concentrated point.

"I am many," a gargled laugh, black blood bubbling from the Daemons lips. "We will Become." A flash of light, a silver glow that radiated from behind his eyes.

"Riley," Alice whispered, a quiet noise, a last breath.

Pushing away from the Daemon as his body eroded into dust Riley turned towards her weak voice. She could barely make out him running towards her, his arms crushing as he pushed the gun away from her slack grip.

"Alice?" He shook her in his panic.

All she heard was white noise, Riley's mouth moving but no sound coming out.

"You can't get attached," the stranger said as he came to stand beside Riley, his hand resting on his shoulder. "She's too far gone."

Alice tried to speak, only a croak coming out.

Riley juddered his shoulder to dislodge the hand. "Xander, go stand guard."

"She's dying."

"I said back the fuck off," he snarled.

"Riley, listen to me." Xander got down on his knee. "You can't. You know what would happen. If The Order…"

Alice tried to speak again, her ears starting to ring as sound slowly came back. "Riley?" she uttered in barely a whisper, her throat dry.

"Hey." He stroked her hair from her eyes, ignoring Xander. "Did you really have to burn the place down? Over dramatic or what." Riley tried to smile, the light not reaching his eyes.

"How did you find me?" she asked.

"Unimportant," he replied, cradling her as if she could break.

He checked her wrist, hand covering her wound even as the fire began to eat away at his flesh. She tried to pull away.

"Stay still."

"Don't boss me around," she moaned as her eyelids became heavy.

The flames licked his skin, her blood continuing to burn her up from the inside out.

"Alice?" He rocked her gently. "ALICE, WAKEUP!"

A groan, her face scrunching up in annoyance.

"Alice listen to me, I need you to expel all the fire. Everything, you need to ostracise your power reserve."

"What are you doing?" Xander asked, his tone deep with worry.

"Alice. Nod if you understand."

A small movement against his chest.

"Ready? On the count of three. One, two, three."

He held her as she screamed, fire pouring from her fingertips, an unpredictable recalcitrant element. The walls creaked, straining against the intense heat.

"We need to move!" Xander shouted over the roar of the flames.

"Give it a second."

A metal beam crashed through the ceiling.

"WE NEED TO MOVE!"

"WAIT!" Another crash as the metal beam landed on the ticket office, smashing the glass into tiny shards. She felt Riley cover her with his body, shrapnel bouncing off his back. Blood no longer poured from her wrist, the fire having died out when she expelled her magic, her energy along with it. She could no longer feel anything.

Riley checked her pulse, feeling nothing.

"FUCK!"

He laid her on the ground, her aura damaged beyond repair as she pushed out everything she had.

"FUCK. FUCK. FUCK," he chanted, hovering his hands over her body.

"What can I do?" Xander asked, remaining calm.

"Pump her heart." Riley started breathing for her, tipping her head back to force air into her lungs. "Come on Alice." He started breathing for her again.

"This isn't working." Xander stopped pumping to check her pulse. "It's not beating on its own."

"MOVE!" Riley pushed him out the way, hovering his hand gently over her heart.

"What are you doing?" Slight panic.

Riley concentrated as he shot a small amount of arcane into her heart, shocking it to restart.

Still no pulse.

"Shit." He repeated the shock, his hand burning as he concentrated it into a small area.

A small beat, faint against her skin.

EPILOGUE

Alice hobbled ungracefully with her one crutch, taking a seat on the dust sheet-covered sofa. She groaned, allowing herself to sink into the cushion, her aches and pains protesting at any sort of movement. Even sitting down seemed to hurt.

She rested her head against the wall with a huff, her eyes tracing the intricate designs plastered onto the ceiling. A few cracks marked the otherwise beautiful work, nothing some DIY couldn't fix.

She could hear muttering from the kitchen, Sam and Dread bickering over something completely ridiculous. They pretended to hate each other, but she knew, deep down, way deep down, that they did at least like each other.

Or it could be more like tolerate.

She couldn't help but laugh to herself as she started to climb painstakingly back off the sofa, intending to go save two of her favourite people from possibly killing one another.

"You don't need this many mugs," Dread grumbled as he put away yet another novelty mug into one of the kitchen cupboards. "I know for a fact you guys don't have enough friends to use all these."

"Aye, but what happens when one of our mugs decides to grow penicillin? Who are we to stop something from potentially saving the world?" Sam commented back, a smirk on his lightly stubbled face.

Alice just leant against the newly bought table, the chairs yet to be made. Sam smiled when he noticed her, rolling his eyes once Dread commented about the bad taste in mugs yet again.

Returning the smile automatically she stared at the deep bruises across his wrists and face, her smile slipping quickly. Shifters usually healed bruises within a couple of hours at most. It just showed how badly he was beaten, torn ligaments, broken bones, all priority compared to a few bruises.

"Alice you need to sit down. You shouldn't be up." Dread put the mug away with the others, trying to hide his concern.

Alice just sighed. She wasn't stupid, she knew she was hurt. The aches she felt a testimony to that, as was her new crescent moon scar that was a constant reminder of one of the worst nights of her life.

Or, at least in the top three worst nights of her life.

The top of the crescent started in the middle of her left palm, curling down to just below her wrist, the thickened skin several degrees colder than the rest of her body.

"I thought I could help." She had been bed bound, poked and prodded for weeks. She was about to lose it. She either needed to stab something or put away some damn mugs. As she stupidly gave up her sword, she was left with the mugs.

Clenching her fist she looked at Dread, wanting to ask the question she had been asking every day. Luckily Dread knew exactly what she was going to say.

"No," he sighed, shaking his head gently. "I haven't had any reports."

Fighting disappointment she just nodded, deciding to look at the badly drawn pictures that Sam drew on her cast one night after too many wines. She knew it was a long shot. When she heard that Kyle was nowhere to be found at the train station she had hope. Hope that she would get answers, that he could help her understand.

Yet, he was nowhere to be found.

She had decided to move back into her family home, use her happy childhood memories to overcome the bad ones. She needed to learn to accept her past, accept the things she couldn't change. Honour their memory. Renovating the house, making it her own was a start. Second was finding her brother.

"Hey baby girl, have you seen Riley recently?" Sam asked almost absently, his attention mostly on unpacking and not on the conversation. "I haven't seen him in a few weeks. He hasn't been to work either."

"No, I haven't," she replied. It had become apparent pretty quickly that she had no idea how to contact him, which frustrated her even more than the cast. She had so many questions about what happened that night, her memory fuzzy to say the least. He wasn't just a druid, he was more, just as she was more.

Dragon. War.

He had disappeared once he had completed his duty, no longer interested.

"Good riddance," muttered Dread. "All he will bring is trouble. Damn druids."

DING.

"I'm coming," she called down the hallway, the cast on her leg hindering her speed dramatically. Her aching wrist wasn't helping either.

DING.

"I'm coming," she called again, dodging around cardboard boxes stashed high around the living room and hallway.

DING.

"Bloody hell, I'm coming!" She continued her painful journey, her whole body aching as she pushed it.

"Are you answering it or not Alice?" Sam shouted at her.

"I'm bloody answering it," she let out a frustrated snarl.

DING.

"Oh, for... I SAID I WAS...!" She opened the front door, her voice shutting off instantly.

"Hello," the man greeted, a black wolf sitting calmly by his legs.

"Hello," Alice stumbled. "Why are you...?"

"I'm Theo. You must be Alice."

"I know who you are," her voice husky, anger growing. She glared at the man standing on the doorstep. "Why are you here?"

She never wanted to see Rex again, his betrayal scorched into her brain forever. Looking at his identical twin was almost as bad. Theo's hair was cut shorter, the strands barely touching his ears compared to Rex's full head of hair. An old scar split his face, starting from his forehead, travelling across his nose and distorting his upper lip. The darkened skin should have made him ugly, yet it gave his face more character. That lip turned up at the corner.

"I thought you would be taller." Eyes laughed at her aggressive reaction, or he could be laughing at her nest of a hair, barely brushed ponytail at least two days old.

"I disappoint myself sometimes too."

"You have a nice house."

"Please get to the point." She wasn't petty. Not petty at all.

He gave her a shy smile. "I wanted to say thank you, for what you did."

"Oh." Her arm shook as she balanced her weight on the crutch. "That's okay."

What else was she supposed to say to that?

"And Roman wanted to say thank you." The wolf by his feet stood up, his tongue rolling out of his mouth in a wolfish grin.

"Where's Rex?" Alice asked, hoping he was nowhere nearby.

"Not here." The smile fell from his face.

"What are they doing here?" Sam came up from behind her with a snarl.

"You must be Sam," started Theo.

"Why the fuck are you here?" Sam's hackles rose, his teeth flashing as a threat. Well, as threatening as a man with a tea towel decorated with kittens draped over his shoulder could be.

"We're here to apologise. To you both it seems."

"It's not you who should be apologising," he snapped. Alice put a shaky hand on his shoulder, calming him.

"No it shouldn't be, but let's not speak of my brother, or about the pride."

Theo seemed to hesitate, trying to find the right words.

"They are no longer an issue." His eyes flashed wolf, the same ice blue as Rex before he turned back to Alice. "Like I said, I just wanted to let you know how grateful I am, as well as my pack. I can't even begin to explain the reasons why Rex did what he did." He flicked a look towards Roman. "He broke so many pack laws in his desperation, once we figured out how he tracked you..."

"Wait, he tracked me?" She looked down at her naked wrist, the leather wrap having been cut off at the hospital. "It was the bracelet, wasn't it?" It all made sense.

"Ironically enough it was with the bracelet they could find you at the train station." He shook his head at the thought.

"Baby girl, you okay?" Sam's concern breaking through.

She ignored the question, instead asking her own. "Was that all it could do?"

She waited for the answer, her eyes appraising Theo as he thought about it. Theo was attractive in the general sense, in the same way she had found Rex attractive, yet she felt nothing.

It made her chest ache, a sour taste at the back of her throat.

"There's no way to know, I'm not familiar with the magic behind it."

She gave a shallow nod, not wanting to speak as she digested the information.

"I have put in the request to take over White Dawn. Unfortunately, it means you might see more of me in the city." He attempted to smile charmingly, but it came off more awkward.

"I hope you do a better job." Maybe just a little petty.

A deep chuckle. "I hope so too." He tilted his head, clearly hearing something she couldn't. "That's my signal to leave."

Theo patted Roman on the head.

"Before I go, I just want you to know if you ever need anything, from myself or the pack please do not hesitate to ask, it's the least I can do."

He turned to leave when Roman nipped at his heels.

"Oh yes, I almost forgot." Reaching back he passed across her sword, her crystal necklace wrapped tightly around its hilt. "I believe these belong to you."

Alice touched the coolness of her sword, happiness at feeling the familiar weight against her palm. With a flash of light runes appeared down the shaft, brightening as she brushed her fingertip down the metal.

"Alice..." She heard the concern in Sam's voice, he knew the sword had never done that before. Unable to comfort him she watched the lights dance, a pain in her gut.

Something had changed. She didn't know if that was for the better or not.

She needed to figure out who she was.

"Thank you," she said as she put down the sword, not wanting to look at it. Not wanting to acknowledge that she wasn't what she thought. What her parents were.

"You're welcome." With a small smile Theo turned away, Roman tight behind. "This really is a nice house."

"Thanks," she replied to his back. "It was my parents."

It's home.

The End of Book One

TAYLOR ASTON WHITE

Druid's Storm

AN ALICE SKYE NOVEL

DRUID'S STORM

BOOK TWO

PROLOGUE

Dread felt like he was on trial.

The box The Council made him stand in was small and confined.

"So it has come to our attention..." a slight pause as Valentina, the head of The Council looked down at her notes. "Alice has come of age."

"Define 'come of age'," asked Dread, slightly anxious. He didn't get nervous, not in his thousand plus years roaming the earth. He had seen kingdoms fall, queens conquer lands and fought the Great War.

Yet, he felt nervous now.

The Council governed all Breed. It was they who made the laws, who had worked out a treaty with humans almost three centuries ago. It was they who publicly executed anyone they believed to have a difference of opinion. Dread had worked hard to keep under their radar, and had run the Supernatural Intelligence Bureau as directed, no questions asked. He'd worked even harder to keep Alice under control, to downplay her power surges as a child. He had hoped, prayed even, that her ancestry was simply an exaggeration.

How wrong he was.

The Council of Five stared, their attention on him absolute. On the left, seemingly uninterested in the situation was Xavier, his orange eyes flashing in challenge as Dread met them. His hip tilted, feet dangling off the side of his wooden throne. A slow smile crept across his thin lips, showing a row of sharp, pointy teeth as his other half, the tiger, shone through. He was very much dressed down in ripped jeans and a short-sleeved T-shirt with a bands name Dread had never heard of.

"Don't be so crass. You know exactly what we mean."

Beside Xavier sat Frederick Gallagher, one of the most powerful witches in Europe.

"Do you think her sudden power flare has gone unnoticed?" He leant forward as he spoke, his velvet green robe opening to reveal a white ruffled shirt.

"As my fellow councilman has pointed out, we know of her recent power incline. You were asked when you became her legal guardian to inform The Council when she started to show the power her heritage gifted her." Valentina pursed her lips disapprovingly. "We will do well not to allow her to succumb to the same fate as her brother."

Dread said nothing, not wanting to inform them that Kyle was believed to be alive, but missing.

The Council craved power.

The children of Dragon were power.

"This is getting –"

"– tiresome." The Fae twins sat to the far right, each sitting on an arm of their single throne. Quention and his sister Liliannia were both faeries with straight white gold hair, oversized lilac eyes and pointy ears. They were identical to the point their androgynous appearance made it exceedingly hard to tell them apart, it was only the slight curve of Liliannia's breast that gave her away. They watched Dread as if he were a bug, boring and unimportant.

"Does she even know –"

"– about her legacy?" Quention finished for his twin, their voices painfully high-pitched.

"No."

He was sure of it. She wasn't ready to understand, wasn't prepared to have that sort of responsibility.

"Do you think us fools, monsieur Grayson?" Valentina tapped her exceedingly long nails against the wooden arm, painted a blood red.

"I would never lie to The Council, Mistress."

He almost choked on the last word, a name he was forced to use out of 'respect' for the leader of his Breed.

"He's telling the truth." Mason Storm was the last member, sitting directly to Valentina's right.

He stood for the druids, completing The Council of Breeds.

"She seems to know nothing of her heritage," he said on a laugh. "Ignorant."

"Careful." Dread felt his fangs release, his eyes darkening in a warning.

"How dare you speak…"

"ENOUGH!" Valentina's voice echoed throughout the room, anger surging across her delicate features as she demanded attention.

She carefully pushed her straight black hair behind one ear, showing more of her delicate porcelain skin. Dread looked at the large ruby at her throat, not wanting to meet her dark, slitted eyes. Valentina was old, older than even him although she looked around fifteen, an undeveloped fifteen-year-old.

"You mock us."

Frederick had sat back in his seat at Valentina's outburst, a ball of pure white arcane rolling playfully through his fingers.

"It was agreed that once Alice came of age, she would be trained. I demand she immediately be turned over to my guidance."

"We had all agreed at the time, that monsieur Grayson would be the most suitable…" Valentina started.

"I did it as a favour to a friend. Not for The Council," Dread stated, watching Valentina's face tense at the blatant disregard.

"This is ridiculous." Frederick extinguished his arcane, fidgeting in his seat. "Her care should have been given to The Magika and me. Not this vampire who hasn't even trained her in basic magic."

Dread growled, unable to stop the sound.

"I have done what is best for her, unlike you…"

"Hold your tongue," Valentina snarled, flashing her fangs. "We have not forgotten that you lied about her survival. We could have executed you on principle but decided it was better for the child to stay with you for stability."

Dread clenched his jaw. He had hidden Alice successfully for years, created a spider web of lies to keep her safe from the people who would use her for their own personal gain. Unfortunately, nothing got past The Council.

"I understand."

"Good. Now, we have been given reports that Alice is unable to control her power surges, can you confirm?" she asked, raising a dark eyebrow.

Dread wanted to hit something, his fingers crushing the edge of the wood he gripped in anger. He knew Valentina had sent a spy to work for him, knew instantly his new recruit was The Mistress' soldier and he was sure the others had sent spies too.

"She's been seeing a doctor regularly, a witch," he added before Frederick could protest, "who is helping her with control."

"You failed as her Caretaker," Xavier's deep, smoky voice said. "You need to be punished." His orange eyes flashed finally with interest, clearly the one who wanted to do the punishing.

"She should be with me," Frederick stated.

"Do you think we do not know –"

"– what you would do with her Frederick?" The twins chimed in. "It is why we decided she shouldn't be with The Magika –"

"– until she could hold her own. We can't have you syphoning off all that power now, can we."

A chuckle as Xavier leant forward, stripes appearing then disappearing on his tanned skin as he played with his beast.

"This little witch sounds interesting." He tilted his head in a feline way. "Mason," he started, turning those unusual orange eyes towards the druid, "is it not your job to deal with Daemons?"

Mason's face flushed a deep red, his eyes hard as he adjusted his necktie.

"That situation has been dealt with."

"Your transgression almost cost us dear little Alice's life. Maybe you're the one who needs to be punished." Xavier tensed as if he was ready to pounce.

"We have called this meeting to discuss the future of Alice," Valentina said sternly, ignoring the tiger.

"Alice should be turned over to myself and The Magika." Frederick shot to his feet aggressively. "We have the ability to train her."

"I disagree, it should be an impartial party that cannot benefit from her." Xavier smiled lazily, loving the friction he caused.

"This is just ridiculous." Frederick sat down again, his long robe floating down to rest beside him.

"We agree with the tiger." Quention settled for the twins.

"I have a suggestion." Liliannia joined in with her brother. "She should have a Warden assigned. One who should train her –"

"– in both defensive abilities as well as magic."

"Interesting." Valentina clicked her tongue. "What do you think, Commissioner?"

Dread tensed, not usually addressed with his proper title.

"If it pleases The Council then a Warden couldn't hurt."

"I will put myself forward." Mason inserted. "As a Druid, we are gifted warriors in both combat and magic."

"This is absurd," Frederick grumbled.

"This is becoming boring," Xavier dragged a claw against the wooden chair arm, leaving a long scratch. "I vote for Mason."

"A druid would be the appropriate choice considering her lineage," Liliannia added.

"I agree with my sister, we vote for Mason," Quention agreed.

"I must disagree." All eyes turned to Dread. "Councillor Storm, you are the head of The Order, or have you forgotten? You could not possibly give Alice the attention she would need for such training."

"The Guardians then." He smirked as if he had won. "They are trained since children with discipline. It's exactly what that girl needs."

"We have voted." Valentina flicked her hand. "Councillor Storm will assign one of his Guardians as a Warden to Alice. They will be in charge of training her in the correct skills to defend herself as well as controlling her increasing power."

She quietened Frederick as he started to object.

"After an initial period, Alice will be asked to prove her skills with a test. If she shows no sign of control, she will be turned over to The Magika. They will decide her fate." That pleased the male witch.

Dread looked over at Mason as he fought not to comment, not wanting any emotion to leak through his words. Alice was his daughter in every way but blood, and he was honoured to bring her up for his late best friend. Yet, he felt helpless as he watched the Council decide her fate.

He just hoped that one day she could forgive him.

Dawn's light woke him as a bird chirped outside the open window, the white curtain blowing gently in the breeze. Opening his eyes he stared at the ceiling, the small imperfections memorised as he checked how his pet spider was doing in the far corner.

Jumping out of bed he grabbed his clothes quickly , pulling them on methodically as he flicked his eyes to the clock above his bed, the only decoration in the stark, square room.

Ten minutes.

He began to pace, it was only a matter of time before he was due to be trained again. Due to be humiliated as the teachers beat him to a pulp.

It wasn't supposed to be this bad, his training. It was supposed to come naturally according to his father.

He was born for this.

Yet he couldn't control his beast.

So they trained him. Trained him beyond what his body could handle until his bones ached and his skin became swollen. The beast controlled him, not the other way round. His beast was better, stronger.

His spirit animal.

The other half of his soul.

Five minutes.

Letting out a puff he sat on the bed, the only piece of furniture in the room beside a clothes rack, which held three identical black outfits. There wasn't even a mirror, strange considering vanity was an asset according to the teacher. Which was crazy. The prey he was being trained to hunt, to extinguish, wouldn't care about his looks.

One minute.

He stood up, making sure his tight black shirt was wrinkle free and that his arms were folded behind his back as he waited for the bedroom door to be opened, for his training to begin.

It was only another four years, two months and twenty days before he would be back home where he belonged. Not that he was counting.

CHAPTER ONE

The black, floor-length dress was modest, high in the neck but low in the back as she posed in front of the mirror. Alice knew as she walked that flashes of her legs would be seen through the almost indecent slits down each side. Not necessarily appropriate for a charity Gala, but perfect for being able to access the twin daggers strapped high on her thighs.

She hated shopping, which was why Sam was the one who went and purchased the dress specifically for the Gala.

He would make a great wife, she mused to herself.

A flash of light caught her eye, her favoured sword sitting where she left it a few months back.

According to Dread, it had been her mother's, a traditional blade passed down through the family. It was still bittersweet that she never received it from her parents, that they would never be able to see her use it. That she would never get to ask why the blade flashed with twinkly lights now every time she touched it, glowing runes that only appeared when she either stroked the steel or held the hilt. Writings she couldn't understand.

It had never happened before. Not to her at least.

Not wanting to think about it, or the man who could also make the steel glow, she faced the mirror once again, glancing at the elegant lines of the dress as she applied a dark lipstick.

Struggling with the zip she strode down the stairs into the living room, surprised to see Sam stretched out on the sofa half asleep in a way only a feline could. He let out a little sneeze, his eyes opening a slit as he appraised her outfit with a knowing smile. He really enjoyed shopping.

"Come here baby girl..." He motioned for her to stand before him, his movements lazy as he reached for the hidden side zipper. "You look delish, all those rich snobs won't know what hit them."

"You know this is a work thing," she said with a grin.

This was her first contract in months. Well, technically it wasn't a formal contract, but that couldn't ruin her mood. She was joining a team of Paladins as security for the charity 'Children of the Moon,' an organisation that helped young children who suffered from life-threatening illnesses caused by the vampira virus.

The Gala was held yearly in the Grande Hotel, a sizeable, flashy event that allowed a handful of celebrities and the local wealthy elite who used the limelight generated to showcase their own personal wealth.

"Does that mean they have cleared you from medical leave?" Sam asked as he started to play with her hair, curling it around his finger before pining it artfully into a bun.

"I've been cleared for weeks."

Her doctor had declared her healthy and strong enough to get back to work.

Dread, on the other hand, had disagreed.

She had asked daily to get back to the hunt, almost squealed in delight when he had said he needed her for that night.

"That's it, you go have fun with the uber-rich while I stay home with Mr Shorty over there," Sam sighed, stepping back to admire his work. "Bloody thing is back, almost gave me a heart attack."

"What?" She looked at him like he was crazy. "Oh, you mean Jordan?"

"Aye," he nodded towards the space beneath the stairs.

Following his gaze, she searched beside the cardboard boxes that still held some stuff they were yet to unpack. At this point, she had no idea what was in them, clearly something unimportant if they hadn't noticed anything missing.

Beside one large box stood Jordan the gnome, his fists clutched tightly around a fishing rod, face frozen into a smile. With his blue coat, green belt and red-capped hat, they had no idea know how he had ended up there. He had just appeared one day and hadn't left since.

She had tried to return Jordan to Al, his rightful owner, on numerous occasions but the happy fisherman somehow always made his way back. Whether it was sitting by the tree in the garden, hiding in a cupboard in the kitchen or lying on the bottom of the bed, the gnome never left for long. They had no idea how it moved, just knew it could when no one was watching.

They tried not to think too much about it.

"What do you think, Jordan?" She twirled for the gnome. "Don't I look sophisticated?"

Of course the gnome didn't reply, just continued to smile wide.

"That good, huh?"

"Stop playing with it, we're trying to get it to go home," Sam scolded. "If you keep acknowledging it, it might never want to leave."

"Don't be so silly. It's an inanimate object."

Just one that liked to move around on its own.

Sam snorted as he tilted his head to the side, his ear twitching.

"Your ride's here."

Sam moved towards the front door, opening it as Dread approached in a full black tux. Alice had been best friends with Sam for years, knew shifters' mannerisms well but their heightened senses still amazed her. Something she wished she had.

Not that she disliked being a witch, but being able to see in the dark and hear over great distances always seemed pretty cool, especially when she was on a contract.

Definitely could have used those skills a time or two.

Although, the whole shifting into an animal whose instinctual personality could take over seemed too much of an effort.

"Sam," greeted Dread before turning his dark gaze towards Alice. "You look appropriate."

"Wow, thanks," she replied, deadpan.

"Now, young man," Sam began in his poshest fake voice. "You will have her home by midnight?"

"Or what? She turns back into a hag?" Dread replied, his face unimpressed.

"A hag?" Alice cried. *That's bloody rude.*

"How dare you insult her," Sam responded, fighting to keep his face stern. "I'll have you know she will turn back into a pumpkin."

Alice noticed Dread's mouth twitch, his dark eyes narrowing.

"Duly noted."

She scowled between them. "We ready to go?"

"Yes, follow me."

Dread walked towards the black BMW where a man dressed in a chauffeur's outfit stood beside an open door.

"Take a seat, and I will brief you."

Deciding not to comment on his abruptness, she slid in beside him, thanking the driver quietly as he closed the door behind her.

"Take this."

Dread handed her an earpiece, a small flesh-coloured ball that fit inside her ear. She adjusted her hair to hide it.

"It has an inbuilt microphone. Once we get to the event, it will be turned on, and you will be able to communicate both ways with Rose, Danton and a few security personnel."

"Okay."

She sat there, fidgeting with excitement.

There had been several months of hospital appointments, physiotherapy and boredom. She knew if she didn't get back to work she was going to combust. Sam had taken some time off to spend with her, for which she was grateful, but he never left her alone. While she had appreciated everything he did to help her while she was recovering, he hadn't given her any alone time to figure out what was next. Even now, she wasn't sure.

"You're squirming," Dread said, frowning. "What's wrong?"

Oh, I'm just trying to figure out what the fuck I am.

She looked away, hoping he didn't catch her internal dilemma from her expression. "It's been a while since I've been useful."

"You weren't ready," he stated, which was his usual response.

Weren't ready, my arse, she hissed inside her own head.

Dread had always taught her to get on with life, regardless of what happened, and a lot had happened. Yet he had stopped her from returning to work, wanting her to 'take time to recover.' As if sitting at home with an overbearing leopard would have helped.

"So what's the plan for tonight?"

"The plan is for you to be my plus one."

He double-checked his silver cufflinks.

"We are to clap at the appropriate moments and pretend to be interested in what everyone has to say."

"Sounds thrilling."

He turned to stare at her, his heavy eyebrows dominating his aristocratic features. His face was slightly flushed, the result of a recent feed that gave him an almost human look. It made him dangerous, even with the obsidian ovals he called eyes, ones so dark she couldn't tell where the irises started, and pupils began.

"A threat has been made against the charity patron Markus Luera, as well as some other members of the board. As a precaution Mistress Valentina has asked for some Paladins to be present."

"Valentina? As in Councilman Valentina?"

"Stay away from her Alice, she's mean and powerful. You would likely upset her."

"Upset her?" Alice questioned before she noticed his slight smile.

Upset her my arse.

"You are to pretend to be interested in the event as a guest, not security. You are to keep your eyes and ears open and communicate with the others without giving yourself away."

The car jolted as it was driven across the cobblestones, getting closer to the red carpet Alice knew would be presented.

"As much of a pain as you are with following orders you have a great eye for detail, which is why I have chosen you to act the part of a rich, charitable woman rather than staff."

Alice fought not to beam at the compliment, had to chew the inside of her cheek to stop from grinning like a maniac. She didn't usually need vocal recognition of her ability, she knew she was good. At least, good enough to have not allowed herself to be killed. But Dread didn't do compliments.

"Tell me more about this threat."

A proud smile curled Dread's lips.

"The threat was received anonymously a few days ago, no signature or prints. A typed warning stating that Mr Luera is the intended target."

"Target of what?"

"That is what we're here to figure out." A friendly voice spoke gently into her ear.

Alice felt herself smile.

"Hey, Rose."

"How come you get to be all prim and proper?"

"Just lucky, I guess."

Alice felt the car slow.

"Bonsoir, ma petite sorcière. I see we are no longer slacking, non?""

"D, nice to hear from you too. You guys found anything yet?"

Lights flashed beyond the darkened window, silhouettes moving behind the glass.

"No, the guests have only started to arrive."

"Radio silence please," Dread said as the car came to a complete stop. "Alice, remember to smile."

The red carpet was already full of tuxedos and evening gowns, paparazzi trying to syphon through the guests to the celebrities.

Walking slowly down the carpet on Dread's arm she stopped and smiled at the reporters asking him questions, her gaze sweeping across the crowd.

Faerie lights had been draped between the street-lamps, creating a fallen star's effect that was eerily beautiful against the darkness of the sky. The red carpet was a darker red than she anticipated, the fine fabric a flutter of activity from the flashes of the photographers.

Gently escaping from Dread's grasp she made her way towards the entrance of the hotel, not wanting to take attention away from anyone else.

The interior was just as beautifully decorated as the outside, a selection of large round tables having been placed around the edges of the grand room, all draped in white linen with silver candelabras. Located at the centre was a large wooden floor placed in front of a pop-up stage. A podium was set up between two display stands, displaying the Children of The Moon's logo as well as a selection of photographs.

Accepting a glass of champagne from a member of the wait staff Alice placed herself with her back against the wall, able to see the entrance as well as all the guests already walking around.

People chatted amongst themselves, ball gowns and tuxedos mingling as each person tried to compare their wealth of diamonds and expensive watches. Alice recognised a few familiar faces from television, a well-known architect as well as a famous movie actress. The Mayor of London was chatting happily to someone beside the stage, his big gut bursting at the seams of his tuxedo.

"You must be the infamous Alice Skye."

Alice spun towards the woman who spoke, her dark hair blending into the black ball gown she wore on her tiny frame.

Standing at barely five feet, Valentina looked nothing like Alice thought she would, her black boatneck dress emphasising her flawless pale skin with a fitted bodice flowing into a floor-length silk skirt. She looked almost like a child playing dress up.

"Councilman," Alice greeted, nodding her head gently.

"Dread has told me so much about you." Valentina smiled, her ruby red lips tipped at the corner. Alice fought her instincts not to step back from the predator's smile.

This woman is powerful.

"All good things I hope." Alice met her eyes, her own smile wavering as she saw the sombre depths. She thought Dread was old, but this was...

"Alice, it is time to take a seat," Dread interrupted, grasping her arm and pulling her toward a table.

"Mistress Valentina, I hope you make time for me later, we have much to discuss about your trip to London."

"Bonsoir Commissioner Grayson, I was just speaking to your Alice." Her smile was full this time, fangs peaking as white tips against her lips. "It is rude to interrupt us women, non?" A gentle laugh. "How is my youngling doing? He only has praise for you and the organisation."

"Your watchdog is doing well."

"As expected," Valentina nodded. "My Danton has been with me for centuries, I do miss him back in Paris."

Watchdog? Alice thought, sipping her champagne. *Danton's her watchdog?*

"If you trust me to do my job, then you should be able to remove your mole from my Tower." Dread forced a smile.

Valentina let out a laugh.

"Mon ami, we wouldn't have put you in such a prestigious position if we didn't trust you," she said, dark eyes narrowed.

"Alice, be careful of the Mistress," Danton spoke quietly in her ear, careful for the other vampires not to overhear. *"Do not underestimate her."*

She fought not to reply in anger, only remembering at the last minute he wasn't actually in the conversation. How long has he answered to Valentina? Where were his loyalties?

Saving the thoughts for later she did a quick sweep of the room, trying to find him amongst the staff.

"Please, take your seats," a mechanical voice asked.

"Ah." Valentina reached out to touch Alice's hand, her palm cold as she gave it a little squeeze. "It looks like we are almost ready mademoiselle, please find me later. I would love to chat more." She let go slowly, her fingertips lingering on the pulse on Alice's wrist before she wandered off towards her seat.

"Alice, we're over here." Dread guided her with a hand to her back, pulling her seat out for her when they got to their designated table.

Questions bubbled up her throat, her mouth opening to ask before she quickly closed it. It was the wrong time and place, there were too many ears. She needed to get her head back in the game, she could interrogate Dread and Danton later.

"Something smells off," her earpiece rattled.

Alice tipped the champagne flute to her mouth, pretending to drink so she could reply. "What do you mean?"

"I smell something acidic, but can't tell where it's coming from," Rose replied. *"I'm in the kitchen."*

Alice thought about that for a second. Rose's nose was closer to her panther than human, could smell scents everybody else didn't even know existed.

"D?" Alice whispered quietly, making sure her head was down. "Go see if you notice anything unusual." Vampires had sensitive noses too, albeit not as good as a shifter.

The reply came swiftly.

"Oui."

A waiter dressed in black slacks and a neat white shirt came up to the table, a blood red napkin draped over his right arm.

"Could I get anybody some drinks?"

"Order me a glass of the Chateau du Sang," Dread replied before anyone else could get a say in. "My companion will just have a glass of water." He quickly added before Alice could order herself. Scowling, she clutched her champagne closer.

You're working, remember. His eyes glared.

Yeah, well technically, so are you. Her own eyes replied before he turned into a conversation with the man beside him. *Fuck sake.* She savoured a small sip of her champagne, enjoying the bubbles as they burst on her taste buds.

There were only two people she could have a wordless conversation with, have a strong enough bond to be able to read their expression. Dread had brought her up, had been her parental guardian since the death of her parents.

"Are you sure you would not like some fresh blood, sir?" The waiter asked Dread.

"Anybody holding a red napkin is available," he said as he tipped his throat, holes marking the lightly stubbled flesh.

"I would like fresh," a man opposite interrupted, his grey hair slicked back in a modern style, a complete contrast to the Victorian style suit he was wearing. His fangs were long and pearl white, a shade similar to his pale, yet withered skin.

The thing with vampires is that you couldn't really tell their age at a glance, he could be ten years undead or one hundred, his aged skin unusual amongst most Vamps. The majority of humans applied to be changed before they became thirty, the wrinkles that the vampira virus couldn't remove were fixed before his turn. From the number of wrinkles, Alice guessed he had been turned before The Change, where vampires, as well as all Breeds, hid among the humans. From the state of his skin, his life before wasn't a prosperous one.

His lady friend, on the other hand, was clearly new, her pupils dilating every time somebody came close, her tongue licking the inside of her lips. She would have been around twenty-five when she turned, as per the law stating all candidates must be in prime health and between the ages of eighteen and thirty-nine.

Before the laws, the death rate of the newly turned was around eighty per cent, the virus temperamental, which was one of the reasons why The Council created the candidate process. The second reason was an agreement with the humans back when they were negotiating Breed citizenship that vampires – who were the only Breeds that were originally human – could only be turned under a strict process. This gave the Norms a false sense of control so they didn't have to worry that they would be overrun with the living dead.

"So do you let your date order for you every time?" a male voice beside her asked.

"Excuse me?" Alice spun toward the dark-haired man. "He isn't my date," she replied before thinking. *Bollocks, yes he was.*

"Well, that's going to make flirting a hell of a lot easier." The stranger's mouth erupted into a full smile, highlighting a single dimple in his left cheek. "The name's Nate Blackwell." He held out his hand, flaring his chi in greeting.

"As in Blackwell Casino?" She felt his chi brush against hers, fuzzy in its sensation.

Blackwell Casino was one of the newer skyscrapers built in the southern district, a beast of a building that stuck out like a sore thumb against the protected Victorian structures that surrounded the expensive area.

"That's the one."

"Alice." She clasped his hand, allowing some of her own chi to reciprocate, just enough to seem polite, but not enough to encourage.

"Alice." He seemed to taste her name on his tongue. "Pretty name. Haven't seen you in these circles before."

"I don't normally get invited," she replied with a genuine smile.

"Well, I hope you get invited to many more."

"One, two. One, two." A man started to tap the microphone on the stage, testing the sound.

"Looks like it's about to start."

Alice continued to sip her champagne, ignoring the water the waiter had placed beside her.

"Then I guess I will be chatting with you a little bit later," Nate said with a wink.

"Welcome everybody to the tenth consecutive charity gala and the first for 'Children of the Moon.' If you could please put your hands together for the charity patron, Markus Luera."

The speaker on the stage clapped, stepping down as another man took his place.

Markus Luera was dressed in a tailored dark blue suit with black bow tie, his white beard was a shock compared to his jet black hair that was spiked up at every angle possible. Holding a cane against his tanned left arm he held his hand over his breast pocket, smiling to the crowd before turning towards the central table.

"Mistress Valentina, it is a pleasure you could join us."

He gracefully bowed, dipping his head before standing straight.

"It is an honour that you would grace us with your presence for a charity so close to home."

Mistress?

Alice studied Markus Luera carefully, noticed the nervous gesture of his hand as he tugged at his cane. Mistress was Valentina's title from other vampires, as a member of The Council she stood for all the Vamps, was essentially their leader, their voice. 'Mistress' was supposed to be a label of respect. Or fear. Which meant Markus Luera was a vampire, one with a tan.

Vampires don't tan.

Valentina smiled at the attention, waving elegantly from her seated position.

"Monsieur Luera, I'm interested to hear from the guest speaker, I hear he has been exceedingly generous."

"Then I will keep this short and sweet, Mistress."

He turned to address the crowd.

"Friends, I have gathered you here today to highlight the great work 'Children of the Moon' have been doing for the local children affected by their horrible inflictions. The actions of my fellow board members have helped over one hundred younglings with their life-changing conditions, building moon rooms for the children to live out their final days safely. As it stands, we are closer than ever to a cure, every donation counts towards a future where children who are born with the vampira virus will be able to live to an age where they can survive the transition."

The room was quiet, everybody listening intently as Markus passionately spoke about the condition that had affected around five per cent of children. They still didn't understand the disease, couldn't comprehend how the virus could attack a child while still in the womb of a parent who wasn't a vampire.

"As you have all paid the £10,000 entrance fee you are all greatly thanked by the children who are still going strong, and by the children who are yet to be born."

Holy shit, this cost £10,000 each?

"But my next guest has gone far and beyond to help out the children. He and his family have donated a total of one million pounds over the last year to help build a research facility here in London. Please welcome with open arms, our guest speaker, Mason Storm."

Alice choked on the final bit of champagne, the bubbles bursting in her throat as she tried to control her breathing. Eyes around the table shot to her in annoyance, sniffing and tutting in displeasure at the disruption. Dread silently handed her a napkin, his attention not wavering from the stage. Coughing into the linen, Alice watched as Mason smiled to the audience, their applause loud and over the top.

Her heart skipped a beat once she noticed the other man who joined him on stage. Anger, embarrassment, and, weirdly, excitement all flowed across her brain too fast for her to really decipher. Her emotions were chaotic as she watched Riley stand beside his father, a beautiful redhead clinging to his arm.

You have got to be shitting me.

CHAPTER TWO

Alice clapped along with everyone else, her ears unable to pick up the speech Mason delivered as her senses concentrated on Riley. She didn't understand why she had this reaction to him, a man who was there when she was at her worst, someone who pretended to care and then vanished. It had been months since she last spoke to him, last saw him, last thought of him.

The man who saved her life.

She still felt the attraction, his black tuxedo blending in with the tattoos that danced across his throat every time he swallowed. She knew his eyes were grey, like a storm that his name represented, that he had a faint, barely visible scar that started high on his cheekbone and finished at the top of his upper lip, the same lips that were once electric against her own.

Yet he had still left, not giving her a reason.

Staring at him now she knew it wasn't him she missed, it was the answers he possessed. She still couldn't recall with any certainty what had happened, her memory of the night she received the Daemon's bite blurred and disjointed. She had hoped he would tell her.

Riley saw her then, his eyes flashing in surprise as his smile wavered. The redhead on his arm pushed her breasts into his arm, speaking gently into his ear as she battled for his attention. Riley responded, his mouth moving silently as he replied, but his eyes never left hers. The redhead was tall, almost as tall as Riley in her red heels and dark pink, exceedingly low cut dress.

"Alice, I think you need to come see this."

Alice blinked, welcoming the distraction from Rose. Quietly excusing herself from the table, she made her way towards the back of the room, following the waiters through a set of double doors. The kitchen was large, full of gleaming stainless steel cabinets. Chefs wearing white aprons worked frantically to prepare the five-course meal that was to be served sometime in the next few hours. A waitress leant against a wall beside the ovens, a colleague holding a white sheet against her throat as red seeped through the cloth.

"Excuse me, no guests are allowed back here." The waiter holding the cloth exclaimed as he applied more pressure. "You need to leave."

"Over here."

Danton's head poked through another door, his eyes a warning as he ushered her though.

"Please, don't," he whispered to her. "I'll explain everything."

Alice gently nodded, understanding. They had been friends since her first day as a Paladin, so she would allow him time to explain.

"We found this." D moved to stand beside Rose, her nose scrunched up as she gripped a white shirt in one fist. Her panther prowled behind her eyes, Rose channelling her beast's instincts.

"What is it?" Alice accepted the shirt when it was held out, not understanding. "It's just a shirt." The same one all the waiters wore, including D and Rose.

"It smells acidic," Rose said, her voice deeper than usual. "We found it in the alley."

Alice couldn't smell anything.

"D, what about you?"

"It smells sweet," he shrugged. "The blood on the wrist smells the strongest, étrange."

Alice glanced at the small mark on the sleeve even as she made her way to the emergency exit. The alley behind the hotel was surprisingly nice, considering it was full of dustbins. The cobbled stones, that were the same as the front pathway, shone as if they had been polished to a high shine. Lights flooded the small area, mostly from the many windows of the guest rooms high above.

"The smell is strong back here," Rose said, her eyes flashing as she took a step forward.

"Wait." Alice held up her hand, making sure they stood by the door as Alice slowly walked forward, following the barely visible droplets of blood.

"Morte," D muttered under his breath.

"There's a body slouched against the brick."

Alice bent at the knee, making sure her dress didn't dip into the pool of blood embellishing the cobblestones, the lights from above making it look like a giant jewel glistening in the night. Rose and Danton wouldn't have been able to see the body from the door, the man hunched enough to be hidden behind the furthest bin.

"He smells acidic," Rose whispered, turning her nose away.

"He smells sweet," D frowned, crossing his arms across his chest.

"He smells dead," Alice added, recognising his uniform as a waiter from the Gala, one without a shirt. Blood stained the front of his bare chest, a sea of red wet against his skin. "It's his neck."

She turned his head, having to use some strength when his muscles resisted.

"He hasn't been dead long." He wasn't stiff enough to be in full rigor mortis. "He must have been killed just as the guests were arriving."

Alice studied the few small holes in his flesh, neat, not what she was expecting considering the amount of blood. "He was a blood donor." She released his head, cringing when it didn't immediately drop back to its original position. "He shouldn't have bled out this much."

"I'll call The Tower, we need to get someone down here," Rose said as she got out her phone.

"He's a Norm, you'll have to call the Met too," D added.

"Do you think I don't know that?"

Alice left them to bicker, not wanting to be away from the party for too long.

Slipping back into the main hall she spotted Dread standing at their table. The speeches had finished, so the guests were mingling amongst themselves as soft music filled the room from the pianist in the corner. A small crowd had appeared on the dance floor, their bodies slowly swaying.

"Commissioner..." She began politely before she felt someone jerk her shoulder.

"Alice." A hand encircled her wrist, pulling her away from the table and into the array of the dancers.

"Riley?" She tugged against him, his grip like iron.

"What are you doing here?" he asked as he pulled her toward him, clasping their hands together until he moved her into a gentle dance matching the rhythm of the piano. She allowed him to lead, not wanting to make a scene as she tried to catch Dread's attention. She didn't have time for this.

"I was invited." Well, technically, she was still a guest.

Riley narrowed his eyes, it was obvious he could not imagine how she could afford a ticket. She tried not to scowl in response.

"What is S.I. doing here?"

He controlled their dance, moving seamlessly between the other dancers. She was lucky he could lead so well, she had no idea what she was doing. His hands started to crush into her hips, his fingers finding their way up the high slits of her skirt.

"You're working, I can feel your knives."

She yanked his hands away, trying not to draw attention to herself.

"Maybe I like always to be armed." She caught a look behind his shoulder, Mason staring at them from beside the stage, his face like granite as he followed them across the dance floor. "Your dad doesn't seem impressed with our dance."

"Wouldn't take it personally, he doesn't like anyone," Riley said as Alice tried to hide her laugh, the noise escaping in a snort. "You look... good, your aura is much better than the last time I saw you."

"Yeah well, growing back most of your aura isn't a fun experience, I wouldn't recommend it," she quipped. "Not that you would know."

"Look, I haven't come here to upset you. I just need to talk..."

"You've had several months to talk. I'm not interested."

She had searched for him, wanting to know what happened with the Daemon. Yet she couldn't find him. He had left her at the hospital once her aura was stable enough and disappeared, left her to figure it all out for herself.

She turned her head away, not wanting to look at his face. Her eyes immediately wandered back to Mason, Riley's father talking to the redhead with pillow breasts. The woman abruptly turned to stare, her eyes shooting daggers as she puckered her cosmetically enhanced lips. Alice couldn't tell from this distance whether it was a permanent enhancer or just a charm.

"Well, this was a nice dance. But if you mind..."

"I'm trying to talk." He gripped her harder. "I've been assigned as your Warden."

"My what?" Rose buzzed in her ear, the noise a hum she couldn't concentrate on.

"Look, this wasn't my decision. The..."

"May I interrupt?" a voice interjected. "I would like this dance."

Riley pulled her against his chest, his arms enclosing her as he spun them away from Nate. "Fuck off Blackwell," Riley snarled, his eyes flashing silver in a warning.

"The lady clearly wants to leave. Go be with your bimbo over there." Nate nodded towards the redhead. "Didn't think you were into forcing women, Storm."

"Excuse me, gentlemen." Alice slipped beneath Riley's arm.

"Enjoy dancing together."

What the hell was a Warden? Her mood darker than before she finally made her way back to the table, her ear still buzzing as Rose and Danton argued.

"For goodness sake just call it through," Rose moaned.

"I thought that was your job?"

"Can't you see I'm a little busy here?"

"His heart stopped a few minutes ago, you can stop holding his throat now."

"Guys," Alice tried to break into their dispute. "What's happening?"

"Another waiter has died, bled out." Rose quickly replied, breathing heavily.

"We need to talk to all the staff," Danton added.

"We need to shut this thing down," she murmured to herself, reaching out for Dread. The man opposite her started to choke, the Victorian clutching his throat as he began to convulse, blood spluttering from his mouth to cover his shirt.

Alice raced towards him, catching him as he fell to the floor while his date screeched beside them.

"Help me!" she shouted at the hysterical woman as she struggled to hold his weight.

Another guest reached over to help, laying the Victorian onto the floor safely away from the table. He suddenly shouted, throwing himself forward as a fountain of black poured out of his mouth. The violent movement pushed Alice away, the black liquid barely missing her as she watched his spine twist at an impossible angle.

"What's happening?"

"Can someone call 999!"

"*Alice, we have a problem,*" Danton said into her ear.

"Yeah, well I have a problem of my own," she muttered into the microphone, scanning the crowd for Dread. He stood with his back towards the wall, his eyes razor- sharp as he took in the chaos surrounding them. A feminine scream brought her head around, another guest convulsing as her eyes bled down her porcelain skin.

Dread began to bark orders, people running in panic as they tried to escape. Among the confusion, Alice noticed a single waiter wearing a smirk. He watched everything unfold while he held a cloth against his throat, the fabric turning a pale pink.

She caught his eye, his own flashing in panic before he turned and ran towards the back of the hotel, towards the lifts. Without thinking she followed, her dress wrapping around her legs as she ran through the crowd.

"HEY!" she shouted after him. "Fuck sake." She kicked off her heels before unclipping one of her knives. Within a few seconds she had sliced off the bottom of the dress just above her knees, leaving the remaining fabric behind as she followed the blood trail quickly up the carpeted stairs.

The hotel's décor was minimalistic, pale grey carpet with white walls and wood panelling, helpful when tracking the blood. Trailing the droplets, she walked down the hallway lined with closed doors, her back to the wall as she listened intently. She had already noted the map by the elevator, knew there was no exit this direction other than the way she had already come.

"Hey, what's happening down there?" a man asked as he opened his hotel door, his face angry as he stepped into the hall in just a towel.

"Get back into your room please, sir."

"What, you a stripper or something?" he said before he spotted her knife she still had in her hand, his face becoming ashen before he ran back into his room. She couldn't really comment, she could feel the breeze on her bare legs.

Red smeared against the wall, leading around a corner.

A woman shrieked, running past her from the direction of one of the bedrooms. The door was ajar, showing the minimalist design flowing elegantly throughout.

The waiter was half crouched, half collapsed beside the bed, the sheets soaked through with blood as if he had tried to stem the flow.

"Are you okay?" Alice asked as she quickly checked the room for threats.

The bathroom door was open, the oversized mirror allowing her to see it was empty from her position. The room itself was large but bare, giving her confidence there wasn't anybody there other than the two of them. She sheathed the knife.

"Why did you run?" she asked as she knelt beside him, watching his eyes glass over as blood seeped from between his fingers. "Let me help you."

With a last burst of energy, he jumped to his feet. "You can't help me." He pushed past her towards the balcony. Unable to stop him in time she watched him disappear several floors below.

CHAPTER THREE

The bus screeched as it pulled up at the end of the road. Alice tried to step off with as much dignity as she could muster, ignoring the open stares from the other passengers.

She looked deranged, wearing a dirty evening gown with the hem badly ripped. Her hair was no longer in its bun, the blonde strands tickling her bare neck and shoulders. She wasn't even wearing shoes, the heels having been lost in the commotion.

Dread had been forced to leave the event early, leaving Alice the option of walking home or public transport. Luckily she lived in London where night buses were a thing, although apparently that was when the weirdos liked to ride. Which proved how unstable she must have looked, as no one would sit next to her, preferring the crazy cat lady or even the man who had chatted happily to himself.

Curtains twitched, letting light leak into front gardens as the curiosity got the better of her neighbours. She's sure she'd hear about her unsocial behaviour from Mr Jenkins a few doors down as soon as dawn broke.

He had candidly introduced himself as the head of the Neighbourhood Watch, one who expected complete decorum from his street. He had almost had a heart attack when he once found Sam as a leopard sleeping in the windowsill, soaking up the sun. The fact Sam was a shifter didn't bother him, it was the fact he decided to shift in full window view to give him a wave.

It was unfortunate that clothes didn't reappear magically once shifters changed back into their human form.

Alice personally thought it was funny, but she was used to shifters aversion to clothing. They liked to touch too, their animalistic personalities finding it comforting while everybody else thought it was invasive.

Mr Jenkins liked to remind her repeatedly he had lived on the street for over fifty years, meaning he had probably known her parents. She had decided not to ask him if he remembered, it didn't matter. She had accepted their deaths, was no longer haunted by them. So she allowed him to moan at her for Sam's indecent behaviour, their loud music and her late nights. He meant no harm, just an old man who needed to fill in the loneliness since his wife passed away.

Alice stopped cautiously by her front door, her eyes scanning the darkness before settling back on the medium-sized box that was sitting in the middle of her welcome mat. Warily she approached, wishing the Neighbourhood Watch that Mr Jenkins gloated about so often actually worked.

"What's that?" a voice asked from directly behind her.

Jumping she turned, not having heard anyone sneak up behind.

"You almost gave me a heart attack!" she glared as Riley stepped out from the darkness. "What are you doing here?" She didn't want to talk with him right now, she had a strange box to deal with.

"I thought you might have needed your shoes back?" he smirked as he held her heels on the ends of two fingers. "I also wanted to compliment you on the lovely legs."

His eyes travelled down past the poorly cut dress, his smile telling her he was messing around.

"What do you want Riley? It's late."

She glanced at the box again, wondering what it was. She wasn't a shifter, so couldn't smell its contents and she didn't know any spells that could check whether it had a curse on it or not.

She didn't have many options, one: kick it, run away and hope for the best. *I'm sure that would amuse Riley.* Or two: pour salt water over the box, ruining the curse and possibly the contents. That's if it even was cursed, which was entirely possible knowing her luck.

"We need to talk," he said as he swung her heels gently. "I'm also pretty interested in why you have something dead in a box on your doorstep?"

"Dead?" Surely he was joking.

Riley stepped forward, bending down to open the cardboard before she could stop him.

"Wait, it could be a trap..."

"What the fuck Alice?" Riley looked at her, mouth agape as the lid of the box flapped open.

"Keep your voice down," she hissed as she peeked inside.

She could barely make out the shape, her crap porch light barely illuminating the dark object. She had only just got rid of the latest ravens that had nested there. They returned every time she cleaned them out, breaking the bulbs every time. It was getting to the point that she might just let them be.

"Why do you have a severed head in a box?"

"A head?" It came out a squeak.

Unlocking her front door she ushered him through, pushing the box past the threshold with her foot. The house was dark, Sam had left for work a while earlier.

"Did you say a head?" she asked in disbelief as she turned on a light.

"You're clearly making friends," he commented as he looked around the living room, his eyes stopping on the gnome that was sitting on the sofa. "A friend who likes to send decapitated heads."

Alice didn't respond, instead looking into the cardboard box at the thick head of black hair. She didn't want to touch it but found herself needing to know who it was. Gently lifting it by the scalp she scrunched her nose, trying not to make eye contact with the pallid white eyes. The head had been neatly sliced off, the skin almost perfect other than some slight third degree burns along the edges.

"Holy shit," Alice dropped the head, cringing at the noise it made when it hit the wooden floor before rolling away.

"Who is it?" Riley picked it back up, studying the face in detail before turning to her. His nostrils flared, an eyebrow coming down as he stared.

How can he hold it so comfortably?

"No one, I don't know her," she replied too quickly, not wanting to tell him it was the Necromancer who had been finding candidates for The Becoming, the same witch that burned away her aura.

"You're lying to me."

He placed the head back in the box, folding his arms across his chest. She had only just realised he was still in his tux, the bow tie slack against his lapels.

"Am I?" She didn't owe him anything.

She knew as soon as she recognised the head who had left her the present. Would do anything to protect him. It was why she would never tell, never want Riley to look in his direction.

She had only seen fleeting glimpses of her brother in the last few months, a shadow that wore dark jeans and black hoodies. She hadn't even told Dread, not wanting to draw attention. Her brother was broken, the slave bands that encompassed his neck and wrists bonded to him on a level she couldn't comprehend, so she couldn't tell anyone, not until she knew for sure he wasn't a danger, to himself or others.

At least, not a danger to people who didn't deserve it.

"Why are you here?" *Please fuck off.*

"We should discuss this Warden thing." His eyes flickered to the box. "And I'm still interested in the head."

"Firstly, that isn't happening," she dismissed him, turning to climb the stairs towards her bedroom. "Secondly," she shouted down from the top, "it's my head, not yours. Now thank you for my shoes, but you can leave."

She wasn't going to be forced into something she didn't want to do, especially with a man who seemed to bring the worst out in her. She could feel it even now, her chi energised as it felt his own unconsciously caress hers. Could feel her fire grow within, desperate to get out, stronger in his presence. It was as if he was a battery, her personal charging cell, a catalyst that she didn't understand.

She didn't have time for him, not when she was searching for her brother, was searching for answers to her ancestry. She didn't need a Warden, a babysitter. He would just get in the way.

She angrily stripped off the remaining fabric of her dress, tossing it on her bed as she unclipped her knives.

Bloody stupid druid.

"Alice, we need to discuss this." She heard his deep voice through her bedroom door.

"I asked you to leave."

"Look, this wasn't my choice," he said through the wood, the door rattling as if he leant against it. "I don't want to do this…"

"Of course, you don't. You have such issues that you couldn't answer my questions before you..."

The door crashed open.

"You need to calm down." His eyes were pure silver.

Fire choked her throat, could taste smoke on her tongue as sparks crackled between her fingertips.

"Alice." Her name came out a growl as his hand clamped down on her forearm, his palm warm on her skin even as the intense heat dissipated. "Calm down." Riley's tattoos gently glowed, the patterns hypnotic. "Don't tell me about issues. You know nothing."

"Exactly. You told me nothing."

She calmed her breath, flame receding as she fought it back down. She hadn't had a flare up in weeks, had thought she had it under control.

"How can you do that?"

She broke the connection, stepping back. He had syphoned her excess magic, taken it into himself. Something he had done before, but something she didn't think she needed. For weeks she had been training, practicing bringing herself to the peak of her power then back again without a flare out. Something that would have taken her a few minutes to calm down had taken him seconds.

He wiggled his fingers, his eyes slowly returning to their usual grey.

"Magic."

"What are you?" she asked, a question that had haunted her for almost as long as she had known him. She always wondered if that's why he had never come to see her, she saw more of him than he wanted to show. "You're not just simply a druid."

She would know, her father was one. Technically her brother was one too, only males inherited the genes to harness ley lines.

His eyes became guarded.

It seemed everyone had secrets, some just more interesting than others.

"Shouldn't I be asking you the same question?"

Alice started to laugh, the sound on the edge of hysteria before she noticed her reflection in the mirror.

"Why am I always naked around you?" She quickly grabbed the closest shirt, the black fabric covering enough to pass for modesty.

Riley's eyebrows shot up before his face crumbled, a smile breaking through.

Her shirt read *'I hope you like animals because I'm a BEAST in the bedroom.'* She tugged the hem down.

"It's one of Sam's," she said in its defence.

"Sure." He didn't seem to believe her. "Cute bedroom."

"It's a place to sleep."

It was her old room, the walls the same baby pink covered in glittery stars from her childhood. She had decided to leave the painting until the summer, just adding accents of creams and greys to help it resemble more of an adult's room. She couldn't think of anything worse than staying in the master, so had allowed Sam to have it.

"Why are you even here?" she asked.

"You invited me."

The fuck I did.

"I vividly remember asking you to leave."

She was getting tired, knew there were only a few hours left before she had to be at The Tower. She had wanted to speak to him months ago, now she couldn't get him to leave.

He ignored her, instead wandering across to her chest of drawers where he picked up a trophy she'd won when she was five before his eyes settled on a photograph.

"Your family?" he asked as he handed it to her.

"Yes." She stroked the glass of the frame before putting it down.

"You look like your mum."

"Why does my dad not have as many tattoos as you?" she said, a lump in her throat.

That had always confused her, she had initially recognised what Riley was from those runes tattooed onto his skin, her father having had similar around his wrists. Yet she had never seen another druid with as many as Riley. She knew they held spells, but wasn't sure exactly what.

"You have something against tattoos now?" He crossed his arms, leaning back against the doorjamb. "That your brother?" His eyes moved back to the photograph.

She nodded, not adding anything further.

"You've never mentioned him."

She didn't say anything, instead her eyes traced the photograph.

"I don't have any siblings genetically, but I have a group of friends who I consider my brothers."

Alice looked at him then, surprised he told her something so personal. He had always been business, prioritising his job as a Guardian for The Order over everything else. Not that she had any idea what that was as, unsurprisingly, he never explained. The only fact she knew were what she was told as a child, that it was an organisation strictly of druids.

"We trained at school together," he continued.

"School?" she echoed. "I could never see you as a schoolboy." No, she could only ever imagine him as he was now. Never a defenceless child.

"It's our childhood that defines us."

"Maybe," she quietly said, undecided whether she agreed or not. "Why are you telling me this?"

"I don't know." He seemed confused himself. "But you need my help…"

He stopped her when she began to interrupt.

"The Council have decided you need to be trained in both self-defence and magic."

"Why a Warden? Why you?"

Why couldn't it be anyone else?

"I don't need any help." She moved into the hallway, forcing Riley to follow her back down the stairs.

"I don't know why me. I was told, not asked."

"So you're The Council's puppet?" Alice said as she played with a flame along her fingertips.

She felt her anger renewing, needed something to help control it. She had never had problems with her temper before.

"Leave."

She began to open the front door, Riley's palm slamming it closed.

"You really aggravate me sometimes, Alice. Stop cutting off your nose to spite your face."

"I'm not." She wasn't. Was she?

"The Council can go fuck themselves. I have no interest in their petty politics."

He watched the flame carefully, his jaw clenched as he towered above her.

"You're an adult, a fucking Guardian. You could have said no."

She extinguished the blue sparks with a light pop, instantly missing the small heat.

"There aren't many people who can do what I do."

"I don't need any help," she repeated, the words sounding less convincing even to herself.

"Really? What was that earlier then?"

He stepped impossibly closer, crowding her against the wood.

"Why do I feel it when you're about to lose control. It's like this intense heat against my chi." He lifted his hand, almost as if he was physically feeling her aura.

"I know what I'm doing."

She didn't want him to touch her, her pulse erratic in his presence. It was overwhelming, especially as she fought for the control she desperately argued she had. She was tired of it, tired of men having an overpowering effect on her. It made her reactions feel forced, unnatural, as they were with Rex.

"Sure you do sweetheart."

"I need you to leave."

Riley tensed as Alice stood her ground, his jaw tight as he looked down his nose at her. This was all her patience had left.

"We're not finished."

"Tonight we are."

Riley growled, his breath close enough to brush her face.

"Stop being a brat. You need my help whether you want it or not. I'm not going to let you combust because of your bloody stubbornness."

Riley let go of the door, allowing her to open it a sliver.

The winter air tangled with her shirt, the coldness separating them, allowing her a second to calm down.

"I guess I will be seeing you around."

She stared at the door, not wanting to know his expression. She didn't want to ask for help but understood she needed it.

It wasn't really Riley she was furious at, it was everything else. The feeling that her life wasn't in her control, that she was helpless in the hands of the universe that laughed at her tragedies.

She refused to fail.

Her eyes landed on the cardboard box that was still where Riley had left it, wondering why Jordan the gnome was curiously peeking inside.

When life gives you lemons.

You squeeze them in the bastard's eyes.

CHAPTER FOUR

Alice exited the lift on the forty-second floor of the Supernatural Intelligence Bureau – also known to the locals as The Tower. The usual drab grey cubicles were a welcoming sight as she made her way to the space she had occupied for the last five years.

She broke into a grin at all the cards and notes welcoming her back, enough to hide the cat-themed knick-knacks she kept on her desk. An unopened bakery box had been left beside her computer, Alice's smile changing to a smirk once she saw the note scrawled on the inside.

'About time you got your lazy arse back.'

From the handwriting, she knew it was Rose.

"Oh, I didn't realise you were back," Michael sneered as he wandered over. "I heard you were still hospitalised."

Alice plastered on a fake smile, hiding her grimace from the coffee stench Michael always seemed to emit. It was like he bathed in it, or used it as fuel. She couldn't stand Michael since she had trained with him at the academy. She wasn't sure why, but had decided long ago it must simply be a character flaw that he was such an arsehole.

"Nice to see you too, Mickey," she said, smiling at his scowl. "How has it been?"

"Oh, you know, the usual. Don't worry though, I've taken up your slack," he said in an ostentatiously pompous tone. He flicked his head back, moving his shoulder-length ginger hair away from his eyes.

She had always thought it was a beautiful colour, but would never tell him that to his face.

"Been working with the big guys recently. There's a lot of change comin' you know." He sniggered, flicking at his hair again. "Ya betta watch out."

"Hey Michael," a squeaky voice said from behind them. "Your latest assignment has landed on your desk. Oh, doughnuts."

Barbara, Dread's assistant, grabbed a jam filled doughnut from the bakery box, biting into it aggressively.

"Don't mind if I do."

"Help yourself."

Alice quickly closed the lid on the box, saving them for later before Barbara – also known as Barbie due to the likeness to the doll, could devour anymore. Alice smiled, waiting patiently for Barbie to finish the treat, which included sucking her fingers clean of the excess sugar.

It had only been a few months since Alice last saw her, but Barbie seemed to have aged, her nickname not as apparent. The once platinum blonde hair had darkened a few shades, especially at the roots and the baby pink nails that were usually well- manicured were chipped, partially bitten. Even her charm, the magically infused necklace that helped to hide her wrinkles seemed to be expiring, her wrinkles blurry but visible against her unusually pale complexion.

"Nice to see you Barbara." Mickey grinned, winking at her blush. "I guess I'll be speaking to you girls later."

"Hope you enjoyed your holiday Alice, it's been so stressful around here recently," Barbie said once Mickey moved back to his own desk, her eyes following his departure for longer than necessary.

"It wasn't a holiday,' Alice sighed, shaking her head. "I was on medical leave."

Barbie continued as if Alice hadn't spoken.

"It's been a nightmare," she whispered, her attention becoming distracted with Michael before returning to Alice. "New rules are being implemented, and The Council keep making surprise visits." She seemed flustered at just explaining.

Maybe that's why she looked so unkempt.

"The Council have decided they want a more hands-on approach with the organisation."

Barb opened the box of doughnuts back up, selecting an iced one before closing the lid again.

"It's become unbearable. Those council suits keep commenting on my job. Bloody bastards if you ask me..." Her eyes darted to Alice, shocked at her own comment. "Please don't tell Commissioner Grayson I said that."

Alice just smiled. "Is there anything I can help you with?" *Like more doughnuts?* "I need to get to work."

"Oh." Barbie brushed the crumbs from her fingers onto the floor. "The Commissioner wants to see you."

"Dread?" Alice frowned. She had only just got there, surely he couldn't find an excuse to check on her already?

"Oh Alice, you really should call him Commissioner. It makes you look tacky and unprofessional when you call him by his forename," Barbie said with an absent wave of her hand. "It's called work etiquette."

Alice was about to reply with a snarky comment but kept it back. It was a habit Alice couldn't break, she had always called him his given name since she was a child. Their relationship wasn't known in The Tower, Dread never mentioning it and neither did Alice. It kept accusations of favouritism to a minimum, not that he ever gave her an easy time because of his parental guardian status. Probably the opposite.

"Thanks, Barb, I'll keep that in mind." Alice grabbed her satchel, tossing the strap over her shoulder as she made her way to the back of the floor.

"Alice, welcome back."

Dread's office was dark, the window that hid one of the most beautiful views of London hidden beneath a specialised blackout blind. He seemed to reflect his mood with the blind, wanting to sit in the dark when he was angry or indifferent. The majority of the time the blind was down.

"Take a seat."

Alice sat down heavily , a frown pinching her eyebrows.

"What's this about? I spoke to you yesterday."

"I have your assignment, I wanted to hand it over personally."

"Why?" she asked, apprehensive. Dread didn't hand out contracts personally. The last assignment he administered directly ended with her being hospitalised.

It wasn't a good omen.

"Fine, I wanted to talk to you before you return to active duty."

He studied her, his gaze creating a chill on the back of her neck. He was angry, but she wasn't sure why.

"I want to make it clear that it wasn't me who signed off on your return. I still don't believe you're ready…"

"How can you not think I'm ready?" She surged onto her feet, Dread's eyes eerily following her outburst. "I have done…"

He didn't give her the chance to finish. "We haven't discussed your recovery."

"I'm healed, what else is there to discuss?"

"You haven't spoken to anybody about it, not even Samion. That's unhealthy, you might be suffering from PTSD…"

"I'm not, and I'm fine."

She truly was. She no longer gave it much thought, had gone past it almost instantly. It wasn't the actual incident that frustrated her, it was who had put her in that position in the first place. She no longer thought of him anymore either, not wanting to waste competent brain cells. Besides, it wasn't like she hadn't suffered accidents while at work before. She had been bitten on numerous occasions by both Vamps and shifters, nearly sliced in half by an irate leprechaun and now almost sacrificed by a Daemon.

"Alice, I'm not going to give you a choice." Dread scowled as his eyes turned dark with impatience. "If you will not discuss it with either myself or Sam, you will talk to your doctor. Otherwise, I will remove your Paladin status."

"You can't do that!" *Fuck. He can do that.*

She watched the warning flash across his face, knew he wasn't messing around. Biting the inside of her cheek she sat back down, tapping his desk with her fingertips.

"I don't want to go back to the doctor."

She had been forced to go weekly for months to become a lab rat.

She had agreed at first, just as interested in what her power could do. It was what kept her up at night, her magic and ancestry an enigma she wanted to understand. She knew nothing of her heritage, had hoped learning about her magic would bring her a step closer to knowing.

But not at the expense of herself, her sanity. Because they weren't helping her, forcing her to do test after test while explaining nothing. She figured out pretty quickly they were only interested in the effects her fire could create, as if she was a weapon they were figuring out how to harness. So instead of reacting, she had kept calm, controlled her chi, much to the frustration of the doctors. Then she stopped going entirely.

She hadn't had a flare up in weeks.

Until Riley.

"Alice, listen to me. It is paramount you keep going. We don't have a choice."

"*We* don't have a choice?" Alice felt irritation flicker.

"Please." That one word broke her. Dread didn't beg. "Keep attending until I say so."

Alice thought about it for a moment.

"It's The Council, isn't it?"

Dread smiled, a slight tug at his lip.

"You were always an observant child. Yes, it's why you have been assigned a Warden. The Council have decided your power flares are unpredictable. They do not like unpredictable."

"Do they know why?" She had never told Dread the names she had been called, wanting to figure them out on her own. Dragon. War. Now she wondered if he actually knew all along, as The Council seemed to.

Dread took a moment to reply, the vein in his forehead pulsating.

"They suspect you're a descendant of one of the Elemental families, a Draco to be exact."

"And what do you think?" she quietly asked, her heart in her throat.

"I think that I have kept that information secret for as long as I could, for your own safety."

Alice closed her eyes, taking a second.

"You shouldn't have kept these sort of secrets from me." Her voice was hoarse when she spoke, her lips trembling. He had known all along.

"No, I shouldn't," he agreed, which shocked Alice. "For that, I apologise. I kept this knowledge from you because The Elementals aren't revered, they're feared for their power. But, after your recent incident, I trust it would be wise for you to understand your ancestry. There's an exhibition on The Elementals in the National Museum, I believe it would be wise for you to visit."

Alice nodded, not sure what to say. Dread wasn't a traditional father, but he had brought her up to the best of his ability, and she loved him for it. She understood the sacrifices he had made to look after her, even more so now. She couldn't be angry at him for that.

"Have you had any reports on Kyle?"

Kyle had visited her a few times over the last couple of months, barely letting her catch a glimpse. She wasn't going to mention the head in the box, she hadn't really thought up an appropriate excuse.

"Short sightings over the city. I have decided to let him be for the time being. He will come home when he is ready."

She wanted to protest, demand he come home straight away. She was becoming impatient, not wanting to leave him to wallow in his own self-pity. She knew first-hand the consequences.

"You going to show me this contract yet?"

"It's an assignment, not a contract."

Dread handed over a manila envelope full of documents and photographs. Flipping it open Alice scanned the front page.

"What you have is all the witness statements and photographs of the recent genocide where a total of eight vampires were poisoned."

"The Gala?" Alice scanned the images, noticing how all the dead looked eerily similar.

Bodies that slumped at abnormal angles as if the spines couldn't support their weight, their skin shrunken, dehydrated with black veins visible through the paleness. Blood covered the majority of the areas surrounding them, the red turning to black.

"I thought this would be handled by The Met?"

The Metropolitan Police handled everything to do with homicides for both the Norms and Breed. They called Paladins – the official name for her role within S.I. glorified bloodhounds as their jobs were to hunt down and track the Breeds The Met weren't trained to deal with. After the Breed was detained, they would be handed back.

"It is. However, new protocols have come into place. The Council believe there is still a divide between humans and Breed, to help close that divide they have implemented a programme where detectives in The Met can ask for Tower assistance. This has been in the works for a while now."

"What does that mean?"

"It means you are on retainer until further notice. You will be working with a team chosen to investigate these murders. The lead detective on the case will be in contact sometime today."

Alice clutched the manila folder to her chest, a grin creasing her cheeks.

"I won't let you down."

CHAPTER FIVE

Checking the motel name, Alice parked next to an unmarked police car, ignoring the disgruntled looks from the men in uniform as her car spluttered to a stop.

She loved her Beetle, the first and only car she had ever bought. Unfortunately, no amount of oil changes or services would save it from the inevitable. It was a miracle the old rust bucket had survived as long as it had, it was old even when she bought it five years ago from a dodgy looking selkie.

It had been cheap, which is what she had wanted at the time. To be fair, that's what she wanted now. Alice loved her job as a Paladin, enjoyed the investigative hunt, the thrill of the chase. She did not, however, enjoy the high mortality rate for a crap wage. Hazard pay was a curse word when brought up to the board of directors directly above Dread. They believed the honour of serving justice was payment enough. There was a reason Paladin enrolment was declining rapidly.

"Excuse me, ma'am, you can't park here," a uniform said from beside the yellow police tape. "Can't you see the area is closed off to civilians?"

"I was invited." She had received a phone call minutes after leaving Dread's office asking her to attend. "I'm the liaison from S.I."

He didn't seem to believe her, even when she showed him her badge.

"I'll handle it from here officer."

A man she recognised as Detective Sullivan O'Neil stepped forward.

"Agent Skye, a pleasure to see you again." He wore a long black trench coat over a white shirt and tie, a packet of cigarettes sticking out of his breast pocket.

"Detective O'Neil," she nodded in greeting. "I'm surprised to be here in all honesty."

Over three centuries of peace between humans and Breed and there was still prejudice. Alice never took it personally, always wondered if it was a subconscious instinct that the majority of Norms tried to limit their interaction with people who could eat, maim or kill them by accident or otherwise. The Met was no different.

"Aren't we all?" He adjusted the single cigarette that was tucked behind his ear before shaking her hand. "I assume you've been briefed?"

"Not really."

She shrugged at his displeased look.

"Well, the basics are you have been selected to be part of a team specialising in the more... abnormal crime cases."

"Abnormal?" she asked. "What do you mean abnormal?"

"You will see." He nudged her to follow him through the car park. "As it stands, the statistics of a human on human homicide is around a sixty-eight per cent charge rate. However, add any Breed to that mix, and the percentage drops dramatically to around twenty-five per cent."

"Why do you think it's so low?" Alice asked as she followed.

The motel was just off the motorway, a large building with around five floors as well as a separate one-storey structure that faced the road. O'Neil guided her past the main building towards the other side of the carpark.

"My superiors believe it's human ignorance."

He shrugged, stroking his goatee in thought as they approached the crime scene, third door from the left.

"I can't say I completely disagree."

"What do we have?" Alice said as she stepped past the threshold, careful to not disturb the blood that had soaked into the carpet.

"Is this our Breed consultant?" A man the size of a wrestler, asked from beside the bed. He wore an identical trench coat to O'Neil, his expression less than friendly. "She's smaller than I imagined."

"Agent Skye, this is my partner Detective Michael Brady." O'Neil shot his partner a warning look. "You'll get used to him."

"Fuck you, Shelly." Detective Brady scowled, turning his dark eyes, almost as dark as the ebony of his skin, towards Alice. "What are you? We haven't been briefed other than we are expecting somebody from S.I."

"I'm a witch," she said as politely as she could. "Are we going to have a problem?" How was she expected to work with someone who was that instantly hostile?

The distrust seemed to disappear, replaced with caution.

"I didn't mean to cause offence. Now let's finish here so I can go home to my wife."

He seemed to take a long look at the body before moving to stand by the open door.

"You should stop calling your hand your wife, it's creepy man." A short skinny man stepped inside the room. He was wearing a full body white plastic sheet, including the hood. "You must be the new member of Spook Squad, the names Jones. Pleased to meet ya."

He went to shake her hand before he pulled back, noticing the red smear across his glove.

"Oh, sorry," he grinned, his brown eyes flashing in mischief.

"Spook Squad?" Alice asked, looking between the three men.

"Ignore it," Brady said. "Stupid uniforms think it's funny," he huffed as if he wasn't pleased with the name, or being a part of the 'Spook Squad.'

"Is this the whole team?" she asked, her gaze sweeping across the room before settling on the body spread-eagled on the bed.

"No, Officer Peyton is dealing with the manager." One of the men replied, from the deep tone of voice, she guessed it was Brady.

"This is a strange situation to meet everyone," she murmured as she carefully moved towards the bed, trying to get a closer look.

The motel room itself was budget, the front mainly glass with a door covered by an ugly green brocade curtain. A woman lay splayed naked across the duvet, her arm at an awkward angle hanging off the side of the mattress. The bed sheets, Alice guessed, would have matched the brocade curtain, the pattern the same but the colour darker, almost black as it soaked the blood.

A syringe had fallen through her fingertips, track marks consistent with the size of the needle decorating the inside of her arms. Blood had seeped from the tiny holes, red and shiny as if it was fresh. Bite marks bruised the inside of her thighs, the bites neat compared to the jagged horizontal scars along both her arms.

"There's too much blood." Almost her entire lifeblood. "She didn't clot."

"We haven't confirmed, but it seems so, the whole of the bed as well as a good circumference of the carpet is soaked through," Jones said. "The wounds suggest feeding."

"A blood junkie?" Alice turned back to the door, noticing how only Detective O'Neil and Jones remained.

A nod from O'Neil. "One of the boys also recognised her from the strip."

"Looks to be dead around twelve hours guessing from the state of the body," Jones chimed in, his suit crinkling as he fidgeted.

"There's no bag." Alice checked the bathroom, careful not to touch anything.

"Bag? Why would she need a bag?"

"She would at least have a bag with spare clothes, maybe even a small suitcase."

Alice searched around the room, bending down to check underneath the bed. The frame was too low to be able to fit a suitcase beneath, and the wardrobe was completely open. Someone had smashed the door from its frame, leaving only the hinges.

"There isn't any makeup. Surely if she were a professional, she would have everything within easy reach?"

"What are you saying?"

"I'm saying she never planned to stay here long." There wasn't even a spare pair of underwear, only the one lace thong that was just outside the blood's radius.

"So she's just passing through?"

"I can't say for sure, I don't have much experience in the field. But if you were a sex worker, surely you would want to freshen up between clients?" Or at least have a packet of condoms to hand.

"It's an interesting thought. Officer Peyton might know more."

"Okay." Alice took one last look at the blood, the previous night's conversation with Danton and Rose giving her an idea. "We need a Vamp."

"A vampire?" O'Neil looked surprised. "Why would we need a vampire? You're the Breed expert."

"Firstly, I'm not technically a Breed expert. Just because I'm a witch doesn't mean I know everything. Secondly, this condition looks similar to an event that happened last night."

"You talking about the Gala? You should have received information regarding the genocide from the Commissioner, but it's the Norms involved we're interested in right this moment."

Detective O'Neil touched his cigarette, almost reassuring himself it was still there.

"Several human waiting staff died of blood loss last night, surprising considering their wounds were considered minor."

"It's called exsanguination," Jones added. "Although an official coroner report hasn't yet been published."

"Why would a team specialising in abnormal Breed cases be called in for blood loss?"

"It isn't the waiters we were originally called in for."

O'Neil opened a breast pocket on his jacket, flipping open a black book and reading his notes.

"Eight vampires died within a small time frame of consuming, what we are assuming, was blood from the blood-waiters. All those affected had severe reactions to an unknown substance found in the blood. The five waiters who were affected all bled out from the bites, wounds that wouldn't normally be fatal."

He snapped the book shut.

"So they bled to death." Alice nodded, confirming her suspicions. "What can stop your body's natural healing mechanism?"

"We're waiting on the lab to confirm, but we're suspecting it's some sort of poison. If it is, it will help explain what happened to the vampires."

"You think they're both related?"

"Why do you think we're here?" Jones smiled cheerfully. "Exsanguination is a pretty common C.O.D. but not like this. It's interesting that we have found another body in the space of twelve hours that has also bled out in suspicious circumstances. So until we prove this otherwise the case is also ours."

Alice looked at the fang marks decorating the dead woman's thighs.

"That would mean we're looking for another body."

"We have uniforms patrolling. The suspected poison was safe long enough in the blood-waiters for a few hours, at least. The vampires that ingested it had symptoms roughly thirty to sixty minutes after."

He seemed to frown to himself before locking eyes with Alice.

"You asked for a vampire, why?"

"One of my colleagues smelled something unusual about the blood of a blood-waiter we found in the alley. It could help to confirm if it is, in fact, the same substance."

"Interesting." O'Neil passed a look to Jones.

"On it," Jones said quickly as he scurried out the door, his white plastic overall creaking as he moved.

"Fascinating team," Alice said as she waited by the door.

"You could say that." O'Neil sniffed as if displeased before allowing a police officer in uniform to pass into the room.

"Detective, how may I be of assistance?" the newcomer asked.

"Officer Dunton, could you please see if you can smell anything unusual about the deceased."

"Sir." Officer Dunton looked surprised but nodded before entering the crime scene carefully.

"You have a vampire on the force?" Alice questioned, shocked. Breed didn't get hired into human law enforcement.

"He's new. Good guy, keen to learn."

O'Neil turned back to the officer as he approached.

"Sir, I'm not quite sure what you need, but the room smells sweet."

"Sweet?" O'Neil turned to Alice, an eyebrow raised.

"Officer Dunton, what does blood normally smell like to you?"

"It usually smells like copper, sir."

Alice stepped outside, allowing the clean air to remove the smell of death from her nose. She nodded as Dunton left the crime scene, his face puzzled as he went back to his post by the small crowd that had gathered.

"You think you can handle this?" O'Neil asked when he joined her, a lit cigarette between his lips. "I know Paladins don't usually deal with this side. You will need a strong stomach."

"I can handle It."

Paladins were usually behind the chase, not the investigative side. Her standard contracts consisted of finding an unruly shifter who pissed in the wrong garden or tracking down a black charms dealer. Not investigating a gruesome murder.

"We heading to the manager's office?"

"Hmmm." He took a drag of his cigarette, savouring before blowing out the smoke. "What made you think of a Vamp?"

"My vampire colleague stated the blood smelled sweet. Yet a shifter who has a stronger nose couldn't smell anything but death."

"That indicates they are targeting vampires."

"That's what I'm thinking."

Alice stepped into the small, stuffy reception. Who she assumed was the manager was sat behind an old desk, his eyes wide in panic as he flashed a look to Alice and Detective O'Neil.

The walls were covered in plastic that looked like wood and the window was partially covered by an off-white lace curtain. A thin key cupboard was beside him, covered in cobwebs. The room stank of tobacco, strong enough Alice desperately wanted to open the window to allow some fresh air in.

"I told you I don't know anything." The older man was dangerously thin with pure white hair. "I just found her there," he said as he nervously patted the sweat from his brow.

"Mr Johnson, my name is Detective O'Neil, and this is my colleague Agent Skye. You have already met Officer Peyton."

Alice glanced at Officer Peyton, his face blank as he appraised her. He was tall yet slim, his height dwarfing O'Neil, who was already four inches taller than her five foot five. His hair was white blonde, the strands just covering his ears while his eyes were crystal blue.

She kept her face blank as she assessed him back.

He isn't human, she thought to herself. Not that she could be sure, just a gut instinct. Fighting her reflex to touch his chi with her own she turned to Mr Johnson with a friendly smile as he paled.

"Why have you brought a witch? What is she going to do?" Mr Johnson licked his dry lips, his hands gripping the edge of his desk to the point his knuckles were white.

"How did you know I was a witch?" Alice asked, stepping back to give the man some breathing space before he started to hyperventilate. You couldn't tell at a glance what Breed someone was generally, especially a witch who just looked human.

"I feel you," he whispered, as if it was a secret.

"So you're a mage?" It was the only explanation she could think of. Mages were humans with witch ancestors. They had the ability to harness magic but generally weren't powerful. He probably felt her aura when she entered the room, hers would feel slightly electric compared to the others unless she concealed it.

"Can you confirm you're the manager here?" O'Neil asked before Mr Johnson could answer her question.

"Yes, sir." He visibly swallowed, his eyes darting back and forth to Alice.

Stepping even further back, she made herself as unthreatening as possible. Considering she was wearing jeans, a fluffy dark purple jumper and leather jacket she didn't think it was too hard. Luckily he couldn't see her Paladin blade strapped to her back beneath.

"How long has the victim been using one of your rooms as an... office, shall we say?" Officer Peyton said with just a touch of an accent she couldn't place.

"I have already told you this. I wasn't aware she was even a..." A cough, Mr Johnson collecting himself. "A lady of the night."

Bullshit.

You didn't have to be trained to see he was lying. His eyes were constantly moving when he wasn't checking to see if Alice moved. Every time he lied, he looked down, even when being directly spoken to.

"When did she hire the room?"

He licked his lips once again. "Yesterday, around three or four? I can't be sure."

"Did she sign anything? Leave credit card details?"

"No, she paid in cash up front," he seemed to sniffle. "She signed the guest book." He opened a drawer on his desk, pulling out a large plastic folder. "Look, here she is. Room three, Stacey Cartman."

"Stacey Cartman." O'Neil wrote in his little black book. "Anything else you can tell us? Did she have any visitors?"

"Surely CCTV would have caught something," Alice added.

"No," he squeaked. "We don't have CCTV here. She was the only visitor in the outbuilding. All my other guests are here, in the main building." He looked around as if he could see through the walls.

Alice froze, her head automatically turning towards the door as she felt something brush against her chi. Frowning she glanced at Johnson, then O'Neil, wondering if they felt something too. When they didn't react, she allowed some of her own chi to release, to explore around the room.

O'Neil was definitely human, his aura bland and unused. When her chi touched Peyton, he shot her a cautionary look. His chi felt human too, yet he knew when she touched it, which was impossible if he wasn't a magic user.

"What are you doing?!" Mr Johnson leapt from his chair, the hairs on his arms standing on edge.

"Sorry." She reigned herself back, giving him an apologetic smile.

Something brushed across her chi again, something hot. Her gaze shot straight to a shadow standing beside a lamppost on the other side of the motorway.

"Excuse me," she said as she felt herself walking past the police tape, almost without thought.

The shadow stood leaning against the street lamp, a black hoodie covering the face as the light flickered ominously overhead.

"Kyle?"

It had been weeks since he had allowed her to catch a glimpse of him and now he was only across the road.

Her brother stepped away, walking down the street in the opposite direction.

"Wait!" she called as she started to panic. "Kyle!"

"Agent Skye, are you okay?" Detective Brady came to stand beside her, his eyes scanning the road. "You almost stepped into traffic."

Catching her breath, she composed herself.

"Sorry, I thought I saw someone I knew." She stretched her chi as far as it could reach, unable to sense her brother who had disappeared into the darkness. She had never been able to feel him, only be able to see him as shadows.

Was he finally reaching out for her?

Or was he starting to lose control?

"We have a lead on Stacey Cartman. She's on parole for drug trafficking so we have a current address. According to the system, it was her husband that originally paid her bail so we're hoping he will be available for an interview."

Alice had one last look down the street.

"Okay, let's go."

CHAPTER SIX

Alice pulled up beside Detective Brady, his expression bored as he leant against his black BMW.

Out of all the members of her new team, Detective Brady seemed the most zealous, as if he took everything personally. O'Neil seemed indifferent, like he didn't care whether or not he was a part of the team while Jones was happy to be anywhere. Peyton, on the other hand, was just... other. She wasn't sure what to think of him just yet.

"Did you get lost or something?" Brady asked as he bent at his waist, close enough his breath misted up the window. "You getting out the car?"

Alice sighed, stepping out of her Beetle, eyes scanning the cheap housing estate. They were still in London, as far out as the Breed district could go before turning into the countryside. The small building was covered in scaffolding, making the entrance to the flats dreary and unwelcoming. The surrounding streets seemed to be deserted, in the way bad neighbourhoods did when they noticed someone from law enforcement.

"What do you expect to find?" Alice said as she allowed him to take the lead. The security door was broken, allowing them to enter into the hallway without being buzzed. The air stank of damp, the carpet squidgy beneath her boots as Brady looked around.

"Hopefully the husband can give us a timeframe," Brady grunted as he knocked on the first ground floor flat on the right.

After a few seconds he knocked again, harder.

"Hello? It's the police, open up." Another knock, this one hard enough to rattle the door, the cheap wood crashing open with a bang.

"Shit." Alice and Brady said at the same time, both drawing their weapons, Alice with her sword and Brady with his gun.

The room inside was covered in darkness, the curtains drawn and the lights off. An intense smell of decaying flesh assaulted their noses as they took a step forward, her blade giving little light as her runes glistened. Brady's eyes flicked to her sword, his lashes covering his expression before he quickly looked away.

"Hello?" he called, his deep voice echoing through the room. "Is anyone in here?"

Alice came to stand beside the overturned sofa, noticing a body half-draped across one of the cushions. The man's eyes were wide and lifeless, a single bullet hole in the middle of his forehead.

"It's clear," Brady said as he came to stand opposite. He reached up to pull at one curtain, illuminating the room in as much sunlight as the scaffolding across the window would allow.

"Bloody hell!"

What was once a standard living room had been covered in a green fluffy film. Almost every available surface surrounding the body had vegetation growing, grass, flowers and even toadstools. A table had been overturned, what remained of a copper spelling pot and crushed herbs scattered across the floor. Glancing back at the body, she noticed the green substance partially covered his flesh too.

"What is all this?" Brady opened the remaining curtain.

"He's been executed," Alice said gently, as if she could still upset the dead, which was debatable depending on who exactly had died.

"What makes you say that?" Brady knelt, taking a closer look.

"Just a hunch." She shrugged, unable to explain her gut feeling. "Can you touch his necklace?" It was costume jewellery, a red jewel encased in gold. She could see from where she was standing it wasn't real, the ruby plastic.

"Excuse me?"

"I can't reach it from here." She made eye contact with Brady, making it almost a challenge. She saw how he looked at her sword, wasn't sure of what it was until just now.

He didn't trust her.

His jaw clenched as he slowly reached for the necklace, hesitant as if it was going to bite him. As soon as his flesh touched the stone the glamour broke, the magic dissipating in a burst of sandalwood.

"Shit!" He snapped his hand back, eyes accusing.

"He's Fae."

Alice pointed to the body's new look, the one he was born with before he wore the charm that altered his appearance. Made him appear more 'normal.'

"Or at least half-Breed." The body looked more human than usual Fae, his skin a pastel green with eyes only slightly on the larger size. His hair – which was sacred to many Fae – was cut short, showing off his pointy ears. "Maybe even a dryad." It would explain the greenery.

"A tree nymph?" Brady looked sceptical. "Why was he executed?"

"Fae can't lie," she said before correcting herself. "Well, high caste Fae can't lie. I'm not sure about the lower caste."

It wasn't known whether they were unable to lie, or had simply been forbidden by the High Lords. It has made the majority of the higher Fae master manipulators, twisting words into half-truths. Just as The Council reigned over all Breeds, each Breed had their own ruler. For the Fae, it was the High Lords, the oldest and most powerful amongst their kind.

"He may have known too much information." Or just a small pawn in a bigger game, they would never know.

"They may be incapable of lying, but they can be perfectly dishonest with the truth," Brady said deadpan, almost as if he were quoting.

"That sounds like something the Church of the Light would say."

The Church of the Light came into existence around the same time Breed became recognised citizens. It was a place humans went to worship a god and condemn everyone that disagreed or was different.

All Breed were classed as different.

"My father was a minister," he said without any emotion. "I was brought up in the church."

"Is that why you don't trust me?" she asked before she even realised she spoke. "If your religion believes all Breed are inferior, then why are you on this team?"

She wasn't angry, just interested. Many different religions were strictly human, The Church of the Light was just the one that craved media attention the most. She didn't see Brady as someone who would follow such a strict faith.

"I never said I followed my father's beliefs." His face was stern, his body language closed off.

Alice decided not to comment further. Instead, she turned her attention back to the fake ruby.

"He's wearing the colours of the Unseelie court." The Dark Fae were a genuinely cruel race compared to their lighter brethren. Although being part of the Seelie Court, also known as Light Fae, didn't necessarily mean they were good.

"Fucking faeries," Brady grunted.

"Fae, not faerie. He isn't a faerie." That she thought, anyway.

"It's the same thing," Brady said as he glanced around the room.

She just shook her head.

"There's been a struggle." He pointed out a dent in the wall, shaped like a fist.

Leaving him to study the wrecked living room, Alice walked down the hallway, her eyes catching on a photograph beside the bed. A young man stood alongside a woman she recognised as Stacey, the woman found in the motel. His arm crushed her against his chest as they both smiled to the camera. Around his neck she could make out the gold chain, the fake ruby hidden beneath his shirt. They were beautiful, tanned skin with bright clear eyes, Stacey's hair was cut at the shoulders, several inches shorter than it was now. They looked like a genuine, kind and happy couple, their smiles not showing the poor choices they were yet to make.

The room was reasonably clean if a bit messy. The duvet cover wasn't made, pillows were tossed across the sheets while a large amount of lace and silk underwear scattered beside the pillows. A cardboard box was half open by the dresser, unopened boxes of condoms and sex toys tossed messily inside.

The moss, Alice noticed, hadn't reached the bedroom apart from a few toadstools that had started to grow beside the door. The greenery seemed to be growing in a controlled area around the circumference of the body. Fae died in strange ways, their bodies not decaying as others did.

This one was turning back to the earth.

Alice began to walk back to the living room when she spotted more spelling pots on the kitchen counters. Hesitating at the threshold, she looked back to see Detective Brady on his phone, his back to her.

Not wanting to interrupt she stepped toward the counter, frowning at the contents thrown across the countertop. Stacey's Breed hadn't yet been classified, the examiner had yet to do a series of tests to determine her true Breed. Even then it was not always accurate. From the herbs, she would have guessed a witch, the spelling pots and utensils not usually used by Fae, their magic much different. Dandelion, galangal and feverfew lay partially crushed as if she was interrupted while she was making a potion. Or she was just messy.

One copper pot was half filled with a dark liquid, and a few leaves Alice couldn't identify floating on the top. A small opaque tube connected the pot to a smaller one placed beside it on a high pedestal. Every thirty or seconds or so the unknown liquid would drip from the top pot into the bottom via the tube. The drop broke the surface of the dark water, creating a ripple effect that smelt of sulphur.

Scrunching up her nose Alice leant forward, trying to guess what she could have been making that would create a sulphur smelling concoction.

Only dark magic...

"What do you think you're doing?" A deep voice growled from directly behind her.

With a jump Alice turned, her arm knocking into the larger of the two pots, making the water slosh down one side. Instantly the countertop started to bubble, the plastic overlay warping as if it was in contact with intense heat. Within a few seconds the liquid evaporated, leaving a fine layer of crystal.

"Fuck sake Brady, why did you sneak up on me like that?"

He narrowed his eyes, his face stern as he looked around the small kitchen.

"What do you think you're doing?" he repeated.

"I wanted to know what it was." She gestured to the setup. "I wanted to see..."

The words escaped her, lungs tightening as she noticed the carvings on the counter. When she had accidentally moved the pot she exposed the pentagram that has been scraped into the plastic.

"Agent Skye?"

"There's a pentagram here."

She moved the rest of the pots gently to the side, exposing the whole pentagram.

"It's inverted." *Fuck. Fuck. Fuck,* Alice chanted silently to herself.

The chances of meeting a Daemon was one in a million, their Breed beyond rare.

The first time she met one, she was barely six.

The second time she almost died.

The chances of meeting one again...

"What does that mean? Don't you all use those stars?"

"It's inverted," she said as if that was explanation enough.

His face said differently.

"It's a sign of Daemonic worship."

Witches pentagrams consisted of a five-pointed star within a circle. An inverted pentagram was identical except it was flipped, the twin bottom points at the top, symbolic of Baphomet, the devil's ram.

"She could just be a fanatic."

"Maybe." She needed to talk to Riley.

"Guys I'm just finishing up!" A voice called from down the hallway.

Alice looked at Brady, his face thoughtful before he turned and left. Following she noticed a man was standing by the body, a large DSLR camera in one hand.

"Oh, hey, Jones."

"Who else would it be?" he said with a grin. "You find anything?"

She told him about her theory with the moss.

"That's fascinating. I don't get to work with many Fae, they don't seem to ever die," he said cheerily as he photographed the room from different angles.

"Agent Skye, you're our resident Breed expert." Brady started with a raised brow. "Aren't Fae immortal?"

"Tell that to the dead." She nodded to the body.

"Seriously though, in my line of work we see many dead bodies. In my fifteen years this is the first Fae." Jones finished his photography, his face screwed up in concentration as he measured something with his hand.

"Yes and no." Alice thought about her answer, her knowledge on Fae far from perfect. "Fae is an umbrella term, a faerie is very different from a troll yet are both are classed as Fae. The majority have longevity, they don't age in the same way as us, and they can't catch diseases."

She looked back down at the body.

"Although, clearly a bullet works."

"You said us. You're not one of us," Brady said nonchalantly.

Alice's response was instinctive. "My DNA would disagree."

It was how the majority of Breed remained undetected before the war. Scientifically her DNA matched that of a human, they didn't understand why witches were born with the ability to manipulate magic. Nor did they understand why shifters had human DNA when human and animal DNA when shifted. Scientists were still trying to figure that particular question out.

"Brady man, careful," Jones warned.

"I didn't mean anything by it." He seemed genuinely confused. "I don't care what you are, or where you're from. I care whether you can do the job or not."

"Ah, there's the usual grumpy old Brady," Jones laughed. "Alice, as you're new you get his extra offensive side."

Brady replied with his middle finger.

"Don't worry about it." For someone who supposedly didn't follow the Church of the Light, he sure thought like one. "You see something we don't, Jones?"

"The blood spatter on the wall behind indicates that the gunman was standing." Jones made a hand gesture of a gun, pointing it at the wall before frowning. Looking around, he opened the front door, stretching his legs to make himself taller.

"Right here. The victim would have been standing a foot from the door. The bullet entered straight through the frontal bone resulting in instant death. The momentum threw him back into the sofa, which overturned and landed him there."

"So are you suggesting the gunman didn't even enter the room?"

"Doubtful. The bullet hole implies it was a small calibre weapon, but it still would have been loud enough to force the shooter to leave immediately. The only other explanation would be if a silencer were used, even though they're not as silent as the name suggests but still quieter than a normal shot. There's no residue around the wound that I could see, however, to really know I would have to analyse the bullet and see if there are any deviations along the metal."

"Then who trashed the room?" Alice asked.

"Well the deceased wouldn't have been able to defend himself, so the abrasions along his right fist suggests he hit something solid..."

"Like a wall." Brady finished for him.

"Maybe there was an argument?" Alice shrugged, it was the only idea they had.

"Entirely possible." Brady got out a little black book from a pocket, identical to O'Neil's. "It would explain why Stacey used the motel to entertain her clients, rather than here."

"That's saying she brought her clients home, which is unusual but isn't unheard of. It might be worth talking to the neighbours." Alice said, moving towards the front door.

"O'Neil already has that covered, although I doubt anything will come from it." He scribbled something down.

"What makes you say that?"

"I find with estates like these all the neighbours have selective hearing."

He tucked away his book, his dark eyes appraising the room once more before settling on her.

"Agent Skye, it seems we're finished here." He gestured for her to follow him out the door.

Saying goodbye to Jones she exited the flat, noticing how O'Neil was questioning a neighbour a few doors down, his sighs audible as the neighbour repeatedly expressed they didn't know and hadn't heard anything.

Selective hearing. Alice would smile if their blatant uncooperativeness weren't helping someone get away with murder.

"So you gonna tell me why your face went white as a sheet when you saw that pentagram?" Brady asked as he walked her to her car. "We're not going to have an issue, are we?"

"What exactly are you suggesting Detective?" Alice stopped at her car door, turning so she was full on facing the Detective.

He didn't reply, his face like granite. If it was an interrogation technique, it was pretty good.

"Daemons haven't been recorded since the late nineteenth century." She opened her car door, throwing in her bag.

"That didn't answer my question." Brady placed his hand on the top of her door, his dark eyes barely blinking. She could tell he used his sheer size to intimidate and manipulate. Luckily she wasn't easily intimidated.

"Thank you for your help today, Detective." Alice smiled, showing teeth. "Now if you would excuse me." She pointedly looked at his hand. "I have somewhere to be."

With an irritated twitch, Detective Brady let go.

"You were right before. I don't trust you, and it isn't because you're a witch." He turned to his car. "Have a good evening, Agent Skye."

"Arsehole," she whispered beneath her breath, her eyes tracking him until his headlights had disappeared down the road.

Darkness had started to fall as they analysed the crime scene, winter creeping in as autumn gave way. She was going to have to be wary of him.

Alice was about to get in her car when she noticed a woman hiding behind an overgrown tree directly opposite the crime scene. She watched for a few minutes, deciding whether to approach. She could hear the woman's hollow cry, her eyes shiny as she watched unblinking from her hiding spot.

Unable to leave Alice cautiously approached, making sure her smile was friendly. "Hello, are you okay?"

The woman, pale as a ghost turned almost mechanically as if she was too petrified to move.

"Do you know what's going on?" She started to scratch her elbows, her nails broken and bit to the quick.

Alice debated on what to tell her, only now noticing how her pupils were huge, not reacting to the lights flashing from the emergency vehicles.

"They found someone in one of the flats." She decided on not enough information for details but enough to gain a reaction.

"Stacey?!" Her voice was a high squeak, her throat scratchy as she started to sob. "Was it Stacey?"

"No, a man." Alice wanted to comfort the woman who had wrapped her arms around herself, almost as if to control the tremble as her cries stormed through her body. "It was a man."

"Steve?" The woman sniffled. "I told her it wasn't worth it. I said we would find something else, try chemo again…"

The woman started to murmur to herself, forgetting Alice was there.

"Chemo?" Alice gently pushed, understanding this woman was not stable. "Was Stacey sick?"

The woman sniffed again as snot dripped down her nose before she wiped it off with a dirty sleeve. In fact, her whole outfit was dirty, mud and grass stains patterning the oversized coat and jeans. The woman's hair was dark and greasy, what was left of her cheap lipstick smeared across her face from the sleeve.

"Cancer." She choked out the word. "Doc's said there's nothing more to do, said they couldn't do anything else. I think they fucking stopped because we're working girls. Didn't want to infect their stupid clean hospitals with the likes of us," she snarled, anger breaking through the tears. "She was desperate, no money to go private. Couldn't figure out dark magic. Even got Steve to start dealing but it still wasn't enough."

She stood staring at the entrance to the flats, almost mesmerised.

"Santa offered her a lifeboat."

"Santa?" Alice stepped forward, trying to read her reactions without startling her.

The woman's head twisted around slowly, her face oddly blank.

"He looked like Santa. Old, chubby with a white beard. Said he could give her a special drink. Make her better again." She started to laugh, the tone on the edge of hysteria. "Santa can do that, you know? He's magic."

Another chuckle.

"Let the light guide you."

Let the light guide you? Alice repeated to herself.

"What's your name?"

"Name?" The woman asked, her eyes now wholly vacant. She had no idea where she was, either the drugs taking their toll or the grief.

"Can I take you anywhere?" *Like a woman's shelter.* "Can I get you some food? A nice warm place to stay the night?" *Anything.*

"Mia, my names Mia."

She started to sob again, the cries racking her body violently as she scratched at her hair, knotting the strands.

"I need to... I need to... go, yeah, go." With that she bolted away, leaving Alice to stare after her.

H e groaned as he held his ribs, the wind knocked out of him as he knelt on the black mat. They were trying to make him angry. Make him release his beast.

But he couldn't, he knew his beast was pure rage. Would destroy all of them, kill them as they had beat him.

They didn't understand. Couldn't comprehend the uncontrollable anger his spirit beast held. He understood, the boy. He no longer showed the anger that still made his blood hotter at the thought. No longer wept openly with grief.

Accepted what he could not change.

His beast could not.

Could not accept the death of their mother, the woman as peaceful as Goddess Gaia herself. The woman who taught him the old ways, of using the earth itself, using the ley lines. Not the way he's being taught now, with darkness and blood. Marking his flesh with permanent glyphs, making him stronger, faster.

Under their control.

They didn't know he didn't need them, he was already stronger, faster.

Choking out a breath he felt his ribs crunch. The teacher had broken them, again.

His beast would kill them.

CHAPTER SEVEN

Puffing out a breath, Alice scowled at the illegible writing scrawled along the edges of the page.
She didn't realise there would be so much waiting around while the investigation progressed. She wasn't used to following The Met's rules and regulations, she wanted to track down the perpetrator immediately, not wait around for the autopsy report.

She knew she was being unreasonable, but weeks of sitting around doing nothing was taking its toll.

So she had spent the majority of the last several days trying to figure out what her mother had written, the notes doodled beside instructions in the leather-bound grimoire.

Each page, Alice had discovered, held different spells, potions and wards the majority of which she had never heard of before, all scripted by hand.

Her success rate was precisely zero per cent. Two days and half a dozen potions later and not one had gone right. So Alice glowered at the writings, wondering if she was just a terrible witch or her mother's recipes were wrong. She had followed the instructions, as much as she understood, exactly. Yet all she had to show for it was one unhappy roommate, a half dead and overgrown garden, a hole in the wall and a smashed copper pot. A pot that, somehow, had exploded into several shards that were still embedded into the kitchen wall and would stay that way for the foreseeable future. Or until she bought a step ladder.

Sleeping Potion

INGREDIENTS:
20 Lavender Stems
100 grams Valerian root
50 grams Hawthorn
50 grams Magnolia Bark
500ml goat milk
Handful of Straw

METHOD:
Bring the milk to a boil then add the valerian root and hawthorn. Meanwhile, burn the bark into fine ash and sift into the mixture. Continuously stirring with a copper spoon add the lavender. Cover and leave to boil for a further two minutes. Once the timing is up, carefully pour the milk into a bottle, making sure to sift out all the remaining lumps using the straw.

Alice re-read the instructions for the eighth time, memorising them before she attempted it.

'Great defensive strike. Pour over the opponent for them to instantly fall into a deep sleep. Chance of death 0%,' was messily written beside the directions, making her wonder why her mum would need to know defensive spells considering she was just a simple gardener before her death. That's what she had always been told anyway. She doubted it now, wondering what her mother or even her father did to be targeted by Daemons.

It was why she was carefully studying the grimoire, looking for answers.

Since finding the inverted pentagram Alice felt a sense of urgency that her house was unprotected. She wanted to set a ward, a spell that helped to discourage evil influences and deflect misfortune. Human superstition believed good luck charms or even hand gestures did the same thing. Unfortunately for Alice, she felt a four-leaf clover or crossing her fingers wasn't going to be enough for her. But before she attempted something as complicated as a protection ward, she needed to master at least one potion.

Sitting back on her heels Alice adjusted her copper pot, making sure it was correctly positioned over the hot coals. This time – unlike the others, she had decided to create the potion within a circle she had carved into the tiled floor, salt teased into the grooves to act as an extra barrier. Big enough she could sit comfortably inside along with her instruments. The five-pointed star within a circle was ready, the candles in place at every anchor point. Lighting them in sequence, first earth, then fire, water, air and lastly spirit, Alice felt the circle materialise with an audible pop.

It always amazed her when she saw her aura reflected on the shimmery surface, the green and blue moving across the opaque surface, the same colours as her flame. Bringing her hand to barely a centimetre away from the barrier, she felt a gentle tingling along her fingertips, the colours swirling to concentrate on the almost connection before she moved away.

Auras were thought to represent you as a person, the colours reflecting your very soul and thoughts.

She wondered what hers said.

Reaching forward she grabbed a mouthful of her katsu curry, nibbling the chicken from the bowl in her lap. Sam was the chef in the house, so when he was home he would cook. When he was out Alice survived on leftovers, sandwiches and takeaway. Baking, on the other hand, she was quite good at but only if you preferred the taste to the look.

Setting down her fork Alice started the potion, waiting for the milk to boil before she added any of the ingredients.

"*Adolebtique.*" She flicked her wrist towards the coals, helping them burn faster so she could begin. Before she added the first herb, Alice checked the instructions, holding her breath as she mixed in the final lavender, happy the concoction didn't explode in her face.

She sifted the milk through the straw, smiling as the liquid settled into the small bottle, even if the colour was slightly purple. *It's supposed to be purple, right?* Popping a cork into the top she tilted it, watching the milk swirl with a gentle glisten. She had no idea if it worked, wasn't sure how she could test it.

BZZZZZ

Alice jumped at the distraction, frowning as she looked around for the noise, wondering if she had set off the fire alarm, again.

BZZZZZ

Her phone beeped from the table, the handset lighting up from the table.

"Shit. Shit. Shit." She scrambled to her feet, careful not to break the bottle that she clutched in her palm.

"Hello, this is Agent Skye," she said as she placed the potion onto the table.

There was a pause at the end of the phone.

"Hello, is this Alice?"

Alice checked the number, realising too late it wasn't any of the team, but an unknown number.

"Ah, yes, that's me. Can I help you?"

"This is the reception at Club X. I've been asked to call you regarding one of our employee's Ranger..."

"Ranger?"

"I apologise, I meant to call him Samion."

"Oh, Sam isn't available at the moment," she said, most of her attention on the bottle. "He's at work."

"Yes," the voice said dryly. *"He works here, that's why I called."*

Alice took longer than it should to understand what was said. Sam had only recently returned to work after taking time off to spend with her while she healed. He was supposed to be working at the Blood Bar.

"You're his emergency contact. The manager has asked for you to come speak to him immediately regarding syringes found in his locker as well as a bag of what we expect is Brimstone."

"You must be mistaken. Sam doesn't do drugs." She didn't believe it. He had promised, that of all his vices, he would never turn to drugs, even though his personality was that of an addict. They were each other's rock, had been since they first bonded as children in their trauma support group.

"Well, be that as it may, he was still found with narcotics. If you do not attend, we will..."

"No, no. I'm coming." Alice felt her pulse race, her nerves on edge at the very thought of Sam using any drugs.

"What's the name of this place again?"

The bouncer looked shocked when he noticed Alice standing before him, her hair messy and curry staining part of her basic grey T-shirt. In her defence, she had been in a hurry to leave, barely giving herself time to squeeze into some jeans and trainers. He was lucky she hadn't turned up in her pink unicorn lounge bottoms and rabbit slippers.

"Hello," she said a little breathlessly. "I'm here to pick up Sam."

She had pretty much run from the car, the traffic light at this time of night, or as light as traffic in a central city could be.

"You the new girl?" He looked her up and down, seemingly unimpressed. "You're not dressed appropriately."

"I'm sorry, I didn't realise there was a dress code for a nightclub," she replied tensely. What would he have preferred, her pyjamas?

He looked confused.

"Well, we technically don't have a dress code, but all the girls dress... erm..." He shrugged as he struggled to find the right word. "You're pretty, but not like we normally hire."

"I'm not a hire," she said sternly, "I'm here to pick up Sam." *What is he on about?*

"What?" he frowned, the fat of his face creasing. "Excuse me."

His hand went to the side of his face, pressing the small headpiece further into his ear.

"Oh, you're here to pick up Ranger. Why didn't you say so?"

Alice felt her mouth open, then thought better of it.

"You sure you don't want to change? You're going to stick out like a sore thumb in there," he chuckled to himself.

"I'm sure it will be fine," she murmured as he escorted her through the reception area. "Oh fuck sake, you've got to be kidding me."

"Have fun," the bouncer sniggered as he left her amongst the throngs of patrons and dancers.

Well, it could have been worse.

Alice had never felt overdressed before, but that's definitely what she was. It wasn't a night club like she had initially thought, but a strip club. The dancers were wearing barely any clothes and neither were the customers.

From what she could see in the dark, the room was all centred around one large stage with oversized speakers and flashing lights standing beside it. Dark wooden tables were strategically placed facing the stage, almost every single seat occupied with people drinking and squealing at the woman dancing provocatively in a latex suit, money hanging out of zips along the sides.

A few private booths were placed against the back wall, each with a metal pole speared through a circular table. Both male and female dancers stood on the tables, dressed in either leather or latex.

"Excuse me, ma'am, you need to find a seat," a soft voice said from beside her. "The show has already started."

Alice turned, her gaze taking in the short, dark-haired man with the most beautiful lavender eyes she had ever seen.

"Huh?" She could barely hear as the music pounded and the audience cheered.

"You. Need. To. Find. A. Seat," he shouted at her, his grip hard as he grabbed her forearm and leant forward.

Without thinking, she twisted his arm, dislodging him as he screeched in pain. "Ow! Ow! Ow!"

"Don't touch me," she hissed as she let go. "I'm here to speak to the manager."

Mr lavender eyes seemed to groan, his face contorted in pain.

"Do that again," he moaned.

"What? Hurt you?" Alice asked, horrified. *Where the fuck am I?*

"Ladies and gentleman..." A voice purred over the microphone. "May I introduce to you the man you have all been waiting for... Ranger!"

Alice automatically turned to the stage as a man dressed in full body leather walked out barefoot. White blonde hair blanketed around his shoulders, long enough to reach the small of his back. Alice felt her face burn as soon as she recognised Sam, his body like liquid as he danced to the music.

The audience went wild, men and women throwing money, underwear and other things onto the stage. As she watched, he started to remove parts of the leather, starting with the corset, allowing the golden flesh of his chest to show through.

Alice wanted to look away, her gaze locked as she watched her friend of seventeen years dance. She had never seen him in any other way than her best friend, their relationship a strong bond that had nothing to do with sex. Yet, even as her cheeks burned, she didn't look away, able to appreciate his beauty, his inner leopard giving him grace in his movements.

As more leather was removed the scars started to appear, getting a loud reaction from the audience, as if they were excited by the history of his abuse.

She watched as Sam's nostrils flared, his fingers curling to the point his claws threatened to break his skin. His ambers eyes scanned the crowd.

"Oh god, he's choosing."

"Pick me, pick me!"

"He's so amazing." People hopped up from their tables, arms raised.

Sam caught her eye, his own confused as he hopped down from the stage. She felt stuck in place as he stalked toward her, people's hands brushing against him as he approached.

"What the fuck are you doing here baby girl?" he whispered, his breath tickling her ear as she stood like a statue. He started to move around her, the crowd going wild behind.

"I got a call," she explained. "What the fuck do you think you're doing?"

"Just go with it," he said as he danced around her. Quickly, he bent her backwards, a hand at the small of her back as he leant towards Mr lavender eyes, their lips locking in a clash of tongue above her. The crowd erupted into a cacophony of noise, each shout barely distinguishable.

"That's it, I'm done." She pushed him away, conscious of touching his naked chest. She had never had any issues with his nudity, had accepted it was part of him being a shifter. But she couldn't handle it right now.

"Alice," he hissed as she started to walk away. "Come here."

His hand shot forward, grabbing her wrist in an iron grip.

"Take a bow." He pulled her down, a fake smile plastered on his face. "Follow me." He guided her behind a velvet curtain behind the stage, releasing her once they were out of view of the audience.

"What the hell was that?" She shouted as quietly as she could, anger bubbling. "What's going on?"

Sam shrugged. "This place was hiring, so I went for it." He crossed his arms, closing himself off.

"No, you don't get to do that." She pulled at his arms. "I don't care that you're a stripper, it's your life to do with it as you choose. I'm angry because of the drugs Sam!"

She felt her heart start to race, a warmth beside her face as her little blue ball of fire burst into a happy existence.

"Fuck sake." She tried to swat the light away, but it happily danced out of reach. Her 'Tinkerbell' as Sam liked to call it was an annoyance, appearing as a physical manifestation of her anger. No one knew what it was or how she did it. All she knew it was one of the most irritating things in the universe.

"Drugs? What are you on about?" He stepped back as Tinkerbell shot towards him. It never used to do that, actually attack people who she was angry with. It was more unpredictable since her power surge but also appeared less often. It took a lot of intense anger for it to appear, unlike before, when stubbing her toe would be enough.

"Someone called me, asking me to come here because they found Brimstone!"

"That's not mine!" He looked worried. "I took it from a friend. You know me, I don't touch that stuff!"

"Ah, you must be Miss Skye. You were down as an emergency contact on Ranger's documents." A man dressed in a dark suit approached, his gaze hard as he looked her up and down.

"Hello." Alice grasped his outstretched hand, her face frowning as she struggled to recognise him.

I've seen him before.

"I'm Mr Donald, but you may call me Mac. Shall we?" He urged them to follow him. "I appreciate you coming down so quickly, Miss Skye."

"It's Alice," she interjected as she closed the door behind her. Mr Donald sat down behind his desk, allowing them to either stand or take the two seats in front of him. She chose to stand as Sam leant against the door. "Why am I here, Mr Donald? I've spoken to Sam, and he has explained the drugs aren't his."

"It's Mac. I know they're not his…"

"Then why have you called me? This isn't school, I'm not his mum."

Mac looked irritated but continued. "I apologise with how we phrased the call, but I was hoping you would help me get the answers from Ranger. He isn't talking, he might see some sense if a friend were here."

"Still seems a bit ridiculous."

Sam smirked in agreement.

"We get the dancers regularly tested. We have a zero tolerance on drugs, recreational or otherwise. We need to know who they belong to."

"They will be gone immediately and will not be brought back on the property, what does it matter who brought them?" Sam said.

A bang, a heavy fist hitting the table.

"It matters because this is my fucking business and I will not let anybody who works under my name fuck that up!"

"I thought you said the dancers were regularly tested?" Alice asked.

"They are. However, I allow some people who aren't hired directly through the club to offer their... own product."

"He allows prostitutes to work with his patrons, he takes a cut of their earnings." Sam stepped towards the desk, anger vibrating his shoulders. His leopard prowled behind his eyelashes, wary.

"It isn't illegal. I give them a safe place to work in exchange for a cut of their profit." Mac started to stand, his eyes changing from a deep brown to a pale blue as he glared at Sam.

Fuck sake, another shifter.

"Calm down, both of you." She carefully stood between them, ignoring Sam's warning growl.

"Your roommate hasn't been helpful in finding out who has been dealing on my property."

"They weren't dealing." A snarl.

Mac went to his drawer, pulling out a large plastic bag full of red powder and a single syringe.

"This looks like a fucking lot of gear for one person." The words came out slightly garbled, his animal reacting to the aggression in the room.

That's when it clicked, she recognised him, had seen him around.

"You're one of Rex's wolves."

"Theo's wolves. Rex has gone AWOL. I was hoping you wouldn't have recognised me considering I'm not a pup, I don't have to do the dirty work." Meaning he was dominant. "I don't tangle in pack politics."

"He wasn't involved. Otherwise, I wouldn't be working here," Sam said as his palm came down on her shoulder, reassuring her.

"If you are so dominant, why did you let him get away with what he did?"

"I wasn't aware." He relaxed back into his seat. "Rex's actions do not reflect the integrity of the pack." He smiled charmingly, completely changing his otherwise hard face. "I hope there aren't any bad feelings?"

"My problem isn't with the pack." Not really, it was with their former Alpha.

"It's..." A set of lights were along the wall behind Mac's head, seven in total, each with their own gold number. The number seven flashed violently.

"I'm sorry, what is that for?" she asked curiously, pointing to the light.

"Fuck." Mac leapt up from his desk just as a woman crashed through the door, throwing Sam out of the way.

"Sir, there's been an accident." The woman said, swallowing tears. "In the Pride room."

"Ah, if you would excuse me." He patted his pocket nervously.

"I smell death," Sam stated as he moved down a corridor, letting Alice run behind.

"RANGER STOP!" Mac shouted.

"It isn't one of our girls." Sam physically relaxed once he peered into room seven. "It's a customer." His eyes were serious when he glared at Mac.

"Fuck." Mac stood in the threshold, his eyes wide. "One of our best fucking clients too."

"You have seven rooms, what are they for?"

Each door, other than the seventh, were closed. Red lights were above each one, some lit and some not.

"What do you think are everyone's most carnal desires?"

"You named your rooms after the seven deadly sins?" Alice tried not to smirk as she read the small inscriptions on each door. Lust, Gluttony, Greed, Sloth, Wrath, Envy and finally Pride.

"Mac named them. They're for clients with money, ones who like to pay for extras with the women he doesn't technically hire."

Sam crossed his arms, face angry. He clearly had some negative opinions about the rooms.

"It smells like a fang face."

"Vampire?" Alice tried to peek in the room, unable to see anything in the dark.

"Please step back, Miss Skye. We need to wait for the authorities to arrive."

"Now that you mention it…"

CHAPTER EIGHT

Alice stood against the wall as Jones eagerly photographed inside the small room, the squeak of his plastic overall setting her teeth on edge. She had been waiting patiently for the forensics to finish while Sam stood beside her uncharacteristically quiet, his leopard analysing the situation with pure focus. She allowed him to stay for the time being, his animal instincts reacting at seeing the dead body. His leopard was always protective of her, regardless if she needed it or not.

"How was your date?" Sam asked as he carefully watched everyone who came in and out the corridor

"Date?" she replied, frowning.

"With Alistair?" He smirked down at her, his amber eyes amused.

He enjoyed telling everybody who asked about his eyes that he was born with them, in truth, they were a constant reminder of his harsh childhood. His leopard protected him the only way it knew how, but in doing so left him with permanent eyes of a predator.

"Al or whatever you want to call him." He brushed his shoulder against hers in affection.

Alice sighed, playing with the hem of her T-shirt before looking up at him. Thankfully Sam no longer wore his leather stage outfit, he had changed into a simple shirt and jeans once the authorities had turned up. His hair was in a high ponytail, keeping the blonde strands off his face. She had always been jealous of his hair, how it was completely straight compared to her natural wave. She had never told him so, didn't think his already enormous ego could handle it.

"Oh, that." She had no interest in going on a date with Al, her local magic shop owner and friend. He was a nice guy, even attractive but she wasn't interested in dating anyone. Unfortunately, Al didn't understand body language and wouldn't stop asking, so eventually, she had agreed, much to Sam's delight.

"That's tomorrow." She checked the time on her phone, the digital clock showing she had been there for hours already. "I have to meet him at Circle Plaza at six."

"The Circle, huh?" Sam whistled. "Fancy."

"Agent Skye, I didn't know you date." Detective O'Neil smiled as he walked over, a small curve of his lip. "I'll have to tell the other guys."

"Is that a joke, Detective?" She honestly wasn't sure, didn't know him well enough.

"Could be." He coughed, his small smile disappearing as he flipped open his black pad to study his notes. "According to Mr Donald, you were here before they found the dead body?" He looked at her over the paper, eyes questioning.

"I was here to pick up my roommate." She nudged Sam, who was staring into the room, arms folded.

"Aye, hello." Sam nodded towards the detective but didn't offer his hand.

"Irish?" Detective O'Neil asked.

"Aye, Galway. Not many people can tell." Sam looked surprised. He had only the slightest Irish twang, his accent having diluted from the amount of time he has lived in England. The only time it really came out was when he was angry, his accent and language changing back to that of his childhood.

"Father's from Dublin." Was all O'Neil said in explanation. "We will have to interview you once we have looked at the crime scene, please remain on the property."

"Aye." Sam waved absently before turning to Alice, his fingers brushing through the loose strands of her hair. "You okay?" *Should I stay?* His face asked.

Alice gently smiled, allowing him to continue touching her. He was calming his leopard, reassuring himself she was okay even though death was thick in his nose.

"I'll catch up with you."

He reluctantly released her. "Meet me after my late shift tomorrow? You can tell me all about your date."

"And you can tell me about your secret career change," she countered, unimpressed.

Sam smirked before disappearing down the corridor.

That boy has way too much interest in my love life. She shook her head.

The 'Pride' room was bright with artificial lighting, the glow harsh as it highlighted every little detail. Jones was thoughtful when Alice and O'Neil entered the small room, his eyes never straying from the deceased on the bed.

"What do we have?" O'Neil asked.

"Looks like we've found our vampire friend," Jones said when he finally acknowledged them.

A male was positioned on his back on the bed, half hidden beneath red furs that were draped across his body. White foam and bile had dripped from the side of his mouth onto the black sheet.

"You think this is him?" Alice asked as she watched Jones touch the thin skin, his fingers almost going through the flesh. "He doesn't even look like a Vamp."

"Yes, pretty confident in the way his body has started to degrade. As you can see..." Jones pointed to the body. "The deceased is suffering from severe dehydration as well as deterioration to muscle tone. He is almost mimicking mummification, which could explain the lack of stench." Jones studied the body closer.

Unlike faerie tales, vampires didn't turn to dust once dead. Instead, they decayed just like everyone else. The older the Vamp, the worse the smell and rot, almost as if their corpse reflected their real age.

The square room itself was floor to ceiling black latex with a drain in the corner. Alice didn't want to know what the cleaners hosed down after a client.

Mirrors covered every wall apart from the one behind the bed, that held shelves with an impressive selection of sex toys, varying from ordinary to ridiculous and dangerous.

"Mirrors for a room called Pride, funny." Alice moved closer to one, checking out the handprints along the glass. The main door caught her attention in the reflection, the light glinting off the solid metal with a single handle only accessible from the inside.

"How long has he been here?" O'Neil asked.

"It's hard to say." Jones shrugged. "An educated guess would be at least eight to twelve hours, maybe more. I would have to check in on the autopsy to make sure, wait for the blood works to match the others."

"Is there CCTV in this room?" O'Neil asked as he scanned along the ceiling.

"No, we do not record or monitor anything that goes on in the private rooms," Mac Donald said from the doorway.

"You must be Mr Mackenzie Donald?" O'Neil politely shook his hand. "Can you please explain to me what exactly happens in this room?"

O'Neil raised an eyebrow, pen poised on his notepad.

"These rooms can be rented privately by the hour. It is up to the clients what they do in here." Mac crossed his arms, closing off his body language.

"What time did he rent the room?" Alice asked, watching his iris flash a quick blue once she made eye contact. If he was getting annoyed at their questions already, he wasn't in for much fun.

"Around two."

"Is that not an unusual time for someone to hire this type of room?" O'Neil looked around, gesturing to the sex toys.

"My establishment is usually only open from eight to six. However, I make compromises for certain clients. Mr Little was a regular and big spender."

"Mr Little as in the Mayor's assistant?" Alice didn't recognise the man but definitely recognised the name, having been in the press several times in the last week alone. Mr Little was the current right-hand man to Mayor Clawford, a mage and spokesperson for 'Breed is Us.' Highlighting equal rights to the lower scale Breeds, such as mages.

"That's correct. We take client confidentially seriously, which is why he frequented so much."

"Tell me, Mr Donald, how did Mr Little seem when you saw him?" Alice questioned, watching him flinch.

"It's Mac," he growled, "and that's confidential. What we do here isn't illegal." He started to get defensive, his shoulder tense as he leant forward. "We don't encourage the women to solicit themselves. However, we give them a safe place to do it."

"We're not judging, but this man has been dead around eight hours, and nobody thought to check on him?" She watched his face flush red.

"The door is solid steel and several inches thick. The handle is on the inside with no way to open from the outside once the door is locked. You have no CCTV to act as a deterrent and have named the rooms after the seven deadly sins."

Alice stepped closer, watching how he automatically stepped back. He noticed too, the anger apparent in his expression.

"Rooms that you have named after behaviours deemed as cardinal vices, that have been tainted into excessive passions. In what way do you think people aren't going to take advantage of that?"

His eyes glowed pale blue, his wolf taking over. She didn't take much notice, shifters generally were quick to anger, especially dominant predators.

"We choose our customers carefully. They're fully vetted before they even step foot in any of our rooms."

"You still haven't answered my original question." Alice stifled her anger to maintain professionalism. She was trying to remain polite, do her job. Yet his aggressive reaction was grating on her nerves.

Predatory shifters were a pain in her arse.

"I didn't see Mr Little when he came in so cannot say how he was. He always books in advance without any assistance from us. The women or men he has chosen meet him in there."

"Who had he planned to meet?"

"All you need to know is that she's safe. Mr Little always booked a full twelve-hour slot. We've always assumed that he enjoyed relaxing on his own afterwards, so never disturbed him."

"What's her name? We would like to speak to her," O'Neil asked.

"Unless you have a warrant I will not speak to you about confidential details. I protect all my staff."

"If that's the way you wish to take it, Mr Donald…" O'Neil left the threat in the air. "I would like you to answer one more question. Do you recognise this woman?"

O'Neil produced a photograph of Stacey, the woman found in the motel. Alice recognised the picture from the bedroom, one that was on the nightstand.

Mac stared at the photograph for a few seconds, his jaw rigid. "No comment."

"Her name is Stacey," Alice said, watching his reaction. "She was found dead. We have reason to believe both the deceased knew each other."

"Stacey's dead?" Mac looked genuinely torn, it made her step back, allow him some space. "Yes, I know her. Knew her." He coughed to clear his throat. "She was a regular with Mr Little, but we let her go over a year ago." His eyes shot to Alice. "We have a zero tolerance on drugs. I wouldn't be able to tell you if they were still seeing each other outside my establishment."

"Do you know if Mr Little liked to use blood whores?" O'Neil asked. Blood whore was the term used for women who got high then allowed vampires to feed off them in exchange for money. Vampires metabolism was too fast, they couldn't even get drunk unless they drank the whole bar. The only thing that seemed to affect them was drinking contaminated blood.

Mac scowled. "So beautifully put. All I know is he asked one of my girls once to do it. When she refused, he never asked again."

"Thank you for your time, Mr Donald." Alice gave him a short nod.

He went to leave, hesitating before looking back.

"Miss Skye..." She caught his eye, was interested in how much control he allowed his wolf to have. "Get whoever did this. Stacey was a good girl who got in with a bad crowd. She wouldn't have hurt a fly."

Mac left the room, his office door slamming shut a moment later.

CHAPTER NINE

This is just my luck.

Alice sulked as she trudged through the busy underground, following the mass towards the vague direction of the exit. Her tyre had blown out earlier in the day, luckily relatively close to her house. She had abandoned it to Sam, hoping he would be able to sort it after his shift.

She huffed out a breath, the air freezing cold in the middle of December. Happy music flowed across the overcrowded tunnel, a mixture of acoustic guitar and violin that fought with the general noise of the crowd. As she walked the music got louder, until she was able to see buskers playing beside the mouth of the exit.

In full winter coats, scarfs and fingerless gloves they played, smiling and tapping their feet as they got into the rhythm of their tune.

Alice stopped by a train map, adjusting her scarf while enjoying the music as it flowed into a well- known musical number. As she watched, the guitarist began to mumble beneath his breath, inaudible against the instruments. Within seconds light erupted around them, little balls swirling and dancing in time with the music as the guitarist continued his silent chant. Alice couldn't help but smile as the children sang and danced along in delight.

"Stupid fucking faeries," someone spat.

"Go back to where you came from." Came another slur.

"Dirtybloods."

Alice turned to the three men, noticing their joint snigger as they kicked debris towards the musicians. They were all dressed in long black overcoats, open to show dark business suits with expensive gold watches.

"You're polluting with all that fucking sparkle."

"Humans rule this city."

"You're not wanted here, bloody faeries."

Alice felt herself get angry even as the musicians ignored the disruption. 'Faeries' was supposed to be a derogative term towards anyone of magic origin, whether they were a faerie or not. She had never met anyone who was actually offended by it, except faeries themselves of course.

"I think that's enough, boys." A tall man approached them, dressed in his own expensive suit. "You're making a scene."

"Who the fuck are..." One of the men began before he quickly stepped back, looking at the floor.

"I think you should all continue on your way now." The man's voice dropped. "Unless you would like to answer to me."

All three men quickly made their way through the exit, barely giving a backwards glance. The tall man started to turn, his eyes a bright gold before settling into a warm brown.

His face shimmered gently, the glamour he wore to make himself look more human reactivating. Alice said nothing as she watched him adjust his coat, brushing imaginary hairs from the lapel.

His eyes shot to hers, the warm brown narrowed as he looked her up and down. Death. That's what she saw in his eyes, endless death.

Deciding she wasn't a threat he gave her a gentle nod before he walked away, heading further into the underground. Alice couldn't help but stare after him, almost as if he was a bug she needed to examine. He must have been a High Lord, the oldest amongst the Fae. Someone she knew not to mess with.

"Thank you for listening." A cheer as the musicians finished their set.

The sudden applause made her jump, shocking her out of the stasis. Laughing to herself, she followed the crowd into the cold night, happy it was only a short walk to the restaurant where she was meeting Al.

The Circle Plaza was an opulent glass conservatory situated on top of a tall, thin tower. A receptionist and doorman greeted her at the entrance to the golden lift, the metal shiny enough to reflect her image back at her.

"Do you have a reservation?" The receptionist asked, her ice blue eyes silently judging Alice's red scarf and worn leather jacket.

"I'm meeting Alistair Medlock."

"Ah, Mr Medlock. He hasn't arrived yet, you may make your way up and wait at the bar. Once your partner has arrived a member of staff will show you to your seat."

"Thank you," Alice said as the lift door closed behind her. Taking off her jacket and scarf, she held them on her arm, studying her reflection in the metal.

If it were up to her, she would have worn a dark pair of jeans and a nice shirt. It was Sam who loudly protested what she should wear, to the point he had the dress already picked out for her. So she ended up wearing a mid-length spaghetti strapped red dress, with her hair lightly styled into waves that draped gently across her shoulders. She didn't know why she was here, why she even agreed to come on the date. It wasn't as if she had any luck with this sort of thing. Besides, Sam had enough sex for the both of them.

"Fuck sake," she mumbled beneath her breath, nerves a flutter in her stomach.

Why do I let people guilt trip me into shit?

She would happily take on a raging blood-lust vampire than a first date.

The lift dinged on the top floor, the doors opening to show a large open floor plan with the bar situated in the middle, surrounding the kitchen. The whole room was made of glass, giving a magnificent view of London in lights. Allowing a waiter to take her coat and scarf Alice settled herself onto a bar stool, ordering the first cocktail she saw on the menu.

Holy shit! Alice accepted the drink from the bartender, staring it as if it was made from gold. *Who pays this much for a drink?*

"Beautiful." A masculine voice said from behind her.

Turning her head, she gave a genuine smile, recognising the friendly face.

"The view? It's amazing, isn't it."

"I wasn't talking about the view." Nate Blackwell smiled charmingly before sitting beside her. His dark hair was shorter than the other day, the dark strands gelled into messy points. "Impressive performance at the gala by the way, I have never seen someone throw off their heels so fast while running." He chuckled, sipping his whisky.

"It's a talent." She smiled, tipping her glass.

"You never mentioned you were an agent, although I should have guessed considering you were chummy with the Commissioner." He tapped a finger against his glass, leaning forward to whisper into her ear. "You here on business, or pleasure?"

"Pleasure," she said with a small shrug. "Yourself?"

"Alas, it is business." He held his palm flat against his white shirt, feigning disappointment. "But I wish it was not."

"Mr Blackwell, how nice of you to make it on such short notice."

A man with long, pure white hair and black wraparound glasses approached. He wore a turtle neck black jumper with leather straps across his shoulders, holding two pistols.

"Mr Storm is waiting for you." The man turned, his mouth a grimace as he noticed Alice.

Alice recognised him but wasn't sure where from, his look unusual enough to stick in her memory. He clearly recognised her, his blatant disregard obvious. She fought not to turn, trying not to give in to her curiosity of which Storm it was. Not that it mattered.

"Ma'am, Mr Medlock has just arrived, if you could follow me..." A waiter happily interrupted the awkward moment.

"It was nice to see you again Nate, I hope your business isn't too boring."

She stood up, grabbing her cocktail.

"It's business Alice, it's always boring." A chuckle.

"This way, ma'am." The waiter guided her to a table beside the window, Alistair already sitting down in his seat.

"Hello," she greeted as he stood up, kissing her on the cheek. She tried not to show her reaction at the seating arrangement, not wanting to create a scene. She hated sitting with her back to the room, especially when she wasn't armed with anything other than a single knife strapped to her thigh, her clutch too small for a gun. Al only had his back to the kitchen with one door, compared to a restaurant full of people.

"I'm sorry I was late," he mumbled, "I had problems closing the shop."

He nervously touched his wine glass, brushing his fingertips across the surface before settling them into his lap.

"It's fine, my car decided to die today, so I had to take the tube." She allowed the waiter to set the napkin across her lap, nodding in thanks.

"Why didn't you contact me? I would have picked you up?" His smile turned to a frown.

"I didn't mind." She did, but it was either that or have no exit strategy if the date went to shit. "This view is amazing," she said, changing the subject. The view really was remarkable, a great vantage point of the city. Festive lights added to the magic, creating a serene scene as the sky threatened to snow.

"I'm glad you like it, one of my regulars mentioned this was one of the best places." His eyes twinkled. "You look, ah, wow."

"Thanks," she grinned, happy she went with Sam's idea and not her jeans and a nice shirt.

Al had dressed in a black suit with algae green tie that matched his eyes, his usual lank brown hair brushed from his face, framing his high cheekbones. She studied his skin for a second, wondering where his freckles had disappeared to until she noticed him nervously turning a black ring around his finger, the onyx glittering.

Complexion amulet, one that hid his freckles underneath a magic shroud.

"You look great too," she awkwardly complimented him back.

I'm so crap at this.

Al grinned in return, tugging his green tie. "I picked it out myself."

He held back a laugh as the waiter arrived and took their orders.

"How's Jordan? He still up to no good?"

"He keeps scaring Sam." She sipped her cocktail, enjoying the fruity flavour. "You ever going to take him back?"

"He's welcome back if he wishes, but I doubt we have any choice in the matter." He shrugged, blasé as if they weren't talking about an inanimate object that moved on its own. "Erm, Alice, do you know that guy?"

"Huh?"

"The man over there keeps staring in this direction."

Alice automatically turned, her eyes scanning the crowd until she settled on the table he was talking about. Mason Storm was charming the waiter as he ordered, Nate's dark head sitting beside him. Business meeting, he had said.

I wonder what type of business it was.

"I don't know him." She turned back to Al.

"Isn't that Councilman Storm? He just bought out one of my biggest competitors." He settled back in his chair, crossing his arms. "Bastards are putting me out of business."

"Yep, bastards," she agreed.

"I appreciate you accepting my dinner date, once Sam mentioned you were..."

"Wait, wait, wait. Hold up." She held up her hand. "You spoke to Sam?"

That weasel, he had put Al up to this.

"Guilty." He held up his palms, smiling before his eyes darted down. "Oh," Al reached forward before she could react, grabbing the crystal she wore tight to her neck. "You still wear it?"

The lapis lazuli was tied to a leather strap, the crystal singing at the sudden attention. Once Al had released it the stone went back to the hollow of her throat, settling down as it retouched her skin. He was the one who helped her unlock her crystals potential, able to create a physical barrier with a single incantation. That crystal had saved her life on more than one occasion.

"Yes," she stroked the cold surface. "I always wear it." Al caught her eye, his genuine happiness shining through.

He really is a nice guy, she thought, continuing to play with her necklace.

"Thanks for the..." She began before a distracting buzz vibrated the table. "I'm so sorry." She grabbed her clutch, unzipping to check her phone that continued to vibrate. "I thought I turned it off." She tried desperately to cancel the call, hitting any button she could in panic.

"That's okay, I know you work for the Supernatural Intelligence Bureau, if you need to answer it, go ahead, I don't mind."

"You sure?" she asked even as the phone started to vibrate once more, noticing it was Detective O'Neil.

"I'll be here once you get back," he winked.

"Thanks, I won't be long."

She left the table in a flurry, politely smiling at the people looking as she made her way towards the large balcony. Opening the door, she stepped into the cold, quickly getting herself under one of the warm heaters.

"Bloody phone," she mumbled as she flicked through her contacts.

"You shouldn't be outside without a coat. You could catch your death," a deep voice sniggered.

"Excuse me?" She glared at the man standing on the other side of the balcony, face hidden in shadow. An orange cigarette briefly glowed, highlighting his hair. "Oh, it's you."

The white-haired man who had a preference for sunglasses, even outside in the darkness of night.

"Seriously, have I done something to offend you?"

"No." Came the slow response.

"Then what reason do you have to dislike me?" she asked, not understanding why.

She didn't care if he liked her or not.

"I neither like you nor dislike you."

"How lovely," she murmured, turning her back. "Where do I even know you from?"

"Xander, what are you doing? I asked you to..." Mason stormed through the glass door. "Oh, I didn't realise you were outside," he sneered at her.

"Oh look, another fan of mine. What a lovely evening, isn't it Mason?"

"It's Councilman Storm." He glared at her before turning his frosty eyes towards the white-haired man. "Xander, get inside."

"I don't answer to you."

Another puff as he held the smoke in before releasing it out his nose.

"So fuck off."

"I'm the Arch..."

"I. Don't. Answer. To. You." Xander took off his glasses, his eyes so pale they were almost white.

Mason's face flushed red in irritation, even deeper once he caught Alice staring.

"Careful boy..." Anger apparent in every line of his body, his usual air of sophistication shattering. "Final warning."

Xander bowed sarcastically at the waist, his guns glinting from the light of the heater. Putting back on his sunglasses, he slowly walked into the restaurant, not acknowledging Alice.

"It's rude to watch another man's argument." Mason turned his impatience on Alice. "Did your parents not teach you better manners?" he sniggered.

Alice saw red, her hand crushing the phone even as the plastic groaned.

"I'm sorry, I didn't realise this wasn't a public place."

"Pathetic, let's hope my son doesn't beat you too badly into submission."

Alice ignored the threat.

"Why have The Council assigned me a Warden?"

"Because you're a liability," he replied as he grabbed the door handle, turning his back to her. "And you are a time bomb waiting to go off. We shall see if your fate matches the rest of your family."

He closed the door behind him, leaving her staring after him through the glass, up until he joined Nate back at the table with his fake smile once again in place.

What did he just say?

The phone vibrated in her hand.

CHAPTER TEN

The sky had begun to glow white as Al drove her across the city, snow starting to fall as the temperature plummeted. Alice hated winter, didn't understand the joy of snow. It was cold and wet, two of the most miserable things. She touched her palm to the car window, feeling the frostbite through the glass.

"Here we are," Al said, putting the car into neutral.

"I'm sorry our date was cut short," she said, turning to face him, her hands freezing as she grabbed her bag.

"Your job is important," he shrugged. "At least we got some fancy drinks." He shot her a side smile.

She felt guilty. Not guilty because the date was cut short, but because she was glad for the excuse to leave early. The call had been O'Neil letting her know about a meeting, something she couldn't miss.

"It was a nice evening." Her eyes darted to the digital clock by the steering wheel, only 6:56 p.m. She hadn't even been at the restaurant for an hour before they had to leave. She really sucked at dates. "I'll make it up to you."

"I have an idea," he said as she turned to face him, his lips stroking across her own before she could even react. She automatically kissed him back, his tongue teasing her bottom lip as she pressed forward.

She felt nothing. No excitement. No attraction.

Nothing.

After a minute Al slowly moved back, his eyes sad as he sighed dramatically.

"You didn't feel anything either, did you?"

Alice awkwardly laughed, shaking her head gently. "I'm sorry."

"Don't be, that's what first dates are for." He rested back in his seat, closing his eyes. "Friends?"

"Of course," she gripped his shoulder, squeezing it gently before opening the door. "It really was a nice night."

"We will do it again sometime," he smiled. "But as friends."

"Friends."

Waving her goodbye, she stepped through the revolving door. She quickly took in the grand atrium, studying the white tiles, high ceiling and large opaque glass behind the front desk.

"Hello..." she started as she approached.

"Just a moment ma'am," the woman said, her attention on the paperwork scattered in front of her.

Alice waited even as she felt eyes prickle her skin. Officers milled around, some leaning against a few desks to the side of the room, their eyes tracking her every movement.

"I'm here to see Detective O'Neil," she said when her patience ran out. "I'm Agent Skye, he should be expecting me."

That caught the woman's attention, her eyes appraising Alice slowly before she frowned. "You the witch?"

"Spook squad." Someone quietly murmured from beside her, followed by a few chuckles.

Alice shot them an irritated look, watching the men's faces turn sober before she gave her attention back to the woman.

What's their problem?

Alice scrambled in her clutch for her badge, holding it to the glass so the officer could see.

"That would be me."

"What's a witch doing in our department?" Another of the men said from behind.

"She doesn't look like a witch, more like a hooker."

"Pretty though..."

Alice felt her ears burn.

"Hey guys," she moved so she all the male officers in her sight, plastering a smile on her face. "Do we have a problem?"

There were three men in total, one at his desk with paperwork stacked high and two who sat on the edge. The five other desks were empty.

"No, ma'am," one of them chuckled. "You going to play with our wands?"

Alice felt a blush burn her cheeks.

"What do you call a clairvoyant leprechaun who escaped from prison?"

The men looked at her as if she was crazy. Which honestly, was debatable.

"A small medium at large," she finished.

One officer broke into a grin with the other two continued to stare at her as if she had lost it.

"No?" She dramatically rolled her eyes. "What about this one. What did the policeman say to his belly button?"

"You're under a-vest," replied a deep, gravelly voice. "Agent Skye, is there a reason you're aggravating my officers?" Detective Brady frowned, crossing his arms across his chest as he glared at her.

"They invited me to play with their wands," she said, her eyes narrowed. "I was just starting with some foreplay."

Brady's' eyes shot to the men, who quickly made themselves busy. "Very funny Agent Skye. You're late, please follow me."

He turned towards a keypad and entered the passcode, consciously making sure she couldn't see. Holding the door, he waited for her to follow, his face impatient.

"I was told to get here for seven." She followed him through the corridor, meeting every set of eyes who uneasily stared her way.

This place seems welcoming.

"Through here." He opened another door with a key card, allowing her to enter before him. Quietly thanking him she passed through, greeting O'Neil, Jones and Peyton. The room smelled of fresh coffee as all three men sat quietly around a circular table, the reason for the smell evident in the centre. Behind O'Neil was a large felt board, photographs of each deceased connected with the case showcased in vivid detail.

"What are you wearing?" Jones chuckled. "You look hot."

"I was on a date." She smiled before sitting down, besides Brady.

"Did any of the boys give you any hassle?" O'Neil raised his eyebrows.

"She tried to bore them with bad jokes." Brady leant back in his chair, a small smile on his lips.

"They weren't bad, they're just a bad audience," she muttered.

"Apologies about cutting your date short Alice, but we needed this meeting sooner rather than later. Jones, as you're the one with the most information, why don't you start?"

"Right-o." Jones leapt up from his chair, his T-shirt crinkled to the point it was entirely possible that it had never seen an iron. "As you can see from the photographs, deterioration amongst the bodies is pretty consistent, with the end results including severe dehydration and muscle loss. Bones become brittle and in some cases have even disintegrated under only a small amount of pressure." Jones pointed to one photograph showing bone fragments, the once white shards now a dull grey.

"Is that in both the deceased vampires and humans?" Brady asked, leaning forward in his seat as he studied the gruesome details.

"Yes. The main difference is the process is much faster in the vampire targets. They start to degenerate within thirty to ninety minutes while the human carriers don't show deterioration until a few hours after exsanguination. We believe the carriers are ingesting the substance rather than injecting as there seems to be a more concentrated amount at the back of their throats. Other than Stacey Cartman, not one of our carriers had evidence of intravenous injection."

"Any luck on I.D.'ing the substance?"

"Yes and no."

Jones reached across the table and opened a black folder, handing out identical sheets with various numbers on.

"So as of yet, we have not been able to positively identify it completely, however, from the concentrated amount found, I have been able to cross match the results with a recent analysis." He pointed to the numbers as if anybody else could understand it. "It's blood."

"Blood?" All three of them said in unison.

"Yes. In fact, it's almost identical to that of a John Doe found in an abandoned warehouse a few months back. It's on record that he has been classified as a Daemon transition."

"What?"

"You have got to be shitting me!"

Alice felt herself go still, her full attention on Jones as he explained the similarities in the blood works.

Daemon. Fuck sake.

"Okay, so for now we will accept that it's Daemon blood until we find any evidence otherwise. What do we know of Daemons?" O'Neil asked, looking expectantly at Alice.

Alice blinked stupidly until Brady gently nudged her.

"What can I tell you about Daemons..." She hesitated, deciding carefully how much she could say. "From the limited information out there, the impression is that Daemons are well equipped with black magic. They're not technically classified as Breed as they haven't been recorded since the early nineteenth century. There is no known data regarding their origin."

"What about the significance of drinking their blood?"

Alice shook her head. "It depends on how you look at it. Vampires exchange blood when they are transitioned. So it's a possibility that drinking Daemon blood is part of the initial ritual, although this is all speculation."

"We need to know more. What's their feature characteristics? How could we identify one?"

"You would know." Alice laughed, the sound empty. "They were named Daemons because of their physical similarities to various religions depictions. Full-fledged Daemons would have to be under glamour if they were walking among the general population."

"What about only part Daemons? Like the ones in transition?" Jones asked.

"There isn't really anything. They could look like you or me." She moved her attention to Brady. "Did you get anything more on those markings we found in Miss Cartman's kitchen?"

"I have them here." Brady shuffled through his stack of notes until he produced some photographs. "I couldn't find anything on the markings other than confirming what Agent Skye said at the scene." He pointed to the top of the pentagram, explaining the significance to the other guys.

"May I have a look?" Peyton asked, his blue eyes serious as he held his hand out for the images. "These look like Brimstone. Some manufacturers like to protect their batch as they cook, she was probably dealing."

"Actually it was her husband who was dealing," O'Neil added, squinting at his notepad. "Steven Cartman. Charged with possession, intent to supply, GBH and ABH."

"That brings me to my next point: Mr Cartman." Jones went to stand by the grey felt, pointing at the right photograph. "I've included him on the board even though he isn't a direct victim. Steven Lewis

Cartman, age unknown. Breed has been confirmed as Fae, however, neither of the Courts have come forward with anymore details on specifics. He had a minute amount of the substance in his system but not enough to be deadly, it's likely his wife transferred it through a kiss."

"Bleeding gums?" Brady suggested.

"Actually that's a possibility, she was suffering from stage four lung cancer. Bleeding gums, as well as coughing blood are common symptoms."

"What about the recent vampire?" Brady asked. "How is he connected?"

"Mr Chris Little was confirmed to have known Stacey intimately for at least a year. Forensics also found his name and details in a little black book hidden beneath her mattress with dates of their meetings."

"So are we suggesting this was a targeted kill?" Alice asked.

"It would be a great coincidence if not."

"Let's hope no other high ranking Vamp likes to sleep with the ladies of the night then, shall we," Peyton mumbled.

"So do we have any other leads?" O'Neil looked around the room. "Surely that can't be it? We can't just sit here until we have another victim to add to that fucking board." His lip twitched, his hand touching his breast pocket as if searching for something.

"Sick, she was sick." Alice stood up, walking over to the photograph of Stacey, naked on the bed. "I was approached the other night by a woman claiming to be their friend. She explained Stacey was sick and the hospital couldn't do anymore for her. Apparently, she had tried every option she could think of, including black magic."

"What's this friends name? She could be our next lead."

Alice had to think. "Mia."

Peyton searched through the paperwork before stopping at one sheet.

"Is this her?" He handed Alice the paper.

Office of the medical examiner
London

Report of examination

Decedent: Mia Simpson
Case Number: RF 14466-882036

Cause of death: Exsanguination
Identified by: *Fingerprints *available from database*
Age: *25 years*
Sex: *Female* ***Race:*** *Caucasian* ***Breed:*** *Human*
Date of death: *(Found) 18/12/2017 (Estimate) 18/12/2017*
....
Date of Examination: *19th December 2017 through to 20th December 2017*
Examination and summary analysis performed by: *Dr Lewis Fisher*
Cause of death: *Exsanguination (Loss of blood to a degree sufficient enough to cause death)*
....
Findings

() Sharp object used to cut with an upwards stroke
() Angle of laceration consistent with self-administration

() Other than throat, no other open wounds
() Blade matched wound
() Scars consistent with self-harm
() Brimstone found in blood sample, 15%

....
Conclusion:
The subject fatally wounded herself by slicing her jugular in one clean movement. The manner of death is suicide.

Alice read the paper silently, the feeling of guilt crushing.

"Agent, you okay?" Jones cautiously approached her, both hands palm up as if she was a wild animal, one that could attack.

Her Tinkerbell floated around her wrist, sparking each time it approached the autopsy report.

"I'm sorry." She fluffed the ball of fire away. "Yes, this is her."

She handed the paper back, trying to ignore the stunned looks.

"Apologies for my reaction..." She couldn't finish.

"Would this put us in any danger?" Brady asked deadpan, his face serious as he cautiously watched her light.

"Sometimes, this happens. I'm sure you understand premature ejaculation Detective?" She tried to smile at her joke, her lips trembling at the effort.

"Do you remember anything else about your conversation with Miss Simpson," O'Neil asked before Brady could reply.

Alice thought back.

"Santa offered her a lifeline." She frowned even as she said it out loud.

"Santa? Are we serious right now?" Brady grumbled, her ejaculation joke having not gone down well.

"Santa had offered to protect her soul. I didn't take much notice because this woman was high and delirious."

"This is nonsense from a woman high on Brimstone, surely we can't take anything she said seriously…" Brady stood up, frustrated. "Fucking Santa for goodness sake."

"Let the light guide you," Alice whispered, finally remembering the phrase the woman muttered beneath her breath.

"What did you say?" Brady stood beside her, his mouth agape.

"Brady, do you recognise that phrase?" O'Neil asked.

"It's a saying from the Church of the Light," Peyton spoke up, his eyes darting to Brady, who had taken on a grey sheen.

"They have nothing to do with this, they're controversial but peaceful," Brady stuttered.

"Is this a conflict of interest?" O'Neil asked. "I have to know if you need to be reassigned."

"No conflict of interest," he glared, nostrils flaring. "I'm just surprised. I doubt we can take anything Miss Simpson said seriously while in her state."

"Either way it's a lead."

O'Neil wrote something down in his little black book.

"Do we know how many churches they have in London?"

"Just the one," Brady confirmed.

"What's our best approach?"

Brady took a second to think. "Undercover would be my guess. I doubt they would talk to the police, never mind a witch."

"Don't worry Detective, they won't know I'm a witch."

CHAPTER ELEVEN

"What are you wearing?" Sam asked as he took a seat opposite her in the small coffee shop. "Please tell me you didn't wear that to your date?" he glared.

"What? No!" Alice started to laugh, gaining her some odd glances from the other late-night customers.

She simply wore a vest with black workout leggings. Sam's eyebrows rose when he read the typography across the fabrics, his initial shock turning into a smirk. The words *'I don't run!'* was printed large across her breasts with *'but If I am, you probably should too as something is chasing me'* written underneath. She thought it was comical. The other customers didn't seem to agree.

The coffee shop was quiet, which wasn't a surprise considering how late it was.

She would never have known the shop existed if it wasn't for Sam's weird career change. The aromatic scents of coffee beans and homemade fruit scones were comforting as she cuddled around her caramel latte.

The place itself was cute, with a varied selection of freshly made pastries and cakes on display plus a chalkboard with over one hundred different coffee and tea blends. Babies, puppies and kittens that were dressed as fruit decorated the walls, which Alice thought was a bit strange but not totally unamusing.

"Then why are you wearing your gym gear?" he asked while he waved his hand for the employee's attention. "You don't normally work out this late."

"Because if I don't hit something soon, I might explode," she sighed, sipping her coffee.

"Was the date that bad?" he asked as he ordered a black Americano from the barista.

"It wasn't awful." *It wasn't exactly good either,* she wanted to add.

But Sam could read her eyes, his own replying, *you're obviously too good for him.*

She couldn't hide her smile. There were only two people she could have a word-less conversation with, able to understand each other's expressions. It took knowing someone better than yourself to understand.

"There was no spark," she explained out loud. "Maybe I'm just destined to be alone forever."

"So sad, baby girl," Sam laughed. "Maybe you could become one of those crazy women with a ton of cats?"

"Well, I technically already have one," she grinned.

"Very funny," he said as his eyes danced mischievously.

"So are we going to talk about the elephant in the room?"

An eyebrow shot up, a smile playing across his lips. "What elephant?"

"What happened to being a bartender at The Blood Bar?"

Sam smiled at the barista when he brought over his coffee, winking charmingly.

"I don't know really," he shrugged. "Saw it advertised and thought why not?"

Alice shook her head. Sam was the most impulsive person she knew.

"I love to dance and enjoy people's reactions when I do. So what that I slowly take my clothes off?"

"I don't care that you strip for a living, I care because you didn't tell me."

Alice looked down at her coffee, staring at the caramel liquid. They told each other everything; it was what they did. A mutual dependency on each other's crap. She knew the reason he never told her wasn't that he was embarrassed, Sam didn't get embarrassed. So why didn't he tell her?

"I wanted to tell you, but you were still healing. You didn't need the added stress of knowing I was working for one of the pack."

"I'm not angry at the pack!" She raised her voice, causing eyes to shoot in their direction. "I don't blame the pack," she said quieter. At least, she didn't anymore. She knew how hierarchy worked, knew that the low-level dominants, as well as the submissive, were compelled to follow their Alphas orders.

"Good, because we had an unwanted guest this morning while you were out."

"Guest?" she frowned. "Who?"

"Theo Wild."

Alice sat back in her seat, staring at Sam as she thought it through. Why would the new Alpha of White Dawn want to speak to her? She had already told him what she thought, wanted nothing to do with him or his twin.

"What the hell does he want?"

"Apparently he had petitioned for you through The Tower. Dread refused the contract and he wanted to personally ask you for your help."

"Dread refused?"

Dread never refused work, the man would accept the last blood covered penny from a dying old woman.

"Wait, what does he need help with?"

"Theo wants to find Rex. Apparently, he's disappeared, refusing any calls or summons. I know there's something Theo didn't say, he seemed worried, desperate even."

"Desperate?"

"Something bad is happening. An Alpha doesn't show weakness, at least, not a proper Alpha. Yet he begged me to ask you." Sam shook his head.

Alphas didn't beg.

"I wouldn't have accepted it anyway," she quietly said, finishing off her drink.

"You sure about that?" Sam asked, his amber eyes seeing through her.

No, she wasn't sure.

"You need to..." Sam stopped mid-sentence.

"Sam? What are you..." she felt it then, the familiar current across her chi. She whipped her head around, mouth open as her brother stood in the threshold.

Kyle stared between them, his movements agitated as if he was ready to flee. He wore all black, his face slightly obscured by the oversized dirty black hoody. She didn't notice Sam move until he was already beside Kyle, he spoke softly, his voice not carrying across the short distance. He waved goodbye before he left, but Alice couldn't look away from her brother.

Kyle warily took a seat opposite her, pushing off his hood. He had cut his hair, darker than she remembered, almost black compared to the mousy brown of his childhood.

"Your cat threatened me at the door," Kyle said, a shadow of a smile creeping across his lips. "I like him."

Alice burst into laughter, feeling a tear burn down her cheek. "Yeah, he's overprotective."

Kyle hesitantly reached over, his hand shaking as he brushed the tear away. His sleeve pulled up at the movement, revealing the silver band that encircled his wrist. Her eyes shot to it before he quickly covered the band back up.

Slave bands, once controlled by a Daemon before Riley destroyed him. She knew he had another on his other wrist, as well as a choker around his neck.

"Why haven't you come home?" she said, feeling desperation grow.

"I can't." His voice broke, making her heart ache. "How can you live there, knowing what happened? How can you survive the memories?"

"You have to learn to accept your past. Accept the things you can't change."

"We shouldn't have to accept them," he growled. His pupils grew, encasing the majority of his eyes before he closed them, breathing heavy.

No, I guess not.

"It doesn't hurt as bad."

Kyle's jaw clenched and his cheekbones grew sharp, his hands clawed as he silently struggled. She longed to reach out and comfort him but knew that would only push him away.

The barista started to make his way over, a friendly smile plastered on his face until Alice caught his attention, silently begging him not to approach.

Relaxing back into her seat once he nodded she cupped her drink, patiently waiting. Kyle had put on weight since she last saw him properly, his face not as gaunt. But he was still too skinny. Too pale.

Alice hitched in a breath, pain resonating through her left palm, her crescent scar pulsating. Frowning, she clenched her fist to try to stop the ache. It had never done that before, not since the bite had healed. She opened her hand, tracing the darkened skin that started in the middle of her palm, curling down to just below her wrist.

"I'm sorry," Kyle said, eerily soft. His eyes were once again green, the same as hers, the same as their mothers.

"It was never…"

"It hurts, doesn't it?" he interrupted as he stared at her palm. "Where he bit you."

"It's fine." She clenched her hand again, hiding it in her lap beneath the table. "None of it was your fault."

"You don't know that," he snapped, his eyes darkening with his anger. He started to shake, his control splintering. "I can't… I need…" His chair crashed to the ground as he abruptly stood. "I'm sorry."

"Kyle, wait…" She reached for him, only grasping air as he left the coffee shop, forcing people out his way.

"KYLE!" She ran after him, stumbling to a halt on the street.

He was gone.

Fuck.

Alice held her breath, concentrating as she watched Bishop's huge bicep flinch, a split-second tell that he was going to move.

She jumped back just in time, barely missing the head-sized fist as she kicked out, catching his knee with her foot which gained her a satisfying grunt.

She was too wound up, needed to vent her excess energy.

The talk with Sam hadn't helped the violent turmoil in her gut, it just added to it.

She should have helped that woman, instead she was dead. Now she had the option to help a man she never wanted to see again, his brother begging for her assistance. Then there was Kyle…

Alice needed to hit something, to process through her emotions just as the doctors had advised. She was grateful she lived in a city, a place where it wasn't uncommon for a gym to be open late.

"Stupid bitch, that fucking hurt," Bishop snarled, spit jumping from his swollen lips.

She ignored the jibe, instead ducking as he launched at her once more.

"Stay the fuck still."

Alice knew she was pissing him off, was watching his face turn a dark shade of red as she kept evading him.

"Take your time, Bishop," she goaded, enjoying his angry grunts.

Bishop was over six foot, double her weight with a face only a mother could love. She knew that one hit from a meaty fist could end her, so she had to wear him down first. As a workout, it was average. Her heart rate was barely up, and she hadn't broken into a sweat. But as a distraction, it was perfect. It forced her to concentrate, slowing down her rage until it was a quiet simmer that she could think past.

Dodging yet another move she kicked out, showing him off balance and into the mat.

"Alice, stop playing with him," Sensei scolded. "You should have had him pinned by now, but you're too busy toying."

He shook his head in disappointment before moving onto the next couple.

"She can't fucking pin me!" Bishop roared, teeth bared as veins pulsated down his thick neck. He was panting at the edge of the mat, elbows rested on his knees.

Alice rolled her eyes, bouncing on the balls of her feet when she felt something tickle across her aura.

She frowned, wondering what it was as she quickly glanced around, unable to find the source. Checking to make sure Bishop was still panting in his corner she turned around, finally spotting the man dressed in dark jeans and a black top, a leather jacket draped across his arm.

He leant against the wall, arms folded across his chest as his razor-sharp gaze watched unwavering. She had no idea how long he had been standing there.

"Fuck sake," she moaned beneath her breath.

She gestured to him, a smile curving his cheek before his eyes hardened to something behind her.

Abruptly she was airborne, the wind rushing out her body in one startled exhale when she hit the mat hard, her lungs struggling to recover as a heavy weight settled on her torso. She twisted, trying to dislodge the pressure to no avail, Bishop's knees pinning her arms down.

She tapped the mat three times, signalling defeat. The weight didn't move, so she tapped the mat again even as she started to struggle harder.

"How do you like that? Bitch!" Bishop spat at her, his full weight crushing.

"GET OFF!" she gasped. She threw herself to the side, unsettling him before he had her arms painfully pinned above her head.

"There's only two places for women," he said with an expression of pure fury. "In the kitchen and on your back, legs spread..."

She didn't allow him to finish.

"Ventilabis," she snarled, throwing her head into his nose as intense heat pricked across their skin.

"FUCK!" He automatically moved to protect his face, giving her the room she needed to kick out from underneath him.

Inhaling a lung full of air, she coughed, bending at the waist.

"What the fuck was that?"

"YOU FUCKING BURNT ME!" Red marks decorated his tanned skin, beside singed hair that was smoking. "That's cheating."

He went to grab her neck, his mouth howling in pain as her knee connected with his groin instead.

"Bishop, get up." Sensei scowled, tapping him with his foot. "You know the rules. Once a partner taps out, you stop."

"But she used magic!" he snapped back, eyes full of hate.

"And you would have let her pass out. This is your only warning, play by the rules or leave."

"It's my turn."

In all the commotion, Alice hadn't heard Riley move towards them, his face devoid of any emotion. He shot a look towards Alice before stepping onto the mat and removing his shirt. Alice stepped back, trying not to stare at the mesmerising tattoos.

"You can leave your shirt on, you know," she murmured.

Riley was a better match to Bishop, their sizes similar, although Bishop wasn't as tall but meatier compared to Riley's toned strength.

"Is that who I think it is?" Sensei asked as they eagerly watched the two men circle each other. Alice noticed many of the other sparring couples had stopped to watch too.

"My stalker? Then yes, yes it is."

"Don't be a wise arse." He smirked down at her. "What's he doing here?"

"Probably wants to kick my arse, just like he's doing Bishop's."

Alice felt the kick as Riley's foot connected to Bishop's stomach, the move winding him completely. Alice tried not to smirk, enjoying the fight.

Payback's a bitch.

"Wow, that man can move," Sensei whistled, his complete attention on the match, "almost as well as myself."

Alice didn't comment, instead analysing everything both fighters were doing. It was akin to a sleek, elegant panther fighting an untrained puppy, Riley counterattacking and dodging every move with ease. His movements even seemed lazy compared to usual, his speed matching his partner when she knew he was faster. Much faster.

"I'm sorry, I didn't know he would be coming."

"Are you kidding? My students need to watch how he moves, and that includes you." He caught her eye, his attention going back to the fight a few seconds later. "Surprising isn't it? Considering who he is. I wonder who he trained with?"

A huge cheer as Bishop crashed into the mat, his breathing laboured as Riley stood above him, barely sweating. "Stay down."

"Fuck..." A sharp inhale as Bishop brushed the blood from beneath his nose. "You." He staggered to his feet, fists lifted.

"Suit yourself." Riley leapt at him, turning into a roundhouse kick that flattened Bishop once again. This time, he stayed down. The room erupted into applause, every student having stopped what they were doing to watch.

"GET BACK INTO POSITIONS!" Sensei yelled, disbanding the crowd.

"I apologise if I was a distraction." Riley stepped forward, shaking Sensei's hand.

"No need to apologise, it was an honour to watch." With a bow he turned back towards his students, turning around only to give Alice a wink.

"What are you doing here?" Alice angrily whispered as she walked towards the changing room. "How much did you see?"

"Enough to know that you can move well," Riley said as he followed. "You had so many opportunities to beat him, yet didn't. Why?"

"I don't have to explain myself to you," Alice said as she pushed open the changing room door.

How dare he just turn up like that.

She punched in her locker code, opening the door when a hand slammed it shut.

"That was lazy fighting, and you know it," Riley glared.

"Bloody hell Riley, this is the ladies changing room."

She quickly regarded her surroundings, relieved that they were alone. From the sound of the adjoining showers and the women's underwear on the bench that separated the lockers they wouldn't be alone for long.

He continued as if she hadn't spoken.

"You move well, fast. But you continuously leave your left side open. You can't always resort to your magic…"

She tried to yank the metal door, before letting out a sound of frustration.

"If you were so bothered, why didn't you step in?"

"I knew you would be able to get out of it." His looked at her with a such pure focus that unnerved her. He pulled his hand away, allowing her to open the door. "Besides, it would defeat the purpose if I just saved you."

Alice had to grit her teeth from snapping back. She wasn't a damsel in distress, she was a trained Paladin.

"What are you doing here?"

"To see you. You're ignoring me."

"That's funny considering I haven't heard from you in months."

She slammed the locker shut once she had grabbed her bag, letting it drop to the floor by her feet.

"Now are you going to stand there and watch me shower or are you going to fuck off?"

His gaze intensified.

"Is that an invitation, sweetheart?" He gave her a slow teasing grin.

She knew he was joking, but she couldn't stop the heat that shot through her.

"Fuck. Off."

His lip twitched as he fought not to laugh.

"That's harsh considering you were inviting me into the shower only a moment ago."

"I swear Riley, I will…" Alice heard footsteps.

Pushing him back, she hid them behind the lockers, her palms on his bare chest. The woman sang as she dressed quickly, the changing room door swinging closed behind her after a few minutes.

She pulled her palms back as if she had been burned.

"You're going to get me kicked out." She caught his eye, taken back by the unidentifiable emotion. His humour had gone, replaced with a stern expression.

Riley reached down to her bag and grabbed it before she could.

"We need to talk."

"Give me my bag." She went to snatch it, but he was faster. "RILEY," she snarled, not wanting to draw attention as another woman who had walked in, her eyes widening as she briskly made her way to her own locker. But not before she gave Riley a long look.

"We need to talk," he repeated. "Not here, it's too public."

"I'm busy."

"I didn't mean right now." He seemed annoyed. "I'll come by tomorrow."

"I'm busy," she replied again.

I don't need this crap.

"Doing what?"

"If you must know, I'm going to the Church of the Light."

"Why?" He handed her the bag before he folded his arms, making her eyes trace the tattoos along his pec. Her eyes shot up as her cheeks began to burn. Riley didn't seem to notice.

"None of your business." She enjoyed it when he clenched his jaw, eyes pinched in anger. He wasn't a man who was disobeyed often.

Riley cocked his head before he stepped forward, crowding her.

"Why?" he asked again.

"I'm thinking of converting," she shrugged, desperately trying not to touch him again. "Can you please put on a shirt?"

"Why, does it bother you?"

"No," she said too fast.

He growled, throwing on his T-shirt.

"I know you're part of that Spook Squad."

Alice just narrowed her eyes in response.

"Meet me at my place tomorrow... after your church," he added before she could protest, "and bring your sword."

CHAPTER TWELVE

Alice stared at the ornate, but tired architecture that was the Church of the Light, the morning sun giving an almost ethereal quality to the off-white brick.

She must have walked past it hundreds of times and never looked up, never studied the gargoyles that crouched beside the tall but crumbling spires or the old bell through the broken stained-glass window.

The grounds, which must have once had fresh flowers and neatly trimmed shrubbery, had decayed into dilapidated courtyard with dead grass and aged headstones.

"The place has let itself go over the years," Peyton stated as he watched her expression. "Strange considering Brady's intel stated they charge an extortionate fee to join." His lip lifted.

"It's fitting they have gargoyles," she mused. "They're supposed to scare off evil."

Peyton's lip tugged again at the corners. "They consider Breed to be evil."

"What do you think?" she asked.

She turned to look at him, wanting to see his reaction. She still hadn't figured out what he was, knew he couldn't be human. At least, not entirely.

"Are Breed evil?"

"Breed is both evil and good, as are humans. That's the way of life," he said, left eyebrow arched. "Is that the response you wanted?"

"I have time to wear you down," she shrugged, smiling at his subtle head shake.

"We're going to be doing this my way."

He tugged at his tie as if he wasn't used to wearing one, the bright red a shock against the darkness of his tailored suit. Alice, in contrast, wore a pair of blue jeans and a slogan T-shirt that luckily her leather jacket covered, so she didn't look too casual.

Nobody mentioned dressing up, she thought self-consciously.

"Why are we here so early?"

His light eyes shot to her, his face impassive. He shook his head again before he crossed the street, confidently walking through the tall gates and towards the door as if insects weren't crawling across her skin. Trying not to squeak, Alice walked rigidly beside him, trying not to draw attention to herself among the other people. As she crossed the threshold, the sensation stopped as suddenly as it started.

"Did you feel that?" she whispered, looking around to see if anybody else had reacted.

What the fuck was that?

"Remember why we're here dear," he tensely replied, his eyes scanning the few people who were setting up extra seating beside the pews.

A woman wearing a yellow checkered jumper approached, a wide grin creasing her face.

"Are you the Noland's?" she said in a preppy voice. "Why you guys are early, service doesn't start for another few hours or so." A woman wearing a yellow chequered jumper approached, a wide grin on her face.

"That's us, ma'am." Peyton grinned, clasping her outstretched hand. "We know we're early, but we don't have time to stay for the service you see? My wife has a doctor's appointment for her fertility check-up."

Peyton grasped Alice's hand, patting it gently.

Alice's face broke into a fake, shy smile.

Bloody hell, he's good.

Peyton was playing to the recent propaganda that human numbers were falling compared to Breed. There was no evidence to suggest their fertility was failing. However, facts have never been strictly necessary to scare the general public.

"It was the only appointment we could manage," Alice politely added.

Peyton started to stroke Alice's hand gently, even giving her a little squeeze of reassurance.

"I appreciate you accepting my call the other evening, we didn't really know where to turn and have heard great things about your service."

The woman's eyes melted at the affectionate connection.

"Oh you poor dears, it's those damn Breeds, cursing us normal folk with poor fertility." She tutted and frowned, creating deep crevices in her forehead. "Feel free to have a look around, the only people who are here other than myself are a few volunteers who are helping to set up."

"Thank you kindly," he winked, before turning away. "Come on dear, let's get accustomed to this magnificent church."

"Yes, honey." Alice smiled appropriately, letting her gaze take in the supposedly 'magnificent' church. The inside was only marginally better than the outside, the walls the same dull brick.

A gust of wind caught her coat from one of the broken windows, the cardboard that had once been taped up had fallen off, dropping the temperature in the already cold and open room.

"Excuse me, can I help you?" Another woman approached, her eyes unfriendly as she folded her arms. "We're not open right now, you'll have to come back later," she said, her tone short.

"Hi, my name's Gary Nolan, and this is my wife, Melissa." Peyton tugged at Alice. "We were invited by your friend to look around. We're looking to..."

"You're not wearing a ring." The woman interrupted, her eyes shooting to their joined hands where neither of them wore any jewellery.

"Oh, that's me," Alice chuckled, tugging her hand. "Miss ole clumsy."

"Ah, yes." Peyton started to laugh too, catching on to the situation fast. "My wife's an artist, gets paint everywhere. She recently knocked over a whole pot of paint, covering both of us completely."

"That reminds me honey, the rings need to be picked up from the jeweller's a week on Tuesday."

"Oh," the woman looked almost embarrassed by her hostility. "It's nice to meet you, my name's Mrs Lucinda Potts. I apologise if I came across as rude, we've had a lot of weird people wander in recently. I could have sworn they were Breed, but you know we can't always tell." She shook her head.

"I know exactly what you mean Mrs Potts, it's the reason we're here." Peyton moved closer, putting a reassuring hand on her shoulder. "Our neighbourhood is full of them, my wife and I are so worried about our souls being affecting by living in such close proximity."

He genuinely looked worried to the point Alice wasn't sure if he was acting or not.

"It can affect you if you're too friendly with them. But in the same breath, you don't want to upset any of them just in case."

Her eyes darted around as if she mustn't speak of such things. "I heard witches have the ability to suck your soul right out of you. So be wise."

"Oh no, really." Alice gasped, trying not to smile. "We don't live near any witches that I know of, it's those blood sucking vampires that worry me. How can they have a soul if they're already dead?"

"Tell me about it!" Mrs Potts said energetically before starting a lecture about vampires, blood and sacrifices.

"Lucy, can you please help out in the office? James is struggling." A deep set man asked as he approached. "I'll speak to our guests."

"Of course, my dear." She smiled shyly before walking off.

"I see you've met my wife, the names Gordon Potts. How can I help you today?" The gentleman smiled warmly, shaking both their hands before resting his own against his breast pocket.

Alice frowned, taking a second to recognise the man who stood before her.

"I know you, you were leading the rally in front of Parliament."

He had wanted public places to segregate Breed and humans. He was removed from the grounds, but not before giving an interview to the local news station.

Mr Potts grinned, the expression uncomfortable.

"That is just some of the work we do here."

Alice smiled but stepped back, feeling something off about him.

On the news footage he came across as confident, his gaze razor-sharp as he addressed the growing crowd. The man who stood before her didn't ooze the same confidence as he did on the TV, but something dark and ugly instead.

He looked genuine, his face clean- shaven and clothes pressed neatly, the only difference was he wore a leather eyepatch. She didn't know why she suddenly felt the need to recall her magic, her fire tickling her fingertips as she choked the urge down.

There's something wrong.

She wished Peyton had telepathy, it would make everything so much easier. But even if he did, she couldn't explain her gut feeling. That the pirate wannabe was a bad guy because the butterflies in her stomach told her so.

"Your Church is wonderful. My husband and I were fascinated by your wife's passion against vampires," Peyton said.

"A personal favourite of hers." He smiled again, the emotion not reaching his one, pale brown eye. "I appreciate you visiting, as my assistant mentioned on the phone we're in need of some new members who reciprocate the same beliefs."

"That's why we're here." Peyton opened his jacket pocket, pulling out a cheque. "Our admittance." He handed over the money.

"Mr Noland, this is triple our fee." Gordon popped it in his pocket before either Alice or Peyton could ask for it back. "Such generosity…"

"Such generosity deserves special treatment," Peyton finished for him. "Our mutual friend explained you have an inner circle, I believe both my wife and I would benefit from that service."

Gordon said nothing for a second, his eyebrows pinched in anger before he visibly relaxed. "Only those invited may join The Leader's circle. Why should I entertain your arrogance?"

"Because that cheque is just the beginning. I believe in this faith, therefore I am willing to invest in our immortal souls."

"Then Mr Nolan, we would be honoured if you joined us tomorrow night to meet with The Leader. The Leader's circle meets once a week, with only the privileged invited to attend."

"So you're not The Leader?" Alice asked, getting her an unimpressed look in return. "We were under the impression you head this church?"

"I'm merely his closest subordinate. He's the one who offers salvation, protection for our souls. You will meet him tomorrow night, and he will decide whether you meet his expectations." He grinned, showing off pearl white teeth.

"That sounds perfect, I look forward to meeting The Leader." Peyton shook his hand. "Melissa, let's go before we are late for your appointment."

He looked expectantly at Alice.

"Yes, we can't be late. It was lovely to meet you." She nodded a goodbye before walking beside Peyton until they were outside the church grounds.

"So, what do you think?" Peyton asked as they walked side by side. His tone back to his usual closed off self while his smile disappeared along with his chipper personality.

"I think the place is toxic." Alice stopped walking once they were a few roads away. She wrapped her jacket more firmly around her, the temperature dropping as the sky above threatened more snow.

"Toxic? What makes you say that?" He stared at her intently, his eyebrows creased before he noticed their surroundings. Cars beeped around them as pedestrians made their way to work.

"We can't talk here, follow me." He guided them to a café, walking towards the back to an occupied booth. Brady turned to them as they approached, a half-eaten bagel clutched in his large hand.

"Brady," Peyton greeted as he waited for Alice to climb into the booth before him.

Alice narrowed her eyes, not wanting to be trapped against the wall. She stood there until Peyton sat down himself, shuffling to give her room.

"Don't you guys look cute," Brady observed as he sipped his coffee. "I'm just finishing up here. What did you find out?"

A large pot of tea was already on the table beside a jug of milk and two spare mugs.

Alice grabbed the mug closest to her, pouring the hot liquid before clutching it in her cold palms.

"What do you know of The Leader?"

Brady sat back, the plastic booth squeaking in protest at his excess weight.

"According to my intel, he *is* The Church of the Light. Back in his youth he had a greater following, but as the years have gone by, he's only left with the single church."

"Who's your intel? Is it reliable?" Alice asked.

Brady shot her a look. "He's an old family friend. Both he and my father used to be part of the faith, believed in the greater good of humanity. They both left when I was a child, but he still pops in from time to time."

"Okay, do we know why the church is in such a state?"

"According to the paperwork, there was an accident around six months ago with the foundation."

Brady handed over plans, highlighting the original structure and grounds. It showed the church in its entirety, a spec drawing of every room.

"An accident? What sort of accident?" she asked, looking up from the images.

"The report doesn't say, but one that can shatter windows and crumble tombstones," he shrugged as he grabbed his jacket. "I have to meet O'Neil in five, can I leave this with you guys?"

Alice glanced at Peyton, who was studying the plans intently.

"Sure Brady," Alice said when Peyton continued to ignore him. "We'll sort it."

Brady grunted his goodbye.

"This might be why they're asking for admission fees." Peyton blinked when he looked up. "Where's Brady?"

Alice shook her head. "He had to leave. What were you saying about admission fees?"

"This might be why they're asking for admission fees, to help cover the recovery costs of the accident."

"Isn't that what insurance is for?"

"Interesting point. They either haven't got any insurance, or there's a reason behind why they didn't want to claim."

"Isn't it illegal to not have insurance for something like that?" Alice asked. Which left the other option.

"You're right, it makes them desperate."

"Exactly, and what do desperate people do?"

Peyton sat back in his chair, thinking, his tea completely untouched in front of him.

"They resort to desperate measures."

He looked down at his mug, frowning before gently moving the teaspoon away with the tip of his finger.

Alice frowned, watching the odd move. Why wouldn't he touch the teaspoon?

"Can you touch iron?" she asked casually as she swapped into Brady's old seat.

"Iron?" his eyes narrowed. "What makes you say that?"

Alice shrugged. "No reason."

Except he had tried to avoid touching the spoon.

Iron was an irritant to the Fae in the same way pure silver could cause painful burns to shifters. It had forced them to move out of cities until the industrial revolution, where steel was mass-produced instead for foundational building material.

Iron was still a small percentage in buildings, but not enough to get a reaction. The teaspoon wouldn't have much if any iron at all, but Peyton didn't necessarily know that.

He frowned at her as he grabbed the spoon, placing it next to his other untouched cutlery. His eyes danced with amusement when he caught hers, a slight smile tugging his lips. He knew exactly what she had asked.

Bastard.

"What do you think about Gordon Potts?" he asked, ignoring the spoon situation.

"He felt... off." Saying it out loud made her feel stupid.

"You saying he isn't human? You keep trying to convince yourself I'm not human, so I apologise if I don't take your word seriously."

"I never said you weren't entirely human."

Not to his face anyway.

"I also didn't say he wasn't human, just something feels off. I can't put my finger on it."

"I'll look into him, see if he has any criminal records." His eyes glazed for a second before focusing on her once again. "You have anything else?"

"No."

"Then I'll see you tomorrow, wife." He smiled, just a small curve of his lips.

He had an odd sense of humour, and she would simply have to add that thought to the very short list of other things she knew about Officer Peyton.

CHAPTER THIRTEEN

Alice knocked gently on the wooden door that was supposed to be Riley's place, her temper flaring when she was made to wait several minutes with no response. Riley must have known she was there, the rigmarole of being I.D.'d at the front desk, glared at by security and then escorted into the private lift just to get to the front door.

She wasn't technically late to his demanded meeting, he never exactly specified a time. He had asked for her to meet him at his place after the Church of the Light, giving her no more information than the address. He didn't know she went early in the morning, then went for a jog, made fresh bread, and did pretty much anything else she could think of that delayed her.

She even spent a good twenty minutes appreciating the gorgeous, glass skyscraper that was in the centre of the Breed District. Each window mirrored, reflecting the city back beautifully.

She didn't want to be there.

She didn't want a Warden.

"About time you got here," a mechanical voice buzzed.

Alice looked around then frowned, not seeing where the voice could have come from considering the door was still closed. Riley's place was the only door on the entire top floor of what she thought was an office building.

When she had entered the atrium many floors below, she thought she had the wrong address. Men and women in suits seemed to be working, talking on their phones and generally looking busy. She even noticed a large board displaying names of a few businesses that operated inside the high rise, the name 'STORM' across the top.

It was peculiar, to say the least. Did he live at his office?

"Get in. We're towards the back."

We're? Alice pushed the door, realising it was unlocked. Closing it behind her she squinted at the darkly lit room, trying to make out the rough shapes of the sofa and large TV.

She tried to have a nosey before she heard a faint clanging followed by a deep growl. Figuring that was more interesting she followed the sound into a large room, just as poorly lit.

Dropping her bag onto the floor with an audible thump she waited to be noticed as Riley and Xander fought with swords, metal clashing violently as they attacked each other at full speed, their movements blurred.

Alice couldn't help but stare, watching both men move as if they were in a choreographed dance. They continued to snarl as they became faster, bouncing off their heels as they pushed and parried in equal shows of power. Both were shirtless with similar tattoos patterned across the majority of their chests, back and arms.

She still didn't entirely understand what the tattoos meant, her father only having a simple design around his wrist. Riley hadn't exactly been forthcoming with an explanation, even though he knew she wanted to know more about her father's heritage.

"ENOUGH!" Riley growled as he threw down his sword, lifting his leg into a quick kick that connected with Xander's stomach. Xander huffed back, fist clenching around his sword as he stood there, chest heaving.

With a quick nod Xander placed his sword into a special frame on the wall before turning to the door. His eyes were the palest blue she had ever seen, almost white to the point she couldn't tell where his iris's began or even finished.

He shot her a glare, grumbling at her from the back of his throat before walking out.

"Light on," Riley said huskily, the light above reacting to his voice command.

Alice had to blink several times before she could see, her eyes taking their time to adjust to the sudden brightness. Riley stood in the centre of the room, arms folded, anger evident in the curve of his brow.

Fuck sake, what have I done now?

Refusing to be the first to speak, she studied the room, admiring the ornate swords and axes displayed on the walls. It was larger than she initially thought, twice the size of her house in square feet, at least. On the far right stood various weight apparatus, running machines and punching bags. The rest of the floor was empty, giving room for movement. For a home gym, it was impressive, although, she didn't understand why he would need so many machines if he lived there alone. There were even seven lockers, clearly well used and decorated with novelty stickers.

"Strip." A demand, not Riley's usual chirpy attitude.

"Excuse me?" she shot back, his attitude igniting her own anger. "What bug crawled up your arse?"

"I said strip, sweetheart," Riley said, dropping his tone as his eyes flashed silver. "Why can't you follow orders?"

"Because..." Alice started, hesitating as she thought of a reasonable response that wasn't childish or petty.

Fuck sake.

Huffing in frustration she ripped open her jacket, throwing it onto the wooden floor beside her bag. She was glad she had already changed into her gym clothes, satisfied she didn't have to give in to his demand. Although she felt overdressed.

Riley wore skin-tight shorts, ones that left nothing to the imagination as they stuck to every muscle possible. Alice fought not to look down, wondering if the tattoos that danced across his hips went lower...

NO! She scolded herself. She did not need that image stuck in her brain.

"What are you wearing?" he asked, his anger not as vivid as before.

Alice couldn't hold the small smirk back any longer. How could he possibly ask her that when he stood there virtually naked?

"It's a shirt," she said, playing ignorance. She watched as he tried not to smile, his anger starting to dissipate.

Her top read, *"I HAVE ABS-olutely no control.'*

She wasn't going to apologise for it. "Why is it so dark?"

"Xander doesn't like the light," he replied quickly, his bare feet making no noise as he walked towards her.

"His eyes?" she questioned, not really expecting an answer. She had only ever seen people with eyes that pale who were sight impaired. Yet, Xander walked confidently, showing no signs his eyes caused him any problem. "So, you live in an office building?"

"It's my building," he said. "I split my time between here and my other place."

"The building? You own the building?"

"Where else would I keep all my investments?" he said, eyebrows low as if the question confused him.

"Bloody hell, how much money do you have?" Alice was embarrassed as soon as the question left her lips. She knew it was rude, but couldn't seem to help herself even though the answer didn't really matter. Riley came from money, but she didn't really understand that he was a businessman.

"Did you come equipped?" Riley said instead, his grey eyes catching hers.

Nodding, she pulled out her sword that was strapped to a specially designed harness between her shoulder blades. As soon as she palmed the hilt the runes along the steel glowed eerily. She didn't acknowledge the flash of light, deciding to ignore it. She still didn't understand why the sword suddenly reacted when she touched it, couldn't find any difference in its performance. The runes themselves were just as confusing, the shapes unlike anything she had ever seen before.

It wasn't of witch or druid origin.

Riley observed the lights carefully, frowning at the patterns that continued to glow. Even he didn't seem to know why the blade shone, or if he did, he wasn't telling her.

"What's the matter?" she asked as he just continued to stand there. "You seem..." Riley leapt towards her, his leg curling around in a wide kick that made her jump back with a shout.

"You didn't react fast enough," he growled, his eyes flashing silver in an instant. She was still mesmerised, watching his unusual eyes turn from a storm grey to a mirrored silver then back again. It wasn't a druid trait, she knew that for certain.

No Breed had silver eyes, not even the Fae.

"Faster."

He threw his weight against her shoulder, disarming her with a quick flick of his wrist.

"Again." He handed back the sword, his features stern, almost disappointed.

"Fine," she said through clenched teeth. This time she lasted around two minutes before he rendered her unarmed, her blade clattering to the ground whilst Riley remained unharmed. The third time she lasted three minutes, then it was five, then seven.

Each time he left her unarmed without breaking a sweat. It was insulting.

"Again." She jumped at him this time, engaging the fight as sweat trickled down her back. Feigning a turn, she waited for him to react, as he spun to grab her she jumped back, turning the opposite direction and hitting out. The flat of the blade touched his hip, enough for her to grin, thinking she had the upper hand.

The sword was tugged from her grasp, thrown across the room as arms enveloped her, crushing. Alice remained calm, breathing in deep as she threw her head back, smashing into his nose.

"FUCK!" Riley roared as he tugged her back, flipping her onto the ground. "ENOUGH!" He put his whole weight onto her hips, pinning her as she breathed heavily beneath him.

"I got you," she smiled, even as blood started to trickle out his nose.

He gripped her wrists harder, holding them above her head as he ignored the slow descent of his blood.

"If this were a real fight, you would've been finished." She wanted to do a happy dance, elated at the small victory after all the times he had disarmed her with ease.

"You honestly believe that?" he said, his eyes intense as he studied her. "You should have made that move within the first ten minutes. You didn't even scratch me and you think you've won?"

He released her wrists, but remained above her, his weight on his arms.

"You seem to think this is a game. Like this isn't life or death." He hopped up, moving away to kick her sword further away. "Even now, you don't even realise how close you are to the edge."

Alice clambered up to her feet, wanting to argue.

"No, I'm not..." Then she felt it, the burning inside, the suffocating heat that was bubbling beneath her skin, threatening to explode.

"Alice?" A trace of concern on his face. "Look at me," he demanded.

Alice flicked her eyes to his, holding the grey spheres as they became molten silver. Those eyes weren't his, weren't Riley.

"Riley?" she questioned even as she started to taste smoke.

"Concentrate on me," he growled, his voice deeper than usual, hoarse.

Alice began to gasp for air, her power beyond her safe level. Flicking her wrist, she released as much of the fire as she could, concentrating on the burst of orange as it burned into a deeper blue. Letting out a breath she felt smoke tickle her nose as her fire started to burn the wooden floor. Sucking it back in she stared at the scorched mark, wondering what the hell happened.

"Hey, are you okay?" Riley was suddenly beside her, his hands holding her upper arms in a bruising grip.

"I haven't had a flare out in weeks." She never even felt her power breach the safety level, had been too busy with Riley. "How did you do it?" She tried to step back, but he gripped her arms harder.

"Do what?" He finally released her, but did not step away.

"It's you, being close to you..." she began even as she felt the fire begin to build once more.

"It might be the ley line. This place is built on one."

"You know I can't feel ley lines," she said angrily.

Ley lines were natural energies that seemed to connect ancient sacred sites around the world, undetectable to anybody who wasn't attuned to the earth. As a witch, she could see them through her third eye, but was unable to harness the natural energy, unlike druids.

"Look at me." Riley's hand shot out to grip her chin. The instant his skin made contact her inner fire calmed, retreating to a manageable level.

"How can you do that?" She stood there, welcoming the sudden feeling of peace. She could feel the pulse in Riley's palm, feel the warmth of his skin.

Riley smiled but didn't answer her question.

"This wasn't as bad as last time," he said, his thumb rubbing circles along her cheek. "However, we do need to figure out what made your power react in such a violent way."

Alice suddenly felt awkward, her cleansing calm being replaced with distrust. Stepping back, she broke their connection, confused as to why she wanted to step back into his hand.

"Your chi is energy, an arcane you can manipulate and control." Riley's hand was suddenly covered in silver, a ball of arcane so controlled it was a perfect misty sphere.

Alice was captivated by it, enthralled. She blurred her vision, concentrating on opening her mind, opening her third eye.

The ability to see more than the mundane was something she took for granted, it showed her perceptions beyond ordinary sight. It showed her the Plethora ley line, one of the largest in the south of England that happened to be swirling around Riley's penthouse. Ley lines usually kept close to the earth, a rainbow of swirls and smoke that flowed from one site to another. Riley had had someone harness the ley line to encompass his whole building, or at least his penthouse, resulting in his own personal power socket.

"How?" she asked, watching the multitude of colours flowing across him.

"It's a secret," he said, eyes sparkling as he smiled. Her breath caught at that smile.

I need to go.

"I have to go," she echoed her thoughts. He was too distracting.

"We're not finished with training. You need to learn how to harness your power."

"Not today, I don't."

"Yes, today." Riley shot his arcane to within an inch of her face, the heat of the power touching her skin. "You have little control over yourself," he said as he began to get irritated. "Your affliction with your fire isn't normal, you need discipline…"

"Stop it, I'm doing fine on my own." She turned to pick up her blade, sheathing it in one practised move. "I'm a grown adult, I don't need to be babysat."

"You need fucking training." Riley raised his voice, the arcane extinguished when she turned back to him. "What about that flare up?"

"YOU were the reason for the flare up," she snarled, feeling her chi ignite.

Fuck sake. It was Riley that brought out these strange feelings, ones she tried desperately to suppress.

"Surely you know you're not simply a witch. You're more, your power reacts more like a…"

Alice cut him off with an empty laugh. "You don't know anything."

"Grow up, sweetheart," he snarled, stepping towards her aggressively. "This is my job, something I have been asked to do…"

"That's right!" she interrupted. "You're The Order's puppet. Or is it The Council's?"

Riley growled, his fists clenched as he began to speak.

Alice cut him off.

"Tell me Riley, have you been given the order to destroy me if this doesn't work?" She held her breath for the answer, his silence all she needed to know.

She began to laugh again, a full belly hysteria.

"Everything is out of my control. I have been told I have a Warden. I have been told The Council are concerned about me. I have been told my life is at risk."

"You think I don't understand?" he said through clenched teeth. "You know nothing of my life. Know nothing of what I've been through." He stormed towards her. "Why do you resist so much? Is it the training? Or is it me?" His nose almost touched hers as he bent forward, his eyes furious as he tried to intimidate. "You need my help. Not the other way around. Remember that."

"Fuck you."

His lips were on hers quick as a flash, their tongues battling for control as he pulled her head towards his. His chi was electric, sparkles across her skin as she absorbed his warmth like a woman desperate for touch, for connection. Her hands were everywhere, touching and shaping his body as his own clenched around her hips. She let out a moan, the feeling...

"Sire?" Xander's voice echoed in the room.

As if they were drenched in cold water they leapt apart, both panting uncontrollably.

"What is it Xee?" Riley didn't look towards his friend, his eyes too intense as he concentrated on Alice.

"Your father."

Alice tried to smile, her emotions raw. "Your duty calls."

Riley said nothing for a moment, just stared. "You have an appointment."

The statement threw her.

"What are you, my secretary now?"

He just glared at her before turning his attention to Xander. "Make sure she attends."

He lined up among the other boys, all shaking as cold water drenched their bodies. They had just finished a five-mile run in the rain. They weren't allowed to speak to each other. Barely even look.

But he glanced anyway, curious. He had been there six months before he saw anybody else other than the teachers. Not even his father, not since he came to tell him of his mother's death. They were all boys, almost men.

He had heard a teacher slip in conversation, saying they were the children of the strongest.

Bred specifically.

Who breeds for a child specifically?

Not his mother. She was peace. Would never have bred him into this world if she knew what they would do. Beat him. Control him.

They thought he was their puppet.

They were wrong.

There were seven of them in total.

Seven boys.

Seven beasts.

CHAPTER FOURTEEN

"**G**et out of the car." Xander leant over her lap to force the door open. Alice slammed it back closed as she turned to scowl at him.

"You didn't answer my question."

"I don't answer to you," he snapped, his jaw clenched as the steering wheel screeched beneath his palms. He had been silent throughout the drive, ignoring any attempt of conversation. She knew he hadn't been pleased with babysitting duty, something they agreed on.

Her gaze wandered to the hospital, nerves attacking her stomach. There was a reason Alice didn't attend her doctor's appointments. She didn't like doctors. Not necessarily the whole profession, just ones who looked over her like a lab rat. Ones who didn't see her as a person, but an equation they were struggling to figure out.

"Why am I here?" she asked him again as he refused to face her, his eyes hidden behind his wrap-around glasses. "Seriously? You won't even answer that?" She let out a noise of frustration. "It's not like I asked you about your special tattoos or why you called Riley 'Sire.'" She had been stunned at the title, wanted to know more.

His jaw moved, showing his irritation.

"Isn't your father a Druid?" he asked, surprising her.

She nodded.

"Then how come you don't even know your ancestry?" he bit out.

Alice didn't miss a beat.

"Because he's dead. Died when I was young."

Xander finally faced her, his expression softening as he murmured words in a language she didn't understand before switching to English.

"I'm sorry."

"What for? You didn't kill him," she said calmly, shrugging. "I don't know much about either of my parents."

Alice gripped the door handle, pulling it gently until it clicked open.

"They're not just tattoos, they're magic infused glyphs. Druids get them around their wrists when they come of age. It helps them to control ley lines, among other things."

Alice held the door, staggered he had answered. Xander had been vocal that he wasn't her number one fan, yet he had answered a question Riley wouldn't.

"Then why do you and Riley have so many?"

Xander remained silent, long enough that she didn't think he would answer at all.

"You're going to be late for your appointment."

Alice opened the door, her feet crunching on the small amount of snow that had settled on the footpath.

"Why am I here?" she asked once more, hoping he would finally explain why they wanted her to attend.

Xander leant across the seat, his face calm as he looked up at her. It annoyed her that she couldn't read his eyes behind the glasses, couldn't decipher his expression clearly.

"You need to be careful. You need to attend as that is what The Council wants."

"Of course, they say jump, and you both ask how high."

He growled, the sound weird as if it started from deep within his chest. "Fuck The Council."

That didn't answer her question.

"What about you calling Riley 'Sire?'

Xander pulled the door from her grasp, speeding off a second later.

"Well, then."

She rocked back on her heels, the cold biting into her exposed cheeks.

What *did* The Council want?

It was the second time The Council had been mentioned when she discussed the tests. First with Dread, when she promised him she would attend and second with Xander. It made her cautious.

It also made her wonder why she was asked to undertake the tests at the General Hospital and not the hospital wing in the S.I. Tower. As usual, the corridors were painted white, matching the white tiled floor and ceiling. The artificial lights glowed eerily above her, guiding her further down the corridor until she came to Dr Richards' office. A man stood outside it, his face in a scowl as he spotted her.

"You're late," he grumbled, his dark eyes narrowing. "Get inside." He opened the door with one of his big meaty fists, pushing her through before locking the door behind her.

"Alice, how nice of you to come today." Dr David Richards smiled uneasily from his seat beside his desk, his eyes flicking to the small window in the door then back at her. "It's been, what, four weeks?"

Three and a half, actually.

"What's with..."

"So let's get started, shall we?" he interrupted, his eyes flicking to the door then back again.

"Okay," she said as she sat awkwardly in the uncomfortable armchair.

He nodded, his hands agitated as he shuffled through his papers.

"As you have missed other appointments, this is just a catch-up from the previous tests."

Dr Dave – as he liked to be called, frowned as he read through the notes, the eagle tattoo above his right eyebrow angrily judging her.

"As I'm sure you're used to now, the video camera will record every test and conversation in the room," he said as he pointed to the professional camera set up in the corner, the red light flashing ominously. "How has your general health been these past few weeks?"

Alice listed everything he wanted to hear, it was like a rehearsed speech she had memorised from the previous visits. All she ever got from these appointments were the facts she was generally healthy, and that they had no clue what caused her power flares.

Pointless.

"What about flares?" he asked, "when was your last one?"

"Over four weeks ago," she replied instantly even as his eyes narrowed at her answer.

He knew she was lying.

"Fine," she huffed, her eyes glaring into the camera then back to him. "It wasn't exactly a flare," she lied again. "I just became overwhelmed."

"Overwhelmed? In what situation were you in?"

Alice felt her face begin to burn, it took all her control to keep her face relaxed.

Fuck you, Riley.

"I was training."

"Training?" Dr Dave repeated, his attention on something behind her.

"Oh, let me get that..." He stood up quickly from his seat just as his arm swung and hit the camera off its mount.

The camera crashed to the ground in an audible thump. He promptly ran to the equipment and placed it back onto its stand, only for the red record light to be turned off.

Alice wanted to ask if it was safe, decided against it as Dr Dave gazed towards the locked door.

"We only have a few minutes or so before they notice the camera feed has stopped." He sat back in his chair, face concerned as he kept flicking nervous glances towards the camera and the door. "I need you to know that I do not work for S.I. nor The Council. I give my findings directly to Commissioner Grayson, do you understand?"

"Yes." Dread trusted him.

"I have only just recently been informed about your ancestry. Unfortunately, that also means The Council know, which is probably why there is so much attention on figuring out your power limitations. I'm hoping they will be satisfied with the video footage, but I can't promise I can keep them from trying to continue their experiments."

"Excuse me?" A man wearing a dark suit burst through the door, someone Alice didn't recognise. The man who pushed her through the door stormed in behind him.

"Can you not see I'm with a patient?!" Dr Dave barked. "You're interrupting."

"Apologies Dr," the man said without any sincerity, "the camera isn't working, so this session cannot continue."

"Oh, is it not?" Dr Dave turned towards the camera, reached over and flicked a switch. "I knocked it over a minute ago and didn't realise it had switched off. Are we working now?"

The man stood there for a moment, his face unfriendly before he nodded. Without a goodbye he left with his friend, closing the door behind them.

"What's with the suits?" Alice asked before she remembered they were being watched.

Dr Dave thought about the question before answering, his head nodding towards the camera.

"I believe they work for the new team that reports directly to The Council. I've been informed you will be seeing them around The Tower too."

Great, just what I need.

"Seems friendly."

"Let us get back to your results. All your tests have come back as expected for a woman your age. At the moment we're running on the theory that your ancestry has given you a greater ability to harness energy than the average person."

"Should I be worried?"

"That remains to be seen. We have been asked to keep a close eye on you until we recognise a pattern with your power flares. Until then I'll be researching other descendants and see if there is any record of anything similar."

"So, this was a waste of time."

Again.

"Forever the optimist," he chuckled. "We need to test your stamina and heart rate again," he said as he turned on the running machine beside his desk. "You know the routine."

"Yes," she sighed, removing her jacket.

Whatever Dread had planned, it better be worth it.

CHAPTER FIFTEEN

Alice stroked her fingers through Sam's glossy hair, the smooth movements comforting as he stretched across her lap in a distinctively feline way.

He chuckled at the movie they were watching, his hand reaching out to grab the popcorn in the bowl by the floor. Alice darted her eyes up to the screen, watching the clearly fake vampire bite into his busty victim's neck. She couldn't see clearly, the mid-day sun streaming through the gaps in the curtain, so she went back to stroking Sam's hair, enjoying the heavy silk through her fingers.

"Watch this bit," Sam laughed. "You can clearly see how fake the blood is."

They both had the majority of the day off, and had decided to catch up with their weekly movie. It was Sam's choice, which was why they were watching a poorly rated B-movie with the worst acting she had ever seen. She loved him, but he truly had the worst taste in movies.

"Hey, did you see it?" Sam moved onto his elbow, his hair pulling from her hands as he turned to check. "Are you even watching?" His eyebrows came down in concern.

"How can I not watch the man with those abs?" she smirked, knowing it would get a reaction. "Remind me again why you chose this specific film?"

He grinned, the leopard showing unrepentant mischief in his eyes.

"You can't say I don't treat ya." He popped another popcorn into his mouth before relaxing back onto her lap, his head resting on her thigh.

As soon as he started to laugh at the film once more she allowed her smile to drop, her hands busying themselves in his hair once more.

She couldn't concentrate on the screen, her brain overthinking every little detail of the past few days. It was actually comforting to sit with Sam, to hear his untainted joy at such a simple thing. He was her rock, kept her down to earth. He knew all her secrets, her nightmares, her worries. And he loved her anyway, flaws and all.

"That was one of the worst films you have ever made me watch," Alice said an hour later. "Not even the abs could make up for it."

"Nah, it wasn't that bad." Sam stretched his arms above his head, turning to look at her. "Your choice next week, you can torture me with one of those sci-fi's," he groaned, pouting.

"I've decided on a superhero one, actually," she grinned, knowing he secretly loved all things fantasy and sci-fi just as much as she did. Last year she had gotten him to dress up as a green monster for a convention, he groaned the whole day but she knew he loved the attention. It wasn't like she wasn't dressed up too, in the matching monster outfit.

"So you've been quiet," Sam commented as he sat up.

"Did you want me to talk through the whole film?"

He poked her nose. "You know what I mean," he smirked. "How was training?"

Alice looked away, not sure what to say. "It was okay."

"You're not telling me something."

"I don't think I want to continue training with Riley," she said as she stood up, stretching her legs.

"Riley? Why?" Sam pulled her back down beside him.

"I... I." She didn't know how to explain how she felt. "I don't trust him." Which was true, she didn't trust him, not entirely at least.

"You need to train," Sam stated, shaking his head. "Don't be an idiot baby girl."

"I can do it on my..."

"No," he said, cutting her off. "You need the help. You know it even if you don't admit it yourself." He sighed as he reached for her hair, tangling it around his finger. "Riley isn't Rex."

Alice couldn't help her flinch. "Why would you say that?"

"Because I know you, more than anyone else. They're both men of authority, you're afraid the pull you feel towards him is being manipulated, like the bracelet."

Alice sat there dumbfounded, staring into his amber eyes. *Shit.*

"You're allowing what *he* did to influence your emotions on the one man that can train you. And you do need the training."

"Okay, who are you and where have you put my best friend?" Alice pulled away.

Sam let out a mock growl before he bounced to his feet.

"Sometimes it's my turn with the helpful advice," he grinned. "Anyway that's enough of my superior guidance, I need to get ready."

Alice couldn't help but smile even though she felt confused. She had to think about what he said. Sighing, she swung her legs onto the sofa, lounging back. "I didn't think you're working today?"

"I'm not." He caught her eye, his leopard flashing across his amber irises. "I have a date."

"A date?" she spluttered. "But you don't date!"

No, Sam was a once, maybe twice casual sex guy. He didn't do commitment.

"Who is she?"

"*His* name's Zachary, and I met him the other day." Sam gave her a slow grin. "You okay on your own?"

Alice felt her smile tighten. "I'm a big girl, I'm sure I can look after myself." She could distract herself.

Sam read her expression, his own smile wavering.

"I can stay," he said, sounding unsure.

"And miss your hot date with Zac? I don't think so." She jumped up from the sofa. ""Go, have fun. At least one of us should get laid."

Sam smirked. "Maybe it should be you," he winked before he moved upstairs, the shower starting a few minutes later.

Alice stood there for a moment, staring at the rolling credits on the screen. She couldn't stay there, moping around. She needed to do something, anything.

Decision made she grabbed her jacket, locking the front door behind her.

Well, I guess this was a good enough distraction, Alice thought as she stared at the portrait of a dragon.

She had already memorised every scale, every flame and curl of smoke. Large eyes, like emeralds glistened as razor-sharp teeth snarled. One claw curled around a pearlescent orb, protecting it while the other clutched at a rock, one that teased the edge of a mountain.

Even as she looked at the painting, her own face mirrored slightly by the reflective glass, she couldn't comprehend how she could be called a dragon, a beast so beautiful it took her breath away.

A beast of mythology, one that didn't exist. But it also made sense, a dragon the symbol for the Draco's, a family name so old it was said they existed around the time of The Goddess, the alleged creator of the witch race.

At the beginning of time she gifted four humans with an element, she gave the ability to manipulate water to a Diluvi, earth was given to a Terra, air was gifted to an Avem and fire was for a Draco. Over the years the original elemental powers became diluted through generations combining, creating modern witches' ability to control magic. At least, that was how the legend went.

Dread had told her to visit the exhibit, she had used as many excuses as she could not to go. She hated to admit that she was afraid, afraid of what she was, afraid of what she could be. She didn't have her parents there to ask, to seek comfort. But she wasn't a child, she was a fully grown- arse woman who needed to understand her heritage if she was to grow further.

No more hiding.

She had felt drawn to the portrait almost immediately, but what really caught her attention was the poem engraved beside it, the same poem that was messily written on a coffee stained napkin in her pocket.

With steady breaths, they ride towards the dawn.
Mortals cower in the dark, defenceless, prepare to mourn.
Shadows move across their souls, as darkness, corruption and power grows.
The four elements, magnets against mortal breath.
Generations of lies, of wrath.
Power in its truest form, made physical with greed.
Are they saviours who wish to lead?
Famine destroys along the path, against Pestilence in his wrath.
Death stares and waits his turn, as War's flames turn to burn.
The apocalypse they bring to earth, destroying it for all it's worth.

It was the same poem recited to her by a dying Daemon, one who called her not only Dragon, but War.

"Excuse me, ma'am," a voice from behind her gently asked. "You've been staring at the painting for a while now, could I be of some assistance?"

Alice gripped the red velvet rope, not wanting to look away from either the dragon or the poem. Peeling her fingers back, she turned to the voice, noticing the balding gentleman wearing a smart suit and lanyard. Behind him only a few people remained, the museums closing time coming up fast. She really had been staring at the painting for hours.

"Do you know much about that poem?" she asked.

"Ah, it's a beautiful one," he smiled as he looked at it. "An old poem with no author." He shuffled closer. "It's the prediction of the apocalypse as believed by The Knights."

"The Knights?" she asked, frowning at him even though his attention was on the poem. She had never heard of them before. "What have they got to do with the Original Elementals?"

"It's because this particular poem dictates that true-blood Elementals were manifestations of the four horsemen of the apocalypse."

He grinned, obviously enjoying her shocked reaction.

"It's also why the original families have been hunted, leaving no known descendants but a room full of artefacts." He gestured to the large room, Alice only just noticing the other portraits and relics on display.

When she had entered a few hours ago, she instantly felt herself drawn to the dragon, completely ignoring the three other portraits placed equally spaced along the wall, each representing an element. The first was earth, a large crystal gargoyle perched on top of a mountain, the sunlight splintering through in a beautiful rainbow. Water was depicted by a three-headed hydra, the scales shimmered as if water physically flowed across the painting. Last was air, a pure white gryphon in mid-flight. Each feather was meticulously painted, the talons and beak dangerously sharp.

Large glass cabinets stood beneath each portrait, holding various memorabilia from crystals, drawings to a few black and white photographs. Alice studied the photographs, scanning them to see if she recognised any of the men and women who posed stone-faced for the photographer. Of course she didn't, the date stamped on them almost two hundred years old.

"Where do you get the items from?" she asked as she pointed to the photos. "Can't these just be anybody's?"

"Donated mostly. Some are lent to the museum by people who collect such things, and some are from historians who can approve their authenticity. The photograph in the middle is the last known picture evidence of any of the Elementals."

Last known picture?

"Why do you say there are no descendants?"

"Well, I'm sure many people originate from them, but there are no known true descendants, ones who have the same ability as their ancestors. The legend is that King Arthur himself was scared of their combined power, so worried for his people he sought out the Celts who predicted that it only took one true descendent in any generation to cause true devastation. If all four true Elementals got together then... well... it would cause the apocalypse."

"That sounds ridiculous."

"Well it does now I suppose, but back then they truly believed it. Believed it to the point the Terra family became known as Death, Draco's became War, Diluvi's became Pestilence and Avem's Famine. The original four elementals became The Four Horsemen of the apocalypse."

He pulled at his lanyard, frowning.

"It caused the families to go into hiding, protecting themselves from the king's obsession. He would get his Knights to destroy towns and villages all from a whisper or even a rumour that an Elemental could be found there, even though only a true-blood could actually control their ancestor's magic."

"I didn't think The Four Horsemen legend was a Breed story?"

"Ah, many renditions of the same tale can be found among most religions and Breeds. In the same way, many religions believe in different variations of a comparable god. It was the same with King Arthur, he thought it was his job to make sure the prophecy could never come to be, so he organised his Knights to hunt down the families and slaughter them."

"So they were made pariahs," Alice said, clenching her fist. "What do you believe?"

"Excuse me?"

"Do you believe there are family members still out there? From any of the elements?"

"It's impossible to tell. It's believed that The Knights are still hunting today, believing that even now, the descendants could bring hell on earth."

Alice kicked an aluminium can away with her boot as she walked to the bus stop.

She felt drained, as if her whole life was a lie which, technically, it was. She didn't know who she was, who her parents were. She kicked the can again, enjoying the clatter it made across the pavement, the snow having already disappeared.

At least I have control over this, Alice thought as she kicked the can once more, *the existence of an inanimate object.*

Alice lifted her boot to kick the can again, hesitating when she heard something crunch behind her. Spinning, she swept her eyes across the empty street, unable to tell where the noise came from. It was late, but not late enough in the city to be so quiet. She flared her chi, trying to sense if she was truly alone or not. Nothing, either she was going crazy or whoever was there had concealed their aura.

Senses on high alert she slowly bent to grab the can, throwing it in the bin before she began walking once more.

Another crunch, closer this time.

It could just be a cat, Alice thought as she forced herself to remain calm, to not hurry her pace.

Crunch.

She flared her chi again, hoping it was just Kyle.

Crunch.

Alice casually turned down a dark alley, luckily London was full of them. As soon as she was out of sight of the street, she ran to a dustbin, crouching behind it. She held her breath, waiting. A few seconds passed before she heard it, someone walking into the opening. She slowly stood up, making sure she was hidden in shadow. A man she didn't recognise stood at the mouth of the alley, his face stern.

Now, who are you?

The man grunted, walking forward. When he passed, Alice stepped out from behind the dustbin, intending to follow him. He stopped in his tracks, his head swinging from side to side as mumbled something beneath his breath. A ball of light shot out of his right hand, suspended in the air for a few seconds before floating towards Alice.

Alice leapt back, the ball of light following. The stranger turned, his eyes wide when he realised she was behind him.

"Who are you?" she asked, watching his light carefully. "Why are you following me?"

"Shit!" He threw his hand forward, the ball of light expanding, lighting the dark alley in an unnatural light. Alice had to squint, the light blinding.

"Hey!" she shouted as her eyes began to water. "Who are you?"

"*BUTIO!*"

Alice rolled away just as the ball burst into sparks, barely missing the spell as it shattered around her.

A hand was around her throat, pinning her to the cobblestones as he rummaged in his pocket, finding a small glass bottle while his knee pinned her shoulder. Eyes narrowed he went back into his pocket, pulling out an identical glass bottle. He pulled out the cork with his teeth, muttering beneath his breath.

"*Somnum ante lucem. Somnum ante lucem. Somnum ante lucem.*"

Alice scratched up his hand, forcing him to release his grip just enough so she could smash her fist forward, cracking his nose. His hands loosened completely, enough for her to fling herself to the side, dislodging his knee.

"Fuck, my nose!" he cried as gripped his face, the glass bottles smashing at his feet. A vapour cloud curled around his legs, slowly crawling up his body before disappearing.

"Who are you?" She gripped his collar, pushing him against the brick wall with as much strength as she could. Luckily he was small for a man, a size similar to herself. "What was in the bottles?"

"You... ca... blllerrrrrrrt..." the stranger slurred, his eyes becoming unfocused.

Alice shook him.

"Pay attention!" When he didn't, she slapped him. "Why were you following me?"

"Bloooo... me... foo."

"Oh, for fuck sake." She released him, allowing him to crash to the street, head slumped back with his legs at an uncomfortable angle. A second later he was snoring softly.

Alice stared at him for a moment, then the shards of glass a few feet away. The hand at her throat hadn't been strong, he never intended to hurt her, just keep her still long enough before he could grab the potion.

The man snored gently, his breath hitching at intervals before he groaned.

A sleep potion.

The glass crunched beneath her boot as she crouched down, staring at the remnants of the two bottles. One was obviously a sleep potion, and the other...

"Fuck," she cursed, recognising the flower on part of a shard. A forget-me-not.

Angry she kicked at his leg, getting her a soft grunt before he continued to snore.

"A fucking amnesia potion," she moaned at the unconscious man. "Really?" She kicked him again, savouring his grunt.

She hoped he had bruises in the morning, or evening, or whenever the spell wore off. Opening his coat, she rummaged through his pockets, finding three more bottles and a wallet. Popping the bottles in her jacket, she opened the wallet.

Burt .P. Lince
The Magika
Department of Magic & Mystery
Officer ID – 74692-6

"Great, just great, He's a fucking Officer for The Magika. Shit. Shit. Shit."

She grit her teeth, tucking the wallet back into his coat. She couldn't just leave him there, not if he belonged to The Magika, the witches' official congregation. While a witch held a seat within The Council, The Magika specifically governed their own Breed on a day- to- day basis. Every witch was supposed to present themselves to the congregation to be ranked into a tier system, something Alice never went to.

What was The Magika doing following her?

Alice eyed the glass shards once more, biting her bottom lip.

Well, at least he isn't going to remember what happened.

CHAPTER SIXTEEN

Munching on a noodle, Alice grinned crazily at the jogger who was giving her an odd look. She didn't think it was weird for someone to sit on a bench eating from a box with chopsticks. Everybody else who walked past seemed to disagree.

She ate another mouthful, ignoring the black wolf that sat and stared from the shadows. It was small, closer to the size of an average domestic dog than a shifter. But she recognised those arctic eyes.

"Go away Roman," she murmured into her box.

He just tilted his head in response. She would have thought it was cute if she hadn't known why he was there. At least she didn't mind this particular stalker.

"I'm not interested." She didn't want to help find his older brother, didn't care what happened to him. Probably. "Tell Theo I say no."

The wolf whined, scratching at the pavement with his claws.

"You been here long?"

Alice jumped up from her seat, having to scramble to catch the takeout box she threw into the air in panic.

"Bloody hell Peyton!" She shot him a scathing look. "You trying to give me a heart attack?"

She had purposely sat on the bench across the street directly in front of the church, allowing her a decent visual of the entrance as well as all road access. He seemed to have appeared from thin air.

"You need to wear a bell," she mumbled into her food, finishing off the remaining noodles.

"You should be more cautious," he said, looking unimpressed. "How long have you been here?"

"Not long." She hadn't realised how late it was when she left the museum, but luckily had enough time to grab dinner – after leaving Mr Lince slouched against a lamppost. He was going to wake up struggling to remember the night before, with all his potions missing. Plus a few extra bruises.

She didn't feel guilty at all.

"Why do you think they have these meetings so late?"

She tossed the takeaway box into the bin beside the bench, glancing up at the gargoyles on the roof. She swore they moved, but knew the thought was crazy. Yet she couldn't tear her gaze away, their snarling faces fascinating. Alice blinked several times before she turned to Peyton.

"Bit suspicious, don't you think?"

"Maybe," he mumbled. "What's with the wolf?"

"Wolf?" she said as her gaze slid to where Roman sat, blended into the shadows. "What wolf?"

Peyton just gave her a pointed look.

"Fine. As long as it doesn't compromise tonight, I don't care."

Alice stared at him, eyes narrowed.

How did he know Roman was a wolf? A human couldn't have been able to tell, in fact, most people wouldn't have been able to tell. He didn't look like a traditional shifter.

"We ready to go?" she said instead of asking the question.

She moved so she stood beside him, hiding her arm that was warning Roman to stay. At least, she hoped it was.

"Hmm," he nodded, his eyes intense. "Your instinct was right by the way, about Gordon Potts. Convicted and served time for ABH to his previous wife, including coercive behaviour and battery."

"Previous wife? What happened to her?" she asked as they slowly made their way across the road.

"Meera Potts disappeared several years ago. He was brought in for questioning, but there was no evidence to suggest foul play. Mr Potts went to court to get her classed as legally dead a year or so after her disappearance."

"She not have any family?"

"If she did, they didn't speak up. In fact, not one person would make a statement against him."

"Sounds like a great guy."

"So what we thinking, is he a changed man under the eyes of their god..."

"Or is he their muscle that deals with the issues?" Alice finished for him.

"Bingo." Peyton smiled gently, the expression softening his otherwise hard face.

He looked relaxed in his jeans and chequered shirt with his white blonde hair neatly brushed. His blue eyes weren't as meanly pinched as they usually were. It didn't suit him, at least, didn't suit the image she had in her head of the hard arse police officer.

"Are you ready?" he asked as they came to the gate.

No.

The last time she had felt like she was being eaten alive. Something to add to her growing list of 'no fucking idea.'

"Of course, dear." Alice accepted the hand he held out, concentrating on the connection as a million insects started to crawl across her skin. Luckily it only lasted a few minutes, stopping entirely just as they entered the church.

Alice didn't exactly know what to expect, her mind pushing out ideas of an AA meeting or even a book club. Disappointingly it was nothing like she imagined, the main hall eerily quiet as they were guided through.

The pews had all been neatly arranged from the earlier session, large copper bowls placed at each end, begging for donations. They followed the green carpet that had been rolled down the centre, towards the stage that had hundreds of melted candles, still lit.

"Through here," a man encouraged them, pushing them into what looked like an office hidden behind the stage. "Please get on your knees before The Leader."

Peyton dropped down, pulling Alice with him. The room itself was too small for the number of bodies, the floor space barely enough room for the twelve or so to fit. A man sat quietly at an old desk, his head framed with inspirational quotes that hung limply behind him on the wood panelling.

'When we put our care in his hand, he puts peace in our hearts.'

'The pain that you're experiencing is nothing compared to what they will get in their damnation.'

'Faith is seeing the light in your heart when all you see is darkness in others.'

Alice would have been amused at the quotes if her knees didn't itch from the threadbare carpet. She wanted to tug at her jacket and scarf, the temperature inside the small room increasing dramatically as everybody settled before the man, Mr Potts standing towards his right.

Each religion had their own ideologies regarding a divine, whether they were one person or more. Witches generally believed in The Goddess, more of an entity than a god while many Vamps kept to their human beliefs.

Alice didn't believe in anything, not since she witnessed her mother's death. She was jealous though, that someone could believe in someone or something that could help guide them. Or someone they could blame.

The man who sat at the desk remained silent as he appraised everyone on their knees, his eyes hard as he studied everyone individually.

This must be The Leader, she thought as she tried not to fidget, her blade feeling exposed under the scrutiny even though it was hidden beneath her jacket.

Alice let out a gasp, the crescent scar on her hand throbbing intensely, the same as it did when she was with Kyle. She fought not to look down at her hand, not wanting to draw attention.

She felt Peyton flick her a look of concern. Shaking her head gently she clenched her fist, fighting a groan of pain as she concentrated on The Leader, noting his similarities to the one and only Saint Nic. His hair was pure white, matching his long beard and bushy eyebrows. He was on the larger scale, with a pot belly that strained the buttons on his pale shirt.

'He looked like Santa. Old, chubby with a white beard. Said he could give her a special drink. Make her better again. Santa can do that, you know? He's magic.'

The memory of Mia describing the fate of her friend was still vivid in her memory. The so-called Leader looked the part, an influential man who could use his words to convince a vulnerable and desperate woman into something she didn't want to do.

"Ah, who do we have here?" The Leader stood up, coming around the front of his desk. The wood squeaked as he relaxed his weight onto it, leaning back. "New blood in my herd."

"They were the ones we spoke of earlier, my Leader," Mr Potts said from beside him. "I thought they would be trustworthy to join us."

"While I trust your judgment, my good friend. I always choose who's worthy of an audience with myself." The Leader sneered, his eyes suspicious when he looked at Alice and Peyton. "Why are you here?"

"We seek guidance," Alice said before Peyton could begin. "We worry for our mortal souls."

"My wife is right." Peyton lifted his hand to grip hers, squeezing it in reassurance. "Breed have overtaken our neighbourhood. We need like-minded individuals who support our views on them."

"And what exactly are your views?"

"That they shouldn't exist. They are inhuman abominations that need to be cleansed so the earth can thrive once more."

"Perfect answer." The Leader smiled, his face softening. "Gordon, my friend. Remind me, why do you believe these two were respectable of the leader's circle?"

Gordon leant across, whispering in his ear.

"Ah."

The Leader turned his attention back to Alice and Peyton.

"Your generosity has brought you amongst us, but you must prove yourselves worthy."

"Of course."

"Friends, please join me in welcoming our new members." The Leader clapped, encouraging the others to join in before he opened his arms wide. "Now, what are the updates?"

Members spoke up in turn, excited as they discussed upcoming rallies and protests. She even recognised a few from earlier, including Mrs Potts who sat towards the front, close to her husband. Her eyes were closed, a silent smile on his lips as she listened to her friends casually discussing disrupting hospitals where Breed were known to work, as well as charity events to raise money for the church itself.

"I would like to thank you for all your noble work, and I would like to discuss some great news," The Leader said, smiling, showing off a full set of veneers. "As we know, the press doesn't understand that we are trying to cleanse the world, but today they have confirmed that those fanged beasts have been cursed, struck down where they stand."

Alice risked a quick glance at Peyton, who just subtly shrugged. She didn't think the information had been released to the public yet. The Gala had been dealt with quietly, the press stopped from reporting.

"I thank you all for your sacrifices in the name of our divine, but our work is far from over. The world is still full of those Breed, and until they have been extinguished, we will continue in his name."

People quietly murmured in agreement.

"Bless you."

"Hail divine."

Alice clenched her fist harder, the pain resonating through her palm as Gordon's expression changed, his mouth set in a grim line. He quietly excused himself, leaving through the door beside the desk.

Where does that go to?

She noticed Peyton checking out to the door too, his jaw set as he watched for it to re-open. That door wasn't on the blueprint.

Alice finally glanced down at her hand, the burning and throbbing becoming unbearable. Almost thinking it was on fire, she gently traced the crescent scar with her fingertip, not understanding why it was reacting in such a way again.

"My Leader..." Gordon Potts stepped back through the door, a strained look on his face. "I would not interrupt if it wasn't important."

The Leader glared for a moment. "My children, unfortunately this meeting will have to come to an abrupt end, I have business to attend." He nodded towards everyone, a friendly smile painted across his face. "Let the light guide you."

Everyone replied in unison, almost perfectly synchronised.

"Let the light guide you."

CHAPTER SEVENTEEN

Alice eyed her car in the driveway, the blue rust bucket taunting her as she shivered in the cold.

"Bloody thing," she cursed as she unlocked her front door, stamping her feet of the excess snow before stepping inside. It just had to start snowing as she walked home, the sky covering her in the delicate white fluff that bit into her skin.

She hated the winter.

"Sam?" she called into the darkness. "You home?"

Alice frowned, her senses on high alert.

The air was still, the house silent, but she couldn't shake the sense of urgency, like she was being watched. Her eyes settled on the corner of the room, the light from the street lamps failing to penetrate the dark space. She slowly reached for the switch, her back pressed against the door.

"I hope you don't mind my visit," a girly high-pitched voice said from the darkness.

Alice flipped the switch as she pulled out her sword, the tip pointed towards the intruder's throat before she even recognised the vampire.

"Valentina."

Alice held the blade steadily, her ears straining to make sure they were alone. Pointless, considering vampires were silent predators.

"I didn't see you."

Why were you hiding in the dark?

"Then I will forget your manners this one time." Valentina stared at the runes on the blade, ones that were alight and glowing. Her eyes flickered in annoyance.

Alice had to make a conscious effort to sheath it, fighting against her better judgment.

"Does Dread know you're here?"

"Nobody knows I'm here," she smiled, causing shivers to rattle down Alice's back. "It's why I'm alone and haven't got my guards with me."

She looked around the room, the darkness of her hair and dress a stark contrast to the pretty white wallpaper Sam had just put up.

"Interesting home, I see you haven't finished unpacking?" She nodded towards the pile of boxes.

"Is there anything I can help you with?" Alice asked, irritated but remaining polite. She wasn't interested in small talk, not even from a member of The Council.

Valentina ignored the question, instead went to touch one of Sam's half-naked men's magazines on the table, flicking through the pages as if she had never seen such a thing.

"How is your training going with Councilman Storm's son?"

"Fine."

Alice dropped her bag, nudging it under the side table so it wouldn't be in the way. She kept her back to the door, keeping the sofa between them.

"Only fine?" She looked up then, the light catching the red ruby necklace that hugged her throat. "It surely cannot be merely 'fine' now, can it? Is this Riley not good enough?"

"No, no, that's not what I'm saying."

"Then it must be more than fine. You need to learn control if you are ever going to be of any use to us," she said sternly, her eyes narrowed as she looked Alice up and down. "You look strange."

"Strange?" Alice looked down, wondering what she was on about. She looked as she usually did.

Maybe she had some smeared makeup?

"Yes."

Valentina finally put the magazine down, her gaze arctic as she slowly moved around the sofa, her fingertips reaching across to trail down Alice's cheek.

"Like a pretty girl next door." Her voice was distant, almost a whisper before she snapped her arm back. "It doesn't suit you."

Alice fought not to flinch at the sudden movement.

Fuck. Fuck. Fuck.

Her hand twitched, itching to grab her sword. Up close she knew Valentina hadn't fed, could tell by the absence of humanity in her gaze. Vampires came from humans, many keeping the same characteristics and personality traits after the turn. Valentina's eyes, when they connected, were old, ancient with a ring of red around the irises. If Alice didn't know any better, she would have said she had never been human, just... other.

"I see your soul, child. You're just like me, dark, full of horrors many people couldn't survive."

She opened her mouth, her fangs elongating to twice their length.

"It makes us powerful, strong."

Alice stepped back, moving away from the door and Valentina's reach while her pulse thumped against her throat, adrenaline rushing through her veins. A normal reaction when faced with a predator, and that was precisely what Valentina was, a predator. Just one that was shaped like a young girl, with dark tresses and large eyes in a pale, porcelain doll face.

Valentina moved forward as if she were a magnet, her face granite as the twin fangs peeked through her lips, too long for her petite mouth. Alice slowly reached for her hilt, wondering how long she could survive against someone as powerful as her.

"Why are you here?" Alice asked, trying to distract her from the hunger.

"I want to know what is happening with my vampires in this city." Valentina's voice was eerily soft when she replied, her eyes no longer as hard.

"That's what I've been trying to figure out."

"Tu es trop lent," she snapped angrily. "Too slow. I want to return to my home, to Paris. I need this absurdity to end."

"We're working on it."

"We're?" The oily black pools of her eyes receded into narrowed points. "Ah, yes. The police force you seem to be working with. Smart move by Monsieur Grayson, getting all the Norms on his side." She smiled, the emotion not making Alice feel any better. "Now tell me why you have been interested in the Church of the Light?"

"How did you..." Alice wanted to kick herself.

"We are watching until you are no longer a liability."

"I thought that was the point of Riley, or should I say, Danton?" *And Mr Lince,* Alice wanted to add but doubted Valentina had anything to do with The Magika.

"You think I would trust those druids?" She let out a high pitched laugh. "A bit of advice, don't trust anybody. You'll survive longer."

"So I shouldn't trust you?" she replied without thought.

"Very clever, Alice." A predator smile, a warning. "Danton was one of my guards before I lent him to Grayson. You're pouting like it was a dirty secret, but Dread knew all along who he belonged to."

"How long have you been watching me?"

How long has Dread allowed it to happen?

"I'm growing bored with this conversation." She gave a dismissive wave. "Now tell me about the church."

"It's a church who hate all Breed, what else do you need to know?" Alice spat, allowing her anger to shape her words.

Valentina spun and hissed, her hands turning to claws as a black wolf growled, his electric blue eyes glowing.

What the... Alice quickly accessed the situation.

"Bad dog," she scolded the wolf, placing herself between them cautiously. "I'm so sorry - he should have been in the garden."

How the fuck did he get in?

"That is not a dog," Valentina said, her voice hoarse, her eyes never leaving the wolf.

"Of course he is, picked him up from the pound only a week or so ago." Alice wondered if Valentina could hear the lie from the change of her heartbeat. She hoped not.

Valentina looked unamused when she finally met Alice's eyes, her face wary.

"Be very careful Alice, remember who your superiors are. My patience is wearing thin."

"We're still investigating. Once I figure out what has been happening to the Vamps, I will be able to make a report."

Valentina stared for a moment, completely immobile as if she were a statue, not one twitch of a muscle.

"I will find out your dishonesties Alice, then you will answer to me."

"I'm invested in this too. I have friends who are at risk."

"Then get results." Valentina reached up slowly, ignoring the wolf's warning as she brushed hair off Alice's face. "Tick tock."

CHAPTER EIGHTEEN

Blood Bar was busy for a weeknight, almost every table taken as music flowed from the band on the stage.

Fighting through the crowd, Alice found a seat beside the bar, allowing the music to calm her nerves. She couldn't relax once Valentina had left, not even with a wolf who seemed to be stuck in his animal form. He wasn't exactly one for conversations, and he just sat, staring. What was she supposed to do with that?

"Can I get you anything?" The bartender asked as he flicked a rag over his shoulder.

"Vodka martini, please."

"Coming right up."

Alice waited for her drink, cuddling it to her palms once it was presented in a flourish. She wasn't sure what she was doing there, didn't know who else to talk to. She couldn't speak to Dread, not yet. Not until she knew more. So it only really left her with one option.

The deep husky voice of the man in question broke through the music, his low rumble pleasing the crowd as he introduced the next band onto the stage. Alice sipped her cocktail, sighing at the delicious burn of the alcohol. The crowd continued to murmur excitingly behind her, forcing her to spin in her stool to face the stage out of curiosity.

Riley Storm was one of London's most eligible bachelors, at least, that's what the magazines had said anyway. He oozed sex appeal as he teased the crowd, his blue-black hair pulled back from his masculine face, his stubble longer than the other day. He wore the same uniform as his staff, the casual form-fitting T-shirt suiting him as much as a thousand-pound suit would.

Alice took another sip of her drink. She hated the fact she couldn't look away, the same as the many females gyrating for his attention on the dance floor. He had something about him, a magnetism that instantly got her back up.

But Sam was right, her wariness of him was because of the past. Riley wasn't trying to manipulate her emotions. He seemed just as confused by their magical connection as she did.

He saw her then, his smile faltering before he quickly recovered. He didn't seem pleased to see her sitting at his bar. She wasn't exactly delighted she had no one else to talk to, so it was mutual. Sad really.

"Hey, do you want a drink?" the man beside her asked, grabbing her attention. "I'm buying." He winked, smiling to show his fangs.

He was dressed pleasantly in a white shirt and smart jeans, his blonde hair combed off his face, highlighting the impossible beauty of his skin.

"No, thank you," she smiled back. "I already have a drink." She nodded towards her cocktail.

"I'll get the next then," he continued, undeterred.

She shook her head. "I'm waiting for a friend."

"You only said friend, not boyfriend." He grinned, sipping his own red drink. "You at least open for donations?" He meant blood, his eyes tracing down the line of her throat.

"Sorry," she shrugged.

She would have enjoyed the disappointment in his eyes if he hadn't been staring at her like a popsicle. She never understood the lure of vampire sex, didn't want to be a midnight snack.

"Do you know I work with a vampire?"

"Oh?" he said, his drink at the edge of his lips.

"Yeah, he's a real pain in my neck."

The man burst out laughing, choking on his drink. "You sure you're not open to donations? Or even a dance?" His eyes glistened.

"Sorry, I'm not your blood type."

"Hey, Will," another man walked up, placing his hand eagerly on his friend's shoulder. "A girl is giving up free sips in the corner. She's wearing this cute little fluffy cardigan."

"Not now Glenn, I'm talking to a pretty girl."

"She's not interested." A tattooed arm appeared between them.

"Riley!" she squealed at his abruptness. "I'm so sorry..." she began to apologise to the man, but both he and his friend were already gone. "Riley, what the hell was that about?"

"Why are you here?" he asked, eyes hard as he studied her. "We haven't got training planned."

"I wanted a drink."

"At this specific bar?" He began to relax, leaning back against the free stool. "You sure it wasn't to see me?" he asked, smug, crossing his arms across his chest. It brought her attention to his tattoos, glyphs as Xander had explained.

A flare of irritation. She had asked Riley on numerous occasions about her father's heritage, but druids were secretive bastards. He had told her barely anything. Yet, a short car ride with Xander gained her that information.

Her eyes shot up, Riley's expression curious as he caught her staring.

"I'm not here to just see you." She was, but she wasn't going to admit it. "Besides, aren't we friends?" The word surprised her, because they were friends, she just hadn't realised it.

Riley just smirked. "Come on, follow me to my office."

He guided her past the dancers towards a set of private stairs, his office on the floor above. Alice had to ignore the death glares from the other females, instead concentrating on not spilling her drink when the dancers bumped her.

They passed through a door at the top of the stairs, the hallway pitch black as she stumbled in the darkness.

"Riley..." She reached out blindly, feeling his hand grab hers.

A spell was on the tip of her tongue as he pushed open another door, allowing a small amount of light to penetrate.

"Now tell me why..."

"Riley darling, about time you came up. I've been waiting."

A redheaded woman was sat cross-legged on the small wooden desk, her short skirt riding up to show baby pink lace underwear, a teasing smile on her magically enhanced lips.

"Mandy? What the fuck are you doing here?" Riley demanded, growling as he flicked on a switch, lighting up the hallway behind them.

"You never returned my calls," Mandy petulantly replied, swinging her long legs to stand. "Your other office said you were at your new bar."

Her eyes slowly judged the room, taking in the small, gloomy space in one sweep.

"I don't know why. It seems... cheap."

Alice finally recognised her from the Gala, the one with the pillow breasts that had been Riley's date.

"Do you want me to come back later?" Alice said dryly. "I seem to be interrupting something important."

"You. Stay!" Riley snapped before returning his burning gaze to the redhead. Alice couldn't confirm if she were a natural redhead or not, the quick flash they received too fast.

"Oh, and who are you?" Mandy glared, flicking her hair over one shoulder. Her short skirt showed off her impressive legs while her top was cut low on the front, highlighting her breasts. A gold chain glittered between them, drawing the attention.

"Mandy, you need to leave." Riley reached past her towards the old handset phone, dialling for security.

"What? I thought you would have wanted to see me?" she whined. "You would rather spend time with... that?" she huffed as she pushed past Alice, standing beside the door.

Alice stepped away, sipping her drink while watching the drama unfold.

"Leave or be removed."

"But darling..." she purred.

"Leave."

"Fine, I'm going." She dropped her voice to a whisper, shooting Alice an evil look. "He isn't in proportion anyway."

Alice tried to hide her smirk behind her glass, waiting until Mandy was out of earshot before turning to Riley.

"Did you want me to leave? You're obviously interested in humping her."

Humping? Did I just say humping? I've been around Sam too long.

"Humping?" Riley burst into a grin, his question echoing her own thoughts. "I think you mean fucking sweetheart, besides, it's you who's thinking about me humping her."

"No, I wasn't." Alice felt her cheeks burn as she started to imagine his sweaty body moving... *oh, for fuck sake.* "Anyway, I assumed she was your girlfriend."

"Why, jealous?" he teased.

"No," she replied a little too fast. "Besides, from what she said, I don't think I'm missing anything special."

Riley erupted into laughter, his hands unbuckling his belt on his jeans. The fabric sagged, dropping to show naked flesh, no underwear.

"Haven't we been through this before? Except last time you were tied to a chair."

"I try to forget." She looked away, having no desire to see whether the redhead was right about his proportion or not.

She considered the room instead, his office small, the overhead fixture missing its bulb, so the only light was from the bar below, the back wall made of glass. Photographs were tapped to the exposed brick, covering the whole available space in small square Polaroids. Posed pictures of employees smiling to the camera as well as some action shots, including Sam, who was shot serving a drink with a smile on his face. On his weathered desk was a single landline phone and a computer. It was basic but had character.

"I have never dated nor have I fucked Mandy," Riley said as he buckled his belt back up. "She was just conveniently available for an event."

"Why are you telling me? You're a big boy, I'm not your keeper."

"Say that big boy comment again," he said, eyes gleaming mischievously.

Alice rolled her own eyes instead.

"What happened with Sam?" She nodded towards his picture.

"He had a better offer." Riley shrugged, coming to stand beside her. "He also dislikes me, makes it hard to work together."

"He doesn't dislike you," she frowned, turning to face him.

He was close enough that she had to tilt her head to see his face.

"He didn't understand why I had to leave. Sometimes the best thing for someone isn't what you want." Riley frowned, his eyes catching hers before he looked away, hiding his expression.

He snatched her cocktail from her hand, downing the last remaining liquid before placing it onto his desk.

"So you going to tell me why you're really here? Or was it simply to scare away my customers?"

"I wasn't trying to scare them away," she glared.

"Then tell me the real reason you're here."

"Valentina."

"Valentina?" He gestured for her to come further into the room before he clicked something that made the low hum of the background music mute. "The room's now secure. Tell me what happened."

Alice began to explain how Valentina had turned up at her house, wanting information on the poisonings amongst her vampires.

"My father never mentioned her still being in the city." Riley sat at his desk, the cheap seat squeaking at his weight. He looked like he belonged, not someone with a multi-million -pound estate. To be fair, he never really acted like he came from money, he seemed to always enjoy doing everything himself, his hands reflecting his hard work. Unlike Mandy, who branded the place 'cheap.'

"Valentina said that she didn't trust the druids."

Riley thought about it for a moment.

"And what about you? Do you trust the druids?"

She knew there was a right and a wrong answer.

"'You are a time bomb waiting to go off. We shall see if your fate matches the rest of your family,'" she quoted instead of answering.

"I don't understand."

"Your father said that to me."

"Did he?" Riley reached to a drawer, bringing out two fresh glasses and a decanter. Popping off the lid, he filled two glasses up with the amber liquid, pushing one glass towards her. "My father says many things."

"What do you know about my family?"

"Other than what you have told me? Nothing."

"Surely your father must have said something."

"Why do I feel like you're implying something against my father?" He sipped his drink while Alice ignored hers.

"My family is the reason for the warden, he must have mentioned something."

"No, I don't need that information, and I never asked. Alice, what are you trying to say?"

Alice moved away, pressing her hand to the glass wall. "Is this mirrored?" The dancers below never looked up.

"Alice..." Riley growled.

"Fine. I've recently found out that I'm a descendant of Draco, one of the original elemental families. I believe that knowledge was one of the reasons my parents were murdered."

Alice hesitated, watching the dancers.

"Your father said I was a time bomb, and that my fate could match that of my family."

She pushed away from the glass, turning so she could see Riley's face, read his expression. He seemed calm, his eyes soft as he listened to her. She couldn't see any recognition; no tell-tale signs he already knew her past.

"So to answer your previous question, no, I don't trust the druids."

A loud bang broke through the tension.

"Excuse me sir," a man shouted through the door. "We have an emergency."

"I'm busy." Riley never took his eyes off her.

"But, sir..."

Riley looked annoyed but opened the door to show a worried bouncer, blood on his hands as he raised a fist to knock against the door again.

"What happened?" Riley snapped.

Moving through the dancers was easier the second time around, most of them outside crowding around the scene.

Alice quickly surveyed the situation, noting how the vampire on the left was already dead, his skin starting to peel and dehydrate in front of her eyes.

"Don't touch him!" Alice barked out the order, making some of the crowd jump back.

She recognised the dead as one of the vamps at the bar, the friend to the one she was talking to. A woman knelt beside him on the hard floor, blood turning her fluffy white cardigan into a pink mess. Blood poured down her throat from the several holes, her blood refusing to clot.

"Stay down," she grabbed the woman when she tried to scramble away.

"Get off me," she snarled, trying to scratch up Alice's arm.

"If you don't stop moving, you'll bleed to death."

"What?" The woman's eyes took on panic, her hands trembling as she grabbed her throat. "I'm bleeding? Why won't it stop?"

Alice almost felt sorry for her, almost.

"Alice, how can I help?" Riley asked calmly, his bouncers working on keeping the crowd back.

"Keep pressure on her wounds."

Riley replaced the woman's hand with his own, trying to stem the flow before the ambulance arrived. Alice stood back, trying to see if anybody else could have been affected. The crowd seemed in equal measures curious and shocked, but no one appeared to have drunk from the woman.

She took a deep breath, noting how many of the customers still clutched at their cocktails, cocktails made with blood.

If the drinks were contaminated...

"Riley, where do you get your blood from?"

"Blood?" He looked at her like she had lost it.

She turned to him, the front of his shirt soaked in red.

"For your drinks, where do you get it from?"

"A local supplier," he frowned. "Why?"

"I have a..." *Shit.* "You need to close the bar."

Sirens drowned out his reply. The paramedics began shouting out demands almost instantly. They ignored the vampire, his death evident as they moved Riley to start working on the woman who still continued to bleed.

"She's going to die," he said gently as he stood beside Alice.

She said nothing as she watched the woman start to cry, deep painful sobs that racked her whole body.

"No. No. It isn't supposed to be like this, they said it wouldn't be like this," the woman bawled.

"Who said it?" Alice tried to reach the woman, her efforts falling short when she's forced back by a paramedic. "Who said it?"

The woman looked at Alice, her eyes glazing over as her lifeblood soaked into the street. "May the light burn you forever more."

CHAPTER NINETEEN

Alice stood outside the supply store, staring at the red neon sign that glowed against the dark brick.

She should have gone home, blood still dried beneath her nails even as she had tried to scrub her hands clean. But she couldn't get the idea of contaminated blood being sold out of her mind; that an innocent person could be infected, dying a painful and unnecessary death. Because it was an infection, a toxic point of view just as much as the physical contagion. If her deduction was right and whoever was behind the genocide had been able to taint bottled blood, the death rate could be catastrophic.

'Blood on the Go' was the only local supply store in the city, part of a larger chain that dominated across England and Wales. Apart from the red sign, the storefront was achingly white, giving it a cold medicinal feel. Alice had been standing there for a while, patiently watching a few people enter the brightly lit store, to be escorted around the side alley towards the back.

"Hello, welcome to Blood on the Go. Are you looking to donate today or purchase?" a clerk asked when Alice finally entered, her perky attitude not reflected in the clock which stated how late it was. Or more likely early.

"I'm not sure yet," Alice replied as she looked around. It was a simple layout, a desk that separated the room in half with several industrial-sized refrigerators full of blood covering the back. Pricing was pinned to the wall, showing that you could buy a single glass bottle of blood type A for £4.99, while blood type B rhesus negative was £7.99. There were also several options for the 'specials' which started at £9.99 per bottle.

Bloody hell, Alice shook her head. *I'm in the wrong trade.*

"Don't worry, it's completely safe. We supply all across the country." The clerk looked sceptical, her friendliness disappearing.

Shit. Maybe she didn't look like a typical donator?

Alice started to scratch along the inside of her arms, trying to appear as shady as she could.

"Do you require medical records to donate?" Alice asked, hoping the answer would be yes. Or, at least they tested the blood for abnormalities. "I need the cash real bad."

"Nope, we don't ask questions. We give twenty pounds for one pint of blood, which you can donate a maximum once per week."

She smiled, showing shiny white fangs. They looked weird, almost fake.

"Is this something you're interested in doing?" She looked smug as she grabbed a piece of paper and a pen, confident.

"Maybe." Alice scanned across the simple contract, noting how they asked for your full name and address. "It says here about photo ID?"

"It's fine if you don't have any, we lose paperwork all the time."

Alice signed the piece of paper, giving fake details. "Do we do it now?"

"A few people are waiting, but I can take you around to have a look."

Alice followed the woman around the back towards the alley beside the building.

A side door was wide open, a beaded curtain concealing inside. Several people hung around the door, glaring as Alice passed through the beads.

"It's just in here." The woman guided her in, pointing out the booth covered by a dirty curtain. Inside was a man wearing a sweat-stained white vest. He didn't look up as he inserted a winged infusion needle into the arm of a painfully thin man, his eyes glassy enough to give the impression that he was high.

The floor was a crusty brown, blood staining the once white tiles to the point it looked like rust. Small refrigerators hummed beside them, blood smeared across the front while used needles were thrown in the corner, beside a full contaminated materials bin.

Alice couldn't believe the health and safety issues.

"How can you be sure the health of your donors if you don't ask for their medical records?"

The clerk looked shocked at the question but answered anyway. Her regular clients must not care.

"We advertise to vampires who can't get infected with anything. It's not our problem if others choose to drink," she shrugged. "Like, we ask you some general health questions, and if we think the blood will be below our standard, we will not pay you the full fee."

She tried to move Alice back, away from the men.

"Why, are you worried about something?"

"So you don't check the blood for impurities?"

"No, why would we?" she frowned, her eyes dashing to the man who had turned to look at them.

"What about storage? How long do you hold the blood before being sold?"

"We aim to sell it in within a few days, but it lasts weeks." A slight frown pinched her eyebrows. "What is this?"

"Do you keep a record of who donates on site?"

"We do as it's the law. We can't accept more than one donation per week, which is why we keep names." She folded her arms. "I'm sorry, you a health visitor or something?"

"Or something." Alice eyed the man with the needle, his gloveless hands clenched as he stood up. "I need to see your records over the past month or so."

"What?" the woman asked, her eyes wide as they flicked towards the man again. Clearly the boss.

"Excuse me, are we going to have a problem?" The man in the vest growled, trying to intimidate. "You can't look at our records without a warrant."

"You need to stop accepting donations immediately," Alice stated. The number of bottles of blood she could see just in the small space worried her, especially blood that hadn't been vetted. She wasn't sure of their client base, buying bottled blood a new concept but if just one contaminated donor got their blood sold…

"On whose authority?"

"That would be the city of London." Detective O'Neil walked in, followed by Officer Peyton in full official gear. "I would like to examine every vial of blood donated in this establishment. While our investigation is going on, you will be unable to accept any donations."

"This is bullshit!" The vested man steamed as he grabbed the bit of paper O'Neil handed him. "We're an honest business..."

"If you're an honest business, you have no need to worry," Alice added. "Although I would re-examine your health and safety."

The place really was disgusting, she wouldn't be surprised if the donators left with infections or even sepsis.

"If you do not co-operate we will come back with a warrant that could result in permanent closure. What would you prefer?" O'Neil stood his ground.

"Fuck sake," the vested man cursed, his face glowing red in anger. "Fine, I will co-operate."

"Oh, hey Alice." Someone wearing a white bodysuit walked in, taping up the room.

It took her a few minutes to recognise the voice.

"Hi Jones, you checking out all the bottles?"

"Don't you know it." He started to whistle to himself, unpacking a bag onto the floor full of different sprays and cotton buds. "Just checked out the front, who'da thought bottled blood would be so pricey?"

"Agent Skye," Detective O'Neil nodded in greeting.

"Thank you for coming so quickly."

"It was a good shout, lucky the owner has agreed for us to take a look. You think we will find anything?" he asked her genuinely.

Alice looked around the room, the different bottles marked with different batches and blood types. There must be at least one-hundred different donors in the back room, not including the ones in the front.

"I don't know. But if we catch just one contaminated bottle, we could stop it from spreading."

O'Neil grunted, his eyes tired. "Either way, we will be comparing samples. Jones has an appointment with someone in The Tower." He sighed, pinching his nose. "Peyton has updated me on the church, but until we get solid evidence we have no chance. You guys have done a great job of getting in, but without a solid ID on The Leader we have nothing. Even then, a dead woman's word doesn't stand in court. You need to find something."

"We're working on it."

She stepped outside, the people waiting to donate long gone once the police turned up. She was beyond tired, the whole day taking its toll. Yet her brain wouldn't quit, she couldn't stop thinking about who was behind the genocide. It was small because they were only targeting vampires, what would happen once they turned their attention to other Breed?

"Agent Skye," Peyton greeted, his face calm. His blonde hair was wet, making it darker than usual. "Did you really have to call us this early?"

"Probably not," she smiled, wondering if there was a coffee shop nearby.

"I get it. I got a few hours asleep at least before O'Neil called. I couldn't let myself relax until I figured out The Leader."

"You find anything?"

"No. Other than the fact he looks like Santa, which is one person's description. Also hard to compare this time of year when many people dress themselves to represent the season."

"Oh, bollocks." He was right. She never celebrated the human holiday, Dread not exactly one for the festivities when she was a child. "That means Winter Solstice is coming." She closed her eyes, pinching her nose. The months had really gotten away from her.

"Without his full name we have nothing. He was only ever called 'The Leader' or 'My Leader.' I even spoke to a few people as we were leaving trying to get his background, but that was useless."

"There's something wrong... something..." Alice couldn't explain it. A feeling? Gut instinct? Then there was her scar, the pale crescent piece of skin that was colder than the rest of her body. It had ached while she was there, then stopped as soon as she had left. "Do you think this is the guy we're after?"

"If it's not, it's a real coincidence." Peyton folded his arms, watching the other officers corner the whole area off as Jones continued working in the small back room. "We need to search that church."

"O'Neil has already said we can't do anything without physical evidence." Stupid if she said so herself.

"No, we can't go in under force," he said, eyebrows creased. "But we need to find evidence before they strike again."

Alice remained quiet. She wasn't hired directly by the Metropolitan Police, wasn't under the same strict rules and regulations. Either way, she had an idea.

"We'll figure something out."

H e pinned the teacher to the ground, a strong grip on the older, more powerful man's neck.

"Let go," the teacher wheezed as he struggled beneath his palm.

He tightened his fist, wanting to end it for them all. This sadistic teacher that smiled at the bruises. Smiled at the broken bones. He had gotten bigger, stronger than they intended. They didn't understand that he wasn't their sheepdog, wouldn't follow their exact order. It confused them which pleased his beast.

"Let go." A voice of reason this time, the voice of a friend. Meeting Xander's eyes gave him clarity. Eyes as silver as his own, almost mirrored so he could see his own reflection.

He glared down at the teacher, watching his face turn purple even though the other instructors quietly murmured from the sidelines. They would let him finish what he started, they wouldn't interfere.

How tempting.

"You're not worth it," he growled as he released his teacher, watching as the pathetic man gasped for breath. He wasn't worth it, wasn't worth the beatings. Wasn't worth the anger from his father who would say it would put their family to shame in front of the Archdruid.

Not that he cared. It was the old man who decided to put him through this training, a great honour for his father who was to become the next Archdruid. So he stepped back, crossed his arms and allowed his friends to stand beside him.

United. An alliance. A force to be reckoned with.

They didn't expect that either, didn't understand.

The total loyalty of all seven.

Brothers.

CHAPTER TWENTY

What the fuck am I doing?
Alice stood at the back gate behind the church, the chilly air dampening her mood as she worked on the lock.
"Stupid bloody thing," she snarled as if scolding it would help. The metal clanged as it fought her picks, the sound echoing across the headstones just beyond.

With an exasperated sigh, Alice scowled. She was running out of time, the sense of urgency fuelled by the man who stood across the street, watching her. He wore complete black, his face slightly obscured by the brim of his hat. He didn't seem to care that she knew he was watching her, wasn't trying to hide when she kept checking to see if he was still there. At least he was open with his stalking, which made a change.

She turned in a burst of frustration, glaring as the man casually leant against a lamppost. She was a fully trained Paladin who was efficiently trained with a blade, yet, she was struggling with an old as fuck lock.

"Typical, bloody typical," she muttered as she waved at the man. She didn't expect a reaction, so was surprised when he waved back as if they were good friends. When she responded with her middle finger he wasn't as pleased. He flashed her a fang, his hiss carrying in the silence. At least it confirmed he was one of Valentina's goons.

Chuckling to herself, she turned back to the gate. She had spent the day studying the blueprints of the church, memorising every nook and cranny until she had fallen asleep at the table. It was Sam who had woken her up after his shift, an amused smile on his face. So she had left later than intended, already behind schedule even before the lock gave her problems.

Luckily it was winter, the sun not rising for a few hours yet.

With a click the clunky lock fell to the floor, allowing her to push the gate open with a squeak. The graveyard was in poor condition, the names of the deceased either scratched off or unreadable as the marble and limestone slowly dissolved from the rain. Overgrown grass and weeds covered the remnants of the graves, making them indistinguishable from one another. It was a shame. The dead didn't deserve the disrespect.

Breed didn't bury their dead, preferring to burn them to ash, that's if the deceased didn't naturally disintegrate on their own. Why bury something that was going to be worm food? You could still grieve a memory.

Please don't let there be any ghouls.

Alice slowly made her way through the grounds, carefully stepping over the graves.

Vampires had a very small success rate. Before protocols came into place, many of the freshly turned became ghouls, a feral fledgeling that only had basic instincts and close to zero intelligence. As part of the transition, humans who had their blood drained and then replaced with their creators' would be buried under the following moon. As cemeteries were already full of the dead, they became prime places to bury the fledgelings.

It was one of the main reasons Paladins were created, to hunt down the feral Vamps and then their irresponsible creators. While it was now illegal to transition without passing a strict test, it still happened. Hopefully, the graves were all empty, no fledgelings waiting to rip out her throat and the bodies moved to a place where they could be mourned properly.

Alice was prepared for the painful sensation, had psyched herself up as the prickling invisible insects bit all along her skin. Gritting her teeth, she concentrated on the lock for the back door. As a deterrent, it was effective. She did not want to be there, would have happily turned right back around, especially when the newer lock was also giving her hassle. Then she felt it, the final pin clicking into place as the door swung open.

Breathing a sigh of relief, she stepped past the threshold into the small, country style kitchen.

Fuck me, that's painful.

She took a minute to collect herself, her skin sensitive even though it looked unmarked. It wasn't real, she wasn't really being eaten alive. That fact didn't make her feel any better.

The kitchen was clean but cluttered. More baking equipment than anyone really needed was stacked up on almost every available surface. An unfinished, hand- painted poster was draped over the table. It was weird to see that the church did regular fundraising when they weren't all protesting about Breeds going to hell.

Alice huffed as she carefully opened the swing door that led into the main hall, the waning crescent moon giving very little light through the windows. The pews were pushed against the walls, leaving a vast emptiness that was creepy in the moonlight, dust in the air giving the echo of ghosts floating across the room. The broken windows were crudely repaired, and floorboards taped back together. For somewhere that charged as much as they did for entry, the money wasn't going back into the church.

She tried to walk slowly, the floorboards squeaking beneath her feet every time she moved. The office was the same as she remembered, the quotes catching her eye even in the dark. The only furniture was the desk, a chair and a bookshelf full of several different well- known novels. The desk was clean of everything, not a single piece of paper, or a pen could be found.

The drawers came up empty, a fine layer of dust inside indicating they had been empty for a while. Alice frowned, checking all the drawers several times just in case.

It's an office, where is everything?

Alice tried the bookshelf, searching through the books finding nothing. Each novel looked brand new as if they had never been used. Some still had their sale stickers. There weren't any folders, no information regarding money or details about the upcoming events that were discussed at the meeting. Nothing.

"Bugger." She slammed her hand down on the bookshelf. "There has to be something." Surely there would be administrative paperwork?

Her attention slid to the only other door in the room, the one Gordon Potts had disappeared into. It wasn't on the blueprints, so was added after the church was built.

It opened without resistance, a strange draft teasing her ankles as soon as she stepped onto the first metal step. She stood at the top, listening intently for any signs of a presence. It was early, but not early enough for her to be confident she was alone.

She slowly took another step, listening intently.

Nothing.

Silence.

Self-assured she continued her descent, noting a harsh light beneath the heavy metal door at the bottom. As well as an electronic keypad a chain was wrapped around the metal, the lock loose with runes engraved inside. She wouldn't have been able to simply pick it open even if it was locked, the design magic infused to stop any intrusion by force.

Either someone was down there, or they had forgotten to lock it, the keypad stating 'OPEN' in big green letters.

"Why would you need a magic lock?" she asked herself. "What are they trying to keep in?" *Or out,* she mentally added.

The door opened, revealing a laboratory around double the size as the office above with several closed doors. It looked newly built, the tiles and surfaces too white, especially compared to the age of the church. There were no records of anything beneath the church, the basement built illegally, without permission. It was probably why the church was crumbling.

What the hell is this?

Shiny cupboards lined the walls with silver pipes crisscrossing the concrete ceiling. A metal table was in the middle, empty glass beakers sitting on the top alongside a computer, the screen dark.

Alice stepped further inside, eyeing the see-through plastic box, a tube with black liquid locked inside. A low hum buzzed, the sound consistent as she searched through the folders and notes left on the side.

Something moved behind her.

Spinning, she let out a gasp, her heart beating a hundred miles an hour as she noticed Roman sitting by the stairs.

"You need to stop doing this," she said quietly, trying to calm herself. *How could he have moved down those stairs silently?*

"Why are you here?" She kept her voice low, quiet.

Roman just tilted his head, his arctic eyes looking at her puzzled.

"This would be easier if you could talk."

He just continued to stare, not even barking.

"Go home."

No response.

Fuck sake.

Deciding to let him be she turned her attention back to the room, finding paperwork in messily written handwriting beside a microscope. Unfortunately, she had no idea what any of it meant, the words and equations gibberish.

A soft snort behind her before Roman pawed at the metal table. Frowning, Alice examined underneath, finding a hidden drawer. Opening it slowly, she noticed the small notebook.

October 26th
The trial will begin in the next few weeks, my followers have all agreed to be part of the next phase. Gordon has already prepared the poison, we now just have to decide our course of action.

November 30th
Another success, the night dweller didn't know what hit him. It seems that consumption is the easiest way to get it into the system, although I was not told the effects it would have on my people. I pray that our sacrifice is enough.

December 10th
It wanted more. Mason promised salvation, but the consequences seem too steep. Have I made an error in blindly accepting a Breed's advice? The very same Breed I wish to cleanse from this earth? Only the holy can judge me now.

Alice read through the notebook several times, a diary of every detail behind the genocide. She couldn't believe it. The hate The Leader had for Breed was beyond comprehension. It wasn't merely hate, it was fear. He feared them.

Fear made people reckless.

'Mason promised salvation.' Alice touched her finger to the name, able to feel the impression of the pen. *Surely it couldn't be?*

A quiet growl brought her head up, Roman staring at the door opposite, his ears flat against his head.

"We're running out of blood," a muffled voice murmured.

Alice froze, panic building as she concentrated on the direction of the voice. She set the book down, making sure it was placed precisely as she first saw it before closing the drawer.

"Now, now. That is your job, I was only supposed to introduce you to it. I have no idea why you have asked me here."

Shit.

She looked towards Roman who was edging towards the stairs. In a split second decision, she made her way through another door, hiding behind it as Roman quickly followed her heel in a huff of annoyance. She shot him a glare before closing the door to a sliver, able to make out some of the lab.

The stench of bleach assaulted her nose immediately, the smell burning as she tried to keep from sneezing. Roman moaned beside her, his nose turned to her thigh.

"Mr Storm, you are a part of this just as much as me. When I have problems, you have problems." The Leader's voice was clear as he stepped inside the room.

"Nonsense," Mason said, his eyes pinched as a metal squeal closed the door behind him. "I introduce you to it, and you organise the removal of as many vampires as you could. That was the deal."

You have got to be shitting me.

Alice watched as one of the most powerful men in London looked around the room in interest.

Shit. Shit. Shit. Does Riley know?

"Well, I want to change the deal!" The Leader barked, shuffling further into the room. "You didn't make it clear how many of my flock I would lose. That alone deserves compensation."

"You want more money?" Mason sniggered. "I thought this was about your belief in cleansing the world?"

"I am but one man. One man that needs money, otherwise I have nothing to help my campaign." The Leader sat at the metal table, his fingers racing across the keyboard. "I'm still recouping the loss of this facility alone." The computer dinged.

"I funded this facility," Mason said, his attention on the beakers on a high shelf. He picked one up, studying the liquid contents then putting it back. "How much?"

"You funded this place but at what cost to me? The damage to the church..."

"How much?" Mason asked again, his voice sharp in irritation.

"One million."

Mason's head shot round, face stern.

"What do I get back for my money? You have only killed a handful of vampires. You didn't even get the Commissioner or my fellow Councilman, and I put them both in a room together for you."

"It wasn't my fault they didn't drink. I can't force it," The Leader growled.

"What about your Summoner? What's he doing?"

"He's been working with it, what do you expect?" The Leader pushed away from the table.

"If he's working with it, then he can get more blood." Mason slammed his hand against a cabinet.

Alice flinched, stepping back as something cracked beneath her boot. Freezing, she waited to see if anyone had heard. Roman tensed beside her, his ear twitching as he concentrated on the conversation. He shot her a warning look, annoyed that she dared to make noise.

"It's asking for more payment."

"Then pay it." Mason patted down invisible creases in his jacket, his face smug.

"I can't just give it…" He seemed to hesitate, his forehead creased in a frown. "They're innocent."

"Then find people that aren't so innocent." Mason smiled, the look making him look evil. "Whatever helps you sleep at night."

The Leader looked defeated as he moved back to the computer. "You at least made any progress with the boy? We need him."

"Are you really in a position to demand anything from me?"

"You know he would be easier to handle. We would be doing exactly the same without the risks."

"Your Summoner thinks he can control him?"

"If the slave bands are not compromised, then yes."

Slave bands?

"My intel says he's still in the city, probably watching his sister." Mason's face sneered. "She isn't going to be a problem, her lack of control will be her downfall."

"Can we not use her?"

Mason thought about it for a moment before shaking his head.

"She belongs to The Council. Besides, it's her brother that we need."

"I apologise if I don't trust your fellow Breed."

"Such disgust in your voice, John."

"It's Leader." A snarl.

"Remember who is paying for all this." Mason turned to leave, stopping at the electronic keypad. "I will give you the extra million, but do not call me again. I want results, not excuses."

"Of course." The Leader put in the code, his body hiding the number sequence before following Mason out. The door clicked closed behind them.

Moving away from the door Alice waited for a few minutes, listening out for anymore voices. Quickly peeking down she tried to dislodge the glass shard without making anymore noise while Roman sat on his hind legs, panting. The room was dark, the bleach stench still burning.

"*Lux Pila,*" she quietly murmured, her eyes taking a while to adjust once the ball of light popped into existence.

Holy shit!

She had found the culprit for the bleach. The floor was stained red, bleach soaked rags left beside buckets full of murky water. The room was twice the size of the lab, half concrete and half tiled. The tiled side held a grey plastic chair that reminded Alice of the dentist, but one with leather straps. The concrete side held two closed metal cells, the red stains fresher inside.

Alice could just make out a faint circle marked across the concrete, the bleach smearing the lines. Stepping closer, she felt her scar start to throb, aching in time with her heartbeat. She ignored the pain, trying to make out the shapes that were once painted.

What are they?

She touched one of the runes that remained, unable to understand its meaning. She could feel power still pulsating from the circle, the magic charged as if it was still activated.

But the circle wasn't anchored, the marks that would have been the five elements destroyed, except one.

Opening her third eye, she tried to suppress the cold heaviness that wrapped around her chest, constricting her lungs. The concrete secreted dark magic, tendrils of orange power shooting out of the ground like lightning.

She didn't understand. A circle had to be anchored to the five elements to work, fire and earth were the two fixed points, with air and water allowing the natural flow of magic through the circle then spirit to close. The fact magic still flowed was supposed to be impossible.

She reached for the bleach, tossing the abrasive liquid over the remnants of the circle, hoping to remove the last symbol, closing the loop. She choked out a breath, the bleach stench unpleasant but better than it was.

"Salt, I need salt." Salt was a catalyst, could break the remaining enchantment.

Roman yipped, nudging a large burlap sack in the corner. He bit into the side, ripping the fabric until salt poured onto the floor. She felt the magic start to dissipate, but too slowly. Smoke sizzled beneath her feet, the vapours black before disappearing altogether.

"I need to get out of here," she cried as the electric sensation became overwhelming, even as the salt fought to break the spell. She opened the door back into the lab, slipping through with Roman quickly behind.

She paused to grab the notebook before she pushed her weight against the metal door, her attention swinging to the keypad.

"You've got to be shitting me!" She pushed it again, knowing it was useless without the code.

They were locked in.

Fuck.

"What do we do now?" she asked Roman, looking at him expectantly.

He shook his head, his eyes wide as he started to shake anxiously.

"Hey, are you alright?"

She reached for him, petting him awkwardly. He calmed instantly, pushing his weight against her palm as his heavy panting quietened. She had forgotten he had been kept in a cage, forced into a transition he didn't want. He was the reason Rex had done what he did, sacrificed her for his brother.

"It's going to be okay."

We're only locked in a secret underground lab behind a thick, key code locked metal door. Casual workday.

Alice snorted at her own sarcasm, gaining her a worried glance from Roman. She scratched behind his ear, analysing the doorframe.

A bang against the metal made her jump up, pushing Roman behind her. Unsheathing her sword, she gripped the hilt, flinching at another loud bang. The metal screeched, a high-pitched shrill that set her teeth on edge.

She stepped back, pulling a snarling Roman with her just as the corner curled in. She knew for sure it wasn't The Leader, a human couldn't physically make a dent, never mind pulling the door from its hinges. Neither could a druid... usually.

Alice gripped her sword tighter.

Danton released the door from his grip, the metal clattering to the floor. He stood there, his dark eyes looking around the room before they settled on her.

"Ma petite sorcière, how nice to see you."

Roman leapt forward, snarling as D showed off his own, impressive fangs.

"What are you doing here?" Alice relaxed her arm but didn't put away her blade.

D looked at her pointedly, his dark eyes holding a controlled anger.

"Why did it take you so long to remove the barrier spell?" His fangs grew longer in his mouth, forcing his lips open. "Merde. It hurts, bâtards sanglants."

"Barrier spell?" *What's he on about...* "Oh, you mean the deterrent?" The horrible sensation of insects biting across her flesh.

"You shouldn't be here, It's dangerous."

"Danton..." A stranger hissed from behind the broken door. "La maîtresse?"

"Non." D shot back in French. "Ne l'essaie pas."

The man tensed, the brim of his hat clutched in his hands. He moved past D to face Alice, his expression tight.

"The Mistress sends her regards," he said in a deep, gravelly voice. Guess he really didn't really appreciate her hand gesture.

D's hand shot out, sending the stranger smashing through the wall, head cracking against the concrete.

"It's time to go," he snarled at Alice.

Alice chased after him, ignoring the stranger as he peeled himself off the wall.

"I need to ask about Valentina..."

"I cannot speak to you of it." He climbed the stairs, assuming she would follow. "Do not make a habit of this, ma petite sorcière. I cannot keep rescuing you."

"But you were watching me because she said so." Alice came to a halt inside the church, begging for D to turn and face her. They had been friends for years, was one of her first partners as a Paladin. Had it all been fake?

D stood in the centre of the atrium, the moonlight giving him an eerie pale aura. He turned his head, his dark hair catching the breeze from one of the broken windows.

"Oui, I'm her soldier. Have been for centuries."

"Tell me D, did you mean any of it? Was it all a job?" She wanted to hurl something at him, the urge to hurt him strong but instead she clenched her fists.

He spun to fully face her, a frown creasing his brow. He appeared in front of her, the speed knocking the wind from her lungs as he gripped her jaw.

"A long time ago, she saved me. She gave me back my life, for that I serve." He gently released her, his skin ice cold. "I help you because you need it, you're reckless like a bad-tempered child. If I hadn't been there over the years..." he hesitated, eyes flashing. "You're my friend. I help my friends."

"Friend?" Alice stepped away, not wanting him to touch her again. Roman stood beside her, his ears pinned back as he watched the vampire. "You didn't help me, you served your Mistress."

"You're too young to understand loyalty, ma petit Alice."

"I know you don't fuck over your friends."

He started to laugh, holding his pale palm over his chest.

"Être juste, I wanted more than simply friends. But you never fell for my la passion." He grinned, the usual flirtatiousness that she was used to back before his eyes hardened. "I was assigned to watch over you, over the years, it no longer felt like a job. You might not understand right now, but you will." He bowed his head, moving away. "Be careful of The Mistress, she is of old and likes to collect unusual and beautiful things."

"WHO'S THERE?" a voice called through the church.

Alice spun to the voice, a flashlight blinding her as it swept across her face.

"PUT YOUR HANDS UP!" the voice shouted.

"Okay, okay." Alice squinted past the light to the officer. "I'm Agent Alice Skye, I heard a commotion, so I came to investigate."

"I SAID PUT YOUR HANDS UP!"

Alice made a sound of frustration, her eyes darting around the poorly lit room in search for Danton, but he had disappeared.

Fuck sake.

"Call Detective O'Neil." Warm fur settled against her leg, the weight comforting as she slowly reached for her ID. "I'm part of the Spook Squad."

CHAPTER TWENTY-ONE

Alice blew into her Styrofoam cup, the aroma of tea soothing as she cupped it for warmth. Morning light streamed through the windows as several officers milled around, flicking her looks of uncertainty when they thought she wasn't looking. It took her an hour to convince them who she was, then another hour of her sitting on one of the pews, forced to wait for her team.

At least they gave me tea, she supposed.

"Agent Skye," a voice barked, strong enough to carry through the church. "What happened?" O'Neil angrily stopped in front of her, his eyebrows pinched and eyes tired. She wasn't sure if he was angry at her, or the situation.

"I decided to stake outside, heard a commotion and thought I should investigate," she lied.

She carefully watched his expression, trying to make out any telltale signs he knew of her deception.

"I hadn't even taken a few steps until Officer Gunner intervened." She shot a friendly wave towards Gunner, with whom she had spent the last few hours chatting. He seemed like a nice guy, relatively new to the force but she wished she didn't know all his ex-girlfriend's names, nor the fact he had one leg longer than the other.

"Why are you just sitting there?"

"I was asked not to move." She tried to hide her annoyance, apparently not well enough by the nudge from Roman. She tried to push him away, which resulted in him settling heavier on her feet instead.

O'Neil frowned at the wolf but didn't comment. Which was good considering there was only so many times she could explain that he was a stray and that no, she couldn't get rid of him. She had tried.

"You have full authority here, you shouldn't have been treated like that." O'Neil reached for a cigarette before fisting his hand. He gave an irritated glance at an Officer who handed over an evidence bag before returning his attention to Alice. "I was told you found this notebook?" He held up the bag, the word *'EVIDENCE'* printed in red across the plastic.

"I found it here, someone must have dropped it." Another lie, but one that benefited them. "It contains journal entries admitting to the genocide."

"Detective, we have a visitor." Peyton cut her a sharp glare as he approached, a knowing glint in his eye.

"WHAT'S HAPPENING?" A commotion as an old man shuffled through the main church doors, his arm shook as he used a walking stick. "THIS IS A PLACE OF WORSHIP, GET OUT, ALL OF YOU!" The Leader waved his free arm angrily as an Officer approached, trying to calm him down.

"Well, isn't that interesting." O'Neil nodded towards Peyton, who unhooked his handcuffs.

"Hello, my name is Detective Sullivan O'Neil, and this is Officer Peyton. Can you please come take a seat?" O'Neil held out his arm towards a pew.

The Leader glared at Peyton for a moment, frowning before he made his way over. He heavily sat down, his shoulder slumped. He looked frail, old. Nothing like he came across before, in the meeting.

"What is this? On whose authority...?"

"Sir, could you please start with your legal name." O'Neil interrupted, bringing out his little black book.

"My name's The Leader." His eyes moved to Peyton again, narrowing. "Do I know you?"

"I don't need to explain the severity of the situation," Alice said as she joined the men, Roman hot on her heels.

"What severity? No one has explained why you are here," he

snapped before he recognised her. His eyes went wide, flicking between Alice and Peyton. "Traitors," he snarled, the weak- old- man- act disappearing. "You... you." The Leader leapt up from the pew before being forced back down. "I knew we shouldn't have trusted you," he spat towards them.

"If you don't calm down I will charge you with aggravated assault towards a police officer," O'Neil warned. "Now, what is your name?"

The Leader hesitated, a note of uncertainty in his eyes. "John Smith."

"John Smith, can you please explain why you have an unregistered laboratory built in your basement?"

"I think I need to speak to my lawyer."

"That indicates you have done something illegal," Peyton muttered. "Have you done something illegal?"

"Answer the question," O'Neil asked.

"I don't know what you're talking about."

"So you have no idea about the lab built underneath your church? I checked, you have no planning permission, which means it was done illegally."

The Leader remained silent, a slight smug look on his face.

"What about the cages? Or the circle you so crudely tried to hide?" Alice added, watching his reaction.

Still no response.

O'Neil eyed him with measured interest.

"Mr Smith, we can do this the easy way or the hard way. We have enough evidence against you with the notebook..."

"You have nothing. Anybody could have written those letters, they don't prove anything."

"No, but the DNA found on the letters will surely match the DNA you have so freely given us." Peyton pointedly looked at the blob of spit by his boot. "Not even mentioning the clear fingerprints from the smudged ink."

"Sloppy if you ask me," O'Neil added, a slow smile creeping across his face.

"It wasn't me. It wasn't. I'm a man of god, only the divine can judge me. I was persuaded for the greater good..."

"The 'greater good'?" Peyton snorted. "I'm sure your god or deity encourages mass murder."

"It wasn't me, it was Gordon. Gordon Potts. He's the Summoner."

"He's a witch?" O'Neil asked The Leader while looking at Alice.

She just shrugged. She didn't know, it was hard to tell someone's Breed by just looking at them. Flaring her chi to see if she could feel someone's aura was the simplest way to know if they were a magic user or not, but that didn't determine the exact Breed. Although, that was only if they weren't concealing their magic.

"He told me he wasn't, that he was normal. But he had ancient knowledge so he could practice magic without compromising his soul."

"You believed what you wanted because it helped you," Alice stated.

The Leader caught her eye. "I believe in what is for the greater good of humanity. You wouldn't understand that," he sneered.

"Who else?" O'Neil asked. "From the state of your church you don't have the funds to orchestrate it alone."

"Mason Storm," Alice said before The Leader could answer. "Was it only Mason from the Storm empire?" Alice asked, panic underlying her tone.

If Riley was involved...

The thought sucked the air right out of her lungs.

"Mason approached me, remember that." The Leader confirmed. "I think I've said enough. I would like to speak to my lawyer."

Alice felt her anger snap. "You pretend to be righteous, but you're just an extremist hypocrite disguised as a religion. You don't deserve the..."

"Agent Skye, step back," O'Neil warned.

Alice moved away before she said anything else. She didn't know what would happen if one of the most influential men in London, if not Britain was found guilty of such a heinous crime. Someone who, in the public eye, had been very vocal in equal rights as well as open about generously donating to various charities.

Shit.

Peyton came with her, his face stern as he moved her away from anyone else.

"What the fuck did you think you were doing?" His eyes flashed in anger, his lips a hard line. "You could have compromised the whole case."

Alice opened her mouth to lie, deciding against it. Peyton saw through her excuses.

"We needed evidence, I found it. Do not tell me you wouldn't have done the same thing if you could."

Peyton's cheekbones sharpened through his skin, his eyes searching hers.

"What are your thoughts?" he asked, voice softer than before, but his eyes no less intense.

"That I want Mason locked up with the key thrown somewhere far away."

Actually, she wanted something darker to happen to him, something that reflected what he did to those innocent people.

"We will never be able to get him."

"What makes you say that? We have all this evidence…"

"We have his name on a piece of paper and a confession that will be thrown out of court."

"I saw him…"

"You saw nothing as you were never there. Otherwise all the evidence will be compromised." Peyton's jaw clenched. "He's going to have the best solicitors money can buy, we won't be able to get this to stick."

"Your rules are ridiculous." Breed authority might have been more barbaric, but in the circumstance it would be justice. Unfortunately, the structure was to inform the head of the specific Breed of the crime – which would be Mason.

"You Paladins have no structure. Just point your sword and stab."

Alice couldn't help but laugh. "You can't say it doesn't get the job done."

Peyton smirked in reply.

As a Paladin, she knew the justice system well. Knew the corruptions and scandals influenced by The Council. They ruled by fear, allowing the human justice system to do its job until they were forced to step in. They wouldn't have agreed to give over their power. They would have said anything to make the Norms happy, even giving them a false sense of entitlement. It was only the extreme cases when the crime was deemed too serious that the Breed's governing body took over. It was the reason why she was allowed to use lethal force. Someone with razor-sharp claws, preference for blood or could turn your skin inside out was a lot more dangerous than the usual human.

"Do you know who he is?" Alice asked.

"If you mean his Council status then yes. Nobody is above the law, not even them."

That's what he thinks.

"What about a confession?" Alice said, knowing he would never see the inside of a cell, at least, not a normal one. She's sure The Council had their own special ones, especially for people like him. Or worse.

"How likely are we going to get that?"

CHAPTER TWENTY-TWO

Alice paid no attention to the beautiful woman who sat behind the glass desk in front of Mason Storm's office, his door closed beside her. The woman looked up, her expression like a fish as she watched Alice push open the door, bursting inside unannounced much to the fluster of the receptionist.

"Excuse me, excuse me!" her red lips gasped. "You can't go in there..."

She came to a halt, her eyes huge, round.

"I'm so sorry Councilman Storm, she just..."

"Louise, it's fine," Mason said calmly, his grey eyes narrowed as he glared coldly at Alice. "Could you please move my next appointment."

"Sir." Louise nodded before closing the door behind her.

"Are you going to explain why you're here?" Mason asked.

Alice said nothing as she looked around the office, analysing his masculine, expensive taste. She knew it would irritate him, her blatant disregard to his question. She needed him angry. To fracture his calm demeanour.

So she remained silent.

His desk was oversized, covered in paperwork with his family name embossed on the front. An oil painting decorated the panelled wood wall directly behind him, what looked like a warped beast snarling. Everything was in masculine shades of navy, pewter and grey other than the burst of green through the floor to ceiling windows. His office was on the sixty-eighth floor that faced directly opposite the nature reserve that was a burst of life in a city of steel and glass.

It would have been breath-taking if she had time to appreciate it.

'*We're live. Try and get him to admit his involvement without leading the conversation,*' Detective Brady said from her hidden earpiece. '*Be careful, we don't know how dangerous he is.*'

"I'm waiting," Mason asked, his tone like ice as he sat down behind his desk. "Why have you made such a rude entrance?"

He relaxed back into his seat, the painted beast surrounding him until it gave the impression they were one. It made him look powerful, a force to be reckoned with. Which was probably the point. She could imagine him there, negotiating his business deals with ease. For the bastard he was, she couldn't dispute him as a businessman.

She gave him a slow smile, enjoying the slight narrowing of his eyes.

"I'm working."

"Oh, yes. Aren't you part of that new inter-breed partnership? Ridiculous, teaming up with the Norms," he sniggered, clasping his hands together.

"I'm surprised you seem so opposed, wasn't it The Council's idea?" she drawled, baiting him.

"Nonsense, why would I care about such a ludicrous concept?" He remained calm, his attention following her as she walked around his office. "Tell me Alice, how is Rexley Wild?"

Alice froze at the name, knew he had said it to gain a reaction, to take back control of the conversation.

"I wouldn't know, haven't seen him." She had done well not to think about him, that man didn't deserve any of her attention, even if it was only her mind. At least, until recently.

"You haven't spoken to him?"

Mason stood up, slowly walking around his desk to stand in front of her. His height dwarfed hers by almost a foot, made her neck ache to look at his face, but she refused to step back.

"Weren't you lovers?"

"Are you asking if we fucked?" Alice asked, using the profanity on purpose. "I don't think that's any of your business." Mason knew exactly what to say to unnerve her, something he could use against her. She wouldn't allow him to get the upper hand.

"How crudely put. I think being betrayed like that is fascinating."

He slowly smiled, leaning forward into her personal space. "Someone who knows you intimately and still chose to betray you, how... embarrassing. Or is it more pathetic?"

Alice didn't respond.

"I don't understand what he saw in you. All I see is a girl who's in way over her head. A pathetic excuse of a witch who can't even control her most basic energy. It's... disappointing."

"Isn't it a shame I don't respect your opinion."

She didn't even see him blur before her head cracked against the glass window, a strong arm pressed forcibly into her throat. She kept the eye contact even as she struggled to breathe, not daring to give him the satisfaction.

'What was that?'

She had forgotten people were listening in, could only hear and not see what was happening.

'Agent Skye, this is your ten-minute warning before we're coming in. Get the confession.'

"I can still feel you leaking energy. Has my son not taught you anything?" Mason asked with a dissatisfied tut.

He released a slight pressure from her neck, giving her the chance to suck in a much needed breath.

"We're not here to talk about me." She enjoyed his frustration as she remained calm, even as fire tingled in her fingertips.

"You're a bomb waiting to go off," he spoke against her cheek, his breath intimate across her face. "You may look relaxed, but I can feel it beneath your skin, your chi's electric. All I would have to do is..."

Alice gave a startled gasp, could feel her chi blazing as Mason touched it with his own. It felt similar to Riley, how he could make it charged just by being close. But it wasn't the same, it was darker, toxic, like a thick tar across her senses.

"Cute trick," she spat at him, not hiding her disgust. He felt... wrong. "Do you do kids parties too?"

"You're like a personal ley line, a power socket that I could syphon," he whispered in her ear. "Maybe that's why everybody is so fascinated with you. It's what made me so fascinated with your mother."

Alice heard the blood rush from her head, her eyes blurring as Mason sniggered. She pushed against him, allowing her energy to coat her palm in a burst of crackling blue. Mason stepped back just in time, an unreadable glint in his eye.

"Don't speak of her," she snarled. She could see her personal Tinkerbell floating from the corner of her eye, the ball of flame sparking at intervals to match her temper. It was times like this when she hated the thing, a physical manifestation of her weakness.

"That's what they want to do, you know. To use The Dragon child. Use you," he said, casually looking her up and down. "Although, you're no longer a child, can't be as easily manipulated. At least, that's what my fellow councilmembers believe."

"You know nothing about my family."

Alice jumped at his burst of laughter.

"Your ignorance is amusing."

'Five-minute warning.'

She wanted to ask him more but knew it wasn't the time.

"Where were you around five-thirty this morning?"

"Why should I answer you?" he smirked.

"Because you've been accused of being a conspirator in a recent genocide."

She watched his reaction, saw a flash of panic before he quickly recovered. Alice tried to hide her satisfied grin.

Got ya.

"This is utter nonsense." Mason walked to his desk to pick up the phone, dialling his receptionist. "I grow tired of this conversation. Leave before you're thrown out."

"Forensics are currently collecting evidence against you for your part in the poisoning," she calmly explained. "I wonder what everybody is going to think…"

"Your uncontrollable surges have clearly affected your mind. I will make sure I report it to The Council Immediately. Your accusations are treason against a councilmember."

"Do you mean the same councilmember that organised the murder of another?"

Masons face turned cold, his eyes guarded. He settled the handset back into its cradle. "What do you want?"

"I want to know why."

Mason stared at her for a few seconds, his grey eyes unreadable.

"Everything I do, I do because it needs to be done."

He moved slowly towards her again.

"Your brother, for instance…"

Alice saw her Tinkerbell sparkle, annoyed that it was giving away her emotions.

"Yes, your brother is very much alive. I've been looking for him actually. He's a danger to the general public."

"You don't know that," she shot at him.

He kept speaking as if she hadn't spoken.

"You know nothing of what I have to do. The decisions I have to make. Valentina has become a threat, she has taken too much power, has become sick with it, her and her night dwellers."

Mason moved closer once again, his movements uncharacteristically rigid. Alice concentrated on extinguishing the Tinkerbell, but left the flame in her palm, not allowing him to get too close.

"It is what I do, it's part of why The Order was created. We neutralise threats to keep the world safe. Are you a threat Alice?"

He stepped closer again, a bare inch away from the magic she coated across her palm.

"Are you following in your parent's footsteps?"

"Don't speak of my parents." Her fire crackled. "You don't deserve to even mention them."

"Druids can become addicted to power, crave it. My ancestors chose power, became corrupted by the darkness of it..."

"Daemons," Alice finished for him as the realisation clicked. "Your ancestors were the first Daemons."

The passage she read months ago flashed across her memory.

'For one to 'Become' age-old one must sacrifice a vessel of clean magic. Doing so will give the bearer the ability to transcend into the next stage, giving unbelievable power over the darker arts, their body reflecting the high power bestowed on them by the mother of everything.'

"The Originals. We're now taught from birth the consequences of choosing dark, choosing power. It's a burden we live with, the curse of our blood."

'One-minute. Keep him talking.'

"Your mother was a power your father craved," Mason continued. "He chose her over The Order, even over The Council. They became dangerous, first when he didn't disclose who your mother was, and then when he refused to hand her over. So they both had to be neutralised."

"Neutralised?" Alice choked out the word.

"It was a shame something as beautiful as your mother got in the way. She would have made a great pet."

"It was you? You led the Daemons to them."

Alice felt her hand start to pulsate, the flames crawling up to her elbow.

"You killed them." The fire began to build in her other palm, an uncontrollable element.

He smiled. "I'm a businessman Alice."

"GET DOWN!" Voice's boomed as the door was kicked open. Three uniformed police including officer Peyton stormed through the door, pointing their weapons at Mason.

"ON THE GROUND!"

Mason was quickly pinned and handcuffed, his smile turning to a snarl as he was manhandled.

"GET OFF ME! DO YOU KNOW WHO I AM?"

Detective Brady approached Alice cautiously, his eyes worried as the fire crackled loudly. She could smell burning, knew if she didn't calm herself, she could suffer a flame out.

"Agent Skye?"

Alice closed her eyes, concentrated on breathing in and out. Smoke tickled her throat, the intense heat decreasing with every passing second before she finally extinguished it. She opened her eyes, instantly searching for Mason, unable to hide her emotion as she watched the sneer carved into his face disappear. Replaced with her death.

Alice wanted to smile, wanted to laugh hysterically as she watched the man who admitted to murdering her parents be taken away in handcuffs, she wanted...

Riley stood in the threshold, his eyes completely silver, unreadable.

An apology instantly bubbled up her throat, one she swallowed. She had nothing to apologise for, the devastating knowledge of what Mason admitted plastered across her face. Instead, she stood there, frozen, unable to break the eye contact.

She felt cold, hollow.

Riley blinked, the captivating silver replaced with steel- grey that darkened with impatience.

"Agent Skye?" Brady nudged her, forcing her attention.

She looked up at him expectantly, having to blink to clear her vision.

"We've got exactly what we need. We're done here."

"Yeah, okay," she replied, voice husky. Lifting up her top she ripped the microphone off, ignoring the acute pain from the sticky tape.

Handing it to one of the officers she turned back to Riley, an explanation on the edge of her tongue.

But he didn't give her the chance.

She quickly searched for him, following back through into the reception where she was met with concerned stares. They had all heard his father's confession, knew one of her darkest secrets, at least partially.

And she didn't care.

Couldn't care while she felt this strange sense of urgency to find Riley, an irrational feeling that something was wrong. Something...

A sharp bark snapped her out of it. Roman whined low in his throat, his tongue lapping at her fingers. She instinctively reached out to his fur, anchoring herself in the warmth. She had no idea how he had arrived up there, but thankful that he had.

"Come on, let's get you home."

CHAPTER TWENTY-THREE

Alice tried not to smile as Roman played with the air currents, his mouth open in a wolfish grin as he caught the wind from the open car window. He was lucky that Sam knew how to replace a tyre otherwise it would have been public transport. Except, even that would have been difficult since shifters were banned from being in public in their animal form. Alice chanced another look at him, his pure black pelt shinier than she remembered.

He was small for a shifter, could possibly have pulled off the deception if no one looked into his eyes. Too intelligent, you could never mistake a shifter for any animal, never mind a domesticated one. Yet, as far as she knew, Roman had not shifted back to his human form, his wolf having taken over back when he had been captured. He should have been showing signs of deterioration, the beast becoming more permanent. However, he didn't. It was peculiar, but she didn't want to jinx it. If Roman needed more time to come to terms with his captivity, so be it.

As Alice drove up the driveway to White Dawn's compound, she felt herself panic, an irrational reaction considering she knew she wasn't in any danger. Anxiety wrapped around her chest, restricting her lungs into panicked gasps.

Roman looked over to her, feeling her angst.

She closed her eyes, shutting everything out. She was still so angry, angrier even more so that she couldn't ask questions of the man who had, willingly, handed her over to a cult. A man for whom she'd had feelings for, with whom she had slept with.

She knew why Roman's quiet whine was reminding her, but she still couldn't control the sudden energy spike. Heat prickled her fingers as she clenched her fists, hard enough she felt her nails cut into her palms.

She hadn't achieved closure, not really.

A warm tongue licked across her cheek. Opening her eyes, she turned to Roman, his own eyes dark with concern. It wasn't his fault.

"It's okay," she murmured, giving him a reassuring smile as she got out the car. She didn't really want to be there. Had no interest in the pack who couldn't, or wouldn't answer her questions.

The old manor house was just as she remembered. Even so, her heart skipped a beat once she saw Theo open the door, her brain seeing his twin instead. Blinking away the illusion she assured herself it was indeed Theo and not the man she never wanted to see again.

"Hello, oh Roman, there you are." Theo smiled at his brother, making the large scar that started from his forehead, across his nose and distorting his upper lip stand out. "Wondered where you had gone off to."

"He keeps popping up," Alice said dryly.

Roman barked before wandering to sit beside Theo, his ears twitching.

"Have you thought about the offer?"

"I'm sorry," she said, her voice humiliatingly hoarse. "I can't." She couldn't face him, not yet. She needed to understand her feelings first, needed to know if they were real. If anything was real.

"We will pay you anything," Theo said as he stepped out of the doorway, a desperate edge to his voice.

"This isn't about money."

Roman snorted, forcing Theo to whip his head towards his brother. He looked at him like he could understand – which maybe he could. Theo growled, the noise disconcerting coming from a human throat. Roman barked in response before moving to slump beside Alice instead.

Theo looked frustrated but didn't say anything.

Great, now she was in the middle of a brotherly spat.

"Look, I need to go."

"Please, you don't understand. We need to find him before Xavier. I can't make you forgive him for what he did to you, but surely you can recognise the reasons behind it."

Alice saw red.

"How dare you say that to me," she snapped, irritation igniting her already high energy level. She took a controlling breath, concentrated on calming her chi. "You go find him."

"Do you not think we have tried?" His eyes flashed blue, his wolf reacting to his own spike in anger. "You're our last option."

Alice opened her mouth to give a retort, but nothing came out. They were desperate. She knew what it felt like to be searching for a brother. Alice wanted to run away, screaming. Wanted to leave Rex to it; a fitting punishment.

But was it though?

She searched Theo's eyes, not sure what she was even looking for. Rex had betrayed her in every way possible. Tricked her. Used her. Yet, she knew she couldn't allow him that fate if she could help it.

"What does Xavier want?" she asked as Theo closed his eyes, his breath coming out in a slow exhale.

"Thank you."

"I haven't agreed yet." She had heard Xavier was one of the most ruthless council members, gaining his position by killing his predecessor. Shifters didn't have The Magika like witches or The Order like druids, where there was a majority panel to decide your fate. They only had Xavier. His decision was final.

"Yes, you have."

Alice looked away, the wind catching her hair as she gazed out towards the trees surrounding the compound.

Fuck. Fuck. Fuck.

She was going to regret this.

"What leads do you have?"

Alice sat in her car, blinking up at the clearly lived in shed.

"This can't be right?" she frowned, checking the crumpled paper map for the hundredth time. "Stupid, bloody..."

Alice smelt smoke, the edges of the paper alight and quickly burning though.

"SHIT. SHIT. SHIT!"

Alice flung herself into the open air, stamping on the map with her boot.

She hated maps. It was her own fault, her satellite navigation unit needed to be repaired, the crystal inside broken, so she had been stuck with the old-fashioned way.

She eyed the remains of the directions, wondering if she was simply born with bad luck. Or it could be that she let her magic go unchecked, which was also her fault.

Great, just great.

She puffed out a breath as she gazed at the crudely made wooden house, hoping it was the right place. She was in the middle of nowhere, the building made from felt, wooden slats and nails which was surrounded on all sides in a thick brush. The only way onto the property was the thin dirt driveway that was clearly handmade. The ground beneath the structure was darker than the rest, the earth charred as if something else had stood there before.

"Well, this is a good place to kill someone," she laughed, the sound hollow.

Why had Theo sent her there? He had given her a vague direction, explained she was to meet with someone who could help. She had no idea what he could do when she couldn't track him. And she had definitely tried to track him. It was like Rex had vanished into thin air.

Or that could be just wishful thinking.

"Hello?" she called, trying to peer through a dark window.

"Who are you?" A man emerged from the forest, his pitch-black eyes guarded as he stayed in the shadow of a tree.

"Oh, hi." Alice tried to approach but stopped when he stepped back. "I'm supposed to be meeting someone here."

"You here for the wolf?"

"Ah, yes. That's me." She gave an awkward wave.

"I told him I don't work with wolves."

"Well, I'm not a wolf."

He tilted his head, staring at her from a distance.

"Your aura is weird," he finally said.

"I'm sorry, what?" She sensed it then, something brushing against her chi. It felt strange, dark.

Where did Theo find this guy?

The man stepped into the light.

"How did you do that?" she asked, blinking stupidly at the vampire. He had just tested her chi. But vampires didn't have magic.

She studied him, wondering if she was simply seeing things. It wouldn't be the first time. His hair matched the darkness of his eyes, spiked in every direction possible with his fangs at full length. He was dressed like a hiker, with heavy boots, jeans and a chequered shirt. Goth meets country. It was a creepy combination.

"I will do this for you because I'm interested in what you are," he stated. "It is not for the wolf."

"I'm just a simple witch." If she kept telling herself that it might be true.

"Just a witch, as I'm just a Vamp," he grinned, emphasising his unnaturally long canines. "But not a wolf," he quickly added, the smile disappearing.

Alice warily watched him, his gaze uncomfortable before he finally invited her inside. She followed cautiously, not really wanting to be too close to him.

The inside was modest, a single camping bed sat next to a chimney and a basic kitchen. Copper pots and crushed herbs covered almost every available surface while dead birds, rabbits and other little critters hung bleeding from the ceiling.

"So what's your name?"

"Unimportant. Unimportant. We do not exchange names. I have no interest in yours. Yet. Maybe? No, no names. Now..." He clapped his hands together. "Your wolf mentioned a bracelet?"

He stood by the chimney, his fingers absently brushing the corpse of a rabbit, his attention never leaving her.

Alice grabbed the leather cord from her pocket, handing it over.

"Do you know what it is?" She hadn't seen the bracelet since it was removed from her wrist, thought it was lost. She was most surprised when Theo presented her with it.

"It's fascinating," the vampire said as he studied it eagerly. "Bought on the black market, incredibly illegal."

His eyes were excited when he looked up, his movements unnaturally jerky as if he had forgotten how to act normal, human.

"The leather would be entwined around the hair of the person they would want to track, then soaked in the owner's blood."

"Hair?" Alice instantly touched her own.

"Yes, yes, hair. It's easy enough to obtain without the victim knowing."

He licked his lips as he held the moon pendant up to the light.

"Now, this is interesting."

Unnerved by the intensity of his gaze, Alice looked at the pendant.

"It would have emphasised emotions towards the person who gifted it, made them heightened. Anger, jealousy..." He made a sound of choked amusement. "Lust."

Alice felt a chill at the back of her neck. Her emotions had been fake, forced. The thought made her skin crawl.

"How heightened?" She held her breath, waiting for the answer.

"The emotions would already be there, but once in the presence of the owner of the bracelet, they would be amplified. General annoyance could become rage while simple attraction could change to intense passion." He licked his lips again, eyes excited.

"So, it can't force emotions?"

"No, no, no. Emotions already there, just amplified. Maybe a little manipulated."

He made a sound of annoyance.

"If emotion isn't already there, the bracelet cannot fake them. That is called Pathokinesis, which this bracelet is not." He snorted, throwing the bracelet onto his bed. "This will be sufficient payment for my services."

"Wait, I never agreed to that."

"Do you not want my help?" he asked, his fingers clawed in a threat. "I'm sure there are many people around that can do what I do."

Fuck.

What exactly could he do?

"What of the effects of the bracelet? What will you do with them?"

"Magic is no longer... it's..." He seemed to struggle for the right word, as if English wasn't his native tongue. "Broken."

Alice thought about it.

"Fine."

She didn't really have any other options. She wanted to curse Rex for doing what he had done, curse Theo for asking her for help.

"This way, this way," he clapped as he pushed his bed over. Beneath was a neatly drawn pentagram in blood, his symbols stylised in a way she didn't recognise.

Alice felt goosebumps break over her skin even as she stepped away, the circle secreting dark magic. It was thick, like oil that clung to her lungs with every breath.

"Stay there," he demanded as he cupped his hands, murmuring incoherently before stepping into his circle. A dome appeared around him instantly, his aura bland, completely colourless.

How can he do magic? It was impossible. It was…

"You're a familiar," she said as the realisation hit her.

Familiars were magical partners to witches, sharing their chi. They were usually a cat or another small domestic animal, the reason being that the witch would borrow their familiar's aura in spells, substantially expanding their own chi. As it caused intense pain and left the creature without an aura to protect themselves, it was ruled as black magic, therefore illegal. The practice of making a person into a familiar was forbidden.

The vampire looked up, his eyes entirely encased by black, his head tilted inquisitively. He would have been tortured every time his master practised magic, something like that would have left many people with a few marbles missing.

Although he had obviously learned a few things along the way.

"You share your master's aura." It was the only logical reason the vampire could practise magic.

He gave her a wicked grin.

"Where is…?" She couldn't bring herself to call the person a 'master' again. It implied he was a servant, a slave. The idea he was seen as an object someone could own made her feel ill.

The Vamp burst out laughing, his shoulders shaking violently as his hands continued to be clasped tightly together. A small light broke through the cracks between his fingers.

"Ladybird ladybird, fly away home," he sang in an eerily detached voice. "Your house is on fire, your children have all gone, all but one that lies under a stone…" He cackled away, the light flickering in his fist before flashing brightly. "All done," he said chirpily as he bounded over to her. "Give this to your wolf, he will be able to track his own blood."

Alice opened her hand as he dropped a small pebble, the surface intensely cold as it hit her skin.

"Blood as in brother?"

"Either or," he shrugged before wrapping his arms around himself, his fingers clawed into his chequered shirt.

Was this all Theo had wanted?

She closed her fist, trying to ignore the fact she thought the pebble had a pulse.

"Thanks."

"That was fun. I haven't done that in a while." His gaze drifted off to stare at the bracelet.

That was her cue to leave.

Even as she transferred the pebble to the glove compartment in her car she felt uneasy, wondering what sort of dark magic had made it. One thing for sure was that she couldn't wait to be rid of it already. She caught herself looking at the charred earth beneath the shed, only just noticing how some of the trees surrounding were also singed.

"Ladybird ladybird, fly away home," she sang to herself, remembering the nursery rhyme. "Your house is on fire, your children have all gone, all but one that lies under a stone, fly thee home, ladybird, ere it be gone."

She really hoped it was simply a rhyme, and not something more sinister. From her gut feeling, she doubted it.

CHAPTER TWENTY-FOUR

Alice smiled politely at the man who swiped her into the basement morgue in the London Hope Hospital. It wasn't a place she often visited, which she was glad about because the place reeked of bleach and formaldehyde. She was trained to track and detain Breed, not deal in dead bodies. Not usually, anyway.

"You're late,' Detective Brady complained once she entered into the room. "You were supposed to be here over thirty minutes ago."

"Traffic," Alice said as if that was an excuse. She didn't get stuck in traffic, but they didn't need to know that. She would have been there sooner if she hadn't stopped back at Theo's, wanting to get rid of the pebble as quickly as possible. She literally threw it at him, driving away to his confused 'thank you.'

She had done what he had asked, it was up to him to find his brother. She just hoped it kept Roman away. She had enough problems, she didn't need to babysit an unstable shifter too.

"If you planned these meetings better, I wouldn't necessarily be late," she whispered beneath her breath as she stood beside Jones and Brady, three sheet- covered gurneys in front of them. Jones lit up when she smiled at him, unlike Brady, who looked unimpressed with her explanation.

"Where's O'Neil and Peyton?" she asked, louder this time.

"O'Neil's busy, and Peyton's an Officer," he said as if that was explanation enough.

"Right, is everybody here?" a man asked as he stepped through the door. "Ah, if it isn't my favourite girl." Dr Miko Le'Sanza grinned when he noticed Alice, his arms wide as he went in for a hug.

"I didn't think you would be on this case?" Last she heard Miko had been hired directly under Dread for The Tower.

"You'll understand why in a moment," he said, eyes gleaming mischievously.

"You know each other?" Jones asked, his attention more on the gurneys than the conversation. It was weird to see him in regular clothes compared to his usual white full-body suit. He wore a pair of worn jeans and a basic logo T-shirt with his brown hair messy, like he just got out of bed.

"Can we get down to business?" Brady crossed his arms, straining his jacket across his thick arms. "We're all here, so why don't you explain why you've had us come down here Dr Le'Sanza?"

"I'm sorry, is there somewhere more interesting for you to be Detective?" Miko asked in a clipped tone.

Alice tried to hide her smirk.

She had known Miko for years, met him on one of her many contracts. He had a fun, flamboyant personality befitting a Brazilian carnival dancer, as was his father's heritage. Until he became aggravated, then he became an icy bastard Alice loved to tease.

Brady clenched his jaw, his skin darkening around his cheekbones, but he remained silent.

Miko glared for a few uncomfortable seconds before he nodded towards Jones, signalling for him to pull off the first sheet on the left. The body was reasonably well preserved, the man looking more like he was asleep than dead. Other than the large Y stitched across his sternum. That was a big giveaway.

"I would like you to bring your attention to patient 'A'."

Jones whistled, admiring the cadaver. "Is this the one we spoke on the phone about?"

"Nope. There's more to come," Miko smiled, his infectious cheerfulness back as he wiggled his eyebrows.

"You mind filling us in?" Brady asked, annoyed.

Alice didn't bother to hide her smile this time, understanding how Miko and Jones would become quick friends. They both worked in a similar field, Miko was a Pathologist while Jones was a Forensic Technician. Both their jobs entailed finding out the cause of death.

Miko pointed to an open wound, highlighting the dying cells.

"Patient 'A' is one hundred per cent human and has been confirmed as being a carrier. We have discovered a lack of platelets and blood glycoprotein, which resulted in severe haemorrhaging, causing death."

"We know this already," Alice said, pointing to the puncture marks on the neck. "The humans fed their victims and then would bleed out when their blood didn't clot."

"Yes," Miko confirmed. "It seemed to start from the access point, in the humans it's ingested. It gets into the bloodstream through cuts in their mouth or once it starts to be digested. The main reason humans don't see symptoms sooner is that the human body can take six to eight hours to fully digest and absorb."

"Why do the Vamps get symptoms faster? If they used to be humans?" Jones asked, frowning.

"Vampires don't have a digestive system as they don't eat. When they are put into the ground to start the turn, their internal organs shut down."

Brady looked over to Alice, who shrugged. She had no idea vampires had weird insides. She had never personally looked.

Vampires were private, rarely sharing their secrets with anyone. The knowledge of the turn was only made public when one fame hungry vampire invited a news crew to witness the whole transition. The newly formed vampire slaughtered the entire crew live on air before anybody could gain control, resulting in a dramatic legislation brought in by The Council. Nobody could be turned without the consent of another master. It made human screening even harder. The newly turned vampires were also connected to their creator until they showed enough control to become their own master.

"Whatever a vampire ingests gets directly absorbed into their cells, which results in a quicker reaction time."

"What about the substance they're ingesting, do we know what that is yet?" Alice asked.

"Ah, that is why it has been flagged by The Tower," Miko's eyes twinkled as he grabbed a clipboard, handing it to Jones who frowned.

"It's blood," Jones murmured, squinting at the paper.

"At least, part blood," Miko confirmed, his eye contact penetrating as he concentrated on Alice. "It's similar to another case where we identified the deceased as being in a Daemon transition."

Of course it is.

Alice instinctively gripped her crescent scar. Brady noticed but didn't comment.

"We knew that already," Jones stated as he studied the paperwork. "But it wasn't one-hundred per cent confirmed until now." He handed back the paper. "So it's Daemon juice?"

"We're confident the other case was a failed Daemon transition, this blood, however, is more distinctive. Defined. It's also mixed with other, unknown materials. Either way it's deadly," Miko nodded. "Okay, let's look under sheet two." He pulled at the fabric, revealing another body, this time female.

Alice recognised the woman from the Gala, a newer vampire who was on her table. She wanted to look away, not wanting the image stuck beneath her eyelids. The woman looked like a ghost, her skin so pale it was transparent. The Y incision hadn't been closed completely, the thread still visible through the ripped skin. Her arms looked wrong, bent at an impossible angle.

"This is one of the first victims, we call her patient 'B'. We have estimated from consumption to time of death being around thirty minutes. The protein started to degrade the cells instantly, resulting in softening of bone and shrunken, dehydrated skin."

He touched the paper-thin skin of the woman, showing how little pressure he had to add to make it disintegrate beneath his fingertips.

"She was found slumped against the table, her spine crumbled."

"This isn't why we're here." Jones eagerly eyed the last gurney.

"No, you all already know most of this, but Patient 'C'..."

Miko pulled off the final sheet, revealing another male body.

"This isn't a vampire..." Alice said at the unveiling. The body was a mixture of the two others, his skin pale and dehydrated but not paper-thin. His jaw was slack, showing regular teeth, no fangs.

"You're right, it's a shifter," Jones said, excited.

"They can be affected?" Brady asked, concerned.

"Apparently so."

"I did some research once you called me," Jones stated. "I don't work directly with bodies, so I had to look into some medical journals, but shifters have the closest physiology to humans. So I'm interested to understand what happened to him."

"Patient 'C' died of haemorrhaging but at a lot slower rate. It is possible he didn't even notice until he was too weak to do anything. Shifters have an incredible ability to heal due to the fact that when they shift from one form to another, their skin rips and bones break. His body was trying to restore even as the substance started to eat away at his cells. It resulted in mild bone deterioration but not enough to cause death. In my opinion, if he had simply ingested it like the humans he probably wouldn't have seen any effect at all, his body would have worked its way through it."

"He didn't ingest it?"

"The substance was found directly in his bloodstream." Miko pulled at one of his arms, showing the small puncture marks.

"He injected it?"

Miko nodded. "Patient 'C', also known as Richard Pail. Arrested for possession of a controlled substance, possession with intent to supply and GBH. We can find no evidence of any other puncture marks other than the ones along his arms and between his toes. We believe he didn't have a chance to spread it."

"They could be branching out, targeting junkies," Brady said, stepping back. "It isn't unheard of that they will swap a feeding for a fix."

"Vampires sometimes seek junkies out specifically for a feed, it's the only way they can gain a high," Alice confirmed.

Brady started to slowly smile, it was uncomfortable besides the bodies. He turned to Miko, who was in a quiet discussion with Jones.

"Where's the case report? We need to know everything about where this body was found."

CHAPTER TWENTY-FIVE

"What the fuck is that?" asked Detective Brady as they walked beneath a motorway crossing bridge just outside the city.

Alice followed his line of sight, silently cringing at the grotesque goblin that was trying to peacefully eat his bowl of unknown meat. It smelt of a mixture of fish guts and stale chicken, the odour strong even through the general aroma of waste and unclean bodies. The goblin snarled when he noticed them, baring the screws he used as teeth in warning.

They were unfriendly creatures generally, keeping to themselves. While they usually were around four foot, the goblin that was watching them with its beady black eyes was taller, around five foot. Alice quickly checked around, seeing if he had friends. They liked to work in groups, using distractions to pickpocket.

Alice politely nodded as they passed, his long green ears twitching in irritation.

"He's nothing you should be concerned about," Alice replied.

At least, as long as we don't piss him off.

Goblins were classed as Fae, and while they had little magic they made up for it in strength. A strength Alice didn't want to go up against, especially as their skin was thick enough to absorb most damage.

"Corvus oculum corvi non eruit," the goblin muttered.

"What did it say?" Brady asked, his eyes narrowed as he evaluated the situation.

Alice shrugged. "Something about ravens, or maybe it's crows."

"Crows?" he frowned. "What the fuck has anything got to do with crows?"

Alice sighed. "He said 'a crow will not pull out the eye of another crow,' or something around those lines."

"That doesn't sound right," Brady muttered.

"Do you want to try and translate then?"

She spoke Latin. Sort of, anyway.

"Well, what the fuck does it mean?"

"It means something like honour among thieves."

"Well that's fucking great," he growled as they walked beneath the large underpass.

The overhead line crossing sheltered the homeless from the worst of the winter weather. In the shadows beneath, the ground was dry of snow, but the wind threatened the flames that crackled in the metal barrels strategically placed around.

It was the home to a mixture of people, some homeless, some junkies. A man shuffled towards them, pushing a shopping trolley full of discarded home appliances and sleeping bags. When he noticed Brady, his face drained of colour, his eyes darting around before he quickly made his way past.

"Did you really have to dress like a cop?" Alice said as a few more people recoiled away from them.

Brady frowned, looking down at himself. "What do you mean?"

"I mean you look like a police officer who also wrestles on the weekend." She pointed to his smart suit and black overcoat. She could even make out the small bulge on his hip where he hid his gun.

"This is how I normally dress." He shot her an aggravated look.

"I think it's best if we split up," she said. "We can cover more ground."

"Fine," he grumbled as he approached a man who was trying to warm his hands by a fire.

Alice stayed back for a moment, scanning the fifteen or so men and women who called the underpass home. Cars sped high above, the disorderly noise irritating even as road debris rained down after every other car.

"Hello?" she asked the man who sat alone in a foldable camping chair, his sleeping bag rolled out ready beside him.

"What do you want?" he asked as he drank from a wine bottle.

Alice guessed his age to be around the late twenties, the dirty beard and sores making it hard to tell. A needle and spoon were carelessly thrown nearby, confirming why his eyes were glassed over.

"I'm not open for business. Come back in eighty-two and a third days," he mumbled.

"I'm here to ask about Richard Pail? Do you know him?"

An incoherent murmur before he licked his lips.

"What about Stacey Simpson? She was a working girl that..."

"Hey, over here." Alice turned to the voice of another man a few feet away. He didn't have the same dazed out look like his friend.

"You talkin' about our Stacey?" He eyed her suspiciously. "You not a reporter, are ya?"

"You know Stacey?" she asked the even younger man, possibly in his late teens. "No, I'm not a reporter."

"A fucking cop?" he snarled, showing cracked teeth.

"Do I look like a cop?"

He squinted at her, taking his time to decide. "S'pose not."

"What's your name?"

He took his time to answer again, a massive grin erupting across his face. "You can call me anythin' ya want beautiful."

"Can you tell me about her? Who she spoke to? Why she was down here?"

"Well, well. It's been a while ya know. The memories all..." He hit his finger against his forehead three times. It brought his arm into clear view, highlighting all the needle pricks against his pale flesh.

"Will this help?" Alice went into her pocket to grab a few notes, handing him the cash. Between her and Sam they could barely make ends meet, yet she couldn't help but want to give the man more money. Just because he made bad decisions did not make him a bad person.

The man appraised the money, licking along the edge before folding it up into a tiny square and tucking it underneath his black cap. "What exactly are ya if you're not a reporter or a cop?"

"I'm a friend."

"Friend? We need more friends down 'ere." He nodded, almost to himself. "It wasn't an accident, ya know. She was tricked."

"Tricked?"

"Yeah, yeah. I liked Stacey, you know? She came down here sometimes, brung us food, sometimes herb," he said, grinning. "Nice gal. She used to sleep down here with us, ya see, before she met that man of hers. Real Prince Charming him."

"You said she was tricked? What do you mean?"

"She doesn't touch the gear anymore, you know? She's clean. Her Prince Charming helped her, got her a flat and everything. The papers said they found needle tracks along her arm." He shook his head.

"Who's her usual supplier?"

"Nah man, I ain't giving that shit up."

His eyes darted around before they settled back onto her.

"But I remember the guy she spoke to last time, before the papers. He's a new dealer, tryin' to push his stuff on us, ya know?"

"New dealer? What does he look like?"

"Fucking weirdo man. I won't touch his stuff, gives me the creeps. He doesn't even accept payment. Just favours."

"Favours? What sort of favours?"

"Don't know man, refused to talk to him. You should ask Ricky, he was chatting with him only the other day."

"Ricky as in Richard Pail?" When he nodded, she continued. "What does this dealer look like?"

"I don't know," he mumbled, scratching along the inside of his arm. "Medium build, dark hair. I think his eye is fucked up or something?"

"His eye? Does he wear an eyepatch?"

"Nah man, but he should though. It's like a prune, all shrivelled and shit. I overheard him saying he can help us all make money."

"Alice, you find anything?" Detective Brady asked as he came up behind them. "They're not talking to me."

"Aw shit man, you said you weren't a cop."

"I'm not." She handed him some more money. "Thank you for talking to me." Alice gently smiled. "There's a shelter not far from here, that money will get you the bus fare as well as some food along the way."

He started to chuckle. "Yeah, yeah, man. I'm sure I will."

"You know that's going to go on drugs, right?" Brady said as they stepped away. "You should never give them money."

Alice just shook her head. "He confirmed Gordon Potts has been lurking down here, and that he talked to our vic several days before his death as well as Stacey Simpson."

"I'll reinstate the APW," he said as they headed to the cars. "It was good that you were here. They wouldn't have said anything to me." He gave her a sideways glance, a hint of a smile. "I appreciate it."

"Aw, don't get all soppy on me now detective," she sniggered.

His small smile tightened. She seemed to be growing on him, probably.

"You coming back to the station?"

Alice thought about it. "No, I have some bits I need to do. You'll ring if you need me?"

Brady nodded, lifting his hand in a half wave as he drove off, leaving her standing by her rust bucket beetle.

"I thought he would never leave."

Alice reacted, her sword in her hand before she even processed the thought, the tip facing Mason Storm as he swaggered from behind a concrete pillar.

"Back off," she snarled.

"Oh Alice, that isn't how to greet a Councilman, is it?" he said, his mouth twisted into an evil smirk. "I thought we were friends." His eyes danced with laughter as he slowly walked towards her, his arrogance overwhelming.

He wore entirely black, the outfit so tight it was like another skin. It was disconcerting, she had never seen him in anything but a power suit.

"I see you made bail."

"Of course," he said as if it was obvious. "As if simple human laws can keep me contained."

"What about Breed laws?"

Mason stopped when he was only a few inches from the edge of her blade, the runes highlighting his face in little bursts of light. He didn't give them a cursory glance, his attention entirely on her as he sized her up.

"I am the law."

Mason smiled as he leapt forward, knocking her sword from her outstretched hand as if it was a fly swatter. It clattered to the ground, the runes disappearing as the blade settled into a puddle. Alice kicked out, her foot connecting with his stomach with enough force for him to growl.

Her fist shot out, catching him in the chin before he gripped her wrist to the point of breaking. Twisting out of it she blocked his punch, his speed and strength nowhere close to Riley, yet faster than a shifter.

"*Ventilabis,*" she shouted as she forced him away, the heat of her chi searing her fingers a second later. Mason dodged the flame, his face screwed up in annoyance. *"Scintillam."* She shot a spark towards his face, using the distraction to run to her sword.

Alice gasped, crashing to her knees even as she reached for the hilt, her fingers trying to grasp it as she was torn away. Her chi was on fire, electric as it felt like it was being painfully pulled from her.

"This is getting tiresome." Mason dug his fingers into her skin, dragging her across the concrete before throwing himself on top of her. His fist hit her in the eye, cracking her head against the floor. "Is this all you got?"

She tasted blood as she screamed, her aura throbbing as Mason manipulated it.

"ADOLEBITQUE!" she spat, satisfied as an instant burn started to bubble against his cheek, the skin darkening before splitting open in a burst of red.

"ENOUGH!" He hit her again even as he pulled her magic. It was like when Riley had done it to help her with control, but this time it was forced from her, the pain excruciating even as she gasped for breath.

Hands restricted her neck, his thumbs digging into the hollow of her throat.

"Why didn't you just die in the first place," he growled. "Then you wouldn't have been in the way."

Alice scrambled against him, her body pulsating in a great wave as she fought for control. She could see from the corner of her eye a burst of flame, her power leaking as Mason syphoned.

"You could have been magnificent, little dragon," he whispered against her.

Alice felt it then, like a dam had broken, an overwhelming energy that had to escape. Screaming through the pain, she shot her head forward to connect with his nose, the crack loud as his hands loosened from her throat. Her fists shot into his chest, sending him several feet in the air before he fell to the concrete in a crash. She shakily stood up, her hands up to her elbows completely encompassed in bright blue flames licked with green. She had never felt it so alive, so powerful.

Mason struggled to stand, the wind knocked out of him.

Bending down she grabbed her sword, the blue flames covering the steel within seconds, the runes flashing beneath. She felt like she was attached to a power socket, the energy burning through her too much.

Throwing out her hand she let some of it loose, concentrating on extinguishing as much as she could as Mason finally came to his feet.

"Arma," she whispered as her breath came out in smoke. Her shield surrounded her, the beautiful film of her aura protection until she could get herself together. The fire still crackled loudly, but no longer growing uncontrollably.

Mason just stared, his face expressionless as he watched. The burn across his cheek looked sore, even more than the break in his nose, the injuries marking his otherwise beautiful face. She didn't feel guilty, her wrist bruised from where he had almost broken it and her eye was already starting to swell.

Neither of them said anything as the wind picked up.

With a nod Mason stepped back into shadows, leaving Alice alone to figure out what the hell had just happened.

CHAPTER TWENTY-SIX

The key turned in her front door when she felt something move behind her, swinging her arm out she threateningly held her keys in her hand, pretending it was something scarier.

Xander stood there, his face furious as a single drop of blood dripped down his cheek where the edge of her key caught him. She didn't apologise, straining to keep her arm from waning as she watched him. His muscles were bunched, eyes hidden behind his glasses so she couldn't confidently tell when he was about to move.

You've got to be shitting me.

He wasn't alone, five other men stood quietly behind him, all dressed identically in black leather. She didn't recognise any of them.

"Where is he?" Xander snarled.

It took Alice a second to understand his question. "How do you know where I live?"

Xander moved like lightning, his hand snapping out to grab her neck, her back smashing into her front door in a matter of seconds. Without thinking she punched his jugular, kicking him in the shin at the same time he dropped her to clutch his own throat.

Dropping the keys, she unsheathed her sword, holding it between them.

The other men moved then, fanning out in a perfect semi-circle. They all were large, at least six foot plus with similar black and red tattoos patterned on any exposed flesh. If any of them moved like Riley, like Xander, she was fucked.

"You fight dirty." Xander choked out the comment, coughing. He lifted up his fist, asking the men to move a step back. They didn't. Instead, they unsheathed their own weapons. Two had swords, thick metal almost the size of Alice's thigh, two went for their handguns while one went for his scythe, as if he was the Grim fucking Reaper.

Alice didn't think before she released some fire in an arch an inch in front of their boots, making them step back or risk being burned. She hid her grimace, her chi still recovering from Mason as her eye ached in time with her heartbeat. She stared at each in turn, she was too tired and sore for this shit and wanted them to know. The fire gradually got larger until one by one they sheathed their weapons.

Accepting that, she extinguished the flame.

"Where is he?" One of the men asked, the one with black hair spiked as if he was an anime character.

"Who?!" she bit out.

"Riley," Xander growled, baring teeth.

"I haven't seen him since I helped arrest his father," she spat back.

"Holy shit, really?" the anime haired man laughed.

"She's telling the truth," another one of the men said, his expression less happy.

"Wait, you arrested Mason?"

All her sudden confidence seemed to disintegrate, she had to relax her arm before the men noticed it shake. She spotted a few curtains twitching across the street, nosy neighbours getting their gossip. They probably thought she was about to have an orgy or some other nefarious thing. Mr Jenkins glared from behind his own curtain, eyes judging.

"He isn't replying to our call," Xander stated.

"I don't know what you want from me."

"You need to tell us exactly what happened," he aggressively took a step forward.

Alice ignored him, kept her ground. "Well, I arrested Mason…"

"No, from the beginning."

She described how she had broken into the church.

"Why did you break into there? It's just full of extremist nutters."

"Shut up Sythe," Xander roared before he turned back his attention to Alice.

I was trying to figure out who's behind the vampire deaths," she explained.

"Who says it isn't natural?" Sythe asked, ignoring Xander. Sythe looked at her like he was examining a rat, his eyes a pale caramel brown that contrasted against his dark hair. One arm was bare, showing off his tattoos while the rest of him was covered in black leather. A gun was on his hip while two short swords crisscrossed his back.

"Let them all die, vermin anyway," another of the men said, his hair a beautiful honey brown that was styled to try and hide the red scar that sliced down his left eye.

"It's not natural," she clarified. "Humans have been purposely poisoning themselves."

"What has this got to do with the boss?" The men started to bicker.

"Is this about his bar?"

"That fucking place? A stupid idea that was," Scar face laughed.

"He had the idea while he was drunk."

"All his ideas come from when he's drunk."

"SHUT UP!" Xander snarled at the men, stopping them from squabbling between themselves. They just sneered back.

"Alice, tell us what happened."

"I found evidence that Mason was involved in the genocide."

The men said nothing, their expressions closed off.

"That doesn't explain why Riley's gone."

Alice began to speak when she caught her neighbours glaring again.

"Look," she said harder than she intended. "I don't know what you want from me, but I need to go." She opened her door, planning to close it quickly behind her before a thick boot pushed past the threshold.

"We're not finished here," Xander growled as he used his weight to keep it open. "We need to figure out where he is."

"I'm not inviting you in," she said as she stared into his sunglasses, wanting badly to read his eyes.

"Please."

Alice clenched her jaw, her face tired.

"Fine." She stepped back, allowing the six men to crowd her living room. Three of them awkwardly folded themselves onto her sofa, their massive frames barely fitting.

Xander and scar face stood by her door while Sythe casually walked through into her kitchen. She heard banging and crashing before he returned holding a bag of frozen peas, throwing them at her with a smirk.

"Your eye looks like shit."

"Thanks," she muttered as she held them to her face. Luckily the swelling had already gone down, her eye open and clear although she felt a bruise.

"Who are you guys?"

They all turned towards Xander, who remained silent.

"You're not even going to introduce yourselves?"

That's just rude.

She sighed. "Why are you here? I have already said I don't know where he is."

"He's your Warden..."

"And?" she interrupted. "It's clear neither of us wanted it."

"I like her," the man on the furthest left of the sofa grinned. His face was movie star beautiful, his lips a little too full. His hair was dark, cut military short.

"You don't need to know who we are," Sythe said as he looked curiously around the room. "All you need to know is we're here for Riley." He started to prod through her things, moving some of the boxes she had stashed under her stairs. She ignored him.

"You think he's in trouble?" She eyed Sythe, watched him tense as he shot a quick glance towards Xander.

They all remained silent again.

"If you're not going to talk, you might as well leave."

"We don't trust you." Xander broke their silence.

"You came to me," she said, frustrated. "Now, what has happened to Riley?"

"Why do you care?" One of the men from the sofa stood up, his movements agitated as he stared her down. He had the most beautiful shade of red hair, like the heart of a ruby. His eyes were dark, hard and angry.

"Are we really going to have a pissing contest now?" Alice couldn't believe it. "I care because he saved my life."

"So you owe him?" he spat it out like it was offensive.

"Kace," Xander growled. "Calm down."

"Well, Kace..." Alice stepped up to him, shaking her bag of peas in his face. It would have been more threatening if she wasn't almost a foot smaller and the peas didn't make little tingling noises every time the bag moved. "I do owe him. But not only that, we're friends." She thought so anyway. Were they? It was complicated. "I help my friends."

A loud chuckle. "I really like her," the man with the beautiful movie star face said as he winked at her. "Come on big guy, come be moody over here." He unfolded his long legs from the sofa before reaching over to Kace's shoulder, pulling him gently away.

"Alice, when was the last time you spoke to Riley?"

"I didn't speak to him, but I believe he overheard Mason's confession…"

"Confession?"

"It was more of a gloat."

"Can you get to the point?"

Alice thought about what to say, decided on the truth.

"He overheard how Mason was behind the death of my parents."

She let that sink in.

"How he led the Daemons to their house. This house, in fact. Where the Daemons murdered them in front of me."

"Fuck."

"What?"

"No way?"

Xander stood rigid, veins in his arms visible as he clenched his fists.

"Everybody out!" he shouted to the men. They all looked at him until he growled, a deep vibration that made them move. Once they had gone he approached her, pulling off his glasses so she could see his eyes. "I need you to stay away."

"Why?" She held those eyes of pale blue, almost colourless.

"Because you're a liability." He breathed into her face. "And I don't like you."

Alice felt herself grin. "I wasn't a liability when you came to me for help."

"Which you didn't provide." He took a deep breath, placing his glasses back on his face. "Stay away from Mason. He's dangerous."

"Is he? My eye wouldn't know."

"Well, he didn't kill you. That's something."

"You seem to think I'm easy to kill."

He smirked, tilting his head like a dog. She noticed because Riley had done it too, something a shifter would do, not a druid. "You have a ghost."

Alice felt ice cold, her spine rigid as goosebumps broke out across her skin. She didn't need to know that. "What?"

"Your gnome is haunted," he nodded towards Jordon who had suddenly appeared on the sofa, his grinning face turned to them. "Be careful Alice, you shouldn't trust the dead." With that he followed his men out, slamming the door behind himself.

"Jordan?" she asked the gnome, knowing he wouldn't answer.

Great, what do I do now?

He looked out into the field they were being made to run in, him and his brothers.

They had all grown, bigger than even the teachers. The last of The Elders had been proud of their progress, had not been upset at the teacher's lack of control.

They did as they were asked out of respect for their people, not the teachers.

His father looked pleased, even if his face was as closed as it always was, even more so since he became the new Archdruid. The opposite to his mother, who was a ray of open sunshine. He allowed her memory to shape him, not let the training shape him into a drone.

His mother had taught him the old ways. Respect for the hierarchy, it's how his people had been for centuries, an old Breed proud of their heritage, yet hiding dark secrets.

He guessed that was why they were created, trained, beaten. A force to take on the ancestors who made mistakes.

Not that they thought it was a mistake.

The wind howled, calling his spirit beast, wanting release. His brothers were the same, yet different, their spirits. All forced on them as children, disguised as a gift. Chosen for a purpose. He wasn't sure what purpose, surely it wasn't just for hunting his prey? He saw the humour in that.

They trained them to be as bad as their prey, stronger, faster. Prey that were ancestors, blood. Someone had to do the job, and it was just bad luck they were chosen.

The sons of the important.

The sons of the strong.

The sons of The Elders.

CHAPTER TWENTY-SEVEN

Alice heard a high-pitched whistle once she had finally convinced the officer to let her beneath the police tape. O'Neil appraised her bruise, his eyes darkening as he flicked a cigarette between his fingers.

"What happened?" he asked on an exhale, smoke coming out his nose like a dragon.

"I thought you were quitting," she said instead.

He just glared at her, the cigarette burning between his lips as he waited. The orange flare highlighted the grey hairs in his goatee perfectly.

"You should really see the other guy," she laughed. She knew he was overreacting, the bruise barely visible anymore. "Seriously, it's fine."

"You been getting yourself into trouble again?"

Alice turned to Brady and Peyton, smiling politely as they joined them on the porch. She had been called to an old mansion in the outer suburbs where there weren't any neighbours for miles around. The place itself didn't look as expensive as it should, the wood around the windows poorly painted black, matching the dirty grey wood cladding on the second floor. Dark red rose bushes guarded the pavement to the front of the house, their thorns abnormally large and sharp. The majority of the windows had been boarded up while some were a spider's web of cracks.

"The whole team here?" she asked, looking around for Jones.

"Jones is inside."

"What's this about?" She tried to hide her chills as they stood on the creaky decking just outside the front door.

"Four dead..."

"Vampires?" She thought The Leader was behind bars.

"No, we believe them to be witches. Although, we think it's connected."

"What makes you say that?" she asked even as she frowned. Something was off, her aura reacting to something she couldn't see. Looking around, she found the culprit hanging from a wooden beam.

The sticks were manipulated around small pieces of bone, tied together with twine. Alice stepped towards it, raising her hand but not daring to touch the talisman. They were held in the position of a full moon between two crescent moons. Skin was pulled across the shapes, making them glow a faint red when the sun hit it at just the right angle.

"What is that?" O'Neil asked.

"It's the symbol of The Crone," Alice answered, fighting the shiver that rattled down her spine.

"What does it mean?"

"It means this is probably a dark coven, they use this symbol to ask The Crone for protection."

"Who is this Crone person? He doesn't sound..."

"She, it's a she." She pulled her hand away as a fly buzzed greedily around the rotting skin. "In witches' lore, it is believed the first humans were given their ability to manipulate the elements by The Goddess, thereby creating witches. She would empower them with her gift if they were to be good, kind. Her sister, The Crone, despised The Goddess. Out of spite she tricked the humans into accepting her gift, the ability to manipulate death and blood, but only if they would sacrifice something to her."

"Sacrifice?"

"Yeah, that's where the origins of black magic come from, although, most modern witches doubt the existence of either The Goddess or The Crone."

"Sounds thrilling," Brady said dryly.

Alice held back a chuckle. "You have no idea."

The men stared at the talisman quizzically for a moment and it worried Alice how little they knew about Breed. Especially considering the general knowledge was taught at school, math, science and 'why is your neighbour eating their dog?' classic classes. Breed had been recognised citizens for almost three hundred years. They had lived and worked alongside Norms for enough generations that there shouldn't be any prejudice. Yet they needed to hire a Breed consultant because none of her team had enough knowledge alone. She didn't know if it was plain ignorance or naivety.

Pursing her lips, she followed them through the door, the smell of meat, blood and rotten eggs instantly striking her nose. The mansion must have been abandoned before it was taken over by the coven, the stairs to the floors above broken beyond repair. Floorboards were missing, leaving gaping hazardous holes and graffiti had been sprayed across a few walls. Two arches on either side of the stairs led off further into the house, the left – Alice could just see, looked like a kitchen with windows facing towards an empty swimming pool. The right led towards a room that was splashed with red, body parts torn apart and thrown across the large space.

"Fuck me," Alice gasped, her brain trying to piece together what could have happened. The room was empty of any furniture, the walls painted over with graffiti, the same as the foyer.

A large pentagram had been scratched into the floorboards, each of the elements drawn in their own circles at each point. Dry blood was splattered across every surface of the room, yet was most consistent inside the pentagram.

"It's a summoning circle," Alice confidently said.

"A what?"

"A summoning circle. It looks… yes," she murmured to herself. "A normal circle is anchored into place using the elements fire and earth with water and air filling the space between. This circle is anchored with all five elements."

"What do you mean, 'five elements'?"

"I mean, there would have been five people, each standing in one of the elemental circles." She pointed out the five separate circles, each touching a different point of the pentagram. "Each person would have represented their element, someone for fire, someone for air… you get the idea. They would light it in sequence before finishing with spirit, which would complete the circle."

"Have you seen anything like this before?"

"Kids are taught this in school, it's how you get students to learn to work together. This is a more brutalised version, made to keep something inside the circle while protecting the people outside."

"What exactly were they protecting themselves from?"

Alice took a second to reply, the scar on her hand aching before she clenched her fist.

"Daemons." The smell was what tipped her off. It's a smell that will be eternally embedded in her brain.

"That's what I thought. Fuck." O'Neil scanned across the room, his eyes narrowing on the body parts that had settled. A large window was towards the back with thick blackout curtains partially pulled. A head sat eyeless, its mouth forever open in a silent scream.

"I thought you said the circle was supposed to protect them?"

"Well... erm." Alice bit her lip, trying to think. There was no literature on Daemon summoning, nothing on black magic in general. Since The Change, everything regarding dark magic was either destroyed or quarantined for the safety of the public.

So who the hell has this type of ancient knowledge?

"The spell either failed or one of the members let the circle drop."

"You need to explain what the hell you mean," Brady remarked as he looked down at part of an arm, his expression open but disgusted.

It was sad that she had gotten over the smell. That actually being this close to a number of dismantled bodies no longer bothered her as much as it clearly did to both Detective Brady and O'Neil. She was more professionally interested than disgusted. Peyton didn't seem repulsed either, neither did Jones when he waltzed in like it was a family wedding rather than a massacre.

"Hey guys, you like the party?" he chuckled.

"You're disgusting," Alice said with a grimace. So she wasn't as affected as others, but she wasn't as bad as Jones. "We're discussing how one of the five bodies could have broken the circle..."

"Four. There are four bodies," Jones chirped, smiling. "We have counted enough times to be confident."

"No, this spell requires five people. They wouldn't have been able to summon anything without all five."

"Well, there's only four people here. Do you think the fifth person made a run for it?"

"There are tyre tracks just up the road," Peyton said.

"Did you know, it was only a month or so ago that I thought Daemons were like unicorns. They didn't exist." Brady mumbled, his dark skin taking on a slight ashen colour.

"Hey Brady, you ever heard of Hansel and Gretel?" Alice said, trying to hide her smirk.

"The kids and bread crumbs?" His wide eyes shot to hers. "You saying it's true?"

"Well, the original Grimm story didn't say that the children were simply human, but changelings."

"Changeling?"

"Yes, Fae children that have been swapped at birth with a human. Probably why they ate the witch in the end..." she let the story train off.

"Alice, stop winding Brady up," Peyton interrupted, but she could tell he was amused.

"What? I haven't even explained Cinderella yet..."

"That's enough," O'Neil stated, a slight smile on his face. "Alice, what do you see?"

"I see four bodies that have been ripped apart. There should be a fifth, but according to Jones there isn't one."

"No, the house is abandoned other than this room and part of the kitchen where there are a few rucksacks full of candles and books. Upstairs is completely unreachable," Jones confirmed.

"So, the only purpose the coven came here was to create the summoning circle?"

"Seems to be. We have four female bodies who have been here long enough for larvae to be implanted in some of the flesh. We have found no toiletries, mobile phones or change of clothes. Nothing to indicate that they planned to stay overnight or for any longer than a couple hours. The plumbing doesn't even work."

"I'm not surprised by the no mobiles. It's known that an electric pulse can break a weak circle, so it makes sense to leave them behind." Alice shrugged.

"So are we believing that the Daemon killed them?"

Alice thought about it. "I can't be positive." She had no idea. She only had the sulphuric smell to go on. "An enraged shifter could deal the same damage."

"Isn't this your job?" Brady frowned.

"I do apologise that I'm not familiar with all forms of dark magic," she said, sarcasm dripping from every word. "It makes the most sense that the Daemon broke free and slaughtered the witches. But then why would it have left one alive?"

"So, the question is," O'Neil mumbled. "Where is the last witch?"

CHAPTER TWENTY-EIGHT

Alice stared at her phone for the hundredth time. It remained the same as it did an hour ago, the same as the last few days, no messages. She wanted to launch it across the grand atrium of Riley's building, allow it to smash into smithereens in a burst of rage.

How dare he ignore her!

Alice gripped the phone, heard the screen screech in protest before she shoved it into the pocket of her jeans. Riley hadn't answered any of her calls.

Petty, so fucking petty, she growled loud enough to make the man in front give her a wary look. She shouldn't have to explain herself, and she shouldn't have had to drag herself to his penthouse because he wasn't answering his damn phone.

Alice took a deep breath, calming her face before she plastered on a fake smile. When it was her turn, she approached the desk clerk.

"He's expecting me," she battered her eyelashes. "Surely you recognise me from before?" She had only been there a few days ago.

"You're not on the list, ma'am." The clerk looked down at his notes.

"He invited me here, do you want me to ring and disturb him?" she huffed, pretending to scan through her phone. "He isn't going to be happy."

"You're more than welcome to wait here in the atrium, ma'am. If you do have an appointment, Mr Storm will make us aware." The clerk said, emphasising that he didn't believe her.

Crap.

"Fine," she grumbled, taking a seat across from the desk beside a bunch of potted plants, giving her a clear view of the whole room. "Riley will hear about this poor service." The clerk just smirked in response.

She couldn't really fault him, he was just doing his job. She undoubtedly should have dressed nicer rather than her skinny jeans and a black T-shirt. Not to mention the slight yellow sheen across her eye, her bruise just hanging on. She really hoped she didn't carry the sulphuric stench from the mansion, she wouldn't be able to explain what it was. Alice subtly tried to smell her arm, the cotton luckily smelling of nothing.

She really stuck out compared the well-dressed men and women who were making themselves busy. The atrium was a hive of activity, the three public lifts packed as everyone seemed to have a place to be. Alice eyed the private lift, the only lift that would take her to the floors high above where Riley's penthouse was situated. She still thought it was weird he lived in an office building, even if he owned the building, and all the businesses inside.

A woman spoke loudly into her phone, her ridiculously high stilettos clicking obnoxiously across the wooden floor. Alice took a second to recognise her, the oversized glasses hiding the majority of her face while her gorgeous red hair had been cut to just above her shoulder blades with the tips dyed black.

You've got to be shitting me.

Alice moved from her seat, trying to hide behind one of the large potted palms. An old man who sat opposite noticed, his wrinkled face creased in amusement.

"Welcome to Storm Enterprise, which business are you looking for?" The clerk greeted her professionally.

"I need to see Riley Storm immediately," the woman said while she hung up her phone.

"Name ma'am?"

"Are you saying you don't know who I am?" she squeaked, throwing her sunglasses onto the desk. "I'm Mandy Marshall of the Marshall family estate."

"Sorry ma'am, you're not on the list."

"I don't need to be on the list you imbecile."

"Unfortunately Mr Storm has strict rules, if you're not on the list, I cannot allow you upstairs."

"This is ridiculous, call him immediately."

"He has asked us not to interrupt..."

"Let me speak to your manager." She looked around for someone else, the other clerks ignoring her existence as they answered questions for other people. "What is your name?"

"Calm down ma'am, or I'll be forced to call security."

Alice couldn't help but smile as she saw the back of Mandy's neck turn red in irritation.

"Tell Mr Storm he will be hearing from me," Mandy snapped, her movements agitated as her heels slapped across the floor in retreat.

Alice smiled, watching her leave before turning to the clerk, his face open with distaste. *What was his problem?*

"Hey, out of curiosity, when was the last time you saw Mr Storm?" she asked politely.

"Why, does he owe you money or something?"

Alice almost leapt across the counter to smack the annoying smirk off his face. She even looked down, making sure she wasn't going crazy. She looked reasonably respectable, the black T-shirt was simple with a regular round neck. It wasn't even one of her slogan shirts, and she clearly didn't have the breasts to make it provocative.

Does he think I'm a call-girl or something? Bloody bastard.

"Why would he owe me money?" she glared, making sure he saw how aggravated she was.

His smirk faltered, eyes slightly alarmed. "My mistake, ma'am."

Does he have many prostitutes over? Great, now all she could think about was if he paid for sex. It wasn't any of her business what a grown arse man did with his money, or time. Alice didn't want to think about it, instead she checked her phone.

Still no messages.

It was like he had disappeared off the face of the earth.

"You waiting for someone, young woman?" the old man opposite asked, his hands clenched around a mahogany walking stick. He looked just as odd sitting in the gold marble atrium as she did with his bright pink Hawaiian shirt. He even wore shorts though the sky outside threatened more snow.

"Waiting for my team," she said loud enough that the clerk could overhear. "Mr Storm's under investigation, he asked me to come to his penthouse for a private meeting to discuss it, but….." She gave an audible sigh. "As Mr Storm has gone back on his word, I have to call in the big boys." She had no idea what she was talking about but hoped everyone else believed her.

"Oh, that young lad surely can't be in trouble? He is always so polite every time I see him." He squinted at her through his round glasses. "What is he under investigation for?"

"Well…" *Shit, what could it be?* "It's very…"

"Ma'am, ah Miss." The clerk waved for her attention. "What was your name again?"

Alice approached the desk with a full swing in her hips.

"It's Agent Skye, thank you…" she tried to search around for his name, but he wasn't wearing a tag. "Clerk man." She leant across the desk as far as she could to encroach on his personal space. He was already slightly nervous, she hoped it would push him over the edge.

"Do you have any credentials?"

"Of course," she replied, showing him her Paladin license.

"Did you say Mr Storm was expecting you?" He visibly swallowed, his eyes darting around in panic.

Alice smiled in victory. "I'm expected immediately. Can you call the lift for me please?"

"Yes ma'am, err, I mean, Agent Skye."

"Brilliant." She began to turn towards the private lift just as she thought of something. "Have you at least seen him in the last few days?"

"No, ma'am, I cannot say I have."

"Doe's he usually go off for days at a time with no contact?"

"Not usually." He licked his lips nervously. "Is he really in trouble? Mr Storm is a great guy."

Alice didn't reply, instead she smiled pleasantly as she made her way to the key coded lift.

Riley's penthouse was the only place on what she assumed was the top of the building, the lift not following the numbers designated to the floors. It had three identical buttons with no apparent marks. She clicked the top one, wondering where the second and third button led to.

Knocking loudly on the door she waited, hoping he would simply be in. Of course he wasn't, even after she banged louder and called through the door.

"Okay then," she mumbled to herself. "Plan B." She produced a small knife and a pin, unlocking the door quickly and slipping inside. "Oh, bloody Hell."

She didn't have a good memory of his living space from her previous visit, the room had been too dark, but she would have remembered if it was in such a state. The open plan living room looked like it had been ransacked, the sofa ripped to shreds, stuffing and fabric making it to every square inch. The TV was smashed, a black hole in the centre with shards of glass glittering on the scratched wooden floor. A shelf had been toppled over, some books strewn underneath while others had been torn apart, flung around in a rage. It looked like a storm had passed through.

Alice made her way to the gym, wondering if his selection of weight machines had made it out alive. As she was about to open the slide doors separating the gym to the kitchen she heard a hoarse voice.

"He's lost it. Look at the place."

Alice could barely see through the small gap, the lights inside dimmed as Xander stood with Sythe.

Fuck. Fuck. Fuck. Of course they would look here too.

Three punching bags had been destroyed, the sand that was supposed to fill them decorating the floor along with some glass shards from the mirrored wall. The room smelt of old smoke, as if one of the running machines had been run into the ground.

It shocked her, the violent display of rage that didn't match Riley's usual humorous attitude. Even when he was angry he didn't feel like he was capable of such a destructive streak. It was as if he had come home in such a craze that he didn't know how to react, his living room getting the brunt of force before he decided on physically exerting his fury.

"Can we bring him back?" Sythe asked his friend, his posture hunched. "I've never seen him rage like this. Axel yes, but not the Sire."

Alice tried to get closer to the gap without casting a shadow against the opaque glass.

He hasn't turned beast," Sythe replied confidently to his own question. "We can bring him back."

"We don't know that yet," Xander declared.

"We would know Xee."

"We haven't been able to get contact."

"He will," Sythe said, confident. "It's his father…"

"Fucking arsehole," Xander snarled. "I haven't even been able to contact him. Complete silence from the Archdruid." He laughed, but it was hollow. "The Order isn't responding to my summons either."

"Fuck them, we don't need them. It's not like they've helped us before." Sythe studied one of the punching bags, kicking it with his boot. "You want us all to go in?"

"Maybe," Xander replied. "I haven't decided yet."

"Who said you get to decide?" Sythe laughed. "Wait, don't say Riley..."

"He's our Sire..."

"No need to get pissy Xee, I know who's the boss." Sythe paced away, his hands fisting. "We need to find him, the boys are getting anxious."

"Do you think I don't know that?"

Alice had heard enough, there wasn't anything here that could help her find him. She tried to move back, her boot slipping on something as she crashed to the ground. Alice clenched her jaw, glaring at the bit of sofa cushion that had somehow found its way into the kitchen. She had been concentrating so hard on moving away quietly from the door that she hadn't looked beneath her feet.

"WHO'S THERE?!" Xander barked as he smashed through the door quickly followed by Sythe.

"Oh, hello," she tried to wave from her sprawl on the floor, ignoring the fact two swords were pointed towards her. "So, how are you?" Red dripped down her arm as she tried ungracefully to stand up. She had fallen onto glass, a shard cutting into her flesh just above her elbow.

"Alice?" Sythe mumbled as he put away his blade.

"I warned you to stay away," Xander said as he helped her up.

"I'm not really good with orders," she shrugged before pulling the shard of glass out and placing it onto the kitchen counter. It was deeper than she initially thought, the cut oozing blood. Alice caught the tea towel thrown at her head, holding it against her elbow.

"For fuck sake, sit down," Xander growled as he started banging through cupboards.

Alice sat on one of the two barstools beside the kitchen island, Sythe was on the other. She hadn't really had a good look at the kitchen, the room darker than she thought was comfortable, but Xander seemed to see perfectly, his sunglasses nowhere to be seen.

"What are you doing here?" he asked, his voice weirdly soft, not reflecting the anger clearly etched onto his face.

"Thought I left something here last time... ow," she scowled as

Xander pulled the tea towel away to look at her wound. "Fine. I was here to see if I can find Riley."

"You not think we would check?" Sythe said around a mouthful of nuts.

Where the hell did he get nuts?

"I don't know."

"Stay still." Xander held her arm as he stuck three butterfly stitches onto her elbow, wrapping it up in a bandage. "Bloody liability."

She ignored him. "So you guys going to tell me more about Riley missing?"

Both the men looked at each other before Xander replied.

"How much do you know?"

"I know Mason is the Archdruid, who happens to be a major bastard and head of The Order." She watched their expressions remain closed. "I also know Riley is a Guardian, as you have been calling him 'boss' I assume all you guys are too." She wasn't going to mention 'Sire,' not until she knew more.

Sythe stopped mid crunch, looking slightly alarmed.

"Your father was Jackson Skye," Xander stated as if it explained everything.

"What aren't you telling me?"

"The Order is in shambles, Mason has gone AWOL since his arrest and isn't answering anybody." Xander looked towards Sythe, his eyes flashing silver before nodding. "Riley disappeared around the same time."

"Is that normal?"

"No. He tolerated his father more than we did, but..." Sythe seemed to struggle to find the right words. "Riley always felt a responsibility."

"But you didn't?"

Sythe let out a laugh. "You have no idea."

"Riley wouldn't leave without an explanation," Xander said, matter-of-factly. "We're a team."

"Then we have to find him."

"Yes, we. Not you." Xander narrowed his eyes. "I can feel you, your energy electric even as you pretend otherwise."

"No, it isn't," she argued. She felt fine, her power under control.

"You need to stay away, you're unpredictable, like a live wire."

"It's not my fault I've been forced to have a Warden. I never asked for this."

"Neither did Riley," Xander stepped away, anger vibrating his shoulders. "You need to learn control, discipline. You're like a child, barely able to stop yourself from killing everyone around you."

"What do you think I've been doing?"

"Learn faster. Before it destroys you."

"Fuck you Xander. You're so far up your own arse you can taste your own breath."

"Like I said, childish." He turned away, placing his sunglasses onto the bridge of his nose. "Sythe, we need to go."

Sythe moved, heading through the house towards the lift. She followed them out.

"Wait, I have more questions…"

"The world doesn't revolve around you."

Alice stepped into the lift with them, a bad decision considering they looked like they wanted to kill her, their faces far from friendly. She had obviously overstayed her visit. Well, Xander's was unfriendly, Sythe just looked at her like she was crazy, which was debatable.

"Look, I just want to know if he's okay."

"Why do you care?"

She paused, she didn't know why.

"I just do." She tried to keep eye contact, although it was harder through Xander's glasses. "Neither of us asked for this, yet we're stuck together."

She could feel it then, her chi charged as it reacted to her anger. A violent surge of energy she couldn't control. Both Xander and Sythe could feel it too, their faces shocked as they tried to step further away into the small space. She wanted to smirk but decided it wasn't a good time. Tinkerbell appeared with a pop, bobbing around her head in a flurry of sparkles.

Xander stood still, barely moving as if he were a statue. When the lift opened at the atrium he pushed past, his long legs carrying him across the floor much faster than Alice could chase while Sythe stayed behind.

"Please," she called as they left the building. "Whether I like it or not, I need him. Now, where do you think he is?"

Xander stopped, his face turned up into the sun, his sunglasses protecting his sensitive eyes. He no longer looked angry, more lost.

"We don't know." With that admission he walked away, leaving her behind.

Alice just stood there in the street. It was then the sky decided to open, snowflakes gently floating down to start covering the ground in white. Cleansing. It was fitting really.

"Go away Roman," she murmured. She had spotted the black wolf as soon as she left the building. If he kept casually walking around in his animal form he was going to get fined, or maybe even put in the pound. "I've already helped you, what more do you want?"

Roman crept from behind the bench, his tongue rolled out on one side in a wolfish grin.

"This would be easier if you would shift and talk."

He responded with a chuff.

"Why you talking to a stray?" Sythe appeared silently behind her.

"Fuck me, why did you sneak up on me?" She tried to control her panicked heart.

"I didn't. You need to learn to listen better."

Sythe approached Roman, his long fingers brushing along his dark fur before snapping his hand back. Roman had tried to bite him, but Sythe moved faster, you wouldn't have been able to see his movement if you weren't watching directly. Even then it was hard.

Fuck. It was safe to assume that Sythe moved as fast as both Riley and Xander. Which meant the other four did too.

"Is there something you want?" she asked. She didn't mean for it to sound so pissy, but she was busy having a one-sided conversation.

"Where's your ball gone?" he frowned.

"It likes to come and go as it pleases," she shrugged. She wasn't going to admit her Tinkerbell was a physical reaction to her strong emotions. It was embarrassing enough already.

"I can see why he likes you."

"Huh?" She looked at Roman who just shrugged, one of his shoulders lifting as he tilted his head.

"Riley. He's fascinated. We're not allowed to be..." Sythe reached forward as if he was going to stroke her face.

Roman snarled, launching himself between them.

Sythe just studied Roman with his caramel brown eyes.

"Guess I'll see you soon, Alice." He winked as he turned back towards the building.

"What was that about?" she asked the wind because it had a higher chance of responding.

Roman didn't move until Sythe was out of sight.

She flicked his ear.

"Hey, you could have warned me he was there you know." He was standing in front of her, he would have been able to see him or even smell his approach. "It would have been better if you were human."

He just stared at her. It was getting harder to believe there was a man in there.

"If you shift, I'll buy you a nice juicy burger," she bribed him, hoping something would work. Surely it wasn't healthy for the amount of time he spent as a wolf.

One problem at a time.

Her stomach started to rumble. *Great.* Now all she could think about was a big juicy burger. Her stomach rumbled again, the vibration violent.

"Oh." She grabbed her phone from her pocket, answering the call.

"Agent Skye."

"It's O'Neil. How fast can you get down to the station?"

CHAPTER TWENTY-NINE

Alice stood and watched through the two-way mirror as O'Neil and Brady tried to interview Gordon Potts. He sat there relaxed with his arms loosely folded, ignoring them as he stared past at his own reflection.

"Has he said anything yet?" Alice asked, frowning. She had gotten to the station as quickly as she could in rush hour traffic.

"Nothing," Peyton answered, his voice dark. "He's mocking us."

"What about a solicitor? Or even his wife?"

"He's made no phone calls." Peyton shrugged, not caring that he didn't have legal representation. "He also hasn't got a wife."

"What? Then who was the woman at the church?" He had said she was his wife, why lie?

"No idea, but he isn't legally married. The last thing on record was his previous marriage, which has been legally dissolved due to the presumption of death."

That's strange.

Alice shook her head, studying Potts as he just sat there freakishly calm. He didn't look like a man being threatened as a co-conspirator to mass genocide.

And that worried her.

She could make out O'Neil's mouth moving, but couldn't hear his words as Brady remained silent, his arms mirroring Potts. She assumed they were doing good cop, bad cop. O'Neil was probably trying to reason with him before Brady took over, using his six foot plus, wrestler frame to intimidate instead. Clearly the good cop routine wasn't working.

"Why was I called?" She had no experience in an interrogation. At least, not one where she couldn't threaten to stab or burn someone. Strangely enough, she didn't think that would go down too well in this particular situation.

"It was my idea," Peyton mumbled as he gave her a quick look, his attention returning to Mr Potts a few seconds later. "Since The Leader disappeared into thin air while inside his cell, I thought it would make sense to have an expert on magic close by."

"I'm not an expert..." she began before she realised what he said, "did you just say he disappeared?"

"No one called you? John Smith, also known as The Leader vanished into thin air. CCTV showed him sitting there one second and the next he had gone. There was no break in the time stamp." Peyton frowned, thinking. "In your experience, what could make a human disappear like that?"

"It's impossible..."

Humans had no connection to their auras, so was unable to harness them into a chi.

"Maybe it was a charm?" Just one she had never heard of.

Teleportation wasn't a common gift, only a small select amount of Fae could travel that way. Even then, they couldn't share it. It has been a power coveted by the many, yet no witch, mage or even other Fae had been able to replicate it.

"I suggested a boggart," Peyton shrugged.

"What have you been reading?" She eyed Peyton, trying to hide her smile. "Boggarts haven't been seen in over two centuries."

They were a type of faerie that liked to cause mischief in the marshes and make things disappear. They were also behind many child abductions which helped a rumour escalate that all faeries feasted on children. While the High Lords never admitted it, they never denied it either. Although, it was probably one of the reasons boggarts had been forced to disappear themselves.

"You could say the same about Daemons."

Fuck. He had her there.

"From my limited knowledge, Daemons can't disappear at will. But they can be forced from one location to another by calling their given name."

"But John Smith isn't a Daemon. His DNA comes back as one hundred per cent human."

"Which leads us back to square one."

Gordon started to move his arms slowly, one hand reaching up to his eyepatch which he flicked up, revealing his blind eye. Alice instinctively took a step back, the movement making Potts smile.

"This isn't a window, right?" she asked.

"No," Peyton confirmed even though he noticed Gordon Pott's response.

"Then how can he see us?" She moved forward, noticing his eye track her movement.

"He can't." He didn't seem convinced.

Alice couldn't stop herself from staring at his right eye, the one he had hidden behind the patch. The eye beneath was shrivelled like a prune, the colour a sickly grey surrounded by the darkness of the socket. It was disconcerting, something you would see in a bad zombie movie with terrible special effects. It didn't look real.

"What the fuck is wrong with his eye?"

Alice thought about it for a moment. "Black magic."

Every spell required a sacrifice in various levels of severity, especially potions, charms and physical circle enchantments. The majority of witches used plants or their own blood to quicken the spell, Gordon was sacrificing his own eye. It was a step before turning to the true dark, where the only cost that was sufficient would be death.

She wanted to feel his chi, understand how he could perform this sort of magic yet remain undetected. It made sense when she thought about it, someone had to be creating the deterrent around the church, yet Gordon didn't have the Breed vibe, never mind a witch.

Gordon remained silent, a knowing smile on his lips as he stared past the detectives towards Alice and Peyton. Brady stood up suddenly, causing his chair to crash behind him before he stormed out of the small room, quickly followed by O'Neil.

"He isn't talking," Brady growled as they approached. "The bastard is just sitting here."

"You guys have any ideas?" O'Neil asked, his eyes pinched as he reached into a pocket for a cigarette. "We can only keep him for another twenty hours before we either charge or release him."

Everyone stepped away from the mirror, whispering even though they knew they couldn't be overheard.

"Hit him?" Alice suggested, laughing at their less than impressed reactions.

"Something legal," Brady replied dryly.

"Why are you time restricted? We know he did it..."

"We can't charge him on an accusation. At the moment, we have no physical evidence against any of the suspects for the genocide. Without evidence, we don't have a case."

"We have the letters..."

"Which aren't concrete. It's known that a court can strike evidence that lacks a proper foundation. That means we need to prove he physically wrote it."

"And not some random person," Brady added. "Those letters don't mention Potts, so without a confession or any evidence we're going to struggle."

"If we don't charge him we're allowed to lawfully keep him for up to twenty-four hours. As it's a suspected serious crime we could apply for an extra seventy-two hours, but we still need something solid to get him on."

"The church is still sealed off from when we checked it over. The tech guys found nothing other than bovine blood."

"Bovine blood?" Alice asked. "That's..."

She sucked in a breath as something oily rubbed across her aura, the sensation similar to pins and needles. She turned the same time as Peyton towards the two-way mirror which had been smeared with blood, hiding Potts from view. Alice beat the men to the interrogation room, kicking the door down and drawing her sword at the same time.

She had never felt anything like it once she stepped inside, the air thick, coating her aura in a sticky substance she itched to remove. The room was washed in red as blood smeared the walls with hand-drawn symbols painted around his chair and partially across the desk.

"STOP, OR WE WILL SHOOT!" One of the men yelled as Alice's head buzzed as if she was underwater. Shaking, she tried to clear her ears, only realising the abhorrent blare was actually Potts chanting in a language she didn't recognise.

"NO!" she shouted, holding her arm out as O'Neil and Brady cocked their guns.

"He's in a circle!" Bullets can't penetrate an aura, they would simply bounce back.

Gordon grinned as he finished his chant, blood dripping down from his eye socket and onto the white floor. Alice took a second to realise the eye that was once in his head was presented to them on the table. He had ripped it clean out of his socket, using the resulting blood to draw the crude spell. Alice studied his circle, his aura a pale grey with flecks of green. It looked sick but strong.

"You mock our religion," Gordon sneered as he clenched his blood-soaked fists. "You don't understand what we need to do."

"How are you doing this?" Peyton asked as Gordon chuckled in response.

Alice shook her head again, the feeling of water still there. She flexed out her chi, wanting to touch his to help understand. She stretched it out for a fleeting second before she heard a snap, it resonating back like an elastic band.

"FUCK!" she yelled as she jumped. It had hurt, her whole body feeling as if she had been stung.

"I wouldn't do that if I were you."

"You do realise you're not human." Alice snapped, the sudden pain fuelling her anger. "Nobody human can do this." Not that she truly knew what he was.

"My Breed status means nothing. It doesn't mean the world isn't corrupt," he growled.

Alice noticed his arm move, almost touching his circle by accident. She needed to aggravate him, force him to pop it.

"We never said it wasn't, but people like you are the reason behind the corruption..."

"It's people like me who have the courage to try to stop it!" Gordon screeched before he started to snigger that turned into a deep belly laugh. "I have my job to do, as you have yours."

Gordon reached for the circle, a toothy grin on his face as he touched the bubble for it to pop. Alice jumped forward, her arm instinctively covering her eyes as smoke erupted around her, choking.

"ALICE DON'T!"

"SKYE?"

"FUCK!"

Eyes watering, she tried to blink through the cloud, unable to see anything. The floor vibrated beneath her feet, the shapes on the ground glowing red before disappearing altogether.

"Nice of you to join us," a voice sniggered.

Spinning she gasped, staring at Mason Storm through a silvery veil. The rest of the smoke dissipated, allowing her to see clearly that she was no longer at the station.

CHAPTER THIRTY

Mason, The Leader and Gordon stood just beyond the silvery veil, a look of smug satisfaction painted on their faces.
Fuck. Fuck. Fuck.
"How did I get here?" she asked, looking around.
Where is here?
"By standing in my circle you followed the pathway," Gordon said as he held his hand to his eye, stemming the blood that continued to flow.
"Just like I knew you would," Mason added, smiling. "Stupid girl."
"My Leader, what are we to do with her?" Gordon asked, seemingly ignoring Mason as he looked expectantly to his right.
"This is not to do with us, my child. Our mission is to continue as we were."
The Leader looked at Alice inquisitively before turning to Mason.
"Mr Storm, I'm sure we will continue with our business shortly. I would appreciate it if you fixed this... loose end."
"Ah, we both know how you deal with loose ends, my friend."
Mason grinned at Alice, dismissing the others. Half his face was bandaged while his nose had a horizontal cut across the bridge and bruising around both of his eyes. At least she'd caught him good. If she weren't in such a highly stressful situation, she would have probably smiled.
"I bet you didn't think you would be seeing me again so soon?"

Alice remained silent, concentrating on her surroundings. She could feel the power vibrating through the concrete beneath her feet as the dark magic oozed from the silver circle surrounding her on all sides. The blood that had painted the floor sizzled, the overwhelming smell of death and bleach assaulting her nose. She wasn't in a pentagram, she was in two circles, one bigger than the other with runes painted in-between. Five smaller circles were equally spaced around touching the outer edge, each with an element smeared inside.

Cold seeped into her bones through her thin jacket as a low beat thumped.

Thump.

Thump. Thump. Thump.

Thump.

"No comment? How unusual for you."

"I have nothing to say," she replied, edging away until she touched the dome, causing pain to sear down her spine. She was trapped.

"Careful," Gordon smirked as he watched her wince. "You're in my circle. Only I can break it."

"I'm sure you're very proud," she said dryly.

Thump.

Thump. Thump. Thump.

Thump.

"This is very tiresome. If you do not mind, Mr Storm, but I will be taking my leave," The Leader said as he held up his hand. "I have no interest in seeing the main show. I will allow Gordon to stay to help you with your... project."

He gave her a last uninterested look before opening a door towards the back, besides two cells. One seemed empty other than a mop and bucket, the other she noticed a topless man kneeling, his face distorted by this dark hair. The cell door was open, the man seemingly stuck by the chains attached to his wrists.

I'm under the church.

She finally noticed the police tape that had been tossed carelessly onto the floor. She licked her dry lips, remaining calm.

Thump.

Thump. Thump. Thump.

Thump.

"You going to explain to me what he meant by 'main show?'" she asked, keeping them in her sight. She had to think of a way out and fast.

What the fuck is that noise?

Mason grinned. "Other than it being good business? I'm sure you would agree with me when I say Valentina needs to be removed from power," Mason continued without pause. "She has become so overwhelmed with her role that she is no longer impartial."

"And I suppose you should take over?"

"Of course. I should sit at the top of The Council, not that child." His face curled up in disgust. "The vampires have too much control under her power, even with their restrictions. Alas, all I needed was to nudge the church in the right direction."

"I thought all members of The Council were equal?"

Mason laughed. "Your ignorance is amusing. How could you possibly compare me to the likes of those animals? Or even a common witch?"

Alice heard a growl, wasn't sure where it was coming from. Her eyes landed on the chained man again, but he remained unmoving. Lights danced across his skin as his whole body tensed, the chains screeching as they were pulled with force. The pattern of the lights she recognised.

"Riley?" she called.

A growl in response.

"RILEY?!" she shouted this time, panic an acid on her tongue.

"My son made an ill-advised mistake," Mason snarled as he hit his hand on the outside of the cell. "I brought him up to trust no one, it's why I was able to chain him. Incompetent. His mother would be so disappointed."

Riley finally looked up, looking towards his father with hate in his eyes. His whole body tensed again, his muscles rigid as the lights flared up across his exposed skin.

Mason struck out once more, hitting Riley across the cheek even as he sagged against the chains. He knelt down, carefully holding his son's face in his hands.

"You were the strongest amongst them all, the leader. You were trained specifically to protect our race, our secrets. Yet your disobedience shames you. It was I who planned The Guardians, it is I who can destroy them."

Riley launched himself forward, making Mason scramble back out of his reach. The chains screeched as they began to stretch, the chain links warping under pressure.

Thump.

Thump. Thump. Thump.

Thump.

"Reckless boy," Mason snarled as he came to his feet. "You shouldn't have questioned me, my son. I have worked my whole life to be where I am, I will not let your conscience ruin it."

He was scared of Riley, she could see it in the way his hands shook, the way his eyes were wide, cautious.

"What have you done?" she asked, wanting to reach Riley as he tensed again, like an electric current was forced through his veins. She watched as a spark crackled through the air, knew it was from the silver cuffs that encircled his wrists.

She needed to get them off him.

Thump.

Thump. Thump. Thump.

Thump. Thump.

"My son still needs to be trained, he must become the Archdruid after me. He will learn. He will sacrifice, as I have."

"Sacrifice what exactly? Your empathy?"

"He will do what is right for our people." Mason turned to Gordon, who had stood there and watched the exchange. "And what is right for our people is to remove you. Permanently."

Gordon smirked, his hand patting against his thigh for another beat.

Thump.

Thump. Thump. Thump.

Thump. Thump.

He was beating her heartbeat.

Alice went to react when she felt the pressure in the bubble change. Gordon mumbled beneath his breath as the blood runes painted onto the floor glowed with an eerie light. A pop of air behind her made her turn, even as the hair on her arms stood on edge.

"*ARMA!*" Alice screamed as a six foot plus man exploded behind her, his face contorted in rage as his red eyes scanned the room before settling on her. She watched him appraise her aegis shield, his expression turning confused as the horns on his head curled towards his brows. He stepped towards her as the wings behind him folded away, disguising themselves in the black Metallica T-shirt that suddenly appeared over his naked chest. His horns disappeared beneath his dark hair and his skin became pinker, less grey. The only thing that didn't change was his eyes, red and slit like a snake.

"What is this?" The Daemon disguised as a man asked in a smoky voice. "Why have I been called again?"

Alice tried to move back, realising if she went any further she would destroy the only thing protecting her. He gave her a last curious look before dismissing her, his attention on Mason and Gordon.

"This is not part of our agreement," he snarled, his fists clenching as dark veins appeared beneath his skin. Alice clenched her own fists, trying to stop the pulsating ache of her crescent scar. She tried clumsily to reach her harness strapped to her back before realising her blade wasn't there. A glint from the corner of her eye, her weapon laying a few feet away at the edge of the outer circle.

She was trapped in her own aegis inside another circle, without her sword.

Fuck.

"It isn't an agreement if we know your name, slave." Gordon grinned.

"I await the time where I tear your flesh from your bones you snivelling little cu..."

"Xahenort," Mason demanded, forcing the Daemons attention towards him. "We have called you to offer you payment."

"Payment?" Xahenort chuffed. "I have just feasted on four females." He moved towards Alice, his gaze evaluating her. "Why would I want this one?"

Alice hurled herself towards her sword, gritting her teeth as her aura rebounded back when her circle dropped. Kicking the blade up she gripped the hilt.

"*ARMA!*" She shouted just in time. "Back the fuck off small horns," she snarled, pointing the blade towards him as he loomed.

"That," Mason began," is Alice Draco."

"Draco?" Xahenort looked over her again.

It was weird considering he looked normal with the band T-shirt, ripped skinny jeans and Converse. Except for the eyes.

"I have no interest in this."

"Do you not know who this is? She was being used in a sacrifice..."

"I know who she is. I'm not interested, I have no such wish as my brethren to create an army."

Xahenort looked at her again, his face frowning as he tested her aegis shield with the palm of his hand.

"Is this the reason you called me?" he angrily asked.

"We are running out of blood, use the girl to refuel."

The Daemon caught Alice's eye, talking in a language she didn't recognise. She held the sword out, the runes dancing across the steel. His red eyes flicked to the sword, then back again before repeating the same phrase.

"Le'meloa nirha shilia."

She had no idea what he was asking.

"Stop talking to her!" Gordon shouted.

"Dricania polir shilia?"

"I don't know what you're saying," she explained, stepping back as Xahenort let out an exasperated sigh.

"How can you not speak the tongue of the ancients?" His red eyes narrowed. "Only those of blood can use Fae artefacts such as the blade of Aurora."

"STOP TALKING TO HER!" Gordon shouted once again before turning it into a chant.

"Daemon," Mason demanded its attention. "I will not ask again. Refuel with the girl. We need the blood samples immediately in the lab if we are to continue with our agreement."

"You can only call me because you have my name. That doesn't *control* me." Xahenort returned his attention to Mason before he pressed his palm to the floor, smearing the blood runes with his fingertips then licking the excess. "If I was to replace the blood of the caster with someone else's, this shield will fall." He shot her a look.

This shield will fall?

Alice considered the five points, able to touch part of them that were under the dome.

Replace the blood of the caster.

Alice sliced her hand, letting the blood drip through her fingertips.

Please let him not kill me.

She dropped her defence.

CHAPTER THIRTY-ONE

Smoke sizzled as her blood mixed with the rune, creating a crack along the veil. Gordon turned white, Latin tumbling out of his mouth as he tried to keep his circle from falling.

She ran to the next one, smearing her hand across the floor before moving onto the next.

"It's almost time..." Xahenort goaded as his horns pierced through his hair. "I'm coming for you." His wings uncurled from his back, taking up most of the space inside the circle. His hands clawed, nails elongating as his T-shirt and jeans ripped. "You're mine."

Ducking beneath the leathery wings Alice moved to the last rune, her fingertips brushing it as the circle collapsed around her in a burst of sparkle. As Xahenort bounded through his wing caught her, forcing her to the ground as her sword clattered out of her palm.

"Riley!" she called as she scrambled to get back up, her hand reaching for her hilt before it was kicked further away by a black boot, closer to the cages.

"You have done nothing but get in the way," Mason snarled as he kicked her in the ribs, causing her to flip onto her back. He held a dark green ball of aura in his right hand, the energy growing as he pushed it towards her.

Alice rolled at the last second, trying to keep from screaming as the energy began to eat into her aura. She grit her teeth through the pain as she kicked out, hitting Mason in the knee hard enough to cause him to stumble. She searched for her own chi, coating her arms in just enough time to dissipate another ball of energy thrown.

"RILEY!" she shouted, trying to find him through the chaos. He was still in the corner, his face contorted in pain as he rode the electrical current forced through his body.

"He isn't going to help you." Mason reached down to grip her by the throat, pulling her up onto her knees. He seemed to ignore the flames on her arms as she tried to push him away, his eyes on the edge of sanity as he bared his teeth. "I'm really going to enjoy this."

He tightened his fist.

A crash as metal rattled, the noise shattering as it brought Mason's face around. In his distraction she pushed with all her weight, breaking free from his hold as fire ate away at his suit. She lifted a fist, punching him square in the nose with an audible crack. Mason's eyes went wide as blood poured down his face, his hands lifting up as Gordon clattered into him, taking them both down into a heap.

"I'm not finished with you, yet," Xahenort growled, his red eyes glowing as he jumped towards the two fallen men.

Alice moved quickly towards Riley, his dark hair covering his face with his body slumped forward. Her hands shook as she tried to touch the cuffs, her skin burning on contact.

"FUCK!" she cried, shaking her hands before trying again.

His chains had warped, no longer attached to the floor with the lock damaged. His tattoos glowed faintly across his skin, moving gently with each shallow breath.

"Please, wake up!"

She picked up a small chunk of concrete, bringing it down on the lock with all her strength. It shattered into pieces, allowing her to tug at the cuff once more, the metal pulsating beneath her fingertips as an electrical current shot through. She snapped her hands back, waiting for the current to pass before she started on the left cuff, her hands began to blister before it finally came free, falling from his wrist to spark against the floor.

Riley's breathing became less shallow, colour returning to his skin as she started to remove the right one. It moved a centimetre, her skin protesting...

A hand wrapped in her hair, pulling her back.

"I've had enough of this!" Mason screeched. "The Council should be thanking me for getting rid of you."

Heat seared her chest as he pushed his green arcane down, aiming for her heart.

Screaming through the pain she released her chi, the tumultuous energy flowing out of her in blue tendrils that surrounded them. Her blue fire scorched the concrete, aiming for Mason as he stumbled back. The blue devoured his green, absorbing the excess as Mason stared, mouth open in a gasp.

"Impossible!" He flicked out his hand, his chi trying to syphon hers. Control.

She felt her power hesitate, fighting the pressure before becoming stronger, the intense burning evaporating as she felt something caress her aura, adding to the torrential energy already flowing out of her. Silver sparked through her blue, pushing through Mason as if he was nothing.

She could feel something warm drip down her face, the copper settling on her lip as her vision blurred, the edges turning dark. She screamed, pulling the energy back inside before she became overwhelmed. Her power stopped like a faucet, leaving her empty, the absence of everything disconcerting as she fell to her knees.

She blinked, struggling to make out the fight in front of her, the Daemon's wing curled around his great body to act as a blade, the spike at the end of his wing arch sharp. She could no longer feel the pain, her whole body numb as she shook her head, unable to make out any of the noise other than the beat of her own heart that rushed through her head.

Sound came back in a brain- searing rush as she heard the screams of Gordon falling to Xahenort. A movement at the corner of her eye drew her attention to Mason who scrambled to his feet, half his suit burned away to reveal pink scorched flesh.

She pushed with her last bout of energy towards her sword, rolling to her feet with the blade turned to where Mason once stood.

But he was gone.

Taking a deep breath her bruised ribs protested, her vision struggling for clarity as she heard something scrape behind her. Spinning, she held the edge of her sword out, her arm wavering as the last of her strength vanished.

"You know my name," Xahenort said as he approached. He was covered head to toe in blood, the liquid soaking every inch of his large frame. His wings curled behind him, the bottom claw scraping against the concrete as it twitched. He had ripped Gordon to shreds, pulled him apart with his sheer strength.

She used both her hands to hold her blade, making sure Riley was behind her as she steadied her pulse. Tinkerbell popped around the edge, gliding along the steel in what she hoped was a threatening way.

"I don't want your name."

"Yet, you know it." He tilted his head, his eyes moving to Riley before returning to her. "I am Xahenort, the original, the master of mistakes. In my thousands of years, I have never quite witnessed something like you, Draco." His attention shot to her sword. "Such power, yet you do not understand."

He started to edge towards her, his gaze fascinated as she stepped back, almost collapsing into Riley.

"I have taken my payment. Therefore I will let you be." He took a last look around the carnage, a private smile on his lips. "Until we meet again, War."

Smoke erupted around him, shrouding the room until he was gone.

Sheathing her sword she returned to Riley, his silver mirrored eyes wide open but blank. She ignored the burning sensation as she to pulled the final cuff off, the metal falling off his wrist just as he exploded into a burst of colour.

"Well, you seem to have been busy." A woman's voice laughed.

Alice stood there, unsure whether to concentrate on Valentina who had walked into the room, The Leader's head in her grasp or the wolf-like creature that suddenly stood before her. The beast nudged her out the way, placing himself between them.

"How, lovely." Valentina eyed the gore before settling on the beast, her expression turning to stone.

"Riley?" Alice croaked, her hand shaking as she reached for the pure white fur of the beasts back. Her hand touched silk, the strands soft but heavy. Black patterns decorated across his spine and legs, glyphs that matched the tattoos of the man. "What are you?"

The beast moved closer, his attention on Valentina as he snapped his long jaws in a warning. His head was the shape of a wolf – larger than a shifter with his shoulder hitting her sternum, but his legs were bigger, closer to a lion. Claws uncurled from his paws, as long as his fangs but serrated.

Alice kept her hand in his fur, using him to centre herself.

"How did you find us?" she asked Valentina as the beast growled, the sound smoky.

"I was coming to burn the place down," she said warily, holding The Leaders head up to show them. "Saw this pathetic excuse running away and thought I would bring him back to watch his beloved church fall to cinders." She glanced at the head, his face in permanent terror before she threw it away in disgust. "Pity."

Alice tried to hide her horror at the noise it made when it landed. Valentina carefully moved forward, never taking her eyes off the beast as she floated to observe the markings on the floor.

"Daemons again?" She sniffed as if disgusted. "Councilman Storm has failed again. Whatever should I do with him? Hmm."

Her eyes were completely black when she turned, her dark dress mopping up the blood as she approached. She was ethereal as she slowly reached up, hesitant to the beast as her pale hand touched the blood along Alice's face before gently licking it.

Riley went rigid as he growled again, his jaws opened to show his impressive fangs. His tattoos seemed to pulsate, almost moving across his fur as his long tail separated into several distinct furry whips. He launched at Valentina, his jaws wide but Valentina had already moved.

"Riley?" Alice reached for him, trying to calm him down.

"He isn't there right now," Valentina said as she sucked at her fingers again. "You should ask him one day to explain exactly what his father did to him. What he forced on his own son."

She cackled, even though she stepped back when Riley moved into a crouch.

She was afraid.

"I seem to have taken care of the situation. Thank you for your help Alice, I'll be keeping an eye on you." Valentina backed out, her gaze never leaving Riley's.

"Riley?" Alice bent down to his level, pulling at his fur. "Are you okay? We need to get out of here."

The stench of blood, death and sulphur was overwhelming. She desperately needed to repair her aura, could feel the ache of its loss.

He erupted into light, multi-colours bursting from beneath her palm. Gasping she wrenched her hand back, watching in awe as fur became skin. The coloured lights dimmed, settling into the black and red tattoos across his flesh.

"Riley?" Her voice quivered as she spoke, her legs wobbling before she fell to her knees. "What the actual fuck?"

"We need to get out of here!" Riley shouted as he gripped her arms, pulling her up.

"What the fuck?" She smacked at his naked chest. "You're a... what the? Fuck."

Riley gave her a gentle smile, the emotion not reaching his eyes. "The church is on fire."

"WHAT THE FU..." She smelt it then.

Riley grabbed her arm, pulling her through the church as fire crackled dangerously around them. A black plume of smoke threatened to cut them off before Riley crashed through a window, landing gently on his feet beside a grave. Helping her through Alice turned to watch the church, fire burning from within, fighting its way through the wood and brick.

Riley began to move away, pulling her with him.

"Wait."

He stopped, but he didn't face her. The marks on his arms were already fading, the burns from the cuffs disappearing before her eyes. His tattoos no longer glowed, no longer pulsated.

"We need to talk."

"Here?" He finally turned, his grey irises edging towards silver. "I need to deal with my father."

"We are not to be blamed for our parent's choices."

Or mistakes.

She needed him to understand that.

She couldn't read the emotion etched across his face. He opened his mouth to speak, but didn't.

She collapsed onto the grass, her legs unable to carry her weight, exhausted. Letting out a sigh she moved onto her back so she could watch the church burn.

It would have been beautiful if Xander wasn't blocking the view.

"You look like shit," he said as he began to pull her up before Riley's smoky growl stopped him. He released her hand, letting her drop back onto the wet grass.

Alice sucked in a pained breath, all her cuts and bruises starting to protest.

"Yeah, well, almost dying can do that to you." She shot a look at

Riley, his eyes more silver than grey. He seemed fine, even for a man standing butt naked in the snow.

Groaning, she came to her feet, checking over her injuries.

Nothing broken, just a couple scratches and bruises. She couldn't help her grin, or the fist she pumped in the air for victory. Xander looked at her like she was crazy, but she didn't care.

"I need to call this in," she said.

"You need to leave, your aura is fractured and your energy is leaking," Riley said, his voice hoarse.

He was right, she knew that. Instead, she stood there, Riley to her left and Xander to her right and watched as the church crumbled into itself, the fire dancing against the wind as smoke billowed into the sky.

EPILOGUE

Alice played with the handwritten note that had been left on the edge of her bed late one night.
To wear if you ever come to Paris – Valentina.

The ribbon wrapped black package sat untouched in front of her, as it had been for the past week. It felt weird to receive something from Valentina, even weirder that she had left it for her to find inside her home. Was it a threat that she could get in without being discovered? Even Sam hadn't sensed her, and she had broken in when they were both asleep.

"That's a pretty box. You going to open it?" Michelle, Brady's wife asked gently. Alice had just met the woman and instantly knew why Brady had married her, a tender person compared to his great force.

"I suppose so," Alice replied quietly. It had been Jones' idea to throw a party to celebrate closing their first case. Nobody wanted to other than him, but he persuaded them otherwise. They all eventually compromised on a winter BBQ, one at her house.

"Back away from the pit, this is my domain," Sam growled at Brady who kept trying to take over poking the meat.

"You're doing it wrong," Brady grumbled back.

O'Neil watched them with a smile on his face, a bottle of open beer in his hand while Jones chatted beside him excitedly.

A light sprinkling of snow covered the garden, bringing the darkness of the box out in stark contrast. Black wasn't a welcoming colour. Alice pulled at the silk ribbon, letting the fabric drop onto the wooden table before she slid the lid off.

"Wow, that is beautiful," Michelle beamed, looking inside.

"Err, yeah," Alice mumbled. Inside on a velvet pillow sat a satin choker, the centre adorned by a Victorian style pearl cameo surrounded by white diamonds.

"Holy shit baby girl, that from fang face?" Sam whistled as he noticed. "You think that's real?"

Alice quickly shut the box, tying the ribbons back up and pushing it away. She didn't know why Valentina gave her such an extravagant gift. She didn't want it.

It had been several weeks since the last victim, all the contaminated blood in the city caught and destroyed. It was good that the contagion didn't keep, the carriers dying off before they had a chance to start an epidemic. The basement of the church held secret rooms that were only found once the building turned to ash. Rooms that held the personal belongings of around fifty sacrifices.

She felt better about Gordon's and The Leader's deaths more and more each day, especially when she thought about the innocent victims. Mason, on the other hand, had disappeared off the face of the earth. His office had released a statement that he would be unavailable for the foreseeable future. Which basically meant they had no fucking idea where he was. The Council only stated they were in the process of replacing the Councilman. Which also gave no information.

Xander or another one of the ninja wannabes had turned up at her house almost every night, just watching. She wasn't sure why but ignored them for the most part. She had invited them to the BBQ but they had all given her the same strange look.

'Why the fuck would you have a BBQ in December?' They had all asked, which she actually agreed with, but Jones didn't give her much of a choice. When Riley turned up she didn't invite him, his face cold when he asked her to continue their training.

She smiled, slamming the door in his face. She knew he had been busy trying to control the fallout of his family name being smeared across the media, all while negotiating with his father's business partners. But he didn't have to treat her like work.

She wasn't anybody's burden.

"What are you two doing up there?" Peyton called to Sam and

Brady, who gave him a dark look in return. He sat beside her, quiet for the most part.

"So, you going to tell me what you are yet?" she asked, sipping her beer. It had become a game between them, she asked him questions that he sometimes answered. She knew for sure he wasn't human, at least, not one-hundred per cent as he claimed. He had turned at the same time as she did back at the station, had felt something as Gordon created his circle. Humans wouldn't have reacted as he did.

He gave her a sideways glance, his lips pressed into a thin line before she saw him smirk. "You want another beer?" he answered instead, standing up.

"Sure," she chuckled, "but be careful about those bloody boggarts." He didn't find it as funny as she did.

"Hey baby girl, can you get the door? I'm worried if I leave, big boy here will take over,' Sam called, scowling at Brady.

"Look, it's getting burnt!" Brady exclaimed as his wife handed him a glass of wine.

"It's probably just Dread," Alice shouted behind her as she made her way through the house. She gave a quick wave to Jordon, who was watching TV from the corner of the living room. Jordan hadn't really done much since Xander had explained he was haunted. The idea that something was moving him around gave Alice the chills, but it wasn't like she could do much about it. He just made his way back home regardless of where she left him.

"Hey, Drea ... oh..." she said as she opened the door.

"Alice," Theo said, nodding in greeting. "I'm glad you're home."

"Hi, can I help you?" She looked around for Roman, couldn't see him skulking around. "Where's your brother?"

"That's what I'm here about, actually," Theo said, sounding nervous. His hair was messy as if he hadn't brushed it in a while, and the shirt he wore was creased.

"Are you okay?"

He looked ill, his tone taking on a grey tinge that didn't look healthy. It brought the scar that sliced through his face out in contrast.

"No." He shook his head, anxiously reaching up to move his hair from his face. "We've found Rex."

Alice tried to hide her reaction at hearing his name. She didn't want anything to do with him, felt no guilt that he had run from his consequences. Especially since hearing what the bracelet he gave her did. For all she cared he could stay missing.

Yet, the look on Theo's face made her feel sick. "What's happened?"

"He's been arrested. They're going to execute him."

Alice stood there, unsure what to say.

Fuck.

The End of Book Two

TAYLOR ASTON WHITE

ROGUE'S MERCY

AN ALICE SKYE NOVEL

ROGUE'S MERCY

BOOK THREE

PROLOGUE

"Surely, even you have noticed how unpredictable she is," Frederick Gallagher commented casually as he drank from his wine glass, his legs crossed and foot tapping tediously against the stone floor.

Valentina watched her fellow councilman carefully, noticed the slight nervousness of his pulse that beat like an invitation against his neck as he swung his gaze towards her or how he repeatedly licked his lips. He stood on behalf of both the witches and mages on The Council, supposedly equal with the vampires and yet he sought an audience only with her.

"You know we don't like unpredictable," he said as he settled down his glass.

"Is this the reason for your visit, mon ami?" she smirked, enjoying his fleeting eye contact. It was amusing how he forced his relaxed posture, how he fidgeted in his seat or how he spoke slowly even as his breath hitched when she gave him her full attention. Especially considering it was only a decade ago he called her a petulant child in front of their fellow councilmen.

Valentina tilted her head as she continued to stare at Frederick, her memory perfect. She may have the appearance of a child no older than fifteen, but she was anything but.

It was why he had flown all the way over to Paris, a city over which he had no influence.

She was the oldest, old amongst even her Breed.

But Frederick didn't stink of fear in her presence, as he should if he realised what she was truly capable of. There was a reason she had ruled over the majority of Europe for close to five centuries. He saw her for what she wanted him to see, a weak female, a child as he had called her. It was an image she had perfected, made it even better when she personally ripped someone's throat out.

Which meant his nervous gestures were caused by something else...

"Mon chéri soldat, what do you say to this?" she asked her personal soldier who always stood silently nearby.

Danton looked at her expectantly, his arms straight at his side as he posed beside her throne.

"Mistress?" he asked, his dark eyes curious. She enjoyed his body when they were in private, but she very rarely spoke to him with an audience. He was her warrior, a show of strength, of power.

He had become too relaxed while babysitting the Little Dragon, too attached. She had seen to it that he remembered who he was when he returned to Paris with her.

"You know Alice Skye well, what do you think?"

Danton hesitated, his eyes flicking to Frederick then back again.

She would make sure he was punished for his hesitation. Warriors didn't hesitate, not when directly spoken to by their queen.

"She has been training. While her actions can sometimes be described as unpredictable, I believe her overall power has been widely exagéré?"

"You think so, mon soldat?"

"I'm sorry Valentina, but I won't take the word of one of your pets." Frederick shot to his feet in a burst of irritation. "That girl, when grown into her power could destroy us. Surely it makes sense to clip her wings now?"

"Are you talking about the prophecy?" She, of course had heard of the ramblings of an old Fae, had heard of the rumours even when she was a human child who didn't believe in anything but a merciless god. But she had never witnessed anything with her own eyes to suggest its truth. Many religions and mythologies depicted a similar end of the world scenario, and yet, they were still there.

"If my intel is correct she is clearly showing signs of becoming War. What would stop her from turning her attention to The Council?"

"What do you suggest, mon ami?" She flicked her hand, signalling for a top up of her wine. A young woman was pushed inside, her eyes open in fear as she slowly poured the red liquid into Valentina's waiting glass. She was beautiful, with eyes the clearest blue Valentina had ever seen and hair the purest red. She was the newest human in her collection, a pretty bauble.

When the glass was half full Danton bowed his head, taking a blade out from a hidden sheath and cutting the wrist of the young woman. He held her as she screamed and fought his iron hold, releasing her only once the glass had filled.

"Ugh," Frederick tutted in distaste as the women collapsed at his feet. "I see you're still collecting."

"When you're as old as I, you appreciate the beauty in things." She looked at the woman on the floor, waited patiently as another one of her people removed her from the chambers. She did indeed collect things, beautiful things.

Now Alice, she mused to herself. *Was beautiful and powerful.*

Someone befitting her court.

"Frederick, before you waste any more of my time what do you suggest?" she sipped at her enhanced wine, savoured the fear that fragranced the blood.

Frederick touched one of the wings mounted on her wall, an original Daemon wing that was one of her rarest in the collection. It flinched, shaking off his touch much to his surprise.

When he turned, he pursed his lips.

Valentina couldn't help her laugh.

"I believe Alice needs to be under more supervision, my supervision within The Magika. It is only a matter of time before she becomes too powerful, even for us."

"Are you describing your weakness to me?"

His eyes narrowed, mouth set in a grim sneer.

"Very well, I shall call a meeting." She turned to Danton, who obediently lifted his head. She began to dismiss him before she had an idea. "And escort Commissioner Grayson personally."

He woke, a scream caught in his throat as sweat drenched his body, soaking through the thin sheets. It was the same dream, same nightmare that haunted him night after night. But it wasn't simply a dream, it was a memory. The memory of his weakest moment in life, of him crashing to his knees whilst a stronger male forced him into an agreement in blood.

Angered, he sat up, allowing the sheet to pool by his hips. He had five minutes before he had to face them, had to reinforce his part of the agreement. An agreement that went against his very nature.

He dragged a hand down his face, the hair coarse beneath his palm, a reminder that he wasn't ready.

Not yet. Not until his skin was smooth, his shirt pressed. His outside must reflect what he was supposed to be, strong, an alpha, even as innocent blood dried beneath his fingernails and his heart turned to stone.

CHAPTER ONE

Alice woke with a startle, a heavy compression against her chest.
"Hey there Lass, nice for you to join us," someone with a heavy Scottish accent said close to her face. "Can ya hear me?" The Scotsman tried to flash a light in her eye before she batted his arm away.

A red glow emitted from the walls, writing that pulsed with the sudden pain that drilled into her skull. She tried to push at the man who was now holding two fingers against her wrist, but the sudden sharp pain once again took her breath away.

"Get off," she moaned, feeling weak.

The man started to open random cupboards before he slammed them shut again.

"Where the fuck is the stuff, Rick?"

"Fuck me Jim, just check her vitals," another voice replied, the sound coming from the glass window directly behind her head. "We're about five minutes out."

"This wouldn't happen if you put everything back where they're supposed to go," he argued as he slammed a drawer this time.

Alice ignored the man, blinking her eyes as she took in her surroundings. The red writing along – what looked like metal walls, no longer pulsed, the words in Latin she recognised as an anti-violence spell. It took her a moment to realise she was moving, not just her, but the whole room.

"Where am I?" she asked, bracing herself on the bed she seemed to be tied to as the room moved violently. One of the cupboard doors flew open, scattering its contents onto the metal floor with a crash.

"Lass, please let me check you over, 'kay?" The man seemed stressed as he went back to holding her wrist, his face twisted in concentration. She allowed him, it wasn't like she was given much choice. Distracting herself from the nausea of motion sickness she examined his clothes, not initially recognising the green uniform. A red cross with wings was stitched to his breast pocket along with the slogan *'Here for your Health.'*

Bloody hell.

She was in an ambulance. Come to think of it, she could now hear the obnoxious sirens in the background.

Shit, shit, shit, she frowned to herself, trying to remember what happened.

"You're alright, you're going to be okay." Peyton appeared beside her head, his face concerned as he reached to grip her hand. His fingers brushed hers before the paramedic smacked it away with a scowl.

What the fuck is Peyton doing here? She shot him an accusing glare as her frown deepened.

"Can you no see I'm working 'ere?" The paramedic gripped her wrist once again. "Rick, I can't feel her pulse." The Scotsman started to work anxiously, his fingers frantically adding pressure to her wrist until he brushed against her crescent scar. "Fuck sake." He shuffled through the cupboards again, finally finding some stickers that he stuck onto her chest. A chest that was embarrassingly exposed considering her shirt had been ripped open all the way to her navel. At least her bra was still attached, she didn't need to give Peyton a free show to her limited assets. Or to the paramedic for that matter.

"Hey, what the…"

"Stay still," he barked as he attached the stickers to the cardiac monitor, her heartbeat appearing in obnoxious blips seconds later.

"What happened? Why am I here?" The bed squealed as the ambulance turned a corner. She thought she heard Peyton chuckle, but when she looked at him his face was stone.

"You're alive…" Jim the paramedic licked his lips anxiously, his pale green eyes examining her full length. "You were dead."

"Dead?" She tried to sit up, the straps keeping her immobilised on the bed. "I'm not dead."

"You were dead." He just repeated.

"Well, I'm clearly not now."

"She wasn't dead," Peyton added, "just passed out." He gave her a pointed look. "From the drugs."

"I'm sorry, who's the medical professional?" the paramedic muttered as he concentrated on the monitor. "No heartbeat means you're dead."

Oh for fuck sake, she cursed herself. She remembered then, knew exactly why she was strapped to a bed in the back of an ambulance with an unhappy paramedic. She was on an active contract, one that paid her to hunt down a doctor who was allegedly selling drugs while on duty to his vulnerable patients. She had drunk a potion that was supposed to give an impression of an overdose without the actual drugs.

It seemed like a good idea at the time.

"Bet you didn't wish you won the bet now, huh?" Peyton said quietly, but loud enough so she could hear the subtle humour in his voice. Peyton was a weird one, a tough cop who took his job incredibly seriously. He was impressive with his undercover work and sometimes convinced ever her, a contrast to his usual blunt and dispassionate demeanour. It was from spending time with him on jobs that she was starting to recognise his subtle moods and the intense intelligence in those crystal blue eyes.

She tried to shrug, but could only move her shoulders an inch. "Just another day at the office." She looked up at him, his face upside down.

Peyton huffed, leaning back in his chair as he pushed the white blonde strands from his face. "Still think you cheated. In fact, I know you cheated."

"You have no evidence." She couldn't help her smile at his grunt.

She hadn't cheated at their game of poker, Sam had, allowing her to win. But she would never admit it. Besides, it was Peyton who had wanted to make the game more interesting.

If she won, Peyton would have to join her on a Paladin contract, if he won she would have to learn to do all his paperwork as an Officer for The Metropolitan police for a whole month. She had enough paperwork herself to contend with, so was ecstatic when she had the better hand.

The contract was the first in weeks, a break from her liaison work for the Spook Squad, where they specialised in solving the more unusual Breed murders. Admittedly, Spook Squad was more interesting than her day to day job as a Paladin, where hunting down magic users who liked to sell cheap illegal charms was more common than a mass genocide. But it was still more interesting than Peyton's paperwork, so it was a win win situation, even if she was bound to a bed.

The ambulance screeched to a stop, the doors opening a few seconds later to allow the sunlight to stream through. Alice had to squint, the glare blinding as she was finally untied from the bed and allowed to step out towards the entrance of the London Hope Hospital. The front of the building was made up of several five-story townhouses that had been connected to the sleek glass and steel structure built behind, blending the hospital with the surrounding Victorian style buildings effortlessly.

"Come one babe, they're waiting for you." Peyton grabbed her arm, guiding her towards the automatic doors, her leather satchel hanging from his arm. "So, just another day at the office?" he said as they stepped through the automatic doors.

"Well, not a typical day..." she started before a bawling woman stepped between them, her mouth trembling as she held up a sliced finger. Alice followed, waiting in line until it was her turn to register. The Accident and Emergency centre was one of the busiest in the hospital, white corridors full of moaning, bleeding people as a strong mixture of copper and disinfectant was fragrant at the back of her throat.

"Hello, welcome to the A&E department, how can I be of service?"

"I'm here to see Dr Pierce," Alice began.

"That's not how this works," the receptionist – Betty according to her nametag, said.

"Here," Peyton handed her over a piece of paper. "We came in an ambulance. The paramedic gave me this."

The receptionist scanned the document with a pursed lip. "Hmmm," she mumbled as she gave Alice a judgmental glare. "Looks like you're the overdose, we've been expecting you. Please take a seat just over there while I organise the room."

Alice followed the instructions, sitting beside Peyton on an uncomfortable plastic bench. She started to rip the stickers off her chest, frowning at the red welts left behind before tying the remains of her shirt to cover her breasts. With a sigh she nodded to her satchel that Peyton still held. He silently handed it over before crossing his arms.

"Thanks," she murmured as she rustled through her belongings, pushing vials of potions out of the way to access her specially designed handcuffs all Paladins owned.

"Your job seems to be a lot of waiting around," Peyton commented a few minutes later.

"And yours doesn't?" She clipped on a charm – a cylindrical chunk of oak that she had already activated. "You literally stand around for hours at a time."

"I still think my job is slightly more exciting," he said as he watched her click on another charm. "What are those?"

"They're special charms for the cuffs," she smirked, rattling them. "One reduces the wearers strength to that of a Norm and another to make it look pretty." Actually they were both strength charms, she just didn't always trust one. Especially when she knew the man she was about to arrest was able to bench press a car if he wanted to. It was unusual for her to get a vampire contract solo considering their aversion to the majority of spells, which was why she doubled up on the charms.

She specialised in tracking and detaining magic based Breeds such as witches, mages and low to medium Fae, although she had arrested several shifters. But never vampires, not without being partnered with another Paladin at least.

Admin at The Tower had really fucked up.

Closing the clasp, she hooked the handcuffs onto the back of her jeans so she could access them easily.

"Alice Skye?" A man wearing a doctor's white coat called into the waiting room. He smiled when she looked up, flashing his fangs. "Please follow me."

Alice held her hand out as Peyton stood up, a frown creasing his brow. "I need you to wait here in case he runs." She didn't wait for his reply, quickly following the doctor into his office.

"Please, take a seat."

Alice surveyed the room, sitting down in the available chair as the doctor looked down at her notes.

The room was simple, if not a bit plain with its white walls, desk and computer. A bed covered in tissue paper was to the side along with a filing cabinet. The only decoration was several certificates written in fancy calligraphy that you had to squint to read. Basic, but at least there were no windows, the only exit the door to her right.

"So it says here you had an overdose, may I ask what substance you took?"

"Does it matter?" she replied, "I'm just looking for... something stronger." She caught his eye when he looked up, a smile teasing her lips. "I heard from my friends that you might know something about that?"

He looked at her a second, his fangs peeking through his full lips in a burst of anger. Quick as lightening he grabbed her by the remains of her shirt, lifting her from her seat and against the wall.

"Who exactly are these friends?" he asked as he tightened his hand in the fabric.

"Just friends." Alice struggled as she was forced on tiptoe. He wasn't hurting her, just trying to scare, figure out if she was serious or not.

She slowly reached behind her back to unclip the cuffs from her jeans.

"So we gonna work something out? I got cash, or something else?" She tried not to gag as she licked her lips seductively. Or as seductively as she could, which probably wasn't very.

According to Dr Joseph Pierce's file, he was only fifteen-years-old in undead terms, which meant he wasn't a master vampire and was the responsibility of his creator. He qualified as a doctor before the change and carried it on once he gained enough control with his more primal urges.

He also liked to work out payment plans with vulnerable clients who couldn't afford his gear. Payment plans meaning sex, violent BDSM sex. It was interesting researching the guy once she received the contract. Although, the internet was not her friend.

Some things cannot be unseen.

He was a regular at the strip club Sam worked at and frequently used the in house 'sin' rooms for his sexual desires. It was how she knew he would respond to her advances.

She let out a little moan, the soft noise making his pupils dilate and his fangs elongate even further.

This is disgusting, she thought to herself. What was sad is it was the closest thing to anything sexual she had had in a while. *Pathetic.*

As quickly as he grabbed her shirt he released her, his dark eyes narrowing.

He was still close, close enough that his arm was barely an inch from her own. Her hand clutched the cold metal of her handcuffs, her arm moving slowly out from behind her as...

She was suddenly airborne, her back hitting something hard enough to rattle her teeth before she crashed to the ground.

"You stupid bitch," he snarled as he crouched over her, his hands clawed. "You not think I can smell an overdose?"

Ah shit.

Alice didn't give him time to think, she flicked the metal cuff over his left wrist and locked it tight.

"What the?" He stared dumbfounded at the metal, the other half open and dangling free.

Luckily only one cuff needed to be on for the charm to work.

"Surprise arsehole." Alice launched up in a move she had recently learnt in her martial arts class, pushing him off balance. He tried to swat her away, but unused to the limited strength it barely moved her. Grabbing his free arm she twisted it behind his back, clicking the renaming handcuff into place.

"What is this?" he snarled, his arms straining as he tried to break the metal with brute strength.

"You're under arrest for selling illegal substances." She moved him so he faced the wall, making sure his forehead touched the white paint.

"You've got the wrong..."

The door opened to reveal Peyton, his eyebrow arched with an expression of impatience. Without a word he stepped inside, closing the door behind him before locking it.

"Looks like you're all done." He surveyed the room, eyes narrowing once he noticed the cracked wall and smashed pictures.

He guessed that was what she had been thrown against.

"So you're telling me, after all this I don't even get any of the action? My job is definitely better."

"Whatever," she murmured as she started to pat down Dr Pierce, his white coat empty other than a cheap plastic phone, notepad and a small coin purse. "Here." She threw Peyton the coin purse.

"What do we have here?" Peyton unzipped the purse and pulled out eight plastic bags full of dark red crystals.

"Is that Brimstone?" Alice asked as she looked over his shoulder. "It looks, weird." The crystals seemed to glow.

"It doesn't look like any Brimstone I have ever seen." Peyton held it to the light, frowning.

"Please, you don't understand what you're doing," Dr Pierce said, panic underlying his tone. "They will kill me."

"Who?" Alice asked, "who do you work for?"

He only grunted in response.

"Hey Alice, you see anything like this?" Peyton handed her over a packet, pointing at the insignia embossed on the plastic. "I worked in narcotics for five years and don't recognise it."

She studied the stamp, pressing her finger to the raised insignia. The snake was twisted three times into a stylised Celtic knot before it swallowed its own tail. "Hey," she pushed the packet into Dr Pierce's face. "What's this?"

He looked at her, his eyes completely encased by his pupils. "Fuck you."

"Nah, I'm not your blood type." She turned her attention back to Peyton, who still studied the packets. "You think your old friends in Narcotics be able to analyse it?"

He squinted at the crystals before putting all of them back into the coin purse. "I can see what I can do."

"Hey Dr Pierce, your next…" The receptionist knocked on the door.

Alice opened it, flashed her Paladin license to her surprised expression. "I'm afraid Dr Pierce will be out of work for the foreseeable future."

With that she shut the door in her face.

CHAPTER TWO

Alice stepped out of the lift on the forty-second floor, frowning at the chaos.

She stood at the entrance, confused as to why her colleagues were rushing around like headless chickens. The large room was busy, a raucous of sound as people chatted, computers beeped and printers hummed.

Odd compared to the usual quiet.

The forty-second floor was the home of the Paladins who worked in the city, consisting of separate felt cubicles that held each Paladin's personal desk and computer. What was strange was that the floor was usually deserted, everybody preferring to use outside resources to track and hunt their assigned contracts. The space was only used as a communal base or for dreaded paperwork. They had an active job, which meant it was rare for more than two or three to be at their desks at once.

She hitched her satchel on her shoulder, quickly side-stepping out of the way as Jay almost walked into her as he concentrated on his notepad. He angrily growled as he passed, stabbing the paper with a pen like a caveman. He looked the part, with his ruffled hair and leather ensemble, his Paladin grade sword strapped visibly in his sheath. Come to think of it, she had never seen him in the office before. From his scathing expression he wasn't happy to be there either.

Alice shook her head as she made her way to her own desk, pushing her cat-themed mug out of the way so she could place down her bag onto the worn wood.

"Oh, there you are," a cheerful voice sang. "Was wondering when you were joining the madness."

Alice turned towards her friend, hesitating when she noticed the tall brunette covered in dry blood. "Hey Rose," Alice smirked. "Have a busy day?"

"Oh, this?" She scratched at the red on her palm, the blood flaking off to fall gently to the carpet. "Had a slight disagreement." Rose grinned, showing off her tiny fangs that highlighted her feline heritage. "I like it when they're rough," she winked.

Alice couldn't help but smile before she heard Jay swear in the background. "What's happening?" She gestured to the room. It wasn't just Jay who looked out of place, she noticed eight others looking just as frustrated as they worked ferociously at their desks. Richard, a newer Paladin Alice didn't know as well was kicking the printer hard enough that smoke started to appear.

"I was hoping you would tell me." She sat heavily on the desk, slouching as she picked at the hole in her jeans. "Only came in to hand in my completed contract when I walked into this lot. I heard the boss is in a bad mood, making people catch up with old paperwork." She shrugged as she poked Alice's cat novelty clock.

"Dread?"

Alice hadn't seen Dread Grayson, Commissioner of Supernatural Intelligence Bureau since Winter Solstice a few weeks earlier. What Rose, and everybody else who worked in The Tower didn't know was that Dread was her legal guardian, taking over parental responsibilities when her parents were murdered almost two decades earlier. They had a reasonably close relationship to the point she teased his hard-arse attitude and he continued to question her clothing, friends and life choices.

She loved him like her father, but he didn't share his work with her. Their relationship at The Tower was strictly professional.

"Hmm," Rose replied almost unconsciously, her attention on the small fire Richard was fighting against as the printer fought back. "Hey, you spoken to Danton today? Bee's just told me he's resigned with immediate effect."

"D's quit?" Alice felt instant guilt. It had only been a few weeks since she found out that Danton became a Paladin to watch over her on

Councilman Valentina's orders. A spy. Yet she couldn't explain that to Rose, who for the last five plus years had been D's partner.

"Yep, and the bastard isn't even answering his phone." Her eyes diluted to slits, emphasising her anger. They weren't just partners, but best friends. "Fuck it, I'm going to hunt him down." She hopped off the desk just as someone ran past the cubicle, paper clutched to their chest.

Alice waved her friend goodbye before facing the chaos once again.

What the hell is going on? she thought to herself, tapping her fingernails against her desk.

"Hey Bee," she called to her fellow Paladin, waving her arm for attention as she walked past. "You know what's going on?"

Bee spun to face Alice, her dark eyes angry before she realised who had called. "Oh, hey Alice." She stomped over, her heeled boots clicking loudly. "You been to see the boss yet?"

"Not yet, I..."

Bee didn't let her finish. "Well you better get in there, he's been chewing everyone up. It's fucked up if you ask me." She turned back away, heading towards her own desk.

Alice stared after her, watching how everyone gave her a wide birth. Bee worked best alone, and made sure everyone knew it. Alice had personally worked with her twice, and enjoyed her no bullshit attitude both times. She was the only Paladin that was one-hundred per cent human and decided from the beginning she had a point to prove. Now no one could doubt her skills as a tracker.

Deciding to take her advice Alice headed towards the back of the room, bypassing the empty receptionist's desk and knocked gently on the large oak door.

"Dread ... I mean, Commissioner Grayson."

"Come in," a faint voice called through the wood.

"Hey, I was going to ask what's going on..." Alice stopped at the threshold, mouth agape. "What the fuck?"

"Language Alice," Barbie, Dread's receptionist tutted. "You shouldn't speak like that in front of the new Commissioner."

"New Commissioner?"

Barbie sat at the edge of the desk, her already short skirt pulled indecently high. She giggled as she stepped down, revealing Michael Brooks sitting there with a smug expression on his face.

"Mickey?" Alice thought she was seeing things.

"It's Commissioner Brooks," he sneered. "It's nice of you to actually turn up to work, Alice. We have much to discuss."

"I'll leave you alone, Commissioner," Barbie giggled once again, closing the door behind her.

"Commissioner?" Alice parroted. "This is a joke right? Where's Dread?"

The room was starkly devoid of belongings. Two cardboard boxes sat open beside the empty bookcase, dust highlighting all the missing books, statues and awards. The pictures that once adorned the back wall had been removed, leaving clean markings where they once were. The only thing that Alice recognised was the chrome lamp that still perched on the corner of the obnoxiously oversized desk.

"Grayson has been removed from his position temporarily while under investigation."

Mickey stood up, tugging the lapels of his suit that was clearly two sizes too big. He looked like a child playing dress up. He had waxed his red hair back, the length cut to just above his collar. Annoyingly it suited him, showcasing his green eyes which were his best feature.

"Investigation?"

"I don't believe you're entitled to that information."

He leant against his desk, a halo of light surrounding him like a smug angel. The blackout blind – that usually would be down, was wound up, revealing the startling beauty of the city.

"I've been assigned to take over," he grinned, the expression unnerving. Reaching beneath his desk he brought up a red folder, slapping it down onto the desk.

She knew exactly what it was.

"I've been going through your contracts over the last few years Alice." He slapped his gums, eyes alight with excitement as he pushed the folder towards her with one finger. "I find you sloppy in your work."

"I have the highest retrieval rate of any other Paladin in the London division, that includes you," she snapped back at him as his smile faltered.

He sniffed, displeased as he moved towards his leather chair.

"I'm going to be watching you closely, if it was up to me you would be gone along with Grayson. But apparently The Council want you to continue your work... for now at least." He dropped into the chair with enough force it began to spin. He awkwardly grabbed the table before it swung a full three-sixty. Once he was happy with its position he clasped his hands together and leant back.

"You look like a bad action film villain."

His eyes narrowed as he nervously flicked his fringe from his eyes. "Careful, I have more power than you think. For example, I have removed you as Breed consultant. You will no longer liaise with The Met."

"What?!"

Shit. Shit. Shit. She hadn't been liaison with Spook Squad for long, enjoyed the change to her usual contracts. The extra pay was also a bonus.

"You can't do that!"

"Oh, but I can." He smirked as the leather squeaked below him. "I'm the boss."

Alice felt her power flare, took a careful breath to bring it back under control. Normally Tinkerbell, a ball of physical frustration would pop into existence in a sparkling show of embarrassment. It did this time, but she welcomed the small twinkly light, enjoying Mickey's anxious glance as it danced around them like a weirdly happy puppy.

"That is all Alice," Mickey spun his chair towards the window, dismissing her. "Get back to work."

She bit the inside of her cheek to stop her next remark.

CHAPTER THREE

The car screeched to a stop outside Dread's townhouse, the wheels throwing up the white stones of the driveway. The end terrace was made up of four-stories, not including the multiple basement levels he had added in the last several decades. Growing up Alice never really understood why a vampire as powerful as Dread lived in the beautiful place, the century old brick covered in purple wisteria that gave it an almost whimsical look. The place looked like a normal human dwelling, except the dark windows that were actually blacked out. Only as Alice grew did she understand that he chose the place on purpose. Who would suspect the Commissioner of the Supernatural Intelligence Bureau lived amongst the Norms?

Over the years he added more security measures. He bought the townhouse beside him, giving him complete privacy while top of the range security cameras had been fitted. The wisteria was grown purposely, covering protection runes engraved directly onto the brick.

Opposite was a church, amusing considering Dread had bought the house over one-hundred years earlier when humans still believed vampires couldn't be near holy ground. To be fair, some ignorant people still believed it now.

Alice stepped out of the car just as a blacked out limo pulled up beside her. She ignored it to lift the heavy lion knocker on the oversized front door.

"Ma petite sorcière, what are you doing here?" a deep voice asked from beside her.

"Shouldn't I be asking you the same question?" she replied as she continued to stare at the intricate knocker. "Rose is hunting you, by the way."

"Ah, I better get myself out of here, non?"

The door opened faster than her eyes could process, forcing her to step back as Dread appeared in the dark threshold, his obsidian eyes staring. His mouth was set in a thin line, the vein in his forehead that pulsated when he was angry visible beneath his pallid skin.

"Alice, it's nice to see you," he nodded politely, his eyes telling her a different story. *You shouldn't have come.* He looked stressed, even more so than usual which worried her.

What's happening? She asked in the same way, using her expression rather than verbal words. It took knowing someone better than yourself to be able to communicate wordlessly, only being able to do it with Dread and Sam.

His mouth tightened before he straightened up, his eyes darting to Danton before returning to her. "I've been summoned to Paris, to Valentina."

"Enough," D cut in, his tone hardened. "We must be leaving."

"Elle doit savoir," Dread shot back in French as he moved towards the limo.

"La maîtresse l'a défendue," D replied in the same language.

"What's happening?" Alice finally turned to D, noting the full black leather ensemble complete with his statement slicked back hair. Twin guns were strapped to his hips, not counting the knives she could see peeking from his heavy boots. He was one of the first Paladins she had ever worked with, had helped her train her skill in the blade. So it hurt when she looked at him, the betrayal he tried to hide in his closed off expression.

"La maîtresse…"

"In English," Alice snapped, her friendliness gone.

She hated not knowing French, wished she had learned it when Dread tried to teach her as a child. She was more interested in anything else, even when he tried seven different languages. Luckily, she understood at least one word.

"What does your Mistress want with Dread?" she asked in an irate tone.

"C'est important qu'elle sache," D said as he stepped back, nodding to the chauffeur who stood silently.

Alice thought he was just the driver, his eyes hidden beneath dark glasses and mouth set in a grim line. So when his hand moved towards his hip as she reached for Dread, she took precious seconds to react. He had already unclicked the safety on his gun and a single shot fired before she had him unarmed, the weapon thrown across the driveway before his arm hit her with enough force to rattle her skull.

Within a second Dread had jumped forward, tearing his throat out with fangs longer than she had ever seen on him. Blood covered his jaw before it dripped down his front, the liquid darkening his already dark fabric before it blended effortlessly into his suit. It shocked her, when she knew it shouldn't. He was a vampire after all, one old enough he controlled S.I. for The Council. Yet, she had never actually witnessed him be violent.

Dread's eyes were obsidian, anger prevalent as he breathed heavily, his fangs still on show.

D slowly walked over before he nudged the body, the driver's death evident as Alice noticed his spine through the ripped flesh.

"We going to talk about what just happened?" she asked as she watched his lifeblood soak the white stones, turning them a gruesome pink. "Who was he aiming at?"

The shot had gone wide, the bullet missing all three.

"It seems you have a traitor," Dread said, his tone deeper than usual as he tried, and failed, to control his continued anger.

"Hmmm." D kicked him again before pulling out his phone. "It will be handled."

"Danton," Dread said calmer than his face expressed. "Tell her what she needs to know."

"You know I can't..."

"Maybe next time if you did your job correctly, I wouldn't have needed to disarm your driver. I wonder what your Mistress would think..." She gave him a baleful look.

D clenched his jaw, his own expression scathing. "This pettiness doesn't suit you."

Alice's comment forced a nervous laugh. "Do you really know me?"

He looked towards Dread, who nodded, his face still painted in red. They were lucky the townhouse was at the end of the street, with the closest occupied house far enough away they wouldn't be able to see the dead body in the drive clearly. Because that wouldn't stand out in the nice *human* neighbourhood.

"The Council have lost trust in Commissioner Grayson. They are no longer trusting his word regarding certain situations."

"What? Why?" She turned to Dread. "Are you in trouble?" Her eyes settled on the body once again.

What a ridiculous question.

She reached for her blade, unsheathing the steel with a quick swish that highlighted the runes that burst into light. She stepped in front of Dread, facing D.

D sniggered, the sound inappropriate. "You think you can take me, Ma petite sorcière?" He moved faster than her eyes could track, his hand snaking out to curl around hers in a bruising grip. With one twist he could have disarmed her, and she could do nothing to stop him. Except, a flash blinded them both, originating from where his hand touched hers. D jumped back with a snarl, his eyes open in shock as he checked out the new burn along his palm.

She had no idea what just happened, but pretended she knew what she was doing anyway. She had enough practice of faking it.

"Alice, leave the youngling be, he's only following orders."

"Dread..."

He reached for her, the affection unusual. She knew he loved her as his own daughter, but they didn't hug or have long loving talks about boys, woman problems or fashion. That's what she had Sam for. Instead he trained her so she could always look after herself, something her parents couldn't have done. So she welcomed his hand as it clutched hers, his skin cold enough that she could tell he hadn't fed even though he must have consumed some of the blood from the driver.

"Stay under the radar, try not to gain any attention from any of The Council until I return."

"But Dread..."

Stay away from any of The Council Members, he interrupted with his eyes, so D couldn't understand their conversation. *That includes the trial.*

Alice smiled as she squeezed his hand back. She wouldn't lie to him, so she didn't reply to either statement. The trial of Rexley Wild was something she was interested in, yet scared of. She didn't want to see him, the man that used her as if she meant nothing to him. But she promised his twin, Theo that she would at least support, try to stop Rex from getting the death sentence for his part in the Daemon sacrifices.

Which meant she was probably going to be in the room with Xavier, the Councilmember that stood on behalf of the shifters.

Dread released her hand as suddenly as he had taken it.

"Be safe," he said as he slipped into the back of the limo.

D moved past Alice, hesitating at the car door before slamming it shut behind Dread. He took a second to look around, making sure they were alone.

"You're running out of time," he said without facing her.

"Excuse me?" She moved towards him, stopping when he held out his hand.

"They're coming. It's only a matter of time before they decide your fate. You need to learn to protect yourself, learn control."

"D, what are you on about?" She felt an underlying panic at his tone. "D?"

He turned his head, allowing only his profile to show.

She noticed his face was tight, his burnt palm fisted.

"Train harder, faster. It's not just your life at stake anymore. A cleaner will be here within five to sort out the mess." He quickly slipped into the driver's side, the long car peeling out of the drive quick enough to kick up dust.

"WAIT!" she called after it, but it was gone. "FUCK!"

Alice slammed her front door with such force she knocked a picture off the wall. The glass shattered, scattering across the floor in a show of glitter. Her boots crunched the tiny shards, scratching the newly laid floor Sam had lovingly waxed only a few days earlier.

And she didn't care.

She stormed into the kitchen, taking out her frustration on the paperwork left on the island counter. She pushed the sheets off, unsatisfied with their gentle descent until her eyes caught the drawings she had been working on over the last few days. Taking out her sword from her spine sheath she settled it next to the many drawings, the runes that glowed at her touch disappearing. She had been studying the runes that appeared at her skin contact for weeks, trying to understand what they meant.

Unfortunately, she was no closer to understanding, the runes never the same. They were always different in one way or another, changing each time she touched it. And now her weapon had a mind of its own.

She had wanted to speak to Riley about the damn thing, as he was the only other person they seemed to appear for. But he was still dealing with the aftermath of his father, too busy to even answer a call.

So she studied alone. Trained alone.

"Alice? What happened to the floor?" Sam stamped into the kitchen, his blonde hair in twin plaits while his neck was covered in a red lipstick smear. His amber eyes took in the mess on the kitchen floor, concern flicking over the anger. "What's wrong baby girl?"

Alice hesitated, wondering what to tell him. In the end she decided on the truth. They told each other everything, were each other's support rocks.

He deserved to know.

Dread wasn't like a father to him, not like he was to Alice. Sam had been too broken when they met as children, had always kept his distance from adults until he was a teenager, even now he didn't trust many people. When he was a child Sam preferred to roam around London homeless, sleeping rough. It was when they saw each other at the support group that it all changed.

He used to sneak in her window at the townhouse when she was small, used to share a bed while in his leopard form. Dread pretended like he never knew, but Dread knew everything. She asked him once, when she was about thirteen and he always said a friendship like theirs should be protected and cherished. If he needed the security, then he allowed it. But if they ever became more than friends he would rip him limb from limb.

Alice smiled at the memory.

"Did Danton say anything else?" Sam asked as he picked up the remaining pieces of paper, placing them in a neat pile on the counter.

"No, that's everything he said." Which gave her no information, nothing. Alice let out a frustrated growl. "It's ridiculous. No warning, I don't even think either of them would have told me if I hadn't turned up."

"Overlord will be fine, you know he will." He folded his arms, causing her eyes to settle on the lipstick smeared across his neck.

"Sooo, we going to talk about those?" She tried to hide her smirk, failed. "Does Zac wear lipstick now?"

"He should, it would really suit him." Sam's eyes glazed over for a second, a secret smile on his lips. "Anyway he was last week's news, this week I'm into Clarice."

"I'm not even going to comment."

"Oh, don't worry baby girl, you're still my number one gal," he chucked as he approached, his arm coming around her in a familiar hug. "Besides, one of us has to be getting ourselves out there..."

"Yeah, yeah," she replied sarcastically, returning his hug.

"So," he started as he leaned back, his hands relaxed on her shoulders. "What are you going to do?"

"Until Dread's home? Train." She shrugged. "Work."

"What, under that fucking Mickey?"

Alice stepped out of his embrace, reaching for her sword. "What choice do I have?"

CHAPTER FOUR

Alice checked her phone for the hundredth time, annoyance making her agitated as she sat in the busy bank. It had been a week since Dread had left with D, and neither had replied to her messages. Neither had even read any. A week of not knowing whether he was alive, in trouble or dead. She clenched the phone, wondering how much force it would take to crack the screen.

When she noticed the woman next to her flick her a nervous glance and timidly move over Alice took a calming breath, cooling her scowl.

Target: 875638
Mr Etton Riox – Male – Witch. Height unknown – Facial features unknown.
Defrauds customers by dressing up as those customers.
Glamour used.
Aggression level – amber.
Retrieval fee – Basic+

Etton Riox was a notorious faceless fraudster who had been on the Paladins hit list for the past six months. Allegedly he would wear full-body glamour, mimicking the real customer, and would withdraw cash directly from The Bank of Dark Griffin in full view of cameras. They say 'allegedly' because so far three Paladins had failed to track him, and couldn't figure out who it was. The only reason they knew it was the same person was because Mr Riox liked to gloat by sending appreciation baskets directly to his victims.

Because nothing said 'sorry I stole your life savings' like a basket of cheap chocolates.

It had amused Alice for a while, until it was her turn. It had taken her only a few minutes to realise Etton Riox was an anagram of 'extortion' which, while amusing, was just another insult.

So she was hunting a ghost, not the easiest thing to do when her only lead was the bank itself, one that refused to install specialised glamour detection equipment like every other rational bank.

Normal banks used special glass in front of their cashiers that was spelled to see through any glamour and cosmetic charms. Cosmetically enhanced breasts would flatten, tans would fade and wrinkles would appear revealing the customer's true self, which would make her job a lot easier if they could actually see the original person, and not glamour. Especially as there was no warning from his victims. They didn't know he had stolen their identity until their accounts were cleared, and then when they complained the cameras said they did it themselves.

Which is probably why he targeted only Dark Griffin, as they didn't have such security. Instead they used a glass orb that was suspended from the ceiling that would glow green when there was no magic detected, and red when there was.

It was always red.

Alice couldn't think of many reasons why someone would use a bank without the state of the art anti-glamour equipment, unless they had something to hide themselves. But who was she to judge?

So she sat there, waiting, watching.

This would probably be something Peyton would enjoy, she mused to herself. This was what he would have been used to, but not Alice. She had been there a few hours and was ready to rip her own hair out. She believed she had patience, but it was wearing thin as she watched the orb in the ceiling carefully, feeling a slight exhilaration when it finally darkened as two people entered past the glass door.

The first was a young mother pushing a pram, the child talking excitedly to its toy penguin while the second was an overweight older man who hobbled in on his cane. The security guards who had been hired specifically since the bank's recent spate of fraud stood there doing nothing other than chat to one another. They didn't even look up to check the orb, nor did they question why she had been sitting there doing nothing for so long.

If she wasn't inspecting so intently she would have missed it. The old man reached towards the young mum, his hand brushing against her bag hanging forgotten on her shoulder as she stood in line.

"So, Alice. How's it going?" A nasally voice said from directly beside her.

"Excuse me?" She turned to the man who just sat down, a grin cracking his cheeks. "MICKEY?" she hissed. "What are you doing here?"

"It's Michael," he sneered before patting down his purple floral shirt pocket, pulling out a five-inch wand. "I've decided that your performance recently is so poor that I'm going to be your new partner." He flicked his wand, the gold top glittering beneath the artificial lights.

She hated wands, the pretentious instrument ridiculously expensive. They were designed to concentrate an arcane spell, resulting in fewer accidents. If a witch needed it to have 'fewer accidents', then they had some serious problems.

"Seriously Mickey?" she scowled as she turned her attention back to the old man, who had disappeared from the line, the mothers bag now unzipped slightly.

"It's Michael," he grunted, his lip curling in annoyance. "Don't make me give you another warning, Alice. I don't trust anyone else to watch over you."

Alice ignored him, instead she stood up to scan the crowd. She found the man in the corner, leaning heavily on his cane while he surveyed the line. He had put on a pair of oversized glasses, the glass an odd pearlescent green colour that didn't match the rest of his clothes.

A heavy hand landed on her shoulder, forcing her back.

"Now listen to me..."

"I'm working you idiot." She pulled him off, causing a small scene that caught the security guards attention.

"Is there a problem here?" the short one grunted at them. "If there's a problem I would have to ask you to leave."

"Yeah, this guy keeps trying to feel me up." She pointed to Mickey, who turned bright red as he spluttered out a curse. While the security guards were distracted she slipped past them, moving slowly through the crowd towards the old man who had moved closer to the line once more. His arm kept brushing bags, which seemed innocent enough except he kept repeating it. He would brush one bag, frown, then repeat. It was if he was searching for something. He hadn't spoken to anybody, nor had he used any of the facilities available in the bank.

Alice walked beside him, pretending to browse the leaflets on the wall when the air moved behind her.

"ALICE!" Mickey stormed over, puffing in anger. "You're supposed to be hunting your target, and you're over here browsing brochures!" He clenched his wand as he pointed it at her face. "What if Mr Riox walked in here and you were too busy with reading material?"

You have got to be shitting me, she cursed to herself as the old man tensed. She saw the cane move in her peripheral, giving her just enough time to move out of its way. Unfortunately for Mickey he was too busy chastising her to notice the heavy wood whizzing through the air, the impact knocking him off his feet and into her, throwing them both against the wall.

Alice scrambled to her feet as leaflets created a fountain of colour in the air.

"STOP!" she shouted after him as he pushed past people to exit the bank, moving a lot faster than he was a moment ago, his need for the cane disappearing. She followed him into the busy high street, his speed and dexterity anything but old.

Well, at least I know he's the guy I'm after, she thought.

She heard footsteps, knew Mickey would be quick on her tail.

She thoroughly disliked Michael, had since she discovered his personality was that of an arsehole when they both trained together at the academy. But he was still a Paladin, which meant he was trained in both offensive and defensive magic.

"He's running towards Langly Street, cut him off through Pillards," she shouted while slowly catching up to Mr Riox.

She had almost caught up to him when she felt severe heat shoot over her head. Her eyes burned as she instinctively ducked, covering her eyes as light burst across the street, powerful enough to scorch through her closed eyelids. She skidded to a halt, Mickey knocking into her as she tried to wipe the pain from her eyes.

"ALICE!" He pulled her down as he fell, causing her to tumble on top of him. "YOU'VE LET HIM GO!" He violently pushed her, his own eyes red and teary when she was finally able to open her own.

"What was that?" she snarled, the pain fuelling her anger. "YOU COULD HAVE BLINDED US!"

"You're blaming me?" He shot to his feet, his eyes streaming. "This is all YOUR FAULT!"

"WHAT?!" Alice crawled to her knees, her eyes clear enough to see, but still painful. "I'm not the one that fucked up a spell."

"It didn't fuck up. I don't fuck up."

The wand creaked in his hand, the end singed. She's pretty confident it wasn't supposed to do that.

"You were reckless, chasing after him in front of pedestrians," he cried.

"What was I supposed to do? Let him go? After you told everybody in the bank who we were hunting?" Alice let out an infuriated growl. "Why are you using a wand if you're not strong enough to wield it?"

"This was an easy tag, and you let him go."

"No, you let him go." She finally looked around the quiet street, her eyes extra sensitive as she squinted against the natural sunlight. He was long gone, using the botched spell as a distraction to get away. She had no idea whether that was his biological look, or one created by glamour. Either way, she was fucked.

Mickey puffed up in outrage, jabbing her in the chest with the end of his wand. "Do you know what? You're suspended, without pay."

"Wait, wait, wait," she said, her voice rising to a screech. "You can't do that!"

"As new Commissioner of S.I. I can," he said in a menacing tone.

Fuck. Fuck. Fuck.

What was she going to do now?

CHAPTER FIVE

Alice angrily tapped her foot as she waited for her coffee, loud enough that the barista looked over with a raised eyebrow. She had already ripped apart her napkin, creating a snowstorm on the table top as well as bending the spoon. She felt guilty about the spoon, hadn't realised how strongly she had been crushing it as she ate the slice of Victoria sponge.

She had hoped it would have cheered her up since cake makes everything better, unfortunately it was just bittersweet on her tongue.

How dare he suspend me, she thought to herself as she pushed away the half eaten cake. *What am I going to do now?*

"Your coffee," the barista said with a timid mumble, putting her mug down carefully. "I hope you enjoy."

She smiled, stopped when he flinched.

Bloody hell, how moody do I look?

"Thank y..." The rest caught in her throat as a familiar presence touched her chi. She looked around the young barista, her jaw dropping open when she noticed her brother standing in the doorway.

She had felt him more over the past few weeks, but he never got close enough for her to speak to him. She watched Kyle carefully, memorising his features as if she would never see him again. Because she never knew if he would come back.

Their childhood was destroyed by the monsters that go bump in the night. They never got to grow up together, she never got to tease him over his loud music and he never got to threaten her boyfriends when she started to date.

Instead they were reminded of their parent's trauma, of the blood and screams of the night that were an eternal memory. Yet she didn't feel despair when she saw him. She felt joy that he had survived. That they could be in each other's lives, maybe.

Alice didn't notice the barista replacing her napkin as Kyle took the seat beside her, his shoulder almost touching as he looked at the remains of the Victoria sponge. His dark hood was pulled away from his face, showing off his healthier appearance. She looked at him from the corner of her eye, pushing the plate towards him so he could finish the sweet treat. His face wasn't as gaunt, the bags under his eyes not as pronounced and his cheeks were fuller. He had shaved, looked reasonably presentable in his dirty jeans and black t-shirt beneath the dark blue hoodie.

Light reflected off the silver cuffs on his wrists when he picked up the sponge, bringing it to his lips. She knew he had a matching choker, a thick metal band that looked closer to a fashion accessory than what it actually was. Slave bands. Ones that he couldn't remove.

His eyes were the same colour as hers when he finally looked up, an emerald green they inherited from their mother. That was where the rest of the resemblance ended, his other features strongly represented by their father, including the dark hair compared to Alice's bright blonde. Although, the brown of his childhood was now closer to black. Other times, however, she noticed his eyes were even darker, the black creeping across his irises to encompass his whole eye.

She desperately wanted to speak, tell him about her awful day whilst asking him how he was. Where he was living and whether he needed money, but she was scared in case he fled. So she remained silent, almost comforted by his presence.

It was progress.

"You look upset," he said quietly as he finished off the cake, brushing the crumbs from his fingers. "Are you okay?" He lifted the empty plate, taking it to the counter and speaking quietly to the barista before returning to the table, this time sitting opposite.

"Oh, err..." She was overwhelmed that he spoke, took her time to reply as the barista brought over a steaming cup of hot chocolate as well as another slice of cake, this time carrot. "I'm okay, my new boss is just an arsehole."

He ignored the cake and drink. "Want me to take care of it?"

She looked at him, noticed his breathing had slowed down as she decided whether he was serious or not. She didn't know him well enough to really tell.

"I'm a big girl, been looking after myself for a long time."

"Yes, you're strong." He picked up a fork, cutting the cake in half. "Stronger than me," he said on a whisper, almost as if she wasn't supposed to hear the last part.

Alice didn't know what to say, instead she smiled as he pushed half of the carrot cake towards her. She hated carrot cake, didn't understand why anybody would want to bake with vegetables when there were sugar and chocolate available. So she scraped the cream cheese frosting with her bent spoon, savouring the flavour as Kyle devoured his own half in two mouthfuls.

"Does it hurt?"

Alice looked up, the spoon still in her mouth. "Huh?"

His eyes flicked to her scar. "Does it hurt?" he repeated.

"Oh, no." *At least, not now,* she mentally added. She traced the crescent scar, a visual reminder of when she was almost sacrificed by a Daemon. It was several degrees colder than the rest of her palm, the rough skin sometimes throbbing in pain for no reason.

"It's a mark. They will be able to sense you through it." His eyes darkened as his voice deepened. "I can feel it."

Feel it?

"How can I remove it?" she asked as she sucked in a breath as the scar started to ache, the sudden sensation causing her hand to clench.

"You can't." His pupils started to grow before he closed his eyes, his eyebrows crossed in concentration.

Reaching out blindly he grabbed his drink, curling his large palms around the mug for a few seconds as he absorbed the heat. The white of the ceramic highlighted the dirt beneath his fingernails, nails that were bitten to the quick and small red cuts that were new enough they glowed against his skin.

His hands shook as he placed his drink back down. "I'm sorry."

When he opened his eyes once again they were green, but darker. She went to touch him, but stopped when he flinched. He started to shake, his whole body vibrating as he clawed his fingers down his face, strong enough to leave faint lines.

"Kyle?" She reached for him again, ignoring his flinch this time. "What's wrong? How can I help?"

"I need help with something."

"Anything."

He slowly went to his jeans pocket, carefully unfolding an old newspaper. In the corner was a crudely drawn design. "I need to find out about this."

"A drawing?"

She took the paper from him, examining the lines carefully. Roughly drawn using pencil Alice studied the snake which was stylised into a curved Celtic knot, the head of the snake swallowing its own tail.

"What is it?" She recognised it instantly, having only seen it a few days ago on the drugs packet.

What was Kyle doing with this? she thought.

"It's an Ouroboros," he said as she touched the indents where his pencil pierced the paper. "It means infinity, a paradox. It's also a signature."

"A signature?" She handed it back, but he kept it on the table between them. "I can't tell you much other than it's been printed on some new drugs found circuiting the club scene."

"So you've seen it?" He raised an eyebrow before pointing to the snake head. "The Master had this insignia."

"The Master is dead." She had seen it with her own eyes. Riley pushed raw power through a gunshot wound. It was a memory she welcomed when nightmares howled in the night.

The Master could no longer hurt Kyle, control him through the bands.

"I know," he said, almost reassuring himself.

"Then why?"

"I need... I need to..." He couldn't seem to get the words out. "The Master was involved in the manufacturing of a highly addictive drug. He was part of the trinity." He pointed to the three curves. "The Master may be dead, but his drugs are still destroying lives. I want to stop the other two partners."

"How do you know all this?"

He made eye contact, the darkness taking over his irises once more. "I was with him almost twenty years, Alice."

She felt a shiver rattle down her spine as her hand continued to pulsate. She never saw her brother as someone who was dangerous, but he looked dangerous now. His chi was electric against her own, sharp enough to cause other magic users to glance their way in curiosity.

"How can I help?"

"There was a lab where they used to experiment on people with the new drugs. Force them to take it until they relied on it to breathe, to live."

"Kyle..." Her voice broke.

He shook his head, looking away. "I remember the facility, but not where it is. I only accessed it through the hidden tunnels. I need you to help me find it."

"How..."

"You know someone who might know." When he looked back his whole eyes were black, no whites or irises. It was unnerving to say the least.

"Who?"

CHAPTER SIX

Alice felt her nerves jump as she was patted down for the third time, her sword, gun and knife already removed and placed into a locked metal box at reception.

"Do you understand the rules?" the man who was getting too personal with her bra strap asked as he finished checking her for contraband. If he pinged it once more she wouldn't be responsible for her actions.

"Your colleague explained."

"Just so you understand, we have zero tolerance on rule breaking. This is a maximum security Breed prison."

No shit, Sherlock, she thought to herself as she tried to smile friendlily at him.

"There will be a maximum of five minutes with the inmate. He will remain in his cell, behind bars. There will be no touching."

"Does he know I'm coming?" She felt sick, panic rising as she fought her anxiety. The only reason Tinkerbell hadn't popped into existence to torment her was the anti-magic enchantments carved every few feet on the thick stone walls.

She didn't want to see him.

But knew she had to.

"He is aware he has a visitor. We do not give our inmates details as it sometimes riles them up."

Well, this is going to go well.

"Please, follow me."

Alice walked behind the guard as he accessed the locked door, the heavy metal bars swinging open with an audible groan as she was ushered through, the door quickly locked again behind her.

The stone walls continued throughout, creating a dark hallway with only flickers of candle light. Open archways opened out into slightly larger rooms that held four separate cells each. She could hear murmuring, crying as well as desperate spells muttered into the dark. Ones that were absorbed by all the anti-magic enchantments and totems that hung from the high ceilings.

The prison was erected inside a medieval castle. While the outside had been modernised, inside hadn't been touched Torches and small candles were the only source of light, the arched windows bricked in to the point they kept the stench of unwashed bodies thick at the back of your throat.

"Hello beautiful."

"Hey, whore."

"Oi, pretty lady. Come over here for a bit, I won't hurt ya. I got something thick and juicy you can…"

Inmates called at her, their faces appearing in the thin gaps between the thick metal bars as they blew kisses and gestured obscenely.

"GET BACK!" the guard shouted as he hit the bars with his metal baton, the resonating noise a horrible high pitched twang that set her teeth on edge. "He's just through here."

They walked through one last archway, the torches closer together to allow more light to penetrate.

"This is the waiting wing," he said as an explanation. "Your guy is the furthest to the left. I'll be back in five minutes. There is nowhere for you to go, and every inmate is strictly behind bars. I would recommend you don't get too curious with the other cells without risking your face being ripped off."

"Duly noted," she replied dryly.

Alice took a deep breath, instantly regretting it before she stepped into the room, ignoring the curious looks from the few inmates who were to her right. As she walked she noticed most of the cells empty, the rooms looking reasonable with neatly made cot-beds and clean metal sinks. The exception was the blood smeared scratch marks that scored some of the floors and walls.

She felt her heart race as she approached his cell, hoped nobody had strong enough hearing to notice. It was weirdly tidy when she stopped, his bed made with military precision and his food bowl and tray washed up by the sink. His back was to her, his black T-shirt dusty and ripped, reminding her of when she had seen him in Dread's office what felt like a lifetime ago.

Alice fought her instant guilt at seeing him behind the thick bars. It was strange considering she knew why he was there, that he deserved it. Yet, after giving it much thought she understood his actions. She wasn't confident she wouldn't have done the same thing in his situation. It was then she knew she would stand with his brothers at the court, stand against Xavier who was the judge, jury and executioner.

She had never met The Councilman who stood on behalf of all shifters, a tiger with a vicious reputation for death.

He sensed her then, his back tensing as a growl resonated across the stone.

"Alice?" Rex turned in a burst of speed, jumping at the bars as his eyes flashed the arctic blue of his wolf before returning to normal. "What are you doing here?" He slowly reached through the bars, his fingertips searching for her face before she stepped back, out of his reach.

"Hi," she replied, her voice embarrassingly weak before she cleared it. "I haven't got long."

His fists curled around the metal, his biceps tensing as he pulled at them violently. "You shouldn't be here."

"Oooo, is that a girly?" One of the other inmates catcalled.

Rex snarled, the loud vibration making her jump.

"I need to ask you a few questions," she asked as he stared at her, his face aged in a tired way. His beard didn't suit him, the hair growing in odd patches as if he had never really grown one before. Even with just candle light she could make out his dirty bare feet and cotton inmate trousers, the same ones she noticed on all the other prisoners. It hurt to look at him, memories of their time together corrupted with the knowledge of what he forced on her.

She might have felt guilty, but she wasn't ready to forgive him.

She carefully unfolded the crudely drawn insignia, allowing him to take it through the bars.

"Where did you find this?" he asked as he crushed the paper in his hand.

"What is it?"

"Alice..." his voice softened in a way she wasn't used to with him.

"No bullshit Rex, I haven't got the time."

His eyes hardened, his expression taking on its usual impassivity. It frustrated her that even now, he detached himself.

"They go by Trinity. An underground drug cartel that specialised in a superior Brimstone called Ruby Mist."

"What has your Master got to do with this Trinity?"

"HE ISN'T MY FUCKING MASTER," he snarled, eyes flashing arctic. He started to pace, calming himself down. "I had no choice. My pack comes first, always."

"I don't care." She caught his eye, noting his clenched jaw as his beast took it as a challenge. If she was a shifter she would have felt an overwhelming instinct to drop her eyes. But she wasn't a shifter. "What about Ruby Mist? Where is it made?"

"Careful Alice," he growled.

"Answer the question."

He remained silent.

Alice let out a sound of frustration, hitting her hand against a bar. "Fuck sake Rex, help me out here. You owe me. How do you even recognise the insignia?"

The silence stretched between them to the point she didn't think he would answer.

"We used to distribute. It's where I recognise it from."

"Your pack?" She shook her head, realising it wasn't an important question. "Where can I find them?"

"Why are you interested?"

"Please, I haven't got much time."

Rex relaxed against the bars, his forehead pressed against the metal. She knew he wanted to touch her, the wolf in him desperate to reassure himself that she was there. She almost stepped forward, almost.

"Rex?"

"Do you think this is karma? I betrayed you," he said, his voice detached, closed off.

"Yes, you did." She felt her anger ignite. "You tricked me, forced my emotions with a spell, and for what? To sacrifice me to a fucking Daemon." She wanted to laugh, forced herself to stop. "And right now, it doesn't matter."

"I forced no emotion, you wanted me just as much as I wanted you. I felt your heat beneath me when I..."

"Bullshit!" She felt her face burn red. "That bracelet..."

"Did nothing other than track you," he interrupted her, his voice quivering with an unknown emotion. His eyes bore into her, tracing her lips. "I had no choice but to give up something I didn't want to give."

"I'm not here about that," she said as her voice cracked again. "I need to know, where can I find them?"

Rex stepped back, hiding his face in the shadow of his cell. "There's a facility on the outskirts of the city that I used to pick up from, a charity or something. It's just off Rudwell."

Alice sighed, closing her eyes. "Thank you."

When he held out the paper she approached carefully. She turned to leave, felt the air disturb before a heavy hand landed on her shoulder.

"I'm sorry."

She rolled her shoulder, dislodging his hand. "I know."

He welcomed the pain-pleasure of the shift as it took over his body, allowing his wolf to overpower his thought. It was a respite, a moment of pure instinct as he looked at the forest surrounding his home through the eyes of his animal.

They were one, yet distinct separate personalities. He could feel the wolf's anger across his subconscious, clearer while in their animal body.

Angry with him, with the situation.

He couldn't disagree, but the wolf didn't understand consequence as the man did. The lesser of two evils wasn't a phrase his wolf could comprehend.

His jaw dripped saliva, a howl building up his throat even before the idea crossed his mind.

Allowing the sound to echo between the trees he surrendered to his wolf, allowing both their pain and their thirst for blood between their teeth to be quenched with a hunt.

CHAPTER SEVEN

Alice swung her legs up onto the wall opposite the run-down cheap hotel 'The Dirty Flamingo.' She stared at the dilapidated off-red brick, noting how the rust was all that was left of the sign's lettering, giving the hotel an abandoned look even though she could clearly see the greasy receptionist through the broken doorframe. The door was completely removed from its hinges and placed just inside, the light above an unusual red that hinted at other business ventures than just a simple hotel.

Several windows were smashed, some covered crudely with cardboard while others were just taped over. Someone had desperately tried to restore the crumbling brick with plaster, but failed miserably making the building look like it was moulting.

She hadn't even known the place had existed, the whole neighbourhood run down with abandoned buildings, empty car parks and an old factory that had no signs they were still open other than the black cloud from the many chimneys high above. Never mind the hotel actually had an online presence. Alice wasn't surprised at the average rating of just two stars, which she thought was pretty amusing considering.

She had wanted to remove Kyle from the hotel weeks ago, from when she first followed him back one night. But, just as she stepped onto his floor she hesitated, remembering something Dread had said.

'He will come home when he is ready.'

So she let him be and hoped the place had running water.

Alice flared her chi, hard enough that he should be able to recognise it from his room. It was strange to flare it so hard when she usually concealed it, not wanting any attention it could bring if other Breed attuned to their auras were nearby. It was also a way to either greet or flirt with other magic users, something she had no interest in. As she ignored the curious looks from the two men smoking against the wall further down she flared again, hoping it was late enough and he was in.

She didn't want to invade his privacy just yet, not when he was still so disconnected, so she had sat there for a while and waited.

"Hey pretty lady," one of the men called, "you open for a good time?"

"Like I told your friend," she said, gesturing to the other man who glared at her. "I'm not interested." He was taking her chi as an invitation, something that made her feel dirty. She had already told the other one to fuck off, her accompanied hand gesture drilling down the point.

Ugh, men.

"Well, I feel it loud and clear." He whistled, taking his time to look at her black T-shirt, down her jeans before settling on her knee high boots. She was thankful she had changed from her gym gear, the fabric a lot more revealing. "How much for an hour?"

"I'm not working, and if I was, you wouldn't have a chance. So bugger of."

"Now lady, that isn't how you talk to a client now, is it?" He approached, a swagger in his step. His breath stank of alcohol, strong enough that she could almost taste it herself. His friend, on the other hand, just stood back and watched the exchange with muted interest.

"Ever heard of the word no?"

His hand snaked out to catch her wrist in a bruising grip. "Whores like you don't know the word no."

She was yanked from the wall, pulled against his sweaty vest before she twisted in his arm, painfully pinning it behind his back.

"I'm sorry," she breathed into his ear, noting his sharp intake of breath when she added extra pressure. "You were saying."

"Alice," a growl penetrated the dark. "What are you doing here?"

"Oh, there he is," she said, smiling at her brother. "My friends here are just leaving, aren't you?"

"Yesssss." A hiss as she released him. He stumbled as he scrambled away, his friend quickly following behind.

"Remember to respect women!" she shouted after him, grinning at his terrified squeak in return. "And no means no!"

"What are you doing here?" Kyle growled again as his eyes darted around. "You shouldn't be here."

"Hey, nice to see you too," she said as she carefully approached, watching his shoulders tense as if he would flee. "Nice place."

"It's fine," he replied angrily, but didn't step back. "How did you find me?"

"Does it matter?"

Every time she saw him he looked younger, healthier. It made her want to hug him, but she knew that wasn't going to happen, at least not yet. They had entirely different childhoods after their parent's death. While Dread wasn't warm, she was best friends with a shifter, who were known for their affection. She highly doubted Kyle was cuddled or comforted when he needed it. If she tried to give him comfort now, he might react with anger or even violence, the action alien to him.

"I spoke to Rex."

His eyes brightened beneath his hood, excitement running across his features. "And?"

"He mentioned a place just outside of the city, was wondering if you wanted to check it out."

"Tell me the details, I can go alone."

"That's not how this works," she said as she watched his excitement change to anger at a flick of a switch. His eyes darkened, something she was now used to. She knew he was about to lose control when his eyes were as dark as the night.

So they had something in common, at least. The idea that they both would lose control made her feel better, in a weird twisted way.

"Fine," he said on an exhale. "But we're doing this my way."

They crouched behind the 'Sun Breeze Health' sign, apparently partnered with the national health service according to the small print at the bottom. Alice wanted to call bullshit with the partnership when she watched the fifth armed guard walk around the well-lit building. It wasn't like any medical facility she had ever seen, not that she had been to many.

"What is this place?" she whispered to Kyle.

He remained silent, watching the guards carefully. They had been there over an hour, studying the timings to the point they were confident they had a two-minute window to break into a back door. They had already scaled the seven-foot-high fence, leaving her car parked along a country lane a twenty-minute walk away.

He hadn't said much on the drive, but she felt his force as they approached their destination. Like a trapped lightning bolt that was desperate to strike.

They both wore black, blending into the darkness of the forest that surrounded the facility for miles.

Completely isolated.

"You see any security cameras?" Still nothing. She risked a glance towards him, taking her eyes off the facility. "Kyle?"

"You ready?" he asked quietly, his voice intense.

"What? Wait... fuck" she cursed as he leapt up, running across the distance to the back door. If she wasn't watching she wouldn't have seen him, her eyes struggling to track him as he disappeared into the night, appearing within seconds under a spotlight. "Shit."

She ran after him, taking longer than he did. As she appeared beneath the light he had already broken the lock on the door, pulling her through and closing it behind them within a few seconds. She remained silent, mentally cursing him as her eyes adjusted to the dimly lit office. She heard his breathing become laboured, his movements agitated as his hand continued to grip her arm, nails digging in.

"Kyle," she whispered, taking the risk before he combusted. "Breathe."

His hand released her as he shook his head, a growl erupting up his throat. "It's this place..."

"Kyle," she said, "look at me." She could feel him begin to panic.

He turned, his eyes boring into her as a snarl curved his mouth. His eyes were almost black, the whites barely showing.

"Don't kill anyone."

His face became passive, but his eyes remained dark. "I can't promise anything." He reached up, tugging his hood in irritation as he moved.

"Fuck sake."

She followed him, his movements like a ghost as he passed through the seemingly normal office until he came to the reception area.

The room was lit up bright, a beacon against the glass front.

"We need to move fast," he whispered. "The security cameras aren't monitored unless needed." He passed behind the desk, picking up paper and moving keyboards as he muttered beneath his breath.

Alice watched out the front, allowing her to call warnings as guards passed the glass in perfect synchronisation. In any other situation she would have been impressed with their consistency, except the two-minute window that left the building open to a break-in.

"Is it clear?" Kyle called quietly, his head barely visible from his crouched position behind the desk.

"Give it thirty," she replied as she hid herself against a wall, carefully tracking the guard as he walked past.

A buzz echoed through the room exactly thirty seconds later, an uncomfortably high-pitched squeal before an opening appeared behind her. She hadn't known it was even there, the door disguised behind a poster advertising 'Children of the Moon.'

"How did you know?" she asked, but he didn't answer.

The room opened into a skinny corridor, with locked doors both sides and metal steps at the end. Kyle pushed past, climbing down the stairs as if she wasn't even there. As she quickly followed the door behind slid back closed, taking with it the only light.

"*Lux Pila*," she whispered, the ball of arcane illuminating the small space before she could trip over her own feet. "Kyle?" she quietly called down, unable to see him.

His face appeared beside her, skin pale and eyes dark. "Down here," he said before disappearing again.

A crash echoed at the bottom of the stairs. Loud enough to rattle the staircase.

"Shit!" She jumped the last steps, her ball of light lazily following to allow her to watch Kyle bang into another door.

"FUCK!" he shouted, kicking at the wall before turning to push over a chair in a burst of frustration.

Her light flickered above.

The room was identical to the laboratory she had found beneath The Church of the Light, down to the table and door layout. Silver cupboards lined the walls with pipes crisscrossing the tiled ceiling, surrounding the fluorescent tube lighting. A metal table was in the middle of the room, empty glass beakers sitting on the top alongside several computers with dark screens.

The similarities made her hesitate, doubt her memory. Surely they couldn't be identical?

Kyle kicked at the wall again, shattering a few tiles that crumbled to the floor.

"Talk to me," she moved in his way, trying to calm him down as his temper flared. "What are we looking for?"

He scratched across his face, his nails piercing skin as he frantically looked around. "I can't remember." His voice broke. "I can't..." His head shot around, nostrils flaring as he leapt over the table, towards the third door on the right. He gently pressed the wall in three places, the third beeping with the tile moving away to reveal an electronic keypad.

His hand shook as he punched in six numbers, the keypad glowing green before the door opened slowly.

A light turned on automatically when he stepped into the room, his whole body shaking as he looked around.

Questions were at the tip of her tongue when she noticed what he was staring at. She moved past, pushing the plastic sheet that hung from the ceiling to take in the silver chair, covered in rust.

She hesitantly reached forward, smearing the red that wasn't rust, but dried blood. Metal cuffs hung limply from the arms, matching the ones attached to legs. Red crystals were on a small tray beside it along with a used blunt needle, red powder and a mortar and pestle.

Alice picked up the crystal, pinching it between her fingertips.

"It's called Ruby Mist," Kyle said, his voice eerily soft.

Alice turned to him as she placed the crystal back down, concerned that his eyes weren't focused.

"A scientifically engineered drug derived from Brimstone. It has the ability to give the user euphoric release for hours, strong enough to affect those normal Brimstone does not."

"Kyle," she began before his eyes shot to her, causing her to pause. "How do you know all this?"

She watched his pupils completely encompass his whites, his cheekbones sharp against his skin. His hands began to spark, green flames covering his hands that was tinged with black.

"Kyle?"

His chi flared, electric against her own as her scar pulsed in pain.

"KYLE!" She felt the heat sear, bubbling the plastic around her. The ceiling groaned as the heat intensified, fire climbing up his arms. She threw herself at him, knocking him back as the ceiling collapsed above them, kicking up dust that choked her lungs.

"THERE'S NOTHING HERE!" Kyle shot a flame back into the lab, causing the glass beakers to shatter. "THEY'RE SUPPOSED TO BE HERE!"

Alice protected her face, feeling the shards hit her arms. She sucked in a breath, pulling out the glass that luckily wasn't deep.

Fire erupted around him, curving around her as it clambered up the walls. An alarm sounded, followed by a red flashing light and sprinklers that failed to touch the growing blaze.

"We need to go!" she tried to shout above the roar of the flames. "KYLE!" A heavy weight hit her, tumbling them both to the floor. She lifted up her elbow, hitting the stranger in the nose with as much strength as she could before he was pulled off her, thrown into the flames.

Shouts followed through the room, bullets flying that forced her to duck. Kyle didn't flinch as a bullet caught his thigh, his attention on another guard.

She surprised a third, pulling his gun from his grasp and hitting him square in the nose, hard enough that he crashed to the floor out cold. She quickly removed the magazine, kicking it across the floor before removing the bullet in the chamber.

Kyle growled, the sound closer to an animal as he raced upstairs, Alice hot on his heels. Her lungs burned from the smoke that made visibility poor as she followed him out, his arms pouring flames as he moved through the rooms.

Alice caught up to him in the reception, her hand reaching out to stop him as he destroyed everything in his path.

"Wait..."

A loud bang exploded, throwing her forward.

Disoriented, she climbed to her knees, her fingers digging into the cold earth before she pushed herself up onto her feet. Kyle was panting heavily on the grass, eyes unfocused as burning debris rained down around them.

"COME ON!" She pulled him up, forcing them to both run towards the forest, seeking cover as she heard bullets whiz through the air around them.

"I need to find them... I need..." Kyle let out a pained scream, falling against a tree. He ripped off the remains of his hoody, the fabric disintegrating to pieces in his hand before he scratched down his face, leaving red marks.

"Hey, come on. We're almost there." Alice frantically looked around, hoping to recognise where they were. She finally noticed her beat up beetle just past a few more trees. "Look, it's just over…"

Alice ran to Kyle, his eyes rolled back in his head while the slave bands glowed angrily against his skin. He convulsed, shaking violently as she tried to keep him still. A heartbeat later he stopped, unconscious.

"Shit, shit, shit," she chanted, tugging him across the dry leaves towards the car. She lifted him awkwardly into the passenger seat, careful with his head as she ran to the driving side, stalling the car several times in her panic.

She made it home just as the sun threatened to waken the sky, her car screeching to a halt on her drive. She flinched when she dropped him out the car, his head awkwardly clanging against the car door before she was able to grip him under his arm.

"What happened?" Sam asked quietly from the front door, his cat eyes night glowing.

He quickly took Kyle's weight, lifting him onto his shoulder as Alice locked the car, following him up to her bedroom where Sam carefully placed him on her bed.

"Bloody hell, he's heavier than he looks." Sam stepped back, his arms folded over his naked chest. His hair was loose around his shoulders, messy as if he had just been asleep. "What are those around his wrists?"

"Slave bands," Alice replied quietly as she removed Kyles boots.

Sam reached to the left band. "Why hasn't he removed… FUCK!" he hissed, shaking his hand before he sucked on his finger. "Fucking, ow."

"You okay?" she asked as she dropped Kyles boots.

"Yeah, it fucking burnt me." He nodded to the floor. "What's that?"

"What's what?" She followed his view, noticed a piece of paper at the edge of Kyles boot. It had fallen on its side when she dropped them. Bending down she picked it up, opening the folded sheet. It was an article reporting the sudden disappearance of Mason Storm, his photograph circled in red several times.

"Why would your brother have that?" Sam asked.

Alice crushed the paper in her hand. "I don't know."

CHAPTER EIGHT

Alice rolled over, the bed unfamiliar, lumpy and uncomfortable beneath her. She frowned, opening her eyes to stare at the posters of semi-naked people that were taped to the walls. She didn't have half-naked anything taped to her walls. It took her a second to realise she wasn't in her room, but Sam's.

She groaned, rubbing her eyes before she swung her legs over, her feet touching Sam's new luxury rug. He had worked hard to decorate the house to the best of his ability, painting walls and repairing the damage until it was their home. Other than the ridiculous posters his room was beautiful, a haven of calming colours and soft furnishings with bursts of his personality.

Alice smiled at the mess at the end of his bed, clothes thrown carelessly even though he had an empty laundry hamper in the corner. It had taken him years to be able to leave a mess in his bedroom, to not make his bed with military precision and to organise his wardrobe by colours followed by style. Years for him to realise his father wasn't there to beat him if it wasn't orderly, to add to the many scars that already decorated his body. The worst was shifters didn't usually scar, their healing ability when shifting from one form to the other repairing wounds. Yet, his chest said another story, one where the damage was either too much, or that his father had used salt to seal the abuse so even when he shifted, the visual scars remained.

Alice was glad the man who didn't deserve to be a father was dead, because not all monsters looked like monsters.

She crept along the hallway, opening the door to her bedroom quietly. Kyle was still passed out on the bed, in the exact same position he was dropped in. He looked peaceful, younger even. Almost as young as she remembered, a lanky teenager that needed to grow into his shoulders. The morning light shone across his chest, causing the pale scars that criss-crossed the majority of his exposed skin to glow.

Sam was gently snoring in a chair, his legs stretched with his feet balanced on the footboard. His hair was draped like a blanket across his chest, hiding his own scars.

Her heart hurt when she looked at them both, her brothers who shouldn't have physical reminders of their traumas. Traumas that hadn't ruined them, but shaped them into who they were today. Strong men, survivors.

She decided to let them sleep, closing the door behind her before she made her way downstairs as her stomach grumbled to life. The TV was playing a cartoon, Jordan the gnome happily watching it from his position on the sofa. He had somehow managed to move the pillows so they surrounded him, the usual massive grin on his porcelain face.

" Good morning Jordan," she greeted automatically, even knowing he wouldn't reply. He never did.

The last few weeks he had become increasingly annoying. Moving around more than usual, changing channels while she and Sam were watching the TV and generally being a nuisance. They knew when he was in a mood as he would leave random piles of red dust. They had no idea where he was getting it from, having realised it was brick dust.

Did he randomly own some stock? Or did he destroy the bricks himself? Also, what did he have against bricks? How passive-aggressive was that?

It was like having an irritating toddler who existed only to watch TV and make them jump when he hid in cupboards. They had discussed calling in a specialist in haunted objects, but felt guilty every time. Especially when he brought them fresh flowers and herbs.

Alice picked up a stale cookie, shoving it into her mouth as she made herself cereal. Her spoon was halfway to her lips when the doorbell sounded.

Cursing she stormed to the front door, swinging it open before the bell could go again and wake the boys.

"Oh, Detective O'Neil." She blinked up at him, the morning light blinding as he stepped over the threshold.

"Good morning, I apologise if it's too early," he said as he frowned at her.

She automatically tugged at the hem of the sleep shirt, trying to cover as much dignity as she could.

"Cute pyjamas."

She looked down, smirking as she realised what she was wearing. "I got it for Winter Solstice." As a witch she never really celebrated the humans' Christmas holiday, but Sam had seen it in a store and couldn't resist it.

Her shirt read *'Santa's favourite Ho'* in bright red typography.

"Would you like tea?"

"No thank you, I won't be long." He cleared his throat, his hand reaching up to touch the cigarette that lived behind his right ear. "I'll get straight to the point. I've been made aware that you have been suspended until further notice."

Alice felt her shoulders sag. She had hoped it wouldn't have affected her work with Spook Squad.

"I have a meeting with my superiors later to argue it, but until then you are not officially part of the team."

"Have they replaced me yet?"

"I wouldn't know, I haven't answered any calls from the new Commissioner." He looked annoyed. "The team have been informed."

Alice just nodded, unsure what to say. She had wanted to talk to the boys regarding Ruby Mist, hiding the questions within a case. Peyton had the packet from Dr Pierce, and was already making enquiries.

"I'll let myself out."

Alice wandered back into the kitchen, staring at her soggy cereal on the counter.

"Shit," she cursed, frustrated. "Shit, shit, shit."

She picked up her bowl, about to pour the cereal away when a piece of paper caught her eye. Settling the bowl back down she reached for the magazine article found in Kyles boot, her eyes settling onto Mason Storm's face.

Why had her brother had his image?

Alice folded the article back up, placing it in her own pocket. She only knew one man to ask where Mason Storm could possibly be, and now she knew where to find him.

CHAPTER NINE

Alice smiled at the receptionist as she approached the glass desk outside Mason's old office. She was even more beautiful than Alice remembered, her eyebrows plucked to perfection with a red shade of lipstick that made the blue of her eyes shine. Her top was cut almost unprofessionally low compared to the last time, where she wore a modest silk shirt and pencil skirt.

It had only been a few weeks, yet the receptionist remembered Alice immediately, her eyes narrowing in an immediately hostile way. Not that she blamed her, she did arrest her last boss last time.

"Do you have an appointment?" she asked, arching an eyebrow.

"Oh, no..."

Alice hadn't spoken to Riley since the church, where they watched it burn to pieces against the darkness of the night. She had watched it for hours in the snow, her knees frozen as fire fighters fought the blaze. He had disappeared when it finally collapsed, leaving her alone with questions.

But time was up.

She knew he would be busy organising his father's empire while trying to defend his family name. Mason had disappeared off the face of the earth, abandoning his business and his son. His stocks had dropped, speculation of where he was, was front page on every major newspaper in the city. Alleged affairs, drug charges and other nefarious rumours were floated around by his rivals, destroying his reputation.

And she didn't care.

He was the monster who had murdered her parents. Who was behind the recent attempted genocide that almost became an epidemic, and who had tortured his own son.

And none of that mattered.

What mattered was why his face had been circled by her brother.

"But I need to speak to him immediately."

"He's busy," she muttered as she clicked on her computer. "I can fit you in sometime next month."

"No, I need..."

The door swung open with a bang, hard enough to rattle the pencil pot at the edge of her desk. Xander stormed out, his mouth curled in a silent snarl. He ground to a halt when he noticed her standing there.

"Alice, maybe you can talk some sense into him." She felt his eyes bore into her through his dark glasses before he left.

She smiled at the receptionist, the friendly gesture not reciprocated. "I guess he's free now?"

"Alice?" the receptionist squeaked. "Are you Alice Skye?"

"Ah, yes. That's me."

"You're on the pre-approved list." She looked confused even as she said it. "Please, go in."

"Thanks," Alice muttered as she gently pushed the door, closing it behind her as Riley stood by the desk, paper clutched in his fist. His back was to her, his shoulders encased in a dark fitted suit, his blue black hair brushing the white of his shirt collar.

He didn't smile when he turned, his expression more perplexed as he raised an eyebrow.

"Alice? What are you doing here?" he frowned as he shuffled the paper.

"Hey," she said, awkwardly waving.

"I didn't think we had training." he said, placing the paperwork down before he crossed his arms, straining the suit.

She shook her head as she fought a laugh. She hadn't been able to contact him, her patience running thin as she stubbornly practiced the routine he had started to teach her.

"You were too busy to see me." She had wanted to help, that he didn't need to deal with his father alone. Except, he didn't want her comfort. He had made that perfectly clear.

"I seem to remember you slamming your door in my face."

"Yeah, well…" She had wanted to speak to him, train, but began to feel like she was distracting him, like she was a burden. She wasn't anybody's damsel in distress. "Like I said, you were too busy."

"Stubborn as ever, I see," he smirked.

Alice ignored the comment. "What's wrong with Xander?"

His smile faltered, face tightening as he leant against the desk. "Trying to talk me out of something."

"Out of what?"

He just smiled further in response.

"Of course you don't answer, you never do."

"What's that supposed to mean?"

Shit, she thought to herself. She needed not to piss him off, at least until after she knew more.

"I like what you've done with the place."

He had moved the oversized desk to the other half of the room, the nature reserve a burst of green through the floor to ceiling glass, a beautiful contrast to the masculine shades of the room. The bookshelves had been emptied and the extra seating had been removed, leaving lighter marks on the carpet.

"It's emptier." She smiled before she noticed the oil painting to her left, where the desk once was. She reached toward it, able to feel the brush strokes through the paint of the stylised beast.

She understood what it was, who it was. Could imagine Mason sitting there, the painting a powerful image that was an artistic representation of his son.

Maybe she had wanted to give him time to settle his affairs, allow Riley some space to deal with his father's betrayal. Or maybe she needed some time to deal with what she saw, an animal that was predominantly a wolf, but its forearms bigger, closer to a lion with serrated claws and fangs as long as daggers. Not forgetting the multiple tails, quick as whips.

A creature that doesn't exist in lore or myth, at least, nothing she could find.

Alice felt his presence beside her, but she couldn't look away.

It was powerful, beautiful in a dangerous way.

Like the man.

"I'm stripping my father's businesses, selling them off," he said quietly, as if he could disturb the image in front of him. "It's taken a lot of my attention recently."

"Well, it's not like he needs them." She tore her gaze away, feeling uneasy. "You had any luck tracking him down?"

Riley caught her eye, his iris' flashing silver that tore a shiver down her spine.

"No," he coughed, clearing his throat as he walked back towards his desk, shuffling the paperwork. "I'm sorry I haven't been there."

Alice shrugged, watching him work. "Don't worry about it, I get you're busy."

They had a complicated relationship, going out of their way to be separated unless forced. But when they were together... Alice shook her head, clearing her mind as her chi automatically reached out to stroke his. His presence unnerved her, confused her. What made it even more complex was that he seemed just as confused by their connection.

"What's with the paperwork?" she asked.

He scrutinised her, trying to read her expression. "Just contracts and blueprints. I'm trying to break up this organisation without impacting the charity."

"Charity?" She looked at the paperwork, noticing the title. "Children of the Moon?" Alice had first heard of them at the charity gala, a local charity that worked on a cure to the children born with the vampira virus, a virus that somehow infected an unborn foetus whose parents weren't vampires. It was an incurable affliction that resulted in around five per cent of the deaths in under-threes.

"That's it. : My father was more than just a regular donor, it seems he's one of the main names behind it." He pushed the paperwork away, his jaw clenched. "The only thing my father could do right was business. Could make money from anywhere, even sick kids."

Alice picked it up, reading the blueprint. "Moon Rooms?"

"Yeah, they were supposed to be the newest additions. Rooms designed for the sole comfort of the children. They were approved but never funded for some reason. It's why I'm going through the paperwork." He sighed, looking tired. "There's so much missing. Documents redacted with the solicitors having no idea. I have records of three facilities that my father has funded for Children of the Moon. One is a basic office that accepts public donations, another is Barretts Hospice where the children reside. The third was the lab that was working on a cure, but was destroyed early this morning."

Alice's eyes shot up over the blueprint. "Destroyed?"

Fuck, fuck, fuck.

"Yeah, apparently there was an explosion. Suspicious, don't you think?"

Fuck, fuck, fuck.

"Ahhh…"

"But right now I want to know where the money is actually going."

"You think your father used the charity as a diversion?"

Riley let out an exasperated sigh. "I don't know. So much doesn't add up. He hasn't touched any of his bank accounts, which means he has more that aren't on record. I need to find them."

His eyes shot to hers, a frown curling his mouth.

"So are you going to tell me why you're here? I don't believe this is a casual visit."

"I just wanted an update on Mason."

Riley stepped toward her, folding his arms. "Why?"

"Because it's my business." She tilted her head up, standing ground as he stood over a head taller. "I deserve to know where he is, where he is hiding."

"You think I know where he is?"

"Do you?"

Riley laughed, the sound hollow. "Trust me, he wouldn't still be breathing if I knew." He made a sound of frustration. "He's a fucking ghost."

"We will find him." She knew he couldn't hide forever.

"We? He's my father. I will find him. I will…" His eyes were heated when his palm touched her cheek. "I don't need help."

Her chi reacted violently before she stepped back. "Barba tenus sapientes," she muttered.

Riley frowned. "Wise as far as his beard?"

"It means you're an idiot."

Probably. She had heard Dread mutter it when she was a child.

"I don't think you understand what that phrase means." He smirked, the expression changing his face.

"Mr Storm," his receptionist interrupted with a breathy squeak. "Your appointment is here."

"Give me a minute, Rachel," he said without looking up.

"Guess that's me being dismissed." Alice turned toward the door, hiding a smirk as Rachel shot her an evil stare when Riley tugged her wrist gently.

"I have to go to this party tonight. Did you want to come?"

"A party?" She turned back at him like, shooting a look like he was crazy.

Did he just say party?

"I need a plus one and can't think of anybody more observant than you."

"Wow, I sound like a ringing endorsement." She tugged at her wrist. "Why would I want to come to one of your rich, pretentious friend's parties?"

"Firstly, he isn't my friend. Secondly, I need you to be my eyes and ears. Think of it as a contract, one where I will pay."

"Contract?" Alice thought about it. "Can't you take Xander?"

Riley growled. "No."

"I don't need your money." She did actually, but she wasn't going to admit she was suspended without pay.

"Then think of it as a favour to me. The party is tonight and I need you."

"Tonight? I can't, I already have plans."

"Look, I'm not asking you on a date. We won't be late and it's not a typical party. Besides, you're curious why I invited you."

Alice narrowed her eyes. *Fuck sake.* He had her.

"What's at this party?" she asked.

He smiled as if he had won.

Alice narrowed her eyes. "This doesn't mean I have forgotten about Mason, he isn't just yours to hunt."

Riley smiled. "We shall see."

Alice felt annoyed as she shuffled in her bag, fighting through her random vials, empty chocolate packets and a sunglasses case in search of her car keys. She had gone to Riley in search of Mason, but was no closer to finding him.

"Fuck sake," she muttered as she knocked her bag over, losing the contents underneath her car. She bent to pick up a runaway mascara when something smacked against the metal. Her head shot up, frowning at the small hole in the passenger side door that she swore wasn't there before.

She spun on her heel, abandoning her bag as she saw a long black coat billowing as someone ran down the busy street, in full daylight.

"HEY!" she shouted. "YOU HIT MY BLOODY CAR!"

She shot in the direction, dodging pedestrians and businessmen as she chased the shadow down an alley beside a busy restaurant. He spun, his floor-length leather jacket catching on his legs as he flicked his wrist, a metal star appearing in his hand.

"*ARMA!*" she shouted.

Just as her spherical shield formed she felt a heavy weight hit her side, pushing her into the circle and breaking the connection before it could complete. She hit the concrete hard, her palms taking the brunt of the force as a man shuffled to his feet beside her, wand pointed as a star pierced through the air above them, embedding itself into brick.

"*Rigescuntius indutae!*" he shouted, a light shooting from the end.

"How many are you?" she asked as she launched herself behind an industrial sized bin as another throwing star sliced through the air.

"He isn't with me," the man snarled as he knelt down beside her, the end of his wand glowing. "We don't want you dead."

"We? Who's we?"

A gun cocked, the click deafening before bullets rained above her.

"*Scutumium praesidium.*" The glow intensified around his wand, creating a shield of light that deflected the bullets.

Just as quickly as they had begun, the bullets stopped.

Alice carefully stood up, the man gone.

"What the fuck was that?" She reached up, pulling the throwing star from the wall carefully.

"It seems you have a price on your head," the man replied behind her. "Can you hand over the weapon please?"

"I think I'll keep it," she replied as she clutched it harder, studying the sharp, serrated edges. Her finger traced the engraved sword across the metal, it's circular pommel depicting a sun. "Now, who the fuck are you?"

She dropped her arm, looking up at the man. He was as tall as her, which made him short for a man. What he lacked in height, he doubled in presence. His face was harsh, his eyes dark as he studied her carefully.

"I'm guessing you're from The Magika?" He was powerful, his wand skills the best she had ever seen. "Were you following me or was this just a happy ole coincidence?"

Why was someone from the Department of Magic & Mystery following her?

"I've been tasked to watch you," he replied, his voice unusually deep.

"Of course you have."

Just what I need, another fucking shadow.

"I take my role within the Magika very seriously."

"How good for you. So who was the other guy?"

He shrugged before folding his arms across his chest, his wand still clutched in his palm. "Possibly an assassin."

"An assassin? Of course." She looked down at the throwing star again. She wasn't going to give it up, not until she researched the symbol. As if she didn't have enough on her plate.

"The Magika have taken an interest in you. You're an asset that can't be damaged, at least not yet."

'Wow," she replied dryly. "Aren't you optimistic."

"I'm more of a realist. Whoever is after you is dangerous, you should watch yourself."

"And The Magika isn't dangerous?"

He smirked, the expression unfriendly. "You'll be seeing me around."

"Great," she replied sarcastically. "I can't wait."

CHAPTER TEN

The car spluttered to a stop, barely making it onto her drive before the exhaust backfired with a loud bang. The heating had broken weeks ago, so Alice made sure she kept spare gloves and scarves in the glove compartment at all times, especially as it was still technically winter. Unfortunately, her new air conditioning in the door was larger than she thought. She hadn't even noticed until she had driven off, the bullet's exit hole in the driver's side double the size.

She needed a new car desperately, but between house repairs, their fondness for takeaway and general living expenses they didn't have much spare.

Alice looked up at the tired brick, noticing all the repairs that were still needed. It was coming along slowly, the house of horror that was slowly turning into a home. It had taken her a while to be used to staying there, to not remember the nightmares, the death, the blood. But now she remembered all the happy memories, of her childhood as well as new ones with Sam, ones she cherished.

The house was messy when she entered, the box of Christmas decorations still sitting there after Sam's half-arse attempt of putting it all away. They were Breed, they didn't celebrate the human holiday, yet Sam turned up one evening with a tree and some baubles. She couldn't tell his grinning face to take it back outside, even when half the needles of the tree fell off within the first day.

"Hey Jordan," she greeted her mute gnome as she retrieved the throwing star from her bag, holding the cold metal in her palm. "You didn't fancy helping out, huh?"

Jordan was half-hidden behind the sofa, his pale face poking out with tinsel wrapped around his head. He looked the most festive, with his blue coat, green belt and red-capped hat.

"Talking to inanimate objects is a sign of insanity," a voice said, amused.

Alice spun, her hand gripping the throwing star hard enough to bite into her skin.

"I'm sorry, did I startle you?" Mason sneered, standing in her kitchen doorway with a cup of tea on one hand and a leather bound book in the other.

His face looked painful, the fire damage she had inflicted barely healed.

"How did you get in here?"

He just sipped his drink, a smug expression on his face. "I'm not here for violence." He dropped her cup, the porcelain shattering at his feet. "If I were, I would have killed you in your sleep." His eyes settled on her throwing star, interested but not commenting.

Alice strained as she tried to hear movement upstairs, not knowing whether Kyle or Sam was still home.

"What do you want Mason?" She needed him to leave.

"Do you see how hard it was to find you, Alice?" he smirked.

"What, you mean at my house? Yeah, real hard."

His face tightened. "I like what you did with the place, you have much better taste than your parents." He looked around before he stepped forward, the broken cup crunching beneath his boot. "I hope you don't mind that I had a curious look around, although, I do prefer the old paint colour."

She felt sick each time he mentioned her parents, how he reminded her that they were old work colleagues, even friends.

Until he betrayed them.

"Well, to the point then," he said as he brought up the book, a white piece of paper taped to the front.

"Mason, what..."

He looked at the paper. "It seems I just missed your pussy cat... and your brother. Shame really, it could have been interesting..."

"Stay away from them," she snarled. "You don't need them."

"Maybe," he grinned before he threw the book down. It hit the floor with a heavy bang. "I'm here with a proposition, I thought you would take notice If I showed you how easy it was to get to you. And to get to your family."

She threw the star, the weapon searing through the air before it indented in the wall beside his head. With her hands free she unsheathed her blade, allowing the runes to glow and for a flame to settle along the steel.

"You seem a bit emotional, did I touch a nerve?" His eyes flickered to the star, almost an anxious gesture which he quickly hid with a smile. "I'll make this quick then. Give me your brother, or I'll take your cat."

"Why do you want Kyle?" Her voice was deeper than usual, her anger vivid. Tinkerbell popped into existence to join her blade, the blue ball of light and fire sparkling. A physical manifestation of her rage. Normally she would have been embarrassed at the show of weakness, but instead she concentrated on it, allowing it to clear her head, think past her anger.

"Because since you have destroyed my facility, he is my only investment. I'm having to rebuild everything because of you."

"How is he your investment? What have you done to him?"

Tinkerbell shot forward, growing in mass before it sizzled to the floor an inch from his face. She felt her chi ache as Mason tested her strength, his face slightly puzzled as he tried to force her magic from her, and failed.

Alice couldn't help her teasing smile, one that dropped from her face when he lifted his hand to show a phone, one with a static image of Sam on the screen.

"Here, this was taken only moments ago." He threw it her direction.

She allowed it to clatter to the ground, screen face up. She could see Sam grinning, several shopping bags in each hand.

"It makes sure you don't do anything stupid with that sword of yours. If they don't receive a call from me within ten minutes they have orders to execute."

"They? Who's they?"

He ignored the question. "I'll give you a few days to decide."

Alice felt herself go cold, panic taking over.

"If you tell *anyone*, I will take Sam anyway and I will make sure his screams are heard throughout the city." He walked closer, unconcerned about her blade, knowing she wouldn't risk Sam.

He slowly picked up the phone, keeping eye contact until he left.

Without thought she dialled Sam, her heart in her throat as she waited patiently for him to answer.

"Hey baby girl, you okay?" he answered thirty seconds later.

"Sam?" She breathed a sigh of relief. "Are you okay? Where are you?"

"Okay? Baby girl I'm shopping, of course I'm okay," he laughed. *"You haven't forgotten about tonight have you?"*

"Of course not." It was Sam's birthday, she knew he would be shopping, he did it every year. She just wasn't thinking clearly. "I might be a little late though."

"Late? Why?"

She could hear him whining, even through the phone. She couldn't help but smile. "I have this thing with Riley…"

"Riley, aye?"

"It's a work thing, nothing else," she assured him.

"Alice, are you sure you're okay? You sound upset."

"Fine, I'm fine." He knew her too well, she needed to distract him. "There's this book…"

"Yeah…" He sounded hesitant, as if he knew she was changing the subject on purpose. *"It's from Dread. Look, I have to go, I'll see you later though, yeah?"*

"Of course, I'll meet you there. Love you."

"Love you baby girl," he said as he hung up.

Her eyes settled on the book, the leather darker than her flooring, almost black. She picked it up, scowling at the deep scratches on the wood from where the book caught the cup shards.

She cleaned the mess, settling the debris in the bin before she finally brought her attention back to the book. It was plain, almost non-descript beneath the paper taped to the front. There were no markings on the binder, no name or date. The paper itself was thick, high quality with a professionally typed letter while a messily handwritten note was scrawled in the corner.

Gone out shopping for tonight. Kyle left just as this was delivered from Overlord's minion.
Sam xx

Alice,

I'm sorry I had to leave you like this, but it's paramount that you continue working on control. You must learn about your heritage to recognise your power. I cannot explain everything right now, not when people are watching. Please understand that I have done everything possible to keep you out of harm's way, to protect you as your parents would have.
I hope I have not failed.
You would have been delivered a book, a grimoire. It was one of your mother's, something I never wanted you to have, but it seems I have no choice. Use it wisely.
Your ancestry is why you're in danger, but also how you will survive.
Dread.

Alice stared at the note, unable to process the words. Dread had always known what she was, or at least suspected. Had chosen not to tell her, to teach her. She couldn't understand why.

Alice touched the leather, the skin softer than it looked as she began to open the first page. A snarl erupted from the grimoire, loud enough she snapped her hand back.

"What the..."

She went to touch it again, but this time it growled.

Alice looked around like something else was in the room, the noises not possibly coming from the plain leather book? She pushed it with one finger, the grimoire not reacting at all to the disturbance. As quick as she could she opened it up to a random page, ignoring the snarl even as a slight pain erupted at the end of her finger.

A small pearl of blood appeared at the tip, the single drop splashing onto the page before being absorbed, leaving nothing behind.

Did the book just bite me? What the fuck!

She waited a few seconds before she touched the creamy page, her mother's familiar handwriting comforting as she felt the indents the pen had made on the paper. She hadn't known this book existed, the fact Dread kept it from her hurt worse than anything else. He knew she craved knowledge about her parents, her childhood memories unreliable, confused with trauma.

But as she read she felt a sense of trepidation, the words wrong, dark, dangerous.

It explained why the grimoire snarled when opened.

A warning perhaps?

Alice was an earth witch, someone who used natural ingredients.

She would use plants and her own blood to quicken spells, not fish, goats or even flesh like some of the spells depicted in the book.

She thought her mother had also been an earth witch, but according to the grimoire she had been anything but. Misfortune, revenge, reanimating, summoning, binding and banishing were just some of the worrying spells and curses hand written with detailed instructions. Everything required a sacrifice, starting from living blood to 'of large mass.'

Many recipes were incomplete while some pages were ripped out entirely or redacted with a pen.

Protection Ward
A superior ward that removes dark energy as well as preventing those who have bad intentions. Must be updated regularly with fresh blood.

WHAT YOU WILL NEED:
Bulb of sage
Salt chalk
Redwood soaked in blood (preferably human, but witch is also acceptable)
Matchstick

METHOD:
Burn the redwood to ash, adding it onto the sage bulb making sure to get it into the crevices. Using the salt chalk, draw the protection symbols below at every open pathway. Using a virgin matchstick burn the end of the sage and redwood mix. Blow it out, leaving the embers glowing, allowing the resulting smoke to cover the symbols.

Alice cursed, the page ripped with the symbols missing.

"Fuck sake," she cursed, flipping through the pages, hoping it was elsewhere. "Shit, shit, shit."

It was incomplete. She needed a ward, needed one desperately. Her home wasn't safe and she wasn't sure a normal protection spell would work. There was a reason Dread had given her the book, knew it would hold stronger spells.

She just had to decide whether she was happy with working with black magic.

CHAPTER ELEVEN

Alice watched the night sky, the stars outside the city brighter, more beautiful. Her mind raced, wondered what Dread could be doing, causing her anxiety she didn't need.

He had sent her the grimoire, timing it perfectly as he did everything. But it was incomplete, dangerous spells torn and missing, spells she was brought up to never use. Warned by her parents, by Dread and by The Magika themselves.

Yet it was her mother's handwriting, spells of death and decay. Black magic that was punishable by death, unless proposed directly under The Magika.

Hypocrites, she thought as she picked at the hem of her dress.

The organisation that governed her Breed made the laws, but could break them if they wished. As most people or governments in power seemed to do, Alice was beginning to understand.

And now they were interested in her. A witch who wasn't even registered with them. She wasn't even classed in any of the magic, never thought it was worth the effort to be tested.

Why should an uptight witch several times her age decide how much of a witch she was?

"Hey, are you okay?" Riley asked, his deep voice breaking through her stupor. "We're here and you haven't spoken a word in the car ride over."

She blinked up to him, the inside of the car dark compared to the glowing lights outside.

"Ah, yeah. Sorry, I was daydreaming."

He let out a masculine chuckle, the sound making her tingle.

Get it together, Alice!

"So," she started, trying to gain her composure. "What's this party for?" She smiled at the attendant who opened her door, helping her out the car.

"A rich arsehole who knows everybody," he said as he handed his keys to the valet.

She hadn't even noticed the ridiculously expensive car when he picked her up, knew nothing of it other than it was ludicrously low to the ground and the inside looked like a space ship. It was also alarmingly yellow, bright even in the darkness.

Pompous yellow, she smirked to herself, gaining a curious look from Riley.

"Is there anything I need to do?" She had left her weapons at home, at his request. Well, most of her weapons. She wasn't going anywhere unarmed after Mason's warning. So she had a small throwing knife attached to her thigh, sharp enough to do damage if she needed it to.

But, if he asked her to be unarmed, he didn't need her as backup.

So why was she there?

"I plan to speak to the host, while I'm there I need you to look around."

"Look around?" she looked at him quizzically. "For what?"

Riley shrugged. "Anything?" His eyes were bright when he caught her attention. "He's famous for holding expensive and illegal artefacts. Thought you might find them of interest."

"Is there really any point to me being here?" she asked, even though it was more of a whine.

"Look out for a gold shield, my father lent it to him a decade ago and never received it back. It's worth millions."

"So you think your father has been in contact?"

"Possible. Bernard knows everyone that's anyone. He's a great collector of the unusual. He sought to buy the shield, but was refused. Instead my father agreed to lend it, for a large sum."

He pulled her towards his chest, close enough she could smell his cologne.

"Pre-warning," he whispered against her ear, "our host is...

different."

She looked at his face, waiting to see his smile that would tell her he was joking.

"Different?"

What the hell does he mean by that?

"You're joking, right?" she said dubiously.

"Trust me," he said as he spun her towards the house, his hand a warm presence at the bottom of her back.

The building was a centuries old manor, with beautiful spiralled columns and large, bright windows. Ivy clung to the brick, covering most of the front from the large double door to the top all the way to the fourth floor, where a balcony protruded. From the lights that illuminated the long driveway she could barely make out the vast grounds, the topiary and greenery pruned to perfection.

A woman stood by the front door, a black lace ball gown hugged to her hourglass figure. She flicked a long cigarette holder when she noticed them, a smirk painted on her light pink lips.

"Riley Storm, didn't think you would be here," she purred. "Does he know?"

"You know how I like to surprise everyone, Anastasia."

"You sure do," she chuckled as they passed her, blowing a cloud of smoke in their wake. "He's in a mood, so good luck."

Riley guided them through the grand entrance, politely smiling at a few men wearing tuxedos and women in beautiful expensive gowns.

Shit.

Alice nervously tugged her hem, the dress ending just below her knee. He had asked her to a party, but didn't specify a dress code so she settled on a simple red silk spaghetti strap ensemble that could easily be worn at Sam's party afterwards. She thought she looked nice, even girly considering her wardrobe mostly consisted of black, shades of grey and novelty T-shirts.

Riley in comparison wore a simple suit, not as pretentious as the tuxedos others wore, but still more formal.

"You have got to be kidding me," she muttered as they entered into the grand hall, all eyes turning to them. Everybody wore black, which made her stick out like a sore thumb.

As if she didn't stand out enough already.

"Don't worry, you look more beautiful than any of these posers," Riley whispered to her, his hand rubbing a small reassuring circle.

The affection caught her off guard. That wasn't their relationship, they didn't comment on each other that way. She admitted they had a weird sexual tension, but they didn't acknowledge it. Did they?

"Riley," a silver haired gentleman walked over, an ivory walking stick in one hand and a beautiful woman in the other. "I wasn't aware you were coming."

"I thought I would surprise you, Bernard."

Bernard strained to smile, his skin barely moving. "Quite." His eyes flicked to Alice, the irises pure black. "Who's your guest?"

"I'm Alice," she said, holding her hand when he offered his own. He grinned when she touched him, miniature fangs protruding from his gums. "I've never seen anything like you before..." he teased, appraising her like a prized horse.

"And I you," she said as she studied his features. She thought his pupils were dilated, hiding the colour his irises once were, and his fangs looked similar to those of a cat. But he wasn't a shifter, she was sure of it. "What are you?" she asked without thought.

Bernard shot a warning look towards Riley. "I see your guest can't hold her tongue."

"Careful," Riley warned him.

"I didn't mean to offend," Alice said as she stretched her chi to touch his, feeling nothing other than a bland aura in response. It ruled out a magic user. "I'm just curious, I've never met someone quite so... unique."

"Unique?" Bernard smirked, amused at her comment. "What do you think I am?"

Alice hesitated. "Your skin is pale, eyes dark and you have fangs, even though they are short. Your characteristics hint of vampire, yet you can't possibly be."

"What makes you say that?" he asked, as the woman on his arm looked bored at the conversation.

"You feel too human." Vampires once turned lose their sense of humanity, Bernard still felt human. She couldn't explain it.

His smile dropped. "Hmmm." He brought his attention back to Riley, dismissing Alice with a flick of his hand. "Why don't you join me in my parlour?"

"After you."

They left towards another room, leaving Alice alone with the beautiful woman who was on his arm. She looked at her with disinterest before she was distracted by another of the guests.

"Champagne?" a waiter asked as he showed her his gold mirrored tray.

"Sure," Alice said as she grabbed one, sipping the beverage with delight. The grand hall was uncomfortably large for a residential home, with guests milling around the waiters handing out drinks and hors d'oeuvres. Everything was white marble brushed with gold, which clashed with the bright art work that decorated the walls, alongside statues and glass cabinets filled with seemingly unrelated stuff.

It reminded Alice of a museum, one that had no theme. Twin staircases curved into a mezzanine balcony above, with even more art work.

Armour, swords, beautifully handcrafted tapestries and jewellery made from the largest stones she had ever seen. But no shield.

Alice stared at a particularly interesting wooden chalice, the iridescent paint a mixture of bright colours. It seemed to glow in the light, giving it an ethereal quality.

"How strange, I have never seen it do that," a delicate voice said from beside her.

"Why strange?" Alice asked the exceedingly thin woman. It took her a few seconds to recognise her as a faerie, her androgynous features making it hard to tell. It was the slight curve of her breast that gave it away, almost bare in the extremely low cut dress.

Violet eyes turned to her. "It's glowing," she stated, as if that explained everything.

Diamonds decorated her throat, tied together with what looked like tree roots, not the usual gold or silver. Fae had an aversion to iron, a popular metal that kept the majority of Fae within their own realm, known to everybody as the Far Side. A parallel timeline consisting of glamour and magic. The Fae kept the doors to their realm a guarded secret, with nobody allowed to enter without consent from royalty.

Half their kingdom was ruled by the Dark King, who held the Unseelie Court, while the other half - the Seelie Court - was ruled by the Light Queen.

Over the centuries only a handful of non-Fae had entered, with even fewer returning.

"Does it not normally glow?"

Those violet eyes stared, an unrecognisable expression across her face. "It is the Chalice of Destiny, an ancient Fae artefact that doesn't deserve to be treated in such a way."

Her face blurred, her glamour shifting with her anger before it settled itself. Alice glanced at the glamour beneath, wondering why the faerie had intentionally made herself uglier. Not all faeries were androgynous, Alice had met a few with very distinct features. It was as if the fashion was to all look the certain way.

"What does it do?"

From the horrified look, it was the wrong question.

"It's the Chalice of Destiny," she snapped. "For whomever the artefact deems worthy, the chalice will fill with a gold liquid. If you were to drink, it is said it will grant you your greatest wish, your destiny."

"Had anybody ever been offered the drink?"

The Fae's lips lifted into a snarl.

Guess that was also the wrong question, Alice mused. *Faeries are so bloody touchy.*

"It should be back home, not here." She reached out to touch it, the glass stopping her. "But either way it shouldn't be glowing. It is said that it only glows in the presence of royalty."

Alice shrugged before sipping more of her champagne. "Maybe there's a Fae prince here tonight?"

"Do not joke about such things," she sneered. "A prince would never sully himself earth side."

"What's wrong with earth side?" That was the problem with higher caste Fae, they had superiority issues. "It seems good enough for you?"

"They would not be able to survive here, not enough magic to sustain them in this realm." She looked shocked that she answered.

Fae couldn't lie. It wasn't known whether they have the inability to lie, or have simply been forbidden by the High Lords, the oldest and most powerful amongst their kind. It meant high caste Fae such as faeries would manipulate their answers, twisting words into half-truths.

"Isn't royal knowledge a secret, Riahlia?" a masculine voice said. "Wouldn't the High Lords be disappointed?"

Riahlia tensed, anger apparent in the lines of her shoulders. "Is that a threat, Mr Blackwell?"

"Would I ever threaten you?" Nate smirked before he winked at Alice.

Riahlia hissed, her eyes narrowed. "I will remember this," she said in a huff before walking off.

"Alice, how nice to see you." He sipped his glass, his tuxedo just as expensive as the others. "I wouldn't take you for a party girl."

"I'm just the plus one, I'm afraid." She gestured to her dress. "I obviously didn't get the dress code."

"Never apologise for being the most interesting in the room," he stated, his eyes intense.

"Alice." A hand touched her arm, the presence familiar. "You ready to go?" Riley eyed Nate, his expression less than friendly. "Blackwell."

"Storm," Nate replied just as frostily. "Shame about your father, he was a powerful man."

"You know better than anyone not to believe the tabloids."

"Ah, but sometimes it's interesting when they hold a grain of truth."

Riley stared for a second, looking like he was going to answer before he turned to Alice. "Ready?"

Alice saw the two security guards wandering closer, their attention trained on Riley. One held his hand cautiously close to the visible weapon on his hip, his finger twitching.

Guess we better go.

She smiled a goodbye at Nate, keeping the trigger happy guard in her sights.

"What was that all about?" she whispered as they were escorted out, his car already waiting before they even stepped out the door.

"Don't worry about it."

"We were escorted out." She could still see the security in the car mirror, even as Riley peeled out of the long drive. "Obviously something went wrong."

"Bernard and I disagreed."

"Do you know what, fuck you," Alice said, annoyed. "I'm good enough to look for a bloody shield, that wasn't there by the way, but not good enough to share information."

Riley clenched his jaw even as his hands screeched against the leather of the steering wheel. "You need to be careful of Nate Blackwell. You don't want him to see you as an asset he can use."

"Don't change the subject." She didn't care about Nate, knew nothing about him other than he owned the largest casino in London and that they seemed to despise each other. She had no intention of meeting him again, it wasn't like he hung out in the cheap coffee shops like she did.

"Fine, he bought the shield from my father over a month ago. You couldn't see it because he has hung it up in his office."

"Doesn't that mean your father has access to money?"

"Wouldn't tell me exactly how much, but it was worth millions. Sold it using untraceable cash."

"Shit." It meant Mason was out there with enough money to sustain himself for a while. "Shit. Shit. Shit."

"So eloquently put."

Alice settled into her seat, her mind back on Bernard.

"So you going to tell me what he is?"

Riley smiled, his eyes darting to her before concentrating on the road. "You were almost right. Bernard is a failed vampire."

"A what?" she asked, surprised.

Vampires went through a strict test before they were even allowed to start the transition, a transition that wasn't reversible. Which made it impossible to be a failed vampire, they either succeeded or they died. There was no in-between.

"He started the transition in the early twenties by a vampire only a few years undead himself. The process failed due to his Creators ignorance but he still inherited a few things. Sharper canines, sensitive eyes and an unknown life expectancy."

"Wow, that's unreal."

Riley laughed. "I knew you would enjoy trying to figure out what he was."

Alice looked away, feeling her skin warm. She didn't know what to think about Riley, whether she just saw things that weren't there because she craved the excitement. Or something else. She no longer trusted her own judgments, not when she had so much to figure out. She watched the car whiz through the night, counting the lights before she started to recognise the outskirts of London.

"Do you mind dropping me off at Club X?" she asked a while later, the silence in the car weirdly comfortable.

"Hmm?" Riley murmured, his attention distracted. "The stripper place?" He shot her a wild look. "Why?"

"I told you when you asked me that I was busy," she rolled her eyes. "They closed early for a private party."

Riley was silent again as he drove, the car loud as it roared through the streets. It wasn't long until he pulled up outside the club, causing pedestrians to stare at the car in awe.

"What are you doing?" she asked as he started to remove his suit jacket and tie, unbuttoning the top three buttons of his shirt.

He smirked when he turned to her. "I'm going to a *proper* party."

CHAPTER TWELVE

"No you're not," she stated as he stared at her. "You weren't invited."

"You helped me with my party, the least I can do is help you with yours." Riley stepped out the car, ignoring the people who were curious about his car.

"I don't need help!" she shouted at him as he forced her door open, holding his hand out for her.

"Are you going to deny me this distraction?" he asked when they stood in the cold. He wanted her to argue, could see it in his expression.

Alice clenched her teeth. She didn't know what their relationship was, whether they were acquaintances with aligning agendas, friends or more. But she knew what it felt like to want a distraction, to not want to wallow in self-pity or doubt.

"Fine," she mumbled, looking back at his pompous yellow car. "But just so you know, It's not my responsibility if your car is vandalised or stolen."

Riley gave a wide eyed look to his car as he pursed his lips. She could make out his tattoos on his chest clearly beneath the neon club lights, ones that had started to creep up his throat. He had more than the last time she saw him, she was sure of it. Glyphs, special tattoos that helped druids control ley lines. Although, she had only seen tattoos like his on The Guardians of the Order.

"Hey Alice, you're late," Ricky the bouncer grinned when she approached. "See, I knew you could look hot. You joining the girls yet?"

"You're so funny," she replied deadpan. Ricky was the bouncer who thought she was a stripper the first time they met. An ugly one with messy hair and stained clothes. He liked to remind her whenever he saw her. "Sam already in there?"

"Already been dancing on the bar," he replied, allowing them to pass the red velvet rope. "Enjoy with your date."

"He isn't my date," she said without thought, frowning when Riley shot her an unreadable look.

It wasn't a date, was it?

She didn't date.

Club X was situated just before the river that separated the Breed side of London from the human. It was a high end establishment, with quality entertainers in a low end area. It didn't seem to cause a problem with customers, the strip club constantly packed, with Sam, AKA Ranger having regulars who came to see him dance.

The inside was just as busy as previous times she had visited, with everybody drinking and several dancers on the bar gyrating to the band that was on the stage. A few women squealed when they noticed Riley, running over to run their hands down his chest. Alice laughed at his wide-eyed look.

"ALIICCCEEE!" a loud voice called. "OVER HERE!"

She abandoned Riley to the throngs of women, who probably didn't realise he wasn't a dancer. She should have felt guilty, but didn't. Surely he knew the affects he had on some females? Besides, he was the one who was gate crashing the party.

"Happy Birthday Sam," she grinned when he ran up to her for a bear hug, his arms wrapping around her shoulders hard enough to lift her off the floor. "I'm sorry I'm late."

"Not a problem baby girl. I'm happy that the best person is here," he said, eyes wide as he carefully held a pink sparkly cocktail in his hand. She was impressed he was able to hug her so thoroughly without spilling a drop.

He eagerly introduced her to a few more of his friends, some she recognised from the club and others she didn't. Sam was speaking excitedly with everyone, sipping his cocktail while she excused herself to sit at the bar, grabbing her own sparkly cocktail.

Sam didn't drink often, so Alice watched him closely, smiling as he became increasingly tipsy. He only allowed himself to let his hair down once in a while, even though he preferred not to. His personality that of an addict. Cigarettes were as far as he would go, and even then she had tried to make him quit. To no avail.

How could she give him a compelling argument when she suffered from random spontaneous combustion?

Once he had almost taken something stronger, years ago when they were out celebrating her academy graduation. She had found him in an alley with a dealer, a broken needle on the cobblestones. Her heart almost broke at the sight, turned to stone right there in her chest. She knew she would lose him if he turned to drugs, something she wasn't ready for. She would never be ready to lose her best friend, the man who knew every painful secret.

She was still grateful he had decided not to take the Brimstone, that instead they learnt to deal with their nightmares and insecurities together.

Riley finally made his way towards the party booth, greeting Sam like an old friend. She couldn't hear their conversation, the customers along the bar noisy, even above the live band. Sam pointed in her direction, his eyes catching hers with a raised eyebrow before he introduced Riley to the others.

You didn't tell me you were inviting Mr Delicious, Sam's expression read, albeit a bit hazy as he headed towards her, leaving Riley behind. *If you don't have him, I will.*

To be fair, she wasn't sure on the last part, her attention distracted by Riley who stared at her, even though he was holding a conversation with someone else. It took knowing someone better than yourself to be able to have silent conversations with them, something she had mastered with Sam when they were kids.

But when she looked at Riley she wasn't sure what she read in his expression, and that was what scared her.

"Why is you're face like a slapped arse?" Sam asked when he jumped on the stool beside her, his legs covered in a black wet-look fabric that hugged every muscle. His chest was bare. "It's a party."

"Sorry, busy day."

She sipped her cocktail, savouring the summer berries as they burned their way down her throat. The sensation replaced the cold anxiety that had lived in her gut since Mason's visit earlier, at least temporarily.

"I thought they closed the place for your party?" she asked when she noticed the customers who were still around.

"Everybody who came to the show tonight was invited to stay," Sam grinned as he signalled the bartender for another round of drinks. "So we going to talk about the elephant in the room?"

Alice pretended to look around. "There's an elephant? Where?"

He flicked her hair before wrapping a strand around a finger. "Smart arse. You know I mean tall, dark and handsome."

"Who's that?"

"Oh for fuck sake Alice, seriously?" He thanked the bartender who gave him four shots and a cocktail. "If you don't use *it* soon, it's going to heal over." He downed one of the luminous green shots, slamming the glass back down. The alcohol made him shiver, getting him some appreciate looks from both male and female customers as well as fellow dancers.

"Stop messing with my sex life," she murmured, eyeing the remaining shots. "You're the only man I need."

"Is that why you call his name when you have sex dreams?"

"WHAT?!" Alice smacked his arm. "I do not."

She hadn't. Had she?

Sam chuckled as he pushed a shot towards. "You're allowed to be happy, you know."

"I am happy," she said without thought, staring at the green drink. She took a sip, gagging at the intense flavour. "How can you drink that?"

"Like this." He downed a second shot. His eyes were becoming increasingly red, his speech starting to slur. "Sex doesn't mean marriage and kids."

"Who said I wanted marriage and kids? I plan to be one of the mad cat ladies."

"That's what you are now." Sam slowly blinked, a smile stretching his cheeks. A purr built up in his throat, the sound comforting as he leant forward. "He's still watching you."

"What?" She automatically scanned the crowd for him, finding Riley standing at the exact same spot he was last time. His eyes were intense, unreadable at the distance. It made her feel warm, fuzzy.

Or it could be the alcohol.

Probably the alcohol.

Alice drank the rest of her cocktail anyway. "Sex complicates things.

And he's also my Warden." Not that she needed a Warden, something she had repeatedly complained about, and was ignored.

"Only you could make sex complicated," Sam dramatically sighed. "Do you need a diagram?" He started gesturing with his fingers.

"SAM!" She grabbed his hands, grinning as he leant forward to affectionately touch foreheads. It was something he did when he was in his leopard form.

"You have so much shit being thrown at you from all angles. Playing around with someone like Riley Storm might be fun."

Her smile dropped. "What have I told you about giving me advice?"

"You know I only give the most superior guidance."

"Hey," Riley appeared over Sam's shoulder, his shirt slightly messy with a button or two missing.

"Great, you can keep Alice company while I go dance," Sam smiled, before he turned to wink at her. *Orgasms are your friend, remember.* He downed the third shot.

Shut up, she glared back, which got her an audible chuckle before he disappeared amongst the throngs of dancers.

Alice pushed her glass away, wanting to stay sober enough to take care of Sam.

"So," Alice started when Riley took Sam's vacated seat. "How do you like the party?"

"They're very welcoming," he laughed as he stole her shot, his face turning to a grimace as it went down. "How can he drink this?"

"Like water, apparently," she replied dryly.

"Okay, come on." He placed the glass back down, jumping to his feet.

"Huh?"

"We're gonna dance."

"Wait, what?"

Riley didn't answer, instead he took her hand and guided her towards the dance floor. His hands clasped hers as he spun, causing a squeal to escape her lips. She allowed the music to shape her hips, her body swaying as Riley kept pace.

She felt herself smile, enjoying the vibration through the floor as the alcohol started to bubble happily through her blood.

It felt like a break, a distraction.

It helped her forget, at least for a while that she had threats hanging above her, that she still didn't understand her heritage and that Dread had left her a cryptic message.

She closed her eyes, savouring the music, the beat that curled around her, causing her to sway with abandon.

Hands pulled at her, forcing her to turn into another man's arms who shimmied down her front. She moved away, backing into Riley whose hands gripped her waist. He growled by her ear, warning the other man away. The noise was strange from his throat, a dark vibration that she had never heard from him before.

She felt his touch through the thin silk of her dress, his palms radiating heat as her chi excitedly jumped at the connection. Her power coiled with pleasure inside her, a weird sensation that heightened her slightly fuzzy brain.

They moved as one, his hands still on her hips as she continued to dance to the music. His hands moved gently down her legs, hesitating when it got to her hem.

"Now how are you supposed to get that knife out without flashing your knickers?"

Alice laughed, forcing his hands back up to her hips before she spun to face him. She had forgotten she had the small dagger strapped high on her thigh. If there was ever a situation in which she would need the knife, she wouldn't care who she was flashing.

"Who said I wear underwear?"

His eyes flashed liquid silver, reflecting her image back at her before he laughed.

A quiver of anticipation ran through her at his beast's eyes, something unexpected.

His beast scared her, a creature she didn't know, didn't understand. Yet she couldn't look away, even when the silver dissipated to the grey of a stormy night.

His breath was warm as he leant down, his voice husky.

"I really hope you wax."

Alice smirked. She did wax, but she wasn't going to tell him that.

"Miss Skye," a voice disturbed them. Mac appeared beside them, his expression annoyed. "Can I have a moment?"

Alice hesitated before Sam jumped towards them, his eyes completely unfocused.

"Sure," she said as she nodded towards Riley. "Can you watch Sam for me?" Riley smiled before he followed Sam who was heading back towards the bar.

"You're a Paladin, right?" Mac asked as she followed him behind the stage.

No.

"Yeah," she lied. Well, technically she was still a Paladin. Just not on active duty.

"I need to show you something." He guided her further down the hallway, past the seven deadly sins themed sex rooms to his office. Inside a bouncer leant on the desk, arms folded across his wide chest.

"What's this about? I'm supposed to be celebrating Sam's birthday."

"I know, and I apologise. I thought you would know what to do with this."

"With what..." She heard a groan from behind the door.

Mac slowly closed the door, revealing a man slumped against the wall, his sleeve rolled up to his elbow revealing pale skin. His fangs were descended past his lips, long enough to indicate a vampire.

"What's this got to do with me?" She didn't deal in junkies. "Call emergency services or something. He's obviously drunk from someone who's high."

Vampires couldn't get stoned the standard way, their metabolism too high. The only way to achieve it was to drink from someone who's taken drugs, but the effects were fleeting.

"Or call his Creator." She couldn't tell if he was his own master or not.

"He has been caught on CCTV injecting, using this." He threw her a packet, the stylised ouroboros insignia familiar.

"Ruby Mist," she stated, studying the red crystals inside the plastic packaging.

"You've heard of it?" Mac held out his hand for the packet, placing it onto the desk beside a blackened spoon, lighter and syringe. "I get a lot of gear through here, but this is the first time I have ever seen a Vamp."

"You recognise the packaging?" she asked.

"It's been around a while, but no idea about this new one." He crossed his arms, frowning at the vampire who started to giggle in his sleep.

"He'll sleep it off," she said as she left them to it.

Hopefully, she mentally added.

She made her way through the dancers, searching for Riley or Sam.

She heard a crash, followed the sound to find Sam lying on the floor, surrounded by several smashed glasses. Riley picked him up by the arm, holding him close as Sam swayed.

"How much have you had to drink?" she asked as she stepped over the glass to grab Sam's attention.

"Oh, hey baby girlllll," he slurred. "I'm just playing with this hunk of a mannnnn." Sam tried to touch Riley's pec, missed and almost fell on his face if Riley hadn't been holding him up.

"Oh yeah?" Alice smirked, having never seen Sam so drunk.

"I think we should get him home," Riley said as he fought a smile.

"You coming home with meeeeeee?" Sam giggled. "I can go all night looooonnnngggggg."

Alice just sighed. "Yeah, I think you're right."

CHAPTER THIRTEEN

Alice removed her heels carefully, her feet aching as she threw the shoes towards the door. The living room was dark, quiet, almost peaceful with Jordan nowhere in sight.

Riley crept downstairs, his shirt open almost to his navel. He looked like he had been ravaged, his hair swept messily to the side as if he'd had to wrestle Sam off it. Which was entirely possible, knowing Sam.

"Your Cat just proposed to me," he said with a smile. Sam had become worse when the cold air had hit him, so Riley had to carry him to his room while he sang at the top of his lungs.

She was probably going to get an angry, passive aggressive letter from her neighbours tomorrow.

"What did you say?" she asked as he approached. His height dwarfing hers now she had removed her heels.

"I said yes of course, we've already settled on a June wedding."

Alice couldn't help her laugh of delight, the sound echoing through the room. He had probably been totally serious with the proposal. While he'd never been interested in marriage, he had proposed to three other people.

A warm hand touched her cheek, cutting off her chuckle. Her chi jumped, sending an electrical current between them that hitched her breath.

"How do you do it?" he asked softly, eyes serious.

"Do what?"

"Smile through it all?"

Her own smile wavered. "Because if I don't smile, don't laugh, who will?"

Riley cleared his throat. "Thanks for tonight."

It took her a second to understand, her attention on his lips that were achingly close. "Huh? Oh, what are friends for?"

"Friends?" he leant forward, a bare inch between their lips. "Hmm." He smirked as he stepped back, looking around the living room with interest. Without asking he pushed at her furniture, placing the sofas and side tables against the wall allowing a larger open space in the centre.

"What are you doing?" she asked, confused.

"Wait here," he said as he went out the front door, returning a moment later holding a short sword with a blunt edge. He placed it beside a side table before he unbuttoned the remaining shirt buttons, pulling the fabric off.

"I repeat, what are you doing?" she asked once again as she tried not to stare at his chest, the tattoos so intricate she couldn't help but study them.

"Do you know what I found out after you left the office? That you haven't been to any of your doctor's appointments."

It took Alice a second to understand what he said, her attention on the tattoos.

"You know how important they are. They're tracking your power..."

"What," she interrupted, her temper flaring. "You my keeper now?"

"No, but I am your Warden."

Shit. He had her there.

"If you're not getting regularly checked then you need to train."

He blurred with such speed she flinched when his arm appeared beside her. Without thinking she immediately bent at the waist, bringing her own arm up to block a side attack before spinning out of reach. A leg hit her hip, forcing her to stumble against the wall with a hiss. Adrenaline pumped as she stood staring at him from beneath her hair, her breath already slightly laboured.

"Are you serious right now?" Alice felt her lips part, teeth bared as she jumped at him, spinning into a high kick that he caught without effort. She huffed out a breath when he released her, flicking the blonde strands from her face as he calmly watched her. She had felt the seam at the side of her dress rip, ignored it.

"What is this Riley?" she asked as an unreadable look flashed across his face.

"I want you to be able to defend yourself so you're not in a situation where you end up dead."

"Well, I'm not dead yet."

He growled when he bent towards his sword, holding it at an angle. "Get your blade."

With a slight anticipation Alice picked up her own sword she had left on the sofa, the mysterious runes glowing as soon as her skin made contact.

"Luck can run out, sweetheart."

His arm swung, the heavy metal clashing against hers as she brought it up just in time. His strength was triple hers, so she knew a full on hit with his sword could resonate down her blade and shatter her wrist. So she used hers with a slashing motion, using his own momentum to move past him so she could dance out the way of a brutal strike.

She felt her cheeks curve into a grin.

She wouldn't admit it, but she loved to play with blades, especially with a man who was as skilled as Riley.

She bounced on the balls of her feet, readjusting the grip on the hilt as she waited for him to pounce. Riley had no tells like others she had fought, no muscle tension or eye darts that signalled he was about to move, or even give her a sense of direction. It was always a surprise when he finally did make his move, something she enjoyed. It forced her to instinctively fight, rather than overthinking.

He feigned a hit, pulling back at the last moment to swing it the other way, slapping her arm with the flat of his blade.

"FUCK!" she seethed, checking her skin. He hadn't hit her hard, the sword blunt enough to feel but not to pierce the skin. In a real fight she would have lost the arm. "Again."

Riley hit out again, but she was ready. Steel clashed with a resonating clang that she hoped wouldn't wake Sam. She jumped back as he swiped up at her stomach, her living room too small as the alcohol in her system made her stumble.

Steel at her throat before Riley helped her to her feet.

"I wouldn't recommend wearing silk in a fight, but you need to use everything to your advantage."

"No shit," she laughed as she yanked the already torn seam, the fabric opening towards her hip. Silk doesn't stretch, which made it difficult to move.

"Aw, I liked that dress," Riley said with a smirk. "Red suits you."

"Shame I don't wear silk often. Besides, in a real fight I would always have my magic."

Riley smirked. "But today, there's no magic, not when it's still unpredictable. This is about your sword when there's no chance to run."

Alice walked over, adding an extra sway to her hips. "I never run," she whispered before she hit out without warning, fast enough that Riley stumbled back with a surprised expression. "I'll have you know I'm very much in control of my magic."

"Yeah?" She felt his chi brush against hers, the feeling electric that made her pause. Magic surged beneath her fingertips, wanting to encase her blade with blue flames.

It was as she concentrated on keeping her magic under control that she put another foot wrong, and Riley's short sword knocked against her arm hard enough this time to bruise while he disarmed her with a quick flick of the wrist.

Her sword glared with light until Riley dropped it with a hiss. The flat of his blade pressed against her collarbone, forcing her back against the wall.

Alice panted as he stood over her, his sword blunt but cold against her skin as he stared. His eyes were liquid silver, mesmerising before they settled into his usual stormy grey. She wanted to read his unusual eyes, understand what he was thinking, but instead he concentrated on her lips, his pupils narrowing when her tongue darted out to lip along the bottom.

Alice cleared her throat when he didn't step back.

"You did that on purpose." He had used his magic to distract her.

"Yeah?" he replied with no hint of a smile. "You shouldn't have reacted." His chi continued to stroke against hers, making her heart beat faster at the sensation.

She let out a frustrated growl. She had never felt an aura like Riley's, had never reacted to any other person in the same way. Even now she wanted it to curl around her, cover her like a comfort blanket as her magic reacted in awe.

Which was pathetic.

"Why did your sword just burn me?"

"Huh?" she asked, confused before she remembered what happened with D. "You disarmed me. It seems to have a weird reaction when someone does that."

He finally looked up. "Who have you been fighting with?"

"It doesn't matter."

"Hmm..."

He pushed closer, until his chest touched the other side of the sword. His height forced him to bend, his head tilted at such an angle his dark hair covered part of his face. This close she could make out the faint scar, the only scar or blemish she had ever seen on his skin.

He pulled his sword away, letting it drop to the floor as his hand touched her cheek. "You sure we can just be friends?"

At that moment she didn't care about anything other than the heat of his palm. When he was there she forgot her problems, and thought that maybe there could be a light at the end of the tunnel. So she closed the last inch, enjoyed the sudden inhale of his breath as she touched her lips to his.

She moaned when he pulled her closer, his hands moving down to crush her hips into his. His chi was electric against her own, an avalanche of sensation that heightened his tongue as it darted into her mouth.

"Please," she moaned when they broke for breath. She wasn't even sure what she was begging for, but knew she needed it, needed him, at least for that moment.

Riley said nothing as he lifted her as if she weighed nothing, her dress straining as her legs tried to spread around his waist. She wiggled, pulling the dress awkwardly over her head, throwing it in the vague direction of the sofa, leaving her in her underwear. His hands ravaged her naked thighs, fingers digging in as his mouth assaulted hers. She felt his erection strain against his slacks, excitement sending a thrill through her veins.

She let out a squeal when her back hit the wall, the cold a shock against her exposed back. She expected the impact, had braced herself but she wasn't prepared with how softly Riley had pushed her against it. His fingers ran little circles on her thighs, slowly getting closer to the place she wanted him to be. With a click her thigh holster was undone, the knife forgotten as it tumbled to the ground with the other weapons. Her hands reached up to his hair, feeling the strands through her fingers as his lips bit gently down her throat. He turned her head, kissing down the other side when she sucked in a breath, her attention suddenly on the throwing star that was still imbedded into the wall.

Riley felt her tense, his eyes instantly settling on the weapon.

"What's that?" he asked, his voice deep with arousal.

"Nothing." She tried to pull his face back to hers.

"Did you just lie to me?" He breathed against her neck, the heat making her shiver in anticipation even as he dropped her gently to her feet. He reached over, pulling the throwing star out of the wall with one tug.

Shit.

"What happened?" he asked.

She went to speak, her mouth snapping shut before she could explain. She couldn't tell him, not with the threat fresh in the air. She couldn't risk it, not when it was Sam or Kyle's life.

She couldn't even think of a reasonable excuse.

"I can't tell you."

"Was it him?"

She remained silent, hoping the darkness didn't betray her expression.

"When?" Riley moved away, removing his heat. "You knew I've been hunting him, and yet you kept this information from me."

Alice wanted to curl her arms around herself, a sudden vulnerability settling in as she stood there almost naked.

But she didn't.

She wouldn't give anybody that satisfaction.

"Please, I can't."

"What has he got against you?"

Alice hesitated, carefully thinking it through. "Sam," she whispered as her voice broke. "He threatened Sam."

Riley let out a sound of frustration, his jaw clenched as he studied the throwing star. "At least he's still in the city."

An obnoxious tone broke through their tension.

Riley pulled his mobile out of his pocket, checked the screen before hanging up.

"I have to go," he stated, his eyes angry when he handed her the star.

"Wait, Riley..."

"Not right now, sweetheart." He opened the door, the winter air rushing through to curl around her bare skin.

"I won't let him hurt Sam." *Or Kyle,* she wanted to add. "You need my help."

When he looked at her his beast shone through, the silver orbs captivating. But it was also a warning. "You need continue training, you can't get distracted." He clutched the door. "Thanks for tonight."

The door slammed shut behind him.

Alice stared at the throwing star, pressing her finger into the slight dent Riley had left behind.

"Fuck."

Alice coughed as she opened the kitchen window, the smoke choking her throat as she turned her face to the open air.

"Ugh, why are you making so much noise?" Sam groaned as he collapsed into a chair, his head in his hands.

"Morning princess," Alice sang as she put the burnt bacon onto a plate, the eggs, sausage and beans only marginally better. "How's the hangover?"

"Ughhhhhh," Sam replied, his face still covered. "Why did you let me drink so much?"

"Yes, because I control how many toxic looking green shots you decided to pour down your throat?" Alice pushed at his arm until he sat up, slipping the English breakfast onto the table before him. "You haven't drunk that much since... yeah."

The last time he had drunk like that he almost turned to drugs to deal with the horrors of his past. She was forever grateful he didn't in the end, but that didn't mean it wasn't at the back of her mind that he could slip. It would only take the once and she could lose the Sam she loved forever.

"It's stupid," he said as he cautiously eyed her attempt at breakfast. "One of the guys I recently... anyway, he said something nasty and instead of kicking him to the kerb like I usually do I decided to drown my sorrows."

Sam sighed, ignoring the cutlery to pick up a piece of bacon and bite into the meat. After a long chew he set it back down.

"What did he say?" Alice asked as she scrambled in the medicine box for a painkiller. She found a small wooden disk stuck to the bottom, already threaded with a bit of twine. Using a knife, she pricked her finger, forcing a single drop of her blood to activate the charm.

"It doesn't matter." His eyes glowed when they caught hers. "Seriously, it really doesn't. You know me, nothing affects me like that. I have no idea why this arsehole suddenly did." He shook his head before he groaned and closed his eyes.

"Here." Alice tied the twine around Sam's throat, making sure the flat of the disk was flush to his chest. Sam instantly calmed, the frowns in his forehead smoothing over as the painkiller kicked in.

"Did you know you're my Starlight in the darkness of night?" he grinned as he tugged her into his lap, shoving his nose into her hair.

Alice couldn't help her laugh. "As you are my Sunshine. Even when you stink of alcohol and loudly woke me up this morning puking." She tugged on his ear before jumping up.

"What can I say, I'm a man who can't handle his drink," he chuckled as his amber eyes followed her around the kitchen. "Speaking of stink, is the reason you burnt my breakfast to disguise the fact I smell Riley?" Sam grinned as he wiggled his eyebrows. "Please, please say that hunk of a man is still upstairs?"

Alice turned to look out the window, arms folded. "He didn't stay. We got into this argument and..."

"Let me guess, it was about his father?"

Alice spun in surprise.

"What?" Sam said around a mouthful of food. "I hear things. I guessed he was why I can smell the pack more often in the club... and when I make my way home." He shot her a look explaining that particular subject wasn't closed, and he wasn't pleased. "It's annoying though, they never tip."

Alice decided not to comment.

"What exactly got Riley mad? He couldn't take his eyes off you in the club."

Alice leant back against the sink. "We both know you don't remember anything from last night."

Sam smirked. "Not the point. Now answer the question."

"He doesn't want help finding Mason. He's so thick-headed he can't see that I need to find him too."

"It's his father..."

"And!" Alice barked as she slapped her hand on the countertop.

"That man killed my parents, destroyed Kyle and is now threatening you. I need to see him burn just as much as Riley does."

"Does he know this?"

"Well, yeah, I guess."

"You guess?" Sam uncurled from the seat, moving over to press Alice against his chest. His purr started a second later, the familiar vibration calming her. "He's just been deceived by someone who brought him into the world. A man who was supposed to protect him against everything. The betrayal is…"

Alice hugged him closer as his voice broke.

"You need to give him time."

"I don't have time," Alice sighed, stepping back from his warmth.

She was against the clock. She couldn't wait for Riley.

"It's not his fault. What his father did… it's not his fault."

"We know that," Sam said as he tipped her head up to look at him. "But does he?"

He watched the woman he had been following, her smile radiant as she laughed at something he couldn't see. Her blonde hair was scraped into a messy bun, strands dancing around her face as sweat created a slight sheen across her skin.

He had no idea why they were interested in her.

She looked normal, like everybody else.

But whatever they wanted, he delivered. And they asked for this woman.

So he stalked, waited.

He was patient, a predator who was used to hunting his prey slowly.

And once they had her, he would be free.

CHAPTER FOURTEEN

Alice lifted her fist, the door opening before her knuckles even made contact.

"I told you not to come here," Kyle said as he stood in the threshold, eyes darting with a slightly wild look. "You could have been followed." Kyle stepped back, urging her inside. His hand twitched, like he wanted to pull her through quickly, but didn't want to touch her.

"I haven't been followed," she murmured as he closed the door behind her, setting three separate locks.

At least, she didn't think she was followed. She was a Paladin, she was the one who tracked down the criminals, not the other way round.

"I need to show you…" she paused, taking in the small space as the overwhelming smell of mould assaulted her nose, the evidence in the corner smeared as if recently cleaned.

It was just as awful as the outside, the room dilapidated beyond redemption. It was painted a sickly yellow, the paint peeling off the walls in clumps that left the brick exposed. The bed in the corner was a small double, with brown sheets neatly made that was at odds with the general essence of the room. The walls were damp from the shower, steam covering the single mirror while the only window was covered in wood and nails.

"You shouldn't be here," Kyle said, voice strained. He kept his back to the door, his hands clawed as he held his forearms against his chest. It made him look like a teenager again, more vulnerable. She could see his discomfort, so she moved to sit on the bed, silently grimacing as the carpet squished beneath her boots.

"I didn't know who else to ask. You might know..." she hesitated, not wanting to finish the sentence.

"Know what?" he asked, his face blank.

"Black magic." She watched a nerve jump in his cheek, but his face remained unreadable. His hands dug further into his arms, almost breaking skin as his nails left red marks.

She leant back on the bed as she opened her bag, pulling out their mother's grimoire.

"Where did you get that?" he asked, eyes wide as he stepped forward, hand reaching out to touch the leather-bound cover, which growled and vibrated at the contact.

He snapped his hand back, almost as if he were scalded.

"Dread had it," she said, ignoring the fact the book seemed to dislike everyone. "What do you know of our heritage?"

"Heritage?"

Placing the grimoire on her lap, she opened onto a random page, quickly pulling her hand back as it tried to bite.

"Alice, did that book just..." Kyle reached forward once again, deciding against it when it growled louder. "Dread had it?"

"Yeah, it was Mum's." Alice pressed a fingertip to a page, stroking the paper gently. It seemed to calm down once open, not that she could explain why. Or how.

"Why would Mum have a grimoire like that?" he asked, confused.

"I was hoping you would tell me," Alice said sadly. "I thought maybe you would remember them better."

She began to carefully flip through the pages once again.

"Do you remember learning about the Elemental families?" Every child learnt the history of magic in school.

Kyle stared at her while he decided what to say. "If you mean that Mum was a Draco, then yes, I knew."

"You knew?" She paused on a page, trying to decipher his guarded expression.

Kyle gave her a weak smile. "I've been on the wrong side for a long time, Alice." His eyes flicked to the book then back again. "She was powerful, I remember, but she wasn't an Elemental. Master had been searching for centuries before he found us. If only she was a descendent, then maybe he wouldn't have..." He shook his head. "Trust me when I say he was disappointed when he figured out our father was a druid and not a witch," he laughed, the sound hollow.

Druids were born when the father was also a druid, regardless of the mother. Their genetics only passed onto sons, which made Kyle a druid, not a witch.

"But I'm not even sure what I am anymore," he said on a whisper, almost to himself.

"Kyle?"

She wanted to reach for him, comfort him as he fought his internal dilemma. But he wasn't ready. She had only just gotten him back, she couldn't scare him away just yet.

"What do you make of this?" She finally found the page, turning the grimoire to face him.

Kyle studied the spell with his dark eyes, not black like she initially thought but a deep red.

"It's incomplete."

"I know that," she sighed. "Do you know the missing symbols for the ward?"

He cracked the book closed, almost catching her fingers.

"You shouldn't be meddling with that stuff."

"I need a ward, I have..."

"Promise me," he demanded, his voice desperate. "Promise me you won't try any of these spells."

Alice remained silent, unable to answer. She would do whatever it took to keep Sam safe, to keep Kyle safe, even if it went against everything she believed in. She placed the grimoire back in her bag before she slung it over her shoulder.

"Why do you even need the ward?"

"Have you always known it was Mason?"

She changed the subject, not wanting to risk him knowing just yet.

Not until she had a plan. She couldn't predict his reaction.

"I know it was his lab we destroyed, I'm guessing you knew."

He just stared at her.

"Did you know it was Mason Storm who killed our parents?"

"It wasn't Mason," he snarled, his demeanour changing.

"He gave the order."

"He didn't kill them." Kyle shivered, the reaction strange as he curled his arms tighter around himself. "He wasn't the one that killed them, he wasn't the monster that came to us that night."

"You need to be honest with me." Alice stood before she carefully approached her brother. "If you believe Mason wasn't behind their deaths, then why him?"

Kyle stood his ground, his dark red eyes unnerving up close. Shifters eyes changed when they were angry, not druids. Well, not typically.

He looked down his nose at her, jaw tense. "I remember his face."

"Remember from what? You need to tell me more, help me understand."

Kyle closed his eyes, taking a deep breath, closing himself off.

She knew he wasn't going to give her much more.

"Do you know where he is?" she asked.

Please say yes.

When Kyle finally opened his eyes they were the same colour as her own. He subtly moved his head, forcing her to follow the movement. Behind him, pinned to the back of the door was a ripped map. Half of it was missing, crude drawings replacing some places while string and photographs covered others.

It reminded her of a crime map, something she had seen when visiting Spook Squad.

"What is this?" she asked, stepping past him to get a closer look. Magazine cut outs of Mason and Riley were pinned to the top, beside a series of other pictures and drawings that had been crossed out. Beneath the map was the ouroboros insignia.

"A map," he stated.

"No shit," she snapped as she pulled the picture of Mason and Riley off the door. "Why do you have a map?"

"There are several secret tunnels built before the industrial period, before the underground even existed. I'm marking them out, but many have been flooded or caved in."

"If they're secret, how do you know of them?"

He warily approached, taking the picture from her hand and pinning it back on the wood. "It's how we travelled and how I escaped the train station. There's hundreds of miles unmapped. I was hoping to find an opening beneath the Sun Breeze Health facility."

He slowly traced a black line with his fingertip.

"Mason owns Sun Breeze, had it built years before he decided to disguise its original purpose with helping sick kids."

"So you knew Mason owned it?"

"I didn't know until we got there," he said. "It's why I reacted like I did." He peeked a look at her before returning his attention to the map. "I have never seen the outside, was only ever allowed in the basement or the labs. Its actual purpose is the production of several Class A drugs, the newest being Ruby Mist."

He pointed to the snake insignia drawn at the bottom.

"Each curve represents one of The Trinity. Mason is represented with one curve, Master was another."

"Who's the third?"

Kyle shrugged his shoulders. "The distributor. Master provided the elements while Mason was the production. I have no idea who the distributor is. I'm going to destroy them all, but first I need Mason."

A knock rattled the door.

"Are you expecting someone?" Alice asked as she stepped away.

Kyle grabbed her arm, pulling her back just as the door shot open, all three of the locks shooting across the room. A white light blinded her, forcing her to cover her eyes as something hit her side, causing her to stumble against the wall. Arms pinned she felt something sharp against her flesh, the cold steel shocking her to react.

Still slightly blinded she kicked back, feeling her foot connect to someone with a grunt.

"KYLE!" she screamed, dodging another ball of light that burned across her aura before dissipating against the wall, bubbling the peeling paint.

The bed shattered into splinters beside her before a woman jumped up from the debris. She ran back through the front door without giving Alice a backwards glance.

Alice unsheathed her sword, moving just in time as another blade came down towards her neck. She rolled out the way, her back hitting the other side of the room just as she pulled her sword up to block another swing.

"KYLE?" she screamed again, unable to see him as she pushed back, pulling her aura around her fist in a burst of blue flames. *"ARMA!"* Her circle started to form before it popped, her aura bounding back as it touched the metal pipes in the walls.

The room was too small.

"VENTILABIS!" Her flames soared, catching the assassin in the face as she saw a glint of light.

As the man screamed she hit out with her sword, slicing his arm before he was able to bring up his weapon. She kicked him in the stomach, forcing him forward so she could hit him square in the nose with the hilt.

"ALICE!" Kyle shouted as he came back into the room, blood pouring from a cut beneath his hair. "GET OUT!" He pulled her towards the door, his eyes once again dark red as he pushed her over the threshold and over the decapitated woman. "GET..."

Alice screamed, blood splattered across her face as the end of a sword erupted from Kyle's chest. She caught him as he collapsed against her, the assassin standing behind with his blade raised. She recognised the quick glimpse of the symbol carved into his steel.

She felt her power surge, a recalcitrant fire that threatened to destroy her if she didn't purge. With a shaking hand she thrust it forward, ignoring her own sword. She allowed instinct to take over.

"ADOLEBITQUE!"

She felt liquid heat drip down her face, blood on her tongue as fire poured from her fingertips, hotter than she had ever felt before. It smelted the sword mid-air, melting the flesh of the assassin within seconds. His hands fused to what remained of his weapon, mouth forever open in a scream as her fire continued to eat through the room.

It continued to grow, uncontrollable as sobs rattled her chest. Kyle stared at her from her arms, face grey as his breathing became shallow. Her flames burned around them, destroying everything it touched as she fought for it not to consume Kyle too.

Pulse in her throat she screamed, absorbing the fire back within her, leaving the room charred beyond recognition.

"Please, please..." she bawled as she reached for her phone, dialling Riley's number. "FUCK!" The call wouldn't go through. Her fingers started dialling the emergency services, halting before she pressed call. "FUCK! FUCK! FUCK!" She threw her phone back into the bag.

She couldn't call an ambulance.

Salty tears mixed with the blood on her face as she sucked in a breath. Calming herself, forcing herself to think past her panic.

"Okay, okay, okay." She sheathed her sword before pulling Kyle to his feet, settling his weight against her shoulder. She carefully carried him down the stairs, ignoring his moans as she placed him in her car.

"I'm sorry," Kyle whispered, his eyes fluttering shut.

"No, no. Don't you do this!" she cried as she put the car into gear.

CHAPTER FIFTEEN

Alice settled Kyle down on the sofa, his wound oozing dark blood as she quickly pushed every other furniture in the living room out of the way. Luckily the sofa was still against the back wall, saving her time.

"Okay, okay, okay," she chanted as she pulled the grimoire from her bag, ignoring the books temperament as she flipped through to a spell she had already noted.

Summon the darkness – part two

WHAT YOU WILL NEED:
50 grams Valerian root
50 grams Mugwort
3 full stems Yarrow

100 ml Milk from the breast, mixed with one's blood (goat will do if unavailable)
Salt
Copper pot
Large piece of paper or cloth
Charcoal
Five incantation candles

METHOD:
Draw a protection circle in salt, reversing the elements with an extra circle connected to spirit. It is paramount the extra circle is large enough to encase you and the copper pot. Set the five candles on the elemental points, lighting them in sequence to close both circles.

Add the ingredients to the pot, allowing them to start to burn before you add the blood and milk. On the large piece of paper or cloth write the name of the one you wish to summon in charcoal before adding it into the mixture.

A sacrifice must be made while calling the name of the person or beast you wish to summon –add their blood to the pot.
Call three times, each will make a separate flame flicker.

She skidded across the wooden floor into her kitchen, grabbing the dry ingredients as well as the equipment.

"Okay, okay," she cried as she re-read the instructions.

She really hoped she didn't need to know part one for this spell, that page was missing.

"Right, are you ready Kyle?" she asked, not expecting an answer when she flicked him a concerned look.

He was still breathing. That's all that mattered right now.

She carefully drew the required symbols with salt chalk, knowing that if one elemental point was wrong the spell could break. A circle was supposed to resemble a pentagram, with earth, an equilateral triangle with a line vertically through the middle placed at the bottom left of the star. Instead she drew it at the top left, followed by fire which was an upside down equilateral triangle with two waves on each of the sides.

Usually she didn't physically draw the anchor points, the candles already carved into the right symbols but she wasn't taking any risks.

She added water, simply three horizontal wavy lines and air which was three vertical wavy lines. Finally, it was spirit, which she drew at the bottom of the pentagram which was simply a circle within a circle, symbolizing infinity and eternity.

She lit the candles in sequence, adding a drop of her blood to each candle to quicken the flames. She started with earth, then fire, water and air before she hesitated at spirit.

A sacrifice must be made while calling the name of the person or beast you wish to summon –add their blood to the pot.

She quickly stripped Kyle out of his T-Shirt, the fabric soaked in blood before she settled back down by her copper pot, the candle for spirit directly in front of her.

"Lumenium." She waved her hand, the wick lighting just as the circle popped into existence around her in a burst of ecstasy. It took a few seconds for her aura to settle back down, the blue and green swirls surrounding her becoming opaque as she quickly checked on Kyle, who was safe outside the circle.

Two domes had formed, one the size of the pentagram, and a smaller one where she sat with the pot, connected by spirit.

"I only have dried ingredients, do you think that matters?" she asked him, speaking out loud oddly comforting as she added the valerian root, mugwort and yarrow.

She made sure the pot was scalding, the ingredients instantly burning so she could add the milk mixed with her own blood.

"What about using cow's milk?" She hoped not, she didn't drink goats milk. "It's whole fat," she said, hoping he understood her reasoning.

She wrote the name on a tea towel, the only clean piece of fabric in the kitchen, before adding it into the mixture. The tea towel glowed before dissipating in the milk.

"Please let this work," she said as she grabbed Kyle's T-shirt, wringing it between her hands so his blood dripped steadily.

The blood broke the surface of the milk, throwing up a sulphuric puff.

"Xahenort, I summon you," she called, trying not to choke on the rotten egg stench.

The first candle flickered.

"XAHENORT!" She scrunched some more blood from the T-shirt.

The second candle flickered.

"XAHENORT!"

The third candle flickered before every candle went out in a whoosh. Alice felt the pressure pop before a cloud of smoke erupted inside the larger circle, obscuring her view.

"WHAT THE FUCK IS THIS?" Xahenort snarled when the cloud dispersed, allowing her to see him in his true Daemonic form. He was tall, the arches of his wings almost touching the ceiling, while his skin was a dark grey.

His red eyes settled on her, his mouth set in a grim line as he transformed himself to look more human, his skin becoming pinker, his wings settling into his back while a black T-shirt and jeans appeared on his body. The horns curled down his face, becoming hidden beneath his thick black hair.

"War, did you know I was cooking a roast? If I go back and it's burnt I'm going to bloody hang, draw and quarter you," he sneered, his hand reaching out to touch the bubble that surrounded him. The molecule-thin sphere shaped around his fingertips, stretching across his skin enough for her to worry.

Alice sat there frozen, amazed it worked as well as cautious.

Fuck. Fuck. Fuck.

What did she do now?

The Daemon frowned. "Why are all your seats over there? That's a weird place to put them. They should all face the TV."

"Xahenort," she started...

"War, why have you called me? I'm..." his words caught in his throat as his eyes settled on Kyle. "Now, isn't this interesting. What are you doing with one of us?"

One of us?

"I need your help, my brother..."

"Brother did you say?" Xahenort laughed, his hand touching the circle again. "He hasn't yet embraced his true form."

"Please, help him. A spell, anything."

"What happened?" he asked, head tilted.

She was desperate to stand up, but her circle restricted her to remain on her knees. "We were attacked by assassins, a blade pierced through his chest."

"What sort of blade? An earth blade cannot damage us like this."

"This one had a symbol, the same symbol as the throwing star over there." She gestured to the side table pushed against the wall.

Xahenort hissed, the noise loud enough to make her flinch.

"I haven't seen this mark in a millennium," he turned to her with a full grin. "I hope the person who attacked you is dead?"

Alice remained silent.

"I can help your brother, but for a price. My services aren't free,

Little War, or do you prefer being called The Dragon?" He started to chuckle, amused at himself.

She thought about it. "What do you want? Blood of a virgin? A fucking unicorn?"

"Such attitude from someone so small." His eyes narrowed to points. "I've never had a War before?"

Alice sucked in a breath.

"I enjoy playing with chains and whips. I find pain... pleasurable."

"No, what else?"

Fucking anything else.

"Stop being such a prude. I haven't even decided if it would be sexual or not yet," he laughed before he shrugged. The expression weird on him, almost alien. "But I think you're too small for my tastes, too breakable. The last time I had a blonde I had to sew her mouth shut from all the whining."

"What do you want? Kyle is dying and all you're talking about..."

"You need my help, remember that Little War." He teased the circle with his hand again. "Let me out of this circle."

"No." She couldn't allow him out, couldn't trust him. "I can't let you out, you eat people."

"I don't hear you complaining about lions eating people, because it's in their nature. Or that vampires require blood to survive?"

"Do you require blood to survive?"

"No, I need very little sustenance. But fresh blood breaks through the numbness," he said quietly before he shook his head.

"You're not a lion, you don't need to kill people."

"Who said I killed my victims?" he snapped.

Alice remained silent.

"Fine," Xahenort smirked. "What if I agree not to?"

Alice fidgeted on the floor as Kyle moaned from the corner. "Are you going to help my brother or not?" She didn't have any other options.

"What If I make this deal sweeter? I'll help your brother in exchange for you dropping the circle, giving me the throwing star and for one favour that may or may not be sexual," he teased.

"No, you will help my brother and give me a protection ward for the house in exchange for something else."

"This isn't how negotiations work," he said, beginning to become annoyed. "If we don't decide soon your brother is going to die. I must take him with me if he is to survive."

"Take him with you?" she asked, feeling herself go cold. It didn't occur to her he would take Kyle. "You can't keep him."

Xahenort growled. "Fine, I won't keep him. I'll heal your brother and let him go on his merry way. I'll give you a ward to protect your house and I will tell you about your sword."

"My sword?"

"The blade of Aurora. I call you War because that is your birth right, as is the blade."

Alice began to ask questions when Kyle groaned.

"Mason, do you know where Mason Storm is?"

"That little piss-stain?" he snarled. "He keeps selling my fucking name, if I knew where he was I would kill him myself."

"Okay then, you will heal Kyle and let him go. You will give me a ward to protect my house and tell me about my sword. In exchange I will drop the circle, give you the throwing star and make sure Mason no longer sells your name."

"I will agree if you no longer call me by my summoning name."

Kyle coughed, his body heaving off the sofa to land on the floor with a wet thud.

"Fine, fine," she said, panic taking over. "What would you like me to call you?"

He grinned. "You may call me..." He seemed to hesitate. "Lucifer."

"Lucifer? Really? The name of the devil?"

"Do we not have a deal?" He almost seemed offended. "I think it's a fitting name."

"No, no. I'm sorry. It's a deal."

Please, please don't let this be a mistake.

Alice slowly reached out, allowing the circle to drop as her aura rebounded back into her chi. Lucifer grinned, his wings erupting from his back, large enough for the horns on his wing arches to scratch the artex above.

"I love a bit of earth air," he breathed in before dramatically sighing out. He went to Kyle, picking him up as if he were a child rather than a full grown man. "I will keep my end of the bargain, however I believe I will concentrate on your brother first. I will return to enlighten you about your lovely sword."

"You can't just pop back when you please?" she said, alarmed as she shot to her feet.

"I can because you opened the circle," he grinned. "But I will call beforehand. I wouldn't want to catch you in any compromising positions." Smoke started to float by his feet. "Also if you fail to destroy Mason, the deal is broken and I will not release your brother from my services."

"Wait, you didn't warn me about any of this?"

Lucifer laughed. "You made a deal with the devil, what do you expect?" The smoke circled up around his waist. "But I will give you this final warning before I leave. Do not abuse my summoning name, Little War. While I find this amusing, I do not have limitless patience."

With his final statement the smoke engulfed him with a pop. A second later the throwing star on the table also disappeared.

"WAIT!" she called. "THE WARD!"

Her grimoire flipped to a blank page on its own, writing and incantations appearing on the paper. She studied the spell, not recognising any of it.

Shit. Shit. Shit.

She really hoped she hadn't made a mistake.

CHAPTER SIXTEEN

Alice finalised the last mark, hiding it beneath the welcome mat just outside her front door. Chalk enchantments surrounded her house on all sides, including the inside of every door and window. She had no idea if they worked, hoped Lucifer was true to his word.

She had no other choice but to trust him.

"Miss Skye, what are those marks across your driveway?" Mr Jenkins barked as he approached.

"'Morning, Mr Jenkins," she sighed as she came to her feet, patting the excess chalk from her hands onto her jeans. "How are you today?"

"I was having a grand morning until I saw the graffiti." Mr Jenkins stamped his foot, gesturing to the chalk marks you could barely see from the road.

Alice tried to smile. For a man who was heading past eighty-odd-years-old he was a pain in her arse. He was the chairman of the Neighbourhood watch, not that she had ever seen them patrol the street. Sometimes she noticed curtain twitches, but that's about it.

"It's just a protection ward, entirely legal."

"I'm old, not blind," he snapped. "But it's an eyesore, you should have made the runes neater." He wore a white shirt with bright red suspenders, his brown loafers buffed to a shine. Thick lensed glasses perched on his nose with his long bushy eyebrow hairs floating across the lenses.

He stood by the brown smudge she had luckily already scrubbed, otherwise she would have had to explain the blood drops on her drive.

Mr Jenkins sniffed as if displeased. Alice froze, hoping she no longer smelt of sulphur. She had showered and scrubbed her skin, the stench lingering even after both Kyle and Lucifer had disappeared.

"Hey baby girl."

Sam appeared from across the road, his chest almost naked in his leather strap ensemble. He rarely wore his costume home, preferring to change into simple jeans and a T-shirt before he caught the bus. Although, she loved the look of horror on Mr Jenkins face at the sight.

"You not ready? We have to leave soon," he said as he flashed Mr Jenkins an award winning smile.

Mr Jenkins spluttered, his face appearing with a red splotch as his eyes bugged out of his head. He turned on his heel, heading to his own drive a few houses down. They could hear him muttering to himself all the way.

"I have time," Alice replied as she smirked behind her neighbours back. "Don't you have to change?" She didn't care that he wore his stripper outfit home, but it wasn't exactly appropriate for where they were going.

"So you been chalking our drive? Why?" He crossed his arms as he stared at her. The temperature was almost freezing, yet he stood there with some leather straps covering barely any of his flesh. In comparison, she wore several layers, a scarf and a thick leather jacket.

She had planned for the question, knew with his shifter nose that he would be able to smell exactly what had happened as soon as he opened the door. No amount of bleach would have helped.

"Are you in trouble? Do I need to call Overlord?" he asked, worry underlying his tone.

"I'll tell you everything on the way."

"You sure this is the place?" Sam asked when he peeked through the window, his hands gripping the steering wheel tight enough for the leather to squeak. He wasn't happy with the situation, but trusted her judgment.

"I'm sure," Alice said as she unbuckled her belt. "I'll be in and out."

"I'll just sit here and poke your holes," he mumbled as he played with the bullet wounds in the doors. She had explained everything, every last detail including the assassination attempts. They didn't keep secrets from each other. "Don't take too long."

She was still waiting for him to react about Mason's threat, something he didn't acknowledge on the drive over to Kyle's. His face was hard to read, his eyes guarded. He was keeping his thoughts to himself which worried her.

Sam was usually very explosive with his emotions. The fact he remained quiet was worrying.

She couldn't deal with that right now.

"You cool?" she asked, serious.

I need you to be cool.

He clenched his jaw, a low growl vibrating his throat. "Yeah, yeah." He sighed before he shook himself. "Yeah, I will be."

She knew he was angry because he couldn't protect her.

But she was the one who needed to protect him.

"I'll be quick. We can't be late."

"I'll be sitting here, baby girl," he winked, a smile curving his lips. One that didn't reach his eyes.

She kissed him on the cheek, knew his leopard needed the affection before she opened the car door, stepping into the cold. The derelict building Kyle had called home was covered with police, as she knew it would be.

"Excuse me ma'am, this is a crime scene. You can't stop here," a uniform said when she approached the tape.

"I'm Agent Skye from Spook Squad."

"The witch?"

"That would be me," she smiled, hoping it looked friendly and unthreatening.

"Alice?" Peyton said as he approached. "I'll take her from here."

Alice nodded to the officer, following Peyton beneath the tape. He remained silent as he walked her up the stairs.

"You not in uniform today?" she asked as they got to the top, the smell of charred flesh strong in her nose.

"Been promoted," he explained when he turned his head.

"Oh, yeah?" She pushed for information. He wore a tidy suit on his tall frame, black, like something he would wear to a funeral.

"Yep." He pulled her to the side as another officer passed. "What are you doing here?" His eyes were ice when they caught hers. "You shouldn't be here."

Typical Peyton, right to the point.

"I need a favour."

"Agent Skye," Detective Brady mumbled when he appeared from the doorway, a handkerchief held to his face to dilute the smoke. "I see you have met my new partner."

Peyton just folded his arms in response.

"What happened to O'Neil?" she asked.

"Still around, but getting himself a nice comfy desk back at the office." He rocked back on his heel, his attention on his notepad. "How did you know about this? You're no longer part of the team."

"You seem glad to be rid of me," she snapped before she could stop it. "Sorry, it's been a bad few days."

"Actually, we're in the process of overturning your suspension," Peyton added. "At least for our part. But enough about that for now, why are you here?"

"We haven't called you," Brady said. "So how did you know about this crime scene?"

"Word gets around," she shrugged, unable to tell the truth. "Decapitations aren't that common."

Someone wearing a white protective overall waved from their position with the decapitated woman. Shaded goggles hid their face while the hood was cinched tightly around their head. She automatically waved back.

"Have you found any weaponry?" she asked.

Peyton watched her carefully before he answered. "A throwing star was found several floors below, wedged in the side of a building. But that wasn't what decapitated the deceased."

"No," Peyton added. "It looks like brute force."

"Brute force?"

Holy shit! Alice thought to herself, hoping the shock wasn't painted across her face. *Did Kyle really pull someone's head off?*

"It's why we were brought in."

"You suspecting a Vamp?" she said, playing along. Not that many Breeds had the strength to pull someone's head clean off.

"We shall see if we can pull up any evidence. Jones is just collecting samples from the hallway, the room itself destroyed."

Alice opened her mouth to query about the fire damage, snapping it shut before she could give herself away. She wouldn't have known the details.

"Call me if you need me," she said instead.

"Hmmm," Brady mumbled as his attention was taken by Jones, who was waving him over.

"You're not here for the crime scene," Peyton whispered so Brady couldn't overhear once he moved away, his expression unfriendly. "What's this favour?"

She was taken back by his hostility, not used to the reaction from Peyton. She stared at him a few seconds, wondering if he knew she had summoned a Daemon. Which was ridiculous.

"I need you to look into some tunnels for me."

"Tunnels? What tunnels?"

"Ones that are under the city, built before the underground."

"There are no such thing," he began before she interrupted.

"According to my intel, there are." She checked to make sure Brady was still pre-occupied before she continued. "I'm hoping there is some rough record in the archives. Caverns big enough to walk through, some may be flooded or caved in."

"What's in these tunnels?"

"Something I need," she responded instead. She hadn't known Peyton long, wasn't even sure how far she could trust him.

Peyton's demeanour changed, his eyes becoming alien for a mere second. She wouldn't have noticed if she wasn't paying attention.

"I'll trade," he said. "If I find this information, I want a trade."

She wasn't confident until then what Peyton was, her instincts from the beginning telling her he wasn't one-hundred per cent human. There was only one Breed she knew of that used trades.

"I'm wary about a trade."

There were six rules when dealing with the Fae, regardless of their class or caste.

One: Names had power, a high Fae would never give you their True Name.

Two: Never thank the Fae; they took it as an admission for a debt owed.

Three: Neither high nor low caste Fae could lie, but they could twist the truth.

Four: Fae did not do anything for free.

Five: Be cautious of gifts given; Fae stuff had a mind of its own.

Six: Fae loved offerings, but care had to be taken not to insult them.

Alice thought about his offer, knowing she didn't have anybody else to ask and she was against the clock. She had no idea what type of Fae he was, whether he was full-blooded or mixed. The majority of low caste Fae didn't usually follow the rules, well, not unless it suited them. They would lie, and if caught, be punished by the High Lords.

From Peyton's reaction she guessed he was on the higher scale.

"I won't ask for much," he stated, his expression not changing. "You may ask for guidelines."

Alice couldn't help but flare her chi, probing his. She could tell he felt it from the slight flare of his pupils, but other than that his chi felt normal, boring. It didn't feel anything but human. Except humans wouldn't have reacted at all.

Shit. Shit. Shit.

She hadn't expected a complication.

"Guidelines?" she questioned.

Peyton nodded.

"Okay, what are the guidelines?"

"This isn't how the trade works, you may agree to the trade with restrictions," he said, almost frustrated.

She hadn't dealt with many Fae, many still preferring to live beyond The Veil in the Far Side. Their race was still very alien, their nature not embracing the changes as did other Breed.

She had never found Peyton more other, even if he was trying to help.

Fucking Fae and their stupid bloody rules, she thought.

Her mind rushed as she tried to think of restrictions. "I will trade you the information regarding the tunnels for one gift, this gift must be an object."

"Fine," Peyton said, his usual indifference returning. "I will trade this information for a single earring."

"An earring?" she questioned.

What the actual fuck.

"Yes," his eyes warned. "A single earring, it must have belonged to you."

"Erm, okay. Than..." The acknowledgement died in her throat.

Rule two: Never thank the Fae, they take it as an admission for a debt owed.

"Does Brady know?" she asked instead. She might have felt he wasn't one-hundred per cent human, but that didn't mean she knew what he was. Technically she still wasn't confident.

"Know what?" he asked, his expression returning to normal.

Alice just shook her head. "Contact me when you have the details."

CHAPTER SEVENTEEN

Sam puffed on his cigarette as he leant against the side of the car, his amber eyes watching her cautiously as she crossed the busy road. He could read her like a book, knew something was up as she had nervously parked in the dedicated space. She was grateful when he explained he would meet her inside.

She needed to speak to Theo alone, without Sam interfering.

He wasn't going to like what she was about to ask.

The Great Court was a beautiful building, the last standing example of original gothic architecture that had survived the wars. The white brick was pristine, contrasting against the colourful stained glass windows that decorated the clustered columns. If it wasn't such an unexpected situation she would have loved to appreciate the architecture.

It shocked her that the trial was in such an official building, Xavier, the head of the shifters was judge, jury and executioner. He wouldn't have needed a grand room with an audience.

Shifters in general preferred to do all their official business on their own grounds. The Great Court was a human building for criminal prosecution, not usually Breed. It seemed pointless unless Xavier enjoyed a show.

Theo paced in front of the two-story double doors, the wood old and damaged with a few historic scars. He looked nervous, his eyes fleeting between the colour of his wolf and his own as he paced. He smelt her before she was in view, his nose scrunched as he turned abruptly.

"You made it," he said, his voice deeper than usual as he relied on his wolf for strength.

"I said I would." She flicked her eyes to the other man who waited by the door. He was on the skinny side, his dark hair streaked with random threads of white. He stared at the floor, not acknowledging anyone as he shook gently. His arms were wrapped around his chest, hands clawed into his white wrinkled shirt as if that was all that kept him together.

"Are you ready?" Theo asked as he took a deep breath.

"Shouldn't I be asking you that?" She rubbed her hands together, the cold biting her skin as she noticed chalk still underneath her nails. "Why is it here?"

"Because I believe Xavier has already made his decision," Theo muttered as he looked up at the tall stone building. "Shifter trials aren't public like this. He's doing it for a reaction."

"Who's reaction?" No one else waited outside.

"I haven't figured that out yet," he muttered. "Why have you brought the cat?" He nodded towards Sam, who was still smoking by the car.

"Moral support, I guess," she said. She also couldn't have kept him away, and for that she was grateful. Her nerves were on edge, she needed Sam to keep her centred. "I also need to ask you something, and you can't ask why."

"Ask me something?" Theo frowned, scrunching up his face.

"I need you to protect him, at least for the time being." She would have asked for it as a favour, but she didn't want him to have the option to refuse. Besides, he owed her. The whole fucking pack did.

"Protect?" His eyes narrowed, the colour at the edge of his wolf. She saw he wanted to ask questions she couldn't answer. "Why would we protect a cat? He isn't pack."

"Just have a wolf watch him while he's at work, surely Mac can sort that? Maybe have someone make sure he gets home safe every night."

"Why didn't you ask Mac direct?" he asked, giving her a wary glance.

She hated pack structure, thought it was archaic.

"You're the Alpha," she said politely. "Hierarchy states I must ask your permission."

"You guys set?" Sam said as he approached, the wind catching his blonde strands to tangle around his throat. "We need to go inside."

"Yes," Theo replied, even though he looked at Alice. "I appreciate you coming Samion."

"I'm not here for you."

"Sam," Alice scolded. "Please."

"Come on baby girl," he said as he grabbed her arm to entwine with his. "Let's go get front row seats."

The inside of the building was just as grand as the outside, the stone structure echoing every footstep. Alice shivered as cold seeped through the walls, forcing her to tug the leather of her jacket closer around herself.

Sam pulled her towards the first door in the grand room, the court smaller than she imagined. Who she assumed was Xavier sat behind a large wooden desk, the microphones that were supposed to catch every word brutally wrecked from their mounts, leaving exposed copper wires that sparked every few seconds. His eyes were a warm brown, ones that flashed a bright orange as he watched them carefully take a seat on a front pew. With a smirk he threw his legs over the table, dangling his bare feet over the side which he swung like a pendulum.

"Is that him?" she whispered to Sam who sat down first, conscious that shifter hearing was better than hers. She knew it was probably a stupid question, the arrogance radiating from the man clear but she needed to confirm.

Sam just nodded, his posture tense.

The court itself was just as cold as the corridors, the stone walls bare of any markings or decorations. Dark, well-worn green carpet was placed without purpose against the edges of the rooms, leaving a large open patch where the seven viewing pews were placed. Two isolated boxes were perpendicular to the grand podium where Xavier still watched them with curiosity, his attention not wavering even as others joined them.

The skinny man from outside sat beside her on the front, his breaths coming out in heavy pants as he began to panic. Theo quickly moved up, forcing him to press against Alice's side. His presence seemed to ease the man's anxiety, at least, enough for him to stop shaking as violently.

She reached out to pull his hand into her lap without thought. When his other hand covered hers she left it there. Shifters were two beings in one body, both human and animal with distinct personalities.

When in their human form they thought clearer, their animalistic instincts not as overwhelming. However, they still wanted the physical affection and comfort that their animal craved.

"Is this all?" Xavier purred a throaty growl, a wide grin curving his cheeks. "How disappointing."

Alice quickly looked back, noting that other than the four of them in the front only a small handful of people attended. No one she recognised.

"Shall we start then?" He pounced onto the desk in one feline motion, landing in a crouch on the balls of his feet. Alice was able to hide her flinch, saw his muscle tense just before he moved.

He was a cat. A predator.

She could see the intelligence behind his eyes, with just a hint of madness. It made him dangerous. Even more so than she originally thought. When she caught his eye he smiled again, showing sharp incisors. Stripes appeared across his tanned skin, a quick flash of the tiger underneath that disappeared after a blink.

"Get him in," Xavier called as the door at the end opened, showing Rex standing with chains linking his wrists. He walked confidently to the dock, his face cleanly shaven with his hair tied back with a leather strap. He looked like she remembered, cold and controlled.

His eyes scanned across the pews, her pulse jumping when they settled on her, his face masked into its usual impassivity. Sam growled in his throat, forcing Rex's attention.

"Rexley Wild, of the London White Dawn pack. You stand before the leader of your Breed, your Alpha and brother Theodore Wild, your other brother Roman Wild and your victim Alice Skye."

Roman squirmed beside her, lifting his face for a second before looking at the floor once more. She squeezed his hand in reassurance as she risked a peek at his bowed head, able to see the brotherly characteristics once she really looked. She was happy he was no longer stuck in his wolf form, but she wasn't sure the cowering man beside her was doing much better mentally.

Xavier leant forward until his palms pressed onto the wood, his legs still crouched like a gargoyle.

"You are accused of treason against your own pack, against your Breed, working with a prohibited Breed, distribution of Class A drugs as well as conspiracy to sacrifice a witch to a cult..." He paused, his eyes flashing orange when he turned to Rex, who still stood with no emotion. "How do you plead?"

The room went still as everyone waited. Alice felt her breath hitch, the tension in the room unbearable as Rex lifted his head slightly, looking up at the leader of the shifters.

He remained silent.

Xavier grinned, the excitement unsettling. "No plea? A surprise considering."

He leapt to the floor, prowling towards the dock. He moved with the grace of a feline, even though he looked unkempt in his ripped jeans and black T-shirt. A single silver ring earring glittered in his right ear, next to what looked like a bullet hole.

Normally Alice didn't care about jewellery, but shifters were allergic to silver which made the choice unnerving.

"I have enjoyed hunting down all your accomplices within your pack. People who knew what you were doing, yet didn't come to me."

"What?" Rex's façade cracked before he instantly recovered. "You better have not hurt my pack," he growled.

"Your pack?" Xavier laughed. "What pack? You gave them up when you joined the Daemons."

"No... I..."

"Enough," Xavier snarled.

He clicked his fingers, the noise bouncing off the walls as the door at the back opened once more. A table on wheels was pushed towards the dock, two boxes spaced evenly on top.

"What do we have beneath box number one." Xavier lifted the box, revealing a decapitated head, the skin peeling from the bone.

Alice immediately closed her eyes. She recognised what it was, the skin that remained still stitched with thick black thread, the mouth forever sewn closed. They had held her down, forced their thoughts inside her head.

She felt Sam tense beside her, enough for her to look. Xavier stood barely a foot from where she sat, his shoulders bent so his face was closer to hers. She hadn't heard him move.

"Miss Skye," he purred, a sensual smile on his lips. "How nice to finally meet you. I have heard interesting things about you."

"I'm sure they're exaggerated," she replied, her voice surprisingly strong considering the sudden dryness in her throat.

"Would you like to tell everybody what my first evidence is?"

"An acolyte," she said without hesitation. "He was one of the acolytes for The Master."

"The Master?" he asked, moving back towards Rex as he directed his next question. "Your master?"

Rex remained silent.

"Box number two it is then."

Alice didn't want to look. Instead she watched Rex. His expression didn't change, not a flinch of a muscle or even a wince as the stench of decaying flesh doubled in the small, windowless room. She wanted to scream, shout and make a scene because he remained so emotionless.

"Rex, can you please tell everybody who was beneath box number two?"

He didn't even react at the question, his expression eerily calm. "That isn't one of my pack."

"That's Coleman Grant," Theo interjected. "He's the Pride Leader of Sun Kiss."

"Correction," Xavier laughed. "He *was* Pride Leader. His wife also met her demise, shame really. I haven't met many succubi in my lifetime."

Alice couldn't help but look once she knew who it was, recognising Cole instantly as the head on the table. She should have been upset, but wasn't, instead she felt a sick sense of satisfaction. He knew what was happening, his cryptic speeches encouraging Rex to betray his own pack. He himself was happily killing his own pride, feeding his lions to his wife in exchange for protection.

Protection from The Master, something Xavier should have been doing.

"Where were you?" Alice asked before she could bite her tongue.

"Excuse me?" Xavier swung his head to face her, less than impressed.

Alice angrily stood up as Xavier approached, close enough that she could smell the wildness of him. She had to stop herself from stepping onto the pew to give her the height advantage.

"Where were you when The Master attacked the pack? Attacked the pride? Isn't that your job?"

Xavier tilted his head, eyes a burning orange as she saw his tiger underneath. Stripes appeared across his already tanned face, darkening his skin further. She wasn't sure what it meant.

"Rexley Wild was an Alpha, one of the strongest in Europe. Yet he was too weak to defend his pack against one simple being."

"What's the point of you?" she said as Roman clinged to her arm, trying to pull her back down. Sam looked alarmed beside her before he also stood up.

"Alice…" Sam said before Xavier cut him off.

"No, let her speak."

"You're supposed to protect them." She met the orange of his eyes, hoping his tiger wouldn't take it as a challenge. Normally she wouldn't have worried, the animals understanding that she wasn't one of them, but a witch who had no interest in dominance. Except Xavier was different, his whole personality more primitive.

"Am I?"

"Alice, sit down," Theo barked, his eyes angry when she looked at him. "Please."

"Tell me… Alice," Xavier purred, as if he enjoyed her confronting him. "When did your lover ask me for help?"

"We're not lovers," she shot back.

"He still smells of you," he laughed. "His wolf might even have chosen you as his mate, yet instead of asking me for help, he gave them what he wanted." He leaned forward, his nose almost touching hers as his mouth opened to show his sharp incisors. "He gave them you."

"Yeah, well," she said. "Everyone fucks up."

Xavier's sharp cackle made her jump. "How beautifully put," he said as he still stared at her. "Theo, please tell your twin how many of the pack I have had to terminate because of your brother's treachery."

Theo coughed, clearing his throat. "Twenty-two."

"That's right," Xavier said, his breath warm on Alice's face before he faced Rex. "I have killed twenty-two of your old pack. That's almost a third, putting the whole pack in a weak position against others who wish to invade your territory."

Rex still remained silent.

"Nothing? Even knowing the consequences of your actions? I killed both men and women, people who blindly followed you out of loyalty."

"Anything I say would be pointless, you made your decision well before today," Rex finally said.

"I will ask you again, "Rexley Wild of the London White Dawn pack, how do you plead?"

Rex remained silent, his face finally cracking before he sighed. "Guilty."

"Rex, no!" Theo jumped up.

"Then before your Alpha and family, I sentence you, Rexley Wild of White Dawn to death."

"Death?" Alice cried as Roman snarled, his body convulsing beside her. She panicked before she recognised his bones breaking, skin shifting as he began the painful transition into his wolf. "You can't!"

Xavier ignored everyone, his fingernails growing until they were sharp claws. Rex did nothing as he was forced to his knees, head yanked back to expose his throat.

"YOU CAN'T DO THIS!" Theo roared. "PLEASE..."

Alice saw the claw touch Rex's neck, a bead of red as the tip was pressed into his skin.

She couldn't allow it to happen. She hated him, hated what he did to her and the consequences suffered by his own pack. But she couldn't allow this fate, because she didn't know if she would have done the same thing herself in his situation. She loved both Sam and her brother, would do anything to save them, protect them.

"Wait," Alice said as she jumped over the small barrier that separated the pews to the dock. "Wait, there must be something else, anything else."

"Are you offering yourself in his place?" Xavier asked.

"NO, no she's not," Sam said as he jerked her back. "Alice, what are you doing?"

"Not death, please," she begged.

Xavier released his claw, his tongue lapping at the blood on the tip. "Mr Wild must be punished for his treachery. What do you suggest instead?"

"I don't know," she said as she began to panic. She didn't know shifter politics.

"Hmmmm." Xavier yanked Rex again, forcing his face to touch his own as he forced him awkwardly to his feet. "I think I need a new pet. Fine, I have decided. I will not kill him, instead he will become my personal... helper. But only on one condition."

"What?"

"I want a favour, anything I want at a time of my choosing. I may someday need a witch."

Alice didn't hesitate. "Fine."

Rex fell to his hands when Xavier released him, his shoulders sagging.

"Excellent. I will allow Rex a week to get his affairs in order before he is to return to me. He will serve me indefinitely. If he has any more traitorous thoughts against myself or our Breed, his life will be forfeit."

Alice didn't look back as she walked out of the court, Sam hot on her heels. He snarled as he hit the stone wall with a fist before he stormed toward the car.

What the fuck have I just done?

Alice stood outside the wooden doors, the cold biting her cheeks as she tried to breath.

Fuck, fuck, fuck. As if she didn't have enough problems, she now owed Xavier, the leader of the shifters a favour.

"You shouldn't have done that," Rex murmured from behind her.

She didn't turn, instead nodding at Theo as he left, followed by Roman who was once again a wolf. He gave her a wolfish grin before he yipped, tangling himself in his brother's legs.

"What choice did I have?" she said. She felt his warmth as he moved closer, sending shivers down her spine.

"You now owe him."

"What should I have done?" she snapped as she turned. "Let you die?" She shook her head, letting out a humourless laugh. "I'm not like you."

His hand hesitantly reached for her before she stepped back.

"It's done now, over," she said.

"No, it's not over. Let me make it up to you."

"Can you go back in time? Before you did all this?"

"Ruby Mist, why were you asking about it?" he asked.

"Oh yeah, you're a drug dealer," she snapped. "Bloody hell…"

"Alice, answer the fucking question. Why were you asking about Ruby Mist? How far involved are you?"

Alice thought before she answered. "I need to find out who's behind it. The Trinity."

Recognition flashed across his eyes. "You shouldn't be in that world."

"And who's fault is that?"

Rex clenched his jaw. "Let me make a few calls, see If I can arrange a meeting."

Alice just nodded, not trusting her anger. She didn't want his help, but he was already further in that world than she was. If Mason was one of the three leaders, following the drugs could lead her to him. With Mason gone, Kyle and Sam would be safe.

As long as Sam didn't do anything stupid.

Or that Kyle wasn't already lost to a Daemon.

Just a typical fucking day.

CHAPTER EIGHTEEN

Alice ignored Rex as he stared at her from the passenger seat, the tension uncomfortable as she pulled into the underground carpark, the parking attendant shooting her a judgmental glare at her pathetic excuse for a car.

"We only offer valet, ma'am," he said as he opened her door, eyebrows raised as she fought him on the handle.

"I can park my own car."

Rex ignored the exchange, instead getting out his side. He came around the front before holding Alice's door open as he waited for her to get out with little patience. She grit her teeth as she gave in, ignoring Rex's outstretched hand to hop out of the car herself. She handed the the car keys to the valet, who in return handed her a ticket. She ignored his worried look when he noticed the bullet holes in the side of the door.

She had no interest in touching Rex, enjoyed the tiny twitch of annoyance he showed before he walked away with a stiff gait. He had been silent the whole car journey, his eyes tracing her face as she carefully drove across the city. It had taken him only an hour to get an appointment with someone who could help regarding Ruby Mist, which made her wonder how much influence he really had.

"Rex," she quietly murmured as he approached the glass door that exited the carpark. "Where did you go? When Theo couldn't find you?" It was a question that had been bothering her since she also failed to find him. It's what she did as a job, track and detain Breed. Yet, he seemed to have disappeared off the face of the earth.

Rex tensed, his hand releasing the gold handle of the door to allow it to close. He turned to stare at her, his eyes paler than usual. His hair was neatly brushed, longer than she was used to with the strands brushing the lapels of his dark blue tuxedo. She couldn't help but stare when she picked him up from the compound, annoyed at herself for wanting to take a double look.

She shouldn't want a double look.

Although, she was grateful he warned her of the dress code inside the casino. She hoped the simple grey lace sheath dress she once wore for an office party shouldn't make her stand out too much. Sam had glamorised it with some costume jewellery, even though he was upset with who she was going with.

"A friend owed me a favour," he replied, giving her little information. Which wasn't surprising.

Alice waited for another couple to pass them before she asked another question. "How long have you been dealing drugs?"

He watched her carefully. "I was Alpha for ten years before The Master came onto the scene. He killed three of my wolves before I took notice." Rex tugged at his hair in annoyance. "It started with small favours, asking me to sort out a few people. Then it became pick up and drop offs."

"Why didn't you ask for help?"

Rex continued as if she hadn't spoken.

"When I was asked to enrol my pack, to become dealers themselves I refused. I was happy to risk myself, but not my pack. He killed three more wolves within an hour of my refusal."

"Rex..."

He caught her eye, holding it long enough she saw his wolf prowling behind his irises.

"The pack was loyal to me, didn't question it when a few of them started dealing on the side. But then I started to notice changes, their wolves becoming sick with the poison he was forcing on them. A transition that was never meant for us. Even now, Roman is affected with the same poison, changing him in ways none of us understand, least of all him."

"I know the rest," she said, wanting him to stop. She could hear the agony in his voice, even if his expression didn't reciprocate. She wished he would drop the façade, allow himself to mourn his decisions. Decisions that resulted in twenty-two deaths within the pack, not including the ones that lost their lives at the beginning. Instead he hid behind his impassivity, something that had always frustrated Alice.

"We better get moving," he said as he cleared his throat. "Our host doesn't like being made to wait."

"Why here?" she asked when she finally walked into the casino. "I thought we were meeting someone who can help us with the drugs?"

He ignored her, instead guiding her through the floor with a hand on the bottom of her back. She tensed when he first touched her, the reaction automatic before she forced herself to relax. She needed him, at least for now.

He was trying to move her quickly, fingers pressing before she stopped to look around the huge room. She didn't know what to expect, never having been inside a casino before. But she couldn't help but stare in awe at the huge space, decorated in regal golds, reds and grey. High above she could make out several floors, each balcony full of different tables from poker and craps to roulette.

An overwhelming sound of coins, chimes and cheers on both sides as rows of slots were lit up with multi-coloured graphics that encouraged the hundreds of customers to try their luck.

"Alice," Rex started as she approached a slot, watching the colours spin. "Come on."

Water cascaded from a man-made waterfall, five stories tall that was the backdrop to the bar. The water was visible beneath the floor, a stream under glass tiles before it opened up into an oasis in the corner. Three beautiful sirens sat on rocks within the pool, their pearlescent tails catching the artificial lights pointed towards them. One stood up when a couple approached, her tail coming out of the water to change magically into an iridescent evening gown the same colour as her scales.

"Mermaids?" Rex asked as he watched the women splash each other playfully. "I've never seen mermaids before, I didn't think they lived in the cities?"

"They prefer to be called sirens," Alice said as they walked closer, fascinated with their outer beauty, but also distracted with the cliché clamshell bras. It was also the first time she had ever seen one herself, their Breed preferring to live in the ocean. Fae in general were few and far between, preferring rural areas outside cities or beyond the veil on the Far Side. At least, that's where they were anticipated to be, nobody had ever actually confirmed. As the majority of the Fae lived for thousands of years their birth rates were low, meaning there weren't many on record to begin with.

The siren closest to her started to sing, the sound nothing she had ever heard before. A few of the men who stood at their poseur tables closest to the oasis turned to watch, eyes glazed as they were transfixed by her song. Leaving their alcoholic beverages behind they approached slowly, much to the delight of the siren who beckoned them further, almost into the pool with her. Perfectly synchronised they reached into their wallets, reaching for cash as well as casino tokens that they tossed into the water. As her song came to an end she reached for the money, slipping it into the decorative pirate's chest that opened at her touch beside her.

"Rex?" Alice called when he stood there staring.

He turned to her, his eyes clear as if he wasn't affected. "They look like cartoons."

Alice began to reply before another siren began to sing. This time Alice concentrated on the song, the music washing over her like an electric current that made her teeth ache. It resonated through her skull, almost painful until she called her magic. The familiar heat of her flame appeared on her fingertips, enough to give her clarity.

"Hey," she said as she approached the oasis. "HEY!"

"You can't use magic here," the siren with the crimson red hair said, eyes alarmed as she swam over. "It's prohibited."

"And you guys can't manipulate people with your song. It's illegal."

"No, she means you shouldn't be able to do magic." The second siren said, even as the third continued to sing. "They have special anti-magic controls." She gestured to the ceiling high above.

Alice followed her gaze, noticing a giant pale orb with symbols patterned around the circumference.

"She means there's an anti-magic spell activated, something similar to what you would find in a hospital," Rex said as he stood beside her. "It stops people inciting violence or cheating." Which would make sense in a casino.

"Then how come you guys can sing?" she asked the sirens, ignoring the fact her chi still burned at the end of her fingers.

"Our song isn't magic," the red-head explained to them as if they were children. "It's just who we are."

"It's still manipulating people for money."

"Is there a problem over here?" A man approached, face stern as he held a walkie-talkie. He frowned when he noticed her flame.

"Actually..." Alice began.

"We have an appointment with Mr Blackwell," Rex interrupted as he moved in front of her, forcing the man's attention. "I'm far from impressed with the amount of waiting considering the importance."

"Mr Wild," the man nodded in greeting. "I sincerely apologise. Of course we expected you, someone was supposed to meet you by the entrance." He turned to the sirens. With one hard look they quickly moved back to their spotlights before beginning to sing once more.

"I guess we will just follow you then?" Alice said as she stepped besides Rex, flicking him a look of annoyance. She clicked her flingers, allowed her flame to distinguish with a pop.

"Just this way." He guided them to beside the bar where he pressed a button on his belt. The waterfall parted, showing a mirrored lift that opened a few seconds later.

"I can handle it from here," Rex said as he guided Alice inside, pressing the correct floor. "Thank you for your help."

Alice waited until the doors closed before she stepped away from Rex's palm. She noticed his blatant controlling behaviour, the Alpha tendencies setting her teeth on edge. He noticed her irritation too, his eyes tracing her expression without saying anything.

That made her even more bloody annoyed.

"You need to calm down before we enter his office," Rex said in his usual monotone voice. "Or this meeting may be short."

Alice ignored his statement. If she wanted to be angry, she could be angry.

"What's Nate got to do with Ruby Mist?"

"Nate? Since when were you on first name basis?" he asked, his tone deeper than usual.

Alice felt herself smirk. He wasn't happy she already knew Nate, well enough to call him by his first name. "You didn't answer my question."

"Just let me do the talking," he replied instead.

Alice clenched her fist, deciding against arguing. She still needed his help, at least until she understood what Nate had to do with it all.

Just think of Sam and Kyle, she thought to herself, even as her nails dug into her palm.

The lift stopped on the top floor, the doors opening straight into a huge office. A metal desk faced towards the lift, Nate sitting behind it with slightly flushed cheeks. He absently waved them in, even as he continued the heated discussion with the man sat before him.

"We're done here," Nate said as he stood up, "I have other meetings to attend."

The man turned, his grey eyes narrowed as he looked at Alice, and then Rex. Alice stared, unable to stop herself from appreciating Riley in a full tux, including a silver tie clip that matched his eyes. She hadn't seen him since he had left her standing at her door. He had been pissed off with her then, and seemed just as pissed off with her now.

"Interesting company you keep," Riley said to Nate, even as his unique eyes flickered back to Alice. She knew the question was aimed at her, could almost see the confusion in his expression as his iris' swirled silver, his beast reacting.

She couldn't even help the slight flutter in her stomach, a ridiculous reaction that she didn't need. All she could see was the man who pressed her against the wall with such care as he devoured her. Then left her wanting more.

Fuck sake.

She saw the instant he knew what she was thinking, his own eyes becoming heated as he said something to Nate she couldn't hear.

A hand hooked on her waist, pulling her gently as Rex growled low in his throat. She tensed instantly, but didn't want to make a scene. Riley noticed too, his jaw clenching as he walked past and into the lift that still waited.

"I apologise about that," Nate said as he came around his desk. "He wasn't expected."

"What was he doing here?" Alice asked as she carefully moved away from Rex, only able to do so now he didn't feel as threatened.

Men and their fucking testosterone.

Nate just smiled, showing off his perfect teeth. "Rex, it's so nice to hear from you."

"It's been some time," Rex said as he stepped forward for a handshake.

"How do you know each other?" Alice asked.

Rex turned, his hand still clasped in Nate's. "I'm Alpha," he said, as if that was explanation enough.

"Was," Nate said as their hands parted. "And now you're here, in my office."

Ignoring the sudden tightness between Rex and Nate she nosily checked out the large office, the feeling of suffocation strong as she moved to the only window. Synthetic lights brought out the dark red of the painted walls that covered half of the room, the other half covered in a dark wood. It would have been heartless if it wasn't for the bursts of green in the many plants, as well as another waterfall identical to the one downstairs, but a lot smaller.

"Alice, I've just been informed you were able to call your chi?" Nate said when she turned back to them. "How?"

Alice bit her lip. "It was just a trick of the light, nothing more."

"So are you calling my staff liars?" he laughed as he settled into his seat, the leather creaking as he leant back. He clicked at something on his desk, a screen popping up from the centre which showed the CCTV footage of her flame by the oasis. "The strangest thing is that my barrier didn't even detect it." He clicked another button and the screen disappeared back into his desk.

"It's probably faulty, I would get someone to take a look at it," she said dryly. She had no idea why she could call her chi, she had felt no resistance when she used it. She hadn't even realised she wasn't allowed. "Did you know it's illegal to manipulate your customers?"

"How are they being manipulated?" he said, eyes sharp. "A sirens song is a gift they were born with and nothing to do with magic. It only works on those who are easily influenced, which is why our friend Rex here wasn't affected."

Rex said nothing as he moved into one of the seats in front of the desk, waving Alice over.

"It has no more influence," Nate continued. "Than a woman who uses her breasts to get what she wants from a male."

"Wow, so beautifully put," Alice replied deadpan.

"We're getting off subject here," Rex interrupted.

"Ah yes, shall we get down to business then?" Nate gestured for Alice to take a seat, remained silent until she did so. "I wasn't expecting to hear from you, and then turning up with a Paladin, or at least former," he smiled charmingly. "So what do you want Rex?"

Alice spoke before Rex could. "What do you know about Ruby Mist?"

Nate looked shocked before quickly calming his face into impassivity. "Brimstone? You're here to ask about brimstone?" He tapped his fingers against the desk.

"We need to know where it's based," Rex said. "We both know it originates from the city. I hoped you would know more considering your... experience."

Experience? Alice pursed her lips, wondering why Rex was being careful with his questions.

Nate stared at them for longer than necessary before he brought his attention solely to Alice. "I heard you're no longer with S.I." He made it a statement. "So I'm interested why? If it isn't for an investigation."

Alice couldn't explain the details, she needed to protect her family. "I have my reasons," she smiled, trying not to seem desperate. "The people I'm interested in go by Trinity. I need to find them."

"Them?" Nate laughed as he stood up, turning to look out the single window with his back to them. "You seem confident that this 'Trinity' is more than one person?"

"Mason is one of the three, he was behind manufacturing."

"That's an interesting statement to make. Also very dangerous."

"Do you know where he is?"

"Mason Storm has a lot of interesting people after him," he said as he turned, his smile turning into a full on grin. "Does his son know?" he asked before he tutted. "Of course he does. The Storms know fucking everything."

"Nate, I'm calling in my favour," Rex said, his voice deeper than usual. When she looked at him his eyes were almost arctic, his wolf taking over.

What's pissed him off now? she thought.

"Very interesting," Nate said as he looked between them, noting Rex's reaction. "Why does everyone assume I know where he is?"

"You were in business with him," Alice said as she caught his eye. She just didn't know what business. "Surely you have investments you need to protect."

"Doesn't mean we called each other to discuss our day. We're not some girlfriends who discuss our nails and hair."

Rex growled. "Get to the point."

"I know you understand what this information is worth, yet you don't want it for yourself, but for a woman?" Nate smirked. "How the mighty have fallen."

"Nate..."

"You know how this works Rex, so answer me this. Why?"

Rex remained silent, no movement other than the slight clench of his jaw.

"He owes me," Alice said instead.

Nate looked between them for a moment before he opened a drawer in his desk. "Fine, but that favour is now paid in full, my friend." He took out a piece of paper and a pen before he scribbled an address on it. "Meet me here tomorrow night. Wear something nice." He handed Alice the paper with a place and time written on. "Only you."

Alice tucked it into her pocket.

"Thank you."

"I wouldn't thank me just yet."

CHAPTER NINETEEN

The lift down was achingly awkward, an unconscious anger radiating off Rex as the mirrored doors opened back into the busy casino floor. He waited silently for her to exit, following closely as she walked out.

"I'll meet you by the car," she said as she scanned the room. She knew Riley would still be there, could feel his chi electric against her own as soon as the doors had opened.

"I don't think so," he replied as he noticed Riley by the bar, his voice deep as his wolf poked through.

"Excuse me?" She turned to him, annoyed when he refused to look at her, instead watching Riley. She poked him in the chest, hard enough that his human half broke through his impetuous wolf.

"What?" he growled as he went to grab her upper arms in a bruising grip.

She felt Riley approach, shot him a warning look before she turned back to Rex.

"You have ten seconds to let go," she whispered carefully. She kept the eye contact, making sure he knew how serious she was. When he moved away blood rushed back to her arms, creating pins and needles that stung.

"I'll be outside," Rex said, face guarded.

She watched him until he was out of sight.

"Are you okay?" Riley asked, voice deep in a controlled anger. A gentle finger touched her arm, forcing her to look down at the visible red marks on her skin.

"Just dandy," she said as she stepped back, not wanting him to touch her. "What are you doing here?"

"Me? What are you doing here?" he asked before he looked around. "Look, we can't talk here." He moved towards the side, assumed she would follow him as he pushed the bathroom door open.

"The men's bathroom, really?" Alice scrunched her nose, the odour unpleasant as they got a few weird looks by two men at the urinals. "Fuck sake," she murmured as she pushed him back into a cubicle, twisting so she could lock the door behind her. It was an awkward space, Riley sat on the toilet with Alice backed up against the door, the hook meant for jackets poking into her shoulder.

Luckily the toilet was reasonably clean, as much a men's could be. Even if the cubicle walls still had rude graffiti written on them, as well as an impressively drawn picture of a certain part of the female anatomy.

"I see Mr Wild hasn't been punished for what he did, surprising," Riley said, eyes hard as he stared at her from the toilet.

Alice couldn't help her smile, then her dramatic laugh. He looked ridiculous sitting there in his exceedingly expensive suit, looking at her angrily while she tried desperately not to step in the weird stain on the floor. Her attention kept getting caught on another drawing, an angry looking penis with more veins than could possibly be healthy.

"Alice..." Riley said, turning to look at what she was smirking at. "What are you doing here?"

"I've never been to the casino, thought I would check it out."

She watched him take a deep breath, his eyes swirling silver as a deep growl rumbled through his chest. He never used to do that, or maybe she had never noticed the small animalistic mannerisms. It made her heart skip a beat, in fear or anticipation, she didn't know which.

And that worried her.

"Alice..." he growled. "What were you doing here? And why with the man who sacrificed you to a Daemon?"

"Maybe I'm a glutton for punishment?" she replied casually.

He just growled louder.

"Fine, I needed to speak to Nate regarding an investigation about drugs, Rex said he would get me an appointment."

"Drugs?" he asked, confused. "Why are you investigating drugs?

That isn't what Paladins do which means you're doing it for some other reason."

Alice hesitated, wanting to be careful with what she said. She trusted Riley, but she knew he wasn't thinking straight when it came to his father. She couldn't tell him about Kyle, not until she knew for sure he was okay, and not a danger to himself, or others.

He was the leader of The Guardians of the Order, a faction specifically created to fight against Daemons and anything that was deemed dangerous.

Kyle was dangerous.

But, so was she.

"I'm looking for details on Ruby Mist," she said. "Apparently the people behind it are called Trinity."

"Why are you investigating Ruby Mist?" His eyes narrowed.

"Have you heard of it?" she asked.

"I've seen it come through the bar, but I don't tolerate drugs." Riley frowned. "I've heard of Trinity, they're the biggest players within the drug trade in the city. But why are you looking for them?" His eyes were sharp as he waited for her answer.

Shit. Shit. Shit.

She didn't want to lie to him, not about something that could possibly help. They both needed to find his father, she just hoped he would work with her, rather than against her.

"Because your father is one third of Trinity. I..." she stopped to correct herself. "We need to find him, and soon."

The door bulged as someone knocked violently, pushing her forward until she collapsed onto Riley's lap.

"OCCUPIED!" he let out a bark at the interruption, his arm coming around to hold her steady across her waist.

"Come on mate," a voice moaned through the door. "Get a fucking room."

Alice braced her arms on both cubicle walls as she awkwardly unfolded herself. She opened the door, squeezing herself through the gap much to the shock of the man who was about to knock again.

"All yours," she murmured as she quickly made her way out of the bathroom.

"What do you mean he's part of Trinity? What evidence do you have?" Riley said when he caught up to her beside the bar, his voice slightly raised as he fought against the noise of people betting insane amounts of money around them.

"I thought I asked you to leave," Nate said as he emerged from beside the waterfall, his mouth curled in distaste. "Do I need to call security?"

"We're just leaving," Alice said before Riley could reply.

"Alice, it's a pleasure as always," Nate winked with a suggestive smile. "I'll see you tomorrow night."

She hated men sometimes, especially when they were trying to get a rile out of each other. Instead of rolling her eyes at his flirtation, because she was pretty confident he wasn't interested in anything other than pissing Riley off, she nodded politely.

"I look forward to it," she replied before she grabbed Riley's hand, tugging him towards the car park exit before security forced them out.

"What is with you two?"

"Don't worry about it," he murmured as he looked down at their joined hands.

"Oh, sorry." She pulled her hand away, feeling her skin flush.

"What did he mean 'see you tomorrow night'?" he asked as he held the door open into the car park.

"Why? Jealous?" she said before he growled.

"Nate isn't a friend Alice."

"I asked for some information, he said he could get it for me."

"You need to drop this, he isn't safe. You're not trained..."

"WHAT?" She felt her anger spike hot, Tinkerbell appearing around her head as she fought the sudden power surge. She had to concentrate, not wanting Riley to have to intervene as people gave them worried glances. "Stop being a bloody testosterone driven... beast!"

Her Tinkerbell shot aggressively towards him with intent to harm. He swatted it away casually, as if it were merely a bug and not a ball of concentrated arcane made from fire. That pissed her off, Tinkerbell too from the way it sparkled.

"Beast?" he laughed, even as his eyes turned to mirror. "You have no idea, sweetheart."

She had to bite the inside of her cheek to stop from replying.

Fuck sake. For an insult, she knew it was shit.

"You ready to go?" Rex said as he appeared beside them, his face hard as he stared at Riley.

Riley carefully watched Rex with his unusual silver eyes. "Guess that's my cue to leave."

"Wait," Alice said as he went to turn away. "Fuck sake, you need my help just as much as I need yours."

"Are you going to start telling me two heads are better than one?" he smirked before his eyes hardened when Rex touched Alice's shoulder. "I'm dealing with it."

"Alice, we have to go," Rex said with a snarl. "Leave this wolf, we don't need him."

Alice wretched her shoulder away. "Give me a minute," she scowled. "You," she pointed at Riley. "Stop being all high and mighty. Remove the bug from your arse and think it through."

Riley said nothing as he accepted his keys from the valet.

"You're not in this alone, he isn't just your problem."

"It isn't your problem, either." He got into his car. She had no knowledge of cars, but at least it wasn't the obnoxious yellow one, even though it was just as annoyingly loud as it thundered away.

"Fucking wolf," Rex growled.

"He isn't a wolf," she automatically replied with a sigh.

Well, technically she had no idea what he was.

"You smell of him." Rex said with a dark tone.

"What are you on..." She couldn't finish her sentence as Rex pulled her against his chest, his lips crushing hers a second later. When she didn't resist he pressed harder, his tongue forcing itself through her lips to dominate.

Alice enjoyed the familiarity, but her heart ached. Tinkerbell sparked almost anxiously, confused at her lack of reaction just as much as she was. When Rex finally let up for air she tried to pull away.

"Rex..."

"You're mine, you have always been mine." He kissed her again, one hand pulled at her hair, while the other gripped her wrists even as she stood there frozen. His teeth pulled at her lip, a canine nipping her skin hard enough to draw blood.

This time she reacted, pushing with all her strength as she threw flames onto the concrete to separate them. His face was a flare of shock before he instantly hid behind his emotionless armour.

"I'm not yours. I was never yours."

"Yes..." He stepped closer until the flames roared higher, warning him away.

Her pulse thumped against her neck, smoke strong at the back of her throat as she concentrated on the surge of power as she battled her anger. Her wrists had red marks where he gripped her, which fuelled her irritation.

"You don't ask, you just take. You always have."

"You're my mate..."

"No, I was just someone you hoped could help. You're blinded by the guilt that you're clearly not dealing with in a normal healthy way."

"You don't know what I'm feeling," he sneered, moving as close to the flames as he could without risk of being burned. "You will never understand what I had to do, what I sacrificed..."

"Sacrificed?" she laughed. "I know fucking well what you had to sacrifice."

"Excuse me ma'am," the young valet interrupted as he nervously looked at the flames. "I'm going to have to ask you to leave."

Alice flicked her wrist, absorbing the fire.

"I've had time to think about what you've done, and your reasons behind it," she continued as if the valet wasn't still standing there. "And I had already forgiven you."

Rex blinked at her, face calm but his iris' flickered towards his wolf. He remained silent, his expression hard to read.

"I'm not your mate. I never was. I'm not some wolf you can manipulate and force. I'm a witch."

"I don't care that you're a witch, my wolf knows..."

"Your wolf is confused," she interrupted. "And do you know what? I deserve better. You're an Alpha, you need someone to control and protect, someone that isn't me."

"You want him," he stated.

Alice just shook her head.

She didn't need anyone.

Soulful howls echoed around him as he stared at the body, anger vivid through his veins as his pack mourned.

He couldn't mourn, wouldn't.

Not until it was over.

He knew it was a warning, that he was too slow. So they slowly took his pack, one by one. Forced them into a transition they never wanted, a transition that killed them because they weren't built for the change.

They wanted results, they didn't understand that he couldn't just grab the woman, not when she was a Paladin. He had been watching her, knew she was more dangerous than he originally thought. He would have to be careful, plan it.

He needed her trust before he sacrificed her for the sake of his pack.

CHAPTER TWENTY

Alice tugged on her long sleeves, conscious that she wasn't dressed appropriately for the high-end restaurant.

"I did tell you to wear something nice," Nate said as he smiled towards the waiter, who poured the red wine with practiced precision. "Normally they wouldn't even let you past the entrance."

"This is nice," Alice shot back in a spark of anger, gaining her a judgmental glance from the server.

It was fine, Alice thought. *Well, maybe not posh enough for this place.*

She wore a long-sleeved cotton black T-shirt with a pair of relatively clean jeans. She thought she looked neat and tidy, just not as fancy as the other women inside the exceedingly expensive restaurant. She hadn't heard of The Vine when he gave her the details of their meeting, assumed it was just another generic place. The fact they were in their own private booth with gold detailing and a personal waiter was a pretty big indication that she couldn't afford the place. Which would be why she had never heard of it.

Nate sipped his wine, the cost unknown as Alice glanced down at the menu, noting how nothing was priced on the extravagant menu. Not that she had a clue what much of it was anyway.

He looked like he belonged, his suit probably worth more than her whole wardrobe and car combined, never mind the gold watch that had delicate diamonds and moonstones embellishing the face.

"Thanks for the meeting," Alice said when he just stared over his wineglass. "I appreciate the help."

"You shouldn't thank me yet," he smirked. "I apologise about my earlier comment. You look beautiful," he said while he tilted his head, appraising her. "You have the loveliest eyes, such a unique emerald green. Have you tried a little makeup? Maybe put your hair down? Are you a natural blonde?"

She had her hair in a high ponytail, with a few unruly strands framing her face.

"This isn't a date," she said, fighting annoyance. "So I didn't think my appearance would matter."

"Who said this wasn't a date?" he asked as he waved over their personal waiter who had taken a position by the booth's entrance. He murmured something before the well-dressed man walked out, leaving them alone. "I don't invite just any woman out, especially to an establishment such as The Vine. I have a reputation to uphold."

"Cut the bullshit," she said before she could stop herself. "We both know you're not interested in me like that."

The waiter returned with another bottle of wine, placing it into an ice bucket beside the table.

Nate cut her a cold look, his eyes not moving from hers until the waiter moved back out of ear shot. "Observant," he finally said. "However, while you're not my usual type, I find you fascinating."

"Do you have the information I asked for?" she asked, patience running out. "We're not here for pleasantries."

Nate burst into laughter. "Like I said, you're fascinating." He nodded towards her untouched glass of wine. "Please, drink."

Alice purposely moved it further away. "I'm sorry, I don't drink while working."

"That glass costs more than what you earn per month."

"That's nice."

Nate clenched his jaw. "I prefer a little casual chat before we discuss the details. Pretend this is a date, I would like to know you a little bit more, humour me."

"Fine. I have my mother's eyes, can't cook for shit and my star sign is a Leo. Is that enough for you or would you like my bra size?"

"Leo did you say? Same as myself. Apparently we like to express ourselves in dramatic and creative ways. Would you agree?"

"I've never really thought about it," she said as she watched him sip his wine once again.

"I would agree that you have great courage and energy, so I guess that's accurate at least," he mused. "So tell me, how are you friends with someone who's in Rex's profession? Or was it just sexual?"

"There's nothing sexual there," she retorted, "and what do you mean profession?"

"We both know he deals in narcotics, has been for a lot longer than he would ever admit. So I'm fascinated why a Paladin is hanging around with him when you admit it's no longer sexual?"

"Why is everybody so obsessed with who I sleep with?" she said before she sighed. "Nate, I really appreciate you doing this, but we're here to discuss business. Or was Rex wrong, and you don't know everything?"

"I owed Rex, but not you. I'm happy to give you some of the data, however I'm in the business of information."

"So you do want my bra size?"

His lip curled as he shook his head. "I prefer to find out those particular details myself, the morning after while the bra is on my floor. Now, tell me what you want Mason for?"

Alice hesitated.

"My time is expensive…"

"Fine, Mason was behind the murder of my parents. I need to speak to him regarding it."

"Now that's interesting," Nate murmured as he leant back, his lips twisting into a smirk. "Tell me more."

"No. Rex has already called in his favour, and yet you want more from me."

"I like you Alice, I don't meet many beautiful women as strong in spirit as you."

Nate tapped the table, the waiter bringing over a piece of paper. He checked the sheet, flicking his eyes over the top before placing it face down on the table.

"How confident are you that Mason killed your parents?"

Alice felt her chi spike. "He confessed. Actually, it was more gloated."

"Mason has confessed to many things, doesn't make them true."

"Do you know where he is?" she asked, her hands clenched beneath the table.

"One final question," he said as leant forward, his arms braced on the table. She might not have been brought up with a silver spoon in her mouth, but even Alice knew his table etiquette was atrocious. "What is between you and Riley?"

"Why is that important?" she asked as he waited. "He's my Warden. That's it."

"Is he aware of his father's so called confession?"

Alice remained silent, instead she relaxed her face to betray nothing. Nate had extracted far more information than she was comfortable giving away.

Nate sighed dramatically. "Mason hasn't been seen in a while, rumours are he's gone underground to try to recoup his losses."

"Rumours? All you have is rumours?"

Shit. Shit. Shit, she cursed to herself. How was that going to help her?

"Be careful, Alice," he warned. "Your spirit will only get you so far. Now they are only rumours because I haven't personally witnessed him in the underworld. However, I wouldn't give out information if I wasn't confident in my own people."

"Do you have anything more specific?"

"He was last seen at the fighting pits." He pushed the paper over to her.

Alice read the address before placing the sheet back down. "A cemetery?" she asked, confused. "Why have you given me the address of a cemetery?"

"That's where you will find the entrance to the Troll Market. Inside there you should be able to find details on the fighting pits, they move around frequently so you would have to be quick."

Alice nodded. "Is there anything else I need to know?" She knew very little about the Troll Market, a notorious place where people bought illegal weapons, drugs, spells as well as a few other nasty things. As a Paladin, she had looked for it along with her colleagues, but had never been close.

He smiled, leaning back in his chair before he nodded towards her full wine glass again. "Drink. Before people judge me."

Alice picked up the glass, sipping the deep red liquid before putting it down. She didn't understand wine, couldn't tell the cheap stuff from the expensive. Sam had taken her a few years back on a wine tasting class. Unfortunately, they where they both asked to leave when they couldn't stop laughing at everybody who spat into the bucket. Who would have thought you weren't allowed to actually drink the wine?

"See, that wasn't difficult," he said, smug. "Now the Troll Market is Fae, which means no metal of any kind can pass through its entrance. That means all weapons including steel, iron and everything in between."

"You seem to be familiar with this market," she commented.

Nate continued as if she hadn't interrupted. "I'm sure in your profession you know enough about the Fae but I will just remind you to never thank any of them. They will take it as if you owe them a favour, and trust me, you don't want to owe anybody down there a favour."

"Even the low caste Fae?"

"Can you tell the difference?" he asked, face straight.

Shit. "No, not really."

"Then I will continue as if you haven't wasted both of our time. The physical entrance is through a mausoleum inside that cemetery, you can't miss it. Once you get there you will be greeted by the guard. He will either allow you through, or he won't."

"What do you mean he won't?"

"He only lets people through who are branded, or..." Nate smirked, pulling a gold coin out of his pocket. "You show him this."

Alice went to grab the coin when Nate closed his fist.

"This is Rex's favour and not the address."

He opened his fingers once more, allowing Alice to pick up the coin. She studied the sigil printed on both sides, a jawless skull. The edge of the coin was rough to touch, runes and markings etched into the side. For something the size of a normal pound coin it was heavy. It reminded her of something found in a pirate's chest.

"If this was his favour, why did you give me the address I needed?"

"Like I said, I'm in the business of information. You answered some of my questions, in return I give you the address to the market. Fair exchange."

"Alice?" A familiar voice whined. "How can you even afford this place?"

Alice spun in her chair, surprised to see Michael standing at the entrance to their private booth. "Mickey?"

Fuck sake.

"Excuse me, you're interrupting," Nate said, gesturing for their waiter to intervene.

Michael strutted in, a sneer painted across his face. "How funny that I have run into you." He stood over her seated position, hands on his hips as he thrust his hips forward. Her eyes automatically dropped to the tacky diamond encrusted belt buckle, which was probably the point.

"I see your new position comes with a pay boost," Alice muttered as she grabbed her wine glass just so she could look anywhere else.

"I'm sorry, and who are you?" Nate asked, annoyed.

"I'm Commissioner Brooks, and you are?" Mickey asked as he flicked his red hair from his face. Most of it was slicked back using wax, but two strands continued to poke across his eyes like little horns. It fit considering his suit was a deep shade of red with a black and grey paisley shirt.

"Mr Blackwell."

"As in Blackwell Casino?" Mickey chuckled as he turned back to Alice. "How funny, you'll need a rich man when I finally get to fire you."

"Do you know what Mickey," Alice said as she stood up, wine glass in hand. "I quit." She threw the wine over his head, enjoying his gasp of shock. It would have been more satisfying if his suit didn't match the colour. "So fuck you."

Nate stood up, just missing it splash across the white table cloth.

"ALLICCEEE!" Mickey squealed, spluttering as the exceedingly expensive wine covered his face. "If you quit, you become rogue. Rogue Paladins don't last long in the real world."

Alice ignored him, instead she turned with an apologetic smile to Nate.

"Thanks for the drink. I'm sorry I couldn't stay for dinner." Alice winked at the two men, ignoring the waiters stunned expression as she left. "I'm sure I will see you around."

CHAPTER TWENTY-ONE

Alice hadn't really spent much time around cemeteries. She had always felt they were unnecessarily creepy with their tombstones and dead bouquets of flowers, especially at night. She had never visited her parent's statue, Breed in general preferring to cremate their dead, that was if their bodies didn't naturally become the earth. She knew where the single statue was, Dread explaining as soon as she could understand that it was there if she ever wanted to speak to them. But she knew, even as a child that it wasn't her parents. Just a lump of concrete.

Besides, she never felt the need to try to talk to them. She still had many unanswered questions regarding their deaths, as well as their lives. Asking a statue that couldn't answer seemed like a waste of time.

"Winter is supposed to be almost over," Alice muttered to herself as she pulled her jacket further around herself. The full moon illuminated the dark cemetery, making the tombstones glow eerily. As a deterrent against grave robbers, it worked.

She tried to suppress the chills that rattled down her spine, either from the cold or the uncomfortable creepiness of standing at midnight near so many graves.

She carefully kept her eyes forward, ignoring the blurry figures that stood in the corners of her peripheral vision. Ghosts or spirits weren't common, most people passing onto the other side, or whatever place they believed in, once they died. The most common place to find them was in the old cemeteries, but the problem was the older the ghost, the more unpredictable and dangerous they could be.

Alice didn't deal in ghosts. She didn't think there was much point in learning about them considering you couldn't charge a dead person with committing a crime, which was the whole point of her job. Was.

Necromancers, on the other hand dealt in the dead, all aspects of it. While it was considered black magic, some witches had been able to specialise under the watchful eye of The Magika. She had met only two Necromancers in her lifetime, one who The Tower used when they needed information from the recently deceased, and one who tried to kill her. Seeing as Alice didn't get on with The Towers red-headed witch on the numerous occasions they'd met, and the other's head was buried behind her old oak she held a decidedly negative view of Necromancers.

They were weird, almost alien. Being able to reanimate a corpse and talk casually to the dead must take its toll on their personalities. While they weren't allowed to sacrifice humans like they were supposed to, or even wanted to, they were allowed to sacrifice animals. The older the corpse they needed to reanimate, the bigger the animal. It took a specialised license to be able to practice necromancy legally, with only a small handful active in the whole of the United Kingdom.

Alice continued to walk forward, concentrating in front of her as the ghosts became more and more curious. They generally weren't dangerous, most just echoes of the person they once were. Most weren't even able to touch, just watch, but sometimes there were one or two that had stuck too much to the earth, and those could touch. She felt eyes creep across her skin, forcing her to walk faster.

She reached the metal gate just as she heard the ghosts' quiet whispers as they fought for her attention. Alice could see the mausoleum she needed just beyond the tall, sharp fence. It was in the dead centre of the large cemetery, and the only area that had no working lampposts. From the dust along the glass, as well as the cracks, it looked like the lamps hadn't worked in a long time.

She didn't know if it was the Fae who purposely broke the lights, or the ghosts. Going from the fact the fence and gate were both made of oxidised metal, she blamed the latter.

"Hello?" she called as she opened the creaky gate. "Hello?"

"Oh, hey there doll, yew lost?" a strangely detached voice replied.

Alice spun back towards the gate, confused where the voice came from. "Hello?"

Something brushed against her hair.

She moved up her hand, hitting out as her skin suddenly prickled with pins and needles.

"Hey, hey, calm down bitch," the ghost that stood directly in front of her said. "Yew have to be careful around 'ere baby doll, especially in dis area," he grinned.

Alice stepped back, even as his slightly opaque hand tried to keep the end of her ponytail. "You the guy I need to see?"

"That depends baby doll, how good are yew between da sheets?"

Alice tried to hide her grimace. The ghost was dressed like a nineteen-twenties reject, with his double breasted suit with a chain pinned across the lapels. He even wore a newsboy peaked cap.

"What yew wearin'?" he asked as he slowly walked around her, his figure slowly solidifying as she gave him attention. "You look peas in the pot. I love a bird in leather."

"Peas in the pot?" she asked, confused.

"Yeah, hot. Yew wear dem tight leather trousers just for me?" he bit his lip, appraising her once again. "Or yew 'ere just for a bit of chin wag?"

"I have a coin," she said as she produced the heavy thing from her pocket. She had changed into the leather as it was warmer than her jeans, along with her leather jacket. If it wasn't for her naturally bright hair she would have blended better in the dark.

"Blimey, I can't Adam and Eve it!" he excitedly reached for the coin, his hand passing through it before he attempted again, the second time his hand almost completely solid. Everywhere he touched pins and needled exploded across her skin. "Yew 'ave a pass. Yew don't look like da nawmal person we 'ave 'ere."

"What can I say, I'm special," Alice said dryly. "I need to pass into the Troll Market."

"Why?" he demanded as he played with the coin along his fingers. She watched it for a few seconds, amazed as his hand seemed to become solid just as the coin passed across his skin.

"To see a man about a dog," she replied with the only Cockney slang she knew.

The man laughed, bending over and even clutching his waist. "Are you takin' da piss?" He chuckled some more before he stood up, the coin having disappeared. "Yew get da token back once yew return, if yew return. No metal beyond me."

"Okay." Alice went to move past when his hand passed through her breast. It made her jump back. "Hey, watch it!"

"Keep your hair on, yew ain't answered da three riddles."

"Nobody said anything about three riddles."

"Yep," he grinned as he held up three ghostly fingers. "Answer three riddles an' I'll open da door, easy peasy."

He didn't wait for her to reply.

"The more you take," he said in a clear voice, devoid of his strong East-End accent. "The more you leave behind. What am I?"

"That's easy," Alice said, relieved. "Footsteps."

"Right!" he cheered before he cleared his throat. "This one's a classic. "What is the creature that walks on four legs in the morning, two legs at noon and three in the evening?"

"That's the Sphynx's riddle," Alice said as the man grinned. "The answer is man."

"Lor' luv a duck! A baby crawls, geezer walks an' an elder used a walkin' stick." He clapped excitedly. "Last one," he began once again without his accent. "What has a head, a tail, is brown but no legs?"

Alice hesitated, having to think about it.

Shit. Shit. Shit.

"Oh, errr."

"I'm gettin' old over 'ere."

"How can you get old?" she said. "You're already dead."

"Alrigh', don't cry over spilt milk." He produced her coin again, flipping it up into the air and catching it while he waited.

"A PENNY!" she shouted as she watched him toss the coin. "The answer is a penny."

With a chuckle he disappeared, the door to the mausoleum behind him opening silently. Alice stepped forward, noticing the pale, shimmery veil that covered the double doors.

"Okay," she murmured as she took a calming breath, placing her hand against the veil and pushing forward gently. She felt nothing as her hand passed through, then her arm, then her whole body as she popped past the glamour and into the raucous of noise that was the market. She stood at the top of the stone steps, hundreds of wooden stalls set up below with loud peddlers pushing their wares. The rows were bustling with customers, with people talking between themselves, faeries, witches and even a few trolls.

Some stalls were full of crystals, ones that screamed at any magic user who was close enough for their attention. Crystals were usually greedy, projecting a beautiful song that only those attuned to their chi could hear. The ones on the black, velvet cloth screeched a gloomy, horrible song that made her teeth rattle. Dark energy pulsated from them, powerful enough to tempt even her as she tried to ignore the witch beckoning her forward.

"Come, come, take a look. Natural, created in the deepest, darkest place on both earth and the Far Side."

Alice's own crystal seemed to warm against her throat, reminding her she didn't need, or want one of those crystals made from minerals she didn't even recognise. She had to shake her head to stop from moving further forward, to touch one of the crystals even as it screamed louder. She concentrated on the obnoxious buzzing of the tattoo gun on the next stall, where a topless, sweaty man sat perched on a wooden barrel tattooing a skull and flames. The tattooed flames seemed to move and flicker beneath the candles that were the only illumination in the cavernous room.

It took Alice a minute to realise that it still looked like she was in the mausoleum, with the walls that she could see made from thick stone. Everything was made from wood, twine and rock, no metal in sight other than the weaponry that was being displayed in the corner, the impressive swords, axes, sceptres and arrows all protected within a spherical glimmering bubble-like shield. The ceiling was covered in cages, some empty, some full of random objects as well as a few birds that judged everyone eerily below.

Among the other wares were tables covered in monstrous meats and fruits, mostly grey in colour that had more flies hovering around than the troll that was trying to sell them. Other stalls held oversized blue vases that held various tomes and spells that were covered in dust. A pile of leather bound books sat piled up high, bathed in a dull orange glow of the old glass lamp that was precariously perched on the top.

A raven squawked when Alice got too close, its large eyes reflective as it watched her carefully. Bowls of newts, snakes, mice as well as many different types of birds were available for pets, or also as snacks as one customer munched on a live critter with a soul shattering crunch.

Accompanying the stall full of live animals was a table covered in crochet and knitted jumpers, cloths, frilly doilies that looked at odds compared to the rest of the marketplace. A delicately made cross-stitched framed cloth stated *'Sugar and spice and everything nice!'* was nailed to one of the wooden posts that held the canopy high. With another frame stated *'Snips and snails and puppy dog tails!'*

"Do you like my signs, child?" the old woman asked when she caught Alice staring.

She wore a colourful shawl that matched her other products, her glasses hung limply around her neck as she squinted. She smelt like what Alice assumed a grandma would, of bitter tea and sweet, sugary sponge cakes.

"I have these too..." she said before she produced a giant blanket with a black crocheted pentagram. "Or maybe you would prefer a decapitated head?" she said as she brought over another blanket.

"Ah, no thank you," Alice politely declined, even though she was morbidly impressed with the small details.

Excusing herself she pushed herself between two tall Fae, their skin a pale blue with iridescent silver hair that fell from their tall frames almost to the floor. It was clearly a place glamour wasn't used or needed, where the more different Breed could come together to be themselves. It would have been a nice thought if she didn't just witness one of them buying a cage full of small flying creatures, then loudly laughing to his friend that he would make a meal out of them.

"Last bets!" a woman with half a skull tattooed across her face called. "The Pits are closing in five minutes!"

"Fighting pits?" Alice asked when she approached, much to the distaste of the woman who looked her up and down with disgust.

"Yes, can I help you?"

"I want in," Alice said, producing a roll of cash she had hidden in her back pocket. She had no idea what she was doing, had hoped all her and Sam's savings were enough to help the façade. It wasn't much, what money they made usually going back into the house that, despite appearances, still needed a lot of work.

The woman laughed at the roll, her long nails, painted a blood-red nudging the cash.

"You've never done this before," she grinned, showing off her set of gold teeth before her hand snapped forward to take the money. "Have you?"

"You have to start somewhere," Alice shrugged. "Besides, I've heard you're the best in the business." She hadn't heard that, but was running out of things to say. The woman, whose head was half shaved to match the skull tattoo, just looked at her as if she were a bug. A man, who looked identical with the skull tattoo the opposite side of his face approached.

"Follow Jerry," she said as she flipped over her wooden sign, explaining all bets were closed. "I hope you enjoy your... experience," she ended on a chuckle.

Alice trailed closely behind as the man quickly manoeuvred through the crowd, moving towards the opposite side of the cavernous room to a door that shimmered much like the door Alice entered. He didn't hesitate as he passed through it, forcing Alice to follow into a hallway that was covered in scars and gouges.

The sound of weapons clashing and animals snarling echoed off the stone, the noise apparent as the wall became glass to her right, showing several floors below a blood-covered dirt pit. Sitting in private booths were what Alice assumed the richer clients, each with their own steward and black podium. On the platform above them were crowds of cheering people, excitedly shouting and sneering at the fight below that was only separated by a crudely made metal link fence. One that dangerously bowed slightly from the weight of the excited crowd.

She remained just as silent as the man she followed. He kept peering back at her with a grim smirk before he stopped in front of an open door. He nodded her inside, holding his arm open.

When she didn't immediately move he growled.

"Inside."

Alice felt a poke in her back, followed by an electric current that brought her to her knees. She tasted blood on her tongue when she was pushed forward into the cold, dark room, the door locking behind her with a loud click.

CHAPTER TWENTY-TWO

Alice groaned as she reached for the wall, the stone cold and wet against her palm.

"Fuck sake," she groaned as she tried to call her chi, her aura pulsating as the floor vibrated beneath her knees.

Probably should have been clearer, she moaned to herself as she tried to get to her feet. The floor burst into light, lines that appeared like cracks across the floor and walls that glowed bright enough to show the tight confines of the room. The door was made from wood, backed up with criss-cross metal bars that looked worn and scratched.

She went to touch one of the lines, the electric current throwing her back with a snap. "Don't touch them," a voice whispered. "They'll drain your energy."

"Thanks for the warning," Alice moaned as she climbed to her feet again. She looked around for the voice, noticing a small vent high up in the wall.

"You're new," the voice whispered again. "Who's your master?"

"Master?" she asked. "I don't have a master."

"Then you've taken one wrong fucking turn," the voice laughed just as the glowing cracks dimmed to barely anything. "Don't worry though, most newbies don't last the first fight."

"Wow, helpful," Alice muttered as she carefully stepped over the lines, approaching the door with caution. She held her hand over the metal keyhole, feeling no current. "Does the electric run through the door?"

"I don't think so," the voice murmured. "I've never really paid much attention as the current doesn't affect me. My name's Ricky, been here for more full moons than I care to admit. Not that I can see the moons, have no windows you see. But you get a sense of time eventually, maybe. Are you a girl? You sound like a girl."

"Does it matter?" she asked as she leaned into her boot, pulling out a wooden stake. She knew she wasn't able to take any metal with her to the market, but she was never specifically told she couldn't take weapons.

"Well, if you win you can be sold as a prize to one of the rich pricks because you're master-less. And you're a woman, so..."

Alice didn't need Ricky to finish that sentence.

"To be honest, even if you lose, some of these guys don't even care. Any hole is a goal and all that, even if it's a gaping wound in your chest. Bloody hell, it's been that long even I would have a go at that..."

"Does lose mean death?" she asked, facing the vent.

"Death, dismembered or severely wounded. Like I said, some of them don't care."

"Great, just fucking great." Alice clicked her flingers, a small burst of fire illuminating the lock enough for her to realise her stake was too big to use as a pick. She sighed as the light fizzled out without her asking it to. She frowned even as she re-sheathed her stake, hiding it in a clever strap on the inside of her boot she once saw on one of the poorly acted B-movies Sam forced her to watch.

"Arma," she whispered, waiting for her shield to pop into existence around her. She felt her chi react, stretch before settle back down. "What the fuck?"

"You a witch?" Ricky asked. "Your magic hooha won't work for a while once you've been electrocuted. It has something in it that stunts your chi or something."

"Any way around it?"

"I don't know, I'm a vampire. The last witch I went against I pulled his head off within the first few minutes. That was only because he couldn't call his magic fast enough."

"Wow, thanks for that story. I really appreciate it," she said dryly.

"Okay, there's no need to be sarcastic you know," he tutted. "Besides, it isn't that bad here. If you keep winning they sometimes give you some comforts."

"Comforts?" Alice glanced around at the empty cell. She was clearly in a holding cell which didn't bode well. "Like what?"

"I don't think your cell has anything, they removed the toilet recently when someone tried to smash their head into the porcelain. The noise his skull made was nasty. Anyway, you can probably see the concrete where they filled in the hole."

Alice noticed the slight discolouration against the stone floor, including the slight copper sheen.

"I have a fully functioning bathroom, even though I don't need it," he chuckled. "I have a bed with sheets, I say sheets, they're like fucking sandpaper against my skin but who am I to complain?"

"Why are you here?"

"Sucked on the wrong lady's neck. Just happened to be one of the organisers many wives. But you know, shit happens. After one-hundred wins you get the option to be released or partnered. Partners continue fighting but actually get paid. A lot of the winners become partners because the pay is sweeeet."

Shit.

"Have you ever tried to escape?"

Alice was about to ask again when he finally whispered an answer.

"Once."

She waited for him to continue, when he didn't she sighed.

She was fucked.

Alice sat with her back to the wall, the vent that separated herself and Ricky directly above her. The cracks in the tiles glowed, the intensity changing every few seconds until she pulled her boots back until they hit her chest, hooking her arms around her legs.

She fought claustrophobia as she rattled her brain. She had no phone, no weapons and no magic. She had no source of communication other than Ricky, and he was already too far gone to help. A vampire was the strongest of all the Breeds, if he couldn't escape she had no hope.

"Hey," Alice said when he didn't say anything further after ten minutes. "Do you have a mirror?"

"A what?"

"A mirror," Alice said carefully. "Above the sink?" There was only one thing she could think of that could possibly help her.

"Yeah, why?"

Alice jumped up, plastering herself to the wall. "I need a shard, can you break a piece off and push it through the vent?" Alice stretched, her fingers barely able to touch the holes on tiptoe.

"I don't know..." Ricky muttered.

"Please, I have an idea." A very rough idea that she hoped could work.

"I don't want to get into trouble, I'm only twenty wins off of being offered partner."

"Please..." she begged. "I wouldn't put you at risk if I wasn't desperate."

She held her breath, concentrated on the absence of noise until she heard a smash, the mirrored shard passing through the vent a moment later. She caught it, the sharp edge slicing her hand.

"What's your plan?" he asked, slight excitement back in his voice. "You're not gonna kill yourself are you? If you do I will definitely be punished, I should have said no... I should have said no."

Alice smiled at the shard the rough size of her palm. "I'm not going to kill myself. I'm going to scry." Well, she hoped to scry anyway. It was something taught to all witches in high school. That doesn't mean she remembered what the hell she was doing.

"Scry you say? I knew a lad that could do that. Think he was arrested for pretending to know the lottery numbers..."

Ricky continued to talk as she sat back down, this time in the corner. The art of scrying had been practiced for thousands of years through many different cultures. It was formally a medium for those who were attuned to the spirit world to receive information from the other side, as well as visual flashes of information believed to be from the future, or the past.

Witches had modernised scrying by using it as a way to call another person they were linked with. She was only connected to two people, and Alice doubted Nancy, the girl she was partnered in class with when she was taught how to scry would be able to help.

That left only one option.

"Ricky, I'm going to try something. Can you give me a warning if someone approaches?"

"Sure thing! I doubt you'll get any attention just yet as you've just got here. They normally like to break your spirit for a while before they..."

Alice let out all her breath as she opened her third eye, zoning out Ricky's ramblings. She glanced at the glass, watched how it became misty before colours flashed in the centre.

She touched her fingertips to the mirror, her blood dripping from the cut on her hand on the edge. The mirror absorbed the red, turning the shard darker.

"Xahenort, I call you through the reflection."

Alice waited, the dark misty glass pulsating beneath her fingertips.

"Xahenort? Hello?"

"You have got to be fucking kidding me!" a voice snarled before a pissed off looking Daemon appeared in the glass. Weird white foam covered half his face, his chest bare. "Why have you called me?"

"Oh, hey Xah..." Alice quickly corrected herself. "Lucifer."

"You shouldn't have used my name," he growled as he took a razor to his throat, scraping off the foam and hair beneath. "I'm not a fucking call service."

"It was an emergency."

"Emergency?" His red eyes pierced her through the mirror. "Where are you Little War? I thought you weren't into kinky things like dungeons?" he chuckled.

"Lucy, I'm stuck and..." The cracks along the floor glowed, bright enough she had to pause and squint until it passed.

"I seem to have lost you Little War, the connection is shit. Seriously, thought you would be able to scry better than this. Witches these days, can't spell for shit," he sighed as he finished his shave. "Brother's alive by the way. If I knew you both would be this much of a fucking effort I would have let him die."

"Kyle is okay?" Alice asked before she remembered there was a point to the call. "Wait, I need..."

"Yeah he keeps fucking off without telling me..." Lucifer paused before frowning. "Oh there he is."

"Hey? I'm stuck..."

"I'M FUCKING BUSY!" Lucifer turned his face off screen, his horn curling around his face in irritation. "WHERE THE FUCK HAVE YOU BEEN? I SWEAR, IF YOU BREAK ANOTHER BLOODY VIAL I WILL PERSONALLY SHOVE IT UP YOUR..."

"Lucifer?" Alice tapped the glass for his attention. "I'm kind of in a rush."

His furious face came back on screen. "I swear I'm never doing this again. Your brother is barely house trained."

Alice watched as a vial of green liquid smashed against the wall directly behind, covering him in the liquid. His red eyes glowed as his skin tightened, shrinking to sharpen his cheekbones. Black veins appeared beneath his off-grey skin as he spun around with an ear-splitting snarl.

"Witch! Witch! HEY!" Ricky's voice broke through. "They're coming!"

Alice jumped up in a panic, disconnecting from Lucifer as she passed the shard back through the vent.

"It's actually surprising considering you've only just got here. Maybe they're running out of bodies today," Ricky muttered almost to himself.

Alice jumped back into the corner, careful to not step on a crack as they glowed strongly once again. She double checked her boot, hoping they couldn't see the only weapon she had, especially if she couldn't rely on her magic or Lucifer for a rescue.

Fuck. Fuck. Fuck.

Well, that didn't go to plan.

CHAPTER TWENTY-THREE

"I would say thirty seconds away," Ricky continued. "They sound excited. Good luck, I hope you don't survive to become a sex doll."

Alice choked down her snappy reply as the door swung open. A shadow stood in the doorway, a long metal stick pointed toward her.

"Out," the shadow snarled as he clicked the stick, the end lighting up in a snap of blue.

"Okay, okay," Alice carefully moved forward, trying not to get poked with the cattle prod. If the blue flash was anything to go by it was the same current that would drain her powers. She felt her chi, stronger than it was but still not at its full strength. It was coming back, but too slowly. She couldn't risk them wiping it out again.

"Over here," he growled as he pushed her down the dark hallway, the windows she saw the first time covered so she couldn't see the dirt pit several floors below. The click of the cattle rod made her jump forward, nerves on edge as he forced her down the stone steps.

She had really fucked up.

"Go through."

Alice hesitated at the metal gate, the lights bright just beyond the threshold. She could barely make out a man who was kneeling in the dirt at the other side of the arena, head bowed as blood was splashed across his bare shoulders and hands.

The sting of the cattle rod pushed her though, the current burning through her back as she fell to her knees, then to her hands before the gate locked closed behind her. Her hair created a curtain around her face, strands escaping her high ponytail as she panted through the pain as her muscles slowly relaxed.

A bang clapped like thunder above her, followed by static.

"Ladies and gentleman, look what we have here…" a man said through the loudspeaker. "A little nameless witch against our current winner. With fifteen wins beneath his belt, please put your hand together for Pluto."

Alice sat back onto her heels, putting the loose strands of hair behind her ear as her eyes settled on Pluto. His head shot up, eyes focusing as he frowned at her.

"This is just a warm up, so it's two-hundred to one for Pluto. Get your bets in!"

Pluto climbed to his knees, uncurling himself from his kneeled position to stretch to his full height.

"Fuck," Alice whispered. "Fuck, fuck, fuck."

Pluto was easily six-foot five, and just as wide. His eyes glowed a honey brown, a colour she had only ever seen on one other person.

"Bear, of course he's going to be a fucking bear." Shifters, in general, were faster and stronger than witches. But bears took it to the next extreme. As if being naturally stronger wasn't enough, the majority of bears also lifted weights and worked well as bodyguards, bouncers and other strength related jobs. Pluto was no exception.

Pluto snarled, his teeth long and sharp. His hand clawed, nails elongating.

Alice moved to a crouch, staying low. Her chi ached as it tried to refill, but too slow. Way too slow. She slowly reached for her boot, touching the end of the stake just as another loud bang echoed above.

"Three, two, one…"

Pluto jumped towards her, faster than she thought someone of his size could move. She tensed, waited until he was almost on her when she pulled the stake out, plunging it deep into his thigh just as she moved to the gap between his legs. Pluto yowled, much to the excitement of the crowd as he stumbled behind her, giving her time to scramble to her feet.

"*ADOLEBITQUE!*" she screamed as she pushed her hand toward him, her palm warming but nothing else. "SHIT!" Her chi needed some more time.

"Well look at that ladies and gentleman, the little blonde witch got the first shot in!" the man over the speaker laughed. "Looks like the odds have dropped to one-hundred to one. Get your bets in quick."

Pluto snarled as he attempted to pull the wooden stake out, the end piercing though his whole thigh to erupt through the other side. He turned to growl at her, even as he attempted to put weight on the leg that shook. He fell to the dirt, a pained expression as he carefully and slowly pulled the stake out of his leg.

The crowds crackled with delight, cheering and taunting from high above as debris such as paper cups and tokens were thrown into the pit alongside them. A faint dinging kept breaking up the cheers, followed by a red light that came from several different viewing windows that circled above.

Alice risked a look up, trying to see if Mason was there. Each window held one or two people, not including the personal stewards who stood stone-faced by the black podiums. One held a man, his face open with interest as he watched them in an oversized armchair, a beautiful woman beside him looking bored. Another window held an old man, tubes coming out of his nose and an oxygen tank posed behind him. He subtly nodded toward his steward, who in return pressed down on the podium. A little ding as a red light lit up below the window.

"Another bet for the wonderful little blonde witch, remember everyone, she's master-less so the highest bidder claims her. That's if there's anything left once Pluto is finished." A chuckle.

Each window showed a range of people, mainly men with only a small handful of women. They took turns betting on her fate.

She wanted to memorise every face that enjoyed forcing people to fight against their will. When her attention turned to one of the final windows she froze, her face probably echoing the same horror as the man who stood leaning against his window.

Riley spoke to his steward, face tense as she tried to see who else was in the room.

It was then she felt claws burning though her back.

Pluto's claws sliced through her cotton shirt like butter, her flesh tearing as she spun out of the way. His other paw shot around, catching her on the top of the arm that left a red smear as it pierced through her skin.

Alice grunted through the pain, ignoring her pulse that throbbed in her neck as she felt her back soak with blood. She called for her chi, feeling it almost back to strength before she ran across the arena, a roar following her as Pluto tried to give chase with a limp, his leg still healing.

"Stake," she murmured as she hit the edge of the arena and spun. "Where's the fucking stake."

It was no longer in his leg, the hole healing. She had hit the femoral artery, Pluto's blood pumping out a lot faster than hers as she evaded his swipe once again. It would slow him down until he shifted, then it would heal the wound completely and she would be fucked.

Alice spotted the stake imbedded into the wall.

She needed to get to it, it being her only chance until her powers returned.

She waited until Pluto was close before she grabbed a handful of dirt, throwing it up into his face before kicking out at his wounded leg, forcing him to stumble to the ground.

"That's right ladies and gentleman, this fight has taken another turn so I'm slashing the bets to fifty to one!"

She raced to the other side, her hand slipping off the stake as she tried to force it out of the wall.

"Shit, shit, shit," she chanted as she heard the crowd react.

She moved just as Pluto charged, his actions becoming sloppier as his life blood soaked into the dirt. He hit the wall head on, disorientating him enough for Alice to hesitate.

"You're going to bleed out!" she shouted at him, even as he blindly swiped at her again, his arm hitting her hard enough to leave a bruise. "You need to stop moving."

His skin rippled as his animal fought to break free. Skin, muscles and tendons ripped as fur erupted through his tanned flesh in a burst of brown. A snout began to stretch from the centre of his face, his nose flattening, warping and straining even as his canines doubled in size. They began to protrude out of his growing jaw, forcing it open as excess drool dribbled down what remained of his chin.

He clawed at his own skin, trying to pull it off faster as Alice watched his bones crack and reassemble into a newer shape.

His leg continued to bleed profusely.

"You're not going to make it!" she shouted as she carefully approached, his eyes glazed over in pain as he forced his shift.

"I'm... sorry," his voice growled from the jaws of a bear. "No..." he panted, "choice."

He was a captive, not a Partner.

Pluto's eyes rolled into the back of his head, his body fighting with itself as it decided what shape he was meant to be.

"Shit." She needed to stem the bleeding.

She pulled off her shirt, ringing it clear of her blood before she attempted to tie it around his thick thigh, just above his wound. The crowd around her had quietened to a murmur as they watched her intently.

"Looks like Pluto is almost gone ladies and gentleman, the odds have changed into the little witch's favour!"

Alice calmed her breath, searching deep down as her chi flared to life. She bent over his leg, feeling her own wounds tug along her back as she held both her hands on each side of his thigh.

"Adolebitque!"

Her palms burned as she cauterised the injury, stopping the blood long enough for him to complete his shift.

Pluto was out cold, stuck in mid-shift as his breathing settled down. Fur slowly covered his exposed skin, his body's natural reaction to healing as he slowly but surely finished his shift even while unresponsive.

"And that, ladies and gentlemen, is why we're the best in the biz," the man over the speaker laughed. "What a fight! Who would have thought this nobody could beat our reigning winner!"

Alice clambered to her feet as the metal door swung open, followed by the electric click of the cattle rod as it was shoved into her. She screeched as it tensed her muscles, sucking her chi back out once again.

"As she's still master-less we will have another round of bids to determine whose home she goes to! Do I hear one-hundred thousand?"

"On your feet," the man who poked her snarled, clicking the rod again in warning. "Back to your cell."

Alice stumbled back to her room, falling to her knees which rattled in pain at the contact with the cold, hard stone. The door locked once again behind her, but she had no energy left to protest.

"Soooo, you won. Impressive," Ricky whispered through the vent. "Who did you go against? Was it Bradley? Nah, it couldn't be, he's a beast in the pit. Maybe you had Lacey?"

Alice attempted to clamber to her feet when her knees gave out.

"They're in the office now, someone's bought you," he mused. "Guy sounds pissed off. What did you do?"

Alice finally was able to climb up with a little help of the wall when the door swung open. Riley stood in the threshold with a man dressed in black close behind.

"She's broken," Riley said calmly as he looked her up and down, his eyes hard.

"You clearly saw how she fought in the pit. She's worth every penny," the man dressed in black said as if they were discussing the weather. His voice matched the tone of the speaker, his dark eyes assessing her like a prized pig. "Remarkable if you ask me."

"She's bleeding. Do you have assurance she won't die before I get her home?" Riley asked.

"The deal is one-point-two, an extra fifty thou if you wish to house her here. No discounts or refunds. If you cannot afford it, I have several others waiting."

"Charge it to the account," Riley murmured before he grabbed her arm. She automatically hit out, dislodging his palm and jumping back as adrenaline pumped through her. His eyes shot her a warning look. "And I will take her with me, I have some training to do."

"Great decision Mr Storm, a brilliant buy for your first time. I hope you enjoy her... spirit," he laughed before he clicked his fingers.

Something sharp hit her in the arm, her head becoming fuzzy instantly as she stumbled forward, into Riley's arms. He lifted her up, settling her head against his chest. Her hands were quickly bound, a hood placed over her face tight enough that it muffled all the sounds.

She sucked in a breath as the cuts on her back and arm broke open, stinging as she felt the warmth of her blood drip down her skin. Her movements were sluggish as she tried to wiggle, but the arms around her just tightened.

She couldn't hear the conversation as she felt herself fly, her head swaying until she was resettled back onto her feet. She started to shiver as cold air attacked her bare skin, her shirt probably still tied around Pluto's thigh and she had no idea where she left her leather jacket. To be fair, she couldn't even remember taking it off.

"What the fuck do you think you were doing?" Riley snarled when he tugged her hood off, his face hard with anger.

Alice went to reply, her stomach recoiling before she lurched forward, gagging as her head swayed. Warmth settled around her shoulders before Riley pulled her up, untying her wrists and throwing the scraps into the car.

Her teeth rattled as she pulled her arms through the oversized jacket, basking in the warmth as her head continued to swim. They stood alone in an underground garage, the cars surrounding them costing more than her house.

"I'm bleeding in... in... in your coat," she slurred as she fought to keep her eyes open.

"Don't worry about it," he replied as he helped her into her seat, slamming the door behind her.

Alice jumped awake when the car roared to life, the heating blasting at her face before she sluggishly turned them off. She blinked stupidly at the bright blue dashboard, frowning as she tried to think past the confusion. She felt weird, empty. Worse than when she was attacked with the cattle prod.

"How..." Alice coughed when she tried to speak. "How did we get to the car?" It was uncomfortable to talk, her throat unpleasantly numb as she thought through the haze of her mind.

"The Pits are run by a few High Lords, they use specialised magic to hide the whole operation, including the garage. Nobody knows the exact destination, you have to be invited through a veil, a passage way. The entrance is different every time." Riley remained silent for a few minutes, his jaw clenched as he continued to look angry. "How did you get in?"

Alice stared at him for longer than necessarily as she racked her brain. "Market. Through the Troll Market."

"No wonder you became a fighter, that's the competitors entrance."

She frowned while she took in the information. If Riley was right, and it was the competitors entrance, it would mean she was given bad intel.

Did Nate know?

"You could have ruined everything," he growled as he hit the steering wheel, leaving a dent. "I have no idea what goes through your fucking head sometimes. How did you even know about the pits?" he asked as he shoved the car into gear, peeling out of the garage.

Alice had to take her time to reply. "I didn't have a choice," she said in a weak voice.

"You should have told me, anything to do with my father you should have told me."

"No..."

"DO YOU NOT THINK I KNOW?" he snarled as he stopped at a

red light, his whole body vibrating with rage. "Your brother told me, the same brother that is apparently dead."

Alice jerked herself awake, even as her body wanted to sleep. "Kyle?"

"He came to me, asking for safety for you and Sam." Riley's eyes were pure silver when he turned to her, the man no longer in charge.

"He... is... is..." she struggled to say.

"You didn't think it through, as usual. You just react without thought," he continued as if she hadn't tried to speak. "As if there are no consequences."

"I...I...I was desperate," she said, stronger this time as her head steadied. "I didn't have any choice, Kyle was dying and Mason was threatening..."

"I was working on it," he snarled as he drove. "You knew that's what I was doing. But no, you had to fucking interfere." He seemed to rage as he hit every red light possible. "You could have died. That's what's going to kill you, your own fucking stubbornness."

"MY STUBBORNNESS?"

She pulled at the jacket, suddenly feeling too warm until she realised she was just in a bra. She sucked in a breath, concentrating on her words as her head continued to swim.

"If you accepted help, maybe we wouldn't be in this situation. You're not invincible, you shouldn't have to hunt down your prick of a father on your own."

"Yes, you almost dying is so fucking helpful, thank you," he replied sarcastically.

Alice grit her teeth, deciding there was no point in replying. Instead she turned to the window, watching the streetlights blur as she breathed through the queasiness. At least she was no longer drowsy, the dart that injected the unknown substance working its way out of her system quickly.

She had fucked up, and she knew it.

"Wait," she said a while later. "Did you just really buy me?"

Riley laughed, the sound echoing in the car. "Yep, and I would be angrier too, if I hadn't won twice as much betting on you."

CHAPTER TWENTY-FOUR

"Stay still," the old woman scolded as she dabbed at the cut on her arm with a cotton ball.

"I'm trying," Alice moaned as her arm stung, the old woman having been patting at the same spot for several minutes. "Are you done yet?"

"Est malumius quod pueri shes, aye?" the old woman cackled as she looked over Alice's shoulder, speaking to Riley in a language she didn't entirely recognise.

Riley laughed from his position against the wall. "Et ideamius habent soliatiami."

"Stop talking about me," Alice said, "It's rude."

The old woman hit her on the head. "You're the worst patient, you know?"

Riley laughed again. "She knows."

Alice silently snarled at his smirk.

"You can leave now Tally," the old woman said as she placed the red-strained cotton into a glass bowl beside them. "Your lady friend is fine."

"Maymal?" Riley asked, his expression apprehensive as he moved away from the door. He had changed into some jeans and a T-shirt, his feet bare. She had never seen him so relaxed.

"Out boy, I will not ask you again." She stood up, her whole five foot and ushered Riley out of the bedroom. "Ay ai, that boy needs a smack. It's all gone to his head," she muttered to herself before she opened her leather bag, pulling out several glass jars. "Acting like a damn teenager."

"What's a Maymal?" Alice asked of the woman who smiled to herself.

"He couldn't pronounce my name as a child, so I became Maymal and it stuck. I call him Tally because that boy grew like a sprout overnight," she sighed. "Although, he was never allowed to be a child," she said, sadly.

Alice remained silent as the little old woman rustled through her bag. Riley had brought them to a large manor in the country, a little drive outside the city limits. From what she saw against the darkness of the sky it was a rustic building, with dark beams and grand windows. The interior – from the little Alice had seen – was just as beautiful, with natural earth tones throughout, thick tapestries, distressed stones and natural woods mixed with vivid jewelled accents.

Very different to his bachelor pad in the city.

The bedroom Alice was in was large, with a modern square four poster bed, pale grey wallpaper and delicate gold detailing. Against the dark furniture were plants, bursts of green that matched the room beautifully as well as a hand knitted blanket that had been moved to the bottle green velvet armchair that was placed in the corner.

Photographs and expensive paintings adorned the walls, mostly black and white landscapes but some were of Riley and a beautiful woman.

"Get on your stomach," Maymal said. "I need to rub some ointment into the deeper cuts."

"The sheets?"

"Can be cleaned. Now move," she demanded as Alice rolled onto the bed, resting her head on her arms.

Maymal disappeared into the adjoining room, returning after a few minutes.

"What was that language you spoke before? It's familiar," Alice asked when the old woman approached. She had recognised it as the same dialect Xander once mumbled. She thought it had a Latin base, but wasn't sure.

"You shouldn't ask questions I'm not allowed to answer," she said as she slapped on a freezing cold cream onto her shoulder before moving it along her back.

"What about, how do you know Riley?" Alice asked, even as she tensed as the cream settled into the claw marks with a slow burn.

"I hope you never lose your curiosity," Maymal chuffed to herself. "So, how do you know my Tally?"

Alice sighed. "It's complicated."

"Every story worth telling is," she chuckled as she produced some scissors and started cutting away at her trousers.

"Hey, what are you doing?" Alice tried to move away, Maymal's hand coming down to pin her to the sheets with more strength than was possible for such an old woman.

"You're bleeding. On your leg." Her scissors sliced through the leather with zero resistance. "I need to check in case you need stitches, my dear."

"I am?" Alice tried to peer around before she was pushed back down. The leather was ripped from beneath, leaving her in her unclipped bra and underwear.

"Just bruises and a small cut, you probably didn't even feel it." With a tap she stepped back. "Okay, up. Through that door is a bath, I have added some special oils that will help the bruises and wounds heal. The marks on your back are the deepest so may scar, while your arm should be fine. Please soak for a while, it will make you feel better."

"Thank you for your help," Alice said as she sat up, swinging her legs over the side of the bed as Maymal collected her jars. She ached all over, the bruises Maymal mentioned starting to appear in a pattern across her paler than usual skin. "I really appreciate..."

Maymal had gone, leaving Alice alone.

The bathroom was just as big as the bedroom, with an oversized copper framed bath that could easily sit six was set into the beautifully tiled floor. A walk in shower was in the corner, beside the double sink that looked barely used even with the collection of men's cologne. The gold-veined marble floor was warm beneath her feet as she studied the room.

"Holy shit." Steam billowed from the pool, the relaxing scent of lavender curling around her as Alice stripped and used the stone steps down. The water was murky, full of oils as Maymal had explained. Alice sighed as she settled into one of the seats, the water deliciously warm against her skin.

"Now, are you ready to discuss what you were doing at the pits?"

"RILEY!" Alice squealed in surprise, covering her breasts with her hands as he stood, arms crossed in the threshold. "What the…"

Riley removed his shirt in one clean sweep, showing off his chest as Alice tried to look away. He stepped down, his jeans soaking in the water as he joined her.

"What do you think you're doing?" She splashed at him in panic. "I'm naked!"

He ignored her, instead moving through the water until he could brace his arms either side of her.

"Turn around," he quietly murmured as he picked up a label-less bottle from the side.

"Huh?" she asked, confused before he gently touched her shoulder, encouraging her to turn. When she did, his hands started to moved gently across her skin, leaving sweet smelling bubbles.

Alice suppressed a moan as she melted under his hands. He quietly lathered up her shoulders, moving down her arms and across her back, being extra careful at the claw marks that already felt better. He tugged at the hairband that kept her hair dry, tossing it across the room as the blonde strands landed on the water.

"Why were you at the pits?" he asked once she turned back around.

"Maybe I'm into watching people fight," she said as he growled, but continued to gently wash her skin. "Fine, what are you?" she countered, knowing he wouldn't answer even as she scooped more water around herself. She was so grateful for the oils that made the water foggy.

She watched him tense, his grey eyes slowly becoming the mesmerising silver so clear that she could see her own reflection in those irises.

"No one has eyes like yours."

He picked up one of her legs, making sure she was stable before he began to massage her calf. "I can count six other men who have eyes like mine," he said, voice husky. "We were made specifically to kill my people's deepest secret. Bred to be the stronger, faster…" Riley laughed, the noise hollow.

Alice sucked in a breath, shocked he answered her question even as awareness of him burned against her skin.

He swapped her legs, massaging the second one. "As children forced to share our bodies with a creature not from this plane."

"Riley…"

"We hunt down our ancestors who chose the darkness. But as it turns out, we're the ones cursed by our own fathers."

Alice reached up to touch his face, her fingers feather soft against the stubble on his jaw.

"So to answer your question, I guess you could call me a Chimera. Someone forced to share their soul, cursed as a child by his own father."

"Riley... I..."

"Now answer the question," he said as he settled her leg down, his arms once again braced either side of her. "Why were you at the pits?"

Alice clenched her jaw. "I was looking for your father, happy? I couldn't tell you he threatened my family."

"Why? I could have dealt with it."

"I decided it wasn't worth the risk." She met his eye, noticed how the molten silver shimmered. It fascinated her, even more so after he explained what it meant. "He warned if I told anyone he would take them both. Once Kyle was safe with..." she didn't finish that sentence, remembering who exactly she was talking to. "Once I had sorted protection for both Kyle and Sam, I decided to hunt him down before I ran out of time."

"You're an idiot for going in alone," he whispered against her lips, his breath just as hot as the water as he moved impossibly closer. Her knees automatically spread beneath the surface, allowing him to nudge between them.

"I knew what I was doing."

Sort of, anyway.

"Besides, I came out of it fine."

"Yeah, your fine and my fine are two entirely different things." He tugged at her hair that settled across her breasts. "Who told you about the pits?"

"I have my own informant," she said a little breathlessly as he moved even closer. Even if that informant gave her bad advice. She could feel his jeans against her thighs, the sensation strange. "You're blinded by your own rage, your own betrayal that you're not thinking clearly," Alice said when Riley studied the hair between his fingertips. "It's not me who's putting themselves in danger. It's you."

"Hmmm." His eyes flicked to her lips, his own close. "Are you trying to save me, sweetheart?"

Save?

She remembered what Sam had said, realisation that Riley blamed himself for it all.

"You need my help, whether you admit to it or not," she said as he tried to look away, but was stopped when her palm touched his cheek. "It's not your fault." She looked him straight in the eye, made sure he understood her words. "What he did, is not your fault. You couldn't have prevented it."

His lips touched hers with the barest pressure, forcing a groan as her arms came up to pull him closer. She wrapped her legs around his waist, his jeans pressing against her with an intimacy she relished in. His hands lifted her thighs, pulling her impossibly closer as he started to grind against her in small circles that made her pant in passion.

Her chi reacted when it touched his, a full body sensation that made her light-headed in a delicious way. Riley must have felt it too, his own breathing becoming laboured as he devoured her mouth as if she was the last women left on earth. His movements became frenzied, hands everywhere as he braced her on the side of the bath, pressing kisses down her neck and across her breasts.

"Riley," she panted when he nipped gently at her nipple, licking across the nub to satisfy the sexual hurt. "Please."

His hands, calloused even beneath the softness of the water, moved towards the inside of her thighs, his thumbs precariously close to where she wanted, needed him to be.

When he finally touched she felt her head fling back, her mouth open as she groaned in delight. It was only them in that moment, Alice and Riley.

There were no deaths, no threats or fucking problems.

Just pleasure more intense than she had ever experienced. She pushed at him, jumping back into the water as she reached for his jeans, fighting with his zipper as the water lapped at her sensitive nipples.

His fingers explored, touching her in the most sensitive place almost lazily. It forced mewling noises from her throat, even as she tried to tug him back between her thighs.

"I shouldn't have come in here," Riley breathed, his face intense as he pleasured her with shallow thrusts. "Being near you makes me go fucking crazy."

"I have that effect on people," she squealed when his thumb and forefinger pinched.

"Nobody has that effect on me, sweetheart," he said, ending on a groan as her hands finally wrapped around his arousal that sprung from his jeans. He pulsated beneath her palms, hotter than the water as she circled her thumb over the head.

"How nice for you," she moaned when he pinched her again.

Her arousal became fevered, almost desperate as his lips found hers once again. When he pushed her hands off him, she let go with resistance. He groaned even louder before sucking her bottom lip, their tongues battling for dominance as he gently lifted her up.

She braced her weight with her arms, holding her breath until the first painful inch squeezed past her internal muscles. The ache amazing as he slowly pushed her down, her body squeezing its resistance like a woman starved.

"Shit," Riley groaned as his arms tensed, carefully holding her in place even as he gently thrust.

"Please," Alice cried as each painfully slow, controlled thrust buried him slowly deeper, the water and wet jeans giving it an unreal sensation. His finger crushed into her thighs, hard enough to add to her many bruises as he pulled her up just as slowly as the decent, before thrusting with such power Alice let out a squeal that was caught by his lips.

She held on to his shoulders as she rode his hips, water splashing everywhere as she felt pleasure build at an unbelievable speed. Her chi danced with his, electric against her skin as it bathed in a power alien to her own.

She was so close, the mixture of his thrusts and the water almost...

"Sire," a deep voice interrupted. "You called for a meeting."

CHAPTER TWENTY-FIVE

Alice jumped as if she had been shot, hiding her face behind her arms as Riley turned with a snarl. She closed her eyes, feeling humiliation prickle itself across her face as she tried to conceal the sudden power surge. Smoke on her tongue she breathed through the power, concentrating on keeping it below a manageable level even as she felt the water beside her move.

"What happened?" Riley whispered, his arms pulling her against his chest.

Alice remained silent, eyes closed. She honestly had no idea what happened, was so caught up in the pleasure that she hadn't realised she breached her own power level.

"Feel for me," Riley said as his hand brushed at her hair. "Your chi may have been overwhelmed when the serum finally came out of your system."

"Serum?"

"The dart you were shot with. It makes you drowsy as well as putting a blocker against your magic."

"Wait, they shot me with a fucking dart?" she asked when her eyes shot open, showing they were alone.

She didn't remember that.

Riley watched her with a controlled expression while his chi reached for hers. She wanted to resist, the familiar feel too overpowering but instead of charging her, it calmed her.

"Yeah, well maybe you will think again about infiltrating an underground fighting ring."

Alice just splashed him, full in the face. She tried desperately not to laugh at his unimpressed expression.

"I don't think your friends like me," she said when he just stared.

Riley's face cracked, a gentle smile creasing his cheeks. "Yeah, well. You're hard to like."

Alice went to splash again, his hand catching her wrist before he gently tugged her closer.

"They're all downstairs, but I need you to understand this. I have no idea what *this* is between us, but if we weren't interrupted I wouldn't have been able to stop at just once."

Heat prickled her cheeks once again, even as Riley looked at her with an intensity she couldn't decipher. She wanted nothing more than to finish what they started, the energy between them confusing but addictive. Even now, she ached with the need for him to be inside her.

But she couldn't act on it, not when they both weren't thinking clearly.

"We better go..." she said awkwardly as she moved past him, quickly snapping up the towel that was left on the counter and covering herself.

Riley followed, leaving a pool of water at his feet as she handed him the other towel.

Water drops slowly descended his chest, forcing her eyes to follow the trail, across his tattoos and abs until it settled in the waistband of his soaked jeans. Jeans that stuck to him like a second skin. His erection twitched when she settled her eyes on it, enough for her to realise that neither of them had finished.

Riley quickly tugged off the remaining fabric, throwing them into the corner where she hoped a laundry basket was before he wrapped the towel around himself. He growled, forcing her eyes to meet his.

"We're not finished here, remember that."

Alice would have collapsed if she hadn't leant against the sink, the cold porcelain a shock against her fevered skin.

"I need clothes," she said, her voice huskier than she wanted it to be.

Riley chuckled as he walked into the bedroom. Opening a door to their right he walked into the large closet, yanking a shirt off a hanger and placing it on the bed.

"I won't have any trousers that will fit you," he said as he eyed the remains of her own leather trousers, which now resembled a pair of arseless chaps.

"So is this your room?" she asked as she looked around with fresher eyes.

"I'll meet you downstairs," he said as he quietly left, allowing her to get dressed alone.

The soft overhead light highlighted her new bruises in the freestanding mirror that was beside the armchair, some already turning a sickly yellow. The mark on her arm looked partially healed already, while the slices on her back looked days old, not hours. Whatever oils were rubbed into the wounds clearly worked, she could barely feel the gashes when she tugged the shirt around her shoulders, buttoning up the front with care.

It smelt like Riley, with the length luckily fitting her almost to the knee. Paired with her boots, which she was lucky enough to have had removed before the scissor treatment, most of her modesty was covered.

The hairband he had pulled was long gone, so she allowed her hair to remain down after she brushed it with her fingers, the ends already curling as they air dried. She looked like she had been dragged through a hedge, but, at least, she wasn't dead.

Alice tried to remember the direction to turn when she left the room, the hallway overlooking the atrium below with an open style balcony. A chandelier hung between the two sets of stairs each side, each separate crystal catching the light in a burst of rainbow that settled on the dark wooden floor below.

It was beautiful even in the night, with the backdrop of the large, dark windows settled behind it.

Alice forced herself to step down, to not go into the closed doors that she desperately wanted to explore.

Boots in hand she padded across the floor, thankful she made no noise as she wandered through the left arch, not sure in which direction everyone was. The earth tones continued throughout, the walls tastefully decorated with a mixture of dark furniture, thriving plants and colourful art.

Hand woven rugs were placed on the floor, mismatched, with colours clashing in a way that fit the room.

Crap, she thought to herself when she noticed the landline sitting on the side table.

She had no phone or keys, having left them at home before she entered the market. She wasn't allowed any metal, didn't want to risk anything going wrong.

Which was an amusing thought in itself.

Alice picked up the phone, dialling Sam's number from memory.

It rang three times before disconnecting.

"Fuck sake," she whispered as she settled the handset down. She wasn't sure on the time, but knew Sam would pick up if he was close enough to his phone. He regularly changed her ringtone to make it unique to others, the last time she heard he had changed it to 'The Imperial March.'

Then she remembered she was calling from a landline, a number he wouldn't recognise and not her own phone.

"Uhhh." She called again, waited until after the beep before she spoke into his voicemail. "Sam it's me, I swear if you don't pick up I'm going to buy you the cheapest kitty litter the shop has to offer. You know the stuff, the bits made from recycled cardboard that makes your arse itch," she threatened before she hung up.

He didn't use kitty litter. But sometimes she bought it to tease him when he pissed her off. The last time she had done it he retaliated with buying her a novelty witches hat.

She called again.

"Your only excuse for not answering is if you're working. You better be working Sam."

She hung up again, waited thirty seconds and called once more.

"Fuck sake, who is this calling at this bloody hour? I'm in the middle of... something," Sam snarled down the phone.

"Oh, there's my Sunshine," Alice chuckled, even as she heard a faint female voice pant in the background. "Am I calling too early? Or am I interrupting something interesting?"

"Shit, hey baby girl." His voice became muffled as he whispered to whoever was in the room with him. *"Sorry, that was, erm..."*

Alice listened as the woman in the background moaned beside him.

"Come on babe, get back into bed. I'm waiting..."

"Okay, okay," Alice interrupted before she could hear any more details. "I just wanted to make sure you're okay."

"Shouldn't I be asking you that?" he replied before his voice muffled once more. *"Look, can't you see I'm on the phone? Go finish yourself off if you can't wait,"* he said to the woman.

"Wow, that's... I can hear you're... busy."

"She can wait. Where are you? You weren't here when I got home?"

"It's complicated. I'll explain everything when I'm back." She paused when she heard more whining in the background. "Are you sure this is a good time?"

"Aye, my cock may explode but never mind."

"Oh Sam, you're disgusting." She rolled her eyes at his chuckle. "Look I'll be back soon, I left my phone and keys at home so I was just making sure you'll be in?"

"Alice, it's like five in the morning. Strippers don't make much money during the day."

"Is it really five?"

Had it really only been five hours since she entered the mausoleum? Where had the time gone?

"Who are you calling?" A voice asked beside her.

She jumped, the handset flying out of her hand before she caught it.

"Bloody hell Sythe, you almost gave me a heart attack!" she seethed when the anime haired wannabe appeared beside her. He was dressed down in shorts and a cotton T-shirt, even though he had his twin swords strapped to his back. It was a strange look.

"Sythe? Did you just say Sythe? Where the fuck are you?" Sam called down the phone. "Baby girl where are you? Give me an address and I'll come pick you up."

"Sam I'll explain when I'm home. Love you," she said as she went to settle the handset down, then thought of something to add. "You better be in your bedroom and not on the sofa again."

"Where are you? Wait, I'm not..."

She hung up. She loved Sam, but his sexual achievements were starting to become more work than she needed. She had caught him twice in the last month in a compromised position. Once on the sofa in a position she didn't think was even possible for anybody to fold themselves into, the other up against the fridge of all places. She didn't care that he cleaned up after himself, it was still disgusting.

"You smell like Riley," Sythe smirked. "And I don't mean because you're wearing his clothes."

"Hello to you too."

"You coming to the meeting or what? We're waiting." He spun, assuming she would follow.

Everybody turned to stare at Alice as she entered behind Sythe, their eyes a mixture of confusion and judgment. It made her hesitate, the almost hostile show as all seven stood.

"Alice," Riley nodded from the head of the table, a plate of pancakes and waffles covered in butter and syrup in front of him. "Glad you could join us." His eyes heated as he watched her approach the table, something the others noticed awkwardly.

"Oh, hello."

Every guardian had a plate in front of them, some had started to eat while others remained untouched. Xander stood to Riley's right, with Sythe taking the seat to his left.

"What the fuck is she doing here?" The one with the beautiful red hair said as she took a seat. "Is this a joke?"

Riley growled, his fist hitting the table hard enough for the plates and cutlery to rattle.

"Seriously?" Red-head stood up, tossing his plate across the large table and storming out of the room. The plate spun at the edge, settling down without making a mess.

The blonde pushed at his own plate, his movements agitated before Riley growled once again.

"Leave him," Xander said with a bored expression. "You know he will be back once he's calmed down."

"Kace is right," the blonde said in a soft voice, at odds against his muscled appearance. "You know the rules better than anyone."

"What rules?" Sythe added as he shoved several pancakes into his mouth at once. "I didn't think you believed in rules, Titus."

"Don't be a dick Sythe," the man beside him added. He caught Alice's eye with a friendly enough expression. His face had perfect symmetry, something you would see on the big screen. His hair was cut military short, dark enough mixed with his tanned to skin to hint at a Mediterranean heritage. "The name's Axel."

The blonde stood up in a burst of irritation. "Causam praeceptia suntion."

"Titus..." Sythe sighed dramatically.

"English," Alice said, harder than she initially intended. It forced all the eyes back on her. "If you're going to discuss anything about me, speak English. Please."

"Jax," Titus murmured, "what do you think?"

Jax sat directly beside Alice, his attention mainly on the table. His hair was a beautiful honey brown, so it took her a minute to realise when he looked back up at her it was styled to hide an ugly red scar that sliced down his left eye.

"Fuck The Order," he said in a deep tone. "Fuck their outdated rules."

"What rules?" Alice asked before they all stood up, just as she felt the hairs on her arms stand on edge.

CHAPTER TWENTY-SIX

The air moved behind her, the snarl barely registering as she shoved the chair backwards with such force it cracked into whatever was behind her. Teeth clashed a bare inch from her throat as hot saliva sprayed across her skin.

The chair was splinters within seconds, the beast that appeared ready to pounce as she jumped up onto the table, spinning to crouch on the polished wood. She called her magic, her palm alighting with blue flames that reflected in the beast's silver eyes. Its head and body was the shape of a wolf, one of the largest she had ever seen while the legs were thicker, closer to a lion. Its claws extended, the serrated edges scratching against the wooden floor.

In a flash it was thrown across the room, another beast that was even bigger growling loud enough it made the table vibrate beneath her feet.

"Shit," Xander spat as he appeared beside her, his hand held out to help her off the table. "Come on."

Alice ignored the hand, instead watching the tail of the beast who stood before her separate into seven distinct furry whips. Its hackles rose as it kept its attention on the other wolf-like creature that bled from several bite marks on its neck, turning its white fur a sickly pink.

"Xee man, get her away from them," one of the men said even as the others crowded around her, weapons drawn.

"Riley?" Alice asked, even as one tail swept back to curl against her waist.

"What the fuck?" Sythe said, eyes wide. "Alice, you need to back off."

Alice tried to move back, instead another tail moved to encircle her. "Need a little help here, guys."

She recalled her magic, using her fingers to try and pry her waist free.

"Seriously, what the fuck is happening?" Titus said as he slowly moved beside what she assumed was Riley. "Hey big guy," he said in a calming tone. "Kace didn't mean any harm, just being his usual attention seeking self."

The smaller of the two beasts snarled, spitting blood. It tensed to attack before it hesitated, shaking his head before exposing its throat.

"Ah, well it's nice to know you can all turn into these big fluffy things," Alice murmured as she tried again to untangle herself.

"You've seen us before?" Jax asked, eyebrows drawn as he tugged at a tail himself.

Riley bent back to snap his long jaws in warning, his teeth almost catching Jax before he jumped back.

"Hey," Alice said as she reached forward to place her hand on his back. She tangled her fingers into his thick pale fur, just beneath a darker mark that glowed in the same pattern as one of his tattoos. "I'm okay, Kace was just playing."

She hoped so anyway, otherwise she would have been toast.

Riley turned his head just enough she could see one eye.

"Keep talking, he's listening." Xander quietly said beside her, his hand brushing her arm.

Riley growled, causing Xander to snap his hand back.

"Fuck! Okay, no one touches her."

"HEY!" Alice snapped at the beast, forcing his attention back to her. "Look, I'm fine, He didn't mean it, did you Kace?" She tried to turn but his tails tightened around her.

Kace burst into a ball of coloured light. His eyes were hard when he looked at her, his naked skin covered in blood but no bites marked his neck.

"Just a game," he replied with a throaty croak.

Riley burst into a ball of light of his own, his tails being replaced with his arms as he pulled her down carefully from the table. She automatically reached up, her palms hitting the warmth of Riley's chest before she met his silver eyes.

"You okay?" he asked, his voice deeper than usual, his other half still in control.

"You guys sure know how to welcome a girl to the party."

Kace, who was just as naked as Riley walked past them like he didn't have a care in the world, his face angry as he took a seat back at the table.

"Erm," Alice sneaked a peak down before feeling her cheeks flush. "You can get dressed now."

"Why, we all know you have already seen it all," Sythe laughed as he collected the plates that had moved.

"Enough," Riley scowled, his hands tightening on her waist before he stepped back. "If you would excuse me," he nodded to the group. "KACE!"

Kace grumbled back, but followed Riley out of the dining room.

"Take a seat Alice," Xander said as he came to stand beside her, expression pissed as he removed his sunglasses. "As usual you ignite a reaction."

"You can't seriously blame me for this?" she said. "None of this was my bloody fault."

"I think it's your cheery personality," Sythe laughed again, eating even more pancakes.

"Sythe, do you ever shut up?" Titus sighed.

"You guys are a barrel of laughs, you know that," Alice murmured to herself.

Kace and Riley appeared, both dressed.

"Shall we start this again?" Riley said to the room, eyes back to their usual stormy grey. "Alice Skye, daughter of Jackson Skye, please meet The Guardians of the Order."

Each one stood up in turn, bowing their heads before turning to Kace, who reluctantly did the same.

"We deserve to know why she's here," Kace said, still angry.

"She has a habit of turning up at places she's not wanted," Xander added as he crossed his arms.

"Do you not trust my judgment, Kace?" Riley asked.

Kace clenched his jaw, eyes shimmering before he nodded in respect. "Sire."

"I'm assuming as you brought Alice back stoned means it didn't go well," Xander started. "Especially considering I smelt fresh blood on her."

"Just a scratch," she said. One that she couldn't even feel.

"My father wasn't there," Riley told the group. "He had been spotted a few days ago, but has since moved underground once again."

All the men growled, the noise disconcerting coming from human throats.

"You're not going alone again." Jax said. "It's too risky."

"Agreed," Xander added.

Riley shot to his feet. "Do you not think I'm capable alone?"

"You know for a fact this isn't about your capability Sire," Xander said to his friend. "We do this together, as one."

Riley rumbled, but nodded, his eyes settling on Alice.

"The Pits, what are you going to do about them?" Alice asked as the rest of the men turned to her, confused.

"What about them?"

"They need to be shut down."

"That's not our area," one of the men said. She wasn't sure, her attention on Riley who watched her intently.

She felt her chi spike, anger shaping her words. "That's not good enough. That evil place needs to end. People forced to be fighters, killing themselves for the entertainment of those entitled, cruel people."

"It's not that simple..."

"Alice is right," Xander said as he spoke directly to Riley. "It will be impossible to close it down completely, not when the market has its claws across the country. But, I will deal with it." He nodded at Riley, who returned the gesture.

"So what's the next step?" Titus asked, changing the subject. "Mason is still our priority."

"I have someone mapping the tunnels," Alice said before anyone else could. "The tunnels beneath the underground. They're supposed to connect to the facilities Mason has been known to frequent. I'm hoping he would be hiding in one of those."

"What facilities?" Xander asked with a frown.

Riley leant back in his chair, his jaw clenched. "Facilities disguised as medical research, when in reality they're fronts for his production of Brimstone."

"You're fucking kidding me?"

"I'm not even surprised."

"Wait, there's tunnels?"

Then men started to talk amongst themselves.

"I have only found two facilities, the whereabouts of the others hidden behind fake paper trails." Riley racked his knuckles against the table. "How do you know about them?" he asked, eyes narrowed on Alice.

Oh shit.

She didn't really want to mention her brother. Not to the group of men who tracked down and killed those that were deemed dangerous. Ignoring the fact she had to summon a Daemon to save him, a being they were specifically designed to hunt.

She was definitely going to keep that little detail out.

"When did my brother come to you?" she asked instead of answering.

Riley tilted his head. "So your brother told you."

Kace's head swung round, eyes flashing silver. "That creature was her brother?"

"Who you calling a creature?" Alice felt Tinkerbell ignite at her sudden upset. She would normally be upset at its appearance, but instead she was glad her chi was back to normal.

"She doesn't know what he is," Riley said calmly, even as his brow creased in anger.

"He's a fucking Daemon," Kace growled before he stood up and began to pace.

"No he isn't," Alice stood up too, causing the rest of them to react. Chairs fell to the floor as they all leapt to their feet, some touching their weapons.

Kyle wasn't a Daemon, he had just spent some personal time with one.

She slowly went across the room, catching each set of eyes. "He isn't a Daemon," she said as calmly as she could even as violence thickened the air.

"How did your brother know about the facilities? When even I didn't," Riley asked as he lifted up a fist. The men who had unsheathed their weapons put them down, but remained standing.

She really wished she had her blade, her hand twitching at the emptiness.

She trusted Riley, but not the others.

"He was taken the night our parents were killed. Forced to work for..." She struggled to say his name. "The Master."

"What's that got to do with Mason?" Xander asked, his expression now unreadable beneath his wrap-around glasses he placed back on his nose.

"They were working together. Part of Trinity who designed, produced and supplied Ruby Mist."

"This is a fucking joke," Kace snarled as he continued to pace. "Her brother is one of them. He needs to be destroyed."

"You will not touch him." Alice let the threat linger. "No one messes with my family."

"THAT IS ENOUGH!" Riley roared. "Enough." He stared each of his men down until they returned to their seats. "Her brother is off limits..."

"What, you can't be serious?"

"Sire, he's a..."

"This is *our* job."

"I SAID," Riley snarled. "Her brother is off limits until we have analysed the situation. Until then, we concentrate on finding Mason."

He clicked the manacles around her wrists, her breathing slow as the drugs worked through her system. He lifted her heavy head, his fingers brushing across her lips as he stared at her face. He thought it would be harder as he turned the lock, especially after knowing her. Falling for her.

She was strong, an Alpha, his mate. His wolf agreed, even though his wolf couldn't understand what he was doing. Giving her up without a fight. Not just giving her up, killing her.

Yet all he could think of was his brother.

He had no other option. His pack would always come first.

So he pressed his lips to hers, feeling her warmth for the last time before releasing her head, allowing it to drop, her hair covering her face. He should have put up a fight. There were more of them, could have overpowered The Master. Yet, he didn't. Because she wasn't worth it. Wasn't worth the loss of his own.

He stepped back, giving her a lasting look before he turned away, in search of his brother.

It was easier than it should have been.

Maybe he was the real monster.

CHAPTER TWENTY-SEVEN

Alice tugged on the hem of the shirt, annoyed that it kept riding up.

"You're angry," Riley stated in a stern tone as he drove her home. "Talk to me."

Alice went to reply, then thought better of it. She was angry, frustration fuelling that anger as she tried to figure out what the fuck she was doing.

"He's my brother," she finally said, feeling panic grow beneath the surface. They wanted to terminate him, something she wouldn't let happen.

"I'm dealing with it," he growled. "You have no idea what's happening, sweetheart. You're blinded..."

"He's my brother," she snapped, turning to face him. "You said yourself that you were made specifically to kill your people's deepest secret. Bred to be stronger, faster and for what? Daemons?"

"He's dangerous." Riley clenched his jaw, the blue lights of the dashboard washing over his face.

"You don't know that."

"The transition into a Daemon isn't straightforward; it takes years to truly transcend. Druids who choose the dark path are corrupted, they..."

"YOU DON'T KNOW THAT!" Alice hit out, slamming her hand

on the dash. "You have no idea what he has gone through, the things he has seen or been forced to do."

"And neither do you." Riley pulled into her road, slowing the car as he approached her drive. "You can't keep ignoring it."

"I'm not ignoring it."

She wasn't, was she?

Alice sighed as Riley pulled in behind her Beetle, his headlights lighting up the front of her house. A man sat on her porch, his eyes dark as he watched them get out the car. As Alice approached he stood, his height only a little taller than her own.

"What are you doing here?" she asked when she recognised the man who worked for the Department of Magic & Mystery.

The man stood rigidly as Riley moved quietly beside her.

"May we speak in private?" he asked as his lip curled up in distaste when he noticed her lack of clothing. "It's important."

Alice tugged the shirt down again, even though it hit her knees and covered all the important bits. "Why are you at my door this early in the morning?" she asked again, ignoring his question.

"That's because I wouldn't let him in the house," Sam said as he opened the front door, leaning against the doorjamb. "Been here for hours," he smirked.

Alice smiled at her best friend before turning her attention back to The Magika's minion. "I'm sorry, I never caught your name..."

"It's Mr Lince." He produced his wallet, flipping it open to show his I.D.

Lewis.R.Lince
The Magika
Department of Magic & Mystery
Officer ID – 74791-5

Alice recognised the name.

"I've met your brother." She had actually left him in an alley suffering from several bruises and memory loss.

She still didn't feel guilty.

"The Council have been made aware you are no longer employed by The Supernatural Intelligence Bureau."

"I quit my job," she shrugged, "so what?"

"An unpredictable decision that worries them. The Magika has been tasked with keeping you in until a decision is made."

"Keeping? What, like a dog?" Sam bounded down the step, flanking Alice's other side. "Good luck with that, mate. Been trying to tame her for years."

"A decision? A decision for what?"

"Whether you're dangerous or not," he replied with no emotion. "That's all I know."

"Not very high in the pecking order, are you?" Sam smirked.

"I'm her Warden, I haven't been informed about any council decisions," Riley said.

Mr Lince looked between them before settling on Riley. "You would have been updated directly through your council leader. Except, we all know what's happened there…"

Riley took a threatening step forward. "I think you should leave."

"Not without Miss Skye in custody."

"Cool, so I haven't got time for this." Alice nudged past Mr Lince.

His hand snaked out to grab, his fingertips brushing her shoulder as she snapped up to grab it in a bruising grip. His face was hard when she released it, taking a step back.

"I wouldn't if I were you," Riley growled.

Alice ignored them as she walked into her front room, Sam quick on her heels. She skidded to a halt when she noticed the woman who watched TV on her sofa, accompanied by Jordan.

"Erm, hello?"

The woman turned to look, huffed before returning her attention back to the TV.

Oookay then.

She pulled a face at Sam before they moved into the kitchen. "What the fuck? Why is she still here?"

"She won't leave," Sam said as she opened the fridge, grabbing the carton of milk and opening it. "She's supposed to watch me or something."

"Wait, that's your protection from Theo?" She peaked through the archway back into the living room. The woman was beautiful, with caramel coloured hair and warm honey skin. "You fucked your protection?"

"Erm, I can hear you, you know?" the woman said, still facing the TV.

Shit.

"Sorry," Alice said as she returned to the kitchen. She hadn't met many females of the pack.

Sam shrugged, his upper lip covered in milk as he continued to drink straight from the carton. "So we going to discuss why you smell like blood, and... is that Riley?" His eyes narrowed as he put the carton down. "I wasn't even going to comment on the walk of shame outfit."

"I had an accident."

"The blood or Riley?" Sam grinned as he sniffed against her neck. "Your back was bleeding," he said with assurance, but also with slight confusion. "But it's not fresh, yet you had no wounds yesterday."

"It's fine."

"Are you sure?" he asked, suddenly serious.

Alice smiled, she would never lie to him. "I got up and personal with a bear, wouldn't recommend it. But, yes, I'm fine. All healed up."

Sam raised an eyebrow as he smirked. "A bear you say? That's interesting, but not as much as I want to know how big his coc..."

"Ugh." She pushed a laughing Sam away. "We're not talking about that right now."

"Talking about what?" Riley asked as he came in.

"Nothing!" Alice squealed while Sam kept laughing.

"You get rid of Mr Magic Dick?" Sam asked as he leapt onto the counter, denim clad legs swinging as he reached for the milk again.

"Returning to The Magika with a bruised ego. It wouldn't surprise me if he returned with reinforcements"

"Reinforcements for little ole me?" Alice groaned.

Sam slurped loudly.

"Stop drinking straight from the bloody carton," she scolded him, confiscating the milk.

Sam snorted before he hopped down. "Peyton left you something." He pointed to the envelope on the table. "Said you were expecting it and mentioned something about payment."

Alice opened the envelope, pulling out a hand drawn map and blueprints.

"This the tunnels?" Asked Riley as he looked over her shoulder.

Alice,

The note pinned to the top started.

I have held up my end, you know what to do.
I have highlighted the best routes to take in these tunnels. Many are inaccessible, either on purpose or naturally flooded. I have found several facilities, all connected with more than one entrance in a confusing labyrinth. One entrance was interestingly connected to the church, which, as you know, was never found even after being investigated.
Another was recently destroyed.
The others have all been dark except one, where a recent electrical pulse has been recorded. I suggest this would be the best place to start.

P.

"The best entrance to try is the one on the outskirts of Presley." Alice pointed to the third mark on the map. "It looks hidden just in the forest with the least resistance."

"I know the place," Riley murmured as he studied the drawings. "We should head out there straight away, give us a better chance to catch him out." He stepped back as he grabbed his phone, turning away to dial.

Alice climbed the stairs quickly, heading to her room to change. She carefully peeled off her long shirt and boots, turning to the mirror to check the claw marks. They looked sore, the gouges deeper than she thought surrounded by bruised skin. But clearly days old, not recent like she knew they were.

"I've brought up bandages," Riley said from the hallway. "I figured it's best to wrap you up so they don't break back open."

Alice turned, noticing how severe Riley looked. "I'm getting changed."

"Are you really worried over me seeing you in your bra?" he tilted his head, void of the flirtatious smile she expected. "Sit on the bed."

Alice wanted to argue, but his intensity worried her.

His hands were warm as he gently pushed her hair over her shoulder, his fingers lingering on her neck before he checked her wound.

"It's going to scar," he murmured as he unwrapped the bandage.

"I have many scars." She flinched when the bandage was applied. "You contact Xander?"

"Hmmm." He finished the bandage.

Alice jumped off the bed, opening her wardrobe to grab her last pair of leather jeans and a long sleeved top. Her boots were scratched up, but protected her legs just as they were supposed to.

"What, you just going to watch?" Alice asked as she carefully pulled on the clothes and reached for her blade. The harness strapped across her back, thankfully missing the majority of the bandages.

Riley slowly stood. His eyes shimmered as he watched her strap on two daggers, one per thigh. "Why has your car got bullet holes?"

Alice finished strapping on the daggers in silence before she risked a look.

"Thought it would make it airier."

He came forward as his hand reached up to touch her cheek. Her chi danced in excitement, the electrical current savouring the connection even as she had to breathe through the sudden spike in desire.

"We're not doing this again," she said, her voice painfully husky, not the rejection she wanted it to be.

Riley finally smiled, just a small curve of his lips. "Tell me about your car."

It seems there are people who know my heritage better than me, and they don't like it."

Riley growled, the sound causing her to shiver. "I need to update my men. Can I trust you not to go in without me?" He leaned forward, his attention on her lips.

Alice just nodded, not trusting her voice.

Riley was intense, power radiating off him in waves that shocked her.

His breath was warm as he moved closer, his lips pressing on hers for the barest second before he turned to leave.

Alice stared for longer than necessary until she shook herself. She needed to concentrate on Mason, on keeping Kyle and Sam safe. Riley was a distraction she didn't need.

She just hoped Peyton was right, that he could get the closure he needed.

"You wanna talk about it?" Sam asked when Alice finally came back downstairs.

"Talk about what?"

"Whatever has put that look on your face, or is that whoever?" He reached for her hair, tugging on the strands until she allowed him to plait it. "We've never had conventional lives, both had to go through more than anyone should in a single lifetime."

"I'm going to keep you and Kyle safe."

"At what cost?" He finished with her hair, pulling her into a hug. His cheek settled on her head, the purr comforting. "You deserve happiness."

"What has happiness got to do with anything?" she sighed, cuddling closer into his chest.

"I feel like it's just getting started," he muttered into her hair.

Alice patted his chest, unable to offer him the comfort he needed. Because she knew it was just the beginning, and she had no idea what to do.

"I'm proud of what you have become," he said as he released her. "And I understand why you need to do this."

Sam knew her better than anyone, better than even Dread. They had no secrets, knew each other inside out. She wasn't surprised by his support, even as worry painted his face.

Alice pulled him back for a hug.

"You are my sunlight in a world of darkness." It was something they were taught as children, confirmation of their love as troubled kids in a support group. It was just as important now than it was back then.

Sam chuckled, kissing the top of her head. "As you are my Starlight."

CHAPTER TWENTY-EIGHT

Considering magic was once believed to be powered by the moon, Alice wasn't a huge fan. She enjoyed the lunar cycle itself, could appreciate Nature's natural energies and the beauty of the night. Especially on the outskirts of the city, where the sky and stars weren't obscured by light pollution.

But she never understood why humans once believed the moon was something to be feared. Witches would pray to it for rituals, shifters would use it to shapeshift and vampires lived beneath it.

Humans were gullible bastards.

She would have loved to see their faces once they realised that witches didn't need the moon to perform magic, that shifters could shift at will and that vampires could live beneath both the moon and sun. It was the fear that caused the war that had killed millions, a prejudice that still existed but in smaller groups. A poison in society.

"You been here long?" Peyton asked as he stamped his feet free of leaves.

Alice looked back up into the sky, noting the pink tinge. "Long enough." She had placed herself against a tree trunk, giving her the advantage of watching the single road. "You got here quick."

"You have a habit of calling ridiculously early," he stated as he brushed his hair away from his face. He wore his detective gear, including the trench coat that was almost identical to Brady's.

"You need a hat," she said, amused at his frown. "A proper detective's hat. Maybe even a pipe."

"Do you have it?" he asked, a slight tension in the air. He looked normal, almost bored, the air of otherness he had previously a figment of her imagination.

Alice smiled as she reached up to her ear to grab a single earring. It was a simple design, a single diamond set in silver. She wasn't sure why he wanted an earring, but she hoped it was in fact one-hundred per cent silver as the salesmen said.

It would do no good giving a Fae something that held iron, at least, partially Fae.

She still had no idea what he was, which seemed to be a running theme in her life lately.

"You hear the latest news?" Alice asked when he didn't immediately leave. "I quit Supernatural Intelligence."

Peyton nodded, his face its usual business serious. "You becoming independent?"

Alice hadn't given it much thought.

Shit.

She had quit her job without realising the consequences. Like affording food.

"Pokers at Brady's next week by the way," he said as he checked his watch.

"Is Sam invited?"

"If he doesn't help you cheat again," he said, eyes narrowed.

Alice couldn't help her laugh, the burst of sound loud enough to scare the birds away who perched high on the tree. "He didn't cheat." He did, but she still wouldn't admit it. "Besides, you enjoyed the loss."

Peyton smiled, which for him was a slight curve of his cheek. "I'll see you around."

Alice waved as he pulled away.

The sun threatened to dominate the sky, the pink in the horizon highlighting that the day was against them. They wanted to get to the facility before Mason had a chance to move, the open daylight not a deterrent as they had hoped, not when he had miles of underground tunnels to travel through silently.

"Where are you?" she muttered as she stared at the only car in the park, which was hers.

"Miss me already?" Riley said as he approached from the side, the man with the too full lips and military haircut beside him. They both wore identical outfits, armour that stuck to every muscle intimately like a second skin. It covered them from head to toe, including partially across their fingers and neck. Riley's thick sword was strapped to his back, as well as two pistols.

"What is that?" she asked as she reached up, unable to stop herself from touching the strange, dark fabric. It felt like scales beneath her fingertips, but warm with a slight sheen that looked wet. Lights danced beneath the surface just under her hand, as if Riley's tattoos reacted to her touch.

She pulled her hand back, watched the lights disappear in confusion.

"You going to touch me next?" the military man said, grinning.

Riley growled, eyes narrowed. "Enough Axel."

"What," Alice said as she spotted the scythe on his back beside a backpack. "You the Grim Fucking Reaper or something?"

"Or something," he laughed as he followed Riley into the forest.

"Where is everyone?" Alice asked after a while, the trek to the entrance longer than she thought.

"There are three entrances to the facility, each with several miles' worth of tunnels. It wasn't clear which one would be the quickest, so made sense to split everyone up and meet in the middle."

Riley looked up at the moon that was barely visible against the trees and impending sun.

"It could take us days to explore if we make a mistake. Time we don't have."

"Boss?" Axel called, pointing towards a manhole that they had been searching for. "This looks tampered with." He nudged a rock down into the metal hole, the protection that would have been covering it gone. "There's blood, looks reasonably fresh." Axel bent down to touch the red, his fingers coming up wet.

"Your father?" Alice questioned. "Or has someone beaten us to it?"

"It would make no sense for Mason to damage this, not when he's hiding." Axel looked around, eyes settling on something in the brush.

"Looks like we're about to find out." Riley jumped down, his grunt following quickly after.

"What's over there?" she asked Axel when he returned his attention to the hole.

"Someone dead." His eyes shimmered before they settled back into the deepest green befitting the scenery. "You're up next," Axel said, nodding towards the hole.

"Great," Alice muttered, peering down.

It was pitch black.

She swung herself down, hands catching her hips to move her out the way as Axel followed quickly behind with a soft splash.

"Ugh, whose idea was this again?" Axel moaned as the mixture of damp, mould and who knows what else assaulted his nose.

"*Lux Pila.*" Alice blew into her hand, forming a small ball of light that shot into the air. She blinked to clear her vision, the walls a dark grey that seemed to absorb the little light they had. Water, deep enough that she was grateful for her boots splashed beneath their feet whilst the biggest rat she had ever seen eyed her up from a floating log.

"So, how much do you trust your informant?" Axel asked when they came to a fork in the tunnel.

"There must be something," Riley said as he opened the backpack on Axel's shoulder, taking out the map and a torch. "We're here." He pointed his light. "Officially there is nothing down here other than another entrance north, but it says here it's blocked."

"How far?" Alice asked.

"This is hand drawn, it's not exactly accurate," he replied dryly. "There's supposed to be a route to our left, but it's not there."

Alice frowned, touching the solid wall. Her little light shot towards the ceiling, taller in this part of the tunnel than before. "What's that?" she asked, noticing a ledge connected to a slim gap in the concrete.

"That's probably where we need to go." Riley folded the map, putting it back in the backpack before jumping at the wall. He caught the ledge, pulling himself up. He was forced to crouch painfully, his head bent awkwardly as it touched the ceiling. "The tunnel continues through here."

Alice knocked against the wall with her knuckles. "Who would have looked up when there were several route options?"

Axel shrugged before he turned to Alice. "You need help?" he asked.

Alice checked the height. Moving as far back as she could she ran towards the wall, using her momentum to push herself up. She barely grasped the thin ledge, Riley's hand catching her arm to pull her up the rest of the way. She shuffled on her knees before she was able to drop back down the other side.

"Careful," she warned as the two men joined her. "This is much slimmer." Her shoulders scraped the sides.

Able to barely turn in the space she laughed at Riley, who was forced to turn side on to fit into the gap. He looked huge, his body taking up the majority of space.

"It should lengthen out soon," Riley said as he shuffled through behind her.

"What did the claustrophobic fungi say to his friends?" Alice said as she slowly walked forward, the cold and damp starting to ache her bones. "There's not mushroom in here."

"Really, claustrophobia jokes, now?" Axel muttered from the back.

"There's a door, just up ahead." Riley said as he ignored them.

Alice had to squint, barely making out her hand in front of her face until she noticed the outline of a high security metal door at the end of the tunnel. As she got closer the walls widened, allowing everybody to comfortably stand.

"We're definitely not the first here," she said, the door barely holding on to its hinges. Wards, scraped into the concrete smoked, the sandalwood thick in the airless hole. "The spells protecting the door have been compromised." She went to reach forward, the bite on her hand pulsating with a dull ache that made her clench her fist.

"No shit," Axel laughed as he touched the door, which opened without resistance. "Not counting the two bodies just through here."

"Bodies?" Alice asked, forgetting the pain in her palm as she stepped through into the dimly lit room.

Axel bent down to the closest body, moving the man onto his back. "He's wearing the same uniform as the stiff in the forest." He reached forward. "This wasn't long ago, the blood's still warm."

"Must be security." Riley stated as he checked out the room.

They seemed to be in a storage unit, the room covered in floor to ceiling mesh shelves and refrigerated units. Many were empty, while others held everything from files, glass tubes to noxious substances and vials.

Blood smeared across the floor with footprints leading out of the room.

"Whoever is here, they don't care for subtlety." Alice stated as she pulled out her sword, the runes glowing gently across her blade.

The hallway was empty, tiles that covered the floor and walls splattered with more blood.

"It looks like a hospital."

Viewing windows showed empty rooms complete with beds and medical equipment.

One was smashed, the spider web of glass shattered inwards into the pitch black.

"What's that?" Alice asked before the light flickered inside, highlighting the room for a few seconds before flicking off again. "Bloody hell!" she gasped.

The light flickered on again, showing three beds, all occupied. Each person looked painfully sick, their bones protruding through their skin and cheeks hollow. She could tell at a glance that at least one of them was already dead. From the colour of his skin he had been dead a while.

Both Riley and Axel remained silent as they opened the attached door, their faces frozen as they approached the beds cautiously.

The light flickered off, bathing them both in darkness before returning with a static wheeze. Riley held a syringe in his hand, the liquid red inside while Axel checked the many tubes attached to one of the men.

The smell began to leak through the window's cracks, decay and death thick in her nose as she turned to look away in rage. She was confident then that at least one other man wasn't alive. She had seen, just from the last flick of light the men all had open sores, oozing infected puss. The ones who still had fingers were tinged black, the end of his limbs having no blood.

She forced herself away from the smell, her stomach recoiling before she noticed a drawing board pinned beside the door. Alice skimmed the notes, anger bubbling through her veins as she noted the last entry was only an hour ago.

1:36am:
Patient 152 – 48hrs since death. Decay has slowed to a halt; RM has settled into crystals within the blood. Looking at possibility to retrieve substance and to test it on Patient 325. Decided to allow another 24hrs before retrieval.

Patient 264 – 12hrs since death. No RM found in system. COD yet to be determined as body has deteriorated faster than anticipated. Exposed to RM for three weeks before structure breakdown.

Patient 325 —Exposed to RM for eight weeks before noticeable structure breakdown. If RM removed, Patient 325's heart and respiratory system fail within twelve hours. Highly positive results.
Check-ups have been increased to assure asset remains alive.

4:15am
Patient 152 and 264 no change.

Patient 325 – Confirmed blind in both eyes. Blood pressure is dropping without an obvious cause and another limb has begun to turn black. Booked in for removal before decay sets in.

6:08am
Patient 152 and 264 no change.

Patient 325 – No viable signs. Marked to retrieve RM from blood. Will test on next batch of patients.

"They all dead?" Alice asked when Riley and Axel left the room. She needed it confirmed, hoped they were no longer suffering.

Riley nodded, his rage creasing his brow even as he touched her gently on the shoulder. "They have been pumped with Ruby Mist."

"They seem to be experimenting with the long term effects," Axel added, his usual happy expression just as enraged. "When I get hold of one of those doc..."

"We need to keep moving," Riley interrupted as he moved further down the hallway. "If my father is here, he can answer for these deaths."

A scream echoed through the hallway, a mixture of rage and pain. Alice froze, the sound shooting to her core. Riley moved faster, following the noise as another bone-chilling cry resonated through a set of heavy double doors.

"Hey!" the guard gargled as Axel thrust his scythe forward, stopping the call before it could alert anyone else. Riley caught the man as he collapsed, setting him gently on the floor.

"Shove him in a room," he asked as Axel pulled him away.

Alice touched the door that didn't match the rest of the décor. It was made of thick steel with a heavy bolt locking it closed. She carefully pulled the bolt back, the mechanism screeching, the sound loud in the quite hall before another scream echoed. Using it as a distraction she yanked it the rest of the way.

"Careful," Riley warned, as she slowly pushed it forward, peeking into the room.

Mason stood flanked by two men, his attention on the man who kneeled before him, back hunched.

"You need to have a look at this," she whispered as she stared.

The man on his knees screamed once again, tearing at his own face hard enough to draw blood. Alice sucked in a breath, her palm burning, pulsating with a deep ache just as the man turned to her, eyes the same colour as her own open in horror before they turned to red.

CHAPTER TWENTY-NINE

An arm shot out, pulling her back before she had the chance to jump forward.

"Wait," Riley whispered against her ear. "They haven't spotted us yet."

She couldn't concentrate on his words, her pulse loud in her ears as she watched Mason kick at her brother, his foot connecting with an audible crunch.

Riley nodded towards Axel, who silently slipped through the door. The sound of Kyle's panting and screams concealed their arrival, the two guards distracted as they stood protecting Mason.

"You shouldn't have run away," Mason sneered, lifting his foot up again.

"Fuck..." Kyle snarled, his voice broken in a way she had never heard. "You."

"Because of your decision you have joined our ancestors in the next life, bound to your name, cursed by it. Do you know how long I protected you? It was I who stopped The Master from making you his pet. He wanted to change you as a child you see, before your body could even be able to control the transition."

Kyle screamed before he began to choke, black spluttering from his lips onto the tiled floor.

"And yet, here we are," he chuckled. "Foolish boy, before you were the patient, and now you are the source."

Alice pushed at Riley's arm, her chi electric as panic built. She thought past her rage, using her instincts and training to take in the situation. There were only two guards and Mason in the centre of the large, open area. A circle had been painted onto the floor, disguised in the black and white tiles.

A summoning room, Alice thought to herself, looking around for other indicators. More wards were painted high on the walls, some even on the ceiling.

Whatever they called, it would struggle to get out.

She reached for a dagger, unclipping the weapon.

Axel used that chance to jump forward, beheading one guard with a quick swish of his scythe.

Mason whipped around, face alarmed before it smoothed over. He shouted at the remaining guard to intervene before he encompassed his hands in green and black energy.

"Protect your brother." Riley stepped forward, unsheathing his sword.

Mason threw a ball of arcane, the sphere crashing into the wall in a burst of piercing light as Alice and Riley barely dodged out of the way.

Alice released her dagger, the weapon soaring through the room and into Mason's shoulder.

"Shit!" She had missed, aiming for his heart.

Mason snarled, his hand brushing the dagger before coming away covered with blood. He left it embedded, instead using his own blood to ignite the circle that exploded around both him and Kyle.

Riley roared, his own arms covered in silver as he tried to penetrate the molecule-thin shield that protected them.

"Kyle Alexander Skye, I, the leader of our Breed curse you with your new name." Mason bent towards her brother, whispering the last phrase directly into his ear.

Kyle violently surged, his back bending at an impossible angle before he clawed at the floor. With a screech he pushed forward, the momentum throwing Mason back hard enough to shatter his own circle.

Riley leapt towards his father, sword clashing with magic as Alice ran to her brother. She landed on her knees, her attention fully on him as war surrounded them in a clatter of sound.

"Kyle?" she called as she reached for him, his skin molten hot beneath her palm.

"I NAMED YOU, I CONTROL YOU!" Mason screeched as he dodged his son. "KILL HER!"

Kyle moaned, arms going limp by his side as he finally looked up, no recognition in his red eyes. His hand surged up to grab her shoulders, nails biting into flesh that caused her to cry out.

She watched in horror as his face began to bleed, dark horns spearing through his dark greasy hair. He made no sound as his shirt ripped, his back breaking open as two wings pierced through his flesh, each arch topped with a large, dangerous spike.

Alice watched in horror, eyes burning as tears poured down her face. She reached up to grip his arms, ignoring his nails that continued to dig beneath her skin.

"Kyle? It's me," she called to him, even as he began to climb to his feet, forcing her to follow. "It's going to be okay."

He smirked, the curve of his mouth a warning before he threw her back, hard enough for her to crash to the ground, the wind knocked out of her lungs. She rolled just as a spike crashed down, barely missing her.

"KYLE?"

He hissed, eyes narrowed to thin points before he struck out again. She raised her sword just in time, the metal clashing with his spike before she was able to twist away.

"STOP IT!"

A scythe pierced through the air, barely missing as Kyle brought up his wing to block.

"AXEL, NO!" She blocked him with her sword the second time, using all her strength in pushing him back as he tried to take another swipe.

"He's a Daemon," Axel snarled, aiming his weapon to strike.

Alice ignored him, releasing her excess energy in a burst of blue flame that surrounded him. The wall crackled in warning, trapping him inside.

Her brother just stood there, face confused as he looked at the fire then back at Alice, his eyes becoming green for the barest second. "Kill me." With a howl he collapsed to his knees, hands tearing at his face as he began to convulse.

"FUCKING BITCH!" A hand grabbed her hair, yanking it back with a dagger to her throat as her blade was knocked from her hand.

Mason snarled as Riley stood a foot away, sword raised with eyes pure silver. He looked calm, his face relaxed as he stared at his father.

"What have you done to him?" Alice asked in the calmest voice, even as she felt fire began to leak at an uncontrollable rate from her fingertips. She saw the wall of flame splutter, spreading further across the floor towards her.

"He's become what he was always supposed to be." Mason's shoulder bled profusely as he yanked her head back again, forcing her neck at a painful angle as the blade cut into her throat.

Her fire broke, the tiles shattering from the heat as it slowly crawled toward her. It opened up enough for Axel to join Riley, scythe held steady.

Mason slowly edged back, pulling her with him as the fire crackled loudly. The ceiling groaned, struggling against the intense heat. Mason pushed his face into hers, his skin rough from the poorly healed burns.

"You're going to flame out," he laughed, his attention on his son who slowly approached, sword held in front of him. "And when you do, I'm going to fucking take all your power."

Alice gasped, feeling her chi surge as Mason tried to force it from her, syphon it into himself. Black invaded her vison as she screamed, feeling her power overload. Her fire hesitated, halting its trail before it roared to life twice as strong. Blood on her upper lip as she blinked her vision, confused as to why there were suddenly seven people standing in front of her.

Mason kept retreating backwards, her own dagger slowly cutting into her skin as she felt him panic.

"LOOK, MY SON!" he shouted above the flames. "If you kill me, you won't know how to save her from herself. She is the Dragon that will end it all. A war is coming, and she will ensure you all will fall."

Alice calmed her breath, feeling smoke choke her throat as she felt fire begin to flow stronger from her palms. She slowly reached up, her fingers curling around the blade that warped at her touch. She thrust her head back, hard enough that it smashed his nose, causing his hand to release the dagger. She spun, hitting out as he collapsed to his knees. Moving around him she held his hair in her hands, yanking it up to force him to face his son.

Mason laughed, spitting out blood. "You will one day understand."

Riley stepped forward, flanked by all his men. With a nod Alice released him, allowing Mason to shoot forward just as Riley swung his blade in a clean arc.

Alice didn't hear the noise his head made when it connected to the floor, or the noise it made when Xander kicked it across the room. She could only concentrate on the pulsating roar inside her own head.

She had never moved as fast as when she tackled Titus, who had raised his weapon to strike a killing blow at Kyle who had stopped moving on the floor. His wings were crumpled beneath him, curled as the intense heat crackled across the room.

Titus jumped back, his skin singed as he snarled at her.

She kicked up her sword, the steel covered in her flames within a few seconds. She noticed her arms were completely encompassed with fire, her power growing faster than she could control.

"Alice." Riley dropped his sword, gesturing for his men to keep back. "Control it."

"You'll kill him," she said, voice strangely deep.

Riley stepped through the flames, ignoring it as it began to eat at his armour. "He isn't breathing. If you can't control yourself he's going to die anyway."

Alice felt her heart stutter, just as Riley's soothing aura touched hers in reassurance.

"Give me your word you won't kill him."

"Look at me," Riley shouted as she felt herself sway. "LOOK AT ME!"

She caught his eye, saw Riley beneath his beast.

"You need to trust me."

She looked at each Guardian in turn, their faces a mixture of shock and awe.

She trusted Riley. But not his men.

With a flick of her wrist she extinguished the flames, keeping her sword pointed in warning.

Riley moved in a flash, his hands pumping Kyles chest in a blur.

"Never mind a dragon," one of the men murmured. "She's like a fucking phoenix."

"Xander," Riley called. "Support his head."

Xander hesitantly approached, moving past Alice with caution before he dropped to his knees. He began to breathe for Kyle, his hands glowing yellow as he touched her brother's temple.

Alice felt her arm waver, her energy destroyed as black began to creep across her vision. "Will he be okay?"

She watched as her sword dropped from her hand, the motion slow as her knees gave out.

Kace jumped forward, kicking the sword from out of her reach before he swung her up into his arms. She tried to reach for her brother just as Titus and Axel started working on him. Riley appeared in her vision, face concerned as he gently touched her face.

"I don't know."

CHAPTER THIRTY

Alice sat quietly in the armchair, Sam curled as a leopard across her lap. She stroked behind his ears, a continuous motion that kept her calm as she watched Riley finish the tattoos around Kyle's throat and wrists.

Kyle was unconscious, his breathing steady as he lay as still as the dead on her bed. His wings were folded beneath him, strangely soft compared to how harsh they appeared. She had carefully arranged them, keeping the spikes away as she had stroked across the dark feathers. They started a deep blue, not black like she initially thought that slowly lightened to a soft grey on the inside. They were beautiful, even more so for the weapon they were.

There was no conversation, no noise other than the steady beat of the tattoo gun or the random noises Sam made as he slept. Xander, Kace and Sythe stood in the hall, eyes judging as they watched their leader tattoo protection glyphs on their enemy. Special designs that helped with control of the ley lines when druids came of age. It was supposed to be a big ritual, a celebration Kyle never received.

But she didn't give them much attention, or the other men who were probably making themselves at home downstairs. Not when her brother lay there, still. She wanted to stroke his hair, tell him everything was okay but every time she got close he seemed to react, moan, move in his sleep. So she sat quietly in the armchair in the corner of her bedroom, waiting for Riley to finish.

He had somehow removed the slave bands, the skin beneath red and scarred from the years he had worn them. The scars on his chest were nothing compared to the red mark in the centre, exactly the same place where she saw a sword almost slice him in half. The skin was a pale pink, the wound looking weeks, if not months old compared to the days she knew it to be.

"He isn't a druid anymore," Kace said, his eyes an intense anger as he watched.

"He's evolved," Riley replied.

"Or devolved." Kace shook his head. "We should have killed him."

"He's still a druid. One of us. Just cursed."

Alice turned her attention to Kace, who wouldn't look her in the eye. He huffed, moving out of the doorway to be replaced with Xander, his wrap around glasses nowhere to be seen as he checked the room with eyes that were almost white.

"You never dealt with the ghost," he said, arms crossed as he leant against the doorjamb. "That might be a mistake."

"Been a bit busy, besides he doesn't do anything." she laughed, the sound on the edge of hysteria. It woke Sam, who blinked up at her with feline annoyance. "Sorry," she smiled, scratching at his chin.

Sam pretended to bite at her fingers, ears flat to his head before he licked across her face. With a stretch he dropped to the floor, checking everyone out with a predatory glance before he stalked out the room.

"So what happens now?" she asked, wanting, needing to fill the silence.

"With the ghost or Mason?" Xander replied.

"Either I suppose."

"The ghost needs to be dealt with before he becomes a problem. He's a mischievous sod that I would be careful of. I don't believe he is as friendly as you believe. Regarding Mason..." he sighed, "nothing. He will be replaced on The Council and his... underground activities will be ignored."

"Forgotten," Sythe added. "He will be forgotten, wiped out of our histories as if he didn't exist."

"So everything he has done is going to be swept under the carpet?"

"It's a cruel world, isn't it?" Xander murmured before he put on his sunglasses.

Alice said nothing as she patted her pocket, feeling the gold coin that she had found on her pillow just as they placed Kyle onto her bed. She had no idea how the token pass for the Troll's Market had gotten there, didn't want to give it much thought.

"Hey Xander," she said as he turned to leave the room. "Are ghosts affected by wards?" The Cockney ghost that protected the entrance to the Troll Market said the coin would be returned.

"Depends if they deem you harm," he replied, crossing his arms. "But mostly no, they require special attention."

The buzz of the gun stopped as Riley stepped back to check the black and red glyphs.

"Are they done?" Alice asked as she sat forward, her attention returning to her brother.

"They will help him with control, but in all honesty, I don't know." Riley moved out the way as Alice approached, cautiously laying her hand against her brother's shoulder. He was warm to touch, his bare chest moving soundly as she kneeled on the bed.

With a shudder he opened his eyes, the iris' the green of their mothers as he quickly assessed the room.

"Kyle?" Alice asked before he shot up, moving fast enough she could have fallen if he hadn't automatically caught her arm.

She watched him, saw the sadness in his expression as he released her.

With a nod he disappeared into thin air.

EPILOGUE

Alice sat at the base of the statue that was supposed to represent her parents, the six-foot-tall cement structure the image of two birds. At least, she thought they were birds. The green surrounding it was dead and mistreated, a contrast to the other monuments and graves that bordered the reasonably nice cemetery. If you could call a place where the dead were buried nice.

She had brought flowers, because apparently, according to Sam, that was what you were supposed to do when you visited someone's grave, and laid them at the statue's feet. She had no idea what to say to them, or to her brother who sat on the fence and watched her pick at the dirt.

"You finding buried treasure or something?" Kyle asked with a slightly curious tone. He didn't know why she was there either.

"Oh, so now you're talking," she muttered as she pulled a long weed out the earth. "You've been sitting there watching me like a weird stalker for the past thirty minutes."

"You looked upset," he said as he stepped down from the fence.

"It's called a resting bitch face."

She dusted her hands of the dirt, turning to look at him. He wore his usual all black, with no sight of the horns or wings. His eyes were green, if not a bit wary.

"You look better," she smiled, genuinely happy.

"I've been working with Lucy, to try to…" He looked away, not wanting to vocalise what he was. "The tattoos too…"

"They working?" She nodded towards the ones on his neck, the red and black swirls barely visible beneath his dark shirt.

"We shall see." When he turned back his pupils had dilated, shadowing his iris' with a dark shade of red. He blinked, bringing them back under control. "Congrats on the new company."

Alice grinned. She had officially become an independent Paladin, working privately doing exactly the same job as she previously did for Supernatural Intelligence. Except she took a bigger pay percentage.

"Not sure on the name though."

Alice laughed, unable to hide her delight. "Sam picked it."

He had registered the trademark 'I Spy With My Paladin Eye – Independent Agency' without her knowledge. Once she saw the tagline 'We Find Em & Bind Em,' she couldn't resist.

"That makes sense." Kyle smiled, the emotion softening his face. He seemed calmer than she had ever seen him, almost at peace.

"You coming home?"

"You know it's not my home. Not for a long time." He shook his head. "Besides, I'm not finished yet."

"With what?"

His eyes flashed red, his face hardening as he watched something move behind her back.

"Good, you're both here," Dread said as he approached, even as Kyle took a step back.

Alice launched herself at him, his arms automatically coming around to crush her against him in an embrace that surprised her. Dread wasn't a hugger.

"What happened?" he asked when he touched her cheek, a bruise darkening beneath her eye.

"Mason's dead," she said instead.

Dread sighed, eyes pinched. "Good." He looked over at Kyle, giving him a nod.

"Where have you been?" she asked. "You weren't answering any of my calls…"

Dread returned his attention to her, face stern as he seemed to memorise the details of her face.

"Dread?" she asked, never seeing him like this before. "Are you okay?"

"No." Dread closed his eyes. "I'm sorry, Alice, I did everything I could. But The Council have decided your fate."

End of Book Three

A personal note from Taylor:
I hope you enjoyed Witch's Sorrow! If you want to show your support, I would really appreciate you leaving a review on Amazon. Reviews are super important and help other readers discover this series!

Need more of Alice? Keep reading for an excerpt of Elemental's Curse - Book Four

Alice clutched her side as she ran, unable to stop and take a breath as she chased the man through the busy streets.

One of the things she hadn't expected that afternoon was first, to eat her weight in pizza, and second, to have to run over a mile through two tube stations and several alleyways to catch her latest contract.

What were the chances he would be at the same Italian restaurant as her? She would say her luck was changing, but the stitch that stabbed her side seemed to loudly disagree.

"Stop!" she shouted, almost out of breath. That was the last time she let Sam convince her to eat a large pizza on her own. The man was pretty fast as he dodged around commuters and cars, and she would usually be faster, but there she was, defeated by a stomach full of cheese and carbs.

With a groan, she forced her legs to move, climbing the fence behind a rundown block of flats a few seconds after him.

"I said stop!" Alice skidded to a halt, breath coming out in pants as Mr Luton attempted, and failed to climb over a seven-foot brick wall. "You're under arrest."

A black cat sat and watched her beside some rotten bins, its reflective eyes eerily stalking her every time she moved into a closer position. The poor thing was small, severely emaciated with clumps of hair missing. One eye was blue, the other green while he was missing the top part of his left ear, the edge raw. By the angry red colour and obvious swelling it was clearly recent, which made it even sadder.

The stench from the bins wouldn't have been as bad if the cat hadn't decided to rip them open, polluting the air with a mixture of rotten food, milk and what looked like a crusty sock.

"Meow."

She ignored the feline, pulling out her phone and taking a few snaps as Mr Luton turned with a wide-eyed look. She had been hired to find the drug dealer who sold the drug HE2 to her clients son, resulting in his overdose. The police had nothing to go on, so it had taken Alice a few weeks of searching amongst the usual dealers to find the one matching the description, as well as photographic evidence for the police. It resulted in an official warrant for his arrest. As she had already fulfilled her contract and sent over the evidence, actually catching him was just a bonus.

"You again!" he hissed, looking around for a way out before his eyes settled on her phone. "Bitch, did you just take my picture?"

"Meow!"

The cat sat between them, casually licking a paw. She tried to wave it away, worried it would be harmed, but clearly cats wouldn't listen when silently threatened with castration. She should have known, she had threatened Sam with it once, and that hadn't worked either.

"Get on the ground!" She held out her palm, looking as threatening as possible. It would have been easier if she still had her gun, but she hadn't renewed her license since leaving S.I.

Her hair whipped across her face, the wind cool against her skin. The ice and snow had all but melted over the last few weeks, but the chill still remained. She was grateful she had taken her jacket out with her, unlike Mr Luton who she had caught unawares and had ran before he could grab his own coat. So he stood in his jeans and tank top, as if he wasn't in a country that barely reached the mid-twenties even in summer. He had gotten soaked by a passing car and a puddle a few streets before, turning his white tank see-through. So not only did she have to deal with his pale-arse arms with the worst tattoos imaginable, she also had to deal with his large burger-like nipples.

"Give me the fucking phone." He took a step forward.

Something brushed against her thigh.

"Meow."

Shit.

She tried to push the cat away, but it just continued to watch her inquisitively before it brushed against her once again. Even a rude hand gesture didn't move the bloody thing.

"Meow."

"Fuck off," she hissed as the cat began to purr surprisingly loudly considering it looked half dead.

"Oi, bitch!"

As if called, the cat walked towards Mr Luton, a slight limp to its back leg.

"If you don't get on the ground, I'll have to use force," she warned.

"You?" he laughed, flashing his gold teeth. "You look like you can barely make a fist. Shouldn't you be in the kitchen, doll?" He pulled out a knife, the blade long and serrated.

Well, that was bloody rude.

"Someone is clearly overcompensating for something," she said, steadying her legs. "It's the Mrs I feel sorry for."

A flush coloured his neck. "Give me the fucking phone."

End of Book Three

I hope you enjoyed the first three books from Alice Skye! If you want to show your support, I would really appreciate you leaving a review on Amazon. Reviews are super important and help other readers discover this series!

Elementals Curse
Book Four

An untamed witch. A forgotten past. An unknown legacy.

The nightmares might have stopped, but it's just the beginning for Alice Skye.
Newly Independent Paladin Agent Alice Skye is just starting to get her life together. She's survived a cult, taken down a corrupt druid and things are just starting to heat up with London's finest bachelor, Riley Storm.
With stolen Fae artefacts, missing hearts and a tight lipped Detective, Alice must break down Peyton's barriers, especially since his secret will help find the truth behind several gruesome murders.

But The Council are still watching, waiting as they're quietly deciding her fate.
Can she survive their judgment?
Or will it be her ancestry that destroys her?

Fancy a FREE short story?

Click HERE:
www.taylorastonwhite.com

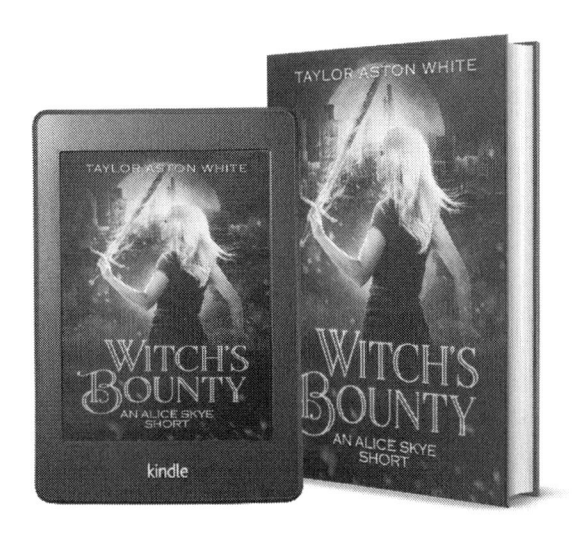

ABOUT THE AUTHOR

Taylor Aston White loves to explore mythology and European faerie tales to create her own, modern magic world. She collects crystals, house plants and dark lipstick, and has two young children who like to 'help' with her writing by slamming their hands across the keyboard.

After working several uncreative jobs and one super creative one, she decided to become a full-time author and now spends the majority of her time between her children and writing the weird and wonderful stories that pop into her head.

www.taylorastonwhite.com

Printed in Great Britain
by Amazon